#2   MAR 09 2010

Also by Joel Shepherd

A TRIAL OF BLOOD & STEEL

Petrodor

JOEL SHEPHERD

an imprint of **Prometheus Books**
Amherst, NY

Inquiries should be addressed to
Pyr
59 John Glenn Drive
Amherst, New York 14228–2119
VOICE: 716–691–0133
FAX: 716–691–0137
WWW.PYRSF.COM

14 13 12 11 10   5 4 3 2 1

Library of Congress Cataloging-in-Publication Data

Shepherd, Joel, 1974–
    Petrodor / by Joel Shepherd.
        p. cm. — (A trial of blood and steel ; bk. 2)
    Originally published: Australia and New Zealand : Hachette Livre Australia Pty Ltd., 2008.
    ISBN 978–1–61614–193–6 (pbk. : alk. paper)
    I. Title.

PR9619.4.S54P48 2010
823'.92—dc22

                                                                                    2009047967

Printed in the United States on acid-free paper

⇜ RHODIA ⇝

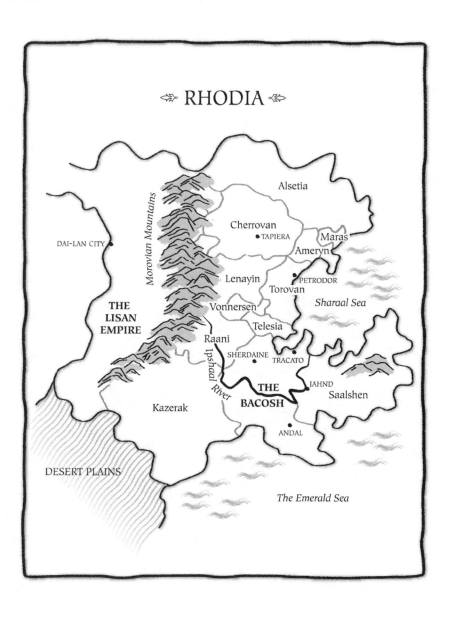

One

SASHA SAT ON THE PROW OF THE BOAT, and saw a number of red and white floats bobbing on the surface ahead. She turned, shielding her eyes against the glare of the sun, and pointed. "That's them," she announced to Mari, back at the tiller.

"Of course that's them," Mari retorted. He was a broad, squat man with powerful arms and a rotund middle, weathered and browned in the sun. He squinted into the glare with no shielding hand, well used to that intensity. Sasha still did not understand how he could know where to find the floats. The sea was slippery calm, save for the rocking of a gentle swell. Off to the right, the hills of the Torovan shoreline loomed brown and green, a series of rocky bays and headlands, small waves lapping at the feet of rugged cliffs. Mari simply seemed to know where he was, out here on the featureless sea, the same way a Lenay woodsman might find his way about the forests and hills of Sasha's native Lenayin.

A gentle, shoreward breeze pushed at the sail, bringing the floats closer. Sasha counted twelve in this cluster. Far off to the right, she could see some more floats, these were green and brown though, not the red and white that belonged to House Velo.

"Sasha, look up," said Errollyn from his post beside the sail. "White-headed albatross."

Sasha squinted into the blue sky, and saw a wide-winged bird far overhead. Clearly an albatross, for its wings were long and thin, and barely flapped. But white-headed? Not only did serrin see better by night, they saw further by day as well.

She glanced at Errollyn—he leaned back on the side of the boat, head tilted to gaze enthralled at the sky. She'd never seen Errollyn more happy than in the last several weeks, coming out on the boat. The ocean was nearly as strange to him as it was to her, and he delighted at its wonders. He wore an old, work-stained shirt and rough pants, dark grey hair falling back in disarray. His arms were bare in the unseasonal warmth, flexed with the knotted muscle of a svaalverd warrior. Very few serrin were given to such casual untidiness, yet Errollyn seemed infinitely more relaxed now than at formal occasions, or in social company. And Sasha realised that she ought to be staring at the albatross instead, and tore her gaze away . . . but not without a small, private smile.

"Forget the damn bird!" Mari exclaimed. "Boy, let out the sail! Valenti, get off your arse!"

Sasha moved back to help Mari's son Valenti, cautiously lest the small boat rock, grabbing the second float to come alongside as Valenti grabbed the first. They hauled wet rope, hand over hand, Valenti racing her with a grin, bare arms straining against the waterlogged weight . . . but it was Errollyn on the other side who beat them both, dragging a wicker cage from the sea with a rush of water. Sasha pulled her own clear at the same time as Valenti, and peered into the round, flat contraption to see if anything had climbed into the hole in the top.

She was lucky—there were two lobsters, flapping and kicking, and she pulled each out in turn, tossing them into the crate at Mari's feet which was already crawling with strange creatures. Valenti added another from his cage, and Sasha turned to watch as Errollyn prised an enormous crab through the hole, holding carefully to its huge pincers. It was red, with a white underbelly and blue trim on its legs.

"Excellent!" Mari exclaimed. "Another that size and Mariesa will have enough for her *crasada dosa*!" Tonight was Sadisi, the birthday of Sadis, a local prophet who had brought Verenthaneism to Petrodor more than seven hundred years ago. Tonight, there would be more seafood than she'd yet seen in nearly a month of living in Petrodor. Her stomach threatened to turn at the prospect. Maybe she could find a good juicy steak.

Errollyn peered curiously at the crab, as it jabbed its pointed feet at him and snapped helplessly with its pincers. Then he dropped it into the crate with the rest and turned to pull out a second, smaller crab. Sasha and Valenti grabbed bait from the bait box, reached in to spear it on the hooks within the cages, and dropped them overboard once more.

"Too small," said Errollyn of the crab.

"It'll do," Mari retorted. "Toss it in."

"Too small, and female," Errollyn replied, peering at the markings. "Throw it back and you'll have many more crabs hatching in years ahead."

Mari was unimpressed. "We need the meat, now throw it . . ." Errollyn did throw it—straight over the side. Mari rolled his eyes in exasperation. "Blasted serrin," he muttered, stomping past the boxes, rocking the boat alarmingly. "It's a blasted crab. I want to eat it—you want to make love to it."

He grabbed a pole from the gunnels and reached for the next float.

Errollyn caught Sasha's eye and grinned, a flash of piercing dark green eyes behind a long, unkempt fringe.

"Aren't there some serrin who won't eat any meat at all?" Sasha asked, making her way up to the bow to grab the next float. The boat's rocking had been a concern at first, but she was getting used to it now. And her balance, of course, was excellent.

"Yes," said Errollyn, throwing his baited cage back in with a splash. "But they're stupid."

Sasha laughed, hauling the rope. Serrin never dismissed alternative opinions so readily. Errollyn had, by serrin standards, a most unusual sense of humour. Rebellious, almost.

"Why wouldn't they eat meat?" Valenti asked, making his way past Sasha. He put a hand on her waist in passing. It might have cost a Lenay man his arm, but Petrodor men were just like that, she was discovering. One learned to avoid unnecessary arguments, and make allowances. Sometimes.

"To avoid killing animals," Errollyn replied, following Valenti up to the bow.

Valenti turned a frown on Errollyn. "But you love animals! Why do *you* eat them?"

"Why do you?" said Errollyn.

Valenti grinned. "You crazy? They taste good! I'm not going to feel sorry for some crab!"

"Then there you are," said Errollyn with a smile.

"Crabs don't feel sorry for the small animals they eat," said Sasha, unwinding arm lengths of dripping rope into the boat. It was hard work, for the cages dragged in the water, and her arms and shoulders ached. But she had strength there that few human women could match, and the sword calluses on her hands kept the rope from chafing. "Why should we feel sorry for crabs?"

"How do you know crabs don't feel sorry for what they eat?" Errollyn asked her. "Maybe they do. Maybe they say a little prayer and beg their gods for forgiveness."

"Now you're just being difficult," Sasha retorted.

"That's what Rhillian always tells me," Errollyn said with a grin, hauling his own rope in. He was faster than any of his shipmates—not only powerful, but certain with his hands, and poised with his balance. He made it look effortless.

"Then explain yourself, *ma'she das serrinim*," Sasha teased, invoking a Saalsi term for serrin debates. "How does your truth flow?"

Errollyn made a face. "That's an awful translation."

"In Torovan, it's the best I can do."

"I think," said Errollyn, as rope fell from his hands into a gathering pile by his feet, "that it is difficult to swim against the stream. Life feeds on life. We are all creatures of nature, and in understanding animals, I try to understand myself. We are what we are, and we need what we need. I need meat. No other creatures feel the need to apologise for that, and I don't either."

"That's wonderful," Mari said with grand gesticulation. "I could burst into song. If you lot worked as hard as you talked, we'd be knee-deep in dinner by now."

The sun was sinking to late afternoon by the time they'd made the rounds to all of House Velo's floats. The wind gave out completely, and while Mari furled the sail, Valenti unracked the oars. Sasha insisted firmly that she should take an oar, and was rebuffed even more firmly by Valenti, the young, sun-browned man quite scandalised at the prospect. Sasha settled herself on the bow once more, unwilling to further the argument in such a small boat, surrounded by deep water.

Family Velo had been incredulous enough that she would wish to go fishing, and not join the other, rare Nasi-Keth women in practice of medicines and herb lore, or educating poor dockfront children. Once again, she'd managed to offend nearly everyone—the womenfolk, for snubbing their very worthy activities, and the menfolk, for thinking to show everyone their work was so easy that even a woman could do it. It was an annoyance, to have to prove herself all over again. But in all honesty, these days, she was caring less and less. People would either accept her as she was, or not. At least this way, she could know who her friends were.

The little boat surged through the water with each stroke of the oars, then glided, then surged once more. The sound was soothing. The water gleamed like glass, and the still air was warm on her bare arms. She rubbed at her left bicep, absently, where the tattoo still itched.

To the right, out into the Sharaal Sea, a great ship was also under oars, its sails hopefully unfurled to catch any returning breeze. Further beyond, Sasha fancied she could see another, a distant smudge of mast and rigging through the sea haze.

Ahead, the Alaster Promontory jutted into the sea, marking the southernmost point of Petrodor Harbour. Beyond it, within the bay's deeper waters, numerous ships could be seen at anchor. Doubtless shore leave would be in great demand this evening so sailors could enjoy the Sadisi.

Once beyond the promontory, the small boat moved slowly into Petrodor Harbour. The city of Petrodor encircled the bay like a giant amphitheatre. The sprawling expanse of clustered sandstone and brick buildings crowded the slopes, a seething mass of human habitation where it was difficult to tell where one property began and the others left off. Roads could be barely seen, as they wound their way up and down the cluttered incline, but Sasha knew they were there . . . along with the maze of alleys, little stairways, back entrances and secret paths known only to local residents or to the shadowy figures who moved only beneath the cover of darkness.

Even now, with the famed Petrodor incline sunk deep into shadow as the sun set at its back, the sheer scale of detail baffled Sasha's eyes. Here and there across the slope, a larger building broke clear of the confusion—here a mansion, there an old fortress that had once stood alone, now consumed amidst the city sprawl, or a Verenthane temple with soaring spires. The incline itself was uneven—sometimes gentle, at other times looming into a cliff face of yellow sandstone that shone when the morning sun struck it directly.

A third of the way along from Alaster Promontory, the Petrodor Bowl was broken by a protruding ridge, topped with a great, multi-floored mansion behind high walls. Cliffs on two sides plunged straight into the mass of buildings below. The ridge was Sharptooth, and the mansion was Maerler House, not to be confused with "House Maerler," which described the family. The Torovan tongue, as well as Sasha knew it, was revealing itself to be somewhat vague in matters of power—the "fog of intrigue," as Kessligh called it. One of the two great families of Petrodor, House Maerler led a collection of allied houses that locals often referred to as the "Southern Stack," in literal Torovan, stack meaning "alliance" . . . or at least as Sasha understood it.

The "Northern Stack," by contrast, was headed by House Steiner, whose residence was less visible from the bay, lost against the northern ridgeline of grand residences. It was no accident, many said, that the northern mansions seemed grander than those of the south. While House Maerler clung grimly to their ancestral lands and trading routes, House Steiner had always pursued expansion. Their preferred method of expansion had been the Verenthane religion.

It was no coincidence either, Sasha reckoned, that further along that northern ridgeline, a rocky path led out onto the Besendi Promontory, where, high above the yellow cliffs, soared the Porsada Temple, the greatest house of Verenthanes in all Torovan. Its four spires flung their star-pointed tips into the sky, in all defiance of the precipitous drop below. The entire, magnificent structure blazed a pure, gleaming white in the late afternoon sun, catching that light even as the rest of the city fell into shadow. A beacon to arriving ships, a watchtower from which to survey the city, the temple reminded all where the true power of Petrodor lay.

The small fishing boat came close by the side of one of the harbour ships now.

Valenti was clearly tiring, his technique with the oar becoming erratic, and Errollyn's effortless strokes threatened to pull the boat around to starboard. "You're dropping your head," Sasha told him. "Don't bend your back, pull through your shoulders." Valenti muttered something, struggling to correct his posture.

"Leave the boy alone," said his father with a frown from the tiller. "Rowing isn't like swordwork, girl. It's harder than it looks."

"It must be," Sasha retorted. "Because it looks as easy as falling over." Errollyn was laughing as he rowed. Where many serrin found human arguments alarming, Errollyn never ceased to be entertained.

"You wouldn't last fifty strokes," Valenti said through gritted teeth.

"How would you know if you never let me try? You're just scared I'll be better."

"Fine!" said Valenti in a temper. He stopped rowing, and climbed from the bench seat as Errollyn also paused, watching with amusement. "Have your turn, little Princess!"

Sasha grinned in triumph, and slid past the young man who for all the youth of his seventeen summers, was still a half head taller than her. She took her seat, pulled her pair of leather training gloves from the back of her belt and yanked them on.

"Soft hands," Errollyn suggested.

Sasha snorted. "My calluses have been carefully crafted over many years. I don't want new ones in the wrong spots." She grasped the oar, braced her boots on the inner hull rib, and began to pull. It was a little awkward at first, but she watched Errollyn, timed her hands to move opposite his, and used her bodyweight rather than her arms as the oar tugged at the water. They gathered speed with each surge, and then the oar flowed through the water more smoothly, and the effort to keep it steady became less.

It felt good, and made use of all the familiar muscles she liked to use. Each unsteady surge of the boat was a strange sensation . . . but then, she recalled that she had found riding a strange sensation, once, as a girl. Mari was frowning at her from the tiller, with obvious disapproval. She liked Torovan people . . . but, good spirits, they believed in some nonsense! Valenti, now seated on the bow, was out of her sight entirely.

She began to sing, a Goeren-yai chant, in her native Lenay. It was something she'd learned as a girl, at her new home in the hills above Baerlyn in the

Lenayin province of Valhanan. Men had sung it while chopping wood. Goeren-yai men of Baerlyn, with their long hair, braids, rings and tattoos of ancient Lenay tradition. Men who had become her friends as she'd grown, and impressed her with their honesty, their courage, and their earthy good humour.

The song's rhythm fitted well with the strokes of the oars, and Errollyn, after listening for several verses, joined in as the words repeated. A little corner of Lenayin they made, rowing and chanting in unison across the vast, wide bay of lowlands Petrodor.

They continued singing, rowing the boat slowly into the fishermen's dock, a section of wood-planked pier that ran in parallel to the main dock, surrounded by a wide, creaking cluster of fishing boats all lashed together. Mari brought them alongside the family's other boat, hulls bumped, and ropes were flung across, Sasha shipping her oar as Mari and Valenti leapt across and began securing them together. Sasha went to the space beneath the bow and pulled out her sword, bandoleer still attached, and began securing it over her shoulder. Then followed the belt knives, and the boot knife. Errollyn did the same. No Nasi-Keth nor serrin went unarmed in Petrodor . . . in these times, least of all.

Then began the task of carrying the crates of squirming, crawling, snapping seafood across the neighbouring boats to the pier's ladder. Sasha carried the bait box across, her balance nimble on the shifting decks beneath her feet. Valenti made to take it from her, but she put it on her shoulder and climbed the ladder one-handed.

On the pier, Mari talked with a fisherman Sasha did not recognise, the two men peering over the catch, their manner coarse and businesslike. Sasha took the opportunity to swing her aching arms and look about.

This was the South Pier, where the fishermen and small-time merchants reserved a portion of dock for themselves. The pier planks were grimy and rotten in places, and littered with a refuse of fish scales and old rope. Facing the pier upon the stone dock was the chaos of docklife, crowds and stalls, folk selling everything that could be imagined, and some that could never have been until you'd seen it. Men and women moved aside for horse or bullock carts loaded with crates or barrels, some carrying armoured guards in colourful house livery. The shouts of the touts and hawkers competed with the cries of various animals, and the squawks and squabbles of the ever-present white gulls searching for scraps with a beady eye, and the air smelled of a chaotic melange of cooking, strange spices, old wood, rotting fish and salt.

Rising above the fray, the brick and stone façades of buildings, their plaster crumbling, their many small windows framed with worn shutters. Beyond, the Petrodor Incline began its steady climb, a pile of crumbling brick and standstone that looked far less impressive from close range. Only the scale of it still impressed.

To the north, the docks broadened, and larger, well-maintained piers hosted the looming masts of great ships. Sasha could see perhaps a dozen currently at berth, arranged so that the hulls could overlap bows with sterns and save space. Men pushed handcarts, or loaded bags or crates directly onto waiting carts. Great piles of cargo were stacked upon the dock, watched by men with weapons. Horse and bullock carts crowded the remaining space, with people somehow flowing through the gaps between, pursued by the ever-present hawkers, beggars and the occasional stray dog. All in all, it was a scene of the greatest, most spectacular human confusion Sasha had ever beheld. She'd been living with it for nearly a month now, and still it baffled her.

"It's a long way from Lenayin," he said at her shoulder. She nearly jumped, not having heard his approach. But somehow, with Errollyn, the alarm never quite registered. She gave him a smile.

"And a long way from Saalshen," she replied.

"*Las re'han as'e baen*," said Errollyn with a shrug. "The world is a place," in Saalsi. Although frequently very blunt for a serrin, Errollyn could also be as vague and obtuse as the best of them. He leaned close, a hand on her shoulder, and added against her ear in Lenay, "The place is where you are."

And he moved to help Mari with the crates, leaving Sasha to consider that. And to consider further that if a Lenay or Torovan man had touched her so intimately, she'd have wanted to rattle his skull. With serrin, it was different, and with Errollyn in particular. Amongst human men, she'd learned by long experience to guard her personal space. Errollyn simply didn't mean it that way . . . or rather he *did*, as all relations between serrin men and women meant something in *that* way . . . but somehow, it was still different. Not disrespectful. Not . . .

"Oh hells," she muttered, and went to grab the remaining crate of their catch, trying to shake free of her confusion. Valenti interposed himself with a look of cold hostility, and grabbed the crate himself. "Hey!" He ignored her. "Oh come on, you're not upset with me?"

Valenti stalked off, carrying his crate. Sasha took up the bait box and walked at Errollyn's side. "You're such a diplomat," Errollyn remarked, watching the lad depart.

"Oh bugger," Sasha muttered. And more loudly, "Valenti! Look, you don't tell me I'm no damn good at something I know damn well I'd be good at! Valenti!"

"Leave the boy alone," said Mari, carrying his own crate. "You upset a man's pride, but he'll get over it."

"What about a woman's pride?" Sasha exclaimed. Mari shook his head and sighed.

"You don't think that maybe a princess could afford to forgo a little pride once in a while?" Errollyn suggested.

Sasha scowled. "Meaning?"

"Even your sister Alythia wouldn't choose to wear *all* her jewellery to attend a court filled with poor dockfront girls in sackcloth."

"Why do you always talk in riddles?" Sasha snapped. "And besides, I'm *not* like Alythia! I'm *nothing* like Alythia!"

"If you say so, I'm sure it must be true."

Sadisi cleared the docks of merchants and their stalls, and replaced them with revellers. Many fires burned along the waterfront, lighting the buildings and sparkling off the dark, heaving waters. There were some chairs and upturned crates for the old folk, but mostly people stood—eating, drinking, talking, singing and dancing. Thousands of them. Sasha could barely believe her eyes, ears and nostrils.

Her own fireplace was near the Velo house, one of many cramped, crumbling buildings near a side alley off the docks the locals called Fishnet Alley. Gathered about the main fire were members of all the neighbouring families, hardy men and women in rough clothes, and largely in the fishing trade. There were maybe a hundred about the central fire, and hundreds more about the smaller fires. *Crasada dosa* steamed upon great, round pans. A jumble of mixed seafood in a vast tomato sauce, garnished with just about everything.

Sasha stood with her tin plate, eating steaming bits of crab with her fingers and wiping excess sauce with a chunk of bread. Nearby, little blonde Aisha fussed about a fireplace where she was preparing mussels in a vast, steaming pan. A young man Sasha did not recognise came to offer Aisha a sip of his wine as she cooked. Mari's wife, Mariesa, shooed him away with a scowl, but Aisha only laughed, while around the fires Mari and his friends burst into passionate song.

Out on the water, moored ships made a mass of lights, long, gleaming streaks reflected on the dark water, above a spidery tangle of rigging. From the serrin ships, there came the occasional coloured streak of a firework, drawing awed shouts from the children scampering along the jetties. To the far north of the bay, the white spires of Porsada Temple gleamed ghostly bright from fires atop Besendi Promontory. There, the priests held service for Saint Sadis. Below, Petrodor celebrated.

A new arrival stepped through the crowd, with several others close behind. Men stared, for her beauty was spectacular. Lean and as tall as some men, she moved gracefully through the press, smiling to those who greeted her. Firelight lit her white hair to a brilliant gleam, as crisp as mountain snow, and tied into a single braid that fell down her back. Her eyes shone a sharp, emerald green, flicking from person to person with that piercing, almost animal intensity that was peculiar to serrin.

Rhillian.

She greeted Aisha with a hug, and her eyes found Sasha's.

"Good evening," Rhillian greeted Sasha with a smile. "Or Happy Sadisi, whatever the proper term." They exchanged a hug.

"Isn't this amazing?" Sasha exclaimed, gesturing to the firelit commotion.

"You think *this* is amazing?" Rhillian's enthusiasm only made her all the more stunning to behold—burning green eyes, flashing white hair and perfect white teeth. "I've just come from the Endurance, it's reached the Slipway now. Crazier a sight I have never seen."

"Mari was telling me about the Endurance! I'd love to see it."

"It goes on all night, why don't we go up and see after you've eaten? It'll come down the Corkscrew after the Slipway anyhow, much closer to here . . . I can't *imagine* how they'll keep those carts from running away and ploughing through someone's house."

"You're here to see Kessligh?" Sasha asked her, chewing on some bread.

"No, you," Rhillian said mildly. And smiled at her. "You seem surprised."

Sasha shrugged in exasperation. "Everything's so political these days. I hadn't thought you and Kessligh had finished your business."

"We haven't." Rhillian picked a prawn off Sasha's plate. "But even the 'White Death of Petrodor' needs some time to relax every now and then." She said it with a faint edge. It was what the rich men of Petrodor's highest families called her, Sasha knew. The "White Death of Petrodor." Rhillian was, by human reckoning, the most powerful serrin in the city. By serrin reckoning . . . well, serrin did not view things in such simple, hierarchical terms. But she had great *ra'shi*, the serrin term for respect and credibility, through all Saalshen. Serrin had no kings or queens, or anything that might say "power" to a human. Kessligh said that Rhillian was perhaps one of the ten most powerful serrin in all Rhodia. Which was about as precisely as anyone had managed to explain what Rhillian actually was, to Sasha's memory.

A handsome young man sauntered between Rhillian and the steaming pan of seafood. "Please, my most beautiful lady!" he exclaimed. "I cannot allow you onto our dock without savouring our hospitality! You must accept some food!"

Rhillian considered him with an elegant tilt of the head, chewing on the tail of Sasha's prawn. The young man was game—he barely even flinched as those green eyes found him. "But I've eaten," she said.

"A drink, a drink for the beautiful lady!" said the young man, in search of whoever now had the wine jug. Quickly a cup was filled, and placed in her hand. Sasha grinned, watching the serrin's dismay.

"Who is that young man anyway?" Rhillian asked as he moved away to pester some other attractive woman. Sasha drained her own cup, and took Rhillian's so she could eat.

"I think he's a Malrini," she said. "There's at least thirty families just in this little block, I'm still learning them."

"Petrodor is so crowded," Rhillian agreed glumly, taking another prawn. Her voice felt strained, having to half shout over the top of it. "I'm not obliged to have sex with him now, am I?"

Sasha laughed. "That's up to you. I'm sure he wouldn't complain."

"Even I must draw the line somewhere, I suppose."

Sasha considered Rhillian with amusement. "You know, you're nothing like what I'd been led to expect before I met you."

Rhillian raised eyebrows at her. "How so?"

"The White Death of Petrodor," said Sasha, teasing. "Errollyn has so much respect for you when he usually has no respect for anything . . ." Rhillian grinned, "and the archbishop wets his bed when he dreams of you, and even Kessligh doesn't push you around. But you're not two spans tall and breathing fire. I must say, I'm disappointed."

"Good," said Rhillian, around her mouthful. Even with juice dribbling on her fingers and chin, she still managed to look poised and elegant. Cat-like, Sasha thought. She'd heard people described like that before. Rhillian was the first who truly matched the description. "Let me tell you a little something about Errollyn."

"Yes?"

Rhillian licked some juice from her finger. "He's insane."

Sasha laughed. "You two are impossible! Can't you just call a truce?"

"No seriously," Rhillian insisted, in a manner that was not serious at all. "I've been thinking on it. Of all the many philosophical inflections of the Saalsi tongue, all the many shades of meaning and description that you're always complaining about . . ."

"I am not."

"They all fail to do Errollyn justice," Rhillian concluded. "He's a raving loon." She managed to keep a straight face for several heartbeats, before she and Sasha burst into laughter.

Errollyn, Sasha had gathered, was different. A *du'janah*, they called him, a term which Sasha still did not entirely understand. All the serrin seemed to have great affection for him, and he for them, as always seemed the case between serrin . . . yet there seemed an unspecified *distinctness* about Errollyn and his position amongst his own people. All of those who served Saalshen's interests abroad—the *talmaad*—were direct and straight talking, by the convoluted standards of the Saalshen serrinim, but Errollyn was even more so. Sometimes, Sasha thought, he enjoyed human company more than serrin. And sometimes, she fancied that some serrin, perhaps including Rhillian, found that . . . disconcerting.

Yet for all their strangeness, Sasha was only too well aware that her new serrin friends were far more at home in Petrodor than she was. She had been here a matter of weeks, Rhillian had been in Petrodor for three years now, and while Errollyn was younger and less experienced, even he was nearing the end of his second year in Petrodor. Saalshen's trading interests in Petrodor were vast, and had deep roots. There had been serrin outposts here for more than three hundred years, it was said. Two hundred years ago, following the invasion of Saalshen by the Bacosh King Leyvaan, Saalshen had expanded its trading range in the hopes of new human allies from other parts of Rhodia. Petrodor, then a simple fishing town, had erupted into unanticipated wealth, size and power. Yet, despite all the serrin had done for the city, its residents were not always grateful.

Some Lisan sailors moved slowly through the crowd, careful not to touch anyone. They had long, dark hair, broad faces and slanted eyes. The swords in their belts were curved, and even their sleeveless undershirts were light skins, to go with their leather pants and hide boots. They stared at Rhillian and Sasha as they passed, with neither friendliness nor curiosity.

Rhillian smiled at them. She waved and called a greeting in the Lisan tongue . . . Rhillian was not much of a linguist, by serrin standards. She only spoke five foreign tongues, besides all the Saalsi dialects. Amongst the *talmaad* that was almost retarded. The Lisan stared, expressionless, and moved slowly on.

"Spies?" Sasha suggested, watching them go.

"Assuredly. The families know their own cronies wouldn't be very welcome down here. So they pay the Lisan to come wandering through, knowing the locals can't very well object to sailors on the docks. There's not much the Lisan won't do for gold."

"You're just so popular with everyone," Sasha remarked.

"Oh, they're here to watch you at least as much as me," Rhillian said cheerfully. Sasha didn't like that. "Uma to Kessligh Cronenverdt, the hero of

Lenayin, returned to Petrodor to reunite the Nasi-Keth. The families always hated the Nasi-Keth, at least as much as the serrin, possibly more. Demon serrin they expect to fight, but for humans to actually join forces with those demon serrin . . . well, that's traitorous."

"That's okay," said Sasha. "I'm used to wealthy Verenthanes hating me. Makes me feel at home." A running child thudded into her leg, stumbled, then kept running, oblivious. Another chased her. "Hey!" Sasha called, spilling some of Rhillian's wine on her shirt sleeve. "That was my leg, if you don't mind!" But she was more amused than annoyed. She'd done far worse at that age.

"Human children can't see in the dark either," Rhillian observed. Her green eyes flashed as the firelight caught them, an inhuman gleam.

"So far I've fallen amongst the commonfolk," Sasha remarked, shaking wine from her sleeve and examining the stain. "I led the first Lenay rebellion in a century and the Udalyn people pronounced me their saviour. Now just look at these indignities."

"It's the indignities that remind us what life really is," Rhillian replied. "Even the greatest king suffers minor indignities. And can be undone by them."

"Only a serrin could find something profound in a wine stain."

Rhillian smiled. Her gaze shifted to the north, as she retrieved her cup to take a sip. "Just look at Porsada Temple." The white walls and spires seemed to shimmer above the dark waters. The reflection on the bay was ghostly, amidst the outline of ships. "Such a beautiful thing. It's almost enough to make one wish to be a Verenthane."

"It's very pretty," Sasha agreed, dryly. "But I wouldn't go that far."

Two

"YOU DON'T THINK IT'S A LITTLE REVEALING?" Selyna asked her princess, dubiously.

"Oh nonsense, I think it looks wonderful." Alythia considered herself in the full-length mirror. The gown was a radiant lime green, with flowing folds and a decorative bustle at the back. The front clasp was a gold and onyx brooch, pinned upon a somewhat lower bust than was typical for Petrodor. The brooch went well with the pins in her waves of dark hair, falling about her partly bare shoulders. "Oh I love these earrings, too. Where did you find them, Vansy?"

"A wedding gift from Lord Nandryn of Valhanan," said Vansy, fastening a lace tie at the back.

"I must go through some of those boxes again," Alythia thought aloud, adjusting the lie of fabric on one shoulder. So many gifts, they'd been piled into an entire cart for the journey from Lenayin. Upon the wedding train's arrival in Petrodor, there'd been a second, even larger round of gift-giving. Most of Petrodor's ruling classes had turned out for the marriage of the heir of Family Halmady to a Lenay princess.

The splendour had been breathtaking. Long processions out along the Besendi Promontory to Porsada Temple. Families in colourful costume, with coloured flags flying in the breeze, before an azure ocean view. The Porsada Temple, as white as polished quartz against the sea, its spires soaring skyward. The ceremony itself, the guests asparkle with more jewellery than all the lords of Lenayin could possibly have owned.

Ceremony enough to allow her to forget the disaster of her train's send-off from Baen-Tar. The turmoil and delays, the fighting, her father's absence when her betrothed, Gregan, had arrived to escort her to Petrodor. It had been a rebellion . . . and of *course* her wretched sister Sashandra had just happened to be leading it. Sasha had always hated everything that Alythia thought best about Lenayin, everything that counted for true civilisation. She had thrown in her lot with the pagan Goeren-yai to fight the Verenthane Hadryn in the north; which had meant that King Torvaal had been in Hadryn when her future husband had arrived in the capital Baen-Tar.

Alythia had been so embarrassed, and so angry. But she was here now, and the wedding had been a wonderful success. For sheer finery, the Petrodor Families were a whole level above even Lenayin royalty. She and her two maids had worked all afternoon to select this dress and its accompaniments. She'd done some extra tailoring herself to get it looking this good. Princess Alythia was renowned as the most beautiful Princess of Lenayin, and that from a good crop, too. She'd show the Petrodor families she belonged.

She turned away from the mirror as Selyna and Vansy continued their adjustments. The chambers' windows were many-paned, and worked into a light, wooden doorway that opened onto a balcony. Glass doors. Alythia had never seen such architecture. How wonderfully sophisticated beside the heavy stone and thick wood of Baen-Tar! The Halmady Mansion's walls were a sandstone brick, creamy yellow in colour, as was much of Petrodor. The chambers' floor was polished floorboards, but downstairs, many of the important rooms were spanned with polished marble.

Beyond her balcony, a firework streaked across the sky. Most seemed to be coming from the ships out on the harbour. Each ship shone with many lamps, and from this height, they seemed like a collection of children's toys, all lit up with festival charm. Alongside Halmady Mansion sat Torgenes Mansion, a beautiful building of three floors, great forward columns, many balconies and a sloping, red-tile roof. And, of course, great perimeter walls topped with spikes and guard posts . . . but Alythia had lived all her life in Baen-Tar, surrounded by enormous city walls as tall as five men, and such modest defences as these took little getting used to. Beyond Torgenes Mansion, the great, curving sweep of Petrodor Harbour continued, alive tonight with even more lights than usual.

A door opened and Alythia turned to find Gregan Halmady paused in the doorway, staring at her. She curtsied and pretended a shy smile. "Good evening, my husband," she said, with a forced effort to get her thoughts back into Torovan. Chatting with her Lenay maids, it was sometimes difficult. How strange to be married to a man who only spoke Torovan. "You look very handsome."

And he did. Gregan Halmady had twenty-five summers (three more than herself) and a breadth of shoulder that was pleasing. He had a round face and curly hair that grew out as much as down. That was odd too. Alythia couldn't recall having ever seen a Lenay man with such curly hair. He had nice eyes, a widish nose, and excellent taste in clothes. He was dressed now in an embroidered dark tunic with a wide Torovan collar and a silver clasp at the throat. There were rings on his fingers, a silver-pommelled sword at his hip and tight pants that tucked into knee-high black leather boots.

Gregan *always* dressed nicely. Most Torovan men did. When Alythia had first seen him, she'd been so relieved. Her father and eldest brother had assured her that she would not be marrying an ugly man, but then, what would *they* know?

"How do I look?" she pressed impatiently when her husband did not immediately reply.

"You look . . . amazing." Alythia believed him. The night following their wedding, he'd made those feelings clear enough. And on most nights since. Alythia smothered a dainty giggle behind her hand.

"I could tell Selyna and Vansy to leave us for a moment, if you wished? The carriages will not expect us *immediately,* will they?"

Gregan, to her disappointment, appeared somewhat anxious. "I . . . well . . . no, M'Lady, I think I really must attend to the procession. Mother will be up to see you shortly."

And he departed, closing the door behind. Alythia frowned. "He's so timid!" she exclaimed, turning back to the mirror. "I wish he'd just *grab* me sometimes!"

"A Torovan man is not a Lenay man," Vansy said knowingly, combing out her princess's hair, with several pins yet to go in. Vansy was tall and sensible, an older girl from Tyree. Selyna was smaller and dark, from northern Banneryd. "Torovan men have more manners."

"Too much so, sometimes. And why must he call on his mother all the time?" Alythia and Lady Halmady were not on good terms. The old lady was a witch.

"Family is so important here," Selyna ventured.

"Hmph," said Alythia. "And he called me 'M'Lady,' did you hear that? He always does that, even when we're alone sometimes. And he's always anxious, like he's scared he'll offend me or something."

"I think he merely needs time to get to know you," Vansy said decisively, sliding in another pin. "Marriage is a big thing to a young man, especially one who's never had much experience with women before."

Alythia frowned. "Don't you think?"

"With Lady Halmady watching over him?" Vansy countered.

"I suppose," Alythia conceded. She was so glad of her maids. Especially Vansy. Not only was it nice to speak Lenay, it was nice to have two people around who weren't afraid to tell her what they thought. So many Torovans seemed afraid to tell the truth to a person's face. Sometimes they were so polite, and so gracious, it became exasperating. "He *is* rather . . . well, let's just say that he fumbles a lot." Selyna giggled.

"And," Vansy continued, "M'Lady can be somewhat intimidating."

"Intimidating?" Alythia gaped at her in the mirror. "Exactly how am I intimidating?!"

"M'Lady is very beautiful, and very headstrong, and in case M'Lady has not noticed, Petrodor is not a city accustomed to beautiful, headstrong women who say what they think."

Alythia had to laugh. Vansy was right, of course. But that only made the challenge greater, and more exciting. "They'll come to like me," she said slyly. "You'll see. I'll win them over. I'll become the talk of all Petrodor. They've never seen anyone like me before."

Lady Halmady, however, had other ideas. "The front of that dress," she said disdainfully, upon entering the chambers, "is disgracefully low. Remove it at once and find another."

Lady Halmady dressed principally in black, as was fitting for a high-class lady of Petrodor whose hair was beginning to grey. Her face was round, and her hair curled like her son's, but her eyes were hard, and tight with little wrinkles. Alythia found her stiff with formality, and utterly obsessed with matters of status and decorum. It made a distasteful spectacle. Nobility and royalty should be graceful, not uptight and insecure.

"Oh, but *really*, Mother," Alythia laughed, trying to make light of it.

"Really nothing." Her mother-in-law's lips pursed together tightly. "The festival celebrations of Sadisi are some of the grandest on the Petrodor calendar. The honour of House Halmady is at stake. I'll not have it said that the heir of Halmady is wedded to a highlands wench of easy virtue."

"You . . . you accuse highlanders of easy virtue?" Alythia asked. "Mother, I assure you, nothing could be further from the truth!"

"From where I'm standing," Lady Halmady said coldly, "and from where countless men shall no doubt also be standing at the festival, with wide, salivating mouths, there seems little truth to your claim."

"At least they're no brothels in Lenayin!" Alythia retorted. "I never even understood what a brothel was until someone who'd travelled to Petrodor explained it to me!"

"You watch your tongue with me, young lady! I'll tolerate none of your highland lip in this house, I warn you!"

"If you have such contempt for highlanders," said Alythia in exasperation, "then why in the world did you allow your son to marry one?"

Lady Halmady slapped her. Alythia's head snapped about, a cheek and temple stinging. The force of the blow astonished her.

"You do not question the motivations of this family's elders, do you understand me?" The older woman's voice was tight with rage. "You are your husband's servant, and thus a servant of this house. You do not question. You obey. I know that you are a princess. It may seem to you that this family is nothing more than commoners. But let me assure you, young lady, that a noble family of Petrodor is of a vastly higher station than even the *royalty* of that highland barbarian cesspit could aspire to. You did not marry *down*, my dear. It is *we* who married down, I am quite sure."

Lady Halmady turned and stalked out, her black dress sweeping the polished boards in her wake. Alythia put a hand to her face, her ears still ringing. Selyna and Vansy hurried to her side.

"Oh, M'Lady," Selyna gasped, "you're bleeding!"

Alythia looked at her fingers and saw that it was true. Lady Halmady wore many rings. Who'd have thought that old lady could wield such a blow? Alythia had little experience in being hit. In fact, she thought dazedly, she'd not been hit since . . . since that little bitch of a sister Sashandra had given her a right hook at their brother Krystoff's funeral. She'd been hitting everyone, then. That was twelve years ago.

"That will swell up," Vansy said matter-of-factly. "Look, you can see it swelling now."

"Swell up?" Alythia felt a wave of panic. She pushed her maids aside and staggered to the mirror, peering close. The cut was as long as a fingernail and, as Vansy had said, already swelling. "Oh that . . . that horrid old bitch! Look what she's done! I'm going to kill her! All this work for nothing . . . I can't go to Sadisi like this! Like a sailor straight from a dockside brawl! What will people say?"

"M'Lady," Selyna ventured in a small voice, "perhaps you should keep your voice down a little . . ."

"What does it matter?" Alythia fumed. "She can't speak this barbarian tongue anyhow!" She yelled toward the door in Torovan, "She wouldn't learn a single syllable of that heathen monstrosity of a language, it's too far beneath her! She married *down*, you see! Down into the sewer, down into the swamp! Well how is *she* such a fucking sophisticate, when *I* can speak four languages and she can only manage one?"

She stumbled on one thick-heeled sandal in her fury, nearly falling. She tore it off her foot and threw it hard at the door. It hit with a loud crack and fell impotently to the floor.

Family Halmady left for Sadisi Festival without her. Alythia stood and watched through a small, barred window as the carriages left. Hooves clattered between mansion walls, and she caught a glimpse of armed guards hanging off the trailing carriages. Half of the house contingent, and many men from loyal, lower families, would be guarding the family's seniors: Patachi Elmar Halmady (her father-in-law), Lady Halmady, Gregan, brother Vincen and his wife Rovina, younger brother Tristi, little sister Elra and her rag-doll, Topo. The rag-doll got to go. The Lenay princess did not.

There were few good views over neighbouring streets, for defensive purposes. Serrin archers were good shots. Soon Alythia grew tired of peering through the little stone window in Vincen and Rovina's chambers, and went back to her own. But there was nothing to do besides sit on her bed and sulk.

This year's Sadisi Festival was going to be thrown at the Steiner Mansion. Family Steiner was the wealthiest, most powerful family in Petrodor. Family Halmady liked to style themselves the second-most powerful, but in Petrodor, such things were always debatable. Steiner Mansion was even more grand than Halmady Mansion, and their celebrations and parties were opulent beyond imagining. Such grand events were Alythia's raison d'être. She loved to socialise. She loved to impress. She loved to be near real power, and feel its warmth radiating through her. She'd been looking forward to this day since she'd first arrived in Petrodor. Now, it was all ruined.

The family would say she was ill. A few might believe it at first, but not later, when the gossip started. Halmady Mansion had many servants, and where there were servants, there was gossip. It had been the same in Baen-Tar. News of the conflict between Lady Halmady and her son's new wife would soon make the rounds. Such conflicts were not uncommon, she'd gathered. No doubt everyone would find it very amusing.

She snorted at the thought and curled her bare feet up on the bed, touching the swelling on her face. It wasn't all bad, she realised. Such gossip could easily hurt Lady Halmady worse than it hurt herself. Men in particular might take the beautiful princess's side before they took that crusty old battle-axe's. Especially if she gave them some extra persuasion. She thought about it for a while, watching the odd firework streak across the bay, and refusing to become too dispirited. She was clever at this kind of thing, she knew she was. It was a puzzle, but all puzzles had a solution.

After a while, she began to wish she hadn't allowed Selyna and Vansy to leave. There was a servants' party somewhere along the lower slope. They'd volunteered to stay behind and keep her company, but obviously their hearts weren't in it. Alythia couldn't blame them. Both would stay with her in Petrodor for a year to help her settle in. The pay was good, some of which would be sent back to their families in Lenayin. There was also the prospect of a Petrodor husband, one reason both were so eager to attend the Sadisi celebrations. But until that husband arrived, or the year was up and they returned home to Lenayin, they were both very much in the same position that she was—young Lenay women abroad for the first time in their lives, and very often overwhelmed by the foreignness of it all.

They were the lucky ones, though, said a small voice at the back of Alythia's mind. They'd either find a husband and stay here by choice, or they'd get to go home. You're stuck here for life, whether you like it or not.

She shoved the voice aside angrily and jumped from the bed. Damned if she'd sit here and sulk, that was just what the old witch would wish her to do. The night air was lovely in the memory of a hot day. She'd go for a walk.

The gardens of Halmady Mansion were terraced as the slope began to descend. And they were truly beautiful. Alythia walked barefoot on the lush grass, then stepped onto smooth, stone pavings. Trimmed bushes waved their leaves in a cool breeze, and the garden lamps cast gentle shadows across the slope. Water tinkled in a nearby fountain.

Alythia paused behind a garden chair. The lower garden fell away beneath, affording her a clear view over the top of the perimeter wall. At the very bottom, where the dark sea met the shore, the lights burned especially bright. Sounds carried faintly from far below; distant celebrations. The docks were full of rough folk, it was said, and they celebrated accordingly. Rough folk, serrin, and Nasi-Keth. Alythia still thought it odd that the serrin, who had so much wealth, would spend more time near the bottom of the Petrodor Incline than the top. She'd asked some of her new family about it, but none of them had an answer. None of them had ever been to the bottom of the slope, save passing through for the occasional sea voyage. And none of them expressed a desire to ever do so.

The mild air felt lovely on her skin beneath a simple, summer dress. The garden air was alive with fragrances, and the view across the fire-lit curve of Petrodor Harbour was more spectacular than even the most wonderful mountain-view in Lenayin. For a while, her face ceased to ache so badly and her frustrations faded from her mind. This transition in her life was full of challenges, but she would face them and make a good life for herself. All royal women had to go through this. Her second-eldest sister, Petryna, had married to the Lenay province of Yethulyn, where there was considerably less culture and excitement than Petrodor. Her eldest sister, Marya, of course, had married the Heir of Steiner . . . and would now be happily entertaining at the Sadisi Festival that Alythia was missing. And her littlest sister, Sofy, would soon have to manage an even more difficult transition than this one when she married the heir to Regent Arrosh in Larosa, the most powerful of the Bacosh provinces. Of all her sisters, Alythia was surely the most in her element in a social cacophony like Petrodor. If she could not survive this experience, then no one could.

The soldiers in the garden watched her as she climbed the gentle terraces back toward the house. There were always soldiers on guard these days—men from loyal houses, mostly sons of Patachi Halmady's numerous cousins, their loyalties carefully vetted.

They watched her as she walked, with just the right combination of anxious deference and obvious lust. Alythia smothered a smile and allowed her hips to swing just a little more, within the breezy folds of her dress. Torovan men were a fascinating puzzle of many contradictions. Intensely selfless in their loyal service to higher families, and yet intensely proud, too, of their own heritage. Very protective of their own female family members, and yet (she'd heard) scandalously forward in their lascivious discussions of other men's wives, sisters and daughters. Devoutly Verenthane and pious when it suited them, and yet utterly obsessed with women and sex. It made a young woman who had the gifts and the aptitude for such games feel alive.

The mansion loomed above, four floors of stone walls, segmented windows and sloping, red tile roofs. It was the most beautiful fortress Alythia had ever seen. She walked the smooth, paved patio past another fountain. Rows of columns and arches lined the patio, and she stepped through the main arch into a lamp-lit passage.

The passage opened onto the inner courtyard, a square patio overlooked with balconies on two sides, and windows on two others. About the patio, great ceramic pots with flowering plants, more water features with golden fish and green lilies, and more columns, lit with lamps. A servant hurried past the columns, but otherwise the courtyard was quiet. At least half the household staff were at Sadisi celebrations. With nothing else to do, Alythia picked a direction she'd not yet walked. She would explore.

The direction she chose led to the southern defensive wall, lined with metal spikes. Alythia walked along the wall, glancing up to see guards atop their posts. So strange to think that a house like Halmady Mansion might consider itself vulnerable. And yet she'd heard some hair-raising tales of what Nasi-Keth fighters had done to several great houses in the past. Night Wraiths, the family men called the Nasi-Keth, and sometimes the serrin too.

Shadows in the night, bloodthirsty and godless. Some men made the holy sign when they spoke of them.

The path ended in a wooden fence. Alythia peered over the gate, inside was dark. A lattice covering made for a ceiling, overgrown with a grapevine. Alythia reached over the gate and undid the latch. Closing the gate behind, she reached up for the nearest bunch of grapes. She popped one into her mouth and it was delicious. Another bunch hung near and she moved to sample it.

A throaty snarl in the dark was the first hint that she was not alone. Alythia froze, her heart pounding. That sounded like . . . She turned, very slowly. Two reflective eyes were watching her, not six paces away. The eyes moved and a chain tinkled. A shadow resolved itself. A dog, shaggy and chained. It snarled again, bloodcurdlingly. It was a big dog, too. Alythia had never particularly liked dogs. Now, that sentiment was reconfirmed a thousandfold.

Trying to stop herself from shaking with fear, she began a very slow retreat to the gate. Dogs, she recalled someone in Baen-Tar saying, could smell fear and see it in a person's posture. They reacted to that fear with fear of their own, and aggression. Best not to let them see your fear, that person had said. Well, it was too late for that, because she was terrified.

As she reached the gate, she began to hope that she might make it out without getting mauled. Then the dog lunged. Alythia screamed, colliding with the gate as she stumbled backward. The dog's chain pulled tight with a snap, its teeth snarling barely an armspan from her throat. Alythia scrambled along the overgrown fence, then fell on her backside. The dog strained, thrashing and darting, but Alythia was out of its reach.

Running footsteps came up the path and the gate rattled open. A man yelled at the dog, running at it. It backed off, then turned and lunged, only to receive a savage whack from the man's scabbard. It yelped and scrambled to retreat. Another soldier grabbed Alythia by her arm and pulled her out of the gate.

"M'Lady, are you hurt?" Other soldiers were running up, and a few servants. Alythia struggled for breath, her limbs trembling. Her knees felt as though they were about to give way. "M'Lady?" From within the enclosure, there came yells, whacks and yelps as the other soldier meted out some harsh punishment.

"I'm . . . I'm all right," she managed, breathlessly. "The chain stopped him short."

"I'm very sorry, M'Lady," said the young soldier, gallantly. He seemed most pleased at his successful rescue. "Someone should have warned you about the wolf. It was an oversight. Someone shall be punished for it, I assure you."

"Wolf?" Alythia blinked at him.

"Yes, M'Lady, it's a wolf. A she-wolf." The second soldier was emerging now, his sword and scabbard in hand, closing the gate behind him. "It was a gift from a merchant just eight months ago. A beautiful little cub it was then, with big paws and big ears, and soft grey fur. Master Tristi and Mistress Elra were very fond of it and it followed them everywhere." The soldier's lips twisted with an ironic smile. "But pretty wolf cubs, you know, they soon grow into big wolves."

"You can't keep a wolf for a pet!" Even Alythia knew that. "They can't be tamed, no matter how friendly they are when they're little! And they grow up so fast!"

"Doubtless M'Lady has much highland knowledge of such things that we lowlanders have not learned," said the soldier. "I think the animal should be killed, myself, for its own sake as much as others'. But the children still recall the little cub, and cannot bring themselves to . . ."

"Wait . . . highland knowledge?" Alythia looked back toward the gate. "It's a Lenay wolf?"

"Yes, M'Lady." The soldier's look was quizzical. "There are few wolves left in Torovan, they kill the farmers' livestock. The dukes of many regions offer great rewards for wolf pelts. The merchant who brought this cub had just returned from Lenayin. What happened to its mother, I do not know."

Alythia ventured cautiously back toward the gate. The second soldier stood aside, with a questioning look to his companion. Alythia ignored them, and peered over the gate. The wolf now huddled in a far corner, mostly invisible in the dark. A Lenay wolf. She'd heard them howling, once or twice, when she'd visited Baen-Tar town nearer the forest at the bottom of Baen-Tar hill. Now it was here, chained in a Petrodor mansion, where no Lenayin wolf had any business being.

Strangely, she found herself recalling a silly argument her wild brat sister Sashandra had had with their brother Damon upon one of her rare visits to Baen-Tar many years ago. "They don't attack people, Damon!" Sashandra had insisted, as loudly as always. "That's a Verenthane myth! They might eat you once you're already dead, but they're scared of people, mostly. They'll only attack if they're scared and cornered, or if they're protecting their cubs!" Sashandra might have been a crazy, selfish tomboy, but she certainly knew animals.

Scared. She'd walked into its enclosure, a stranger in the dark. Those snarling teeth, those laid-back ears . . . they'd certainly scared *her* well enough, but it'd been the wolf who'd been terrified first. Perhaps it had cause to be terrified. Perhaps it had learned to be. Now it huddled in the dark, beaten, bruised and chained.

"Perhaps," said the small, dark voice in the back of her head, "in a few more years, that will be you."

The narrow path climbed steeply up a flight of crumbling stairs, then took a sharp turn past a garden wall. Sasha moved quietly in Rhillian's wake, hoping she could be half as quiet as the graceful serrin. Errollyn followed and Aisha brought up the rear, their blades drawn. The alley narrowed, then opened and suddenly there was a marvellous view of the harbour, and light enough to see the path clearly. The three serrin and Sasha pressed close to an uphill wall, and the protective shadow. Directly below were people's yards, small vegetable gardens. From here, agile people could climb onto roofs, run along walltops, and into courtyards. For people who knew Petrodor's alleys, and had the vision to move through them at night, the city lay exposed.

The alley turned uphill again; a steep, ragged stairway between walls so close Sasha had to keep her arms tight to her sides. A cat sprinted before them in panic, and leapt a wall. Rhillian jogged easily, leaving the steps where they curled around a large tree growing from the rock, finding foot holds on its big, exposed roots. Then she paused, and pointed at the step ahead with her blade, for Sasha's benefit. When she hurdled the step in question, Sasha vaguely saw a trip-string in the gloom, doubtless rigged through a gap in the neighbouring wall, where it would ring a bell and warn of wraiths passing in the night. Petrodor's alleys were full of such devices, more use against night-blind humans than serrin. Sasha pointed to the step for Errollyn, hurdled it and jogged onward up the steep, winding stairs.

They crossed several narrow roads that wove their way across the slope, past brick and stone buildings with shutters tightly closed. The din of voices and music seemed to grow louder as they climbed. Further along one road, Sasha saw a great mass of people gathered outside a bar, with fires, music and dancing. At another crossroad, a stray dog barked madly and charged them, but Aisha hit it with a stone from her pocket and it sprinted yelping in the other direction. Its companion, however, chased them up the alley, growling and barking, and another of Aisha's well-thrown stones only seemed to infuriate it.

Aisha prepared her blade, but Errollyn pushed back past her, fake-stepped left, then hook-kicked with his right, crunching the dog so hard to the head it fairly spun about and rebounded off the wall. It lay still, then tried to rise, then fell again.

"Errollyn!" Aisha said with annoyance, moving back to kneel by the scraggly, bony animal. She felt its neck, then made a face, drew her blade and cut its throat. "Why not just use your sword? It's kinder."

"My *tel'shan'til* needs practice," Errollyn explained easily. It was a form of unarmed combat, mastered in Saalshen, like the svaalverd. Aisha wiped her blade on the dog's mangy coat and waved them onward, irritated. The path was briefly wide enough for two and Sasha fell back to Errollyn's side.

"And here I thought you loved animals," she remarked. She had no great love of the stray mutts of Petrodor, but Errollyn's methods seemed needlessly callous. Sometimes, he just seemed . . . unpredictable. Dangerous, even.

His green eyes flashed in the dark as he looked at her. He was not a small man, nor a weak one, yet his presence seemed to fill more of her awareness than mere size could explain. "The strays around here are diseased," he said. "The aggressive ones are either so hungry they're insensible, or possibly rabid. In the wild, nature culls the weak and sick. Here, they are kept alive."

"You could have used your sword," Sasha echoed Aisha's scolding.

"When a mouse attacks a bear in the woods," Errollyn continued, "and the bear swallows the mouse whole, do you feel sorry for the mouse?"

"If one happens to have a soft spot for suicidal mice, I suppose one might."

"There's a great difference," Errollyn replied with a smile, "between those who say they merely love nature, and those who proclaim to learn from it." Sasha gave him a long, wary look . . . but then the path was narrowing again and she had to move ahead to keep in single file.

Finally, as the noise ahead seemed at its peak, Rhillian paused beside a wall where the growing trunk of a tree had cracked the bricks outward. Rhillian climbed with ease while Sasha sheathed her sword and clambered over branches in Rhillian's wake, then along the wall to a flat rooftop. Along the hard tiles of the rooftop, then a stiff-fingered climb up a short length of vertical, stone wall, and pulled herself over the top.

Here was a wide, flat roof of paved tiles, flanked on all sides by plants in clay pots and walls made light with patterned holes. There were also some chairs, a little table and a trapdoor in the centre of the roof.

The noise from the street below was deafening. Rhillian sat on a bench behind the low wall, and peered over. Sasha, Errollyn and Aisha gathered alongside. The street was broad enough for two carts, and cut diagonally up the slope. Its sides were lined with crowds of people. Directly below, a team of shirtless men were manoeuvring a big, open cart down the hill, backward. Towering within its tray loomed a great, stone statue of a half-naked man with enormous muscles, a sword in one hand, a staff in the other. The statue looked to be solid rock, and more men stood within the cart to keep it from toppling on the sloping cobbles.

The statue stood adorned in a giant, purple cloak with golden arrowheads, and had a huge, eight-pointed Verenthane medallion about its neck. Around its great, muscular arms were flower garlands, silk tresses and silver bells. The men on the ropes heaved and yelled, muscles straining, while others moved ahead downslope, directing the way or helping to steer. Several carried great wooden blocks to jam under the wheels and the cart tried to run away. The crowd yelled and threw things. Musicians followed the descent, a colourful, unholy racket of trumpets and drums.

"House Firis!" Errollyn shouted over the noise, grinning. "They look to be struggling a little! The night's young yet, perhaps they went out too hard on the first climb!"

Sasha stared down in wide-eyed amazement. Behind the musicians trailing House Firis, another cart was descending into view between close, roadside walls. What happened if one of them lost control? The thought didn't seem to bother the roadside crowds, many of whom moved alongside their chosen team yelling encouragement. The Endurance would go on all night. Surely not all of these teams would have enough fit men to make the final, dawn climb back up the incline.

The statues, Sasha knew, were of Saint Sadis himself. It had astonished her when she'd first seen them. Her knowledge of Verenthane saints was limited to Saint Ambellion, the man who had brought the faith to Lenayin. He was depicted as an old man in robes, walking in worn sandals with the help of a gnarled staff. Saint Sadis was, by comparison, sexy.

When Saint Sadis had first come from the Bacosh, Petrodor was just a little fishing village ruled by a local duke who lived in a castle atop the incline. Legend had it that Sadis's preaching had insulted the duke, who sentenced Sadis to ten days of the worst labour in Petrodor—hauling carts up and down the slope from the shoreline below. In those ten days, the story went, Sadis had borne incredible loads with tireless determination, and had shown no sign of weakness. Men had asked for the secret of his strength, and had learned that it came from the Verenthane gods. From that inspiration, the Verenthane faith had grown strong in Petrodor. Every Sadisi, men spent one day, and all of the night, hauling laden carts up and down the slopes to commemorate Sadis's efforts, and to demonstrate their own faith-through-endurance to the gods. They'd been going since dawn, and the strain was showing.

"Whose house are we standing on?" Sasha thought to ask.

"Friends," said Rhillian, with a vague shrug. Despite her usual directness, Rhillian could be as obtuse as any serrin where questions of security were concerned. "I don't see any of the Firis sons present."

"Busy elsewhere, no doubt," Errollyn agreed. "The sons are usually the most eager to represent their house. I see a few cousins I recognise, some uncles, lots of minor related houses. No, wait . . . there's Georgy Firis. At the end of the second rope."

"Only a grandson," said Rhillian, with a faint shake of the head. "Not a great commitment from a senior Steiner ally to the Endurance. Evidently they have matters more pressing."

"More talks?" Sasha asked, frowning. "Even on Sadisi?"

"House Steiner holds a great festival celebration at the Steiner Mansion," said Rhillian. "Everyone shall be there. Your sisters included."

Marya and Alythia. It felt strange to be so far from home, and to know that two of her sisters were so near. Marya was wife to Symon Steiner, the eldest son of Patachi Marlen Steiner. Once the patachi died, Marya would be the wife of the most powerful man in Petrodor. There were four children, none of whom Sasha had met. It had been fourteen years, in fact, since she'd last seen Marya. Sometimes she hoped, perhaps forlornly, for a reunion. She doubted that the grand house of Steiner would be pleased at the prospect.

She'd beaten Alythia's wedding train into Petrodor by ten days. The wedding had been five days after that . . . two weeks ago now. She'd only seen the wedding from a distance. She was not insulted at having been excluded from the invitations. She greatly doubted that House Halmady would have been any more thrilled to see her than House Steiner. And, unlike Marya, Alythia would most likely have shared the sentiment.

By such ties did the greatest trading city in all Rhodia bind itself to the highlands barbarian kingdom. Houses that were not even royal—made noble only by their colossal, garish accumulation of wealth—wedded various princesses of Lenayin in order to ensure the loyalty of their uncivilised neighbours. Sasha had never been one to place much store in the divine rights of noble birth, and yet she still found something about it all distasteful. Well, she thought grimly, watching the men of House Firis straining against their burden, this is one Princess of Lenayin who's not for sale.

"You didn't just invite me up here to watch the parade, did you?" Sasha asked Rhillian, warily. Rhillian gave her a brilliant, faintly dangerous smile.

"*Ar'mahler t'eign*," she said, reproachfully. *Arnai*, meaning "indelicate" or "graceless," elided to *leimahler*, meaning "opinion" . . . but very close to *leimas*, meaning "view." And *eign* from *rhe'leign*, meaning "future" . . . but elided to the omnipresent *tas*, implying the subjective, rather than the objective. Implying, perhaps, that the holder of such an indelicate opinion (suspicion?) was . . . paranoid? Was not thinking clearly? Had struck close in her suggestion, but not accurately? Or all of the above . . . or none?

"*Ny as'sere sa'toth khan*," Sasha retorted. "Don't play games with me." Saalsi was poetic, and obtuse, and could be read backward, forward and any combination in between. A language of poets, philosophers and dreamers, for whom the form was often more important than the function. She'd learned it well, by human standards, in her twelve years in the Lenayin wilds with Kessligh. When she was younger, he'd sometimes insisted they spoke nothing but Saalsi for months. But it still confused her at times, to hear those familiar forms upon the lips of serrin. Serrin who used words as a dockside juggler tossed knives, a dazzling play of surprise and misdirection.

"You can often tell who's plotting what just by watching people," Aisha said cheerfully in Saalsi, gazing down on the road. Aisha was usually cheerful, and had the good manners not to twist her Saalsi into knots that strained a poor human's comprehension. Being half-human herself, she had more sympathy for their shortcomings. "For instance, look . . . up the road here, at the next cart. That's House Esheron. And here carrying the wheel blocks is Ellot Esheron, Patachi Esheron's brother . . . only his arm is in a sling, and he appears to be limping, which explains why he's carrying the blocks instead of manning a rope. An accident, or has he been fighting with someone?"

"It's rumoured he and his brother don't get along well," Errollyn said thoughtfully. "There was that missing Ameryn shipment, and the short-changing of the moneylenders."

"Perhaps the moneylenders tried to get even," Rhillian suggested.

"Or perhaps his wife beat him up again!" Aisha laughed. "She's a fierce one!"

The three serrin continued the commentary as house after house passed with their laden carts down the Corkscrew. Their knowledge of the inner doings of the Petrodor families seemed inexhaustible. But then, the *talmaad* served Saalshen. It was their business to know, and they had plenty of gold to spend for the knowing.

Sasha's interest increased considerably as the cart of House Halmady came into view. The livery was black and red, the statue of Saint Sadis pointing with one accusing forefinger, eyes intent above a flowing beard. The crowd of followers about the Halmady cart seemed particularly large and vocal. The trailing musicians made a din that could barely be described as music.

"You'd think the second-most powerful house in Petrodor could afford some decent musicians," Sasha suggested with a wince.

"Look," said Rhillian, with a deadly straight stare. "By the left wheel. He wears a silver bracelet."

"Oh yes," Aisha agreed, leaning on the wall to peer closely. Errollyn, Sasha noticed, was watching the windows and rooftops of surrounding buildings. His vision was even sharper than Rhillian's and he'd strung his bow. His skill with that bow had to be seen to be believed. "That's a silver chain. Pretty."

"So what?" Sasha said.

"Duke Tarabai's men have a liking for silver jewellery," Aisha explained, her blue eyes not leaving the scene. In the confusion of men, alive with shadows in the light from many torches and lamps, Sasha had no idea how they could make out individual pieces of jewellery. "Danor has some marvellous silver mines. We trade for silver quite frequently, there's not much in Saalshen."

"Thieves," Errollyn added. "We've not had a fair price from them yet, since there's so little competition. Tassi was the only one who came close." There was a sadness in his voice. Aisha looked sad, too. Sasha remembered their friend Tassi, and then the sadness was hers as well.

"To his left now is Daneri Belary," Rhillian added.

"Truly?" Aisha peered more closely. "Errollyn, can you see?"

Errollyn spared the approaching cart a brief glance. "Daneri Belary, and Jonti Maer," he said.

"Where?" Rhillian searched. "Oh yes, in the cart, supporting the statue."

"Daneri Belary would be Duke Belary's heir?" Sasha wondered.

"No, second son," said Rhillian. "Duke Belary and heir will be at the Steiner Mansion. The Endurance is a boy's adventure. A symbol of trust and allegiance between the dukes and House Steiner. Jonti Maer is the heir to Family Maer, another of Vedichi's most prominent."

"Steiner's allegiance grows wide," Sasha observed.

Rhillian nodded. "The question is how wide?"

Duke Tarabai was the feudal lord of the northern Torovan province of Danor. Duke Belary was the lord of western Vedichi. Sasha knew little enough of Torovan lords and their doings, except that here, the land was worked and owned in feudal ways that had not yet been successfully introduced in Lenayin, and spirits willing never would be. Sasha had led a rebellion, in part, to prevent such a thing. And had been exiled from her homeland by her own father, King Torvaal of Lenayin, for her trouble.

The relationship between the city of Petrodor and its feudal provinces, she was gathering, was curious. Most of Petrodor, when drawn upon a map, fell within the province of Coroman, but two hundred years of accumulated wealth and power had made the city a power unto itself, far beyond the control of feudal dukes. Petrodor was also the seat of Verenthane power in Torovan, and indeed in all northern Rhodia. Most of Torovan's wealth found its way through Petrodor at one time or another, and regional dukes and nobles who knew what was good for them paid homage, and were rewarded.

Until recently, the great houses of Petrodor had needed the Torovan dukes for one thing only—trade. Now, with war afoot in the Bacosh, the houses discovered that the dukes had one other thing that Petrodor could use.

Soldiers. At the bidding of the holy brotherhood in the Porsada Temple, House Steiner and its allies were trying to raise an army to reclaim the "holy lands"—the Bacosh provinces of Rhodaan, Enora and Ilduur, which had fallen under the sway of Saalshen two centuries before. When the then-king of all the Bacosh, Leyvaan, had failed in the invasion of Saalshen, Saalshen's counter-invasion had taken the three nearest Bacosh provinces for a buffer, and changed them beyond recognition. That change had profoundly disturbed Rhodia's holy brotherhood, leading finally to the Archbishop of Petrodor's most recent declarations of Holy Crusade. And the Petrodor *talmaad*, under the archbishop's very nose, now attempted to disrupt those preparations for war by any means possible.

Rhillian drew a deep breath, a hand on her stomach. She belched, softly. "Too many prawns?" Sasha suggested.

Rhillian smiled. "Humans can claim most follies as their own, except excess. We serrin invented that."

"And arrogance," Errollyn added. Rhillian shrugged. "Indecisiveness," Errollyn continued. "Self-importance. Complacency. Lust."

"Oh no," said Aisha, shaking her head, "I like lust."

"Ambiguity," said Errollyn. "Moral equivalence. Laziness."

"Never knowing when to shut up," Rhillian added, with a sharp glance. Errollyn met her gaze with a half-smile. For a brief instant, the air between them seemed to crackle.

A loud crash from upslope interrupted. Music and shouting on the road below paused. Then came distant yells from around the uphill corner. The crowd began to surge in that direction.

"There was bound to be at least one," said Errollyn, sliding to his feet, bow in hand. "Come on."

They abandoned their rooftop and made their way along the dark back alleys parallel to the road. When the shouting grew louder, Rhillian led them up another winding stairway. The alley mouth opened onto the road. Rhillian took the left corner, Errollyn the right, with Sasha in the middle. Aisha remained behind, to cover their backs.

To the left, now downslope after their climb, a confused crowd pressed about an overturned cart. The Sadis statue had clearly fallen, injured men were carried from the press, some clutching broken limbs. Others yelled and gave directions, frantically, searching for family or friends.

"House Ragini," said Rhillian. "Another of House Steiner's lackeys."

Errollyn, Sasha noted, was once again searching the surrounding buildings, with barely a glance at the chaos. He held his enormous bow like a staff, one hand lingering by the quiver of arrows at his hip.

Now from the crowd, a man was being carried, arms limp, head lolling. His hair was wet with blood. "Looks like he broke more than just his arm," Sasha observed.

"That's Randel Ragini." Rhillian's voice was hard, with suspicious certainty. "Patachi Ragini's heir. How convenient."

Sasha frowned. "Convenient?"

"In Torovan it's *maradis nal-maradis*," Rhillian explained. Fortuitous ill-fortune, Sasha translated. She almost hadn't noticed they were still speaking Saalsi. "The convenient accident. Like when the Endurance statue topples over, and it just happens to be the family heir who's killed."

"How do you know it's no accident?" Sasha replied. "This whole crazy festival's just an accident waiting to happen!"

"Those are the best kinds," said Errollyn, his eyes not leaving the surrounding buildings. "Welcome to Petrodor."

"Come," said Rhillian, watching as the men laid the body by the side of the road. Some were weeping, gesticulating with both hands to the night sky. "We'd best go. This one will have repercussions."

"Why?" asked Sasha. "What was House Ragini involved with?"

Three

DUKE ALEXANDA ROCHEL watched the stone walls pass his carriage window, as the wheels clattered over cobblestones. It had been a long bumpy ride on bad roads, climbing switchbacks through some truly bad neighbourhoods of crumbling hutments and outright slums. Now, the cobbles jarred his teeth and bounced the wide-brimmed hat upon his head.

On the seat opposite, his daughter Bryanne peered wide-eyed through the window, trying to see above the high walls that lined the ridgetop road. Bryanne had never seen Petrodor. Like all Torovan noble children, she had been raised on stories of its wealth and grandeur. Alexanda saw the faint bewilderment on her face, the surprised dismay. So far, she'd seen slums and walls topped with sharpened spikes. Not to worry, child, Alexanda thought grimly, it only gets worse from here. Gods how he hated Petrodor. He was so pleased to be invited to Patachi Steiner's Sadisi party, he could just hit something. Preferably Patachi Steiner.

"Don't look so *grim*, dearest," said his wife, the Duchess Varona, from his side. She was dressed in her finest gown, a tight-waisted, shoulderless, velvety black and sequinned silver piece that displayed a figure well preserved for her thirty-eight summers. The curls in her black hair, and the pale powder and red paint of the makeup, had taken her and her maids since lunchtime to arrange. "I'm sure it shall be a lovely evening. Bryanne, I'm so looking forward to introducing you around. You look truly lovely."

Bryanne, a pale, slightly pudgy girl who at fifteen had yet to grow properly into her womanhood, bit her lip. Her hair, dress and makeup only added to her father's sour mood. This was not the little girl he knew. All dressed up to impress some boot-licking little Petrodor mummy's boy. Bryanne was a quiet, obedient girl who liked to paint flowers in the garden on a warm summer's day. He'd have more gladly thrown her into a den of hungry wolves than the pack of insolent, insufferable masculinity he was sure to find at Patachi Steiner's but Varona had insisted. She meets so few eligible boys in Pazira, she'd complained. She needs to broaden her horizons, instead of sitting around all day painting and daydreaming.

Alexanda recognised the walls of several great mansions from the crests beside their huge, metal-barred gates. Here was House Halmady, headed by the particularly vile Patachi Elmar Halmady. His heir Gregan had recently married a Lenay princess. Lenay princesses were apparently all the style these days, in Petrodor. Royalty—the latest accessory for the fashionable elite. Alexanda snorted to himself. Lenay royalty only, however. It had the sad desperation of the nouveau riche, buying gaudy jewels from the worst dockside merchants without questioning their true origin or quality. Still, any royalty was impressive enough for Torovan, whose last true king had been some seven hundred years ago. Or rather, it was impressive enough for families whose wealth and power barely dated one and a half centuries. Family Rochel, on the other hand, was old money. Alexanda Rochel traced his noble claim to the Dukedom of Pazira back through twenty-three generations of forefathers. Petrodor wealth and promises might have impressed others of the Torovan dukehood, but it certainly did not impress *him*.

The carriage clattered to a halt. Ahead, there came shouts from the leading guard cart to Steiner soldiers manning the gate. Immediately there were Pazira soldiers to the left and right of the carriage, maroon and gold colours over armour, eyes watchful beneath crested helms. These days more than others, a heavy guard was required to travel through the City of the Night.

A loud squealing from ahead, and the forward carts resumed their clatter. The carriage followed, and then the walls of Steiner Mansion were passing, manned by watchful Steiner guards. The cobblestone path descended, turned, and then there were great, stone columns on the right. Soldiers opened the carriage doors, and Duke Alexanda Rochel of Pazira took a deep breath and stepped into the warm Petrodor night.

He turned to help his wife and daughter from the carriage, and was then greeted by a handsome, thin-bearded man with a pointy chin and dagger-sharp eyes, splendidly dressed in a tight, embroidered jacket and colourful shirt with a wide, angular collar.

"Duke Alexanda," said Symon Steiner, heir of Family Steiner. He bowed, as did Alexanda, then clasped hands. The man wore enough rings to make a woman blush, the duke noted acidly. "A great pleasure to greet you once more. My father shall be so pleased that the duke of Torovan's most beautiful province has managed to attend our little function."

"The pleasure is mine," Alexanda said gruffly, but Symon had already moved to kiss his wife's hand. Varona loved it, of course.

"My beautiful Duchess, you look ravishing this fine evening."

"Oh Master Steiner, you flatter me." Alexanda made a low growl in his throat, but no one noticed.

"But not at all, my Lady. Your beauty defies even Master Time, you grow only more radiant each time we meet. And this lovely creature must be Bryanne." He kissed the girl's hand as well. Varona shot her husband a stern glance, silencing his impatience. Alexanda grunted. "Dear girl, I can vouch that there will be many, many young men desperate for your hand in a dance tonight. Please do not disappoint too many of them, we have not the medicines in our house for so many broken hearts."

Bryanne blushed bright red and mumbled a reply. Symon looked about in further surprise. "Duke Rochel, you have only brought your lovely daughter? But where are your handsome sons?"

"My husband felt that the household should not be left unattended," said Varona, smoothly intervening. "The rains shall be on us soon, and the planting, and Carlito can use the experience of managing affairs on his own."

"Oh, a great pity," Symon said sadly. "I had looked forward to seeing them both again."

Do you think I'd bring my heirs to this treacherous snakepit? Alexanda fumed silently. With whatever devious poison you and the priests are no doubt conniving? If disaster befalls on this journey, you'll only get me, *not* my sons.

The entrance hall of Steiner Mansion was imposing. A huge, wide floor of polished marble so smooth it gleamed like ice. Overhead, five great chandeliers blazed the incandescent light of a hundred candles each, refracting from many thousands of crystal beads.

Some Steiner cousins attended them across the floor, Duchess Varona leading the way, Bryanne staring about in awe. *This* was the Petrodor of her bedtime stories. Everywhere were bustling servants and watching guards. Ill-gotten gains, all of it, Alexanda thought darkly, surveying the surroundings as he walked. Serrin wealth. In his great-grandfather's day, merchants had held a station little above that of prostitutes. Now, they built preposterous monstrosities like this to intimidate the true nobility, and make stars in their wives' and daughters' eyes.

They were led along the main hall through the mansion's centre, one magnificent, gleaming room after another. Finally they emerged onto broad steps opening onto a vast patio and expansive gardens beyond, crowded with people. Jewellery flashed, and embroidery glimmered under the light of ornamental torches. A small orchestra played and perhaps a hundred elegant ladies and gentlemen made slow, spinning circles on the pavings. There were long tables, piled with luscious food, and servants darting amidst the guests to replace all that was consumed with new dishes from the kitchens. Draping the tables, the columns above the stairs, and even some trees, were colourful festival decorations. Beyond, and about, lay the vast, glittering expanse of Petrodor Harbour.

"Excuse me, Duke Rochel?" Alexanda turned to find a woman approaching up the stairs, a little girl in her arms. The woman had long, dark hair, tastefully arranged to a knot at the back, and wore a rich, green gown. She seemed perhaps thirty-five, with a round face, a pleasant smile, and a weight to her hips and bust that was typical of a wealthy Torovan woman. "Oh how lovely to see you once more. My husband is performing his duties well at the door, I trust?"

"Lady Marya Steiner," said the duke, gravely, and kissed her offered hand. "Your husband was most eloquent, as always. I believe you have not made the acquaintance of my wife, the Duchess Varona?"

"A true pleasure." Unlike most wealthy Torovan women, with Marya Steiner, one could almost believe she meant it. Though married to a Torovan for fourteen years, she still spoke the tongue with a thick, musical highlands brogue. As Duke of Pazira, the western half of which was one long, uphill climb into Lenayin, Alexanda had had plenty of experience with highlanders. There were those who said that the accent was so strong it was infectious and could be caught when the wind changed from the west, like a cold. Once caught, it stayed for life.

"And you must be Bryanne!" Marya exclaimed. "Aren't you pretty!"

"Thank you, Princess Marya," Bryanne said shyly. "Is that Shyana you're carrying? She's very pretty."

"Yes, this is Shyana." Marya said, kissing the sleeping girl on the hair. "She's only two, she's very tired. I was just about to take her upstairs to sleep. Would you like to come?"

"Oh could I?"

"Lady Marya, you're too kind," Varona interrupted, "but I had really thought to introduce Bryanne to the dance at the earliest—"

"Oh, dear Duchess," Marya laughed, "I'll make certain she's introduced to all the most handsome boys personally. But first, she can help me put my little girl to bed, yes?"

"Oh . . . well, of course." Varona smiled, thinly.

Marya appeared not to notice the discomfort, took Bryanne's hand, and swept toward the big, guarded rear door. "Do you know any lullabies, Bryanne? Tell me which are your favourites?"

"All these servants and nannies to take care of the children, but she takes her girl to bed herself," Alexanda said approvingly, watching them leave. "That's a true Torovan woman for you. Pity we have to go to Lenayin these days to find one."

"Oh, Alexanda, really," Varona huffed. "It's all very well for her, all the most eligible men will be falling over themselves trying to marry *her* daughters."

"My vast apologies for *only* being the Duke of Pazira," Alexanda growled.

Before long, the senior men were invited to gather in Patachi Steiner's study, on the third floor overlooking the celebrations. The room was grand, its walls lined with books in polished bookcases, a large writing desk in a corner, with a view of the harbour. Alexanda stood before the open balcony doors, a glass of wine in hand, and gazed out at the view until Patachi Steiner himself had arrived. The pompous git had to be the last one in, of course.

Reluctantly turning, Alexanda considered the gathering. Patachi Marlen Steiner was looking old, his broad shoulders now stooped, his white shoulder-length hair thinning on top. Where once his beard had accentuated a fine jaw, it now hung sagging upon loose folds of neck. But his eyes were watchful, and full of knowledge.

Symon Steiner stood talking to Duke Tarabai of Danor, a tall man with a square face and big ears. As far away as possible, examining books on an ornate shelf, was Duke Tosci, a man as solid and squat as a statue. Tosci and Tarabai continued the tradition of hatred between Coroman and Danor provinces. Surely even a man as dull as Duke Tosci knew that the families liked to play Coroman and Danor against each other? Or then again, Alexanda pondered, perhaps he was the only thinking duke in Torovan.

Also present were four other patachis. Alexanda recognised only one— Patachi Elmar Halmady, Marlen Steiner's right-hand man. He had far better things to do than memorise the faces of this quibbling crowd. Duke Belary of Vedichi, fat, bearded and stupid, sidling now to Steiner's side, Alexanda knew only too well and he loathed him most of all.

"My friends," said Patachi Steiner, "a toast to Saint Sadis." He took a cup from a nephew, there were no servants in the room tonight, and held it aloft. All drank.

"A toast to the archbishop!" said Patachi Halmady, and all drank to that as well.

"A toast to our gathering of families," Patachi Steiner finished. A nephew made the rounds with a wine decanter, refilling the men's cups. Even the boys had swords at their hips. "I shall begin proceedings by relating the latest news from my good friend King Torvaal Lenayin. The rebellion in their north has truly ended. Lenayin stands ready to serve the Verenthane cause, and preparations are being made even now to muster a great army."

"That is good news," said one of the patachis. "Our forces grow strong. Even the Saalshen Bacosh cannot stand against us."

"Good news?" exclaimed Duke Tarabai of Danor. "It's phenomenal! The only thing in all the world those barbarians are good for is fighting! Usually they just fight each other or the Cherrovan, but now! An entire, united army of Lenayin! Good gods, should they march with us on our crusade they'll wipe the Bacosh clean of serrin single-handedly. The rest of us will just need to watch and applaud."

"And what of the girl?" asked Duke Tosci of Coroman. "Is it true that she's come to Petrodor?"

"Assuredly," said Patachi Halmady, gravely. "And her uman."

"Then Kessligh Cronenverdt truly led the Lenay rebellion?" asked another patachi.

"No," said Symon Steiner. "It seems that the great Nasi-Keth left Lenayin for Petrodor well before the rebellion. Sashandra Lenayin led the rebellion on her own, and survived."

"And fled in terror for her life!" Duke Tarabai added.

"She was expelled from Lenayin by her father," Symon Steiner corrected, elegantly fingering his wine cup. "After producing from him some very reasonable terms, sparing the lives and fortunes of those who followed her."

Some of the men appeared disquieted at that. No one questioned the heir of Steiner's information. Family Steiner, it was well known, had a great many sources, in all the most unlikely places.

"Well, better her leading the rebellion than Cronenverdt," said another of the patachis. "That man has too much standing already, Lenay Commander of Armies and hero in a land that loves war and heroes more than most. If the Nasi-Keth unites beneath his leadership, we shall have trouble."

"No," said Duke Tosci, somewhat gloomily. The expression suited his dark, downcast features. "Not better. Much, much worse. A Nasi-Keth uman draws much status from his uma . . . his pupil, if you will. It was said of Kessligh Cronenverdt that his achievements in Lenayin are so formidable, the only thing he lacked was an uma to match them. And now, his uma has become legend by her own hand. And she's a *princess*. This will complicate King Torvaal's position. And ours, when Cronenverdt's prestige rises even higher, with the girl now at his side, here in Petrodor."

Alexanda saw the dark look that passed between several of the dukes and patachis. Being of Coroman, Duke Tosci was the best informed of all the dukes on affairs in Petrodor. His knowledge gave him an advantage, and the others didn't like it.

"Duke Rochel," said Patachi Steiner, his gaze settling upon Alexanda. "You know the highlanders well. What think you of this outcome?"

"Outcome?" Alexanda said dryly. "There is no outcome, Marlen." Several men frowned at that informality. Alexanda did not care. "The matters that divide the men of Lenayin divide them still. I believe this rebellion was overdue, in truth. King Torvaal is an honest and trustworthy man, but his circumstance makes him a poor ally. Lenayin is unstable, it always has been, and always shall be. Only a fool would hope otherwise. Should an army of Torovan march into the Bacosh to fight with the Larosa, the army of Lenayin could just as likely prove our doom as our victory, you mark my words."

"If you don't wish to fight, Alexanda," Duke Tarabai said loudly, "just say so. Rather than invent these pitiful excuses to frighten us all."

"Only a fool, I said," Alexanda repeated, with a glare at the tall Duke of Danor.

"Will you not fight, Alexanda?" Patachi Steiner asked. His tone was still, his eyes unreadable. This man had ordered more men killed than Alexanda had drunk cups of wine. The gaze of such a man held a great weight, regardless of his expression. "I am informed that you have come with a guard of four hundred soldiers?"

"Five hundred," Alexanda replied, matching Steiner's gaze. "These are but a token. Archbishop Augine himself has called for men of faith to make war in the Bacosh, to reclaim the holy lands of Enora, Rhodaan and Ilduur from the serrin. I have many more men of faith in Pazira who stand ready to join such a quest. I merely state that no battle was ever won by wishful thinking. Should the men of Pazira join an army of Torovan in the march south, we should be fully prepared for all eventualities."

"And beneath whose *banner* shall you march, Alexanda?" asked Duke Belary. His jowled, bearded face was pink with the pleasure of his insinuation.

"I am here, aren't I?" Alexanda said coldly. "Where are the Dukes of Songel and Cisseren, might I ask? Why not aim your barbs at them?"

"They accepted other invitations," Patachi Halmady said coldly. Family Maerler, he meant. The rivals. The enemy. Family Steiner were not the only ones who knew how to throw a Sadisi party.

"As is their right," said Patachi Steiner, mildly. "Family Maerler have stronger holdings in the south, it is only natural that Songel and Cisseren should accept their invitation. More talks shall be had. We shall see if there is an understanding to be reached between us."

Which, Alexanda thought darkly, could mean anything from innocent dialogue to mass slaughter. He had not brought five hundred soldiers merely to demonstrate his readiness for war—he'd brought them for protection, too. Patachi Steiner, for reasons that eluded Alexanda, saw a profit in this mad war. If an army of Torovan was to be formed, Family Steiner wanted command. House Maerler most likely wished the same. Gods prevail upon them all a rare common sense and civility, Alexanda thought. Or else there'll be trouble.

"The girl," said Duke Belary, scratching at where his beard failed to cover his second and third chins. "She should be killed."

"And Cronenverdt too," agreed Duke Tarabai, nodding vigorously.

The patachis, Alexanda noted, showed little enthusiasm at the suggestion. "Easier said than done," said Patachi Halmady. He was a tall, thoughtful man of a mild temperament. It was said he had a taste for books and learning. It was also said that his interests sometimes made the brothers from the Porsada Temple uncomfortable. He did not show any outward sign of ambition, and was said by some to lack the spine of Patachi Steiner and his ilk. It made Halmady a safe, reliable ally for Steiner—a rare thing in Petrodor. "The Nasi-Keth are formidable warriors, and they have much support across the lower slopes. We do not venture there lightly, my Dukes."

"Allow entry for two hundred of my best men," Duke Tarabai boasted. "I have swordsmen in Danor without equal. Tell us where they live, and we shall storm the place and have their heads."

Amongst the patachis, eyes were rolled. "Are you that eager to lose two hundred men, Duke Tarabai?" one asked.

"Such has been tried before," Symon Steiner said coolly. "There are many hundreds of Nasi-Keth, my Duke. Perhaps as many as fifteen hundred. They fight like demons, and they own the alleyways as surely as the cats. The poor love them and will warn of any move in force. Worse, the poor will barricade, and spy, and drop flaming jars from the windows. And, in all likelihood, the serrin will help them. There are at least two hundred of the *talmaad* in Petrodor, probably more of late. Senior Nasi-Keth also move from house to house and rarely stay in the same lodgings for long, so their location can hardly ever be guaranteed. Even should your two hundred men survive long enough to reach the target, the house would likely be empty . . . and very few of your men would live to escape back here to the higher slopes."

Duke Tarabai drew himself up, bristling. "You underestimate my men, young Steiner—"

"There shall be no such attempt," said Patachi Steiner, with a sharp gesture of his hand. "The forces of the provinces shall not operate in the city without the consent of the families. And we do not give it."

Duke Tarabai paled a little beneath the patachi's stare. "As you say, Patachi. I meant no offence."

"You are correct in one thing, though," the patachi continued. "Cronenverdt and his girl make matters complicated. It shall be difficult to raise any army and come to an understanding with the Maerler, with the Nasi-Keth suddenly militant and interfering beneath Cronenverdt's command. But one must know the city, Duke Tarabai. You are a foreigner from the countryside. I—" he raised a crooked forefinger, "I have lived in this city for all my sixty-four years. I have done business here, and I have made fortunes here. I tell you that there are other ways, Duke Tarabai, to resolve a problem, than the brutal force of a direct assault. Such is not the Petrodor way."

Duke Tarabai made a small bow. "I concede to your wisdom, Patachi. What are your plans?"

The great man of Petrodor gave the Duke of Danor a lingering, watchful stare. "When I need you to know," he said simply, "I shall tell you."

"Well it wasn't me," said Rhillian, sipping a cup of water. "It's the usual Petrodor tangle. Anyone could have killed Randel Ragini."

The bar was dingy, old plank walls lit with dull lamps, small, scattered tables frequented by a few quiet patrons. Most of The Fish Head's usual customers were outside.

Sasha sat alongside Rhillian, watching Kessligh's expression. Aiden, one of Kessligh's closest allies amongst the Nasi-Keth, wore a thinking look. They spoke Saalsi, as was common between Nasi-Keth and serrin in Petrodor. Very few who were not one or the other could speak it with any fluency. It made spies less of a problem.

"I hear Randel Ragini was actually a good man," Aiden volunteered. He had a homely face, with a wide neck and unremarkable chin, black hair slicked back from his forehead, and friendly brown eyes. But he wore the sword at his back svaalverd-style and had passed the *useen* of the Nasi-Keth—the graduation ceremony, from uma to uman, student to teacher. Such men were not to be taken lightly, no matter *what* they looked like. "He gave money to the Riverside Brothers, and helped fund an orphanage at Cuely. It's sad."

"Good men usually die first amongst the families," said Kessligh. He looked grim, and just a little tired. The dull lamplight seemed to weary his features even further. It seemed to Sasha that, for the first time in all the years she'd known him, only now did he truly look the fifty years she knew him to have. A craggy face, sharp-edged and worn. Her uman for twelve of her twenty years. The nearest thing to a father she'd ever have. Certainly her true father, King Torvaal of Lenayin, would never qualify.

It was strange to see him in this environment. Kessligh was born in Petrodor, the son of poor dockworkers who'd died young from the then-rampant infestations of disease. The Nasi-Keth had become his family, and their teachings had granted him hope. He'd been a loner even then, desperate for escape and wide horizons. When Torovan volunteers had come calling for men to go and fight the Cherrovan warlord Markield, young Kessligh had leapt at the chance.

Fighting in Lenayin had been vicious, and casualties high, which had afforded a brilliant young officer opportunities for rapid advancement. Kessligh had demonstrated a rare genius unmatched in that conflict, and had risen right to the very top—Lenay Commander of Armies—and inflicted upon the Cherrovan a thrashing from which they had still not recovered. It was a post he had held for the following eighteen years, over which time he had become known by many as the second most powerful man in Lenayin. But then King Torvaal's heir, Krystoff, whom Kessligh had been training as uma, had been killed, and Kessligh had resigned his post, and taken Krystoff's grieving, tomboy sister into the wilds of Valhanan to live on a wild hillside and breed horses.

Twelve years of training, and now they arrived at this. Kessligh had great status still, despite his thirty-year absence from Petrodor, and, as his uma, so did Sasha. She saw in his face now the accumulated strains and frustrations of a man who was not particularly happy to have been forced back into this old life once more. Kessligh had never particularly liked Petrodor, nor appreciated the petty squabbles of its residents. Sasha, for her part, was finding more to like about the place than she'd hoped to dare . . . but still it was not difficult to empathise with her uman. All this intrigue became exasperating.

"Randel was rumoured to have had an affair with a servant girl," Rhillian offered. "Surely someone's honour was offended, if true."

"Yes," said Errollyn, "but they'd usually kill the servant girl, not the heir." His finger traced a scar on the table's surface, absently. "Wasn't he to be betrothed to one of Halmady's girls? Maybe Halmady took the affair for an insult."

"More likely it was Family Maerler," Aiden disagreed. "All kinds of things go on in the trade that even the Nasi-Keth don't know about. Maerler and Steiner are always killing each other over something."

"My coin's on Steiner," Kessligh said grimly. "Murder is one thing. This was public, made to look like an accident. When Maerler and Steiner people kill each other, no one bothers to disguise the knife wound. They want each other to *know* it was payback. Payback is currency in Petrodor, and merchant families understand currency and trade all too well."

"You think they killed their own ally's heir?" Errollyn asked. He found such things intriguing.

Rhillian's frown was more typical of serrin confronted with such tasteless human cruelties. "Why?"

Kessligh shrugged. "As Aiden says, we only see a fraction of it. It could be anything. Outsiders might not guess it was murder, but I reckon Patachi Ragini will have no doubts. A warning to him, if you like, from Patachi Steiner."

"The stack rearranges itself," said Rhillian, her emerald eyes thoughtful. "There is power in the offing. Torovan raises an army, but who will lead? Patachi Steiner no doubt fancies himself the general, but Patachi Maerler will disagree. The dukes are all in town, pledging the support of their men and coffers to one or the other, and each receptive to temptation. Perhaps Ragini flirted with the wrong maiden. Perhaps this was his leader's warning not to stray too far from the flock."

Sasha snorted. "If straying from the flock was enough for murder, we'd have nothing but corpses all across the upper incline. They're all doing it."

Aiden shrugged. "Some more than others."

"They're doing more than just raising an army," said Kessligh. "The weapons trade now accounts for perhaps one in every ten gold coins the houses make. Almost all of it's going to the Bacosh. And there's talk of larger shipments on the seas even now. We're trying to find the time and place, but no luck so far."

"All weapons?" Sasha asked. "The Larosan armies have no want of weapons, surely?"

"But Lenayin does," Kessligh replied. "Lenay warriors have plenty of swords, but not much else. Lowlands fighting is different than highlands. They'll need shields, helms, heavier armour."

"And the Petrodor families will buy all this for Lenayin?" Sasha asked. Armoury on that scale would be horrendously expensive. That the families were willing to spend lives for the cause of a free, Verenthane Bacosh, there was no doubt. But gold?

It seemed too generous by half.

"There's a lot of trade between Petrodor and Lenayin," said Errollyn, shaking his head. "Lots of ways for the families to receive return payment. Probably your father will be sending many large wagon trains down to Petrodor to pay for it all."

"Money that should be spent on feeding the poor and keeping the roads open," Sasha muttered. "One bad flood can wipe out half a province's harvest, and he's wasting gold on chain mail."

Footsteps approached, and all about the table looked up. "Now what are you lot muttering about over here in your evil foreign tongues?" said the cheerful barkeeper, dumping a new jug of water on the table. "A recipe for cooking small children, perhaps? So do you fry them? Or boil them in great, steaming pots with lots of onions?"

"Fuck off, Tongren," Sasha told him in Lenay with a broad smile. Saalsi had its sophistication, and Torovan its clever turns of phrase, but, for swearing, no tongue beat Lenay.

Tongren laughed. "Oh ho! The little princess has a foul tongue. Stop scratching the damn arm or it'll swell up all red and nasty-looking, I'm warning you."

Sasha looked in surprise at her right hand, which was scratching the tattoo on her left bicep again. She smiled, sheepishly. "It itches."

"Of course it bloody itches! It's three days old; it's supposed to itch." His dark, lively gaze fell to Rhillian. "I don't suppose I could interest the lovely lady Rhillian in an ancient marking of the spirit world? Sasha can tell you my prices are quite reasonable, and my quality unmatched."

"I know," said Rhillian, "she's shown me. But no, I'm afraid not."

"Ah, but M'Lady, it's said all across the highlands that the wise folk of Saalshen are as one with the spirits! Have you not felt the tug of the ancient highland ways that have drawn so many of your ancestors into the hills and valleys?"

"I have," Rhillian admitted, and flashed him a stunning smile. "But even you, Master Tongren, cannot improve on perfection. No tattoos."

"Modesty, thy name is Rhillian," Errollyn remarked.

"In the highlands," said Tongren, with a glinting smile, "we say that perfection is the light, but all light casts a shadow." He gave a short bow and swaggered back to his rickety bar.

Rhillian gave Errollyn a sideways stare and remarked something to him in dialect that no one else at the table could possibly understand. Errollyn only grinned. Sasha reflected that if any person had the right to be immodest of her appearance, it was Rhillian. Although Errollyn was surely not far behind . . .

To Sasha's undying embarrassment, the day she'd first met Tongren she'd mistaken him for a fellow Lenay. In fact, he was Cherrovan. It was the first time in her life she'd come face to face with the mortal Cherrovan enemy and not had to kill him. Petrodor had many folk of highland origins, Lenay and Cherrovan. Some had come in search of work, others in search of adventure, but most were outcasts of one sort or the other. Highlanders, Lenays and Cherrovans alike, were fiercely tied to the land of their origins and few left willingly. Tongren had never fully explained why he and his family had made the long trek to Petrodor, nor why he showed little enthusiasm for returning to Cherrovan. He did not, he'd said, find the Cherrovan of today very welcoming. Hearing what she'd heard herself, Sasha had some idea what he might mean.

"You met with Patachi Maerler today?" Kessligh asked Rhillian, returning to Saalsi. Rhillian did not reply immediately. For a brief moment, Sasha thought that she might refuse to answer.

Then she nodded. "We had lunch." Eyebrows raised at that admission. Lunch implied trust. Trust well placed, it seemed, since Rhillian had evidently not been poisoned.

"Did you have an interesting talk with the Dukes of Songel and Cisseren?"

Rhillian gazed at Kessligh for a long moment. Kessligh, who was far too wise in the ways of serrin to flinch at the piercing gleam of those eyes. Then she smiled, a slow spread across her face. "My dear Kessligh," she said mildly. "Have you been spying on me?"

"We were agreed, Rhillian," said Kessligh. "We were agreed that Saalshen and Nasi-Keth would work together. We both seek to prevent a war against the Saalshen Bacosh. We were agreed that neither would take action without consulting the other—"

"I have taken no action," Rhillian objected. "I seek to talk to all the game's players, that is all."

"You seek to make common cause with Family Maerler against the Steiner," Kessligh retorted. "Don't you?"

For a moment, Rhillian's gaze was undaunted. Then she looked at the tabletop with a heave of her shoulders. Finally, she looked up at Sasha. Sasha watched her, cautiously. "I cover all my options," Rhillian said quietly. "I tell you this, although there are many of the *talmaad* who would not wish me to, because you are my friends. But Kessligh . . . the Nasi-Keth cannot even agree on who leads them—"

"Kessligh leads the Nasi-Keth," Aiden interrupted, with a flash of temper.

"Do you?" Rhillian asked Kessligh, earnestly. "When will you tell Alaine? Or his followers?"

"It's not Alaine who causes the biggest trouble, it's Gerrold," said Aiden, his voice rising. "And that's *your* fault Rhillian, not ours—"

"Aiden." Kessligh held up a hand. "Let her finish." He folded his hands on the tabletop and waited.

"They all gather, Kessligh," Rhillian said sombrely. "All the dukes. Most are with Steiner. Steiner has the most money, and quite possibly the backing of the temple. The momentum is with him, and if it continues, he shall surely lead an army of Torovan to the Bacosh next spring. Our friends in the Saalshen Bacosh can withstand the Larosa alliance, and perhaps the army of Lenayin . . . but if the Torovans march south as well, I fear it shall be too much."

"I agree," said Kessligh. "Danor alone can give perhaps eight thousand. The others, somewhat less . . . but if Songel and Cisseren come on board, it will be at least thirty thousand men, possibly more. The Larosa have perhaps sixty thousand. Lenayin could muster as many as forty, although thirty seems more likely given the ongoing instabilities . . . but thirty thousand Lenays, well equipped, are worth twice that many Torovans. Perhaps more than twice. At least one hundred and twenty thousand men, and possibly as many as one hundred and fifty . . . and perhaps Telesia and Raani will send a token force as well.

"Enora, Rhodaan and Ilduur can between them muster perhaps forty thousand. They comprise the most formidable army in all human lands, but even with their defences, odds of three- and four-to-one against are treacherous. Saalshen can add great numbers for harassment but, against all logic, Saalshen has refused to create heavy forces, despite two centuries of warning that they must.

"We must win the conflict here, Rhillian. If the army of Torovan can be held up, or split, or prevented from forming and marching entirely, we can win the war before the forces even take the field in the Bacosh. Better yet, if we can intercept these weapon shipments to Lenayin, that will give the Saalshen Bacosh more time to prepare. But it can't happen if the Nasi-Keth and the *talmaad* cannot work together here in Petrodor. If we get in each other's way, or work toward conflicting ends, it will be a disaster. And I'm telling you that forming an allegiance with House Maerler is a crazy risk to take—"

"Riskier than putting all faith in a Nasi-Keth leader who does not command all of the Nasi-Keth?" Rhillian's tone had hardened. "What will you do, ask them nicely? And which of the families will listen, when they know you do not have the force to back up any threats?"

"I'll *get* the force," Kessligh said shortly. "I am getting it."

"You play politics while my entire people are threatened with annihilation! We have tried playing politics with humans before. We tried with King Leyvaan two hundred years ago. He repaid us with slaughter. These people hate us. These Verenthanes, they think we are the demons of Loth incarnate, and they wish us nothing but death, right down to our smallest children . . ."

"Not all Verenthanes," Aiden said quietly.

Rhillian's emerald stare found him, and flicked down to the eight-pointed star medallion upon his chest. "Of course, Aiden my friend." She reached to him across the table and grasped his hand. Her expression was pained. "Of course not all Verenthanes. But the priests, and the powerful, and the fanatics . . . it is enough, Aiden. It is the majority, in fact, in all places except amongst the Nasi-Keth and the peoples of the Saalshen Bacosh itself.

"Humans hate so easily. I think you need to. It tells you who you are. Such hatred is visceral. We serrin . . ." she shook her head, helplessly. "We do not understand it. We try, but it is beyond us. We are not so territorial. We *know* who we are, and such hatred has no use for us. We only understand one thing, a thing in which we have been two hundred painfully slow years in the learning. These people, these haters? They only stop when we kill them."

Her gaze travelled about the table, stopping at one after another. There was no imploring search for understanding now. Only a cold, deadly certainty. Serrin, Kessligh had said often enough, were peaceful by choice, not by nature. It was, to say the least, a significant distinction.

"Saalshen shall not allow Patachi Steiner to form this army," Rhillian said coldly. "We shall prevent it however we have to. If our Nasi-Keth friends can offer a better solution, we'll take it. Only know where we stand. If the Saalshen Bacosh falls, the fanatics will not stop at the border. They'll march on into Saalshen, and they have all the mercy of death itself. We do not fight for an ideal, or a king, or wealth or land. We fight for the right to exist. And we refuse to fail."

Four

JARYD NYVAR CIRCLED, flexing his left hand against the grip of his stanch. Opposing him circled Teriyan Tremel, long red hair tied into various braids down his back. Shouts and yells filled the air, and the clash of wooden stanches, followed by the thump of a landing blow. Jaryd barely heard them, watching only Teriyan's feet, and his centre, as old Lieutenant Asheld had taught him long ago in the yard of Nyvar Holding.

Teriyan attacked, a deceptive, sliding approach preceding a vicious slash from the right. Jaryd parried, danced back, knocked the next attack sideways and nearly caught Teriyan's padded banda as the taller man leapt aside. Teriyan grinned, sweat dripping, and gave a nod of approval, wrist-spinning his stanch. Jaryd's face never moved.

Teriyan attacked twice more, and both times Jaryd faded, the second time clipping Teriyan on the shoulder. His left forearm throbbed where it had been broken nearly two months before, but it felt strong beneath splints and a wooden guard. Teriyan favoured the right-foot half-step, he decided. It preceded most of his attacks, just for an instant. When the next attack came, Jaryd parried and cut hard for the left, just where the transition from high defence to low was most difficult . . . but met a firm defence, followed by a hard blow to his midsection.

He fell hard in the dirt, jarring his old injury. Teriyan grinned again, spinning his stanch as he stood over the fallen man. "Nice try, lad, don't think that half-step hasn't been obvious to four dozen other opponents too." He reached down, but Jaryd ignored the hand, and got back to his feet.

"Again," said Jaryd, stonily, resuming his stance. Teriyan shrugged, and did likewise. Two exchanges later, and Jaryd's next hard cut also met with firm defence and a killing blow.

"You're leaving yourself too far open," Teriyan advised, shaking his head as Jaryd once again struggled to his feet. "It's no good going for the kill all the time if you get killed in the process. You don't have to risk so much when you attack."

"All war is risk," Jaryd replied, wiping sweat from his forehead, and dust from his pants. "Again." His forearm was throbbing now. He'd been first to arrive for evening practice and intended to be last to leave. It was a pattern he'd been repeating since his arrival here in the small Lenay town of Baerlyn one and a half months ago. Back then he'd been restricted to basic drill, strength-building and technical exercises. Only now was his arm recovered enough that he could match himself against the village seniors. But, after so long without sparring, his form was rustier than a farmer's scythe.

Twenty exchanges later, and he'd been knocked down another four times. Each time, he dusted himself off and resumed his stance. The sun now sank below the lip of the Baerlyn Valley, casting shadow across the training hall, its surrounding grassy paddocks and the long, winding strip of ramshackle wooden buildings that was the town.

"Enough," said Teriyan, finally, as the tachadar circles about them were abandoned by the other combatants, and the outdoor yard grew cool and silent. "I've a hard day tomorrow, and you'd best be riding back before dark."

"The dark doesn't frighten me," said Jaryd. "Once more."

"I said no, lad."

"Perhaps you grow too old for fighting," said Jaryd. "Perhaps your wife could find better use for you in the kitchens."

Teriyan just looked at him for a moment. Then resumed his stance, wordlessly. The next time he attacked, it was faster and harder. Two blows had Jaryd reeling, and the third took his leg from under him. Then he was on his back, blinking into that darkening blue sky, with Teriyan's stanch pressed point-first into his chest.

"You're an angry little bunny, aren't you?" Teriyan observed. "You really think your grand revenge will come sooner for all your puffing and blowing?"

Jaryd knocked the stanch aside and climbed slowly to his feet. He ached and throbbed all over. He'd run that morning, performed the most tiring stable chores after that, then practised taka-dans and knife throwing beneath the old vertyn tree at the ranch, then gone hunting with bow and arrow for game in the wild hills. He'd only managed a rabbit, but it was all experience. When he had been heir of Tyree, he'd always believed that enemies were most honourably killed in single combat, preferably when challenged to a duel. Lately, however, he'd become less fussy. If the Great Lord Arastyn of Tyree died by formal challenge or by an arrow shot from the bushes in the dark, he cared not either way. Arastyn had invoked Sylden Sarach, an old law, and had dissolved Jaryd's family, stripped him of noble title and perhaps, though no one was certain, even murdered his father.

Jaryd cared little for his lost title. He had not relished the prospect of becoming Great Lord of Tyree in the first place. He had never loved his father, nor had his father loved him. His sisters and younger brother had seemed to accept their fate willingly enough, and Jaryd found in their willingness nothing but contempt for them. Wealth was often nice, but now that he lacked it, he found that he did not miss it particularly. And as for status, every Lenay man worth the name knew that the only true status in Lenayin was honour, and the only true honour came from courage, steadfastness and skill with a blade.

Jaryd did not seek revenge for any of these lost, petty things. When they invoked Sylden Sarach, Arastyn's men had killed Jaryd's little brother Tarryn. For that, all would die.

"Lad, look at you," Teriyan sighed. "You're a mess. Even Sasha didn't work this hard, and she's harder to keep still than a bobcat with a bee up its arse."

"I'm fine," Jaryd muttered, straightening with difficulty. His back was suddenly stiff, and his shoulders hurt—muscle, bone and all. "I grow stronger."

"Aye, you do. One day soon you'll be so strong, you'll be dead." Jaryd stretched, gingerly, trying not to wince at the various accumulated pains. Teriyan shook his head. "Look, why don't we grab a meal at the Steltsyn instead? I'll bet it's a damn sight better than whatever mess Lynnie's cooked up for you, and I'll tell you how I read that last overhead cross so easily—"

"I don't need your pity!" Jaryd snarled at him. "I can feed myself, I can train myself, I can claim revenge myself! And I will!"

He stalked off, trying not to limp. Teriyan watched him go, eyes faintly narrowed, stanch across his shoulders, muscular arms hung on the ends.

As Jaryd rode back to the Baerlyn main road, he could smell dinner wafting through town, or smoke that rose from stone chimneys above brown slate roofs. Children looked at him as he passed, guardedly, which was most unlike Lenay children anywhere. Jaryd thought they'd been warned not to bother him. Which suited him fine.

He passed Parrachik's, the moneylender where wagons were waiting down the side lane, and Torovan merchants in bright shirts and broad hats were seated about a table on the verandah, sipping wine with Parrachik himself. All looked at the once heir of Tyree as he passed. All nodded, cautiously, as Jaryd's dark stare passed over them. He felt that he would burn alive from the heat of his shame. He wanted to strike the heads off those smug bastards, but none of it mattered. He deserved his shame. His little brother Tarryn was dead. He, the big brother Tarryn had so looked up to and adored, had been incapable of protecting him. The men who had killed Tarryn would all die screaming, and until that blessed day arrived, all other concerns were as nothing to him. For that day he worked, and strove, with every fibre of his being.

Past the Steltsyn Star, the inn bustling as the meals were prepared and the fires lit, and Jaryd dug in his heels. His horse was a fine chestnut gelding, taken from a fallen Hadryn cavalryman at the Battle of Ymoth after Jaryd's own horse had been felled. It was good to have a horse of his own. He wanted as little of Baerlyn's, or Sashandra Lenayin's charity, as he could possibly accept.

It was nearly dark by the time he reached the ranch, and he saw lamplight glowing from the house windows as he galloped across the open, grassy slope, and then came the barking of the boarhounds. Jaryd skirted the huge, broad vertyn tree, and its surrounding vegetable gardens and chicken run, and headed for the stables.

He stabled his horse in the empty place once reserved for Sashandra's big black, and trudged on weary legs down the grassy slope toward the glowing lights. On the rear verandah, the boarhounds, Kaif and Keef, sniffed at him and wagged their tails—Jaryd gave them each a scratch between the ears, and pushed through the rear door into the kitchen.

Beyond the kitchen, a visitor stood before the fireplace, a cup in hand. He was a young man, dressed in plain travelling clothes, yet even that could not hide the refinement of his bearing. There was a silver clasp at his collar, and a neck chain too. His short red hair shone faintly in the firelight, his skin pale, his features fine, a light dusting of freckles across nose and cheeks. He looked at Jaryd, and his light green eyes registered at first surprise, and then caution. Finally, he gave a weak, sheepish smile.

"Jaryd," he said.

"You," said Jaryd. "You get the fuck out of this house." The young lordling's face fell. The extra horse must have been stabled with the others, Jaryd realised, but he hadn't noticed. Damn he was tired.

"You can't boss him about," said Lynette from Jaryd's side in the kitchen, "this isn't your house." Jaryd stared at her, blankly. Stupid pest of a girl. He hadn't seen her either, there at her kitchen bench chopping vegetables. She had long, tangled red hair, a flaming red unlike this new arrival's pale rose. She was skinny and freckled, and a pain in the neck. Worst of all, she was Teriyan Tremel's daughter, a dear friend of Sashandra's, and was in fact, if not in title, the person-most-senior for the entire gods-damned ranch. At sixteen summers.

Jaryd didn't mind taking instruction from a woman beneath a roof, least of all in the kitchen. That was the way through most of Lenayin—men ruled outside, and women ruled within. But this brat was a horsewoman too, and an annoyingly good one, even if she couldn't see the point of lagand. Around the ranch, all of his victories at grand lagand tournaments, all of his fame as a rider and a horseman and victor in countless swordwork contests, all counted for nothing.

"Aeryl, don't mind him," Lynette called, returning attention to her vegetables. "He's just grumpy all the time. You've my invitation to stay, and Andreyis's too."

"M'Lady," said Aeryl with a light bow. "Jaryd come, share a drink with me." Earnestly. "It's so good to see you, I can't tell you how . . ."

He stepped forward, and Jaryd drew his sword. "They sent you, didn't they?" Aeryl stared at the naked steel. "They sent you to *talk* with me, just like they sent Rhyst to *talk* with me while they murdered my little brother!"

"Jaryd, you stupid fool!" Lynette yelled at him. "Put it away right now! Andreyis!"

"Jaryd, I swear, I wasn't even *at* Rathynal, my sister was ill in childbirth, we were not certain that she would live—"

"Liar! You're all the same, all the Tyree nobility, all a mob of liars and murderers and honourless thieves!"

"Andreyis!" Lynette yelled again and then Andreyis was there, stopping between Jaryd and Aeryl, tall and dark, his hand on the hilt of his sword.

"Put it away," said the younger man. He was awkward, this lad of eighteen summers, not yet grown into his gangling frame. But there was a confidence in his young eyes, and the effect was not entirely spoiled by the big ears that stuck out from under his ragged mop of dark hair. Rabbit ears, the other Baerlyn boys sometimes called him. And other names besides.

Jaryd snorted. "What are you going to do, draw that thing? You couldn't take me in your dreams."

"I could too," Andreyis retorted, but Lynette was advancing on Jaryd in fury.

"You stupid, idiot bonehead!" she shouted, stirring spoon waving in one hand. "What's the matter with you? Is everything a war to you now? Do you solve every argument by killing someone?" Jaryd's lip curled, and he tried to think of some suitably cutting riposte, but he only knew the language of men, all threats, insults and bluster. A redheaded girl with a kitchen spoon was nothing he was equipped to handle. "You're five years older than me, but at least I'm aware that being a great warrior is far more about who you kill and why than just whether or not you can! When are you going to grow up?"

Jaryd stood where he was, sword trembling in his hand. He couldn't recall it feeling this heavy before. It seemed to be made of iron, dragging his arm toward the floor.

"I mean, when are all you young men of Lenayin going to—"

"Lynnie," Andreyis interrupted and shook his head, dark eyes watching Jaryd warily. "Enough, Lynnie." A moment passed. Jaryd sheathed his sword and leaned a hand against the wall. The world was spinning. "Jaryd, come and take a seat. I'll get you something to drink."

Jaryd went, because there was nothing else to do. A chair presented itself and he collapsed into it, somehow managing to avoid tangling the sword. He could hear Lynette and Andreyis in hushed conversation in the kitchen and, quite unexpectedly, he felt a sudden affection for the lad. Andreyis remembered what Jaryd had been, even when everyone else seemed to have forgotten. Andreyis still looked up to him.

For no particular reason, his hand strayed to his chest, feeling at the rings beneath his shirt. There were two of them, slim metal, gleaming with a hint of gold when observed in the firelight. They would bend and come apart to pierce through an ear, or sometimes a nose—Goeren-yai rings, decorations for men, not for women. He had declared himself Goeren-yai to free himself from the restrictive practices of Verenthanes. Those practices would not allow him his revenge. But the old ways of the Goeren-yai knew the tale of blood and steel all too well.

Princess Sofy had given him these rings. A dying man had pressed them into her hand on the battlefield. But a warrior's decorations belonged in battle, and so she'd granted the rings to Jaryd in turn. He wore them now on a chain around his neck. There was no expectation of such decorations amongst Goeren-yai—Teriyan himself, as fiercely proud a Goeren-yai warrior as one could meet, wore neither rings nor tattoos. Yet somehow, Jaryd felt like a fraud, that he could not put the rings in his ear. It was one thing to declare oneself Goeren-yai, and to throw the Verenthane medallion to the floor before his king. But to come here and live amongst the Goeren-yai themselves, to feel their gaze upon him, watching his every move, considering his every foreignness, his every misunderstanding . . .

Andreyis pressed a cup into his hand, and he drank. The wine reminded him once more of Sofy. *Princess* Sofy, he corrected himself. One did not abandon that formality as one abandoned the Verenthane gods, for the Goeren-yai loved the youngest Princess of Lenayin as much or more than the Verenthanes. In the two days after Sashandra's parley with her father, Sofy and Jaryd had shared wine and talked. What they had talked of, he could no longer remember. Probably, he realised, he'd not been lively conversation. In the battle, he'd wished for death. That denied him, he had only revenge left. But Sofy had evidently not found his morbidity too off-putting. She'd granted him the rings, had sipped wine that no Verenthane princess was supposed to sip, and had wished him luck.

Then Sashandra had come and told him that, since she and Kessligh would be absent from the ranch, there was a place available for someone prepared to work hard. A place amongst townfolk accustomed to controversial outsiders in their midst. A place, no doubt, where they could keep an eye on him. His old resentment resurfaced, dark and brooding.

He looked up and found Aeryl watching him from the chair opposite, a cup in hand. Aeryl managed another faint smile. "Your hair is growing," he observed. "Perhaps soon you'll have to tie it in braids."

Jaryd sipped his wine and took a deep breath. "Enough with the small talk. What did they send you here to tell me? What threats?"

"I did not attend Rathynal because my sister was ill," Aeryl said quietly. "She died, Jaryd. I played no part in the great gathering of provinces, nor the events that befell you there. I had my own grieving to attend to."

"I'm sorry." Jaryd stared into the fire. He did not want to look at his old "friend." Amongst those people he had once called his own, he had no friends.

"Your brother Wyndal has been adopted by Family Arastyn," Aeryl offered. "He is most well. He sends his regards."

"Did he send word that he wished me to surrender myself?"

Aeryl paused for a brief moment. "No," he said, then carefully, "no, he did not."

"Good. Because then I'd be forced to kill my own brother for a traitor."

Jaryd sipped his wine again. Aeryl stared for a moment. "Galyndry's marriage preparations are nearly complete," he tried again. "Family Iryani are pleased. Your sister Dalya sends word that she would like you to be there."

"I bet she does," Jaryd muttered. "Just so long as her precious banquets and dances are not disturbed, I'm sure her little brother's murder won't bother her a bit."

"Will you attend?" Aeryl was nothing if not persistent. He'd assisted Jaryd with his studies, when the words and symbols had refused to make sense. The fifth son of Family Daery, he'd always been quiet and studious, excelling in studies, while having much less interest in Jaryd's passions of swordplay and horsemanship. In all their studying together, he'd never voiced exasperation or contempt at Jaryd's complete inability with letters. He'd just made him repeat the same phrases, again, and again, and again. Jaryd had found his attention span with such tedious things astonishing.

"No," he answered. "I've no interest in seeing the last of Family Nyvar abolished before my eyes."

"And so you mean to live out your days here?" Aeryl looked about. "A fair place . . . but something of a fall, wouldn't you say?"

"It was enough for a Lenay princess. Besides, I'm not planning to sit here for long."

"You plan revenge," Aeryl said flatly. Andreyis came from the kitchen and sat beside Aeryl, placing a plate of sliced bread and a bowl of hashal on the table between the chairs.

"I mean to kill them all," Jaryd said darkly.

"That's real smart, that is," Andreyis announced, dipping some bread in the bean paste. "Tell them all about your plans. That'll improve your chances no end."

Aeryl looked incredulous. "Jaryd . . . there are a hundred and seventeen noble families in Tyree alone. They have allies and family through marriage with many other provinces. All have accepted Great Lord Arastyn. How can you possibly think to best them all?"

Jaryd said nothing, and stared at the flames.

"He has a death wish, that's what," said Lynette, coming from the kitchen with bowls of grapes and plums. She pulled up another chair. "He's too damn stubborn to imagine an alternative."

"If I killed you," Jaryd said, "would your father be any different?"

Lynette snorted, tossing her wild hair back. "If you killed me, most of Baerlyn would chase you to the ends of the world. But you're all alone. No one came with you, Jaryd. You've no allies, no support, no army. You'll die, it'll be messy, and it'll be a great waste."

"I used to hear all these great stories from the men in the Falcon Guard," Jaryd muttered. "Stories of Goeren-yai heroism. Now I arrive here, I find they're all cowards."

"I'd think twice before using that word around here." Andreyis said warily.

"What else would you call a people who dissuaded me from taking revenge against those who murdered my eleven-year-old brother!" Jaryd shouted.

"Your honour is your own," Andreyis said. "What you choose to do with it is your concern. No man in Baerlyn will stop you should you choose to continue this path. But neither will we assist or approve if you give us no cause to."

"Listen to your friends, Jaryd," Aeryl pleaded. "They're young, but they speak with great wisdom."

"Growing up in Kesslgh's shadow will do that," said Andreyis. Lynette rolled her eyes a little. Now that Andreyis was a warrior, blooded in battle and successful in his Wakening, she thought him far too big for his boots.

"Jaryd," Aeryl tried once more, "Great Lord Arastyn does not want your head. He's willing to grant you a pardon, if only—"

"The only reason he no longer wants my head is that he's not entitled under the king's law to punish a Goeren-yai who has in turn challenged him to a duel," Jaryd snarled. "My challenge stands, and so long as it stands, his claim and my claim cancel each other. It shall stand until either he accepts, or one of us dies."

"For you to challenge a Verenthane great lord to a duel will require a lord of similar stature to endorse your challenge!" exclaimed Aeryl. "Not just anyone can challenge a great lord, Jaryd, and you might not have noticed, but you're no longer the heir to Tyree!"

"I noticed. My brother died in a pool of blood that made me notice. Princess Sashandra will support my claim."

"Aye, no doubt she would, but she's not here, is she?"

"So will Kessligh Cronenverdt," Jaryd said stubbornly, although he felt less certain of that.

"And he's not here either. Very good, Jaryd, you've named two people who can't possibly speak on your behalf . . . and Kessligh, although a very heroic figure, has no actual noble pedigree whatsoever, and is in fact well known to be in opposition to the very concept."

Prince Damon, Jaryd nearly said, but didn't. Prince Damon was in trouble enough, being perceived to have had some sympathy with the rebellion led by his sister Sashandra. Endorsements from Jaryd Nyvar would do him no favours at all.

"Princess Sofy," he said, with a glare. "Princess Sofy will support my claim."

Aeryl blinked. "Princess Sofy? Do you honestly think she would publicly support your right to chop the Great Lord of Tyree into very small pieces?"

"She said she would." Actually she hadn't. But it had been implicit, he thought.

Aeryl took a deep breath and looked elsewhere for a moment, gathering his thoughts. "Well, Princess Sofy is a woman, so I don't know . . ."

"She's nobility. No, she's far more than nobility, she's royalty. Her claim would stand."

"She's about to be married to the heir of the Regent of all the Bacosh, Jaryd—"

"And she's not happy about it." That was common enough knowledge, and Aeryl didn't contradict him. "Or she wasn't. She's suddenly the most important woman in all Lenayin. Maybe even the most important royal. Without her, there's no marriage, no alliance and no war. She can say what she likes, no one will dare touch her."

"I am quite certain, Jaryd," Aeryl said with the beginnings of impatience, "that if Princess Sofy were here, she would counsel you against this foolishness, and tell you not to throw your life away so cheaply!"

"It won't be cheap, I can promise you that."

"Princess Sofy is a kind and gentle woman," Aeryl persisted, "with no great love of battles and bloodshed. If you think she will support you on this blind insanity of yours, I fear you're deluded."

"If you're so certain, why don't you ask her?"

Aeryl stared. Jaryd knew he had charged well beyond the bounds of common sense or caution, but he could not stop himself now. Princess Sofy *was* a kind and gentle woman, but she was also a just one. She had braved the battlefield and comforted the wounded and dying soldiers until she had dropped from exhaustion. Sofy had been appalled at Tarryn's fate, and infuriated by the actions of the Tyree lords, Great Lord Arastyn in particular. Surely she'd not deprive him of his justice.

All the world wanted Jaryd dead. That suited him fine. Just so long as he could take Arastyn and a few of his rotten, scheming friends with him.

Sasha woke the next morning to the sound of the ocean swell against the pier. Sunlight peered through the shutters of her small room.

From the floors below came the sounds of footsteps and muffled voices. More voices on the docks, fishermen greeting the morning. On the roof above, a gull's feet scrabbled. Then a piercing cry. Another gull answered, circling nearby. The creaking of ropes, as boats strained at their moorings. The air smelled of salt, and the skin of her hands was still dry and taut from the previous day's fishing.

Strange sounds, and strange smells. So far from Lenayin. And yet peaceful, in the strange way that dangerous, overcrowded Petrodor could sometimes spring on a person, right when she least expected it. If she relaxed on her back in the warm morning air, and listened to the rise and fall of the ocean, she could just about drift off to sleep once more . . .

The door creaked open before her eyelids could close entirely. Sasha jerked awake, a hand moving fast to the knife beneath her pillow. But it was only Fara, wrapped in a towel from her morning wash and holding two mugs of tea.

"Thanks," said Sasha, as the other girl placed the mug on the floor beside the bed. Fara returned to her own bed and began dressing.

Neither being a princess, nor the uma of Kessligh Cronenverdt, had been enough to gain Sasha a room of her own. She didn't mind. She and Fara shared the best upstairs room at the Velos, a crumbling little brick-walled space with floorboards that creaked, and rickety wooden shutters that let in the rain in a storm. At least they had a view of the docks—Liam and Rodery were stuck in the back room with only a dingy courtyard to look upon.

The tea was spiced something fierce. Sasha winced as she sipped it, opening the window shutters enough for a view. Already there were small fishing boats heading out past the large ships at mooring. Men clambered over boats along the piers, tending to ropes, nets and sails. The sun glared several hands above the ocean horizon . . . someone had been nice to her, Sasha realised, and let her sleep in past the dawn. Quite likely some of the men would be back from their first fishing trip soon, having set out before sunrise. Others would be off to North Pier to work at the warehouses, shifting the rich families' cargo. Another day in Petrodor.

Serrin put something in their tea that woke a person up real fast. She sat on the floor and did her stretches. Then came the exercises, fast sit-ups and push-ups in her underclothes. Then she lifted her chin repeatedly above the crosswise ceiling beam, with relative ease.

"You should do more exercises," she encouraged Fara, who sat on her bed and arranged little parcels of medicines in small leather pouches, along with other implements Sasha did not recognise, and placed them carefully in a wooden carry box. "Then the boys won't beat you up at training so bad."

"I do enough," said Fara. Fara was a quiet girl with long, light brown hair and eyes that never quite met a person's gaze. Her uman was a healer, skilled primarily in the serrin lore of medicines. Her uman was also a woman; and that, in Sasha's estimation, was where the problems began.

"You could do better," Sasha suggested, stretching her arms.

"Not everyone has to learn to fight with swords," Fara said with irritation, her eyes not leaving her precious medicines. "Fighting was the *last* of the serrin's skills the Nasi-Keth learned to do."

Sasha shrugged, extended her arms, and leapt for the beam once more. "The last and most important," she added, lifting herself up and down, breathing hard.

"Important to you, maybe. Not everyone's a muscle-bound warrior like you." There was an edge of sarcasm to her voice.

Sasha snorted. She completed several more lifts, then dropped to the floor and pulled off her sweaty undershirt. "Do you know your problem?" she told Fara, tossing the shirt on her bed. "You enter the Nasi-Keth, the home of all open-mindedness and learning, yet you cling to old prejudices like a child to a mother's skirts. All these serrin women, and now me as an example, and no Petrodor woman wants to admit that women can fight."

"Oh, you're a wonderful example," Fara said with gritted teeth, uncomfortable now that Sasha wore no top.

Sasha knew that her physique made the locals edgy. Her new tattoo, even more so. Tongren had made it curl expertly about her upper bicep, three interwoven strands, like the tri-braid on the side of her head, dark like forest vines against the pale skin.

"I'd much rather heal people, thanks."

"Most male healers can do both," Sasha reasoned.

"I'm an exception," said Fara, testily.

"Look, why don't you at least come on a run with me? It'll do you good, I find *all* my skills improve when I'm fit."

"Sashandra, why don't you leave me alone?" Fara retorted, looking up for the first time. Sasha could see the alarm in Fara's eyes, to observe her muscular arms, her hard stomach, her compact breasts. "I'm not a highlands warrior princess! Now why don't you go off and . . . and eat raw lizards, or rub sand in your hair, or whatever it is that you do in the mornings to stay so warriorlike!"

Sasha took her towel off the end of the bed. "You think I'm uncivilised, don't you?"

"Heavens forbid I should think such a thing," Fara said beneath her breath, eyes down once again.

"I've met sheep with more character," Sasha muttered in Lenay, putting the towel around her neck and taking her sword and scabbard.

"What was that?" Fara asked suspiciously.

"Just a little something in barbarian-speak," Sasha told her in Torovan once more. "Never you mind your civilised, cultured little Torovan head about it."

She nearly ran into Liam in the narrow hall. "Hey!" the young Nasi-Keth protested, spinning about to avert his gaze. "Sasha! For the gods' sakes, put a shirt on!"

"What!" Sasha snapped at him. "You don't like it either?"

"Like it?" Liam tried to look at her, but propriety kept dragging his eyes away. He seemed caught, like a puppet with two masters each pulling in separate directions. "Sasha, you're naked!"

Sasha laughed. "If you think this is naked, kid, you're in for a nasty surprise on your wedding night." And gave him a playful kick on the backside before strolling to the washroom and shutting the door.

Sasha's morning run took her through narrow lanes until the bottom of the slope where alleys snaked up precarious stairways between crumbling walls.

She ran with several local Nasi-Keth as it was always safer to move in groups, even across the lower slopes.

The run ended in Fishnet Alley by a nondescript lane between buildings. Squeezing through, the lane opened into a broad courtyard. Within it, men wielded practice stanches in single combat and the air echoed with the sharp crack of wood on wood, and the grunting exertion of combatants.

Sasha walked to the courtyard's north side and crouched to splash cold water from a bucket on her face. She grabbed some breakfast from a table under the awning, apologising to the lady for being late. There were door-ways leading from the training courtyard into neighbouring houses, and people came and went.

A little girl with tangled hair and a brown-cloth dress watched her shyly as she ate, seated on an old footstool. Sasha smiled at her. In Lenayin, there were no children allowed in the training hall. And no women, either . . . her-self, the exception. Here amongst the dockfolk, everything was communal. People had no choice but to cooperate, she supposed as she chewed, watching the men fight. They all lived cheek by jowl and space had to be shared.

Finishing breakfast, she strode to the opposite side of the courtyard, strapped on a padded banda, took up a stanch and stepped onto the pavings.

"Rodery," she said, interrupting the boy's taka-dan. "Your quarter-step is mistimed, I've been watching. Here, I'll show you."

Rodery was a big lad of nineteen summers with broad shoulders and dark freckles across his square face. He turned and frowned at her, displeased at the interruption. "Uman Torshai says my footwork's good."

"It is good," Sasha agreed impatiently, taking stance opposite. "I can make it better."

She took him through his moves. To Rodery's credit, he watched and lis-tened, regardless of the occasional dark stare coming from other parts of the courtyard. The svaalverd—the serrin martial art—was all about balance, technique and timing. She demonstrated Rodery's slow adjustment to a roundhouse strike, and gave him some bruises to prove the point. Then she drilled him until his feet adjusted properly, and comprehension dawned in the big lad's eyes, as he deflected her attacks with new poise and speed.

Sasha grinned at him, twirling her stanch. "You see? Much better."

"I'd never thought of doing it like that," Rodery conceded, repeating the steps. "The timing's complex."

Sasha shook her head impatiently. "No, there's no complexity in svaalverd. Look for the simplicity, every time. It's just basic balance, see?" She demonstrated the six basic stances that every five-year-old learned. "And the balance dictates the stroke, see? It's all the same thing. Kesshgh tells me that improving at svaalverd is a constant quest to make everything as simple as possible. There's always one thing that drives everything else. Look for it."

"But . . ." Rodery shook his head, with a spreading half-smile. "But there's so many things . . ."

"*Ele'sherihl*," Sasha told him.

Rodery winced. "Wait, I know that, that's . . . um . . ."

"Study your Saalsi!" Sasha said in exasperation. "Petrodor is full of serrin and they could all talk a stone to boredom! Ask them a question, they'll go on till sundown! *Ele'sherihl* means 'the product of many things' . . . terrible translation, of course, but if you learn the tongue you'll realise how it works. Some things are made that are made up of many things. Like a boat—the hull, the mast, the sails, all are made separately. But, once completed, it's just one boat. *Ele'sherihl*. When you fight, make each stroke just one stroke, not a combination of feet and hands and torso. One thing. Simplicity. That's the key to svaalverd."

There came a *thud* from nearby and a cry of pain. Sasha looked and found a teenage girl clutching her arm. Liam, her opponent, looked exasperated.

Sasha strode over. "Liam! Go easy! The object is to help her improve, not break her bones!"

"I'm okay," the girl protested, shaking her arm. It was Yulia, a slight girl a little shorter than Sasha. She wore her auburn hair in a ponytail and her banda looked a little too big for her. She'd only started attending the training regularly after Sasha had arrived in Petrodor. "It's not bad."

"It was a simple move!" Liam protested. "It's not my fault if she's no damn good!" Yulia, to Sasha's disappointment, only stared at the ground. Damn it, was she the only human girl in Petrodor prepared to fight back?

"Would you beat up a child?" she asked coldly.

"Look . . ." Liam turned to face her, slinging his stanch over his shoulders with a swagger. Cocky, like so many young Torovan men. "She's not a child. She has fifteen summers. And for that age, she's pathetic. Or are you going to tell me otherwise?"

"She needs work," Sasha retorted. "So do you. Girls in this city don't have access to male umans, and they're usually the ones who can fight. And, what a surprise, I find girls aren't made to feel welcome in the courtyards, either. No wonder they fall behind the boys when fools like you try to break their arms whenever they try to learn!"

"Bah!" said Liam, with a dismissive wave. "You make excuses like all the others."

"You truly think women can't fight the svaalverd?" Sasha asked dangerously.

"Sure! Serrin can! And you can, you're a wild, crazy highlander, they fed you raw sheep's bladders in the crib and you grew up strangling wild wolves with your bare hands!" There was laughter from watching men. Many had stopped their sparring to observe the confrontation. "But it's not our culture! And *you*, you should know better than to come into Petrodor from your mountain kingdom and try to turn all our women into wild amazons like yourself—"

"Ha, you're just scared of women." She could see Uman Torshai circling behind to her left, tapping his stanch with one hand, appearing to watch the argument.

"Scared of women!" Liam thought that hysterical. "Truly, do I look scared?"

"Most of you Verenthanes are scared of women. Your entire world revolves around controlling women: make them marry, make them cook, make them make babies until they burst . . ."

"You're crazy!" Liam retorted.

"And all sin comes from women," Sasha continued, "and all lust, and adultery's always a woman's fault, and husbands' tempers . . . all your faults! All your faults, but don't take responsibility, oh no! Just blame your mother, your wife, your daughter. You're just a spoiled little brat who never had his ears boxed and thinks the stars all circle his arse. You couldn't take responsibility for your own fart. And you can't let your women do what they want, because then who'll you have to blame all your failures on?"

It was too much. Liam levelled his stanch at her, his face flushed red. "You watch your mouth."

Sasha snorted. She'd been putting up with this for weeks now, and she was finally sick of it. "Did your mama not raise you properly, or do you just have a really small cock?"

Uman Torshai's stanch whistled at her knees from behind, to Sasha's little surprise. She swivelled, deflecting, and smacked Torshai viciously hard across the banda. The older man staggered and fell.

"Hey!" Liam yelled in fury and swung at her. Sasha performed a simple deflection, which flowed into a sidestep and strike, hitting him across the shoulder. Another attacker aimed angrily for her head and Sasha overbalanced him with an angled parry, twisted for maximum power through the same motion of feet-through-shoulders, with a *crack* that sent him flying.

Torshai came back to his feet and at her, but his timing was off and predictable with anger. Sasha crushed it, sending his stanch flying and neighbours ducking for cover, then took an arm with a downward strike. Liam stood bewildered, wondering what to do. Sasha jabbed, dancing forward. Provoked the awkward parry, and disarmed him with a flick to the wrist, then stabbed hard to the midriff with her full weight of momentum behind it. Liam fell hard on his backside, clutching his wrist and stomach.

About her, all was silent. Men stared. Torshai was on his knees, holding his forearm and grimacing. The third man was half sitting some distance away, feeling his ribs. Little Yulia stood wide-eyed and aghast. Sasha held her final pose, stanch poised, and glared at them all.

"I am the uma of Kessligh Cronenverdt!" she announced, in case there was any doubt. "I am not just his plaything, whatever some may say! You call yourself Nasi-Keth, and enlightened, but I see nothing but superstition and prejudice here! If I find one amongst you who is even *half* my standard with a blade, I'll let you know!"

She turned to leave, tugging the straps of her banda . . . and found Errollyn, leaning against a post regarding her.

"Oh, very subtle," he said in Lenay, apparently very amused. "Kessligh *shall* be pleased."

From the end of the longest pier on the fishermen's dock, Sasha could see all along North Pier, where the big ships moored and cargo moved from their holds to the warehouses and back. In the other direction, Sharptooth jutted into the water, blocking all view of Angel Bay—the southernmost half of Petrodor Harbour—save for Alaster Promontory, further beyond.

"Randel Ragini was one of *Rhillian's?*" Sasha asked Errollyn incredulously.

Errollyn nodded. He sat with his back to the pier's corner post, facing away from the ocean's glare. Partly, Sasha thought, so that he could keep an eye on the docks, and partly because a serrin's sensitive eyes were no friends of the bright sun. He carried no bow today—it would have been too conspicuous in the daytime.

"They're not all bad, the families," he said tiredly. He looked dishevelled, dark grey hair falling haphazardly about his face. Sasha wondered how much sleep he'd had. "Randel Ragini had a taste for serrin things. Probably if he were poor, he'd have become a Nasi-Keth. But, being wealthy, he confined himself to trading curious artworks."

"Patachi Steiner killed him for *that?*"

Errollyn shook his head. "No. Rhillian offered him things. Probably the patachi found out. I don't know how . . . I only just found out."

"Offered him things?" Sasha squinted at him. There were men clambering on nearby boats, preparing to set sail. They were barely within earshot and unlikely to know Saalsi even if they heard. A swell rose beneath the pier as mooring ropes creaked and groaned. Wooden hulls clunked. "What things?"

"I wouldn't tell you if I knew," Errollyn said with a faint smile. "I'm in enough trouble with Rhillian as it stands. If she finds out we talked, anyhow."

"Things." Sasha gazed past Errollyn to the North Pier. Heavy loads dangled in webbing from rope pulleys. Men and mules pulled carts loaded with more freight. Trade from Saalshen. Trade from Ameryn. Trade from the Bacosh, the Lisan Empire and far distant Xaldia. Trade made power. Trade made Petrodor, and the families. No move was made in Petrodor, and no blood was spilt, without it. "Rhillian offered Ragini good terms of trade with Saalshen," Sasha ventured. "Didn't she?"

Errollyn shrugged. "It's possible."

"But good terms to do what? Side with Saalshen against Patachi Steiner? It would be suicide. Surely Randel Ragini did not love Saalshen so much?"

"You're asking the wrong man," said Errollyn. "Rhillian is my friend but, on some things, she trusts me little."

"Well you're here talking to me," Sasha observed, "so I suppose that's logical."

Errollyn smiled, and gazed away at North Pier. "We didn't know what it would do, you know."

"I'm sorry?"

"Trade," he said. "Two hundred years ago, Saalshen left humans alone. We thought it unwise to interfere. Then King Leyvaan invaded and we realised we had no choice.

"And so we began trading. Petrodor seemed a good place to start—only a sleepy village back then, but well positioned on the mouth of the Sarna River with access to inland Torovan and Lenayin beyond. Saalshen knew many skills and crafts that humans did not. Our medicines were in great demand, and our steel even more so. For a while, Saalshen was influential. There was so much wealth in the trade, and every human was desperate to please us lest we stop the supply. The great serrin thinkers who led the push for trade with humans were commended. This way, it was reasoned, we could control humans without having to resort to human concepts of empire and conquest. Empire and conquest sits with us very ill. Even today, much of Saalshen remains vastly uncomfortable with our role in the Saalshen Bacosh. Despite all the good we've done, still many wonder if we did the right thing in occupying those lands and changing them as we did.

"And today . . . well." Errollyn locked a bare muscular arm about an upraised knee and sighed. "The Saalshen Bacosh trades many of the items that were once only available from Saalshen. Those skills, too, are spreading. Today we threaten the families with boycott, and they merely shrug. Worse, I fear our threats of boycott are only encouraging them to make war on the Saalshen Bacosh. They feel the Saalshen Bacosh, once captured, will be ample restitution for the trade they shall lose from Saalshen itself. Trade is no longer a potent weapon of Saalshen. Some say we should withdraw trade now, to punish those who move against us . . . but then, we lose leverage entirely.

"I tell Rhillian every day that we do not understand humans well enough to move against them as we do. Two centuries ago, not a soul predicted what has come to pass today. Humans are a dynamic society, fast to change. Serrin are not. And yet serrin, with our superior talents, refuse to accept our own ignorance. We are digging a hole for ourselves, Sasha. Rhillian insists that it is a tunnel with the bright light of hope at the far end. I say it is our graves."

"Not all humans stand against you," Sasha said quietly.

Errollyn gazed at her. His green eyes were not as sharp as Rhillian's. They were deeper, more jade than emerald. But still, they were brilliant and far from human. "I know," he said simply. "If only someone would tell Rhillian."

"Surely Rhillian does not consider all humans her enemy?" Sasha asked, incredulously.

"No." Errollyn shook his head. "Rhillian believes . . . it is the philosophical precept of the *rhan'ist* and the *tula'shan*." Or that was what Sasha thought he'd said. Errollyn was the most plainspoken serrin Sasha had ever met and yet, when he switched to serrin philosophy, even he sounded alien.

"Go very, very slowly," she told him.

Errollyn made a face. "It's too difficult in Saalsi," he said instead in Lenay, "most of the words lack even basic translation. Rhillian believes that there is no problem with humans at all. She likes humans." A massive overtranslation, Sasha knew—serrin were rarely so simple in their feelings toward anything. But such was Errollyn's style. "She believes the problem lies in human society. Buy her an ale one night and I'm sure she'll be happy to explain it to you."

Sasha frowned. "You mean one human is good, but a hundred humans is bad?"

Errollyn smiled. "Exactly. One human is just a person. A hundred humans make a society. And societies have kings, and religions and priests, and all these other things serrin completely fail to understand."

Sasha shrugged. "Sounds quite sensible to me. I mean, look at Master Tongren in the The Fish Head. I've only dealt with Cherrovan before as a society, and they're no fun at all. But one Cherrovan . . . well, he's just Tongren. A decent, good-humoured man."

Errollyn nodded. "Rhillian believes that human societies always define themselves by their narrowest possible interests. That they are exclusive, not inclusive. She likes humans, but distrusts their societies. And so she expects no help at all for Saalshen from humans. She feels Saalshen has been too forgiving and gentle for too long. She has a good heart, Sasha, but she is convinced that the time has come for Saalshen to take hard actions and make difficult choices."

Given what she knew of Saalshen's enemies, Sasha did not feel she could blame Rhillian particularly for that. "And what do you believe?"

Errollyn sighed. "I believe that the fate of Saalshen is in humanity's hands," he said quietly. "Humans shall either be our salvation, or they shall be our destruction. And Rhillian, I'm afraid, may make the latter all the more likely."

He looked up, seeing someone approaching. Sasha looked and found Kessligh striding along the planks. He wore a loose shirt, rough pants and a floppy hat like Sasha's own, but she'd have recognised that stride anywhere. His approach gave her an unaccustomed feeling of trepidation deep in her stomach.

Kessligh sat cross-legged in the middle of the pier, straight-backed and perfectly flexible, whatever his fifty summers. "I've just come from the Fishnet Alley Courtyard," he said, without preamble. "Some of your peers were a little upset."

"I'm sorry!" Sasha exclaimed. "I just couldn't take it any more! They say they're enlightened, but they're all bigots!"

"Bigots?" Kessligh asked, an eyebrow raised.

"Yes, bigots! They treat women like the bigots treat the serrin, or the Xaldians! And worst of all, I'm a Lenay *and* a woman . . . I know I promised I'd hold my temper, but how are they ever going to learn otherwise if I don't prove them wrong?"

Kessligh exhaled hard and glanced at Errollyn, who seemed as amused as ever. "They have been a little slower in accepting the notion of a female uma than I'd hoped," Kessligh conceded. "It's been thirty years since I was last here. I'd hoped things had changed, at least a little."

Errollyn shook his head. "They're worse," he said. "The rise of pagan ideas has alarmed the priesthood. There is a campaign for morality in all the temples, including the proper behaviour of women. Petrodor Nasi-Keth are open-minded by local standards, but they are also Verenthanes. Many attend temple services. The Nasi-Keth have never tried to shove serrin teachings down people's throats, they understood that the teachings would only succeed if people were allowed to pick and choose."

"Maybe that was a mistake," Kessligh said grimly. "So many people can't see their own hand before their face. No wonder Rhillian doesn't see much hope in the Nasi-Keth when she sees them moving backward."

Errollyn shrugged. "If the Nasi-Keth do not reflect the values of the local population, how can they ever maintain their support? When balancing upon a high wall, one must sway both forward *and* backward."

"I'm sorry I made them angry," Sasha said earnestly. "But people like that are always going to be angry, one way or another."

"It's all right, Sasha," Kessligh said tiredly, holding up a hand. "I'm not angry at you. Many Nasi-Keth do respect you. The others just require some work." He seemed more frustrated than Sasha had ever seen him, as if something gnawed at him, deep inside. In Lenayin he'd always seemed so calm, so certain. Perhaps Petrodor had always made him feel this way. Constrained. Limited by other people's petty prejudices.

He had left her in Lenayin, whilst she remained embroiled in her homeland's squabbles, to come to Petrodor, leaving the brewing war in the north. That had come to rebellion. She'd come to forgive him his absence for she knew that his loyalties to the Nasi-Keth were as inseparable to him as her love for Lenayin was to her. Now, however, she occasionally wondered if he regretted the decision himself.

"We have the name of a vessel en route from Ameryn," said Kessligh. "It should arrive shortly. There's a large weapons shipment aboard. We're going to stop it."

"You think this will win support from Gerrold and Alaine?" Sasha asked warily.

Kessligh shrugged. "I can't control that, their people will either follow me or not. We'll stop that weapons shipment because it's what we need to do. It's what I came to Petrodor to do."

"But you want me to take a leading role?"

Kessligh gazed at her for a moment then smiled. "It would help," he admitted. "The tradition here is that the uma's deeds reflect well on the uman. If I'm to build a following, it'll take a little more than a few bruises to some thick-skulled swordsmen in a training session."

"Leading Lenayin's first rebellion in a century and defeating the Hadryn armoured cavalry in battle isn't enough?" Sasha asked, edgily.

"To these people, Lenayin's a long way away."

Sasha snorted. "I'll help," she said. "I don't want to see this war any more than you do. But there's something you should know first." She looked at Errollyn.

Errollyn told Kessligh about Randel Ragini. Kessligh made a face and squinted off toward the ocean horizon. "Rhillian is too clever for her own good," he said. "A sailor told me once that he'd known men who were brilliant at tying knots. But the real trick, he said, was to know *when* to tie them, and which knot went with which situation. Rhillian's tying her clever knots all over the city, but all she makes is a tangled rope."

"The question is why Ragini?" said Sasha. "Is she trying to break up the Steiner alliance from within?"

Kessligh looked at Errollyn warily. "I rode all the way to Lenayin," Errollyn said, "against Rhillian's wishes, to fight in a battle she said was none of my business. She no longer includes me in her plans."

"Kessligh . . ." Sasha took a deep breath. "I have a contact. A potential contact, right at the highest level of Family Steiner."

Kessligh shook his head. "It's too dangerous. And it's been fourteen years, you've no idea how she's changed . . ."

"Look, everyone says information is power, right?" Kessligh looked decidedly reluctant, but did not argue the point. "How stupid would we be, to have such an important contact and not use it at all? Just one piece of information! Marya's possibly the nicest person I've ever known, she wouldn't hurt a beetle! Maybe she doesn't even *know* half of what her new family does. Surely we should at least try?"

Five

JARYD HAD NEVER SEEN A TRADITIONAL LENAYIN WEDDING BEFORE.
The main road before the Steltsyn Star was a mass of dancing, cheering,
feasting people. The inn's tables had been arrayed in a rough circle across the
road, and serving boys and girls ran back and forth, hauling trays of roast
meat, vegetable raal, breads, wines, fruits and cheeses. Musicians played and
drums thundered as the sun disappeared behind the far valley ridge and the
bonfire at the centre of the circle was finally lit, to the delight and shouting
of all.

Jaryd sat on a far railing of the inn's verandah, eating from a tin plate, a
cup resting on a nearby post. There were more people present than he'd ever
seen in Baerlyn before. Half of neighbouring Yule had arrived in town with
the bride, to accompany her to her husband's home, and her new life. This
entire celebration had already been performed yesterday in Yule, as the village had sent off their girl. This was the welcoming ceremony, and it had
been going since the bride's arrival in midafternoon.

Jaryd saw Lynette arrive, plunging into the crowd to where Teriyan was
in animated conversation with friends. Teriyan handed off his cup, picked up
his daughter and spun her around. They looked so happy as they danced
through the firelit crowd, talking and laughing all the while. Jaryd swallowed a mouthful, and looked somewhere else.

Suddenly there was a pretty girl standing close, directly beneath the
railing to his side. She had light brown, curly hair and wore the plain dress
of a village girl . . . yet decorated in the Goeren-yai style, beads and braids in
her hair, a knotted red sash about her waist, rings on her fingers and bangles
on her wrists. She curtseyed prettily.

"Master Jaryd," she said demurely, "I would be most honoured should
you choose to dance with me."

Jaryd stared down at her. In Algery, they'd had rude names for girls who
asked men to dance. Here in the villages, women were more forward. She *was*
very pretty, no more than sixteen, he reckoned. He recalled many pretty girls,
from that other life. When he'd asked them to dance, they'd rarely refused.

When he'd asked them to do other things as well, they'd rarely refused that, either.

"I'm sorry," he told the girl. "I no longer dance."

The verandah rail shook and a hand reached onto his plate and stole a piece of cheese. "Why are you even here?" Lynette asked him around that mouthful. Her red hair was all tangled from her ride into town, and she smelled of horses. "I mean, why come to a wedding if you're just going to sit here away from everyone and look morose?"

"Jaegar told me at training I should come," Jaryd said stonily. "Jaegar is village headman, I do what he tells me."

"Pity he didn't tell you to have some fun too."

Jaryd ground his teeth and did not reply. She'd never had a brother murdered in cold blood, and she had precious little respect for his grief. It was an effort not to strike her.

"Have you welcomed the bride yet?"

"No."

"You should. I'm sure she's heard all about Jaryd Nyvar. She'll be expecting a greeting and good wishes. That's what Sasha and Kessligh always did."

"Aye, well, they're not here now, are they?"

Lynette sighed. "I so wish Sasha was here now, she loves weddings."

"She does?" It didn't sound like the Sashandra Lenayin Jaryd knew.

"So long as it's not her own," Lynette added with a grin. "But, oh yes, she loves traditional weddings. If she were here she'd be feasting and dancing, and telling all the boys how handsome they looked. She could be such a tease sometimes."

Jaryd exhaled hard. "I wish I'd had the chance to come to know Sashandra a little better," he conceded. Sometimes he envied Lynette and Andreyis that. The entire village, in fact. "She's a remarkable warrior, and she won a great victory at Ymoth. Kessligh himself could not have done better."

Lynette shrugged, chewing on her cheese. "She's Kessligh's uma, after all. But the most remarkable thing about Sasha is how she became brilliant while still managing to be such a pain in the arse."

Jaryd looked at her. He almost smiled. Lynette put a hand on his arm. "You're nice when you smile," she told him. "Hold on, I have to go and talk to the *other* most morose-looking man in Baerlyn for a while. I'll be back."

She jumped off the rail and slid through the crowd. The other man was, of course, Andreyis. Jaryd spotted him on the far side of the bonfire, sitting with two other lads, drinking and looking gloomy. Becoming a warrior didn't change all things, then. He could grow his hair long, get tattoos if he wanted, and move away from home as he pleased, but Andreyis remained awkward and ill at ease, with girls in particular. Except Lynette . . . but she was more like a sister to him, complete with name calling and hair pulling.

Jaryd almost felt sorry for the lad. He missed Sasha, that much was obvious. Perhaps he'd even fancied her a little . . . and what lonely, awkward young man wouldn't have? But she'd been more like a sister too, and so dominantly, ferociously overbearing that the poor boy must have known from the start he had no chance . . .

Neither did Andreyis have many good friends among young Baerlyn men. Lynette conceded that Sasha had first grown to like Andreyis precisely because he *wasn't* one of those arrogant, rude little boys whose ears, knees, ribs, backsides and finally skulls Sasha had had to box to gain some respect . . . and some fear. Jaryd did not know letters, but he knew young men as he knew swords and horses. They'd have resented Andreyis his friendship with someone who had humiliated them. They'd have resented him further his friendship with Kessligh. It was remarkable that a friendship with the greatest warrior in Lenayin could actually make someone *less* popular . . . but Lenayin was like that. Men who gained respect by becoming friends with the powerful were mistrusted. Men should gain respect by gathering honour for themselves.

Some men in colourful Torovan dress were walking up the main road, talking with Parrachik and skirting the children playing games at the edge of the bonfire's glare. Parrachik was an unremarkable man to look at—bald and slim, he wore only a knife at his belt and smiled when local men would taunt him for his lack. A Torovan like the merchants who so often called on him, he'd arrived in Baerlyn fifteen years ago and adopted the local customs sparingly yet for all his success, he wore little finery.

He led his Torovan guests now to the feast, where they looked on with curiosity. Wine was pressed upon them and soon they were talking and laughing with rowdy locals, Parrachik providing translation where local accent or general noise proved too great for the traders' Lenay. Soon the merchants were clapping along to the rhythm with the rest of them, and being invited to dance by local Baerlyn women, all eagerly accepted.

Lynette was dragging at Andreyis's arm, trying to get him to the dance, but Andreyis was resisting. Jaryd pushed himself off the balcony railing with a thud of boots on the deck . . . and nearly missed the second thud on the wall behind. He turned, frowning, thinking someone had thrown something. Instead, he saw a crossbow bolt protruding from the wall.

He dove flat, but no further shot came. Then he scrambled for the inn's doorway and crouched there, staring up at the opposing row of rooftops, bright and dancing in the glare of the bonfire. There was a flash of movement . . . or was it merely a shadow? No one had noticed his little commotion, one more flailing, dancing man at a wedding was hardly an event. If he yelled warning to them, none would hear.

Besides, warning of what? They were not in danger. The assassin was after him. Maybe, the cold thought occurred to him, as he edged back into the cover of the doorway, one of the locals had arranged it. Maybe they felt his presence threatened Baerlyn's relations with the lords. Or maybe Great Lord Arastyn had partisans, or at least paid help here in Baerlyn. If he shouted warning, he would only advertise that their attempt had failed, and perhaps invite a second or third attack. No, he had to capture the assassin himself. Only then could he know what he was dealing with.

He strode through the inn, adjusting his swordbelt where it had twisted in his dive. Through the main room, stripped of chairs and tables, Jaryd found the side exit and pushed out into the paved lane to the stables. Then he ran back toward the road, where the fringe of the crowd milled across the lane's mouth hoping any waiting crossbowman on the surrounding roofs would have far too brief a sighting to take a shot. He ran fast, hand on his sword hilt, to keep his legs free, taking a wide route through the crowd. He skidded between two men, hurdling a running child, collided with the arm of a lady, her drink spilling.

Then he was down a narrow lane between two houses, unscathed and, as far as he knew, untargeted. He hurdled a fence between the houses and took shelter beneath the rear verandah roof. Crouched against a wall, he drew his sword and listened. He heard only the raucous music and laughter of the wedding. He moved as lightly as he could across the verandah planks, pausing with a wince each time one began to squeak. He stopped and listened again.

Nothing. Then a muffled slide overhead. A creak. Two thumps. Then nothing. Jaryd reached to his belt and drew a throwing knife. Reversed it with a flip, catching the blade, his sword now in his left hand. Someone jumped from the verandah roof, thumped into the grassy yard and rolled, pausing to retrieve a fallen crossbow.

"You missed," Jaryd told the crossbowman. The figure spun in shock. Jaryd threw the knife and took him in the thigh. The man yelled, dropping the crossbow again, and fell, clutching his leg. Jaryd stepped from the balcony and walked to him, sword ready, his grip tightening. This must be one of those who had schemed to kill Tarryn. This, he had waited for for a long time.

More movement from the gloom of orchard trees in the neighbouring yard. Jaryd's eyes widened as he saw the questing muzzle of a crossbow through the branches. He threw himself flat. Frustratingly, the crossbowman held his fire. Jaryd rolled desperately for the fallen man, holding him as a shield. The bowman emerged from the orchard and cursed, darting one way, then the other, seeking a shot over the fence. Jaryd rose, his hostage sobbing and holding his leg. A rush of footsteps from behind told him a third man was coming.

Jaryd reached for his boot knife—not really a throwing knife, but he threw it anyway. The bowman ducked, the knife deflected off the crossbow and Jaryd charged. The bowman dropped the crossbow, scampering back as Jaryd hurdled the fence, drawing his blade. Jaryd swung hard, the other man defended desperately, fended the second and third with a clash of steel, yet was simply overpowered by the fourth, lost his hand on the fifth, and was sliced through the chest by the sixth before he could scream.

Jaryd turned and found the third man staring in horror. This man had no crossbow, just a sword. Evidently he did not relish the prospect of using it now. This was no hired blade. This man knew exactly whom he'd been sent to kill. The assassin turned and fled. Jaryd chased, his heart pounding, blood singing in his ears. He hadn't felt this alive since Tarryn had still been in the world. He pursued the fleeing shadow past a chicken run, then hurdled another fence onto a vegetable patch. Another fence, and he was out into an open field in the middle of the Baerlyn Valley. The light of the wedding bonfire grew dimmer behind and the stars overhead were bright and clear. His boots sank into the grass as he ran, stumbling on an uneven patch in the dark. The fleeing shadow before him was slim, and fleet of foot. Jaryd was a powerful young man, and knew how to use that power to intimidating effect with a blade. But now, his legs grew weary, and his breathing came hard, and the light figure ahead seemed barely troubled when he hurdled the next fenceline and raced on into the dark.

It was two fencelines later before Jaryd finally gave up. He'd headed up-valley, past empty farmhouses, tripping on plough furroughs and splashing in irrigation ditches as he went.

"Come back and fight, you horse-fucking coward!" he roared at the dark, with the last of his energy. Now that he'd stopped, the night air chilled his sweat. He was exhausted from the effort, and barely able to keep his feet. The unfairness of it infuriated him. He swung his blade at the dark, smiting invisible foes. Gleaming in the night sky, he saw Ambellion's Star, bright and clear. Cathaty's Eye, the Goeren-yai called it. In the lowlands, and amongst Lenay Verenthanes, it was the Verenthane Star. "You!" Jaryd yelled, pointing his sword at the star. "You saved him! You defy me once more, you bastards! Well I've *had* it with you! I've rejected you, do you hear? This isn't your land, and you can't *fuck with me any longer*!"

A sharp wind blew upon the Cliff of the Dead. Marya Steiner put a hand to her hair and hoped that the pins would not tear out from the force of it. She walked with her other hand in that of her nine-year-old son, and her husband by her side, with a pair of guards to their front and back.

"I absolutely forbid it, Symon!" Marya insisted in a low voice. "This is my sister, she would never put me in danger."

"I hear stories, my love," replied Symon Steiner, edgily. He looked good in black, with a gold-pommelled sword at his hip. A little slimmer and shorter than a Lenay bride might typically have hoped, but he was handsome, and clever, and kind. "This particular sister of yours—and the gods know you have so many I am frequently confused—has a reputation that would insult the good breeding of a rabid dog—"

"Oh, Symon, don't be like that! The Sashandra I remember was a gorgeous little girl, always full of life and mischief . . ."

"There are many definitions of mischief, my love." Symon threw a glance up and down the terraced incline. "One might think that leading an armed rebellion against Verenthane patriots in the north, against the wishes of her father the king, goes a little beyond simple mischief."

Marya sighed, not halting her stride. "Sashandra *always* went a little beyond simple mischief," she admitted. "But . . . oh Symon, you never knew her like I did. You don't know how much *fun* she was! She was a delightful little scoundrel."

Behind them, toward the end of Besendi Promontory, the funeral for Randel Ragini was dispersing. The seniors of Family Steiner, and all their allies, bereaved and sorrowful in black. Marya had never liked that silly Endurance that the men all insisted upon every Sadisi. Three days ago now. Every year, someone was hurt. This year, just like she'd warned would happen, it was someone important. Young Randel, such a nice boy. His father had seemed in shock, barely looking at anyone while the priest had recited the last rites. Doubtless losing a son in such pointless circumstances was difficult, to say nothing of an heir. When she'd taken Patachi Ragini's hand to offer her condolences, it had been shaking.

"Look," said Symon, "at least allow me to place some extra men on the upper terrace. Just in case."

"Symon, she is Nasi-Keth," Marya said reasonably. "And from what I hear, quite talented. Your own sources say she has friends among the serrin, she's been seen frequently with that Rhillian woman . . ."

"All the more reason to—"

"Her note said to come alone!" Marya insisted. "If she has serrin friends, don't you think there might be serrin archers hiding somewhere?"

"Where?"

"If I knew that, dearest, they wouldn't be hiding, would they?"

"It's very windy for archers, Mummy," said Krystoff. He was watching a big gull soaring just above, using the updraughts to hold almost motionless against the overcast sky, save for twitches of its tail.

"Not for serrin archers it's not, darling," Marya corrected her eldest son. Even *she* knew that. "And if your papa insists on moving some men where they're not supposed to be, those archers might use his men for target practice. Mightn't they, dearest?"

The path rounded a bend, and now they could see it—a small, wooden hut where the terrace ended and the sheer cliff resumed. Beyond, where the slope became more gentle, Petrodor began, a mass of buildings up the incline. Upon the docks, men looked like swarms of ants.

"At least you should leave Krys with me," Symon attempted, one last time.

"No," Marya said firmly. "He should meet his aunt, it will do him good."

"For all damnation, woman," said Symon, with the beginnings of cold temper, "would you put your own son's life at risk?"

"No." Marya stopped, and gave him a cold look of her own. "No, I would not."

"I'm not afraid, Papa," said Krystoff earnestly. "I'd like to meet her."

Symon spared the ocean an exasperated stare. "I know you're not afraid, son. I never doubted it."

"Symon," said Marya, her tone softening. "You claim to know something about my sister. Our son's name is *Krystoff*. If you know *anything* about her, you'll know why she of all people could never harm a hair on his head." Her husband just looked at her, for a long, calculating moment. Marya had seen him give that look before, making deals with powerful men. Wondering if all was, in fact, as it appeared. "You Torovans," she said with exasperation. "Truly, one might believe you thought you were the only people to whom family mattered. You have so many family here, Symon. I see so few of my old family. Please."

"Go," he said. "I'll be right here."

Marya kissed him on the cheek gratefully. She clutched Krystoff's hand all the more tightly and walked toward the wooden hut.

Krystoff took the door's latch, well trained in the ways of gentlemanly conduct. The rusty iron squealed and Marya stepped in behind him, eyeing the gloom with trepidation, a hand on her son's shoulder.

"Hello?" she called. Her heart was beating very fast. Surely Symon could not be right? Much of his information came indirectly from Alythia, she knew, and Alythia . . . well, she was prone to making up all sorts of accusations about people she didn't like. Alythia and Sasha . . . Sofy had said, in her occasional letters, how truly alike they were in their high-strung tempers, and how ironic it was that neither could recognise the fact. Surely Alythia had not been more than just tale telling?

Krystoff closed the door behind them, and the wind ceased. Marya's eyes adjusted, and she saw that there were headstones and pavings stacked in stone piles, with shovels and spades to maintain the small flower gardens that grew between the stones. Wind shook the walls and lifted the roof planks against their nails. The panes in two small windows rattled.

"Hello," said a voice to her right, and Marya spun. There was a dark figure there. "Is that your husband? He's a bit small, isn't he?"

"Dear gods," Marya exclaimed, with a hand to her chest. "You startled me."

"Sorry," said the figure. "It happens."

A female voice. But the gloom was too deep for visible detail, and Marya's eyes had not adjusted. "Sashandra?" Marya ventured, a little breathlessly.

A small laugh in the darkness. "You never used to call me Sashandra," said the voice. The Torovan was excellent, yet the accent very broad.

"Gods, come out of that dark corner!" Marya exclaimed, backing toward the windows, her hand still on Krystoff's shoulder. "I want to look at you!"

The dark figure followed, a lithe, soundless movement. Then she emerged into the silver light coming through the glass panes. Not a big girl, especially not for the reputation she had attained, victorious rebellion against the Hadryn and all. The clothes were scandalously unfeminine, yet really quite well made. A jacket of soft leather, neatly fitting pants and snug boots. And a bandoleer, of course, worn over the jacket, the hilt of a sword protruding above her left shoulder. Her short hair had been mussed by the wind, her tri-braid dangling free down the left side of her jaw.

And her face . . . Marya put a hand to her mouth. Big dark eyes, formerly full of mischief. Now watching her, curiously. The same, slightly wicked slant to the eyebrows. The same impudent nose. All grown up, and oh-so-different . . . and yet, to a degree she'd not dared hope possible, clearly the same girl from her memories, all those years ago.

"Sasha?" she said softly. "Is that really you?"

Tears came to Sasha's eyes, unexpectedly. Marya's eyes also filled. The sisters embraced as the little wooden hut above the roaring surf shuddered in the howling wind. How silly to have worried, Marya managed to think past the happiness and relief. How silly to have worried about my little sister. Good lords, she felt absolutely *solid* beneath her leathers! A little less than average size, perhaps, but made of rock!

"Oh here, Sasha, look!" Marya disentangled herself, wiping her eyes. "Here's someone I'd like you to meet! Sasha, this is my eldest boy. Krystoff."

Krystoff bowed. Sasha gazed, her eyes still wet. Such a pretty girl in her own curious way. But then, it had never been *looks* her family lacked. "I am honoured to meet you, Aunt Sashandra."

Sasha grinned. She changed expressions fast, Marya observed with fascinated remembrance. The same little Sashandra. Temperamental, even now. "And I am likewise honoured to meet my nephew," she said, returning the bow. "Do you speak any Lenay, Krystoff?"

"A little." Krystoff gave his mother a cautious glance. "Mother teaches me. And she says bad words in Lenay when she's angry."

"Oh I do not!" Marya exclaimed, but smiling.

"That's good," said Sasha. "It's good to know where your parents come from. *Both* of your parents." With a knowing glance at Marya.

"Papa says the Lenays are fierce warriors," Krystoff agreed. "Grandpa says all of Lenayin shall some day make fine Verenthane allies. I think it's a good language for me to learn."

Sasha's face fell. Not angry, but the smile disappeared as fast as it had come. "Well, your grandpa's not perfect, I suppose." There was an edge to her tone. Krystoff frowned, not understanding.

"Krys," Marya said, "you go and wait outside with your father. Sasha and I need some time alone to catch up. We haven't seen each other in a long time."

"A long time," Sasha repeated with a laugh. "Fourteen years! I was a little brat up to your knee!"

"It was very nice to meet you, Aunt Sashandra," said Krystoff. "Perhaps we can meet again another time."

"I'd like that," said Sasha. Marya thought she meant it. "Oh, and Krystoff?" she added as the boy opened the hut door, letting in a swirl of wind. "Best tell your father that I'm not alone here. Tell him we're being watched by people with excellent aim. He'll understand."

Krystoff nodded, warily. He understood, too. One was not born the heir to the Steiner Empire, of any generation, to not understand such things. The door closed.

"He seems a nice boy," said Sasha.

"He's very sweet," Marya agreed. "He'll make a fine patachi one day."

"Hmm," said Sasha.

"And really, Sasha," Marya scolded gently, "you needn't worry about Symon. He's just worried about me, that's all. There's no need to threaten him."

"I'll never threaten anyone who doesn't threaten me first," Sasha said coolly.

There was a look in her eye as she said it that gave Marya a chill. *That* hadn't been there, in the eyes of the little girl she'd known. The little girl was now a young woman, and this young woman had killed people. Quite a few people, if the tales were true.

"He doesn't look very much like Krystoff," Sasha added, thoughtfully watching the door where the boy had stood.

"Well he doesn't really have to, does he?" Marya countered. "It's the thought that counts."

"I suppose," said Sasha. Marya did not tell her that Patachi Steiner had encouraged her to use the name of Lenayin's deceased heir and Sasha's most beloved brother. The patachi encouraged strong relations with Lenayin wherever possible. Marya did not think Sasha would be pleased to hear it.

"But look at you!" Marya exclaimed, changing the subject. "You look just amazing! Like a hero from some story that has yet to be told!"

Sasha actually appeared to blush, just a little. "Serrin think I'm pretty," she admitted, with just a hint of shyness. "It'd be nice to find a human who thought so."

"You look wonderful."

"You don't seem very surprised. When I first returned to Baen-Tar after I'd left to live with Kessligh, people stared like they were seeing a ghost. They only remembered a little girl with long hair in dresses, I guess . . ."

"I think it suits you," said Marya. "Anyone who'd seen you sliding down staircase railings, and chasing terrified little boys with a stick and yelling, would recognise you now." Sasha laughed self-consciously. "This is the inner you, perhaps. Not many people grow up to become the thing they've always desired. You should be proud."

From the way Sasha smiled, Marya could tell that she'd pleased her. "And look at *you*!" she said. "You're looking very . . . well, motherly."

"I know," Marya sighed, placing hands on her hips. "But they feed me so well, and the food's so excellent . . ."

"Oh, no, no," Sasha protested. "You look wonderful! Motherliness suits you. I always . . . I mean, all my memories of you are of you being kind to me. I remember whenever I'd hurt myself, you were always there to clean my scrapes. You were like the mother I never . . . or rather, almost never had."

You really never did know mother like I did, Marya thought sadly. You don't know what she suffered. You were too young.

"Oh, Sasha," Marya said kindly, "I always wanted to tell you—I'm so sorry that I was not around when Krystoff died. It must have been so terrible for you. How lonely you must have felt."

Sasha gave a small shrug. "It's the fate of Lenay princesses that they be married when their father deems it convenient. How could that be your fault?"

"Even so, when I received the news, I felt so terrible. I cried for days. But mostly, I was thinking of you. I did not know that you would survive."

The kinship between the heir of Lenayin and his little sister had been cute and lovable in many ways. And yet, Marya recalled an edge to the friendship that others did not. Krystoff had been driven, largely by forces known only to him. He had not understood how others did not share his passions and impulses. Only little Sashandra had understood.

"Did you enjoy growing up with Kessligh in Baerlyn?" Marya ventured.

The younger woman's smile flashed. "I loved it. I finally got to run wild." She laughed. "But with some discipline too."

"You did not miss your family at all?"

"Did you?" Sasha countered.

"Oh, of course! But . . . well, I had a new family. And the Steiners treated me wonderfully from the beginning. Symon is a perfect husband, and I have children of my own now. I was homesick for a while, it's true, and I missed you and Krystoff and the others terribly. But I don't know that I can say I was lonely. I always had company and things to do. I always felt included. This is my home now."

Sasha sighed. She walked two steps to the small window and gazed through the cracked, clouded glass. "My home is in Baerlyn," she said. "The townsfolk are my family. And Kessligh. He was the father I never had. He taught me so many things, things I failed to appreciate until recently."

"And so . . ." Marya paused, wondering how to put it. "You feel the . . . the Nasi-Keth are your family now?"

Sasha bit the inside of her lip, thinking as she gazed down on the windswept docks below. "I get tired of all these divisions," she said finally, and decisively. She met Marya's gaze. "People are always telling me that I have to pick one side or the other. I have loyalties to many sides. I won't pretend that I love all my family, but I certainly love Sofy . . . and Damon too, I think. I love Kessligh. I love Baerlyn and the ancient ways of Lenayin. And I love the serrin too. The serrin believe that this human instinct to pick one side and fight all the others is the cause of all humanity's troubles. I think I agree with them."

"Have you spoken to Alythia since she's arrived?" Marya ventured, knowing the answer in advance, but . . .

Sasha gave a short laugh. "I'd get a more friendly response from one of the sea lions on Alaster Promontory, I'm quite sure."

"Have you tried?"

"I ruined her wedding, Marya. Surely you heard?"

"Well yes, but . . ." Marya wrung her hands in exasperation. "Oh, it's so frustrating, Sasha! I mean look at us! Three sisters, all together in the one city. Surely this is fate, to bring us all together so!"

"Tempting fate, maybe," Sasha said, warily eyeing the Verenthane medallion about Marya's neck.

"You don't believe in fate?" Marya asked sadly.

"There's many old notions I no longer believe in," Sasha replied. "And many others I'm starting to. Fate's not high amongst them."

"Wouldn't it be nice if we could all be a family again?" Marya persisted. "I'm not entirely naive, I do know that Petrodor can be a . . . a cold and cruel place at times. But Sasha, it's exactly in such places that the bonds of family matter so much! And I'd so love for you to meet your other nephews and nieces . . ."

Sasha looked at the ground. "I'd like that too," she said quietly. "But with things as they are, I don't know how welcome I'd be."

"Sasha." Marya placed a gentle hand on her sister's shoulder. "Family is important to everyone in Petrodor. If you came to House Steiner with an open heart, you would be entirely safe there. Whoever your friends, and whoever your uman."

"Safe like Randel Ragini was safe?" said Sasha sombrely.

Marya blinked at her. "Randel? Sasha, Randel was killed in an accident . . . they happen all the time during the Endurance, I've been warning people about it for years, but do they listen to a woman? Of course not."

"Your father-in-law ordered Randel Ragini killed," said Sasha. Marya blinked again. Sasha's gaze was direct, searching, as if studying her response.

"And who told you that?" said Marya, unperturbed.

"People who know."

"Look, Sasha." Marya put her other hand on Sasha's shoulders too. "Petrodor is full of rumours. People say nasty things, about Patachi Steiner most of all. I know him quite well. I won't pretend that he's the gentlest, kindest man in Petrodor, but believe me when I tell you this one thing—he's not half of what his enemies say he is. Not a quarter, even."

"He killed Randel because he suspected Randel, and possibly Patachi Ragini, were dealing with the serrin," Sasha continued, equally unperturbed. "My sources say the priesthood were possibly involved, they're the ones most upset by senior Petrodor families dealing with the pagan serrin. Randel collected serrin artworks, including some the holy fathers found blasphemous . . ."

"Sasha," Marya said sternly, "you've been listening to men with evil tongues, the holy fathers do not go around ordering people killed!"

"Seriously, Marya," Sasha said tiredly, with the air of a woman suddenly twice her age. "Your father-in-law is building an army to go and fight a war entirely on the behest of the priesthood. It will assuredly kill many, many thousands of people. The priesthood don't order people killed? Do you honestly believe that?"

Marya stared at her for a moment. Gods, how she hated politics. She half spun, a hand to her forehead. Then spun back. "And is that truly why you smuggled a message to meet me here today?" she asked, woundedly. "I mean . . . seriously, Sasha, what do you want from me?"

"And do you think Symon Steiner would risk his wife and his heir to meet with his sworn enemy in a darkened hut if he didn't see some kind of advantage in it?" Sasha replied. "Or if Patachi Steiner didn't? Marya, we're both being used. People on both sides are looking for some advantage, and perhaps some information." She stepped forward and took Marya's hands gently. Her eyes were earnest. "I came because I desperately wanted an excuse to see my sister again. This was the first and best excuse I've had. But also, I wanted to tell you what I know. You don't have to believe me . . . it's hard, I know. But I wanted you to think about what I've told you. That's all. What you choose to do about it . . . well, that's none of my business."

"Sasha," Marya said quietly, "don't pick a fight with Patachi Steiner. Please."

Sasha's eyes narrowed, head cocked to one side. Fearless, Marya saw despairingly. Of physical danger, at least. This, too, confirmed the memories of the little girl she'd known. "I thought you said he was a good man?"

"Amongst a good man's many duties are the elimination of his enemies," said Marya, sombrely.

Sasha's gaze was long and level. Studying her.

"Patachi Steiner wants this war," she replied, finally. "If it concerns you, tell him to stop."

"Sasha, I'm his daughter-in-law," said Marya, reproachfully. "I can do no such thing."

Sasha shrugged. "Then there's not much I can do."

"You would truly fight?" Marya pressed, with desperation. "Against your own flesh and blood?"

"He's not my flesh and blood," Sasha said coolly. "You are."

Dear lords, Marya thought helplessly. She doesn't understand a thing. "Krystoff is too," she tried. "He's old enough to wield a proper blade in training. He's very good."

"Marya, what the Larosa want to do in the Bacosh is evil, do you understand me?" Sasha's tone betrayed the first sign of impatience. "Not merely misguided or unfortunate, but *evil*. The serrin have done nothing but good for the Saalshen Bacosh, and the Larosa would kill them all if they could, right through all of Saalshen. If your father-in-law brings a huge Torovan army to Regent Arrosh's side, along with the army our true father intends to bring him, they might just finish the serrin off once and for all. The serrin are a bright light in this dark world, Marya. I'll not allow that light to die if I can do anything to help it."

"There are those who say that evil is the human who would fight for the strange folk against her own kind." Marya refrained from making the holy sign as she spoke. The tri-braid in her sister's hair was not just an innocent decoration back in Lenayin. It was pagan. "It would be a sin, they say."

"My own *kind*?" Sasha's stare was incredulous. "What in the world does that mean? I fight for what is right against what is wrong . . . how do evil slugs like the Regent Arrosh suddenly become imbued with holy virtue simply because they're of 'my own kind'? As if humans have never fought humans before and called each other evil?"

"Family is always right, Sasha," said Marya, with a shake of the head. "Family is always good. The betrayal of family is the greatest evil known."

"Tell that to Patachi Ragini," Sasha said firmly, a hard light in her dark eyes. "Your father-in-law murdered his son!"

"Oh, Sasha," Marya sighed, gazing sadly at her little sister. "That's what I'm afraid of."

Six

RIVERSIDE STANK. The Nasi-Keth moved quietly along the narrow streets and alleys, trying not to tread on anything foul in the dark. There were no sewers here on the bank of the River Sarna, on the opposite side of the Petrodor Incline. Only streets with small, open channels of running filth on either side. A few streets were cobbled and firm beneath Sasha's boots, but most were just hard earth that would turn to mud in the winter rains.

The only light came from within the dirty hovels that passed for houses. Firelight flickered between broken boards, and from behind soiled curtains of rough cloth that served for doors. The walls were so thin and irregular that Sasha could hear the voices within: the women scolding, the children crying and many folk coughing—a horrid, sickly sound. The accents were coarse, and not all spoke Torovan. Many were outcasts from neighbouring regions, Kessligh had said. Poor, unskilled and desperate, they came to Petrodor with little more than the clothes on their backs, and threw together ramshackle dwellings with whatever scrap they could find.

Here, they worked, begged and stole, eeking out a living along the overcrowded river docks in conditions unfit for animals. The Nasi-Keth's latest count put the number of tortured souls in Riverside at more than sixty thousand. They had tried to gain converts here, but the people were mostly of superstitious country stock and clung to Verenthane ritual for comfort. Many called the Nasi-Keth witches, and it was not merely for protection from the families that the Nasi-Keth and serrin carried weapons in Riverside.

Soon the slums gave way to large wooden warehouses. Several Nasi-Keth took positions on the corner, while Aiden led the way down a tight alley alongside an old warehouse. Blades drawn, they came to a halt in the confined, garbage-strewn dark, while Aiden peered about the corner. Then he dashed, and disappeared in the gloom. Kessligh was next, and then Sasha. One look about the corner and she saw that they were directly on the River Dock, with water glinting in the darkness ahead and a great mass of barges and ships tied to piers.

Sasha ran, low and fast to a pile of broken wooden crates, and arrived beside Aiden and Kessligh, crouching on the pavings. "Can you see it?" she whispered, peering above the pile. Along the dock, shadows moved against sporadic firelight and she could make out the shape of a spear, or the point of a helm. Guards protecting the boats and their cargo.

"The fourth warehouse along," said Kessligh, squinting into the darkness. "But I can't see the guards."

A fourth set of footsteps arrived behind, and then Errollyn was at Sasha's side. No other serrin had come on this mission, but Errollyn had insisted.

"I see two guards by the Torack warehouse," he said. "They wear Torack colours and the Torack emblem on their coats."

"That's them," Kessligh said grimly. The quarter moon had already been and fled, leaving the night black save for the flickering guard lights. "Can you see any carts? Any sign of transport?"

"No," said Errollyn. He did not squint into the night—he gazed, eyes wide like an owl. Sasha watched him, faintly disconcerted. "Perhaps all the weapons are still on the boats."

"They were supposed to start moving them off this afternoon," said Aiden.

Kessligh gnawed at his lip. It was the only nervous gesture Sasha knew him to have. Steiner knew better than to unload weapons bound for the Bacosh or Lenayin on the main Petrodor Dock, with so many Nasi-Keth and serrin around. Instead they transferred cargo to smaller boats out at sea, which in turn came up the Sarna to unload in Riverside.

"Errollyn," said Kessligh, "how many boats on the Torack pier?"

"Looks like . . . three square sloops and four barges. Barges at the far pier, sloops at the near."

"Do we even know for certain those are the ships?" Sasha wondered.

"Yes," said Aiden. "Three sources, all paid. None knew the others existed so they could not have coordinated their stories."

"It's a high pass in hostile territory," Sasha observed. In mountainous Lenayin, a high pass meant a narrow place where advancing forces could be trapped, and slaughtered. "I don't like it."

"There's never anything to like about fighting in cities," said Kessligh. "If there's been no unloading, it should all be on the boats still. We'll go with plan five for now, but tentatively. I need a scout. If we commit ourselves to the Torack warehouse entirely, we'll need to know what's in the neighbouring ones."

"I'll go," said Errollyn, flashing a smile in the dark. "I'm the only one here who can see."

"Good," said Kessligh. "And . . ."

"Me," said Sasha. "I'm small and I'm sneaky."

"But in a nice way," said Errollyn. Sasha grinned.

"Sneaky in a Lenayin forest and sneaky in a city are not the same thing," said Kessligh. "Better one of Aiden's lads should go."

"I've ridden on campaign with Errollyn and fought two battles with him," Sasha said firmly, giving Kessligh a firm stare. "We'll move better together."

Kessligh's lips twisted unhappily. As if he felt guilty for pushing her into such a position. Sasha felt her heart swell at the sight of his concern. She knew it was stupid, but she couldn't help it. That concern, however, was not evident in his voice. "Stay low," he said, "and pull back immediately if there's trouble."

Sasha took the lead, moving between the old warehouse front and more piles of old crates, where little light penetrated. The warehouse looked abandoned, with nothing stored near that might require a guard. Errollyn followed, his bow in one hand.

The next alley provided cover, and the old warehouse's warped sides provided foot and hand holds for a climb to the roof. Errollyn covered Sasha, then slung his bow over a shoulder and climbed—the bow was nearly as tall as him, but it seemed to give him no problems. When he was up, Sasha pointed to the beam at one end and indicated up the sloping slate roof where it should run. Errollyn nodded, and Sasha moved up that line, careful not to put a foot to either side where the poor construction could plunge her straight through both roof and ceiling.

She paused at the roof's apex and peered across. The next warehouse was guarded. She could see figures standing watch along the riverside dock. From this high angle, she could see others seated behind crates and sacks, their crossbows leaning nearby. Some played dice by lamplight, and she could hear muted conversation and laughter. To her left, away from the river, Riverside sprawled, with only a few lights to break the desolation. Higher beyond rose Backside, referred to by the higher classes as the arse-end of Petrodor.

A hand came down on the tile to her side, and she realised that Errollyn had crawled almost directly on top of her to gain a view without abandoning the support of the beam beneath. The Torack warehouse was still three further along.

"The next roof," he whispered in her ear. "We can jump the gap. Even I can't see enough from here."

His knee was between her own, his body nearly pressing on her back. And she was amused at herself for noticing, with all else that was important in the night. She slithered over the apex and crawled down the opposing roofside, careful to disperse her weight lest she dislodge a tile and bring guards running to investigate the clatter.

At the gap between warehouses, she paused and peered down. She could see nothing below, but there was a guard on the corner. The gap ahead was two armspans—simple enough in daytime, but at night, onto loose tiles, not so easy. She gathered to a crouch, then uncoiled and leapt. She landed comfortably enough, not even displacing a tile.

She crawled onward, feeling very pleased with herself—years of sneaking about forbidden places in Baen-Tar Palace, or climbing trees around Baerlyn, had not been in vain. She paused to wait for Errollyn, only to see that he'd already jumped behind her. She hadn't even heard him land.

Atop the apex of this rooftop, he crawled over her again. "I count nine guards," he murmured in her ear, "but there could be plenty more. We should wait awhile, and see what comes."

"Like this?" The thought was not unappealing. If Errollyn rolled to one side, the tiles would quite likely give way. If he crawled forward above the roof's apex, he'd risk being seen. No choice, really . . .

"You could slide down," Errollyn suggested. "I see more than you."

"Two pairs are better than one," Sasha said quickly. "I might see something you don't recognise."

Errollyn simply lay on her back, taking part of his weight on his arms. Sasha bit her lip. "Don't get too excited," he told her. "This is strictly business."

"Business can be fun too," said Sasha. Dear spirits, they were twenty paces from men who would gladly kill them and she was flirting.

Sasha knew that however nice Errollyn's gentle bodyweight felt, and however his supporting arm seemed to half wrap around her in a partial embrace, she should not take it too personally. She'd seen serrin exchange even more intimate physical affections without appearing to mean very much by it . . . or not as a human might understand such things.

"Look," he said and pointed down at the riverside dock. Some figures walked along a narrow pier lit with the dancing light of a torch. One was a lordly man in fancy clothes. Behind him walked a man in a dark robe and hood . . . strange for the night was warm. Several guards walked with them. "Symon Steiner," Errollyn murmured.

"Really?" Sasha peered more closely. The lordly man wore a broad-brimmed hat, lowlands style, with a plume in the band. The brim cast a shadow, obscuring the face. "Are you certain?"

"Of course. I can see the family resemblance."

"Don't remind me," Sasha muttered. Her own brother-in-law. Dear spirits. "Who's in the hood?"

"Someone who doesn't wish to be recognised, I'd guess. I'll bet you three quarters it's a priest."

"Three quarters? Serrin are so cheap."

"Only because humans fleece us so often."

"Besides, a priest?" Sasha said as the implications of that began to sink in. "Why?"

"Who better to supervise a holy war than a priest?" Errollyn said.

"You think the priesthood has that much control over the preparations for war?"

"Moral guidance," said Errollyn, staring at the figures on the dock. They'd stopped at the beginning of the pier and were discussing something. Their hands barely moved as they spoke, so they were in relative agreement. When Torovans were agitated, their hands waved around a lot. "Steiner provides the money and trade, the dukes and your father provide the men, and the priesthood provides the moral justification."

"And puts the fear of eternal damnation into them," Sasha murmured.

"Exactly." Errollyn moved against her back, and that was an interesting sensation too. "Someone's coming." A soldier jogged across the dock to Symon and the hooded man, and murmured something in Symon's ear. The hooded man turned to look about as they spoke . . . and even Sasha could see the torch-light catch the black robes beneath his cloak, and the glint of something large and gold about his neck. "You owe me three quarters," said Errollyn.

"I don't recall agreeing to that bet," Sasha said.

"Humans are so cheap."

"Only because serrin keep screwing us all the time," Sasha retorted.

"You wish," said Errollyn, with a playful pat at her hip.

"So who sent him?" Sasha wondered. "The archbishop?"

"Perhaps," said Errollyn. "Though the priesthood has factions too."

"Everyone in Petrodor has fucking factions," Sasha muttered in Lenay. She only realised then that they'd been whispering in Saalsi. "I bet even Mari's crabs have fucking factions."

"The nippers against the biters?" Errollyn seemed amused at the concept. "Do you think crabs frame political arguments in terms of steps forward and steps backward, given they all walk sideways?"

Sasha tried to give him an incredulous gaze over her shoulder, but found it difficult in that position. "You're crazy," she told him.

"And you're lying beneath me," said Errollyn. "What does that make you?"

"Female," Sasha nearly replied, but refrained. "Trapped," she said instead. Errollyn muffled a laugh in her hair. Sasha nearly missed the look that Symon Steiner gave to one of his men. She stared as the man pulled something from his belt. Errollyn stiffened. "Oh no," she murmured, aghast.

The garrotte encircled the priest's neck from behind, and tightened. The man flailed, frantically. Sasha could nearly see it, that horrified instant when he realised that he was about to die, and nothing in all the world could stop it. A priest had his gods. A priest should not have feared death. Yet he flailed and kicked all the same. And, sinking to his knees, was finally still.

Men set about stripping the body. Symon Steiner went to talk to another man, with some urgency. With large piles of crates to either side, there was no chance of the dockfront men having seen.

"What just happened?" Sasha asked.

"I'm just a poor serrin lost in the woods," said Errollyn. "Don't ask me." He sounded edgy. His body, once warm and comfortable, now felt tense and hard against her. No serrin had killed another for over a thousand years. A cold chill flushed Sasha's skin as she glimpsed a very familiar human phenomenon through serrin eyes. It scared her.

"Why do you like us?"

"I like *you*," Errollyn corrected tautly, watching the limp white body emerge from the priest's robes on the dock. Sasha felt both warm and cold at the same time.

From off to the left, amongst the jumble of slum roofs, there came a yell. Then another and a clashing of metal . . . not weapons, Sasha thought, but a duller steel.

"That's a signal," Sasha muttered. "Let's go." Caution abandoned, she slid onto the rooftop ridge and ran at a crouch away from the river. On the slum side of the warehouse, she peered down on the opposing street. Dark shapes ran through the shadows, carrying weapons. They were heading downriver, toward Kessligh and the Nasi-Keth. "Shit."

"Mudfoots," said Errollyn. "Looks like an ambush."

It didn't make sense . . . the riverside gangs usually didn't care if Nasi-Keth, serrin or the families came sneaking around their territory, so long as they were only intent on killing each other. But she didn't have time to ponder that now. "Let's get down there."

"Wait." Errollyn pulled a roof tile aside and made a hole. He pulled a ceramic cylinder half the length of his forearm from a belt pouch Sasha hadn't even realised he'd been wearing. He gave it a good shake, then threw it hard down through the hole. There was a blinding white flash, then a whoosh of yellow flame. The white light faded, but the flame remained, and grew. "Go," said Errollyn.

Sasha slithered down the roof. There were no guards at the mouth of the alley below. Now she heard the yells and screams of battle. The mudfoots had run into one of Kessligh's perimeter traps, and the ambushers had become the ambushed.

Sasha found a toehold on the plank wall and began to climb. She was halfway down when a running shadow on the street paused. Then stopped and came over, staring upward. Sasha swore beneath her breath and prepared to drop the remaining distance. From above came a heavy thump, like the high note of a big, Lenay bassyrn drum. A projectile buzzed and the dark figure staggered backward, clutched at his shoulder, then fell and began screaming with pain.

Sasha found several more fast hand and footholds, then dropped the remaining distance and drew her blade. Above, Errollyn was descending . . . he dropped his bow for her to catch, which she did one-handed. She pressed herself to the wall, peering out at the street. There were lights appearing amidst the ramshackle huts opposite and raised voices. The whole of River-side seemed to be waking up.

Two men and a woman came to check on the screaming man, one holding a burning torch. "Come on!" Sasha muttered beneath her breath as Errollyn descended. Errollyn should have shot to kill. But then, she could hardly blame him. Several more runners came along the street, and paused. Looked at the arrow wound, and then looked about, staring up at the sur-rounding rooftops. There was no way out down the other end of the alley, Sasha realised. That way was the docks and family soldiers. If it was a fight, the odds against the mudfoots were far better.

Errollyn dropped to the ground beside her, took his bow from her hand, and said, "Let's go. I'll cover us, I don't think they'll have any archers."

One saving grace—bows were expensive in a big city where good wood was rare, and all expensive things were rare in Riverside. They ran out together, Sasha in the lead. For a moment, their emergence met with no response. Then a yell from behind. Errollyn spun, an arrow from his hip quiver abruptly on his string, even moving backward. The pursuers flinched, breaking away in fear . . . one charged and Errollyn's bow thumped. The man spun like a top, knocked clean off his feet, a shaft through his shoulder. Errollyn had another arrow on his string almost immediately and the pur-suers fled for the cover of walls.

Sasha slowed to let him catch up, more shadows fleeing their approach. Further ahead was a confusion of running, shouting, hand-waving men amidst a dancing chaos of light and shadow. They seemed to be departing away from the river, and now there were large numbers of men running straight toward the crowd, from the far end of the road. They'd been out-flanked, Sasha realised in that instant, the primary escape route downriver had been blocked. It would take a very large number of men to do that. The mission was well and truly off; escape now the only path left, and the only way was south, straight through the swarming, stinking, angry slum.

Sasha turned right and ducked into a dingy alleyway. It was nearly too dark to see and she stumbled over some debris before her eyes adjusted. A dog fled, barking madly, as the alley wound back and forth between squalid dwellings and piled refuse. A girl screamed in fear from a doorway as they ran past. Ahead, Sasha could hear fighting . . . although it seemed to be coming from many locations. The alley joined another, became larger, and Sasha paused, crouching by a wall that stank of urine.

Footsteps and shouting came past, very close. Sasha wiped sweat from her eyes, staring furiously into the dark. They could be ambushed around any corner . . . Errollyn covered the way they'd come with his bow. She briefly considered letting him lead, considering his eyesight, but then thought better of it. Whoever ran into a mudfoot in the dark had better be holding something sharp. Her breath was coming in hard gasps. There was no room, no light and no fresh air.

A little boy ran from a doorway not five paces away, stopped, and then stared at her. He was ragged, his hair a mess, and there were sores about his mouth. Sasha moved past him, Errollyn following, and the boy just stared at them dumbly. Another bend, and a darker patch of shadow . . . she stepped in some foul water, then froze to see some men gathered ahead in a patch of light. Their weapons were rough—rusty knives, some clubs with nails or spikes, an improvised spear. Crude, but effective enough at close quarters.

Movement behind the wall at her right caught her ear, and she stepped back a little . . . then dived as a spear thrust came fast through a gap in the wall, fending with one arm. Ahead, the men saw and yelled. Errollyn shot one as Sasha raced back past him, her forearm stinging. They ran toward the little boy once more, his mother emerged to grab him and screamed . . . Sasha saw a narrower alley to the left and took it, Errollyn in close pursuit.

"Keep right!" he shouted, and she hugged the right wall, missing some obstacle she could barely see in the gloom. The alley's end was blocked so she darted through an open door, to the horror of residents—a pregnant woman clutching a sickly infant, an old man lying on a dirty blanket on a bare dirt floor, a small fire for light and the air thick with smoke. In the adjoining room, a huddled family leapt screaming for the walls. Sasha hurdled their little fire, spying a doorway beyond, and went through it. Rats scurried in the lane, squealing as she passed, and into a wider alley.

Several men ran by, then halted at the sight of her. They were ragged and dirty like the rest, but better armed. One had a long staff, with a rusty blade jammed in the end, another held a genuine sword.

Sasha moved before they could decide what to do, cutting the man's staff clean in two. He stumbled and another tried to dart past, but she slashed his arm and he fell, clutching a shallow wound. The big man swung his sword, but his terrible technique was made worse by his panicked fury . . . she knocked it aside, kicked him in the groin, then cracked his skull with the hilt.

The others ran, but now there were rocks flying past—someone behind her was throwing stones. She made another turn and ran, desperately trying to recall her bearings . . . a woman ahead fell to the ground and covered her head, Sasha simply hurdled her. "Which way?" she yelled to Errollyn.

"Next left," he said, close behind. He knew cities better than she did. She'd always thought her sense of direction excellent, but now she had no idea which way she was going.

She took the left and realised that somewhere near, something large was burning. Light danced on rooftops and shadows wavered. There were many voices yelling. And fighting, very near.

Peering about the next intersection, she found trouble. Three fighters, clearly Nasi-Keth, were trying to move down the alley. At least twelve mud-foots pursued. Two Nasi-Keth turned to slash at their pursuers, keeping them back, the third coming ahead . . . and now, three more mudfoots emerged from a door between Sasha and the Nasi-Keth. The twelve charged, embold-ened. Sasha ran. Errollyn shot one of the near three in the back, the arrow hissing past Sasha's ear.

One of the remaining two did not notice—wielding a big axe in fury. His Nasi-Keth opponent was small and not particularly good, awkwardly dodging one blow, barely parrying a second. The second man noted his com-panion's fall, and spun about, his club raised. Sasha feinted left, sprang right and slashed him across the middle. The axeman disarmed his opponent with a slashing blow and aimed the next to kill, only for Sasha to drive her blade through his middle before the axe could fall.

"Move!" Sasha yelled at the besieged Nasi-Keth behind. Both were fighting desperately, several bodies on the ground and another falling as the big Nasi-Keth felled him. And suddenly Sasha recognised Rodery and Liam. Errollyn shot one mudfoot, somehow finding a gap in the confined space, Liam barely parried a blow from a sword, retreating as he went, and then a spear thrust found Rodery's leg. He stumbled and a mudfoot bodily tackled him, pulling him down. Another angled a long knife for a killing blow—Errollyn's bow thumped, and arrow punched through skull like a melon.

Sasha charged, but already there were more mudfoots coming from fur-ther along. A wall of them, yelling and waving weapons. Liam took the hand off one attacker, then Sasha arrived at his side, and killed the next two with fast, simple blows.

"Go!" she yelled at Liam. And looked back to Rodery, to find a mudfoot had already driven a spear through his throat, and was twisting it viciously. A girl behind her screamed—the disarmed Nasi-Keth, a rare woman. But the wave was almost on them.

Sasha ran after Liam, and Errollyn sent another arrow past her, felling the leader of the wave whose fall tangled those behind. Someone tried to club Sasha from a doorway as she ran, Sasha replied with a slash that took the club and half the wielder's face with it. Only as she ran on did she realise it had been a woman.

Stones came at the four of them as they ran, ducking along new alleys. A stone struck the top of Sasha's head, stinging but not felling her. Children on the roofs, she realised, glimpsing a small shape against the firelit sky. All of Riverside was trying to kill them.

She did not know how far they ran. Gloomy alleys and lanes became a blur, the occasional stone thudding nearby, the yells of pursuit and other, nearby fighting. Sometimes they would come across bodies, corpses dealt by some other group of Nasi-Keth. Several more times they had to fight clear— Sasha killed two more men, Liam one, and wounded several more between them. Errollyn began to run low on arrows, sometimes firing into the dark at targets Sasha could not see. His earlier mercy, it seemed, was all evaporated. The girl was Yulia, and she'd not recovered her lost sword. Mostly, she was crying and terrified, and tried hard to keep up and stay out of the way, with little more than her belt knife for a weapon.

Finally they emerged onto the banks of a dark lake. Its level was low, and the water putrid, afloat with debris. Sasha, Errollyn, Liam and Yulia ran along the muddy, exposed lake bed headed toward the eastward hills of Backside and the high ridge beyond. Shouts and yells pursued them, armed men gathering on the lake edge beyond, waving weapons and torches. Some threw stones and bits of wood, but their aim was poor in the dark.

"Walk!" Sasha gasped to the others, her boots sinking in the foul mud. "Walk. They'll not venture beyond Riverside." Above the lake, and beyond, larger houses rose, several of them grand and old, surrounded by fields and trees. Old lands, not yet claimed by the expanding city.

A stone made a wet smack nearby, another splashed in the water. Yells reached a crescendo and men began pouring off the lip and onto the muddy lake bed. Sasha swore, pulling a knife and noting that Errollyn had only three arrows left. He shot the most well-armed man first—a sword—drew fast and shot the next squarely through the chest. Her target struggling slowly through the mud, Sasha had plenty of time to aim and throw, and hit her man in the gut. Several of the attackers faltered, save one who came straight at

Sasha, and died immediately after from the simplest of swings. The others turned and ran back the way they'd come.

Sasha shook her head in disbelief and trudged through the mud to reclaim her knife, sidestepping stones as she went. The screams of abuse grew louder. The man she'd struck was still alive. Then she saw his face, wide-eyed and panicked, and barely more than thirteen. She swore and pulled her knife clear—it would increase the bleeding, but there was no choice if the wound was to have any chance of healing.

"Here," she said in Torovan, and barely recognised her own voice—hard, tired, devoid of emotion. She bunched up a handful of his ragged shirt and pressed it hard onto the bleeding gash. "Press hard. *Hard*, understand?" She placed his hand over it and made him press. A stone hit her shoulder, another hit the boy's leg. Shit-eating fools didn't care who they hit.

"Sasha, come on," said Errollyn, directly behind her. He swayed aside from a stone lazily. The last arrow was on his bowstring. "The kid has no chance, not in this cesspit." He was right, of course. The wound would turn nasty and the kid would be dead in two days. They couldn't take him with them, that would just invite pursuit, and the look in the kid's eyes as he stared at her suggested he would fight any attempt to save him, if such help came from the likes of her. "Witches!" they screamed on the rim of the lake. "Demons of Loth!"

Errollyn yanked her backward as a stone whistled through the spot where she'd been. She staggered to her feet and stared darkly at the gathering line of hysterical slum dwellers. A new man arrived in their midst, holding a makeshift spear with something dark and hairy on the end. A human head. He lofted it skyward and there were screams and shouts of furious, frightened triumph. Sasha could not recognise the head in the chaos of fire and shadow, but she was certain it was someone she knew.

Errollyn raised his bow as the spear holder turned side-on to address the crowd. The bow thumped and thrummed, and the arrow skewered its target in one ear and out the other. People scattered in panic as body and spear-stuck head toppled. Sasha stared at Errollyn. Grey hair wild and matted, his face wet with sweat, his green eyes burned like the torch fires themselves. A demon of Loth indeed.

"Who was it?" she asked him quietly.

Errollyn looked as though he'd like to kill several more. He took a deep breath, and lowered his bow. "Never mind. Let's go."

"Errollyn," said Sasha, in rising alarm. Her heart stopped. "Surely it couldn't be . . ."

Errollyn saw. "No," he said, shaking his head. "Not Kessligh." Her heart restarted. "It was Aiden."

The foursome limped tiredly across a field, headed for some tall poplar trees along the next wall. A farmhouse loomed near—three floors, like no farmhouse Sasha had ever seen in Lenayin. The night was dark and shadowy against the dim background light, occasional hung lamps and lit windows on the Backside slope above. Grass felt wonderful underfoot. How long had it been since she'd walked on grass? All in Petrodor was stone. Across the vast arc of sky above, a swathe of stars.

Yulia walked quietly, except for an occasional, shaking inward breath. Errollyn had unstrung his bow and walked now with sword in hand. Liam limped on a twisted ankle, but said nothing and refused to slow down. As the heat of battle left her, Sasha felt aches and injuries that she did not recall accumulating. Her head was cut from a stone, her temple swollen from where she'd bashed it on a corner in the dark. Her shoulder ached from that last stone and her right forearm had been gashed from the first spear thrust through the wall. But mostly, she was worried about the other Nasi-Keth, scared for Kessligh, and her other friends. They'd not seen anyone else on this walk away from the battle. Surely many others had taken different directions. Riverside was large and there were many, many routes of escape, she told herself with each aching, worrying step.

When they reached the low wall, Sasha leaned against a poplar and considered the rising Backside slope, dotted with light. "See anything?" she murmured to Errollyn.

"Just the same lights along the ridgetop," he replied. All of the big family houses along the ridgetop were awake, having seen or heard the commotion down in Riverside. Along the riverfront, there was a big fire burning —probably started by Errollyn's little whatever-it-was that he'd thrown into the warehouse roof. She could see several other fires in the near distance. Further west, there were more lights from the river port town of Cuely, a short distance upstream from Riverside. When Riverside erupted, all the neighbours became alarmed. It gave her little comfort to know that she was not alone in having a sleepless night.

"We should go up," said Liam, tautly, gesturing up the slope. "All this walking around is pointless. We could walk for leagues."

"The families will guess it was Nasi-Keth that caused the commotion," said Sasha, shaking her head. "There'll be a big line of them, all along the ridgetop, waiting for us. It's the perfect chance to catch some scattered Nasi-Keth trying to make it over the top to dockside."

"So where do we go?" said Liam, unimpressed.

"I know a place," said Sasha.

"And where the hells is that?"

"Let her alone, Liam," said Yulia, quietly. "She saved our lives."

"After you got Rodery killed!" Liam hissed. Yulia's young face was stricken. "You're useless! We had to fight twice as hard to make up for you, and it killed Rodery! The first thing we should have done is thrown you in the river . . ."

"Liam!" Sasha snapped furiously. "You arrogant shit, you're not half the fighter you think you are! It's just as likely *you* got Rodery killed!"

Liam might have swung at her, but Errollyn grabbed him from behind, twisting an arm while locking an elbow about the young man's throat. The hold was effortless and held Liam as helpless as a fly in a spiderweb. He struggled, twice, then held still, breathing heavily.

"The mudfoots killed Rodery," Sasha told him. "I don't know why they attacked us. Maybe some traitor tipped Symon Steiner off and he told the mudfoots some lies about how we were coming to attack them. Put your blame where it belongs, Liam. Be useful because I've no time for baggage right now, d'you hear?"

"So the warrior princess has herself a pet serrin to do the hard work for her," Liam spat.

"He's saving your life, idiot," Sasha retorted. "Don't fight me, Liam. I'm not big enough to box your ears. If there's fighting, all I have is this—" and she patted the hilt of the sword over her shoulder. "And you've seen how I use it."

Liam blinked at her, finally disconcerted. He looked at the ground. "Let go," he said. "I said, let go!"

Errollyn let loose his arm, but took a hard grip on Liam's throat. "Pet serrin?" he said, leaning close, staring the young man in the face. His green eyes seemed almost to glow in the dark. Liam grabbed his wrist, but could not dislodge the fingers. Sasha was not surprised—a lifetime of archery had made Errollyn's grip like steel.

"You don't scare me," said Liam, clearly scared. "Serrin don't kill in cold blood."

"Doesn't mean I can't break a few bones," said Errollyn, his voice low with threat. "I'd never killed anyone for just waving a spear in the air before tonight, either. Now you drop your selfish whining and pull yourself together. The night's not over yet and there's a fair walk ahead of us. Can you do that?"

Liam nodded stiffly. Errollyn let him go, with a last, deliberate pat on the shoulder. Liam had the makings of a strong young man, but Errollyn was all quickness and all muscle.

"Did it work?" said Errollyn in Lenay as they set out across the next field in the dark.

Sasha spared Liam a glance. He walked with his head down and did not look likely to make more trouble. "I think so," she said. "Did you mean it?"

"I'm not certain," said Errollyn. "Maybe. If he'd tried to hurt you."

"I can look after myself."

Errollyn shrugged. "Even wolves hunt in packs," he said.

Sasha looked at him sideways. "Are you proposing to be my mate?" she suggested. "Or just commenting on my table manners?"

Errollyn smiled. "I thought you liked wolves?"

Sasha sighed. "I do. But not everyone has the luxury of such a close-knit family."

"Serrin do."

"Is that how you describe the serrinim? A pack?"

"Every analogy is fraught. But we share many things amongst ourselves. We hunt together. We raise young together."

"You don't pair-bond for life," Sasha objected.

"Some do," said Errollyn.

"Truly? I've never heard of it."

"There's much about the serrinim you've never heard."

"There's much about humans you haven't heard," Sasha countered.

"I know," said Errollyn, sombrely. Tiredly. "One day, I'd like to learn more."

Nearby, some sheep bleated. There was a pen over by the farmhouse. This near to Petrodor, it was not safe to leave livestock unattended in the fields at night. Not with so many hungry Riversiders so near.

"What are you talking about?" asked Yulia in Torovan. Her voice was small in the darkness. She walked close, thumbs in her belt, in obvious distress.

"Oh, just things," Sasha replied in Torovan. "Serrin things."

"Lenay sounds so different," said Yulia, bravely. "My father thinks it's an ugly language, but I think it's pretty."

"I've had the same argument with Lenays about the Torovan language," Sasha admitted.

"To say nothing of the Torovan people," Errollyn remarked. Sasha gave him a wry look.

"Is Lenayin very beautiful?" asked Yulia.

"Oh yes," said Sasha, wistfully. "It's stunningly beautiful."

"Tell me about it," said Yulia, with faint desperation.

"Maybe later," said Sasha, squeezing the girl's shoulder. "There's a road approaching. Be on your guard, we're a long way from safe yet."

The grand gardens of Pazira House were surrounded by a stone wall, but here, away from the treachery of Petrodor, the walls were not rowed with spikes, nor guarded by watchposts. Errollyn ran first across the road and took position at the base of the wall. Sasha followed, placed her foot into Errollyn's cupped hands and was propelled upward. She lay flat atop the wall for a moment, searching the ground below in the dark, and then jumped, landing on soft grass.

Yulia came second, and fell heavily as she landed. Sasha helped her up, but the girl refused attention. Liam and Errollyn followed.

Ahead, its outer walls lit with lamps, stood Pazira House, a grand mansion of three floors and several turrets. The turrets, Sasha had gathered, were only ornamental—this was a house for living, not a castle for defending. All of the Torovan dukes owned such properties about Petrodor.

Sasha took a stone from the garden and followed Errollyn between tall, trimmed hedges. Beneath the branches of some tall trees, Errollyn gestured them flat, and Sasha pressed herself against a tree trunk. She heard a dog bark somewhere across the gardens, but the wind was blowing into their faces and the dogs would not smell them. Not immediately, anyhow.

Errollyn gestured them up once more and they moved into a maze of waist-high hedges. They stayed low and finally arrived at a wide courtyard with a long, rectangular lake. The house loomed nearer, its outer lights reflected in the dark water between lilies. Sasha could see guards by the main doors, with still more patrolling the perimeter. Soft footsteps approached alongside the lake.

Sasha peered about the hedge and saw a guard in armour with the obligatory broad-brimmed hat, the Pazira maroon and gold colours barely discernible in the gloom.

The guard strolled past them, oblivious. Sasha hefted the stone in her hand, measured the throw, then lobbed. It sailed past the guard's hat and splashed in the water. He spun. Then spun again, searching the night, a hand on his sword hilt.

"The duke prefers mint tea!" Sasha hissed at him. The guard spun a third time, finally facing the right way. But relaxing somewhat, to hear the password. Sasha stood up and he came over cautiously.

"What do you want?" the guard hissed back.

"To see the duke."

"He's abed."

"I'll make it worth his while."

Errollyn, Liam and Yulia were held in the vestibule while Sasha advanced alone down the main hall with two guards. Candles lit the checker-tiled floor—the household was roused if the candles were lit, Sasha realised with little surprise. Riverside was burning and everyone was on guard.

Sasha and the guards waited at the hallway staircase as servants hurried past. The guards' swords were sheathed and they did not seem particularly afraid of her. Wary, perhaps, but she'd not been a complete stranger to these grounds over the past few weeks.

Finally Duke Alexanda Rochel thumped down the stairs in a thin maroon robe and eyed Sasha with displeasure.

"Damn fool of a girl," he rumbled. "What have you and your crazy uman gone and done now, set half of Riverside ablaze?" His white hair was rumpled, his eyes bleary.

"We were betrayed," said Sasha, hooking her thumbs into her belt. "Someone told the mudfoots we were coming and that we meant to do them harm. Lies, of course."

"The only part that wasn't," the Duke of Pazira snorted, reaching the bottom and stopping before her. He fixed her with a beady eye. "Did it ever occur to you that not everyone in Petrodor views the Nasi-Keth as the source of all moral rectitude and goodness? You declare yourselves the saviours of the poor while ignoring the simple human truth that not everyone wishes to be saved. You of all people, Sashandra of the Goeren-yai, should know that."

His stare was knowing. Sasha drew a deep breath. "I've information for you," she said. "The doings of Symon Steiner. I think you'll find them—"

Duke Rochel made an irritated face and waved his hand. "You don't have to play favours with me, girl, you know damn well I'm still in your debt."

Sasha blinked at him. "And on my side, too, I'd hoped," she ventured.

"Damn fool," Rochel muttered. "How did you ever rise so high with so little wits?"

Soon enough Sasha and Errollyn were seated on a sofa before some open windows on the mansion's first floor. The cool night breeze was a welcome relief from the stuffiness of the house. Sasha grimaced as Errollyn washed the wound on her forearm. It was shallow, but it hurt.

"So explain to me this relationship," said Errollyn as he worked. A servant hurried across the central carpet, placed steaming cups on the table, and departed once more. "Sasha never has. Or at least, not to me."

"I'm very pleased to hear it," said Rochel darkly from a sofa opposite. He sipped at his tea. His eyebrows were as bushy and wild as his hair, and he had the habit of raising just one, beneath which to fix a suspicious stare. "Perhaps six years ago now . . . is it six?"

"Six," Sasha agreed, reaching for her tea with her free arm.

"Six years ago, I had some trouble with the villagers of eastern Valhanan in Lenayin. There was a dispute over land boundaries with the earls of western Pazira, some silly nonsense that goes back at least five hundred years. Word spread to the great warrior Kessligh Cronenverdt, who rode from Baerlyn with his skinny, cantankerous fourteen-year-old uma at his side. The Lenays were very angry and I'm quite sure they would have attacked, as Lenays are wont to do at the slightest provocation—" Sasha snorted, "had Kessligh not persuaded them otherwise. And made quite certain I knew about it. That man's a devil in negotiations."

"And so you owe Sasha and Kessligh some gratitude," Errollyn concluded to Duke Rochel. "But I hear you also oppose this coming war."

"Oppose," the duke snorted. Glanced about the room, and the lovely old furnishings, the bright walls, the ornate ceiling. "You speak as if I had any choice."

"A man's choices are his own," said Errollyn. The duke gave him a stare. Errollyn gazed back, green eyes intent within a dirt-stained face.

"The war is a fool's adventure," the duke snapped. "But this is the city of fools, and this city rules all Torovan with its foolishness. It's your fault, you know." With a hard, accusing nod at Errollyn. "You serrinim."

"I know," Errollyn said mildly.

"You gave Petrodor all your trade and you created a monster. Two hundred years ago I could have spanked the patachis' insolent backsides. One hundred years ago even. The dukes ruled Torovan then. My grandfather was such a man. I recall him to this day, despairing at the growing tide of wealth from Petrodor, the promises of trade and fortune that bent one duke after another to the will of the greedy, bloody-handed patachis. Those men don't deserve such power, they've neither the wits nor the breeding. For hundreds of years Torovan has been peaceful and prosperous beneath the rule of the *oldest* families, and we raised our sons with the skills and wisdom to rule wisely, and not for simple profit. Now we are reduced to mere vassals, competing desperately for the right to lick the patachis' boots."

"It seems the way of much human power," Errollyn observed, "that those who deserve it least acquire it most."

"Don't you make sniping jousts of your lofty serrin wisdom with me, boy," the duke snorted. "It was the wisdom of the serrinim that led to these dire straits in the first place. Fancy building up a band of fishermen to be the great power in Torovan and not foreseeing the consequences. Fancy occupying three wealthy, holy Bacosh provinces and not foreseeing that the priesthood would one day want them back, and would bend every man of faith to do so."

"The serrinim have always tried to act with mercy," said Errollyn.

"And exactly!" exclaimed Rochel, waggling a finger. "What do the serrinim know of human mercy? Is it merciful to show visions of the unattainable to the hopeless? Is it merciful to show a starving man only the smell and the promise of food, but never an actual meal? Is it merciful to tell the poor folk of Riverside that their gods are frauds, and thus deprive them of their one small comfort?"

"Most Petrodor Nasi-Keth are practising Verenthanes," Errollyn corrected, "no one ever told them that their gods are frauds . . ."

"You play with human society as if it were your toy!" exclaimed Rochel. "You understand nothing, none of you serrinim, yet you seek to remake us in your own image."

"Duke Rochel, the Nasi-Keth are a human movement. Saalshen holds no reins of power there."

"That's not what I hear," Rochel said darkly.

"Then why—"

"Oh please," Sasha cut in with exasperation, "this is *exactly* the wrong time to start a debate about it."

Rochel sipped his tea. "Women," he snorted. "Never had heads for politics. Another thing to blame the serrin for. Crazy ideas."

"How many Lenay rebellions have you successfully negotiated, Duke Rochel?" Sasha snapped. "I've been breathing nothing *but* politics the last few months, most of which is trying to get me killed. I'm trying to maintain some kind of logical focus, here."

"Dear girl, setting Riverside ablaze does not constitute a logical focus, nor a political nous, nor the general common sense the gods gave a dead, smelly herring."

"We were trying for an arms shipment bound for Lenayin," said Sasha, trying to keep a hold on her temper.

"*Trying* seems to be the operative word."

"Oh, look you smug, self-important git, if you don't wish to know about the goings-on we saw between Symon Steiner and an important-looking priest, just say so!"

Duke Rochel blinked, his cup frozen halfway to his lips. "A *priest* was at the Steiner docks at Riverside?"

"The Torack dock," Sasha corrected.

"With Symon Steiner?"

"They appeared to have just completed an inspection of a boat's cargo."

"You're certain it was Symon?"

"Errollyn saw him clear enough."

The duke looked suspicious. "In matters of Petrodor politics, the priest-hood are neutral. It is tradition."

"Huh," Sasha snorted, "and you think me naive."

"Dear girl, naivety has nothing to do with it. All of the families give sons to the priesthood, do you understand? The balance was agreed long ago, and the ceremonies decree that the gods are neutral. Of course it would be utterly naive to believe that the holy fathers abandon all previous family loyalties upon the taking of the oath, but for the archbishop to take sides openly would be to begin a civil war within the priesthood! And Archbishop Augine is not such a fool as to . . ." The duke stopped, to see Sasha and Errollyn exchanging looks. "What?"

"I don't think you'd be interested," Sasha sniffed. "Such information from a silly, witless girl like me with no head for politics . . ."

"Thank the dear gods for granting me a daughter of pleasant and modest temperament," Rochel said with exasperation. "*What?*"

"They killed the priest," said Errollyn. Watching the duke carefully, awaiting a reaction. "Murdered him."

Duke Rochel stared. Seemed about to say something, then stopped as if lost for words. Then, finally . . . "Symon Steiner . . . killed a priest? Himself?"

"Not by his own hand," said Errollyn. "But facing him as you are facing me. He ordered it with his eyes, to the man with the garrotte."

"Who else saw? Besides yourselves?"

"Some Torack guards on the dock. Several family men I did not recognise."

"Yet you recognised Symon Steiner?"

"Duke Rochel, even Sasha recognised Symon Steiner. My eyesight at night is considerably better than hers. The families have many men, and I do not know them all, despite my years here in Petrodor."

"Who else?" Rochel was more intense, and more serious, than at any time that evening.

"There were piles of crates on the dockfront. I doubt anyone else along the dock saw."

"What did they do with the body?" Rochel pressed.

"Stripped it. We saw no more, we became rather busy just about then."

Duke Rochel took a deep breath. "Damn," he muttered. "Damn, damn, damn."

"What does it mean?" Sasha asked, too exhausted for any notion of subtlety. "Why the hells would my sister's lovely husband murder a member of the highest authority in Petrodor?"

"I don't know," Rochel rumbled. "I only know this—any hope that this power dispute between Steiner and Maerler could be settled peacefully is vanishing fast. Now, there'll be Loth's ransom to pay."

Sasha poured cold water over her head and scrubbed. Pazira House was not poor, and there was soap and hair oils on a tiled shelf in the washroom. She discovered yet more bruises and scrapes as she washed, but was too tired now to recall from where she had earned them.

She recalled the confusion of the Riverside alleys, and the fear. The light in Rodery's eyes as she'd taught him some new techniques. The big lad had had three brothers and two sisters. One morning, Liam had been teasing him that a neighbourhood girl fancied him. Most unlike the majority of cocky Torovan lads, Rodery had blushed.

Aiden, sitting with Kessligh by the fireplace of her home in Baerlyn. Cheerful, principled Aiden. He'd had a family that she'd never met. The Nasi-Keth were his life. He'd believed they could help all humanity, as they'd helped improve the lives of thousands along the Petrodor dockfront. He'd had hopes for the wretched poor of Riverside. He'd not expected them to parade his head on a spear. He'd only wanted to help.

Suddenly she was in tears. She steadied herself against a wall, sliding to the floor as sobs wracked her body. It was a while before she could stop. Never had she felt so helpless as now, confronted with a horror already passed, that she could do nothing to prevent or undo. She sat naked against the cold stone and cried. It could have been Kessligh's head on that pole. Or Errollyn's. A true warrior should surely cope with such fears, and continue regardless. But she had no idea how.

When the sobs had passed, she rinsed herself, dried, wrapped herself in the robe provided, and gathered her clothes and sword. The hall outside was quiet and dark, but for a sole lamp on a side table. She looked in Liam and Yulia's chambers, even sleeping, they looked exhausted. The weariness was a blessing, she reckoned. Without it, sleep would be hard.

She pushed into her and Errollyn's chambers, and found Errollyn lying on his bed, looking at the ceiling. Light from the lamps outside cast a dim, flickering glow upon the decorated ceiling. He looked beautiful. Calm, in a way she envied more than words could describe.

Errollyn took one look at her in the gloom and got up, pushing his bed across to hers, a squeal of wooden legs on floorboards. Sasha dumped her clothes, hung her sword and bandoleer over a bedstead, slid a sheathed knife beneath the pillow, and then fell into Errollyn's arms. She cried some more, and his arms were comforting in a way that no words could possibly manage. He smelled nice and his chest was more comfortable than any pillow. They spoke not a word.

Seven

THE MAN WITH THE WOUNDED LEG hung in his chair, breath snorting through his bloodied nose. When Jaryd entered the room and saw the council's handiwork, he was not impressed.

"That's what you call an interrogation?" he exclaimed in disbelief. "That's it?" Raegyl the stonemason was unwinding strips of cloth from his knuckles and flexing his fingers. The prisoner's face was swollen, and there was blood all down his shirt, but it didn't look like Raegyl had been striking very hard. Even the ropes that tied the prisoner to his chair did not look particularly tight.

"You'll address your accusations to me," said Jaegar, Baerlyn headman. He leaned by one window, massive arms folded, long hair tied into a single, knotted braid that fell down his back. "This interrogation shall go as far as I wish it to, and no further."

Teriyan was there too, and Ryssin, Geldon the one-handed baker, and Byorn from the training hall. Old Cranyk sat in a chair near the fireplace, his cane between his legs, and watched the prisoner through narrowed eyes.

"Let me question him," said Jaryd and pulled a knife from his belt.

"No," said Jaegar, unmoving.

"He has transgressed on the honour of Baerlyn," Jaryd said incredulously, "and now you grant him favours?"

"No man of Baerlyn will stick a blade into a defenceless opponent and consider Baerlyn's honour unsullied," Jaegar said bluntly.

"I'm not a man of Baerlyn," Jaryd retorted.

Jaegar's stare was flat and level within a face set like granite. One eye dark within a maze of intricate black tattoos that covered half his face. "While you live here," he said, "you are."

The prisoner groaned and moved his legs. Blood dripped. Raegyl's fists had made a mess, but it was a mercy compared to the fate of such a man in other parts of Lenayin. In Isfayen, Jaryd had no doubt, the man's face would have been his prettiest feature by now.

"Look at him!" Jaryd exclaimed in frustration. "He knows this is the worst you will do! He's survived this far, he probably thinks he can survive the rest!"

"Betraying the Great Lord will gain him far worse," Cranyk agreed. "But should he hold his silence now, his reward will be even greater. Such are the moments that can make a man's life. He grasps his chance with both hands, with the honour of a whipped dog whining at his master's feet."

"No," Jaegar repeated, this time to Cranyk. "Not while I am headman."

"When I was a boy," Cranyk replied, his aged voice high and thin, "I saw Cherrovan prisoners flayed alive on the road."

"That was revenge," said Raegyl, still massaging his knuckles. "Revenge is different."

"The young *daylthar* has claim for revenge," said Cranyk, nodding at Jaryd. *Daylthar*, good gods, that was an old word. Jaryd had heard it only in recitals of Tullamayne epics, and similar old tales. It meant "stranger," in that very Lenay sense that could mean the person from the next village, or the invading Cherrovan warlord, or the travelling serrin from Saalshen. "All the rest of the world," in totality. Jaryd hadn't thought anyone still used the term. "If the Great Lord had any honour, he would meet the honourable challenge with a blade in his hand. Instead, he sends gold and trades favours to buy the likes of this . . ." with a disdainful nod at the slumped prisoner, "and a cowardly shot from a distance. All who fall outside our honour are no longer protected by it."

"The serrin fall outside our honour too," Jaegar replied, as unmoved as the rock his face and build resembled. "They share none of our beliefs and convictions. Should we then accord them no respect either?"

"The serrin," Cranyk replied, "would never stoop to such an act. They have their own honour, whatever they might call it."

"So do the nobles," said Jaegar.

"Why are you defending them?" Jaryd demanded, folding his arms, his knife still in hand. "What have they done to make you so enamoured of them?"

"It's not a question of liking them, kid," said Teriyan. "It's a question of law. Our laws exist because they are what we have decided is right and just. If others don't share those values, that's no reason to just ignore it all. Honour is honour. End of discussion."

Jaryd shoved his knife back into its sheath in disgust. "This is why civilisations are destroyed," he said darkly. "They lack the conviction to defend themselves by every means possible against those who would destroy them."

"Aye," Cranyk agreed, nodding slowly.

"If we must defeat dishonour by becoming dishonourable," Jaegar replied, "then what have we won?"

Jaryd stared at the men. Teriyan looked sombre, but in general agreement with his friend Jaegar. Raegyl too, and Ryssin. Geldon looked more troubled, his round face etched with a frown. Byorn, too, looked uncertain. Jaryd gave a slight bow to Cranyk. "I thank you for your support, Yuan Cranyk," he said.

Cranyk looked up at him shrewdly. He studied Jaryd's dripping sweat and the weariness of his posture. "You train hard, young Jaryd. Most likely this quest of yours will kill you. But I wish you an honourable death, and the blood of your enemies. Perhaps we shall sing songs of it."

From a man such as Cranyk, Jaryd reckoned, that was great praise. He gave another slight bow, turned on his heel and departed the room.

At the ranch Jaryd went to the stables to see what needed doing, and found Parrachik there looking at some horses with the Petrodor merchants who'd attended the wedding last night.

Lynette had saddled one of the fillies—Felsy, Jaryd saw, noting the white-socked hindleg—and was showing her off to the merchants as they leaned on the enclosure fence. Jaryd stood back, unnoticed for the moment, hands on his head as he tried to stretch his aching shoulders. After watching awhile, he found he could only admire, however grudgingly, the sheer audacity of the skinny red-haired girl who commanded the men's attentions in the manly business of horses. She moved quickly and expertly around the filly, handling her with the surest touch, lifting a hoof with the easy pressure of a hand, reciting breeding and conditioning from immediate memory.

Soon Parrachik glanced back and saw him. "Jaryd!" All present turned to look. "I was hoping to find you here. Tell me, have we found that last scoundrel yet?"

Jaryd shook his head, moving wearily to the fenceline. "Not yet." There was a party of woodsmen out looking for the escaped assassin. Such woodsmen were the reason Kessligh and Sasha had never particularly feared an attack—travelling on the roads in these parts would get you spotted, and travelling off them would get you tracked.

Jaryd exchanged greetings with the merchants and leaned on the fence to watch as Lynette held Felsy's bridle and the prospective buyer climbed astride. A nudge of heels and the buyer moved off, walking the filly at a gentle pace.

"She's a nice horse, that one," Jaryd remarked to the men. "Quick like lightning, she'll be a racer when she's filled out. Hasn't quite the temperament for lagand, but then most mares don't."

"There is no lagand in Petrodor," one of the merchants assured Jaryd in a thick lowlands accent. "We race. And we hunt . . . ah . . . foxes. Big hunts, lots of dogs. We like a good horse. Very pretty, very fast, very . . . well-behaved, yes?"

Jaryd nodded at Felsy. "Well then, that's your girl. She's very sweet."

The rider nudged Felsy up to a canter, and the filly responded briskly. Clearly she wanted to run and the rider obliged – they took off at a gallop, heading upslope.

"We heard the captive and the man you slew were dressed as Torovans?" Parrachik said, looking concerned.

"Aye."

"Most alarming," said the elder of the merchants. "Should you uncover this dishonourable person's true identity, and his employers, you must instruct us. We shall sever ties and do no more trade with these people. We will not have the goodwill between Lenays and Torovan merchants damaged in such a manner. We are appalled."

There was a chorus of agreement from the others, and much nodding of heads. Jaryd wondered if Lord Arastyn had figured that into his plans or not. Certainly Arastyn was as beholden to the wealth of Petrodor as any other Lenay noble family. Jaryd wondered if there was more to it.

He excused himself and took his place beneath the vertyn tree to practise taka-dans. His muscles protested, and his form was terrible. He could barely manage three precise strokes in a row. He stopped, a hand against the tree, breathing hard. Parrachik's eldest son was watching, having more interest in swords than horses. The lad looked nothing like his father—tall with dark, curling hair in Goeren-yai custom. He dressed like any other Baerlyn boy, wore a sword at his hip and was reputed to be one of the better lads at the training hall. What his Verenthane, lowlands, sword-shunning father made of it, Jaryd did not know. Surely he did not disapprove, or else why did the boy dress like this so openly? And Parrachik seemed to have nothing but fatherly affection for him.

Jaryd gave up the taka-dans, called his gelding from happy grazing on the hillside and rode to a rock pool with a waterfall, which Sasha had told him was her favourite place. He left the gelding to graze near the pool, pulled off his clothes and all but fell into the water. The cold hit him with a welcome shock. It was so calm and still, with nothing but the trickle of the waterfall to break the silence. He drifted while river trout flitted amidst the rocks below.

When the cold became too much, he climbed out and lay on a patch of sun-warmed rock. He thought again of Parrachik's son—a boy nothing like his father, yet his father loved him all the same. Parrachik was a good man, he decided. An outsider who made no attempt to copy Lenay ways, but neither caused them any offence. And now his eldest son was more Goeren-yai than Torovan.

His own father was dead, yet Jaryd did not miss him. He supposed that made him a bad son, which was fitting because the old Great Lord Nyvar had been a terrible father. Some rumoured he'd been poisoned by Arastyn. Jaryd couldn't see that it mattered. If his father had died naturally, then he was now with his gods, and out of Jaryd's life. If he'd been murdered, it was just another thing for Jaryd to avenge himself of when the time for revenge came near. Jaryd just wished he didn't feel like a fraud, to be claiming revenge for his father who would certainly not have done the same for him.

His father had always liked Wyndal better. Wyndal was clever, could read in three languages and had a head for treasury sums. He was also thoughtful and rarely answered back. Memories assailed him . . . Wyndal's reproachful stare above a stack of papers as Jaryd came strolling in from another lagand practice. Wyndal all red-faced and embarrassed over a village girl at a dance. He'd rejected Jaryd's advice on how to handle an insistent, buxom young maiden . . . "Not everyone can be like you, Jaryd. A lord should have manners."

Wyndal teaching Tarryn to read before the fireplace. Tarryn had been delighted and intrigued at the beautiful calligraphy. He'd learned fast, to Jaryd's dismay. It had been a battle between him and Wyndal over Tarryn. Thankfully, Tarryn loved his big brother's books and sums just as much as he loved his biggest brother's horses and swords. He'd always been so pleased to see either of them, running out with a grin and a hug . . . Jaryd and Wyndal had become friends almost by accident, mostly because of Tarryn. Because Tarryn loved stories and Tarryn loved horses, and Tarryn was always laughing and exuberant and drawing everyone else into his little circle of sunshine. So many conversations he'd started between Jaryd and Wyndal simply because one of them would be playing with Tarryn first. And then there was the incident with the lame puppy that Tarryn had tried to hide in his room to save from the knife, and the scandal over the hole in Lady Heryn's expensive gown, and the whole uproar about Tefyd the gardener's ruined flowerbeds . . .

Jaryd felt the tears coming, and did not fight them. He curled up on his side, naked on the rocks beside the peaceful rockpool, and sobbed like a baby. About him, the pines stood tall and proud like the columns of some magnificent cathedral, and golden rays of sunshine speared through the branches.

By the time he returned to the ranch, the weather had closed in with a rush. Wind snapped and tossed at the treetops, and drizzling rain threatened to turn to heavier squalls.

Lynette was bringing the horses back and Jaryd helped her stable them. The merchants had departed, taking Felsy with them. She'd sold for thirteen crowns and fifty-seven shingles . . . a small fortune in local terms. Lynette's money pouch rattled at her belt as they ran down to the house in the first drenching downpour. Kessligh had taken the finest horses from Baen-Tar's royal stables as a gift from the king, and the Torovans knew good bloodlines when they saw them.

Jaryd ducked under the house to get some more firewood, while Lynette set about preparing dinner. Andreyis was still out with the hunting parties searching for the assassin. Rain rattled against the shutters, wind heaved at the roof timbers, and Jaryd was glad he was not in Andreyis's boots this evening.

He'd just relaxed in front of the kitchen fire, when there came a thumping at the kitchen door. Lynette spun with a gasp. Jaryd climbed from his chair and took up the scabbard he'd hooked over a chairback. Usually the dogs barked when strangers arrived, but Andreyis had taken them with him. And with many of the woodsmen also out on the hunt, the ranch was less protected than usual. Jaryd pulled the sword from its sheath and advanced toward the door. Lynette took up a kitchen knife, evidently thinking the same thing.

Jaryd stopped a stride from the door, recalling the crossbow bolt that had gone half through the Steltsyn's wall. Could a bolt go straight through this door? Could the house be surrounded?

"Who's there?" he called.

"Someone who's very cold and wet," came a thin, female voice, "and who would very much like to come in!"

Jaryd blinked at Lynette, then grabbed the door latch and pulled it open. A cloaked figure stood in the doorway, dripping wet, holding a hood in place with one hand against the wind. The stranger carried a lamp and lifted it now to face level . . . it shone within the hood, and Jaryd stared in disbelief. He swore.

"Oh dear gods . . . Your Highness, please, come in from the rain at once!"

"Your Highness?" said Lynette, disbelievingly. Jaryd sheathed his sword, took the lantern, then hurried to grab the dripping cloak as it was removed, revealing a slim female figure in pants and jacket, with long brown hair in a bedraggled ponytail. "Your Highness!" Lynette squeaked. "Is that . . . I mean . . . are you . . . ?"

Princess Sofy blinked at the red-haired girl and her weariness seemed to lift as a delighted smile crossed her face. "Oh, you must be Lynette!" She embraced the stunned younger woman. "How wonderful to finally meet you! Sasha's told me all about you. Even though we've never met, I feel like we're related!"

"Hardly," said Jaryd, hanging the cloak and blowing out the lamp. "That would make her a princess."

Lynette grinned in disbelief . . . then realised she was still holding the kitchen knife and put it on the bench. "Oh lords," she said excitedly, peering at the new arrival, "I can see the resemblance! You have Sasha's eyebrows, and her eyes a bit too . . . oh!" She clamped a hand to her mouth and curtseyed quickly. "Forgive me, Your Highness, I shouldn't be so forward."

"I'm very pleased to have Sasha's eyes and eyebrows," Sofy agreed happily. "I'm also rather pleased I don't have her shoulders and terrible haircut . . . I mean, I suppose it's useful sometimes . . ." She pulled at her bedraggled ponytail. "But it's still such a shame. You haven't felt compelled to cut yours, I see," Sofy observed, brushing at Lynette's red tangles with a hand.

"Oh, my father would *kill* me!"

"I rode with your father on the way to the Udalyn Valley. He's a wonderful man!"

"He is a lovely man, and he'd still kill me! This hair is a Tremel family heirloom, he tells me. 'My father and his father's father went into battle with this red hair flowing in the sunlit breeze . . .'" It was a fair approximation of Teriyan's rough inn-talk, an imaginary ale clasped in one hand.

Sofy laughed delightedly. "You're *exactly* like Sasha described! What a delight . . . we're going to have some stories to—"

"Uh . . . girls?" Jaryd interrupted from the doorway. Both young women turned, each with a hand on the other's arm in midconversation. Women were astonishing sometimes, they could establish love or hate at first sight. "I hate to spoil something so beautiful as friendship, but I think I'm missing something here. When last I saw Princess Sofy she was about to agree to wed some horrible shit in the Bacosh . . . someone by the name of Arrosh, I recall, Regent Arrosh's first son and heir. There was this whole war thing depending on it, and the future of Lenayin or something. Now she's turned up here in Baerlyn in a storm, a long way from where she should be, with no apparent guard or escort. What am I missing?"

Sofy blinked at him, then looked at Lynette. "Is he always this sarcastic?"

"Oh sarcasm is an improvement," Lynette returned drily. "Usually he just snarls, or communicates in animal grunts."

Lynette refused to let Sofy tell her tale until she'd had some food. Sofy ate ravenously, sitting before the fireplace, her clothes only a little damp thanks to the heavy cloak she'd worn. Jaryd and Lynette ate too, as the fire leaped and snarled.

Sofy, Jaryd noted, looked different from the way he remembered her. How was that possible, when it had only been a month and a half? She wore different pants and jacket than she had on the ride to the Udalyn Valley. Those had been hurriedly borrowed from the spare clothes of men in the column, clothes intended for younger brothers or cousins. These were tailored, the pants a thick, soft cloth with a leather belt and a light black leather jacket with designs and filigree stitching weaving down its front. She even had a lowlands-style hair clasp to hold her ponytail, although it was carved with Lenay craftsmanship.

Lynette noticed too. "Where do I get a jacket like that?" she said enviously between mouthfuls.

"It is rather nice, isn't it?" Sofy balanced her plate on her lap and moved to the edge of her chair, offering Lynette a feel of the leather. "I've been riding quite a bit since I returned to Baen-Tar, and I found that dear Sasha was right after all—it's just impossible in dresses. But of course there are no riding clothes for women. No women ride save for you and Sasha. I had these made especially, so that I had something nice to wear while riding."

"And what's made you so interested in riding?" Lynette pressed, clearly fascinated.

Jaryd could tell what she was thinking; another woman in Lenayin who rides! And not just any woman, but Princess Sofy!

"Well, I became very attached to my little horse, Dary," said Sofy with a private smile at Jaryd. Jaryd remembered Dary well, he'd been tasked with protecting the horse and his royal rider for much of the journey north, being capable of little else with his broken arm. "I went to see him in the stables every day, and of course he needed exercise, so I would ask stablehands if they could take him riding . . . but it was so sad not to be riding him myself. And after a few days back in Baen-Tar, facing the grim displeasure of the world in general," and here her tone took on a sombre maturity, but only for a moment, "I began to miss the open fields and the wind in my face. There's nothing more amazing than trying something entirely new that you never thought you'd be good at or interested in, and discovering that you're both."

"And the king let you ride?"

"The king," Sofy said primly, the sobriety returning, "is not the problem. Koenyg is the problem. Koenyg blames me for the rebellion, in part. After a few animated discussions, I grew tired of arguing with him and sought refuge elsewhere." She took another mouthful and chewed thoughtfully, then washed it down with some wine. Jaryd might have blinked at that, too. Before the ride north, Sofy had never drunk wine in her life. "He forbad me from riding when he heard of the preparations I made with the tailors. He said it would be a disgrace to the crown and a reminder to all Lenayin of the rebellion and my part in it."

"And what did you do?" Lynette asked breathlessly.

Sofy shrugged, but gave a faint smile. "I ignored him. I truly don't know why I hadn't thought of it sooner."

"Did that work?"

"Oh, wonderfully!" Sofy said with enthusiasm. "I mean, what can he do? If I'm unhappy or upset about something, it doesn't take very long for the staff, servants, stablehands and all to be spreading rumours throughout Baen-Tar, and those rumours spread to the cityfolk who then carry it all over Lenayin. I told Koenyg that the only way he could stop me from riding was to lock me in my chambers. I mean, I'm about to be wed to the heir of Regent Arrosh—" with a meaningful glance at Jaryd, "and the future of Lenayin depends on it . . ." She raised her eyebrows as Jaryd smiled faintly, "and the heir to the throne and the princess in question are having a blazing row, and now he's gone and locked her in her chambers with armed guards to restrain her from doing or saying anything she shouldn't . . . I mean, can you imagine? It would look terrible, just as he's trying to recover people's faith after a rebellion, too. He dare not lay a hand on me, and he knows it.

"So we compromised. I would ride when and where I pleased, and he would give me a Royal Guard escort to ensure my safety. And, wouldn't you know it, it worked wonderfully. People were actually pleased to see me . . . I mean, they don't get to see princesses very often, we're always holed up in the palace. So I would ride through the fields and farmers would wave, and their children would chase me, and then I'd ride through Baen-Tar town and people would actually come out and cheer. I began stopping to talk with them sometimes, and that went down very well . . . some had complaints or petitions, but others were just pleased to talk. Recently I went out to Mesheldyn to see the new temple they're building on the king's coin, and I found the temple looked grand, but the irrigation channels from the river were falling apart and farmers were complaining their water was low and crops were dying, so I told Damon about it and he's seeing it fixed.

"So Koenyg doesn't bother me about the riding any more, I'm sure his spies tell him the people like it and it seems to be helping them forget the rebellion, not remind them of it. I wouldn't be surprised if he tried it himself, just riding out and meeting people. Gods know it would do him some good."

It was the same Sofy Lenayin, Jaryd decided, she'd just grown up a bit. She could still talk endlessly without prompting, and her eyes and voice would sparkle at every point of fascination, which with Sofy meant several times a sentence. And yet, it seemed there was something different about her manner, even if her character remained unchanged.

"Good spirits," Lynette exclaimed, her eyes wide, "you're probably the only person in Lenayin who'd dare defy Prince Koenyg!"

"Someone has to," Sofy said cheerfully. "And he's not so scary really. Lenay people just have this way of building everyone into a legend, good or bad. Koenyg's just Koenyg and, however annoying, he's still my brother."

Doubt, Jaryd realised. Sofy's character was the same as he recalled, but she was missing something, and that something was doubt. The girl he remembered from the ride north had been quiet and uncertain, her eyes darting, worried that she was making an inconvenience of herself simply by being there . . . which she was. But that girl had also ridden in a rebellion, slept on hard ground, shared meals with warriors, cared for her horse, minded a pair of headstrong Udalyn children, learned as much as she could of a forbidden language, and tended the grievously wounded upon the field of battle. She'd also risked death, defied her father, drunk wine and had even got her hands dirty in a Udalyn garden. Such experiences might change a girl, even a princess. They had certainly changed some men.

"Highness," said Jaryd, drawing her attention. She met his gaze, then lowered her eyes for the briefest moment. The same, uncertain flicker. Then back again, with firmer resolve as princessly dignity reasserted itself. It disappointed him that she should fall back on form with him of all people. "Why are you here? Koenyg would never have let you ride here without guard. In fact, I can't imagine him allowing you to ride here at all."

Her eyes darted away again, and he knew he'd hit the peg on the head. "I'm tired of doing everything he tells me," she said churlishly, suddenly an eighteen-year-old again. "To say nothing of father. I've hardly *seen* father since the Udalyn ride. Some of us thought maybe he would assert himself more, but no, he's retreated into the temple and Koenyg seems to handle even more affairs now than he did before. I know I'm not the only one unhappy about it."

Jaryd had often been accused of not being very bright in lordly politics, he'd hated all that pointless, puffing sophistry, and hadn't understood why people couldn't just talk straight to each other. But he thought, just maybe, he could see where this was heading.

"Did you discover something?" he asked. "Something about me?" Sofy met his gaze, sombrely, chewing slowly. "Sofy, what are they up to?"

Sofy swallowed and sipped her wine. She took a second, larger gulp, and stared into the fire. "Jaryd," she said then, "I hear lots of things. It was always just fun before. People like me, and I've always loved gossip, I can't help it. Only recently have I started to realise what power it gives me . . . and how worrying that power is for someone like Koenyg. He's been worried about my love of gossip for years, when I thought it was all just a game . . ." she shook her head in disbelief. "Seriously, I can't believe I've been such a naive little girl.

"There was a lot of talk after your father died." She met his gaze firmly once more. "They need Tyree, Jaryd. The lords. The rebellion was strongest in Taneryn, Valhanan and Tyree . . . and Tyree is central, wealthy and close to Baen-Tar."

"And most of Lenayin's bread is made there, I know," said Jaryd impatiently. Maybe Sofy thought he was stupid too. "I didn't spend my *whole* life as Great Lord-in-Waiting ignoring everything important about my own province, I do know a few things."

"I didn't mean—"

"What are they up to, Sofy? Just tell me straight." He said it hard and blunt. Sofy looked somewhat crestfallen at his response. Perhaps she truly hadn't meant it like that. Jaryd told himself firmly that he didn't care, even as his heart told him he did.

"Well," she said, gathering herself, "there's a big debate amongst the Tyree lords. Some say Family Nyvar's removal was poorly done, because it's set a precedent. Many are quite upset, and not just in Tyree either. They're all suddenly watching their backs and double-checking their alliances, just to be certain their own family is not the next one dissolved by ancient clan-law.

"That debate is making Arastyn nervous. I hear he means you dead, Jaryd." Her gaze was concerned. "I've heard rumours of hired assassins and all kinds of things. The longer you remain alive, the more you fuel the debate and ensure no one forgets what's been done."

Jaryd smiled, humourlessly. "You're a day late."

Sofy frowned at him, uncomprehending.

"Three men dressed as Torovan merchants tried to shoot Jaryd with a crossbow at a wedding yesterday," Lynette explained. Sofy's hand went to her mouth. "Jaryd killed one and captured another, but the third got away. Men are searching for him now."

"So if you rode all this way to warn me that the new Great Lord of Tyree was trying to kill me," said Jaryd, "I thank you for the concern, but I'm already aware." Sofy took another breath, and did not reply immediately.

"That's not the only reason you rode, is it? Tell me."

"Your brother Wyndal," Sofy said bluntly, looking him straight in the eyes. "Arastyn means to have him killed too."

Eight

SASHA AWOKE AT DAWN, hearing guards out in the hall and men talking outside beneath the window. Still she was exhausted, and knew she'd had hardly any sleep.

"Sleep," Errollyn murmured alongside. "The house is quiet. There is no hostility here." He sounded so certain. He had no reason to trust Duke Rochel, nor her relationship with him, and yet he lay on his back, eyes closed, seeming to know that she was awake without looking.

How do you know? she wanted to ask. Who are you? And why do I feel so safe, with you lying at my side?

Sasha awoke again to find the day bright and sunny beyond the window shutters. The bed beside her was empty. Furthermore, her robe was open, and she was naked beneath. No doubt Errollyn had had an eyeful. The thought did not displease her.

She crawled over and peered through the strange shutters—thin wooden slats that opened and closed when one pulled on a string. She'd never seen their like before. Beyond, the broad gardens of Pazira House glowed in brilliant, multiple shades of green and the lake reflected sun and blue sky.

Sasha stretched, and ignored her weariness. There was nothing like a close brush with death to convince a fighter to work on her condition and technique, no matter the discomfort. Her forearm wound was scabbing over nicely, she noted as she did her taka-dans, and the big, tender lump on the top of her head no longer throbbed without provocation.

Sasha made her way through the house and then out into the bright morning. She walked down to the stables where a boy was shovelling muck from the doorway of a stall. He paused to see her coming, wide-eyed. "Lady Sashandra!"

"Hello Mikel," Sasha said with a smile. "Did he hurt anyone while I've been gone?"

Mikel nodded vigorously, wiping sweat from his forehead. "He threw off Ralin, but he wasn't hurt bad, just a few bruises. Master Faldini can ride him, but no one else dares."

Sasha frowned. "Master Faldini?"

"The Earl of Shashti, M'Lady. He's Captain of the Pazira Guard; for now, anyhow."

Of course, Sasha realised, Duke Rochel had brought a good five hundred men or more to stay in Cochindel, the town on whose outskirts Pazira House lay. Pazira families owned most of Cochindel, Sasha understood, and the Pazira Guard consisted of earls and their families, as well as regular, professional soldiers. Beneath them, each province could muster militia from peasants and small landholders. Those would only be raised when the war was imminent. Their quality was not much compared to Lenay militia or regulars, but still, one did not say so too loudly in these parts.

Each of the Torovan dukes had brought forces with him to this present gathering and those forces were now barracked around Petrodor wherever the dukes held ownership. It seemed like a lot of soldiers for some simple meetings, but then this was Petrodor and paranoia spread worse than a Riverside cough.

"Is Master Faldini a good horseman?" Sasha asked. She didn't like the idea of some man she'd never met riding Peg. In fact, she didn't particularly like *anyone* else riding Peg. As luck would have it, neither did Peg.

"Some say he's the best horseman in Pazira," said Mikel. Further ahead, there was a loud familiar whinny, then a crash. Peg had heard her.

Sasha saw a huge black head peering over the gate, a muscular chest shoving hard against the barrier. She hugged Peg, and her enormous, petulant warhorse snorted big, horse-smelling breaths all over her. "Oh here, look," she said, fishing some breakfast fruit from her pocket. But Peg seemed less interested in the fruit than in her. He pushed at Sasha with his nose, with force enough to jolt her backward, and sniffed at her hair. Sasha found she had tears in her eyes. "You never realised you loved me until I left you for a while, did you?"

She rode him out across the mounting yard and through the open gate onto a worn track beyond the walls of Pazira House. Immediately opposite was Cochindel Lake, its banks thick with reeds, willows and waterside bush. Sasha took off along a track to the right, which headed around the lake.

On the far side of the lake, the trail ran into thick trees and she rode through dappled shade. Some of the broad leaves were beginning to change colour, adding a tinge of yellow and red to the green. It was a distinct change from Lenayin's pine forests, but it was beautiful, even at speed.

Before the forest ended, she passed another rider from the duke's stables, and gave a wave as she took his lead. Now heading back around the far side of the lake, the vast, high slope of Backside rose up before her. It was green at the base, but that soon disappeared as the hill grew higher and buildings took over. Atop the high ridge, against the bright blue sky, she could make out the small shapes of great mansions. Beyond them, unseen, lay the Sharaal Sea.

Approaching now on the right, as the trail turned for home, was the village of Cochindel, a tight cluster of brownstone walls and red tile roofs. There were folk out tending the fields where crops grew thick. In one, a harvest was underway and several villagers waved as she passed. The Cochindel temple spire soared high above, a beautiful structure of simple stone. Such lovely buildings, the Verenthanes created. It made her sad.

She returned to Duke Rochel's stables and set Peg loose in a paddock. Sasha removed the sword from her back and sat on a bench beneath a tree, facing the horses. Peg did not stray far, grazing happily in the sunlight, and looking up at her occasionally.

Movement at the stables caught her eye—some new horses mustered in the mounting yard. Nearer, a lithe figure was walking, long-legged in pants, with a broad-brimmed hat on her head. She seemed to see Sasha and broke into an easy jog. Only then did Sasha recognise Rhillian.

Rhillian embraced her with evident delight. "Sasha! I was worried, no one knew of you!"

"You've news of the others?" Sasha pressed, pulling back to look Rhillian in the face. At such close range, Rhillian's brilliant eyes sent a chill up Sasha's spine.

"I've heard news this morning," said Rhillian, "they were speaking of perhaps fifteen missing from Kessligh's party, with you and Errollyn amongst them—"

"Is Kessligh well?"

"Oh yes."

Sasha gasped with relief. She'd never truly doubted it, but still . . . Rhillian smiled, hands on her friend's shoulders. "I haven't seen him, but I'm told he's fine. I don't know much more, I've been busy with other matters."

"Errollyn's fine too," Sasha assured her. "We were separated from the main group, he's—"

"I know," said Rhillian. "He joined us this morning while you were asleep."

"Joined you? Joined you where?"

"Cochindel." Rhillian pointed back past the stables toward the town. "We had a meeting there. Errollyn's arrival was a most pleasant surprise."

Sasha blinked at her. "You . . . a meeting?" Then she realised. "With Duke Rochel?" Rhillian nodded. "My word. He does get around, doesn't he?"

"It appears. Come, let's sit . . . you still look exhausted, Sasha. And your eye is swelling."

Sasha put a hand to her temple, feeling the light swelling there. "I've had worse." They sat together on the bench. "I ought to be jealous," Sasha said wryly. "I'd thought I was the only woman the duke was two-timing with."

"In Petrodor today, almost everyone is unfaithful. I've met with numerous folk who would deny knowing me on their mother's grave. The duke seems a good man, in his way. He wants no part of this war, that's certain. All that remains to be seen is whether he feels he has the option to say no. The ramifications for his province and his family could be dire."

"I know," said Sasha, gazing across the paddock. "He does not lack courage, to flaunt his relations with us so openly. Both of us. Surely word has spread."

"He keeps the patachis guessing," Rhillian agreed. "The patachis are strong collectively, but know better than most that such collectivity is an illusion. Individually, they fear Saalshen, and they fear the Nasi-Keth even more. By announcing his relations with both, Duke Rochel gives the patachis more reason to fear him. It's all a game, Sasha. For now, it suits all sides to maintain an equal balance of fear. But when the time for balancing ends, and the final act is made, be certain you know where you stand, and who stands with you."

More horses arrived at the mounting yard. Soldiers, by the look of them, with broad hats and gleaming buckles.

"Sasha," Rhillian ventured, a little cautiously, "Kessligh's position is seriously weakened. He meant this strike in Riverside to bolster his position within the Nasi-Keth and unite them behind him. Now it's failed. It seems that Alaine is now the strongest of the Nasi-Keth leaders, and—"

"Don't bet on it," Sasha said darkly.

Rhillian sighed. "I try only to be realistic, Sasha. Alaine is friendly enough to Saalshen, perhaps it would be better for the Nasi-Keth to unite behind his leadership, if anyone's."

"Aye, you'd like that, wouldn't you?" Sasha said with temper. "You've been trying to split us from the start, play Kessligh against Alaine and Gerrold . . ."

"No, Sasha, that's not it at all . . ."

"Some will say it was you that betrayed us in Riverside. We didn't tell you everything, but the *talmaad* knew enough."

Rhillian stared at her, her emerald eyes intent. "Do you seriously think that I would?" Her voice was hard.

Sasha shifted uncomfortably. "Not you, personally. But the *talmaad* . . . Rhillian, you've said yourself this is a battle you will do anything to win!"

"I never said that," Rhillian said shortly.

"You did! You said that your people's very existence is at risk and that you refuse to fail!"

"Curse this clumsy tongue," Rhillian muttered. And in Saalsi, "We have our limits, Sasha. I warned only of our determination, not of our cruelty. Trust me that I would never hurt you. Never."

Sasha just gazed at her, helplessly hypnotised by that emerald stare. "I killed people in Riverside," she said quietly. "I lost friends. I saw Aiden's head paraded atop a spear." The intensity vanished from Rhillian's eyes, replaced by shock. "You didn't know."

"No," said Rhillian, with sadness. "I'm sorry. Aiden was a lovely man."

Sasha took a deep breath. "Serrin are so logical, Rhillian. You do not become attached to your arguments and you waste no emotion on your philosophies. It's why you're such a peaceful people; amongst yourselves, at least. But I'm not serrin. And I'm not about to give up on Kessligh, not when it would mean all those people died for nothing . . ."

"No, Sasha, you misunderstand me." Rhillian placed a firm hand on Sasha's arm. "Kessligh is a great leader. I disagree with him on some matters, but he is committed to the betterment of all humanity, and I respect that intensely. I wish only that he would not continue this futile fight amongst the Nasi-Keth, Sasha. If we could only work together, we may stand a chance of ending Torovan involvement in this war entirely.

"Duke Rochel is our friend . . . or at least he would be, given a chance. Other dukes feel the same. We can split them from the patachis, Sasha. We can prevent this great Torovan alliance from forming. We should not be bickering amongst ourselves as to how we should achieve it, not when we are all truly fighting for the same thing."

"You want me to persuade him?" Sasha asked incredulously. Her voice was pained. Everything hurt—her body, her head and her heart. Petrodor was too confusing, even for someone raised on fractious Lenay politics.

"No," said Rhillian. "I want you to think, that's all. Together, Saalshen and the Nasi-Keth are strong. We should not be divided. Think about it, Sasha, that's all I ask. You cannot convince Kessligh of anything if you do not believe it yourself."

"In my experience," Sasha said quietly, "he's usually right about most things."

"He abandoned you in Lenayin," Rhillian said sombrely. "He thought the Udalyn a lost cause. He thought a rebellion would lead to civil war. And he was wrong."

"He thought the Udalyn a peripheral cause," Sasha countered, "not a lost one. He had conflicting priorities."

"So do we all. So did you. It doesn't make him less wrong. Everyone's allowed to be wrong sometime. He's only human."

"As you're only serrin," said Sasha firmly, looking her friend in the eyes.

Rhillian smiled. "I am. But on this, I'm not wrong. I can't afford to be."

Sasha leaned back on the bench and watched the horses. She felt lost. Rhillian copied her pose, took Sasha's hand in her own, and squeezed.

"That must be Peglyrion," she said.

"It is."

"He's every bit as beautiful as you described to me. See the way he stands to keep you in view? See his ear flicking in our direction? That's love."

"You're suddenly an expert on horse behaviour?" Sasha asked. "You're a city girl."

"I know love when I see it."

"Oh go on," said Sasha. "It's not even a serrin term."

Rhillian shrugged in the vague, all-encompassing way of serrin. "Yes, it's a strange human concept. It's intrigued the serrinim for endless centuries because it translates into so many Saalsi words that all mean very similar things, but not entirely. Usually it's the Saalsi terms that have trouble finding precise translations in human tongues, not the other way around. 'Love' has obsessed nearly as many serrin as it has humans over the years."

"I doubt that," said Sasha, with a faint smile.

"Ah," said Rhillian, holding up a warning forefinger, "don't make the mistake of assuming we don't know what it means. Serrin love. We just have a hundred words for it, and a hundred concepts of deep affection, not one. I think humans struggle so greatly with their singular concept because they refuse to accept that there are so many different kinds."

"Huh. Where's the romance in that? Humans like mystery, Rhillian. Mystery is . . . well, mysterious."

"So is ignorance," said Rhillian, smiling. "And humans love ignorance all too dearly." A bee buzzed to some flowers nearby. Peg swished his tail, chewing contentedly. "You could have left him with Saalshen's holdings in Eldin. Kessligh left Terjellyn there."

Sasha shrugged, a little warily. As much as she liked Rhillian, there were some concerns she was less eager to share with her. "It gives me an excuse to visit Rochel. Kessligh approved—I always got along better with Rochel than he did. He's a conservative, aggravating old grouch, but he admires spirit. He seems to think that I'm an example of character over common sense, which appeals to him."

"You probably are," said Rhillian.

Sasha smiled. "Aren't we all?"

"*En'ath*," said Rhillian, with another shrug. The universal truth. Or, in simple human parlance, "well spoken." Sasha did not add that neither she nor Kessligh had wanted *both* their horses in Saalshen's Petrodor stables. There was that old Lenay saying about too many eggs in the one basket.

"Sasha? Did you seriously think it might have been me who betrayed you?" Rhillian sounded hurt.

"No," Sasha sighed, "not you personally. But some of the serrinim . . . they're not all as nice as you, Rhillian."

"Kiel," Rhillian said shortly.

"Aye, well, there's him."

"He's a principled man," said Rhillian, without conviction.

"Aye he is," Sasha agreed. "Most serrin are. So's Patachi Steiner. I just don't like any of his principles."

Rhillian twisted her lips in wry assent. "I just . . ." she began and paused. Sasha gazed at her in surprise. If there was one thing serrin very rarely did, it was begin a sentence and not finish it.

"What?"

"I did not want to make you doubt Kessligh, Sasha," Rhillian said earnestly. "I just thought that it would be truly grand if I could join with some of my closest human friends in fighting for a common goal. And I would be honoured to fight with you."

Sasha blinked at her. Honour, another of those human concepts that barely translated. And this one was far less well received amongst the serrinim than "love." Rhillian was trying to say . . . something. Trying to escape the bonds of language that separated them, however many words they shared. Did Rhillian doubt? Did she wonder, perhaps, at her own strategies, even as she insisted she did not? Did she wish for human guidance? Or did she simply fear that it could be as Errollyn had warned, and that the moral, principled, high-minded serrin could be driven so hard by the need to survive that they would become everything that they despised and were fighting against?

Sasha smiled at her and grasped her hand more tightly. "I would be honoured too," she said simply.

Rhillian disappeared for the rest of the day, taking Errollyn with her, and leaving Sasha with little to do. It had been a long while since she'd had a genuinely lazy day. She practised taka-dans, and walked in the gardens and chatted with Bryanne Rochel.

Rhillian returned after the evening meal and, as dusk fell, they began the long trek up the Backside slope toward home. The journey would be safer now, with a day between them and the events at Riverside. Serrin company now that Rhillian had completed her meetings, would make it safer still. The Backside slums were an improvement on Riverside. They were still rickety and cramped, but the slope ensured the water flowed downhill and did not accumulate in poisonous puddles. Some folk actually waved to them in the dusk and called greetings. Women washed clothes, or prepared meals on exposed kitchen ledges, chatting with their neighbours or scolding rowdy children. Sasha knew well from Lenayin that people did not need to be wealthy to be happy and decent. It was a relief to see that in at least this part of Petrodor, the harsh lessons of Riverside did not hold entirely true.

Further up the slope, signs of wealth grew more pronounced. Houses had hard foundations and brick walls were held together with mortar. Dwellings overlapped, or loomed one above the other, as the slope increased. They mingled with the run-down shacks of more recent squatters, all jumbled together with the planning and forethought of a messy, forgetful child. Roads and trails began to multiply, and the party left the larger path they were on and made headway on narrow steps and winding paths. The serrin took the front and rear of the group as night fell and they progressed by the half-light of a fading moon.

After a long climb through winding alleys beneath ever-heightening walls, they found themselves in a narrow street leading onto a courtyard. Above loomed the spires of Garelo Temple, the second largest temple in Petrodor and a rare break in the almost impenetrable barrier of heavily guarded mansions that separated Backside from eastward Petrodor. Even so, it was a dangerous bottleneck to pass through if they did not wish a long trek around the entire city.

Rhillian murmured to one of the three other serrin Sasha did not know. Liam and Yulia waited—Yulia still without a blade. A nice present that would make for some mudfoot, although they would probably sell it to one of the merchant houses soon enough for a handsome price. Serrin did not sell their swords outside the Nasi-Keth. Any Nasi-Keth could make a small fortune by selling their blade to humans who couldn't get it any other way. Losing a blade cast great suspicion upon the dedication and loyalty of any Nasi-Keth. No wonder Yulia looked so guilty.

Sasha peered past Errollyn to the dark wall that rose at the edge of the courtyard. "Can you see anyone?"

"No, they've all got arrowslits." Errollyn had a shaft on his string, but did not draw. That was House Belis, over there, behind that wall. They had a view of all comings and goings through Garelo Temple. The patachis had once tried to mount a joint guard around the temple, to stop the nightwraiths passage. The death watch, its unfortunate members had called it. Life expectancy on the death watch had been measured not in days, but in hours. At night, no part of Petrodor outside the fortress walls of the great mansions did not belong to the Nasi-Keth. At Garelo Temple, they had written that message in blood.

The walls of Garelo Temple were lined with arches, like ribs along the temple's sides. Errollyn looked that way now, and even Sasha saw movement by one pillar. Hand signals in the dark, too indistinct to make sense of.

"We'll have to run," Rhillian said grimly. The signals had meant nothing good, Sasha gathered. She peered to the right where buildings overlooked the courtyard opposite Belis Mansion. There was no telling where a man of the families might be hiding with a crossbow, this dangerous night . . .

"I'll go," said Liam, with intensity. "I'll draw their fire."

"Adele will go," said Rhillian, nodding to a serrin woman with gleaming, pale hazel eyes. "She sees better. You'll follow. We go rapidly from then. Give them no chance to reload."

One of the other serrin also had a bow, and took position behind and to one side of Errollyn. Adele whispered some last-minute advice in Liam's ear, hands gesturing the way ahead, then she readied behind Errollyn and the other archer. Both men drew their bows with creaking force. Adele sprinted, a lithe shadow fading into the dark, her soft boots making barely a sound. Sasha held her breath, but no arrowfire came.

Rhillian gestured and Liam set off in pursuit. "Damn, I hate archers," Sasha muttered to herself. All her training, and she had no defence against archers but to move fast, hide silently and pray. It wasn't fair.

"I'm sorry to hear that," came Errollyn's voice. Sasha blinked. She hadn't meant *that*.

Another serrin ran, and still no firing. Sasha peered across the courtyard gloom, seeking the shapes of people. Adele seemed to arrive at the temple, Liam gaining behind. Another signal from Rhillian and Yulia took off running. Two thuds from the Belis wall and a frightening hiss. Yulia fell. Errollyn and his companion fired, and Rhillian sprinted into the courtyard. Sasha watched in horror as Rhillian reached the fallen girl, hauled her to her feet and dragged her stumbling onward. More thuds from the wall, and a clatter of crossbow bolts off pavings as Rhillian threw Yulia flat, falling together.

Another thump from Errollyn's bow, and a scream from the Belis wall. One of the crossbowmen had evidently stuck his head up too high.

"Go!" Sasha told the other serrin bowman. He loosed another arrow and sprinted.

"You next," said Errollyn, drawing his third arrow and seeking a target. Pitch black, firing at hidden archers at a hundred paces, and Errollyn was actually seeking targets, expecting to hit someone. Just ridiculous.

Sasha checked the narrow road behind them, to be certain there was no one sneaking up. Errollyn fired and cursed in Lenay. Sasha sprinted across the courtyard. Dark shapes along the way were flower gardens, she realised as she ran, every sinew dreading the imminent hiss of arrowfire. A shot came, and she flinched in midsprint, but the hiss-and-clatter fell some distance behind.

Ahead, the temple and its surrounding protection of arches and pillars approached. She heard another two thuds, but again, the bolts were far away. And then she arrived, skidding to a halt behind the pillars. Immediately there were footsteps and then Errollyn arrived. He must have been fast to have nearly overtaken her. She was quick but her legs were not nearly as long.

Against the wall of the temple, Yulia sat. Sasha ran across. "Yulia! Are you hit?"

"She's fine," said Rhillian.

"I'm sorry," said Yulia, miserably. "I . . . I heard the shot and I flinched, and then I tripped up . . ."

"It's okay," said Sasha. "I flinched too. We don't have to do that again, do we?"

Rhillian shrugged. "I don't actually go *looking* for trouble, you know."

"If you shout loudly enough, and wave your knickers in the air, trouble will find you," Errollyn remarked. Rhillian gave him an emerald stare that might have pinned a more timid person to the wall.

"You actually missed back there," Sasha told him, waiting for her heart to slow once more.

"You imagined it," said Errollyn.

"His second shot did not miss," said the second serrin bowman, covering the courtyard with his bow from a neighbouring pillar. "He's the only one who actually found the arrowslit."

Sasha stared at Errollyn. "You shot a man *through* the arrowslit? I thought he just stood up too high."

"Those wall posts have roofs," said Errollyn. "You can't stand up high."

There were several more serrin already waiting at the temple. One was Terel, tall with red-brown hair and deep bronze eyes. "Nice to see you well," he said at Sasha's side as they made their careful way around the temple, away from the Belis Mansion.

"And nice to see you," said Sasha. Like Errollyn and Aisha, Terel had fought with Sasha in Lenayin and she knew him quite well from their time together on the road to Petrodor. Unlike Errollyn and Aisha, Terel was quite the traditional serrin . . . if "traditional" was any sort of word to apply to a people who did not practise traditions in the sense that most humans meant them. He was formal and reserved, but no less likeable for it. "Been waiting long?"

"One waits," said Terel, in eloquent Saalsi. "One lives, one ponders, one counts the stars."

"Quite," said Sasha, repressing a smile.

There was a passage between the temple and the rectory, and the party slipped down it, gathering again beneath the columns on the temple's far side, directly upon the main ridge road. The ridge road ran along the top of the Petrodor Incline, from one end of the city to the other, connecting the most powerful properties in Petrodor. Here, the opposing walls were high, but without guard posts—only the most powerful families willingly picked fights with the nightwraiths. The nearest off road was to the right, Sasha knew, having come this way a few times before, though never on a night like this.

"Errollyn, Adele, Marlen, Liam, Yulia," said Rhillian, "you go ahead. I'll guard the rear with Sasha, Vinae, and Terel." She was more worried about House Belis than whatever lay ahead, Sasha realised.

Errollyn leapt the steps from the temple grounds down to the road and ran softly beside the opposing wall. The others followed, spreading out to avoid giving wall archers an easy shot into a bunch. Vinae—the second archer—watched back toward the Belis Mansion, an arrow at the ready. There would be other serrin in the temple grounds, Sasha knew, invisible in the shadows, or on rooftops, securing these strategic grounds from the families.

There came a noise from the right, the sound of a gate creaking open. Then yells as men poured forth from a property in Errollyn's path, a stream of waving torches and weapons. Rhillian swore. "House Therold," she muttered. "And so the ground shifts once more."

Errollyn's bow thrummed. Vinae launched a shot into the dark, then more shots came from temple shadows, and from the roof overhead. Men screamed and swords flashed, a chaos of fighting in the firelight.

"Come on!" Sasha urged, desperate to assist.

Rhillian held up a firm hand. "Wait!" As if expecting something more. From a property much further up the right-hand road, more men with torches came charging. And then, to the left, the Belis gate squealed and ground. "Vinae, we'll take the left," said Rhillian, as calmly as if she were noting the warm weather. "There's a lane opposite Belis House, we'll never make the right-hand lanes now."

Sasha saw immediately what Rhillian had in mind. They could not go right, the odds were against it. They had to stop Belis's men from hitting Errollyn's group from behind. May as well go through them.

Men were streaming from the Belis gate, some armed with swords, others with polearms with wicked heads, and a few with axes. The Belis men looked like no family soldiers Sasha had yet seen, with steel helmets and metal breastplates that glinted in the torchlight. Plate armour. Sasha, Rhillian and Terel crouched while Vinae held fire. To the right, Errollyn's group seemed to be winning through.

The Belis soldiers ran past the temple and Rhillian charged. Sasha and Terel followed, and arrowfire tore from the grounds. Six men fell in an instant. Sasha and the others tore into their side, diving into the sudden gaps in their ranks. She slashed low across one pair of legs, parried a blow and removed a head. She was about to parry a new threat, but he fell to Rhillian's flashing blade, and another dropped with an arrow in the throat.

In an instant, a charging formation of twenty-plus men were transformed to a fleeing, shrieking band barely half that number. Rhillian was already charging up the road toward Belis Mansion, from where more men were emerging. Perhaps these had expected to follow behind their braver fellows, or to harass the serrin archers in the temple grounds. Surely they did not expect to see one lone, female serrin come charging at them with blood on her mind.

Rhillian, too, was faster afoot than Sasha, and arrived well ahead. She faked a strike, spun past, and felled one and then another with magnificent precision. Another aimed a halberd for her head, but Rhillian skipped back like a dancer, killed his companion who tried to outflank her, deflected a stab for her middle with a downward, vertical blade which miraculously changed to a horizontal, upward cut with a twist of wrists and elbows. The halberd-wielder fell, gushing blood from the throat.

Four dead before Sasha and Terel even arrived, the men from House Belis did not know what hit them. Sasha cut through one and found the others already scattering, those on the periphery falling as serrin arrows found them. Rhillian was already running to a dark gap in the walls opposite the corner of the Belis Mansion. Atop the mansion walls, Sasha caught a glimpse of activity within the guardpost arrowslit, confused crossbowmen not knowing who to shoot in the melee. She dived through the gap as Rhillian waited behind for Terel and Vinae.

There were steps in the narrow alley, leading downward, and Sasha risked her poor human eyesight, hoping to secure some distance for those behind to follow. She found a corner where a second alley ran off to the right and the slope dropped sharply. Above the next house, there was suddenly a view of the harbour well below, agleam with the last light of a half moon upon the horizon. Little ships, in silhouette against that silver light. Now, they just had to survive the descent.

Soft footsteps behind, above the ongoing yells and screams of men on the ridge road above. Terel emerged on the stairs, half carrying Vinae who seemed to have caught a crossbow bolt in the shoulder. Damn. Rhillian came past at speed, feet flying on the steps as Sasha would never have dared in the dark. She took the lead and Sasha fell behind, guarding the rear from any pursuit. It seemed unlikely. An open road was one thing, but an alley in the dark meant single combat with serrin for whom the night was as bright as any day.

They continued down the steps for a fair time, slowed by Vinae's injury. Rhillian took twists and forks with what Sasha presumed (or hoped) was local knowledge, occasionally turning back uphill, or over a short rise of stairs. Many times they passed rear gates in the walls and Sasha suffered bad memories of Riverside, spears and clubs lashing at her from unexpected dark corners. One time Rhillian actually missed a tripwire and triggered a nearby bell, which set a dog barking madly behind its wall. Rhillian seemed not to care, but Sasha could not escape the feeling of unseen eyes upon her back, aiming crossbow bolts in the dark.

Finally Rhillian paused atop some steps where a big tree grew against one wall, spreading thick roots through the surrounding stone. Terel helped Vinae to rest against the tree and tended to his injury. The bolt had struck him from behind, lodging through one shoulder blade. Terel took a knife to his clothes and began to relate his findings to Vinae in some Saalsi dialect Sasha could make no sense from at all. Vinae seemed somewhat reassured, pale and gasping, but alert.

"Those didn't look like family soldiers," Sasha murmured to Rhillian as both of them crouched atop the uneven stone stairs. "All that clumsy armour, and silly weapons for city fighting. Halberds."

"They were men of Danor Province," said Rhillian. She seemed barely even out of breath, her green eyes sharp and calm, cutting through the dark. "That fool Duke Tarabai has been itching to have at us within the city for a while now. He disdained Patachi Steiner's warnings. Now he learns the patachi's wisdom."

Sasha raised an eyebrow at her. "That's the only nice thing you've ever said about Patachi Steiner."

"Nice? The wise are rarely nice, in this city. Petrodor wisdom is the mother of Petrodor brutality and intelligence its father. These terms are strange to serrin philosophy. No, I'm sure Patachi Steiner was pleased to set traps along the ridgetop after Riverside, and in light of the increased Nasi-

Keth and serrin activity. But I don't think he'll shed tears for his upstart duke to learn his place, either."

"I'm sure he'd rather have killed us all even more," Sasha remarked.

Rhillian shrugged. *"Tian'as fahr."* One could have said, "that meant, if one could know everything." "Although captured for torture might be even more preferable to him."

"Serrin are very good at assassinations," Sasha remarked. "Why not just kill him?"

Rhillian shrugged. "Patachi Steiner is not the easiest target. Our numbers are not enormous. And there's no guarantee Symon Steiner will be any better. Patachi Steiner is at least open to more subtle forms of persuasion, and he is not yet in a state of total war with Saalshen."

"Just limited war," Sasha muttered.

"A perpetual state in Petrodor," said Rhillian. "Today is just another day of business to the Big Patachi." She eyed Sasha sideways. "You show distaste."

"Say what you like about we highland barbarians," said Sasha, "but at least we take war seriously. Here, it's just another transaction."

"Honour," said Rhillian, dubiously.

Sasha nodded. "Yes, honour. It's not such a bad concept, Rhillian. It imparts a price for every action."

"And a reward for every crime," said Rhillian, taking some dead leaves off the top step and wiping her bloody sword with them. "Lenays place honour on codes of behaviour in order to maintain the social order and hierarchy. Patachi Steiner places honour on power and wealth. It is a flexible concept, this 'honour,' neither inherently good nor evil. Like your blade, it depends on the hand that wields it."

"At least Lenay honour is gained from the means rather than the ends," Sasha insisted. It seemed important that Rhillian should understand. This woman was the most powerful and influential serrin in Petrodor. So much rested upon her decisions. The fate of humanity, in many ways. "In Petrodor, the ends can impart any crime with honour, should they be rewarding enough."

"If you're asking for my personal preference of Lenay honour above the Petrodor variety," said Rhillian, "then you have it. But I shall always dislike 'honour' as a concept. Too often it serves to impart respectability upon the most vile of crimes. King Leyvaan's men gained great honour murdering serrin children two centuries ago. Even your wonderful Lenays have a long, bloody history of pillage, murder and rape, all in the name of honour. You are better behaved these days, and honour means different things to you, but that only proves the dangerous ambiguity of the concept."

Rhillian's emerald gaze fixed onto Sasha with spine-tingling force. There was a droplet of blood trickling down one pale cheek. These beautiful people, this beautiful civilisation, was a shining light for all the world, Kessligh insisted. They are peaceful and good because they are philosophical, and do not to leap to conclusions. They neither hate nor fear easily. They do not kill on a whim. They are frequently long-winded, gentle and indecisive.

But what if that changed, Sasha wondered, staring at that terrible, beautiful vision of luminescent eyes and trickling blood. What if we pushed them too far? What it we made them so angry, and so scared, that they lost their indecisiveness and replaced it with determination? There was determination in Rhillian's eyes now. Determination and focused, deadly intensity. Sasha had now seen Rhillian fight. She'd seen Errollyn fight, and other serrin too. Saalshen would be a terrible enemy for humanity. Terrible for the damage they could do, and terrible for the simple tragedy of such good and decent people forced into conflict with those who should do far better to befriend them. She could not let it happen. She would not.

"You need honour to confirm your identity," said Rhillian, unblinking. "Your honour tells you who you are. We serrin don't need it. We *know* who we are."

"*Vel'ennar?*" Sasha asked quietly.

"*Vel'ennar,*" Rhillian agreed. "The one soul," literally translated. A concept of serrin unity. Whether it was real or imagined, cultural or merely philosophical, no human seemed to know . . . and no serrin had yet definitively explained. Not to Sasha's hearing, anyhow.

Vinae hissed in pain as Terel applied something to the wound. He was not removing the bolt, Sasha saw. Probably there were better facilities available to serrin than a dingy alleyway for that. "Do you need any help?" she asked Terel.

"Do you have any skills with medicine?" Terel asked as he worked.

"Um . . . not for something like that, not really."

"Then I don't need your help."

Rhillian's eyes flicked uphill, back the way they'd come. Sasha spun in alarm, but saw nothing. Then, after a moment, a small, indistinct shadow crossed the path. A cat.

"Do you see better," she asked Rhillian warily, "or do they?" Meaning the cat.

Rhillian shrugged. "I've never asked one. Possibly they do. But do they know what they're seeing?"

"Do you? Maybe the cat knows everything and we're all fools."

"A serrin answer," Rhillian said coyly, with an impressed smile. "You're spending far too much time with us. We'll corrupt you."

"Too late. You remind me of a cat, sometimes."

Rhillian's grin seemed to light up the dark, flashing white teeth and gleaming eyes. "Meow," she said with her entire, lean, poised body.

Further down the winding alleys, the party finally arrived at a nondescript gate in the rear wall of a narrow passage. Rhillian reached into a hole beside the gate and pulled something. Faintly, Sasha heard a bell ring. A moment later, a hatch slid aside, and something whispered in dialect. Rhillian replied. Several latches were undone and the gate opened on silent, oiled hinges. Sasha waited until last, passing a serrin she did not recognise, who shut the gate behind her. They made their way through a stone passage with arrowslits at the end, and another gate, reinforced yet open for now.

A turn and then they emerged into a patio centred by a fountain, with gardens about the surrounding wall. The house had broad, slatted doors opening directly onto the patio, behind a row of pillars supporting an overhead balcony. More serrin were waiting, and took Vinae into the house. Sasha followed Rhillian and Terel, and found herself in an adjoining sitting room, chairs about a tiled floor and bookshelves against the walls. Most welcoming of all, Errollyn, Liam, Yulia and Adele were all waiting there.

"Where's Marlen?" Rhillian asked immediately.

"Inside somewhere," said Adele. "He's fine." Rhillian looked relieved. Sasha looked questioningly at Errollyn. He'd leaned his bow against a wall and was cleaning his sword. Evidently he'd had to use it. He met her gaze and gave a faint smile. "I never doubted I'd see you here," that smile said. Somehow, she knew what he meant.

Servants brought them drinks . . . human servants, dressed much the same as serrin—plainly, with few frills or trinkets, but with quality and style all the same. Upon first visiting a Saalshen property in Petrodor, Sasha had been astonished to find human servants in the house. Errollyn had explained to her that the first serrin *talmaad* in Petrodor had resisted it at first—service was not a profession nor a social condition of any sort in Saalshen—but it had been a waste of resources for well-trained *talmaad* to be doing household chores.

The Nasi-Keth had suggested the solution. There were plenty of folk on the Petrodor lower slopes who needed work. Folks with deformities, that often led to them being rejected by their families as cursed. And so the *talmaad* had taken in many such folk as houseworkers—a term the serrin preferred to "servants." The houseworkers were undyingly loyal and the serrin were happier. The houseworkers would surely be in a dismal state were they not "serving," and so "serving" became an alternative no serrin could begrudge them from having.

A bald, round-faced man with an anxious smile handed Sasha a drink and then shuffled off, one leg stiff, one hand and arm curled tight. Yulia was slumped in a chair in a corner. Liam paced, anxious to be on his way.

Rhillian addressed her fellows in Saalsi. "I must meet with Patachi Maerler tonight," she said. "Words were exchanged with Duke Rochel. There are possibilities."

"Shall we send a message ahead?" asked one serrin. "I'm not certain of his whereabouts tonight."

"He'll be home," said Rhillian, with assuredness. "He'll be expecting me."

"What did Rochel say?" asked another man, newly arrived into the room. His jet black hair fell with stylish disarray about a well-formed face. His eyes were a pale, almost colourless grey. Kiel.

"Another time awaits," said Rhillian, in the most abstract form that Saalsi allowed. "Not with others listening," Sasha interpreted that. "Adele, Marlen, stay and rest. Kiel, I want you along. Errollyn too."

"Must he?" said Kiel. The question was blandly put. Much about Kiel was bland, and expressionless. Most serrin were disconcerting to basic human instincts, as was Kiel but in a different way. Rhillian startled with her intensity. Kiel startled in his impassivity. He was the only serrin Sasha had ever met toward whom her instinctive reaction was dislike.

"Must I?" said Errollyn.

Rhillian's stare was displeased. "You know humans better than most. You read Patachi Maerler well. You may notice things others will miss."

"I don't know humans as well as Sasha does," said Errollyn. He sheathed his sword over one shoulder. "Why not ask her along?"

Rhillian's stare became even more displeased. She said something in dialect.

"Rhillian says that I'm being difficult," Errollyn translated to Sasha. "She says I know very well why she cannot ask you along." Rhillian made a sharp gesture of exasperation. "Why don't you tell us all, Rhillian, why Sasha cannot come along? Why is it that you plot things, in a human city, that do not concern our human allies?"

"He becomes more and more human every day," Kiel said mildly. He sounded almost amused.

"Sasha has her own people to return to," said Rhillian, glaring.

"And I'd so much rather go with her."

"Are you *talmaad*, or are you not?"

"Do you define the *talmaad* now?" A human might have folded his arms in defiance. That pose, however, seemed foreign to serrin. Errollyn stood calmly, a thumb in his belt. "You're right, I do read Patachi Maerler quite well. You're a fool to trust him, I said so from the start, and I'm sure I'll tell you the same after this meeting too. What more can I add to your expedition?"

"Loyalty," said Kiel, in Torovan.

Errollyn snorted. "Well may you change tongues," he told Kiel, in Torovan. "And you accuse *me* of becoming more human?"

"We serve the serrinim," said Kiel, in Saalsi once more. "The serrinim cannot be disunited, or we shall fall. Such have we decided, and such does our *vel'ennar* tell us. Will the *du'janah* follow? Or do we have to drag you?"

Errollyn gave Kiel a look that was almost . . . anger. Amongst serrin, in debates, it was rare indeed. "When charging headlong toward a cliff, disunity is no bad thing."

"When the cliff charges toward *us*," said Kiel, utterly unmoved, "then disunity will kill us all."

"And I tell you that debate has saved us in the past," Errollyn said firmly, "and shall do so in the future, if we are to survive at all."

"No one doubts your conviction, Errollyn," said Rhillian, more gently this time. "Your opinions have always been respected." Kiel, Sasha saw, nearly smirked. "But these are not the councils and teahouses of Saalshen. This is Petrodor, and I lead. We are *talmaad*. You swore an oath."

"Another foreign concept," said Errollyn. "You accuse me of foreign thinking, but your own is worse. I learn sarcasm. You learn fear and cynicism."

"Come down from your lofty mountain, great mind," Rhillian said more coolly. "You're right, we do live amongst humans and their ways at times dictate ours. I can give an order if I must, Errollyn. Do you say that I must?"

Nine

SEVERAL QUESTIONS TO DOCKSIDE RESIDENTS told Sasha of Kessligh's whereabouts quickly enough. She walked along the dock, with only Liam for company, and listened to the creak and heave of the boats tied along the piers. Some folk wandered in the warm evening, unaware of commotions elsewhere in the city. Here, some wealthy types with a foreign look about them—Ameryn, perhaps, walking with several prominently armed guards. There, some rowdy sailors, singing as they wandered from bar to bar. Some men played a loud game of dice before their doorway. Some others sang songs to the accompaniment of guitars. They paid little attention to a couple of passing Nasi-Keth.

"You did well," Sasha told Liam as they walked. "Up there, and at Riverside. I was impressed." Liam said nothing. Sasha thought she knew the cause of it. "You were right about Yulia. She should not have come."

Liam gave her a hard, suspicious stare. "*Now* you admit it. After Rodery's dead."

"And what good would it have done to admit it at the time? We were stuck in a situation, Liam. Yulia was there, frightening her further would have only made matters worse."

"Kessligh should never have selected her for the mission," Liam said darkly.

"It wasn't entirely his choice. His seconds chose the personnel, Kessligh cannot know the standard of every Nasi-Keth on the dockfront. Besides, her technique in training was not so bad; she should have been all right against mudfoots. But she panicked and her technique deserted her. That's one thing training can never tell. But now we know."

They arrived at the entrance to The Fish Head where some sailors and locals were having a loud, drunken disagreement, with much shouting and fingerpointing. Sasha and Liam slipped past, down some steps and into the gloomy, lamplit interior.

The space was crowded, with as many Nasi-Keth as Sasha had ever gathered in one place. From the stairs, she could see that there appeared to be three sides to the gathering—a triangle, some fancy, serrin-educated folk called it. Near the middle, men were sitting, tables shoved aside. Further back, men stood, perhaps fifty in all. The air smelled staler than usual, hot and musty. The conversation was loud and animated, and so intense that no one saw her enter.

She left Liam, pushed past men along a side wall and headed for the bar where Tongren the Cherrovan waited and watched, a scowl on his dark face. Sasha nearly smiled. She rapped on the bar and his face lit up. Sasha put a finger to her lips to quiet his exclamation.

"What's going on?" she asked him as he leaned close.

"You're alive!" he exclaimed softly. He clapped her on the shoulder—her sore shoulder—and she winced. Tongren ran a finger on her swollen eyebrow. "What man dared do this to your pretty face?"

"Probably some kid with a rock," Sasha murmured.

He made a dismissive gesture. "You're always beautiful to me. I worried so much for you! Though not as much as one I could name . . ." He jerked his head toward the group. Sasha looked, but could not see Kessligh amidst the crowd. "Kessligh's in trouble. Alaine and Gerrold made lots of noise. Now they challenge him, say he made a big mess in Riverside, lost precious men."

"How many did we lose?"

"One less now we have you back . . . Who else?"

"Liam and Yulia, two more," said Sasha. "And one confirmed dead. Rodery."

Tongren shrugged. "*Sharl*," he said. "War," in Cherrovan. One of her small handful of Cherrovan words; the ones every Lenay knew from four centuries of occupation. "That would be thirteen dead, I think five badly wounded and still two missing." Sasha exhaled hard. It was not as bad as she'd feared. But it was still bad. The whole thing had been bad; there was just no way around it. "Alaine blames Kessligh. Gerrold doesn't blame anyone . . . he's a good man, sensible. But still, he argues. You'll hear."

Sasha pulled herself onto a bar stool. "Get me a drink, will you?"

"Ale?" said Tongren, brightening.

"Juice, please."

"Bloody Nasi-Keth," Tongren muttered, going to do that. "Take over my bar, scare away my customers, but you don't drink. How can you be real fighting men if you don't drink?"

"I never claimed to be a real fighting man," Sasha said pointedly.

"Just my point."

"The plan would have worked," one of Kessligh's men was saying. It sounded like Bret. From her seat, Sasha could not see him. "I'm telling you, our plans were sound, we had good numbers for the assault, Steiner's men would have had no chance against us . . ."

"Would have this, could have that!" That was Alaine, loud and angry. Alaine was always loud and, for a Nasi-Keth, frequently unreasonable. "We hear excuse after excuse from you and your great warrior hero!" Sasha bristled. "Did he make this many excuses when he drove the Cherrovan invaders from Lenayin? You complain like an old woman, and make up fantasies like a child! I don't care what you *could* have done, it only matters what did happen! And this attack was a disaster!"

"Because we were compromised from within," said Bret, from between what sounded like gritted teeth.

"So you say! How long have we been trying to expand the Nasi-Keth's influence into Riverside? The poor, the hungry and dispossessed are our natural allies, and yet you kill them in their dozens, and set fire to their houses—"

"Rubbish . . ."

"And now you sit here and declare before us that you have done nothing wrong! Riverside is lost to us now, for years at least . . ."

"And a great pity," said someone else, sarcastically, "because you were making such wonderful progress there too. Its inhabitants positively reek of wealth and enlightenment."

"You make fun," Alaine retorted, "but thanks to you, now they likely never will!"

"We do what we can for the poor," said Bret, attempting reason. "The odds against our success are huge, yet we make small progress every year. Not every poor child's blistered feet, nor his mother's hacking cough, is our fault."

"Normally, yes, I would agree!" said Alaine. "But now, with Kessligh at your helm, you make a bad choice of priorities. The Nasi-Keth has whatever power and support it has in Petrodor thanks to the poor. Most of us are drawn from the ranks of Petrodor's poor. It was the sons of poor families who died in Riverside in this ill-advised attack. They support us because we do good things for them. We give them knowledge, and medicines, and ways to improve their living so they don't get sick. And we defend them from the cruelty of the families.

"*That* is a wise use of force. That is the only use of force we should contemplate. Not this . . . this brash, dangerous action against the most lucrative arms shipments of the greatest family in Petrodor! Yes, we should help the serrin to defend the Saalshen Bacosh as best they can, but our first priority should always be to our own!"

"If the Saalshen Bacosh falls," came a retort, "then Saalshen itself is threatened. If Saalshen falls, the Nasi-Keth shall wither on the vine. We *do* fight for our own, it's only that your vision is neither broad nor perceptive enough to perceive it!"

"We have neither the strength," said Alaine, decisively, "nor the strategy to contemplate this course of action. We are many, yet not so many that we can afford to waste man after man against the power of the patachis. Have you seen the forces they gather from the provinces? The dukes swear their loyalty and they command entire armies. If they attack us here, we can defeat them, for we own these streets and alleys and no force can take them from us. But to waste good men on such foolish diversions is pointless!

"Look at the good people we have lost! Galthraite, one of our best swordsmen. Aiden, a fine leader. My friend Bron, the mason. Even Kessligh's own uma, legend though some claimed her to be . . . if even *she* cannot survive such folly, what chance do the rest of we mere mortals have?"

"Why, Alaine!" Sasha said loudly. "That's the nicest thing you've yet said about me. Legend? That sounds much nicer than whore, or fool, or pagan barbarian!"

The room stopped, and everyone turned to look. Men she knew, Kessligh's followers, stared in disbelief. One grinned. "Sweet Sadis, girl! I didn't even see you back there!"

Sasha climbed up on the bar and walked across mugs and hands to the thick of the group, her temper at a slow boil. Alaine, further from the bar, stared up in disbelief. "It's nice to know you'll respect me so much more when I'm dead," she told him.

Nearer the bar, men moved aside to clear a space. And there was Kessligh, risen from his chair, and looking at her with . . . a look of as great an emotion or relief as she'd ever seen him wear. She struggled to contain her own emotion, and jumped down into the space. And grinned up at her uman. He nearly grinned back, a smile of wry, twisted delight, and took her arms. "You'll be the death of me," he said, attempting gruffness.

"That seems only fair," Sasha retorted and hugged him, hard. Kessligh hugged her back, harder. "I'm sorry I'm late, but I got cut off. Yulia is well, Liam is back there . . ." and she pointed back toward where she'd seen him last, "and our serrin friend Errollyn is also well. Our friend Rodery died with great honour, against formidable odds, and took several of his enemy with him. He shall be remembered with pride."

Men turned to find Liam and shake his hand, or clap his shoulder. He took it sombrely, with little apparent joy.

"You speak the brave words of a Lenay warrior," said Alaine as the commotion died. Alaine was a man of memorable appearance and no little charisma. He had shoulder-length black hair in light curls. His nose was big, his cheekbones pronounced, and his eyes were deep and dark beneath prominent brows. On his pointed chin, he wore a black goatee. "Yet it is not for you, Lenay princess, to speak of how our fallen men shall be remembered."

"Does honour mean nothing to you, Alaine?" Sasha asked sharply. "It certainly meant something to Rodery."

"Honour means as much to the people of Petrodor as it does to you!" Alaine retorted, dark eyes flashing with anger. "It is not for foreigners to try to tell us what our honour means!"

Sasha recalled her recent conversation with Rhillian in the alley. "A dear friend of mine told me recently that honour, like most human concepts, has no fixed meaning and should thus be distrusted. I say that *all* human concepts have no fixed meaning, and yet, should we distrust them all, we shall be left with nothing. I am Lenay, yet should you choose to confer Torovan honour upon me, I would be flattered. It would be most *enlightened* of you, Alaine, to accept my Lenay honour in the same spirit."

"Oh aye," said Alaine, imitating her accent, "and would it also be enlightened of me to die for your highland honour? If I'll die for any honour, it shall be for the honour of Petrodor, not for the glory of Lenayin!"

"This solves nothing," said Kessligh, pulling Sasha back before she could advance on Alaine. "Alaine, you say that as Nasi-Keth our primary loyalty should be to Petrodor."

"And have always said so!" Alaine said proudly.

"Your argument is sound—your path is indeed a path we could follow." Kessligh spoke with none of Alaine's loud passion. When Kessligh spoke, each word mattered and men listened intently, whatever their personal persuasion. "Yet Petrodor is no island. Neither is any of the powers of Rhodia. Petrodor's current wealth was granted it, unwittingly perhaps, by Saalshen. Lenayin's current stake in Verenthane politics was inflicted upon it by Petrodor. The Bacosh invaded Saalshen two centuries ago, and Saalshen replied with a considerably more successful invasion. Now, the fates of both Saalshen and the Bacosh are inextricably interwoven.

"The fates of all the powers of Rhodia are likewise interwoven. You state that we should not place the fate of the Saalshen Bacosh, nor of Saalshen herself, above our own fate. Yet you fail to see that these two fates are in fact one, single fate. Indeed, were it not for the occupation of the Saalshen Bacosh, the Nasi-Keth would not have been granted such a safe haven from which to grow and spread across Rhodia—in particular here, to Petrodor. You attempt with your arguments to isolate what cannot be isolated.

"Should a united Verenthane army march against the Saalshen Bacosh, the patachis would strike perhaps their greatest blow against the gravest threat to their own power here in Petrodor—us. They will surely attack on into Saalshen, and the serrin will find themselves with more pressing matters at home than the fate of the Nasi-Keth in Petrodor. Imagine, no more cheap serrin blades. No more medicines. No more friendly advice, and occasional military assistance. No more precious information. Then, Alaine, we should truly be alone, and it would be no good thing at all."

Alaine shook his head with a grin of disbelief. "You argue just like Gerrold!" he exclaimed, pointing to a man seated upon the other side of the triangle. Gerrold was older, of more than sixty summers, with long white hair and a kindly lined face. "Why not just join with him, should you love your serrin brothers and sisters so kindly? Why pursue this madness against targets that even Gerrold does not support?"

"Gerrold loves the serrin," Kessligh said calmly, "and the serrin surely love him. He would follow their lead, especially the lead of Rhillian. I say that Rhillian does not know humanity as well as she thinks. She tries to make House Maerler and House Steiner fight, and thinks to side with Maerler. It is the *worst* thing she can do. If *either* of the great families actually wins, and wins conclusively, it shall be a disaster for us. Rhillian does not understand that it is not final conclusions that are essential, but a continued balance of power. Such a balance keeps the great houses constrained, too scared of each other to take great risks. But one of the great families, victorious and unconstrained, will have no such hesitation. Maerler would happily lead a Torovan army to Saalshen to slaughter all the serrin it could find, they have no greater love of Rhillian and her cause than Steiner does."

"Your solution is to do nothing," said Gerrold, with a helpless shrug. Sasha thought it sad that he and Kessligh should find themselves opposed. "Saalshen have had enough of doing nothing. Rhillian does not trust human politics, and I agree with her. She wishes that Saalshen should finally demonstrate its power, and its willingness to use it."

"I say we contain them," said Kessligh. "We play the houses against each other and allow neither to gain the upper hand. We attack their arms shipments and make clear to them that such trade will not be tolerated. We make them stew in their own incapacity and frustration. We show them that we control this city, not they. We give them enough rope and let them hang themselves."

"Worked wonderfully, didn't it?" said Alaine sarcastically.

"If he weren't endlessly undermined from within," said Bret, "perhaps it would have."

"He's all talk," said a new voice to one side. Sasha looked and saw Liam, pushing his way to the front. His young face was set, his lips thin with determination and anger. "He comes to us from a foreign land with great legends of his warlike deeds, but it's all just talk." Sasha stared in utter disbelief. "I was there, in Riverside. I was taken in by all his talk. So was my friend Rodery. The whole attack was a disaster. We didn't know where we were going, there was no planning and everything went wrong.

"He tells us that women should take a greater role in the Nasi-Keth, just like his uma! But he chose Yulia to come with us and Yulia can't fight! Her incompetence got Rodery killed! And then we had to protect her, and Kessligh's uma's no damn better; she can't fight a jot either! All the tales they tell about her in the highlands are lies—she might be good in the training courtyard, but in battle she's just another useless girl! And then she tries to blame me for Rodery's death, her and her pet serrin, and—"

Sasha charged him, getting in a solid blow with one fist before she was grabbed and dragged backward. "I'll fucking kill you!" she screamed at Liam, who hung upon the supporting arms of neighbours, clutching his bruised cheek. "You scum-sucking traitor!" As men wrestled her backward, and more men restrained Liam as he tried to come back at her, and the whole room exploded in uproar.

"Right here, you stupid pagan bitch!" Liam yelled.

"A duel!" Sasha yelled, wrestling an arm free to jab a hard finger at him. "I want a duel, right now! I'll show you who's the useless girl, I'll cut your fucking head off!"

Gerrold took station in the space between the combatants, with a cold stare for them both. Sasha gave up struggling, heaving for breath. "You're not in Lenayin here," he said firmly to Sasha. "There can be no honour duel. We don't do that here."

"I'll start a new tradition!" Sasha blazed. "He insulted my honour, and I'll have his head!"

"No, you will not!" Gerrold shouted.

"Stupid pagan fool," someone else remarked.

"I'll have you too!" Sasha shouted, glaring in that direction. "You think I'm no warrior? Prove it, you fucking cowards!"

"Kessligh!" came another shout. "Control your bitch! She's gone mad!"

"Sasha!" Kessligh stepped before her, darkly furious. But his fury, to the mild surprise of that part of her mind that could still think clearly, was not solely for her. "Calm down." The room quieted somewhat. Sasha calmed, with difficulty, the grip on her arms relaxing a little. "Liam makes allegations without proof," said Kessligh. Sasha recognised that pose, and that tone. It was a fighting stance, but without the blade yet drawn. Men near him became quiet and careful. They might doubt *her* abilities, but they knew better than to doubt his. "There must be some recourse."

"Liam is entitled to his say!" said someone, angrily. "We are the Nasi-Keth and we welcome truth in all its forms, not merely that which you find convenient!"

"All Nasi-Keth are entitled to their say," Kessligh agreed, "but Liam does not merely voice opinions. He makes allegations. That's different. It is the nature of our truth that allegations must be backed by evidence. My uma merely claims the right to contest these allegations."

"We don't fight barbarian honour duels amongst the Petrodor Nasi-Keth!" Gerrold insisted crossly. "We're more civilised than that!"

"Aye," snarled Sasha, "there's no provision for duels because all your enemies are dealt with by a knife from behind in the dark! How *civilised*." She was somewhat astonished that Kessligh was defending her. Usually when she lost her temper and caused trouble, he'd give her a whack about the ears, metaphorically or otherwise.

"You work out the best solution," said Kessligh to those opposite, "because this is presently an impasse. For truth to out, lies must be given their chance to be exposed. Liam's allegations hold no truth until proven, and they can only be proven if challenged. Such is our way."

"Not this way!" Gerrold insisted.

"Then find another," said Kessligh firmly. "Liam entered onto this ground of his choosing. He knows Sasha well enough, and Lenay honour. I have lived in Lenayin for thirty of my fifty years. You cannot *imagine* the gravity of Liam's insult to a warrior of her standard. Sasha's response is truly most restrained. Most Lenays would not even ask for a duel, but would have simply killed him on the spot."

"Well you're not *in* Lenayin!" someone shouted. "This is Petrodor and we do things our way!"

"Sasha is my uma." With an unwavering, deadly stare. "She is Nasi-Keth, and the Nasi-Keth belong to no single city, nor race, nor kingdom. Her truth is her own. Such is our way. Some have accepted her. Liam chose to fight at her side. He placed himself within her truth, by choice. And then, he pissed on it. It was his choice, and so the consequences must also be his. Sasha's origins have naught to do with it. She merely follows her truth. Who disputes?"

"Errollyn," said Aisha, "you're going to make Rhillian really angry one of these days." They walked along a narrow lane that wound parallel to South Pier. The rise was growing steeper as they approached Sharptooth, its sheer cliff wall rising straight from the harbour waters. The lane cunningly ducked beneath the foot of a wall, descending and climbing narrow steps, with a view of the harbour beyond waterfront buildings. Errollyn often wondered at the mindset of a people who had built such a clandestine network into their city. And wondered further if they now regretted it, since its takeover by jumped-up paupers and serrin devils.

"Oh come on," Errollyn replied, "you enjoy making Rhillian angry as much as I do." They spoke in the customary Petrodor-whisper, Errollyn moving close behind his friend, whose pale-blonde head came barely level with his armpit.

"I'd feel so much more comfortable if I actually believed you *didn't* enjoy it so much," Aisha stated, padding lightly down some steps carved into the sandstone cliff. The path now had a wooden fence on one side, Errollyn kept his bow ready and Aisha moved with her blade drawn.

"Patachi Maerler will kill us all at the first opportunity," said Errollyn.

"All the more reason why you should be with her," said Aisha. She paused, pressing herself to the rock on their right. They listened. Nothing moved. "Rhillian does actually desire your guidance, Errollyn." They resumed, cautiously, as the lane rose once more. "Why don't you want to give it to her?"

"She's ignored it so many times before," said Errollyn. The entire situation frustrated him. The Nasi-Keth would determine the outcome of events in Petrodor, not Rhillian. He was certain of it. "She did not even see that outcomes in Lenayin would be important."

"Neither did Kessligh," Aisha reasoned. "He came here instead."

"He has not our advantages," Errollyn replied. "Rhillian does."

"I didn't go to fight in Lenayin because of *that*," said Aisha. "I went because I did not wish to see the Udalyn destroyed in Lenayin. It would have destroyed the entire Lenay equilibrium—the entire balance of cultures, languages and powers. Lenayin has great beauty, and great potential. If the *talmaad* do not exist to further the interests of beauty in Lenayin, then we do not exist for much." The lane dropped into an alley between two property walls. "I defied Rhillian then, but I do not doubt her, as such. She is quite brilliant, Errollyn. You should not give up on her."

"There was a great Torovan painter, a man named Yonaglese . . ."

"I know Yonaglese," said Aisha.

"Perhaps a century and a half ago, he painted the ceiling of a big temple in Songel. Serrin who visited at the time said it was a masterpiece. But within ten years, the plaster had begun to crack, and soon, despite efforts to preserve it, the plaster had crumbled entirely and the painting was lost." They paused at an intersection of alleys and listened. Aisha peered one way and then the other. "Rhillian has masterful strokes, Aisha. But she paints on poor plaster. She has superb detail, yet her broader scope is missing."

"I understood the analogy the first time," said Aisha, with a faintly reproachful look. She smiled mischievously. Not an uncommon expression for Aisha. "I think you're just worried for your little dark-eyed beauty."

"I don't really care *what* you think," said Errollyn.

Aisha grinned. "You should. I'm half human, I see the things my serrin siblings miss."

"Would you stop chattering and move?"

Tall, ugly buildings bordered the base of the Sharptooth cliff. Rock had been cut away to make space for the buildings, and then bricked up to prevent the sandstone collapsing. Down a narrow, bad-smelling alley they crept, until at a sharp zigzag, they paused.

Rhillian emerged from the shadow of a wall overgrown with tall, thorny redberries, then Kiel. "Hello, Aisha," said Rhillian, seeming both pleased and surprised to see her. And a little annoyed. "Errollyn said he needed to fetch something on the way here. I'd no idea he meant you."

"He does know how to make a girl feel wanted, doesn't he?" Aisha said brightly.

"Four people may be too many for the patachi, Errollyn," said Kiel.

"Too many diverse opinions is never too many, Kiel," said Errollyn. Kiel gazed at him with unblinking grey eyes. Perhaps Rhillian thought herself the impartial middle to Kiel and Errollyn's two extremes. But to Errollyn's mind, there was nothing impartial about Rhillian's mood lately. She stood more and more with Kiel, and less and less with him. He trusted Aisha's impartiality far more. As serrin and human both, Aisha saw both sides.

Kiel knocked softly at a rusted metal gate amidst the thorny vines, while the others stood guard. A plate moved aside and whispers exchanged. The gate opened, but it did not squeal—the ancient, rusted appearance was for disguise, Errollyn knew, and the hinges were well maintained.

Kiel led them into a narrow passage cut in the rock, then a man with a lamp led them up some stairs, past a guardroom and into the depth of Sharptooth. The climb was long—the most elaborate back entrance that Errollyn knew of in Petrodor—and old. Surely it had cost House Maerler a lot of money and time to chisel it from the rock, but then sandstone was not difficult to tunnel, and House Maerler lacked neither money nor time.

After a very long climb, from almost sea-level to near the top of the Petrodor incline, they finally arrived at a trapdoor, which opened to reveal a grand cellar, stocked with barrels. Some stairs led up to the great Maerler

Mansion above, but the guardsman took them instead to another door in the wall and through another corridor. After a short flight of stairs, the guardsman knocked on a door and it was opened from the far side.

They emerged into a square, ornate room with a high ceiling. Grand cabinets full of expensive ornaments lined walls hung with intricate tapestries and paintings. From the centre of the floor sprouted a multi-levelled fountain, above which hung a huge, glittering chandelier, alive with at least fifty candles. The room had no windows, but was designed to impress and awe its visitors with ostentatious wealth. And it was designed to be visited directly from the tunnel, without any chance of observation from nosy house servants, or nosy neighbouring houses.

One guard stayed by the door, while another left to alert the house of the arrivals. Errollyn, Kiel and Aisha spread themselves about the room, leaving Rhillian alone in the centre before the fountain. There was only one other doorway at the far end. Only a fool would assault four *talmaad* through one doorway. Or two doorways, counting the one behind.

They waited, not speaking. Perhaps the patachi was in bed, Errollyn thought. Or perhaps the patachi had other, more pressing business. Finally the door opened and the second-most powerful man in Petrodor walked into the room.

Alron Maerler was young for a patachi, at thirty-nine summers. He was tall and slim, with dark curly hair, a trimmed curly beard and blue eyes. His boots were tall, and his clothes cut to suit his lean figure. He moved with an air of sophistication and elegance that was lacking amongst Family Steiner and their allies on the northern slope. Those were merchants, nearest the trading North Pier, and their manner was that of merchants—brusque and blunt, always ready to haggle, to strike a deal, to shake your hand or cut your throat.

Here on Petrodor's southern slope, Maerler headed the other half of Petrodor's power elite—the half that fancied itself more sophisticated, and more well bred, than their northern cousins. Errollyn did not know from where they took that particular pretension—the oldest money in Petrodor was barely two centuries old. But Maerler claimed lineage to old lords, and even to an old king, back in the ancient days when Torovan had had a king. Rhillian thought Alron Maerler more trustworthy than Marlen Steiner, perhaps for that reason, perhaps for others. Errollyn was as suspect of such a judgement as he was of anything.

"Patachi Maerler," said Rhillian, with a bow.

Maerler inclined his head. "Lady Rhillian." Two house guards remained by the door at his back. Otherwise, he was alone and unprotected, save the ornamental sword at his hip. Doubtless he could use it, like most Torovan nobility. And equally doubtless, as a realist in the game of power, he knew himself severely outmatched by even a serrin woman, to say nothing of four *talmaad* all at once.

Errollyn gazed at the man, eyes faintly narrowed. Patachis were always well-protected, yet Maerler made a statement with this defencelessness. Trust, he said. I trust you. And Errollyn recalled what a *talmaad* veteran had advised him upon his first arrival in Petrodor two years ago: "When they smile at you, and call you brother, and use words like trust, and bond, and family, that's when you look for the knife in the hidden hand."

"My good lady," said Maerler then, having surveyed the room. He walked to her and extended his hand. Rhillian gave hers, and the patachi kissed it, like a true gentleman should. "I do look forward to our little visits together. A beauty such as yours is quite a thrill in such proximity."

"The patachi is too kind," said Rhillian with a flashing smile. Oh, she was so good at this. Errollyn had known many women in Saalshen who would have simply stared in puzzlement at such odd human customs. But Rhillian knew just what to do. "I would have come alone, but the streets of Petrodor are so dangerous these days."

Maerler smiled, genuinely amused at the outrageous flirt. Or at least, his amusement seemed genuine. Errollyn had yet to figure the young patachi out. Either he was simply a very good actor, or he truly did enjoy these fun and games. Neither possibility made him at all trustworthy.

"But not at all," he insisted, glancing about at the other serrin. His gaze settled on Aisha. "In fact, I do not believe I have been introduced to all of your party." Rhillian gestured to Aisha. Aisha came, and bowed somewhat lower than Rhillian had. Human customs gave her no difficulty either.

"This is Aisha," said Rhillian.

"Another serrin beauty," the patachi sighed. "I swear there must be something in the water in Saalshen. Please, you *both* must come and sit with me. It shall be my evening's entertainment. Guards, another chair, if you please."

"My dear Patachi," said Rhillian woundedly, following him to the chairs. "I fear you shall make me jealous."

"A-ha!" Maerler turned in midstride, levelling a playful finger at Rhillian. "I have been informed that serrin do not suffer jealousy as humans do. Do you deny it?"

Rhillian gave a sultry smile. "I do not."

"Oh the possibilities!" Maerler exclaimed, looking first at Rhillian, then at Aisha. The women gave each other a sultry smirk. Errollyn nearly laughed.

They sat, Rhillian and Aisha to one side, the patachi to the other. "And to what do I owe this pleasure?" the patachi asked.

"I have news from Riverside," said Rhillian, crossing her legs. "And I have spoken with Duke Rochel."

"My dear lady, everyone has news from Riverside," said the patachi, lazily. "Your Nasi-Keth friends causing trouble again. You should really keep them on a shorter leash."

"The patachi knows very well that there is no leash. And I greatly doubt that you have heard *this* news from Riverside."

Maerler looked at her, cautious for the first time, but hardly worried. "And what do you offer, with this gesture of information?"

"Cooperation. On matters of common interest."

The patachi looked thoughtful. "There is a priest missing from the Porsada Temple," he said then. "The cousin of Gregan Halmady. He has not been seen for a day at least, my sources tell me."

Rhillian smiled faintly. "The patachi is most perceptive. My sources tell me that Symon Steiner had a priest murdered on the Riverside dock last night. A coincidence, do you think?"

"Sources?" There was no doubting the sudden light in Maerler's eyes.

"A witness," Rhillian assured him. "You know how we see in the dark."

A slow smile spread across Maerler's face. "Well, well," he mused. "So the great allies of Steiner and Halmady are in conflict. Your little ruse worked."

Rhillian inclined her head. "Randel Ragini was not a ruse, I had intended him for an ally. But discord within the Steiner ranks serves just as well."

"M'Lady has the makings of a great patachi."

Errollyn hid his expression with difficulty. Randel Ragini, killed in the Endurance. Rhillian *had* been cultivating him as an ally. Errollyn had been witness to several of those meetings. Surely Rhillian had not had him . . . ? No, he dismissed the thought. Rhillian had been with him and Sasha when it happened, and had been genuinely surprised. But not dismayed. Nor had she let on to Sasha or Kessligh her relationship with young Randel. Errollyn had actually liked Randel. But Rhillian saw him only as part of a game for power.

It chilled him. The Rhillian he'd known was a kind person, if a determined one. Now she was changing. Family Ragini had close ties to Family Halmady by marriage. Steiner had come to suspect Ragini, and now evidently Halmady, too. Rhillian and Patachi Maerler were conspiring to bring down the Steiner alliance from within, by setting their most powerful families at each other's throats.

"It seems the conflict has moved to include the priesthood," Rhillian observed. "A curious development for a body that does not take sides."

Alron Maerler smiled. "The priesthood are on the gods' side, M'Lady. Symon Steiner had better hope they don't find out."

"I'd thought the Verenthane gods were omnipotent?"

Maerler's smile grew broader. "Like the serrinim, it seems. The priesthood wishes for a war, M'Lady. They'll support anyone who can bring it to them. Who that might be, however, is a matter for conjecture."

"Even amongst priests?"

"Even amongst the gods, I'm sure."

"And you, Patachi Maerler?" said Rhillian, fixing him with her most penetrating emerald stare. "Do you too desire this war?"

"No more than the last time you asked me. War is bad for business, M'Lady. It is no secret that the Maerler alliance is on the decline in Petrodor, relative to the enormous wealth of the Steiners. I would do well for my family merely to hold onto what we have, and perhaps reverse our decline in this city. I have no time to worry about foreign empires and old religious relics the archbishop insists should be returned to Enora. I have better things to worry about."

"Then why have the priesthood not discarded him entirely?" Errollyn pressed as they followed a guard back down the long, dark stairway to the base of Sharptooth. "Clearly he offers himself to them as a potential leader of this army, or they would have abandoned him by now and thrown all their support behind Steiner."

"It makes no difference," said Kiel. "Steiner moves against us. They should be punished, as should all who would threaten Saalshen. We should make of them an example, as Maldereld once made an example of King Leyvaan and his army."

They spoke in the *alderese* dialect, used mostly amongst the serrinim to discuss scholarly matters.

"You fear that I shall allow Patachi Maerler to win a decisive victory," said Rhillian. "I know it is Kessligh's fear, he's expressed it to me often. But the balance here is fixed. Errollyn, you see the way the houses balance each other. It is *kel'an tai*." In *alderese,* the term meant a symmetry of numbers. "Maerler may desire to win, yet the obstacles before him are vast. Even he cannot overcome the symmetry."

"You're thinking like a serrin," Errollyn retorted in profound frustration. "This . . . this symmetry, it's not a concept easily applied to human civilisations—"

"All the universe is a symmetry, and such symmetries encompass all," said Rhillian with certainty. "Besides, even should Steiner fall to ruin, his lesser allies would survive. Maerler would face continuing opposition from trading families determined to preserve their fortunes. And Patachi Maerler is right in one thing—Maerler is much weaker than Steiner."

"You think to control him?" Errollyn knew that Sasha sometimes suffered from the urge to strangle someone. His current frustration was not so intense, yet it was profound nonetheless. There had to be an angle of attack through Rhillian's carefully constructed logic, yet he could not find it. "We have neither the power nor the influence to control anyone! You cannot put a great grey bear on a leash and take it for a walk, Rhillian. It walks *us*. Or worse, turns and eats us."

"There are always risks," Rhillian said as the stairs turned a corner, and switched back the other way. "But they are less than the risks of doing nothing. We cannot value stability above change, Errollyn. For too long, we have attempted to purchase peace with the stability of tyrants, and achieved neither peace nor stability."

"Errollyn does not speak for stability," said Aisha from behind Errollyn. She spoke the dialect with greater delicacy than any of them and there was concern in her voice. "He speaks for change. He merely observes that a serrin perspective is an imperfect platform from which to view human society and thus judge the nature of impending change."

"He would hand over the direction of the *talmaad* to the humans," said Kiel, distastefully. "Into the hands of those who wish us dead."

"You think the Nasi-Keth want us dead?" Errollyn snapped.

"I'm quite sure that Alaine would not care if we all dropped dead tomorrow."

"Kessligh's friends lost lives in Riverside," Errollyn said coldly, "fighting to stop the armament of forces preparing to attack the Saalshen Bacosh. You give precious little respect to their sacrifice, Kiel."

"I did not ask them to make it," said Kiel, unconcerned. "Saalshen has for too long placed the fate of the serrinim in the hands of humans. That time has passed. Either we show that we act for ourselves, or we admit weakness and invite our enemies to destroy us."

"I agree," said Rhillian. How surprising, Errollyn thought bitterly, with a stare at the low, rock ceiling. "I gained this post because I demonstrated to the councils that I could act, and act fast. As did we all, to varying extents. We follow the course, Errollyn. Should Steiner continue these preparations, he shall pay."

"You dress up these ignoble thoughts with pretty words," Errollyn muttered. "Your independence is just another word for bigotry."

Rhillian not only stopped, but came back up the stairs at him. Errollyn stopped as Rhillian put her nose to within a hand's breadth of his own. Her gaze was hard. "That's one hell of an accusation," she said, putting a finger against his chest, all trace of subtlety vanished from her tone. Further down the stairs, their guard paused with his lamp, surprised to have lost his charges. "You think I don't care about these people? I'm hoping to *save* these people. Kessligh is right. Saalshen is a good influence on humanity, we've demonstrated it often. If we don't survive, humanity's future is bleak. Worse, if we and they end up locked in constant war, we may well destroy each other. But I will not sacrifice Saalshen's greatest hope for survival because your objections make you uncomfortable!"

"And if we gain victory at the cost of everything that makes serrin serrin?" asked Errollyn. Finally, Rhillian looked troubled. But whether that was at the fact of his objection, or its content, Errollyn could not tell. "Will we truly have won?"

"Failure is annihilation," Rhillian said softly. "Anything better than that is serendipity."

Alythia entered her father-in-law's private chambers with trepidation. Patachi Elmar Halmady, her husband Gregan, Gregan's brother Vincen, and their uncle Raymon watched her enter, food half eaten on their plates. Alythia had heard loud voices before she'd knocked on the door. Now, the air seemed strained, and Gregan looked uncomfortable.

"You asked for me, Father?" said Alythia, with a curtsy before the men. Elmar Halmady's usually calm face now wore a frown. Vincen's look was unpleasant, almost leering. Alythia pitied Vincen's wife Rovina and was glad she'd been wed to Gregan instead.

"Daughter," said Elmar. He was nearly blond, with a lean face and blue eyes beneath drooping eyelids. "Are you well this evening?"

The question made Alythia uncomfortable. Uncle Raymon's eyes bore into her, as if suspecting her of something. He was a big man, with a beard covering his second chin, and heavy, dark brows. "Quite well, Father," she said. She'd been dining in her own chambers with her maids, feeling angry, and lonely, in truth. She'd been almost relieved to receive this summons, if only for some insight into the events that caused turmoil in the hallways of late.

"Do you like this family, Daughter?" asked Patachi Halmady. "Are you happy here? Or do you regret your wedding day?"

Alythia blinked, astonished. "Father?" The patachi was usually reserved and intellectual, preferring to discuss the arts or trade, rather than engaging in anything emotionally taxing. But his lips were pressed thin and sour, and he seemed displeased. Alythia tried her best, disarming smile. "Have I done something wrong, Father? I may speak the language, but I am still very recently from Lenayin—I'm never entirely certain when I've offended someone. Please tell me if I do. I am trying very hard, I assure you."

"Jasin Daran has been released of his service to House Halmady," said Uncle Raymon bluntly.

Alythia frowned. "Jasin . . . ?"

"Of House Daran. Handsome lad. Patrolled the walls for us." Alythia's breath caught in her throat. Surely they could not have . . . She held her composure with an effort. "You were passing him messages to take to Patachi Daran. You met at his sister's wedding feast, but a week ago. You were observed to make eyes with him."

"I did nothing of the sort!" Alythia exclaimed, genuinely outraged.

"Jasin confessed," Raymon continued, his eyes dark with suspicion. "He took your correspondence to Patachi Daran, who would reply in turn."

"Patachi Daran is an ally of this house and of House Steiner!" Alythia exclaimed. "He and I had an interesting conversation at the birthday feast, and he insisted we should correspond . . ."

"Oh-ho, is *that* all it was?" said Vincen, with amusement.

Alythia glared at him. "I'm never allowed to do anything, I've been cooped up in my room for the better part of the last week, and I'm only allowed out of the house for formal occasions . . . what do you expect? I want some friends! I want some company! At least I'd like to entertain some of the other ladies . . . and I could be so useful too, you've no idea how much information there's to be had from women's chatter! Why won't you let me be a full part of this family?"

"You sneak behind my back," Gregan said quietly. He sounded hurt.

"Oh no, my love! I just . . ."

"They say you are a whore." Still Gregan did not look at her. "My mother has always said so, and now it seems her words are true."

"You think I *bedded* Patachi Daran? How would that even be possible, given that I'm never allowed from the house?"

"You are disobedient!" Gregan shouted, his voice trembling. "A woman of virtue shall always obey her husband." Dear gods, Alythia thought to herself in despair, I've married a child.

"Who else have you been contacting behind our backs?" asked the patachi.

"Who else?" She was missing something here. Suddenly, she could feel it—the cold, creeping sensation that something was going on that she did not entirely understand. Something dangerous. "What . . . why do you suddenly accuse me?" She forced a laugh at the ridiculousness of it all. "What do you think . . . ?"

"Cousin Gilbrato is missing," said the patachi. "It seems almost certain that he has met some foul end. Someone seeks to damage us. Someone with knowledge."

Gilbrato . . . the priest? Alythia recalled the man at the wedding feast. A young Halmady man, groomed from childhood to represent the interests of his family in the most powerful institution in Petrodor. The priesthood took men from each of the families, and was influenced by each in turn. Now . . . Gilbrato was dead? How could that possibly concern her? Unless they thought . . . unless they thought . . . Alythia stared at them in horror. "Surely you don't think that I . . . ?"

"You show disloyalty. You pass messages beyond our walls. Someone seeks to undermine us. There is a rumour that Lady Marya Steiner has recently been in contact with your feral sister, the Nasi-Keth. Have you been passing messages to her also?"

"To Sasha? Good gods no! Sasha and I have always hated each other! We can barely stand in the same room without a fight breaking out!"

"You claim to be nothing like her," Gregan said hotly, "yet you both come from the same highland stock! Treacherous, uncivilised and lacking in womanly virtue!"

Alythia swallowed hard, and stared at the wood-boarded floor. "You accuse me unfairly, my husband." She struggled to keep the emotion from her voice. This was not going at all the way she had planned. "I am hurt."

Gregan looked away, tore a piece of bread and wiped his plate with it to cover his emotion. For a moment, Alythia thought he might apologise. "Jasin will live," Uncle Raymon said darkly. "He is Patachi Daran's nephew, and they each have uses. But the scars will take a time to heal. Have a care, dear niece. It would be a shame to tarnish so royal a beauty."

Alythia swallowed hard. For one of the few times in her life, she felt fear, cold and hard in her gut. "As you say, Uncle."

Alythia wandered the garden, the grass cool beneath her bare feet. She breathed deeply and tried to dispel the awful memory of fear. She was born into Lenay royalty and she knew what power was. Baen-Tar had always been full of armed men, but she'd never been afraid. Home was the place where a person felt secure and comforted. She'd hoped that House Halmady could be such a place, but her dreams were turning to dust.

She'd dismissed the attentions of Selyna and Vansy—she did not wish to explain what had happened. It was humiliating. In Baen-Tar, she'd been so popular. It was usually so simple to wind men and women around her little finger. She'd assumed that the exotic charms of a Lenay princess would be enough to win popularity in Petrodor. But, instead, there'd been whispers of "easy virtue," and the attention of men at feasts, which had inspired envy from women in Lenayin, gained only evil stares from the ladies of Petrodor.

She stood behind her favourite garden bench for a moment, gazing out at the nighttime view of the harbour below. There was a lump growing in her throat, a great, inescapable despair. It advanced on her like a dark wave, threatening to drown her within its cold, churning depth.

She'd never meant for Jasin to get hurt. He'd rescued her from the wolf that night. Ever since, he'd been friendly. Evidently it had suited him to be on terms with the beautiful Princess Alythia. No doubt he'd boasted about it to other men, and implied something more intimate. She'd found it amusing. He'd introduced her to his Patachi at the wedding feast, and . . . and, well. Perhaps she'd simply wished an adventure. Or perhaps she'd truly been seeking companionship. Or, she admitted now to herself, she'd done it simply to get back at her new family.

But they'd harmed Jasin. Possibly tortured him. Whatever she tried, it turned out wrong. She wondered how Marya had managed to become the very image of a devoted Torovan mother so soon after her arrival. Marya had become pregnant, for one thing, she realised. Not immediately, but soon enough. Perhaps she should think about a child. Her maids kept the serrin's white powder for her, safe from Lady Halmady's pryings—it would keep her belly from swelling for however long she wished. But Lady Halmady had not even spoken to her about a son. Perhaps the Halmadys considered there to be no rush.

Or perhaps, the cold thought occurred to her, this was merely a marriage of convenience, for the duration of the war. Halmady secured its ties to Lenayin and the Lenay army until the Saalshen Bacosh was once again free, and then she'd not be needed any more. Perhaps they'd dispose of her, like refuse after some great feast.

The fear returned. She was going to cry any moment now. She'd cry like a little girl, here before the garden guards. Most of them had surely known Jasin, and some probably blamed her for his fate. Her own weakness sickened her. For the first time in her life, she felt truly helpless. None of her talents would help her here, and she did not know what to do.

She turned from the view and walked back toward the house. Guards watched her beneath their broad hats—the stares that had seemed so playful just weeks before now seemed intrusive and unfriendly. After a short walk, she found herself at the gate to the wolf enclosure. Her heart thudding, she peered over the gate, but could see nothing inside. She reached over, feeling for the latch . . . and withdrew her hand in sudden fear of a lunging grey shape. But no such shape emerged.

Frightened little girl! she thought to herself, furiously. Coward. Sasha would laugh at you. That made her angry. What did she care what Sasha thought? She never had before. But then, Sasha had *always* thought her a coward. She remembered Sasha laughing at her in the stables when she'd been scared to get close to the horses. And again, when she hadn't liked the kennel dogs any better. In fact, she'd never liked animals very much at all. It had not bothered her then that Sasha thought her a coward. It only bothered her now, when it seemed events might finally prove Sasha right.

She had an idea. She made her way briskly to the kitchen. Even late, there were meals being prepared, an entire bench full of ingredients being chopped, a vast pot of soup bubbling over a flame, the delicious smell of baking bread. The kitchen hands did not pay her much attention—there were always family wandering through the kitchens, investigating tomorrow's meals, or in search of a snack.

Alythia found a bone largely stripped of its meat, but still with some good chunks attached. She took it and walked from the kitchen with no attempt at concealment. It was a trick she'd learned long ago in the halls of Baen-Tar Palace—if you looked like you knew where you were going, no one would question you. And a princess *always* knew where she was going.

Back at the wolf enclosure, she looked around, but the path between house and outer wall was empty of guards. She reached inside and undid the latch.

The gate moved slowly open. She peered anxiously into the shadow, the bone clutched in one hand—part temptation, part weapon. "Hello?" she called faintly, prepared to leap back at the slightest movement. "Hello puppy?" She was speaking Lenay, she realised, and nearly laughed, in sudden, hysterical humour. Why would a wolf pup be more likely to speak Lenay? It had lived in Torovan most of its life.

A chain tinkled. Two ears appeared, a faint silhouette in the dark. Two eyes glinted. Alythia froze, but the wolf did not move. Her eyes adjusted further, and now she could see it, lying near the enclosure's far side, as far from the gate as its chain would allow. It wasn't really that big, she realised . . . and was pleased that she remained calm enough to notice such things, despite her pounding heart, dry mouth and trembling hands. In Lenayin, they grew much bigger. She remembered Jasin saying that the wolf had been brought just recently . . . cubs were born in the spring, and it was now nearly autumn. This one would be four, maybe five months old. Huge, for a puppy. But not for a wolf.

The wolf growled, but did not charge. Instead, it crawled further away, low on its stomach. Its tail was down, tight between its hind legs. It was terrified, Alythia realised. Perhaps it remembered her and the beating it had received afterward. Or perhaps it merely expected beatings from strangers who wandered into its enclosure on a late night, probably reeking of wine.

Shakily, Alythia sank down on her haunches, rearranging her dress. The chain would pull the wolf up short if it charged again, she told herself firmly. She was safe here. She reached back and pushed the gate shut behind her. The wolf stopped crawling. Perhaps it registered something was unusual. Or perhaps its chain had pulled tight. Its nose twitched, sniffing furiously. Alythia remembered the bone in her hand and threw it. The wolf flinched, growled . . . and paused, sniffing.

"Oh there, you recognise *that* smell, don't you?" Obviously someone fed the wolf, for it did not seem starved. But she doubted they gave it fresh bones.

The wolf wriggled forward, quite pathetically, straining for the bone yet held back by some invisible force. It was really quite pretty, Alythia saw with surprise as it came closer. There were some evil legends about wolves in Lenayin, but some good ones too. The latter would be Goeren-yai tales, it occurred to her now. Goeren-yai always liked wild animals, especially the dangerous ones. This wolf had thick, dark grey fur, big ears, large paws and round eyes. Still young, with the ears and paws all out of proportion.

Suddenly it lunged, and Alythia stifled a scream . . . but it only grabbed the bone and scampered back to the far wall. But not all the way, Alythia saw as her heart started beating once more. It settled, with some slack still left in the chain, and began savaging the bone. Surely it would damage its teeth, Alythia thought. *Crack!* went the bone. Dear lords. Just as well this half-grown puppy hadn't gotten its teeth into her when it had tried to.

Alythia sat down properly and watched the wolf eat. It was strangely relaxing to focus all her attention upon something else. Something strange, and not human. The wolf had its own problems. Alone of all the residents in Halmady House, it cared not a jot for the Princess Alythia's trials and tribulations. The wolf did not begrudge her anything, and would not pass judgment, it merely counted itself lucky to have been fed, and not beaten.

"You need a name," she said to the wolf, smoothing the dress over her legs as she sat. "I mean, if I'm going to sit here and get grass stains on my dress for someone, they'd better at least have a name." The wolf watched her sideways as it cracked on the bone. "I could call you Sasha. She's a bitch too." It amused her for a moment, but it was too immature and spiteful, even for her.

But there *was* a name she recalled a palace tutor using for Sasha. "Tashyna." The tutor had been from Isfayen and in his native tongue a tashyna meant a great commotion, or something crazy and out of control. "Tashyna," he'd said, with a shake of the head, every time Sasha would come tearing into the room, a noisy little whirlwind in a dress. Once, Sasha had heard him mutter and had confronted him. "Why do you always call me Tashyna?" she'd shouted, stamping her foot. "My name's Sasha!"

Those in the know had laughed. Alythia found herself smiling now to think of it. But sadness came with the humour. Her old home seemed so near, she could taste it, could hear the echo of conversation in the grand stone halls, and smell the waft of flowers from the gardens. Familiar faces. Familiar routines—feasts, play recitals, Verenthane ceremonies at the temple. Her brothers playing lagand upon a broad green field at festival time, the snorting of horses, the shouting of men, and the cheers of the onlookers. Her old maids and her many dresses. The view from her bedchambers, across courtyards and flower gardens, overlooked by lovely stone walls and windows. Flowers in the vase her mother had given her before she'd died.

"Tashyna," she said softly, with tears in her eyes. "I don't know if you're from Isfayen. I doubt it, it's too far away. But why don't we make this enclosure a little corner of Lenayin for just the two of us?"

Tashyna chomped on her bone and seemed content.

Ten

ALF OF BAERLYN'S COUNCIL sat about the dining table in the ranch's main room as morning sun spilled through the windows. The storm was gone and Lenayin was shining once more. Jaegar, Teriyan, Ryssin, Raegyl, Geldon and Cranyk all sat about the table. Princess Sofy had the head chair—a sight not often seen in Lenayin, a woman leading a village council meeting. Jaegar sat at the far end, Cranyk to Sofy's right was the esteemed elder, and Jaryd to her left. Lynette and Andreyis served breakfast, Andreyis weary-eyed from his long night in the storm, having returned at first dawn to report that the assassin was still at large. "Surely the king shall not allow the murder of Jaryd's surviving brother."

All eyes came to Sofy. She gazed at the tabletop for a moment, a slim hand wrapped about the warmth of a mug of tea. "I'm afraid there's not much the king can do," she said. "With war approaching, the king needs the great lords and the nobility more than ever. The last thing he needs now is more trouble in Tyree."

"The lords claim power over their own domains," Jaegar added. "It will cost the king a great deal to intervene in Tyree, the great lords are already smarting at what they see as the king's capitulation to the Udalyn rebellion—"

"But Princess Sofy comes to us herself with news of the other great lords' disquiet at events in Tyree!" Ryssin insisted. "Surely there will be those who would support the king in any action against Great Lord Arastyn . . ."

"Precisely the problem," said Teriyan, with a shake of his head. "This could become a fight between great lords, when the king needs everyone united. He won't do it."

Sofy did not disagree.

"All this politicking is dishonourable," Cranyk said. "Warriors do not seek solutions through parley. The Great Lord Arastyn means to murder the brother of a resident of this village. Clearly our honour compels us to act in his defence, as warriors should."

"We have no proof of Arastyn's intentions," Jaegar countered. And looked at Sofy. "Begging Your Highness's pardon."

Sofy gave him a somewhat imperious look. "My sources are quite specific, Yuan Jaegar."

Jaegar nodded his respect, but his hard features remained unmoved. "This village has just partaken in one grand rebellion against the king's authority. To partake in another, on a matter yet unproven, might seem disloyal." Typically for Jaegar, his tone held a flat, dry irony.

"Dishonourable, I say," Cranyk replied. The two men locked stares.

Jaegar blinked, the only motion discernible on his face. "In Lenayin today," he said firmly, "one does not charge into every grievance with swords drawn. Perhaps we did once, but Lenayin has changed. I believe it's called civilisation."

"Dishonourable, I say," said Cranyk, his eyes half-lidded within a maze of wrinkles and faded tattoos.

Jaegar sighed. "Civilisation comes hard to some Lenays."

"Honour comes hard to others," said Cranyk. Jaegar gave the old man a warning look. Cranyk snorted.

"Begging Your Highness's pardon," said Teriyan, "but what might the king do when he notices the Princess Sofy is missing?" All eyes turned to Sofy again. She blushed. "It's four days ride from Baen-Tar." *When can we expect the armoured cavalry to descend on our heads?* he meant. Everyone watched the princess, and waited.

"I didn't tell anyone where I was going," she said, attempting an even, reasonable tone. "I took Dary out for an evening ride, just around the walls, no need for a guard. Then I just kept riding. There was a festival in town, lots of people and horses, it covered my tracks and scent."

"Aye," Teriyan said wearily. "I reckon we've got a day, at most. Best we decide what to do before they arrive."

Sofy frowned. "I'm not sure they could track me through that festival . . ."

"You don't think they'd guess?" Teriyan asked. "Smart men like your father and brother?" Sofy looked crestfallen. "There'll be riders here soon enough, just to check, even if they don't track you directly. I'd imagine Baen-Tar is in an uproar."

Sofy bit her lip, and looked both embarrassed and stubborn. Clearly she knew the uproar her disappearance would cause. Clearly she thought it served her father and Prince Koenyg right. And would, perhaps, serve to demonstrate why she shouldn't be bossed around any longer. Teriyan empathised, but still, it was a reckless thing to have done. It seemed a common trait that ran through more of the Lenay royal sisters than people had guessed.

"I say we ride," he continued, looking about the table. "I say we go and solve this one ourselves, quietly. No invoking any grand rebellion, no great statements, just a few men on horses through the woods. We grab Wyndal, we get him out and we leave—Arastyn and his fools can kick up all the fuss they like, but Wyndal belongs with his brother. There's enough disquiet about the whole affair that Arastyn won't find many friends in his outrage, especially if we then have some kind of proof of what Arastyn was trying."

"He just tried to kill Jaryd," Geldon pointed out. "Don't need no more proof than that, suspicion will do just fine. No one'll blame us."

"Aye," said Jaegar, nodding slowly. "It'll be a regional affair, the king won't touch it and it needn't touch the king. The princess can stay here and sweet-talk the king's riders when they come, and deny she knows where we went . . . they can't force information from a princess."

"No," said Sofy firmly. "I'm coming too." About the table, the men stared at her. Jaegar took a deep breath, but Sofy cut him off before he could start. "If Father's riders find me here, they'll know for certain I came this way for a reason!"

"They'll know for certain anyway," Teriyan objected, "they're not daft. Some of us will be missing, there'll be tracks in and out, perhaps they'll have dogs . . ."

"But there'll be doubt!" Sofy insisted. "They'll have to ride back to Baen-Tar—four days—with an incomplete report, and Koenyg hates those, he likes to know everything before he acts. And he'll have no clues, no idea of why I came riding out here, if I did at all . . . you men, with all respect, you simply don't know Koenyg like I do! I can guess what he's thinking, but he knows me that well too. If his riders bring me back with them, he'll guess all kinds of things. I'm a good liar but not with him, and he knows it. He'll send riders to Tyree, Tyree's closer than Valhanan . . . he's even got birds now! Pigeons, they carry messages and—"

"Pigeons?" Ryssin looked baffled. "What are pigeons?"

"Lowlands birds," said Teriyan, looking glum. "They can carry messages. They don't last long up here because our hawks and eagles are so hungry, but if you sent two to a target, I'd guess one might get through. Lenayin will seem like a smaller country if everyone starts using pigeons. Imagine, one day for a message to Baen-Tar. Two from here to Isfayen."

"Lowlands nonsense," Cranyk muttered. "I'm glad I'll not live long enough to see my land completely spoiled by their inventions."

"I'll not want to take the future wife of the heir to the Bacosh throne on a hunting expedition," Jaegar interrupted. "This village is in trouble enough with Prince Koenyg as it is."

"I *am* your royal princess, you know," Sofy replied, chin raised. "I *could* just command you."

"I'm village headman of Baerlyn with my boots on Baerlyn soil," Jaegar replied. "I *could* just ignore you."

"Or," Sofy continued as though she hadn't heard him, "I could just ride there on my own. I rode *here* on my own."

"You don't know where Algery is," Jaegar retorted.

"I'll find out," said Sofy. "If I travel on my own, three or four strides behind you." Jaegar pressed his lips thin, and looked to be repressing a mutter of something rude. Sofy smirked.

"No," said Jaryd, when the building frustration and anger became impossible to control. All turned to look at him.

"No what?" said Teriyan.

"You're not going. Any of you." Silence about the table. Jaryd unclenched his fist, it had been steadily tightening as the discussion had progressed. "This is my affair. I swore to resolve it myself, and I shall. I shall accept no assistance."

"Even if it kills Wyndal?" Jaegar said flatly.

Jaryd jumped to his feet, his chair toppling with a clatter. "I never asked for all your assistance!" he shouted. "This is *my* honour, not yours! I won't let you ruin it!"

"Ruin it?" Jaegar raised his eyebrows. "We make it happen. You declared yourself Goeren-yai, Master Jaryd. That is the only reason your head has not been removed from your shoulders by the king's law. You come to live here among us, you make use of our isolation, of our hospitality, and now you think to refuse our assistance in return?"

Jaryd stared at him, unable to speak. This was turning out all wrong. All his life, others had tried to dictate his future. Always they got it wrong, always they expected from him that which he could not give, or snatched his most precious goals and turned them to their own ends. He needed to do this for himself, for his own sake, for Tarryn's, for Wyndal's, before these meddling fools made a mess of everything once more . . .

"Tell me," Jaegar continued, "when you gave yourself to the old ways, did you have it in your heart to actually learn something of them? Or are the ways of the Goeren-yai simply a convenience, to be followed when it suits your purposes and ignored when they do not? To be of the village means to abide by the decisions of its elders. We make these decisions in the best interests of Baerlyn and its people. You have brought these troubles amongst us with your presence, and now we shall deal with them as we see fit. And if you are truly Goeren-yai, you shall abide by that and be grateful."

Jaryd stared at the tabletop, quietly fuming. He wanted to sit, or to turn and stride out, but he could not decide which. Neither seemed appropriate. He was trapped.

"To be Goeren-yai is not to wear a ring and mark your face with lines," said old Cranyk, grimly. "Myself, I could not care if the boy knows a passing spirit from a horse's fart. He has mad courage, he is a warrior and he knows revenge. These, and these alone, are the soul of the ancient ways. All that he has done, Yuan Jaegar, has been in pursuit of his revenge. If you did not wish the troubles that come with his presence, you should have refused him hospitality. I say it is a sad day for this village when the concerns of selfish custom, and the fear of others' opinions, even that of the king, should rule our honour."

Jaryd blinked at Cranyk in mild surprise. The old man's continued support astonished him in its ferocity. He could not recall the last time any elder from his past life had supported his headstrong urges to any degree. Only . . . only Cranyk did not do it for the love of Jaryd Nyvar. Cranyk did it, it seemed, because Cranyk saw something in Jaryd Nyvar that reminded him of that which he valued most in the Goeren-yai. Jaryd could not deny that his decision to cast off the ways of Verenthanes had been driven entirely by selfish rage and the opportunism of revenge. But now, could it be that one of the Goeren-yai's most respected would look at him and find approval for his decision?

Jaegar looked at Cranyk for a long moment, lips pursed in consideration. Then he nodded. "So," he said, not contesting Cranyk's words. "The matter is laid out. Now we all must decide."

Sasha was sitting at the end of the pier near Family Velo's boats, gutting fish. It had been five days since the meeting at The Fish Head. The day was perhaps the hottest she'd ever experienced, and the air was thick enough to drink. She fairly dripped with sweat, in long sleeves to keep the sun off her arms.

Footsteps approached up the pier planks, a middle-aged man with a white beard was coming toward her. Not a docksman—he did not look work-worn, nor did he swagger with a working man's gait—his tunic and pants were plain yet good. He wore his hat low on his brow, his eyes hidden in shade.

He stopped nearby and gazed out to the horizon where thick stormclouds were building, a dark shadow on the sea. Now, a flash of lightning. "It's coming this way," said the man. "We could use some rain, the reservoirs run low."

"Aye," said Sasha, scaling a fish from the tail to the head, as Mari had shown her. "I wouldn't like to be out on one of those ships when the lightning comes. Not beneath those masts."

"It's said that lightning strikes the highest point because the gods discourage the immodesty of height," said the man.

"Is that right?" Sasha glanced up at the Porsada Temple, high atop its far promontory, its spires reaching for the sky.

The man followed the direction of her gaze and smiled. "The temple has never been struck. The gods are selective."

"And here was I thinking they were impartial and fair." She remembered priests boasting the same thing once about the Saint Ambellion Temple in Baen-Tar. Until one stormy night a bolt had blasted the iron star right off the left spire. Then the priests pretended they'd never made the claim in the first place. She would have had so much more respect for Verenthanes in general, she thought, if they didn't make such silly claims.

"No," said the man, turning back to the distant storm. "No Verenthane ever claimed the gods impartial."

"Pity," said Sasha. She laid the fish flat and chopped its head off, then its tail. "Bias is no blessing."

The man looked at her oddly as she scooped the head and tail into a basket, and the meat into another. "You're very handy with that knife," he observed as she took up a new fish. "You must be Sashandra Lenayin."

Sasha smiled. "And I'm sure you only just figured that out now."

The man shrugged. "There are only so many sworld-wielding women on the dockfront who can dissect a fish in the blink of an eye. And you have that lovely accent."

"A *lovely* accent," Sasha repeated, scaling fast. "That's far nicer than I've heard it called recently."

"And what do men call it?"

"Barbarian."

"My dear girl, I would never."

Sasha slit the fish, scooped out the guts with her knife, turning to drop them into the water behind. Chopped its head and tail, disposed of them, and looked up at the man. She gave a final, fancy twirl of the knife for effect. "So now you know my name, stranger. What's yours?"

"I am Father Portus," said the man. "Father Portus Ragini."

"Ragini?" She blinked. "So you're Patachi Ragini's . . . ?"

"Younger brother."

Sasha nodded, considering. "And what do you want with me, Father Portus?"

Sasha walked the docks, a short time after Father Portus had departed. Enough time for her to wash, in the vain hope of scrubbing some of the fish smell from her hands, and deliver her fish to the Velo family stall. She'd been planning to go out on the evening boat, but that was before the storm arrived. In bad weather, Mari would want experienced sailors only. The Nasi-Keth being what they were, it was difficult to make time to help on the dawn boats—at that time, most Nasi-Keth were asleep, recovering from long nights. And so, she helped however she could, to pay for her free board.

She walked with a small waterskin under one arm, weaving her way through the early afternoon chaos. Here were a mass of fish stalls, the morning's catch on display with buyers haggling over price. There, a small mountain of octopus, a squeamish writhing of tentacles. Everything smelled of fish, including her. Seagulls wheeled overhead and occasionally scrabbled underfoot, daring the forest of moving legs for a few smelly scraps.

Sasha sipped from her waterskin as she walked, making certain never to let anyone brush against her, keeping her right hand free for the knife at her belt. Despite the crowds, it was unlikely that too many of the wrong sort of people could infiltrate here with ease—upslope men were rarely welcome and could be spotted by their hair, the trim of their beards, or their lack of fish smell even if their clothes were plain. Locals had an unerring eye for such folk, and for every Nasi-Keth amongst the crowds, there were ten more with family who were Nasi-Keth. Still, Sasha had never felt entirely at ease amongst so many people. She'd seen crowds before, at Baen-Tar festivals and the like, but those were nothing compared to this.

Nearing the big ships of the North Pier, she saw a building of white-washed brick with a single, simple spire above its doors. Rows of vegetable stalls stood in front, doing a brisk trade with dockfront wives and their big wicker baskets. Sasha ducked through the stalls and slipped inside.

Inside was the typical high ceiling and many pews of a Verenthane temple. The entire right wall was a labyrinth of wooden scaffolding, where the pews had been moved to make way. A number of great white sheets now lay across those pews, spattered with coloured paint. Where the scaffolding neared the ceiling, it branched outward, seeming to defy a certain fall. On planks beneath the ceiling, men moved and mixed paints. Sasha walked down the central aisle, gazing upward. Goeren-yai or not, she loved this place. The air smelled of wet plaster and the men's murmured, almost reverent, conversation echoed off the high ceiling. This was a creativity she had never witnessed before coming to Petrodor, and it was mesmerising.

Father Portus stood by the first pew before the altar, gazing upward. Sasha stopped beside him. "You've never been here before?" she asked him.

Portus shook his head. "No. It is . . . remarkable." A priest of the high slopes would rarely visit those of the lower. The priesthood of the Porsada Temple were wealthy men of the families. These small, dockfront temples interested them as little as did the poor, uncivilised labourers who frequented them.

"The artist's name is Berloni," said Sasha. "That's him up there." She pointed to one man, high on the scaffold. "He drew the original outlines. Now he's filling them in, and his assistants do the details."

Across one side of the ceiling, a beautiful mosaic was unfolding. Half-naked figures, scenes of the Verenthane Scrolls of Ulessis, in majestic, sensual poses. Sasha recognised no more than a third of the scenes, but it hardly mattered. The mosaic background was blue, like the sky on a warm summer day, and the figures seemed to fly. Indeed, some had wings—angels, the Verenthanes called those.

"I love this fellow here," said Sasha, pointing to a figure high on the wall opposite. A muscular man with a great beard, mostly naked, holding a babe in the crook of one arm. Both seemed to be emerging from the sea, draped in bits of seaweed, while a beautiful lady in a flowing dress looked on with love in her eyes. "He looks a bit like some Lenay men I know."

Father Portus gave her an odd look. "You must know these men well. He wears so little. They all do."

Sasha shrugged. "It's the style in the Saalshen Bacosh. You recognise the scenes?"

"Of course!" Father Portus looked somewhat . . . uncomfortable. "That's Ronard, God of the Oceans, and his son Trione. The woman is Deyani, Goddess of Love."

"I didn't do so well in scripture class," Sasha admitted. "But if classes were this beautiful, I might have done better. Don't you like it?"

"It's . . . it's . . ." the priest shook his head, helplessly. "They wear so little! Archbishop Augine would turn green."

"I knew there was a reason I liked it," Sasha said edgily. "Who cares what they wear or don't wear, look how beautiful they are! How godly!"

"I fear . . . I fear these may be considered indecent," said Father Portus. "The indecent cannot be beautiful. Indeed, it cannot be art."

"And yet here they are," said Sasha defiantly. "Beautiful, naked, thoroughly indecent, and most certainly art."

Father Portus shook his head, and made a holy sign with one hand. "Such thoughts come out of the Saalshen Bacosh," he murmured. "Whatever shall they dream up next?"

Sasha repressed a smile with difficulty. If he disliked *that*, what followed would be amusing indeed. "Come, we can talk in private, just through here."

She led Father Portus through a door at the back of the temple, where the priests' private quarters might be expected to be, but instead they stepped into a wide, open space of bare brick walls and a plain floor littered with statues. The high ceiling echoed to the rhythmic taps of chisels.

Directly confronting them as they entered the room was a man-sized nude—bearded, muscular, and hauling a great rock on one shoulder. Father Portus stared. Statues of Saint Sadis were common enough in the Endurance, but those were naked only to the waist. Here, even his manhood was lovingly carved in fine detail and (to Sasha's amusement and appreciation) considerable proportion. Father Portus made another holy sign.

"Oh please," said Sasha, stepping about to admire the statue of Sadis from another angle. "Look at the balance, the shift of weight on his hips from the stone he carries. I fight with the svaalverd, Father—trust me, I know all about balance. He captures it beautifully."

"Most ingenious," said Father Portus, averting his eyes. But there was nothing more to see but many other statues in varying degrees of nudity. Some were women, but most were men, fighting, posing, wrestling and stretching. Stone transformed into flesh, so real and sensual in form that it seemed it should feel soft to the touch and not stone-like at all.

"Father Berin loves his art," said Sasha as she led Father Portus on toward the nearest, loud chiselling. "He could have extended the temple with this space, but instead he lets the artists use it. The serrin love it, and some of the Saalshen Bacosh traders now are taking interest, they say Petrodor forms are unique, and demand grows there as well. Father Berin takes a share of commission for upkeep of this and other temples, and the artists support their families with the rest."

A man appeared behind several statues, working on a large block of haggard stone. He saw Sasha and stopped his chiselling with a grin. "Sasha! When are you going to pose for me?" He was a young man, in his mid-twenties, with long, wild hair that would have been entirely black were it not spattered white with stone dust. He wore a long leather apron, and little more than a loincloth beneath that, his limbs slick with sweat from the heat.

"Just as soon as you learn to do women, Aldano," Sasha teased.

Aldano gaped. "What do you mean? Have you seen my fine Princess Felesia? Look, look here . . ." He pointed to a nearby statue—a lady clad in little more than a silk scarf that wound around one outstretched arm and curled languidly down one shapely hip. Elegant, high class and . . . a little bored, Sasha reckoned.

"Hello there, are you a collector?" Aldano asked, suddenly noticing Father Portus.

Father Portus cleared his throat. "An appreciator," said Sasha, smiling.

"Of course you are, of course! Tell me, sir, have you ever seen as fine a pair of breasts as these? And what an arse! Have you ever seen as fine an arse?" He slapped the statue on the backside. Father Portus looked as though he'd swallowed something the wrong way.

"Every time I look back," said Sasha. Aldano roared with laughter, and slapped his thigh. "Only better . . . look, look, your women, Aldano . . . they all sag." She gestured with a hand, across one stone hip. "This is formless, all . . . all soft and pudgy."

"I believe the term is 'womanly,'" quipped Aldano, highly amused.

"No! No, you live on the dockside of Petrodor, you have all these serrin women around, and Nasi-Keth like me—"

"Very few Nasi-Keth like you, dear Sasha."

"Look! Look at this!" Sasha pulled up her shirt to expose her midriff. Father Portus nearly toppled over. "Do you see this? Six equal portions. Flat and hard, and accentuates the line, here, to the hip, and the thigh . . ." She indicated, but not quite at the point of having to remove more clothes. "Now look at her." Indicating the statue. "Shapeless, no form or tone of muscle, nothing. You have the frame right, but there's nothing on her bones."

"You'd rather I did her as a man?" said Aldano with consternation.

"No!" Sasha nearly laughed for sheer exasperation. "This is exactly my point . . . this is womanly, Aldano! I am a woman and this is what I look like!"

"You're an amazon!" Aldano protested.

"So do a statue of an amazon! That's what you can call it! 'Amazon with a Sword'! You've . . . you've done gods, and muscular heroes, and old men, and young boys . . . all these different types of men . . . why aren't women allowed to come in different types too? Some women look like this, sure . . . but why do they *all* have to look like this?"

Aldano looked at her for a long moment, unconvinced. "I'd be laughed at," he said reproachfully.

"You'd be the first!" Sasha retorted. "You'd be original! No one would have seen anything like it!"

That caught the young sculptor's attention. Everyone wanted to be at the forefront of the new trends in Petrodor. "You would pose for me?" Aldano asked. "If I did this?"

"Of course! If I can find the time, and if the gods don't sink Petrodor into the sea for its many sins."

Aldano laughed. "Oh, but carving is all about sin, dear Sasha! It is all form, and shape, and my hands all over your body, feeling its curves, testing its firmness . . ." Sasha only grinned, enjoying the teasing. With Aldano, that was all it was.

She found a quiet space behind several rough, uncarved blocks of stone as Aldano took up his chisel once more. "Young lady," said Father Portus, somewhat grimly, "I do fear for your soul. You should seek absolution."

"I am a Lenay pagan, Father Portus," Sasha told him. "I don't need your absolution." Father Portus seemed to swallow whatever he was going to say next. He was a tallish man with a homely face, a large nose and a narrow chin within a thin white beard. "Now of what did you wish to speak with me?"

Thunder rumbled outside, a long echo beneath the high ceiling. Father Portus looked about, but there was no one to see them hidden behind the stone blocks. "I carry a message from your sister Marya," he said in a low voice.

Sasha blinked at him. "Marya sent . . . Why?"

"She fears that you were right about her family. She knows that her husband had Father Gilbrato Halmady killed. There is tension between Halmady and Steiner. Steiner suspects Halmady of plotting against them. Now, some of Halmady's key allies are meeting with accidents, particularly within the priesthood. Everyone blames the old enemy Maerler, but not everyone believes it. Father Andrel Tirini is missing, and Father Jon Amano has fallen down some stairs and is yet to wake. I am an old friend of your sister's. She fears I may be next, like my nephew Randel. I ask for your help, in her name."

Sasha took a deep breath and wiped sweat from her brow. She took a sip from her waterskin, needing the time to think. Conflict between Steiner and Steiner's closest ally, Patachi Halmady. It did not seem likely that Halmady was seriously plotting anything. Kessligh thought it was Rhillian's work, sowing seeds of suspicion between the two, weakening Petrodor's strongest alliance from within. She'd used Randel Ragini's interest in things serrin to form a relationship with him, thus making Steiner suspect all of Family Ragini, and all of Halmady too, by connection. Halmady and Ragini remained close. Circles within circles, as ever in Petrodor. Had Rhillian truly set up poor Randel for the fall? She didn't want to think about that right now.

Father Portus Ragini. One priest per family, sometimes two for big families. Portus was Family Ragini's representative in the Porsada Temple. So why would Steiner, or anyone, want to start killing priests?

"The priesthood is supposed to be neutral," she said. "It's only useful to get rid of priests if they're planning something. What's going on up in that damn temple, anyway?"

"Dear girl," said Portus with irritable temper, "you really must watch your language! If I knew *why* my life was in danger, I would hardly need your help, would I?"

Sasha folded her arms, unconvinced. "And what could I do to help?"

"Meet again with your sister. She is wife to the heir of Steiner. She has access to information and she says she knows what the killings are in aid of."

"And she'd tell *me?*" Sasha did not know whether to believe it.

"You are her sister."

"I'm her crazy pagan sister. I've no doubt she loves me, but love and trust are two different things entirely." She narrowed her eyes at the priest. "You say she sent you? Prove it."

The fishing boat of Family Darno was somewhat larger than most and had a covered hold. Sasha and Kessligh sat on benches near the bow, above a pile of bundled nets and folded sails. Rain thundered on the wooden roof as a light chop rocked them from side to side against the moorings. Outside, Darno men prepared nets, stowed rigging and made ready for the afternoon run, in hopes that the weather might clear.

"He knew all about it," she said to Kessligh. "I don't know how he could have known if Marya hadn't told him."

"Krystoff's exploits were common enough knowledge in Lenayin," said Kessligh, unconvinced. "Anyone could know that."

"Not that incident, and not with that detail," said Sasha, shaking her head. "And not my part in it. I found the girl in Krystoff's chambers, Krystoff sent me out and I told Marya about it. Marya explained some things to me, and I wasn't so angry with Krystoff for sending me out then. Father Portus recited it in detail."

Kessligh made a face and glanced at the hold doorway. Beyond, men were bailing water overboard in the downpour. "Your memory's amazing."

"I remember everything about Krystoff," Sasha said faintly. "Everything."

Kessligh frowned at her. "You were more angry with him for sending you out of his chambers than for bedding some courtly slut?"

Sasha shrugged. "I didn't know what they were doing. Krystoff only explained that to me later. I was just mad that he preferred her company to mine. And you shouldn't use that language about her, whatever she did. I've been hearing that talk from too many Torovan men, and I'm sick of it."

"Petrodor's not growing on you, I see," Kessligh observed wryly.

"It was," Sasha said. "It was, then it stopped." No one had resolved the dispute with Liam. No one seemed to truly believe his claims about her swordwork, but it made little difference. People sided with him, or with her and Kessligh, based upon their previous inclinations. Liam's defiance was a symbol, and the facts counted for nothing. Sasha hated it. What could a person do when others cared nothing for facts? Her credibility, and thus Kessligh's, was at stake, and yet there remained no recourse. In Lenayin, such lies and accusations were a lethal offence, trialled by lethal means. Sasha could not see how a society such as the good and honest one the Nasi-Keth were trying to build here in Petrodor could survive if truth had no recourse, and thus no value. It made her doubt if there was anything in Petrodor worth fighting for. Anything besides Kessligh, that was. And the serrin, Rhillian and Errollyn in particular.

Liam had moved out of the Velo household and travelled with Alaine's group these days. Some others who had followed Kessligh now did the same. Kessligh's following shrank, and some of those Sasha saw would not speak to her. Lately, when not helping Family Velo earn a living, she'd spent more time with the serrin. Errollyn seemed angry and disillusioned too. Of Rhillian, there'd been little sign.

"I don't like it," said Kessligh. "It might be a trap. You might go there to find Marya and discover a hundred Steiner soldiers instead."

"On that cliff? There's no way to hide from our approaches, we can scout the area in advance. Kessligh, she was concerned. I think she might have even been scared of what she'd married into."

"I don't see how someone as smart as your sister could live in that household for any period and not grasp what her beloveds do for a living," Kessligh said bluntly.

"The way men treat women in this city?" Sasha retorted. "She's little more than a servant, she does what she's told, she raises the children . . . Marya's never been political, she was never interested in which lords were doing what things to whom . . ."

"You were six when she married," Kessligh reminded her.

"Yes, but I used to talk with Krystoff about her, she was Krystoff's friend too."

"And you were only eight when Krystoff died."

"And my memory is amazing, you said it yourself." Kessligh exhaled hard. "I know her, Kessligh," Sasha insisted. "I know her well. It wouldn't surprise me at all if she didn't have a clue the way her family go about business in this city. Look, she's very devout, I remember that very well, the only times I recall enjoying temple services were with her, she'd take my hand and explain all the devotions as we went, and who all the saints and gods were, and I'd think that if Marya thought it was important, then I'd do it just to please her. Someone's killing priests. If it's her family that's involved . . . she'd be horrified, Kessligh. Father Portus says she's his friend. What if she's scared for him? Who could she turn to? Not her own family, obviously. Not Maerler, that's treason, and she's too loyal."

"Halmady," Kessligh suggested. "They're supposed to be allies."

"And right now that might be considered treason too." Kessligh made a face as if conceding the point. "Or proof that Halmady really *are* plotting something against Steiner, with Marya their first recruit within Steiner walls. Who can help? I'm Nasi-Keth, but I'm also her sister. Nasi-Keth can sneak into all sorts of places, and the docks could be a refuge for priests whose lives are in danger—they'd be safe here, even fat-bellied Porsada Temple blue-bloods. They might be high-slopers, but they're priests, and—" *Boom!* a nearby thunderclap cut her short. Sasha swore as men outside cursed and laughed. "Damn I hate lightning."

"That's because you're superstitious," Kessligh said unhelpfully, having barely flinched.

"And," Sasha resumed her train of thought, "dockfront labourers are Verenthanes too. They'd not harm a priest, and would probably protect him from any outsiders who sought to do so."

Kessligh thought about it for a moment as the boat rocked and heavy boots thumped overhead, and the rain fell even harder. It seemed suddenly absurd—the two of them sitting here plotting such grand things. Two little people, alone in a boat in a storm. They could be struck down by a lightning bolt at any moment. And yet they sat, and plotted, as if they thought to change the fate of the entire city. And many things beyond.

Kessligh's lips twisted, a humourless grimace. He kicked lightly at the bench alongside where Sasha sat. "I'm sorry I dragged you into all this," he said then. And met her gaze, sombrely.

Sasha stared back. "No, you're not." And then, as the portent of his words struck her, "No, you're not . . . gods! Don't say that! You said it yourself, all my life has been leading up to this, in one way or another! Don't you dare tell me I've wasted it!"

"I didn't mean it like that," Kessligh said simply. "I'm just . . ." He sighed and shook his head faintly. "I'm just sorry, that's all."

"There's a lot of things in the world to be sorry about," Sasha retorted, somewhat disturbed by this uncharacteristic display of uncertainty from her uman. "It changes nothing."

"On some big matters," said Kessligh, businesslike once more, "the archbishop's council will be sought. Exactly how he arrives at his decisions is a guarded secret. Rumour has it that there is a vote of some kind, amongst the brotherhood. Other rumours say the archbishop decides alone, or waits for signs from the gods."

"Like lightning strikes," Sasha muttered, glancing toward the hold door.

"Exactly. Killing priests could be a precursor to something. A big decision. If we knew what that decision was going to be, perhaps in exchange for the protection of a few priests, it could be worth a lot."

Sasha nodded. But, "You still don't sound very certain."

"I'm not. Suspicion is wise, Sasha, when everyone's trying to kill you. Who will you take with you? I cannot offer anyone, our numbers are too small now as it is. Time spent on missions for the Nasi-Keth is time away from work and livelihoods."

"I'd thought maybe Errollyn," Sasha admitted. "But I've been told he's away. Saalshen's been spread even thinner than we have. Rhillian tries to watch everyone and trusts few other sources of information these days."

Kessligh nodded. "Take whoever you can find. When did Father Portus say?"

"Tomorrow."

Sasha climbed a paved path at the foot of the incline. The rain was light now and rays of sunlight speared orange through broken black cloud. Recalling the directions she'd been given, she turned left into a narrow alley overgrown with thick tree roots and knocked on a door.

"Who is it?" came the call from inside—a woman's voice.

"A friend of Yulia's!"

The door opened readily enough—once upon a time, folks in these parts had been too scared to open doors to strangers, but that had changed as the Nasi-Keth's power had grown and law came to the streets. The people's law, not the families'. A woman peered out at her suspiciously. Sasha adjusted her hat, now wet with rain. "Nasi-Keth," the woman snorted. "What do you want?"

"To speak to Yulia," said Sasha, attempting patience.

"Yulia doesn't speak to Nasi-Keth any longer!" the woman snapped. "Go away!"

Sasha put a hand on the door to stop it from closing. "Are you her mother?"

"I'm her aunt, and I'm telling you to go away!"

"That's not your decision," Sasha said firmly.

"What are you going to do?" the woman shouted in anger. "How dare you come here and tell me what should happen to this family? Who do you think you are, you damn Nasi-Keth, pushing people about—"

Sasha lost patience and pushed past her, into the dingy room. The woman grabbed her arm, but Sasha twisted free and shoved her hard at a wall, one hand hovering warningly near a knife.

"Thief!" the woman shrieked. "Help me! Somebody help me, I'm being attacked!"

"Would you just shut up?" Sasha said incredulously. "There's rules here, not even family can intervene on Nasi-Keth business."

"It's you, isn't it?" The woman jabbed a finger at her. She wore a scarf over her hair, as did many Petrodor women, and her dress was plain and brown. Her eyes were squinted with hard lines. "You're that scabby Lenay bitch, the one who got our Yulia in all that trouble!"

Sasha wondered if it would be bad etiquette to remove the hag's head from her shoulders in her own house. "Yulia!" she called instead. "Are you here?"

Already there were footsteps overhead and shouts from outside. A girl of perhaps ten summers arrived on the stairs and a baby started squalling. Sasha glanced about the room, it was typically spartan, a paved floor and brick walls, a bare bench for a table and a few chairs.

"Why don't you just get out of here!" the woman shouted. "We're honest Verenthane folk here, we don't need your pagan type!" Several men appeared in the doorway, one was holding a chopping axe.

"What's going on here? You, what's your business?"

"I'm Nasi-Keth," said Sasha, trying to keep her temper even. "I want only to speak to Yulia, as is a Nasi-Keth's right. Her aunt tried to stop me, and now calls me names."

"Right enough she'll call you names," said the man with the axe, dangerously, stepping in through the door. "You're standing in her house!" He was bald and bearded, with thick forearms and a rough manner. Perhaps he might have intimidated other people, but Sasha had grown up in Lenayin and had seen plenty of men more scary than this. Perhaps the contempt showed in her eyes, for the man seemed suddenly wary and did not advance.

"You've no right, Rena," said the second man, also bald, but fat and somehow intelligent-looking. "Nasi-Keth are a family unto themselves, that's the rule. You can't keep her out if she wants to see Yulia."

"I'm sick of the Nasi-Keth!" shouted Aunt Rena, hands waving. "They cause nothing but trouble! We used to live like good, honest Verenthanes until they came along! Everything was better then, we didn't have all these demon serrin telling us what to do!"

"Don't you say that," retorted the fat man, edging in front of the man with the axe, as yet others gathered in the doorway behind. Why was it that everything in Petrodor became a drama, Sasha wondered. "I lost five brothers and sisters to the water sickness, and my father was a half-cripple who could barely use his legs until the serrin fixed him! When he was dying, I walked in and saw him on his deathbed, surrounded by healthy grandchildren. He died with a smile on his face, and hopefully so will we, and I thank the serrin and the Nasi-Keth for that, Rena. And so should you."

"Yes, yes, all right!" Rena retorted. "That's all well and good, but it's not right, these other things they ask! It's not natural!"

"Who are you to say what's natural? The families think it natural that we slave for them like dogs for no pay, and lose our heads to the sword should we dare to complain of it! The gods cursed you with a short memory, Rena— I remember my father's stories well."

Sasha turned to the stairs as the argument continued at high volume, and found Yulia standing behind the younger girl. She looked pale, Sasha thought. Pale and drawn. Sasha walked to her, remembering her hat suddenly, and took it off as was the custom indoors.

"Hello," she said to the younger girl. "Are you Yulia's cousin?" The girl nodded. Yulia's mother was sickly and her father dead, Sasha had learned some time ago. Yulia lived with her father's sister and, rather than burden the family with another girl, she'd chosen the Nasi-Keth. Yulia had never told Sasha how that decision had been received amongst her family. Somehow, this reception did not surprise her.

"She's Marli," said Yulia, meaning the cousin. "What do you want?"

"To talk," said Sasha. "Can we go upstairs?"

Yulia nodded mutely. They ascended and came into an untidy upper floor. There were a number of beds, and no privacy or separate rooms. A wooden trunk for clothes, some half-repaired linen, and washed clothes drying on racks. In one corner, the baby's cries came loud from its crib, a simple wooden box on a small table. She counted seven beds . . . eight, if one included the baby, and there was barely enough space between the clutter to walk.

She'd seen poverty in Lenayin, but never with this overcrowding. In Lenayin, there was plenty of space. If a family grew, one built a new room, or an entire new house.

Cousin Marli went to the baby and gathered it up. Yulia sat on a bed by a window.

"I haven't seen you at training," Sasha remarked.

Yulia shrugged, cross-legged and fidgeting. "I haven't been."

"You're giving up?" Sasha asked with a frown.

"Not on the Nasi-Keth, no." More fidgeting. She wore a plain dress, such as ordinary Petrodor girls might wear. Even in the Nasi-Keth, some people frowned on girls in pants. "I just thought maybe I'd do better studying medicines. Like Fara."

"You thought? Or your aunt thought?"

Yulia looked up, and there was desperation in her eyes. "I have nightmares. About Riverside. Do you have nightmares?"

Sasha wanted to tell her yes, that she understood. But that would be lying, and lying was dishonourable. She'd lied before, on occasion, when need had required it. But lately, her Lenay honour had seemed even more precious than usual. "No," she said.

"Liam was right," said Yulia. "You were born a warrior. I wasn't."

"Liam," Sasha said sharply, "now insists that I'm not a warrior either."

Yulia shrugged and resumed fidgeting. "I heard. Liam is upset that Rodery died."

"It's no excuse." Sasha was still angry. She knew herself to be a basically good person, if a little hot-tempered and self-centred. She angered easily, but she did not hate easily and was always quick to forgive. But something about what Liam had done still made her fume. Such things, one expected of an enemy. But of a friend, or one who had called himself a friend . . . it was betrayal. Dishonour. A Lenay warrior did not go against his word or his friends. A Lenay warrior would rather die. Liam, it was clear, was no Lenay warrior. Even now, he did not appear to believe that he'd done anything wrong. Worse, many Nasi-Keth appeared to agree.

Honour, Rhillian had said, means different things to different people. My wise friend Rhillian, Sasha thought sourly. You may yet be proven right.

"I . . . I think maybe Liam's right in other things too," Yulia said quietly. "I . . . I panicked. I lost my sword. Rodery and Liam had to protect me. If . . . If I hadn't lost my sword, maybe Rodery wouldn't be . . ."

"Or maybe he would," said Sasha. "Or maybe Liam would be, or you would be. I don't claim to be the most hardened veteran of war, but I've seen my share of battles. There's just no predicting it, Yulia. Yes, Rodery and Liam had to protect you once you'd lost your blade . . . but then, they're supposed to. As you're supposed to protect them, should they lose theirs. Yes, you panicked. It happens to all kinds of warriors. Many survive and go on to become great regardless. They learn from their mistakes and improve. They don't just quit, Yulia."

"Sasha, I'm not very good, all right!" There was temper in her tone now and tears in her eyes. Across the room, the baby's wails had lessened somewhat. Cousin Marli watched on, wide-eyed, rocking the baby. Privacy would be too much to expect, Sasha knew, and didn't bother to ask. "Even at training, I . . . I only started going that regularly because of you!"

"Don't you try and pin this on me," Sasha said warningly. "Your actions and your choices are your own, that's the first thing your uman told you."

"No, I . . . I didn't mean it like that." Yulia shook her head. "I just meant that . . . gods, Sasha, look around." Sasha did, reluctantly. Downstairs, she could hear the continuing argument through the floorboards. "Do you see why I wanted to be Nasi-Keth? I wanted more, Sasha. More than this. And no one ever rises to great prominence within the Nasi-Keth without some talent in the svaalverd. I wanted to work on it more, but the boys always teased me, and some of the girls too, but then you came along. A human girl, and Kessligh's uma, and you're good! Staggeringly good. Men here couldn't believe it—trust me, I heard what they said when you weren't around. They were shocked. But about half came to accept it, and that gave me hope. Half is enough, for some respect at least.

"So I went to training more regularly. I practised a lot even before, but always on my own . . . and it's not the same. I can look good in training, sometimes. Better than I actually am, I think. Maybe that's why I was picked to go on the mission to Riverside. Kessligh was short of fighters and people thought I was better than I am."

"What does your uman say?"

"She . . ." Yulia sighed, hanging her head. "She didn't approve. I didn't see her as much after I started attending training more. It's not for girls, she said. I pointed to you and she just snorted. She'd rather I studied and learned to teach children. It's good work, but . . ."

"I know," Sasha said sombrely. "I'll tell you this, Yulia—in all my life, nearly all of my greatest supporters, and greatest friends, have been men. Women don't wish to see other women doing something different because it makes them feel less of themselves. Women have too little pride because they are taught from the cradle to be weak."

Yulia nearly smiled. "Maybe," she said, reluctantly. "But then, look at Aunt Rena. She's very proud of what she is, that's why she's yelling at you."

Sasha shook her head. "That's not pride. That's fear. Pride is being so certain in yourself that you're not intimidated by the strangeness of others. Pride is being so certain that you can look after yourself that you don't need to threaten or complain or make malicious whispers behind others' backs. I see too little pride here in Petrodor, from men or women. Only fear and anxiety."

"Pride has many meanings to many people."

Sasha sighed. She'd been hearing that kind of thing a lot lately. "Yulia, I need you to help me with a job."

"A Nasi-Keth job?" Sasha nodded. "You'd trust me? After . . . ?"

"There shouldn't be any fighting." Yulia looked a little panicked. "There *won't* be any fighting," Sasha corrected. "I'm going to see my sister Marya. I need someone to help keep watch, and there's no one else available. Kessligh can't spare a more seasoned fighter when there are so many other threats to cover, and neither Alaine nor Gerrold's followers will be likely to help me."

"Surely there's someone?" There was fear in Yulia's eyes. "I'm . . . I mean . . . I'm just not sure if I can . . ."

"It's your choice," Sasha told her. "I'll go alone if I have to. I just need someone to watch my back, you can do that, right?" Yulia looked at her lap, fidgeting furiously. "You're not a bad fighter Yulia. I've sparred against you, you're not *that* far behind Liam. You just froze up in battle. That's understandable, you've not the experience the others do. But you'll not need to fight anyway. Will you come?"

Eleven

ASHA SAT ON THE BOW of Mari's boat and blinked wearily into the light of the rising sun. A breeze came from the south, filling the little boat's sails, pushing them northward across the harbour. Ahead loomed Besendi Promontory, its cliffs gleaming gold in the low light from across the sea.

"You look tired," Mari observed from his seat beside the mast. Valenti was at the tiller, and handling the mainsail rope—no great affair in the light breeze. Opposite Mari sat Yulia, her slim arms bare, her back to the sun.

"I was never the earliest riser," Sasha admitted, stifling a yawn. "Baerlyn farmers tease me about it, but they don't have to run up a mountain and back before breakfast. And now I'm rarely getting to bed before midnight."

"Bah," said Mari, waving a dismissive hand. "Try working for a living."

"How many thoroughbred horses have you hand-reared and sold to Torovan and Lenay nobility?" Sasha retorted. "All you do is fish; I run a stable *and* train as a Nasi-Keth warrior."

"You want I should hold her close off the shore for a while?" he asked her.

"It'll look suspicious. Just let us off at the steps, then go your own way. You've pots out beyond the bluff, by the time you fetch them we'll be finished."

"Right confident are you," said Mari dubiously as he gazed ahead at the Cliff of the Dead. Its terraces rose most of the way from the sea to the sky. "What if you strike trouble?"

"Look, there's no hiding places." Sasha pointed across the terraces. "If we get attacked we can descend, there's shelter from archers and there's the rocky shoreline along here . . ."

"That's damn slippery," said Mari, shaking his head. "You can't move far along that."

"We won't need to, just long enough to find shelter. Let them come at us along those rocks—I could hold off thirty men on my own." Mari looked at Yulia, presumably to judge if she was boasting. Yulia shrugged, to say she didn't think so. "Sure, if you see us in trouble, hold off and we'll swim to you.

Or head back and get help. But for the men it'd take to catch us here, it'd be a silly waste of effort. Even Steiner don't have that many men. They're all guarding their properties, expecting violence."

"Can you swim?" Mari asked Yulia.

"A little," said Yulia, uncertainly. "Can you?" she asked Sasha.

Sasha nodded. "There was a nice big pond near the ranch in Baerlyn," she said. "A waterfall fell into it. Ten strokes from side to side, and river trout at the bottom. The most crystal water you've ever seen."

"I live right next to the ocean," Yulia muttered, "but you even swim better than me."

There was no movement along the gravestone terraces in the early morning, save for the gulls. Out further toward Porsada Temple, recent stonework marked where terraces were being extended along the cliff face. This was where the wealthiest families buried their dead. The temple priesthood owned the land, and a plot was said to be exorbitant. But there was so little free land in Petrodor, save for that on rises far too steep for dwellings. For Petrodor families, paying respects to the ancestors was a matter of importance, and it would not do for them to be buried too far away. Sasha wondered what they'd do when, in several more generations, the stoneworkers ran out of cliff.

Steps rose from the water, carved in stone and encrusted with barnacles. Mari let out the sail as Valenti steered them alongside, allowing Sasha and Yulia to jump easily to a step, then the boat regathered speed, steering out, away from the rocks.

Sasha and Yulia ascended the terraces, past rows and rows of little stone blocks.

It was a long climb up many flights to reach the undertaker's shed where she had met Marya previously. The cliff face curved here, hiding all view of the temple. On the terrace below the shed, Sasha sent Yulia past the end of the terrace, onto the narrow trail she remembered from the last time she'd been here. Yulia edged her way along with ease, and soon disappeared as the cliff face turned again.

After a while of watching and listening, Sasha edged her way up the narrow stairs to the next terrace, keeping close to the inner wall. Peering over the lip, she saw nothing but headstones, and the little wooden shed, just as it had been last time. Then the door opened and she ducked down a little. A young woman in a dress emerged, but not Marya. She appeared to be looking and waiting for an arrival, wringing her hands nervously. A maid, Sasha decided. Openly displayed, no threat intended.

Even so, she waited a while longer, peering occasionally over the terrace rim. Finally, when convinced it was safe, she moved. She'd seen the terraces from way out to sea, and there was no cover to hide an ambush. The shed itself was the only place where men could hide, and neither she, Yulia, Mari or Valenti had seen anyone. Besides which, the sheer gall of anyone, to make preparations for ambush in a cemetery was beyond imagining.

The maid stopped fidgeting when she saw Sasha walking toward her. When she arrived, the maid curtsied. "Lady Sashandra, I am Tesslyn. My mistress awaits inside."

"You're Lenay?" Sasha asked in surprise. The accent was unmistakable.

Tesslyn smiled. She seemed perhaps the same age as Marya. "Aye, M'Lady," she said in Lenay. "I came out with Princess Marya in her wedding train, fourteen years ago. I decided to stay."

"Fourteen years," said Sasha. "That's a long time."

"Your sister's service is most rewarding," said Tesslyn. "And I found myself a lovely husband and now have children of my own."

"Where are the guards?" she thought to ask Tesslyn, turning to survey the terraces eastward. Always a good idea to take a final look at the surroundings before entering a building.

"There is an old Steiner cousin who is buried just there," said Tesslyn, pointing to a gravestone not ten plots away. "Princess Marya made a great fuss when she discovered none of the present family had come to pay their respects for several years. She said it should be private for the deceased cousin's soul would surely be angry. The family soldiers are a little superstitious, they're waiting well beyond the curve in the cliff here."

"Clever," Sasha observed, smiling.

"Princess Marya is never anything but sincere," said Tesslyn mildly.

"You're not superstitious?" Sasha asked.

"I'm quite certain Princess Marya's prayers have consoled her cousin's angry spirit."

Sasha gave her a sideways look. "Right," she said. She turned to open the cabin door and allowed it to swing, creaking, so she could observe the gloom within. Paused in the doorway, a hand on her knife, looking for ambush. There was nothing, just piled headstones, shovels and other work gear. And Marya, standing by the same little window with the view across the harbour. Sasha smiled at her. "Sorry," she said. "I have to be careful. Kessligh would kill me."

"Oh, Sasha," said Marya with evident emotion. "It's so good to see you!" Sasha went to her and hugged her. And felt a sting on the back of her neck as they embraced.

"Ow!" She pulled back and looked at Marya in puzzlement. Marya looked pale, she realised. Suddenly frightened. Then the dizziness began.

"Oh no," Sasha exclaimed incredulously. "Oh no. You didn't!" She put a hand to the back of her neck and found blood on her fingers; grabbed Marya's wrist, twisted, and found a small needle protruding from a ring about her middle finger.

"Oh Sasha, I'm so sorry!" There were tears in Marya's eyes. "I'm so sorry, I didn't want to do it . . ." Sasha's knife came out fast and Marya's eyes widened. "It's not fatal, Sasha! Oh gods, I'd never . . . it'll just make you sleep!"

Sasha thumped her left hand against the wall, trying to hold her balance as her vision swam and faded. There was strength in her right arm yet. Marya's figure swam close, then far, hot then cold. One thrust. One . . . She hurled the knife at the window instead, but her arm was weak and the glass cracked without breaking. No warning to Yulia. Yulia wouldn't know. "Family!" she gasped. "I'm . . . family!"

"It's been fourteen years since I came to Petrodor, Sasha," Marya said sadly. "Steiner are my family now."

Sasha awoke with a perfect recollection of what had happened. And cursed herself for the greatest fool in all the history of fooldom.

She was lying on her back. On a bed, by the feel of it. And it was hot. She tried to raise her head, and found that was possible, if awkward. She had a nasty headache, a stiff neck and the distant sensation of nausea. Distant, but ready to roll over her like a tide if she moved too suddenly. She lay in a small, stone room. Sunlight shone through a tall, slit window. Despite the discomfort, she was surprisingly clearheaded. The potion had been a serrin concoction, no doubt. The most effective ones always were.

She stretched and found herself thankfully free of other injuries or stiffness . . . except that her legs were bare. Where were her boots? Or come to that, her clothes? She slapped hands to her waist and found, to her alarm, that she was wearing . . . a dress! Damn. She'd spent most of the last twelve years avoiding the prospect of ever wearing one of these horrible things ever again. Now, her efforts had finally been foiled. It was nearly funny, and she fought back an exasperated laugh.

A new, unpleasant thought occurred to her and the laugh died on her lips. She pulled the dress up, and found to her relief that she was still wearing her old, thigh-length woollen underwear. Thank the spirits. She'd not have put it past some Steiner soldier to take liberties with an unconscious woman. Nor a dead one, came the uncharitable thought. She felt herself, but found no irritation, no soreness. Just as well. The serrin's white powder she always carried was with her clothes, and they were . . .

She rolled on the bed and looked around the room. It had three walls—one curved, the other two straight, with a door in one. There was no furniture but for her bed, and no sign of her clothes. Nor, obviously enough, her weapons. Beside the bed, a bucket of water stood on the flagstones with a clean cloth draped over the rim. She dipped a finger in the water and tasted it, suspiciously. Nothing happened, and it tasted good. She was thirsty as all hells. She lowered her upper body off the bed, not game to try squatting just now, and drank directly from the bucket. She wiped cool water on her face as she lay back.

From beyond the slit window she could hear the cries of gulls. She strained her ears, but heard nothing more. Was she in the Steiner Mansion? It would be busy, surely, with guards and servants. Her window opened onto sky, yet she could not hear the clatter of a passing cart, nor the distant commotion of the docks. Just gulls. She thought about getting up, and trying to see out, but she didn't feel up to that just now.

Marya. Marya had betrayed her. Except that now, so soon after the event, it did not surprise her. How could she not have seen? Fourteen years. She'd said it herself, to Marya's maid, just before she'd gone inside. Fourteen years was a long time. Marya had always been traditional. Conservative. She cared for people, and had always conformed her own needs to the needs of the family. And now Marya had children of her own, heirs to the great power of Family Steiner. Of course they mattered more to her than a long-lost sister. Sasha had made the mistake of assuming that Marya's simple compassion would override that family loyalty at least to a small degree, when she discovered that her family were doing bad things. But no . . . that would mean Marya placing herself, and her own opinions and wants, ahead of those of her immediate family. And Marya never had. And now, it seemed, probably never would.

Sasha put a hand to the back of her neck. It hurt, and was swollen. She hoped Marya had at least heated the needle first, for her sister's sake. Probably Patachi Steiner had ordered it, and Father Portus had been the bait. Why her? Had she been in danger of discovering something? Or were they looking for leverage on Kessligh? A cold knot formed in her stomach. As a hostage, they could threaten her with things, if Kessligh did not do what they wanted. How Kessligh would respond, she could not guess. Did not want to guess. Kessligh would not take kindly to blackmail. But then, surely he would not wish her in greater danger, either. Sasha had heard of the families' methods in such matters, the fingers or ears sent to the loved ones . . .

She hit the mattress in a rush of frustration. All her life she'd fought the natural expectation of weakness that came with being what she was—a girl, and a princess at that. Now she was a weak, pitiable hostage. Well, she thought grimly, not for long. The first chance I get, I'm either getting out, or I'll die trying. Better that than for them to use her as a knife at Kessligh's heart. Even if she lived to tell of it, she wasn't certain she could survive the shame.

Soon enough, a plate slid aside on the door and a man peered in. Then the door unbolted and an armoured guard stepped in, carrying a tray. Sasha eyed him from her bed. If she was going to try something, it was better she scouted a little first. The guard wore black over chain mail that covered head and arms. There were metal gauntlets for gloves and extended forearm guards, to say nothing of shin guards and helm. He even carried a shield— square on top, pointed at the bottom. Emblazoned in silver on his black vest was an eight-pointed Verenthane star.

He set down the tray and left the room, with barely a glance in her direction. Sasha sighed as the bolts clacked shut once more. At least now she knew where she was. She'd not seen a man of the Holy Guard before, but she'd heard them described. They were heavily armoured after a little incident half a year back when Rhillian had managed to sneak inside the temple and confront Archbishop Augine directly. Exactly what she and the archbishop had discussed, Rhillian had never exactly said . . . but she had admitted to killing three of the Holy Guard before making her escape. There would be no tackling one of the Holy Guard bare-handed, that was certain. But all that armour slowed a man down. If she could deprive him of a weapon, perhaps . . .

Then she would have to think of a way to escape from within the confines of the Porsada Temple. Once again, she'd only heard it described. The Holy Guard were numerous these days. Even if she stole a guardsman's sword, it would not have the balance of a svaalverd blade, nor the sharpness. Fighting her way out single-handed was possibly not the smartest plan.

She ate the meal, figuring that light bread, soup and water meant it was still lunchtime. The lack of shadow from the window seemed to confirm that. The food was plain, but not bad. At least it seemed the priests did not wish her punished in any way. Yet.

To better absorb her lunch, she sat cross-legged on her bed, and meditated. Kessligh swore by it, but Sasha was more sceptical; she'd never been one to sit still and think of nothing for any period. Still, it made her feel better to be doing something, an activity she could control toward her own ends. And, when thinking of nothing lost its appeal entirely, she thought instead of everything she knew about Porsada Temple: which way the road came in along the ridge, the nature of its cliffs, the proximity of its walls to the sheer drop below.

After her headache had cleared somewhat, she sat on the flagstone floor and did stretches. It was common Nasi-Keth knowledge that poisons or potions of any sort could be hastened from the body by exercise. When she felt up to it, she tried sit-ups and push-ups, and then jumps and running on the spot . . . which felt a little ridiculous with the dress bouncing around her legs. The air inside the cell was stifling and she was soon dripping with sweat, making unsightly dark stains beneath the armpits of her dress sleeves. Take that, horrid thing.

She turned her attention to the slit window, but it seemed entirely out of her reach.

She shifted the bed directly beneath the window—the bedframe was heavy wood and squealed on the flagstones. Jumping from the end, she came close, but not enough.

She examined the mattress, which seemed to be stuffed with straw. Beneath, the bed frame was wooden slats. Easy solution. She wrestled the mattress off the bed, with some effort, and set about turning the bed frame on its end. Her balance was still not fully recovered, but she finally managed it and pushed the frame as close as possible to the wall. Then she climbed the slats.

Peering through the window slit, she could see nothing but ocean, and the sun seemed to be now to the right . . . so she guessed she was facing roughly east, straight out to sea. Right at the tip of the promontory, perhaps. If she were not, she should be able to see the huge temple spires. Perhaps she was directly beneath a spire. Or in one.

The door bolts squealed and clacked, but Sasha didn't bother moving. The door swung open and she looked down to see a guard blinking up at her. "Hello," she said cheerfully. "Have you come to look up my dress?"

"Get down from there."

It would have been too much to ask for the Holy Guard to have a sense of humour, Sasha supposed. "You think I'm going to escape through this little thing? I can barely get my arm through."

"Get down or I'll knock you down." If he risked physical contact, she could grab his sword, or his knife. But there was his companion behind, and doubtless more outside. She'd do better to wait.

Sasha sighed and climbed down the slats. "You could have at least put me in a room with an accessible view."

"The archbishop wants to see you," said the guard.

"The Archbishop of Torovan?" said Sasha, feigning astonishment. "Gosh. But I have nothing to wear!"

The guard tied her wrists with tight cord first. Sasha decided against resisting or refusing—they could have beaten her senseless first, had they chosen. Besides, she wanted to get out of her cell and take a look around. The guard escorted her out of the door, which opened onto a downward spiral of stairs. She *was* in of one of the spires then. One guard led the way, another at her back, each with a shield and a sword at the hip.

The stairs descended into a grand room, high-ceilinged with great, gilt-framed paintings on the stone walls. Gold filigree traced patterns across the ceiling, from which golden chandeliers hung. On the right, large windows looked onto Petrodor Harbour and a warm breeze whispered at white, billowing curtains. At a table before the windows sat an old man in black robes. He sipped at a golden winecup and gazed out at the harbour below. He had white hair about a bald spot and a big chin that had surely once been square, but was now developing jowls. Upon the stand behind him hung a tall, black hat. A cane rested against the wall beside his chair.

He studied Sasha with sharp blue eyes and smiled thinly. "Dear girl." His voice was educated, and condescending . . . and yet, somehow, not entirely convincing for a man of his stature. "Please, do sit." He gestured to the chair opposite.

Sasha walked, a guard at her side, testing her bonds as she went. They were tight and her right hand was going numb. The guard pulled the chair for her and she sat.

"It is customary, my dear, to first kneel before the archbishop, when entering his presence. Even for a princess."

"Is it also customary to bind the hands of your lunch guests?" Sasha retorted.

The archbishop made a vague gesture with his winecup, sunlight shining upon his many gold rings. "You are not my lunch guest and I'm certain you can kneel with your hands tied."

"And get back up again? Not when I'm dizzy from that needle."

The archbishop looked at her, his blue eyes cool. "You are a pagan. That is why you do not kneel. You have rejected your gods."

"Not *my* gods," said Sasha. They regarded each other. This was the most powerful Verenthane in all Rhodia, she knew. With the holy temples of Enora, Rhodaan and Ilduur in the Saaalshen Bacosh out of direct Verenthane control, Petrodor had become the centre of Verenthane faith in Rhodia. For no better reason, Kessligh said, than it was where all the money was. This was Archbishop Augine himself, one of the very greatest men of all the lands. And yet she was not impressed.

He tried to look at ease. He tried to look comfortable. Yet unease lurked behind his smile and the comfortable remark. Perhaps the archbishop simply suffered from being compared, in her mind, to great Lenay men she had known. Men who wore power comfortably, and indeed radiated it as a cloak of honour. Or perhaps he was simply not a very impressive man. In Lenay opinion, there was nothing more contemptuous than a fraud, except perhaps a coward. Sasha resolved to find out.

"Regard this view," the archbishop offered, gesturing with his winecup. "It is magnificent, is it not? The best view in all Petrodor."

Sasha looked, and found that it was. The city—every dwelling, every road, every detail, in sprawling profusion about the harbour. The high sun, sparkling on the waters, and the silhouette of ships and rigging against that golden light.

"I've been out fishing on that harbour," Sasha volunteered. "Have you?"

"In my youth," said the archbishop. He flicked her a sideways glance. Then up, about at the walls. "Do you recognise these paintings?"

Sasha half turned in her chair and surveyed the walls. "That one would be the Enoran High Temple. And that's Saint Tristen on Mount Tristen. And that's Saint Sadis, and that's Saint Ambellion, of course. Not the others, though." She was supposed to be impressed. And intimidated. The cumulative weight of Verenthane history pressed down upon this grand chamber. As though all of the gods and saints were watching.

Sasha stared at the archbishop. "You're drinking wine? Is that proper?"

"It is the Torovan tradition, even amongst clergy," said the archbishop with a frown. "Tell me—"

"Is it proper that I should be here?" Sasha continued, not missing a beat. "I mean, this is Porsada Temple, the holiest temple in all Rhodia."

"Second holiest," said the archbishop, with the first trace of temper.

"Ah yes, the Enora High Temple comes first, doesn't it? These are your private chambers." Sasha glanced around. "The archbishop's quarters? When was the last time a woman set foot in these quarters? When was the last time you even spoke to a woman? In Baen-Tar, even the new priests would run away from me. But now I'm being held in a secure room in your chambers. Tell me, are you in the habit of holding young women hostage in your chambers? Does anyone else even know I'm here?"

There was no mistaking the temper in the archbishop's eyes now. "You should recall to whom you're speaking, young lady."

Sasha shrugged. "I'm just wondering how seriously you take this 'holy vows' stuff here in Petrodor. I mean, we hear all the stories in Lenayin—all the little boys buggered behind the altar, that kind of thing. And now you're drinking wine and holding pretty girls hostage for your private amusement . . ."

"You are being held here as a direct favour to your dear sister Marya!" hissed the archbishop between clenched teeth. "I did inform her that it would be highly improper for a woman to be quartered in the temple, but she did insist! You should be thankful for my mercy that you were not given directly into the hands of Family Steiner, I doubt they'd have arranged such comfortable lodgings for you as we have."

"What would they do?" Sasha asked darkly. "Start pulling out fingernails?"

"At the very least. You cause great difficulties for Family Steiner, young lady. Have you no sympathy at all for the difficult position into which you put your sister?"

"Oh poor darling," Sasha muttered. "I'm sure her fancy clothes and jewellery are just chafing right now."

"Your love of family seems wanting," the archbishop observed, recovering some of his poise. "Do you hold as much disdain for *all* the tenets of Verenthane morality?"

"Marya made her choice," Sasha said shortly. "I've made mine."

"Be aware, Sashandra Lenayin, that your position here is most tenuous." The archbishop sipped at his wine and considered the view. "I could hand you to Family Steiner at any time should your behaviour displease me. As you have observed, it is not proper for you to be here at all. Do not grant me an even greater incentive to unload this burden with which I am presented."

"Unload?" Sasha said with contempt. "Or sell cheap, like the cheap salesman you are? You don't practise morality here, the priesthood of Petrodor never has. You just buy and sell like all the other merchants. Buy off the families to keep you happy. Trade favours when it suits you. Peddle influence. I may be Goeren-yai, but I've known many good Verenthanes in Lenayin, priests amongst them. Their gods were never so short of gold and treasure as yours seem to be."

"You doubt my resolve," said the archbishop icily. "We have already disposed of one Nasi-Keth girl this morning. My guards found her hiding near your meeting place on the Cliff of the Dead. I'm told she put up a stubborn resistance and would have escaped had it not been for an excellent crossbowman. If you wish to join her at the bottom of the harbour, please just say so, and we shall dispense with these tiresome games and insults . . ."

Sasha lifted the table with an explosive heave. The archbishop toppled backward and Sasha rushed forward, but a guard threw her to the ground. She fell awkwardly, struggling to rise with tied hands, but a shield crashed into her side, throwing her further from the archbishop. She rolled fast, but an armoured boot in the side stopped her, and then one crashed into her head and stunned her. It was several kicks later before her head cleared. A kick in the back was agony and one in the stomach drove the breath from her lungs. She curled up and braced as hard as she could, arms over her head to protect what mattered most. Then the kicks stopped.

She lay still, breathing hard, trying to listen past the pain. She heard the archbishop's voice, disappointingly calm and reassuring, talking to the guards. The squeal and crash of the table being returned to its place. Candle-holders resettled. Then a hand grabbed her under each armpit and hauled her up. Her feet barely touched the floor until the guards dumped her in the chair once more.

Sasha tried licking her lips, but it hurt to move her jaw. Her ear stung and her mouth was tender. When she dared to move her tongue past her lips, she tasted blood. She couldn't quite manage to sit straight on the chair, her back and ribs hurt and the world kept trying to tip sideways.

"That was ill advised," said the archbishop. A servant came scurrying to put a new cup of wine in his hand. He sipped it, trying hard to look unper-turbed. Smug shit, Sasha thought. She nearly rushed him again, just to prove her contempt. Only the thought of injury stopped her. If she were injured further, she'd never escape. "You seem a little dense, although given your reputation, that is hardly surprising. Let me explain to you how this arrange-ment will work.

"You will tell me things about the Nasi-Keth. Or not me, not precisely —my interrogators. Where they live, how many they are, what the current political situation is like—and I understand it is quite fragmented—all of this. Should you not, I shall change my more polite interrogator for a less gentlemanly variety with ingenious inventions to make even the stubbornest Lenay princess talk. And then, you shall be very sorry."

"You hurt me," Sasha half mumbled with uncooperative lips, "and Kessligh will kill you. No . . . he'll gut you and make sure you live long enough to see what colour your insides are."

"Kessligh's followers are Verenthanes, even if he himself has lapsed," the archbishop said confidently. "If he wishes to retain any of his fast-fading sup-port on the dockfront, he'll not dare touch a hair on my head."

It didn't make sense, Sasha reflected, back on her bed in the cell. Her hands had been untied and she lay on her back with arms above her head to stop her bruises from stiffening.

The archbishop only wanted her for information? Not likely. He seemed very concerned about Kessligh, that was certain. It was more likely black-mail, she reckoned. Blackmail to keep Kessligh from interfering in whatever came next. Probably they would not risk harming her, as long as she remained useful—which would be for as long as Kessligh remained powerful. Kessligh would not remain powerful for very long if blackmail prevented him from acting . . . or, if in acting, he lost his best guarantee of prestige within the Nasi-Keth—his uma. However she figured it, she had to get out of here.

So what came next? Priests were being murdered. Something was afoot within the brotherhood. Something concerning Family Steiner. Something for which those involved wished Kessligh neutralised in advance. She knew she could not begin to guess. Possibly Kessligh would . . . but she doubted the plotters would leave much advance warning. Just long enough to let Kessligh know they had her. No fingers—probably Marya had made them swear they would not harm her. Marya was important enough that even the archbishop didn't dare break faith with her. Perhaps Marya herself would tell Kessligh. Kessligh would believe her with no severed fingers necessary.

Soon. Whatever was coming, it would come soon.

They'd killed Yulia was her next thought. Grief and horror threatened to surge and overwhelm her. No, she thought desperately. No. Perhaps it was a lie to upset her. But how would they know where Yulia was if Yulia had remained hidden? And how would the archbishop have known Sasha's accomplice was a girl? There weren't many female Nasi-Keth. Yulia alone would not have been able to outmanoeuvre them. In all Sasha's plans, she'd assumed she would be there herself to help Yulia out of trouble. It had never occurred to her that she would be the first to fall and Yulia would be left all alone.

She'd led Lenay men into battles in which hundreds had died. More recently, she'd come to know Rodery of the Nasi-Keth quite well, and he had been killed before her eyes. All was different to this, though. Those men had volunteered. They'd known exactly what they were getting into. But she'd gone to Yulia's *home*, and asked her to come, knowing that the girl half worshipped her, telling her she was not a bad warrior and assuring her that it would not be particularly dangerous, certainly far less dangerous than Riverside . . .

Less dangerous for Sasha, perhaps. Priests and powerful families could ransom Sashandra Lenayin. She was worth something. But what use would such powerful people have for a raggedy Dockside girl with dreams of becoming a warrior? For those people the likes of Yulia were barely worth the cost of the crossbow bolt that killed her.

Sasha knew that she was sometimes arrogant. She knew that she could be self-centred, and could at times fail to consider things from the perspectives of others. She'd thought she was getting better. More worldly and more mature. Wiser. She'd thought she was on her way to becoming the kind of uma that would raise Kessligh's prestige throughout Petrodor. The kind of uma who would make him proud. But now she'd got a nice Dockside girl killed for no better reason than she'd been too damn impressed with herself to consider how it wasn't all as easy for some people as it was for her. She'd been too damn certain that Marya would never betray her.

People like Sofy told her. Oh dear spirits, Sofy. Sofy would have told her not to trust Marya, not now, not in this situation, where her own children's futures were at stake. Sofy would have told her that it wasn't fair on Yulia to pressure her to do something she didn't particularly want to. Sofy would have told her not to get the poor girl killed because Sasha was too damn selfish to stop for a moment and consider other people's problems.

The ceiling began to swim in her tears. She stifled the sobs, as they hurt her bruises, but that felt like penance, and richly deserved. Tears ran down her temples and into her hair. "Oh, Yulia, I'm so sorry," she sobbed. "Please forgive me."

But she didn't deserve forgiveness, and she knew it.

Twelve

WHEN ALYTHIA WALKED INTO THE GARDEN that night with Tashyna on a leash, the guards on the patio stared. The wolf heaved at the leash, straining toward the open grass.

"Hey, steady!" Alythia scolded, pulling back with her entire body, hoping the wolf didn't wrench her arms off. "Steady, steady! Calm down, you crazy fool, you!"

"M'Lady?" asked a guard, approaching uncertainly. "What are you . . . ?" Tashyna growled, backing away as fast as she'd lunged forward, tail down, ears flat, neck bristling.

"Stop!" Alythia commanded the guard, holding out a firm hand. He stopped, a wary hand on the hilt of his sword, eyes wide on the wolf. "Don't approach her, she's not used to it. Just stay back." To her delight, the guard obeyed. At last—power! The guard looked a little scared, as did his companion further away. How wonderful. Alythia crouched, offering a hand to the wolf. "It's all right, Tashyna," she said in Lenay. "It's all right, I'm here. I won't let him hurt you." Tashyna let her stroke her neck and scratch her head. The ears rose and the growling stopped.

"M'Lady," said the guard cautiously, "is this wise? That's a wolf!"

"It's a Lenay wolf," said Alythia imperiously. "Her name's Tashyna. She listens to me." The guard blinked at her. It had been six days since she'd given Tashyna her name. Since then she'd visited the wolf every day, sometimes twice a day, always with food. Alythia was astonished how little time it had taken for the wolf to come to trust her. Probably, she thought, Tashyna remembered a time when she'd been an adorable puppy and humans had been nice to her. Probably she'd only wanted some of that affection back again and had no idea why the exuberance that her human masters had once found so charming was now met with fearful exclamations and beatings. Alythia thought she knew how that felt.

Now, Tashyna had one human in Halmady Mansion who was nice to her, and flung herself upon that protection with desperate hope. Wolves, Alythia recalled her brothers saying, were proof of the natural order of kings. They wanted to be commanded. They needed a dominant ruler to obey. Perhaps Tashyna now believed that dominant ruler was her. It gave Alythia a strange feeling of pride. Someone needed her. Someone enjoyed her company. That someone had four legs, smelled poorly at the best of times and had terrible eating habits, but it was better than no one at all.

Alythia pulled Tashyna onto the grass, where the wolf quickly regained her enthusiasm and began hauling desperately on the leash. Alythia struggled to keep up, her sandalled feet slipping. She tried to keep left of a row of garden bushes, then slipped and fell on her rear, losing the leash from her hand. Tashyna shot off across the grass, rounded the central fountain, half tripping on her lead, then came bounding back, a sinister, lunging shape in the evening torchlight. For a brief moment, Alythia recalled her previous fear, to see that ferocious outline coming straight toward her. But Tashyna slowed, then jumped on her playfully and tried to lick her face.

"Oh get off! You're too heavy!" Alythia struggled to her feet and tried to regain the leash, but Tashyna was off once more, with boundless energy. Alythia sighed and brushed the grass from her arms. This was most undignified, and irritating too. The guards were surely laughing at her. Her heart was thumping with exertion and half-fear, and the stupid animal would simply not do what it was told. But Tashyna had been her only friend for the past week, and deserved this brief freedom. And Tashyna was . . . well, really quite funny too, she thought, watching the wolf weaving between the flowerbeds, tongue lolling, a mad excitement in her eyes. She arrived at the far wall, skidded to a halt and came back the other way, nearly falling. Much to her own amazement, Alythia found herself laughing.

Tashyna came back to Alythia and dodged around her, jumping and snapping at her skirts. Guards on the patio came to stare, and some house staff too. Some looked anxious, but others were laughing. "The Lenay wolf-girl!" someone exclaimed loudly in good humour. Alythia had the grace to turn and curtsey, and gained more laughs. It was more goodwill than she'd experienced at any time since her wedding, she thought, with a surge of happiness. The next time Tashyna returned to harass her, she managed to grab the wolf and give her a big hug. Tashyna whined, struggled and licked.

And raced off once more. Alythia turned back to the onlookers and found that little Tristi Halmady had emerged from the house, escorted by a pair of maids, one of whom carried even littler Elra in her arms. The maids looked anxious, but Tristi was wide-eyed with amazement.

"Alythia's friends with the wolf!" Elra said loudly. She was a pretty girl, her black hair done up at the back, rosy-cheeked and clutching Topo, her favourite ragdoll.

"Alythia, Papa says the wolf is wild and dangerous!" exclaimed Tristi. "He told us we weren't to go near it!"

"Well I assure you," Alythia announced primly to them all, "he demanded no such thing from me!"

"How did you make friends with the wolf?" Elra demanded.

"She fed it," said one of the cooks, who knew.

"I spoke Lenay to it," Alythia corrected. "Tashyna's a Lenay wolf, she only speaks Lenay."

"Her name's not Tashyna, it's Dessi!" Tristi insisted.

"Ah, but that's where you're wrong!" Alythia said brightly. "You see, all Lenay animals have true names. They have old, pagan spirit names—Goeren-yai names. But you need to speak Lenay, and you need to speak it to them nicely, or they won't tell you their true names." It was utter horse manure, all of it, but the crowd on the patio all stared with a look somewhere between discomfort, amazement and respect. Alythia nearly laughed. Perhaps now, finally, she'd found a way in. A way toward respect. Through a wolf, of all things. A wolf that they were all scared of. Perhaps that was it. Perhaps the only way to gain respect amongst wealthy Petrodorians was through fear.

"Can I pat her?" Tristi asked wistfully. "I've wanted to keep seeing her, but Papa wouldn't let me. I'm sure she'll remember me."

"Did you ever beat her?" Alythia asked doubtfully.

"Oh no, I never did! I was always nice to her, honest!"

"Master Tristi," said a maid, "I really don't think that you should . . ."

"Nonsense!" announced a guard. "The third son of Halmady isn't scared of some stupid wolf! If a girl can do it, so can Master Tristi!"

Alythia turned to look back at the garden. She caught only a brief glimpse of Tashyna, a fast shadow against the far, downhill wall. "Come quickly," she said to Tristi, who came running. Alythia put her hands on the boy's shoulders when he arrived and turned them both downslope. Tashyna seemed far more interested in racing from one side of the lower garden to the other as fast as her legs could take her.

"Look how fast she is!" Tristi exclaimed. "I bet she'd make an excellent guard dog. Maybe we could let her loose in the garden more often. Maybe all night. She'd deal with any sneaking nightwraith!"

"I think that's an excellent idea," said Alythia. In truth, she wasn't sure at all—she knew from her brothers that wolves did not bark, so she wouldn't make much of a guard dog if she couldn't raise the alarm. And she was still so wild, probably even this huge garden would not be enough for her. But anything would be better than that little enclosure against the side wall. "Now just remember, move very slowly and be very careful. She's really very sweet, but she gets scared easily. And scared wolves are dangerous. Understand?"

Tristi nodded. He was nearly nine now and curly-headed like her Gregan. Also like Gregan, he was a bit of a mummy's boy . . . or a daddy's boy, at least. Fancy not visiting the pet wolf just because daddy had forbidden it! It would never have stopped her brothers, not even Wylfred.

Tashyna leapt through some bushes, tongue lolling, now slowing as she loped past the fountain. She looked tired and happy. Tristi stiffened anxiously and Alythia squeezed his shoulders. Tashyna saw him and pricked her ears. She ran about them in a circle, head poised, more curious than alarmed.

"It's all right, Tashyna," said Alythia, forcing confidence into her voice. "Come and say hello to your old friend. He's missed you."

Tashyna stopped circling and trotted closer. Stopped, ducking her head nervously, trying to go sideways. "Oh here, come on!" Alythia crouched beside Tristi, a hand out. "It's all right, it's only me!" It astonished her how easily she could read the wolf's thoughts. Fear battled yearning, self-preservation struggled against risk. She'd seen it in people, in the courts of Baen-Tar Palace. The young noble from the provinces, uncomfortable in his newly bought clothes, sighting a glamorous Lenay princess and torn in two directions—backward, toward safety; and forward, toward opportunity. And she'd seen it in the palace girls upon sighting some particularly handsome arrival. For herself, the instinct had always been forward. She'd never known what it was to retreat, until she'd come to Petrodor. Perhaps it was a common affliction for Lenays in Petrodor, walked they on four legs or two.

Tashyna came close enough for Alythia to pat. "Let her sniff your hand," she told Tristi. Tristi did so, breathlessly, and Tashyna sniffed. And licked, as if remembering a familiar taste. Tristi grinned. "Pat her. Scratch her neck, she likes that."

Tristi did that too, his smaller hand sinking into the wolf's thick fur. Tashyna whined, wriggled on her stomach, then rolled on her back.

"That means she likes you," Alythia laughed, rubbing Tashyna's chest.

"She's very pretty," said Tristi, matter-of-factly. "Sister, would you help me ask Papa to let me see her more often?"

Alythia climbed the stairs with more energy and purpose in her legs than she recalled since her wedding day. Finally, she had a reason to go and see her father-in-law. Only a little thing, to be sure, but perhaps that was best . . .

and, besides, the patachi doted on Tristi. If brave Tristi had befriended the wolf, then surely his father would find some pride in that.

Perhaps Gregan would be in his father's chambers, she thought as she walked the polished boards of the ornate upper hallway. She'd barely seen Gregan for a week. For some of that time, he'd gone to pay respects to the various dukes gathered in their properties neighbouring Petrodor. The short while he'd been home, he'd slept in a separate room and spent his time at great luncheons for Halmady and Steiner allies, or plotting in his father's chambers. Alythia began straightening her hair as she walked . . . and considered the grass stains on the sleeves of her dress. She nearly turned for her room to change, but she dared not lose this opportunity. And besides, soon word would spread that the barbarian daughter-in-law had dangled dear Tristi's head in a wolf's jaws for sport, and she preferred to be the one breaking news of events, instead of always reacting to them. That lesson, she'd learned long ago.

Arriving at the patachi's chambers she made a final adjustment to her hair and necklace, and knocked on the twin wooden doors. There was no reply. No footsteps either. Perhaps he was out . . . but there was typically a commotion when the patachi left the residence and there had been none tonight.

It frustrated her, to have such an opportunity, only to turn back now. She knocked again. Come to think of it, there was usually a guard outside this door. Where was he? Concerned, she opened the door. At the far end, glass doors opened onto a balcony, and a broad desk faced the view. Candles and lamps were lit. How odd that it should be empty. Perhaps the patachi was in his adjoining bedchambers . . . but if he were preparing for an early night, where were the private servants?

She walked forward past the table . . . and saw something odd on the floor beneath the desk. Only when she was nearly at the far windows did she recognise the shape in the shadow cast by the chandelier. It was a body. The body of Patachi Halmady, his face to one side, staring at her. Face down in a spreading pool of blood.

A hand clamped over Alythia's mouth before she could scream, and a knife pricked at her throat. "Not a word!" hissed a voice in her ear. "The signal's been given. It will be over soon!"

The man dragged her backward into the patachi's bedchambers. She was thrown onto the bed, and recovered to find herself staring at a man she recognised as a servant, in black tunic and lace collar, levelling a wicked looking knife. "Make a noise and you're dead," he snarled. He was sweating, and seemed highly agitated. Through her terror, Alythia realised there was a weight on the bed to one side. She looked, and found Lady Halmady, her face pale and expressionless, eyes wide with shocked disbelief. Beneath her, the bedcovers were soaked red. On the floor beyond lay a maid, likewise unmoving.

Another man entered the patachi's chambers, giving a small whistle for recognition. He talked with the first in low, hushed tones, giving quick glances in Alythia's direction. Alythia saw that they had both armed themselves with sword belts—most unservantlike. Assassins.

Suddenly she could hear yells from beyond the balcony. Her heart leapt, hope and fright in equal measure. Someone had discovered the treachery. Any moment there would be armed men battering down the door and she'd be in the middle of the fighting. But, as hard as she listened, she could hear no running footsteps in the hallway. Instead, there came a faint metallic sound then a shriek of pain. The yells and clashes grew louder, seeming to come from all about the house. A battle, Alythia realised. Halmady was betrayed. The entire house was falling.

Alythia lay on the bed, frozen with fear. Only a few times in her life had she been truly frightened for her safety, but those had been nothing compared to this. She could not bring herself to move, barely even to breathe. Her left elbow was wet with Lady Halmady's blood. As much as she'd hated the old lady, she'd *never* wished upon her anything like this. Or if she had, she surely hadn't meant it. Nor imagined it so horribly, gut-wrenchingly awful a sight. Inexplicably, her frantic eyes fixed upon an ornate, golden sword in its sheath above the doorway. She'd seen such swords in her father's chambers in Baen-Tar and knew that, for all their decorative value, they were as sharp as any armoury weapon. But what could she do with a sword, even if she could retrieve it? Against two well-trained, professional murderers?

Footsteps rushed along the hall outside. A hammering at the door to the patachi's chambers. "Patachi! We are attacked! You must get to safety!" Alythia heard the door open, followed by a scream of pain. Then yelling in the chambers and the clashing of weapons. More screams and yells of rage. Through the doorway, Alythia saw a man fall, crash and roll. He struggled to rise, but seemed to register a helpless horror, for the sight of all the blood that poured out of him. Then to panic, tears in his eyes, a young man sobbing at the prospect of his own death, slashed from breast to navel and soaking in blood. Alythia nearly vomited, and then the world went black.

She awoke barely a moment later, for now the screams and howls of combat rang in her ears. Beyond the balcony windows, she could hear fighting in the garden. Vansy and Selyna! The thought of her maids thrust her from the bed and she leapt for the decorative sword above the door. It didn't come down the first time, so she knocked it upward instead, and it clattered to the floor. She picked it up and stared into the chambers beyond. There were bodies on the floor, Halmady soldiers, perhaps five. A bookshelf had collapsed, chairs overturned and the floor awash with blood. Beyond the central table, a struggle continued on the floor with desperate gasps and shouts. There was a final, horrifying scream, then a gurgle, as an arm thrust a knife repeatedly into a body.

A man rose—one of the assassins, his black servant's tunic bloodied and torn, a dripping knife in his hand. He turned, surveyed the carnage, and saw Alythia. Alythia's heart nearly stopped. The man's eyes were wild, yet cold. He saw the sword in her hands and snickered.

"You're not your sister, little Princess," he said. "Put it away. I'll not lose my reward so easily."

"I'm a princess of Lenayin! My father will double any reward you've been offered!" The words were out of her lips before she could think. She was aghast at herself.

Something hit the bedroom window behind from the outside, a shatter of falling glass. "What good is Lenay gold to me?" said the assassin, limping about the end of the table. He held his bloody thigh with one hand. "I live in Petrodor. So do you, *Princess*. The favour of Patachi Steiner will carry me further than your father's ever shall."

Alythia stared at him. Patachi Steiner? They were attacked by *Steiner*? Their great and powerful ally? *Marya!* was her first thought. Her sister would save her. Marya would not see her harmed. But the roar of battle came loud and near from all about the mansion now and she was scared for her maids, and scared for Tashyna, and scared for little Tristi and Elra, and Halmady were so powerful, and there were so many guards, and surely they could not lose this fight in a direct assault . . .

She tore the sheath off the sword and circled the table, about the motionless body of the dying boy. She tried to hold the sword as she'd seen Lenay soldiers hold them, but this was a Torovan sword, thinner and lighter, made more for stabbing than cutting. There was only really room on the hilt for one hand, but she held it with two anyway, having no idea how it was done, otherwise.

The assassin blocked her way to the door. He held only a knife against her sword, yet to get past, she would have to go through him. It was clear from the look on his face that he didn't believe she could do it. Neither did she.

Suddenly there were new footsteps in the hall and a figure appeared in the doorway. The assassin half turned and Alythia saw a lithe man in embroidered tunic and tight leggings surveying the scene with horror, a sword in his hand. Gregan. In an eye blink, the assassin scooped up a fallen blade and threw the knife at Gregan. Gregan ducked aside before Alythia could scream, the knife slashing his sleeve, and charged the assassin. Blades clashed and Gregan half stumbled on a body, struggling to defend himself as he staggered sideways. Before she knew what she was doing, Alythia had charged, her blade upraised. The assassin cut at her and she jumped back just in time. Gregan took that chance to slash, taking the assassin across the forearm. He spun away with a strangled yell and Gregan was on him before he could recover, hacking once, twice, three times before the fourth finally exposed the man's defence and the fifth stabbed him clean through the ribs. The assassin fell into a wall and slid down, leaving a bloody trail behind.

"Papa!" cried Gregan, dashing immediately for the body behind his father's desk. He stared down at it, then spun and ran into the bedchamber as Alythia stood in helpless tears. When Gregan reemerged, he was ashen-faced. He stared at Alythia with haunted eyes.

"I'm so sorry!" Alythia sobbed. "I just came to talk to him about Tristi. Tristi wanted me to ask him if he could spend more time with the wolf, and I found that . . . that man here, and them already . . . already . . ."

Gregan embraced her. He looked her in the eyes and Alythia was surprised at the strength she saw there. And the fury. "He nearly had the better of me," he said, jerking his head toward the dead assassin. "Your attack saved me. Today, I am Patachi Halmady. And you are Lady Halmady." Alythia could only stare through tear-filled eyes. "Come, my love. We shall fight and defend our home."

Petrodor was burning. Errollyn stood on the balcony and watched the flames and smoke rise from across the lower north slope. The house was a nondescript residence, humble for its position, upon the upper stretch of the Corkscrew, hemmed in on either side by crowded neighbours. But the balcony afforded a good view of the great houses of the upper ridge and a figtree ensured some privacy.

The door opened behind, but he knew it was Rhillian well before she spoke. "Word from Family Velo," she said softly. "Mari Velo fished a body from the waters off the Cliff of the Dead this morning. It was Yulia Delin." Errollyn recalled young Yulia from the Riverside raid. Strangely, he could not recall her from the fight itself. Rather, he saw her now in his mind as he'd found her that following day at House Rochel, curled in a chair, reading a book. His hands tightened on the railing. Rhillian stood against his side, a gentle warmth. "I'm sure they won't harm Sasha. I've not heard from Kessligh whether he's received a ransom demand or not. He's not talking to me."

Errollyn gazed into the night. He felt no presence at his side, beyond the immediate warmth. Only emptiness. Such was the world of the *du'janah*. He did not feel it. He could not. Rhillian could not understand. Only Sasha could. He wanted her back so badly it hurt.

"Halmady's allies burn," he said. "I count six fires. You've done your work well."

"The northern stack turns on itself," said Rhillian. "The predominant alliance of Petrodor is weakened. We are safer now."

"No," said Errollyn grimly. "They consolidate, that is all. The loss of six houses will weaken the Steiner alliance only a little. All you've done is give them an excuse to eliminate their internal divisions. They will rise from this stronger than before."

"This is not all my doing." Rhillian's emerald eyes were cool as she gazed out at the fires. "The divisions were real. Do not blame me because Sasha took a risk. I love her like a sister, but in truth, she is reckless. Probably her capture had something to do with this assault. But I can't be responsible for Sasha's wild urges, Errollyn."

"This isn't about Sasha. It's about you not seeing what you've done." Rhillian folded her arms and leant against the balcony railing. With her eyes, she challenged him to explain himself, as she'd done so many times before. "The Princess Alythia. What happens to her?"

Rhillian shrugged. "Events will tell. More importantly, the Steiner alliance shall be weakened from within and take many casualties."

"No, *not* more importantly," said Errollyn, frustrated. "She is royalty, Rhillian. Only Lenay royalty, but even that counts for something in Petrodor, however little the families like to admit it. Steiner already have Princess Marya, and Steiner's heirs have Lenay blood. Steiner has forged an alliance with Lenayin for at least three generations, and likely well beyond. Lenayin is the greatest fighting force of Rhodia, save for the Saalshen Bacosh. I've fought in Lenayin, and I've seen it. Warrior for warrior they are formidable, and if Lenay kings ever manage to bring the provinces to heel, they will grow more powerful yet.

"Rhillian, it's not just the serrinim who have miscalculated. King Torvaal miscalculated in wedding Princess Alythia to House Halmady. One daughter married to the powers of Petrodor did not seem sufficient, as power in Petrodor is spread so wide. He judged that wedding Alythia to Halmady, the second most powerful of the Steiner alliance, would strengthen those bonds further. Instead, he created a rivalry."

"There are rivalries everywhere in Petrodor. Everyone assumed Halmady and Steiner were friends . . . what surprise that it turns out otherwise?"

"No." Errollyn shook his head firmly. "Alliance to Lenayin could be the single most significant possession any great house of Petrodor holds. Alliance to Lenayin grants power with the priesthood, who are in search of an army, you may have noticed. And lately, priests have been disappearing. Primarily those from Halmady-allied families."

"The thought had crossed my mind," Rhillian admitted.

"We've been looking the wrong way," Errollyn insisted. "This is not just another Petrodor power game, this is about Lenayin. Rhillian, we cannot allow Steiner to have possession of *both* Lenay princesses. Surely Steiner will take Alythia alive, and probably then find some way to wed her to one of their own . . ."

"That would run against all the Verenthane traditions of marriage," said Rhillian, frowning.

"Who cares? They don't, not when there is this much power in the wind . . ."

He was interrupted by noise from within the house. He pushed through the door, Rhillian following, and found Aisha leaning against the fireplace, gasping for breath and covered in sweat. A woman of the local family who owned the house poured her a cup of water from a jug. Aisha drank thirstily.

"Halmady Mansion's gone," she said, as her breathing recovered. "The fighting ends. They have not put the house to fire. I think they mean to keep it."

Errollyn pictured what he knew of Halmady Mansion's layout. He added the length of time since the fighting had started, and the time it must have taken Aisha to run here with the news . . . "That was fast," he concluded. "Well planned."

"It's not as though they don't know Halmady's defences," Rhillian reasoned. "Friends are easier to spy on than enemies."

"There were Danor soldiers involved," Aisha added, wiping blonde hair from her forehead. "And Vedichi. Adele reports seeing Coroman soldiers involved further down the slope against Family Ragini, but I did not see those myself."

"How many would you estimate?" asked Rhillian.

"Oh . . . I think there's at least four hundred provincial soldiers in the city tonight," said Aisha. "They play their hand early."

"They are confident," said Errollyn. "They do not fear Maerler, nor us."

"Or desperate," Aisha cautioned. "Halmady has many friends. Six houses were struck, the bulk of the force against Halmady Mansion, but the total force looks to me perhaps two thousand or more. That is no small commitment."

"Petrodor politics are the art of using the small threat to imply the large," Rhillian agreed. "There's no need to kill ten men when you can kill one and frighten the other nine into doing what you want. No one wants to show the other how big their knife truly is because nine-tenths of the fear is the uncertainty. Now Patachi Steiner has been forced to pull his knife and show all Petrodor just how big it is."

"It's big enough," Errollyn muttered. "I'd have thought Halmady could hold out twice as long."

"But Danor and Vedichi have declared their allegiance to Steiner for all to see," Rhillian countered. "Perhaps Coroman too. Things become clearer. Only three provinces have declared for Steiner. It's not enough. And now the others see how Steiner treats its so-called allies."

"It won't shock them," Errollyn said firmly, shaking his head. "This is their world. Aisha, did you see anything to tell the fates of Patachi Halmady or Princess Alythia?"

Aisha shook her head. "No . . . we've no spies in Halmady, sadly. Or fortunately, perhaps, given this. I know that Halmady had plans to save the patachi in case of an attack, but most families have those, and secret passages or compartments for the family to hide or escape in. I'd guess that Steiner would want Halmady dead—a former best friend alive would pose too many discomforting questions. My guess is that Steiner had some assassins on Halmady's staff and used them before the family could escape. There's always some men of low station in Petrodor desperate enough to take such risks for huge rewards.

"There were some carts moving along the Sawback Road, though. Likely to transport any important prisoners."

"They'll move Alythia out that way, if she's still alive," said Errollyn. "I have to go."

"And rescue her?" said Rhillian incredulously as Errollyn picked up his bow. "Such prisoners will be heavily guarded, we cannot spare any *talmaad* for such a deed . . ."

"No, these days we can't spare the *talmaad* for anything useful at all," Errollyn muttered.

"There are two thousand Steiner soldiers loose in the city and you think we have nothing to defend?" Rhillian retorted.

"If Patachi Steiner gains a second Lenay princess, he will at the very least gain extra bargaining power with King Torvaal," said Errollyn. "How can you just allow—"

"No," said Rhillian firmly. "The issue is Petrodor. The Maerler alliance has at least ten thousand men under arms within the city alone. This two thousand of Steiner's is nothing, even with three provincial dukes taking Steiner's side. The other dukes are not committed—Pazira, Flewderin and Cisseren are openly hostile to Steiner, Songel is little better. If we keep them all divided, there will be no Torovan army marching south next spring.

"Patachi Steiner can make whatever alliance he wishes with Lenayin, he can ransom back King Torvaal's daughter, he can marry her to one of his other allies, send her to a holy convent to consolidate relations with the priesthood, whatever he chooses. It will all make no difference if Patachi Steiner commands nothing more than merchants and coins. Armies make leaders, Errollyn. If Patachi Steiner has no army of Torovan to command, then he's nothing more than a moneylender for this cause. This action will shake Steiner's base of power to its core, it will increase suspicion, kill many of their men, and make all Steiner allies consider their position. No one will follow this man, Errollyn. If we deny him that, then we stop the army of Torovan from ever forming. Without the army of Torovan, the Saalshen Bacosh is safe."

"And if the pendulum swings so far the other way that Patachi Maerler takes power instead?" Errollyn asked, stringing his bow with a powerful heave on the string, fitting the loop over the notch as the wood creaked and groaned. "Friendly Patachi Maerler with his ten thousand men under arms?"

Rhillian sighed and went to the table to pour Aisha another cup of water. "Errollyn, where are you going? You're needed here . . . what if Steiner's men attack this house? Our other properties?"

"If you're smart, you'll run away." When Errollyn plucked the fitted bowstring it made a deep, satisfying thrum. "Aisha, a second pair of eyes would be useful."

"I forbid it," said Rhillian, handing Aisha the cup. "Either of you. We are in danger, the *talmaad* cannot split in the face of it."

"This is stupid," said Errollyn fiercely. "I've listened to your horseshit for weeks. You've set half the city on fire, you've set forces in motion you have no idea how to control, and now the only decent advice you're receiving, you're determined to ignore. I'm tired of it. I'm leaving." Rhillian blinked. Errollyn had spoken that last in Lenay—as Sasha always said, the swear words were far superior to anything in any Saalsi dialect. "Aisha?"

Aisha looked at Rhillian for a long moment, then at Errollyn, then back again. "I'm . . . I'm sorry, Errollyn. I can't."

"Errollyn," Rhillian tried again, "I understand you're upset about Sasha . . ."

Errollyn nearly laughed at her, humourlessly. "If the sane are irrational, then the irrational must be sane?"

Rhillian's expression hardened. "I give you an order, Errollyn. I make a habit of it."

"And I've made a habit of submitting," said Errollyn bluntly. "No longer."

Rhillian just stared at him. As did Aisha. *Vel'ennar.* The one truth. Beyond a certain point, serrin simply could *not* disagree. The one truth united them. The eternal presence. The light in the dark. It was each other. It was all serrin, their common beliefs and lives, aspirations and dreams. All serrin shared it. Except the *du'janah.*

"Errollyn," Rhillian protested, almost plaintively. "You can't just leave!"

Now Errollyn did laugh in helpless exasperation. "I can't? Watch me." He walked to the stairs across the rickety floorboards.

Rhillian caught his arm halfway there. "Don't you care about us?" There was temper in her voice now, a fire in her emerald eyes. "Doesn't it matter to you if this place is attacked? If innocent residents are killed?"

"You." Errollyn jabbed a finger in Rhillian's chest. "You understand nothing. You accuse humans of prejudice, yet in the years you've known me, you've never once understood what it feels like to *be* me."

"You're playing the victim, Errollyn," Rhillian said warningly, "it doesn't become you."

He could have hit her. He stepped back with a deep breath, snatching his free hand back lest it betray him. "You know what? Fuck you. Fuck all of you." He spoke in Lenay and the strength of his anger scared him. He backed up, wanting only to escape.

Rhillian shook her head. She seemed at a loss. "You've almost become human," she said in Saalsi.

Errollyn felt something snap. "Don't you dare use that like an insult!" he shouted at her, still in Lenay. "You fucking bigot! I don't feel what you feel, Rhillian! I don't feel what most serrin feel! You're supposed to be big enough to accept that, of *course* you are, you are the serrinim! The great and godly, the intellectual, the sophisticated who accept all truths because it is your nature . . . well how sophisticated is this, you can't even understand a single *du'janah!*"

"I cannot confront this," Rhillian sighed. "You are emotional, you complain like a child . . . I don't know what to do with you, Errollyn."

"I know. I know you don't. You never did. From the moment I arrived in this city, I've been alone." He used Saalsi now. The word meant far more than just *solitary,* in that tongue.

"That is unfair," Rhillian said firmly.

"Yet you have no idea why I'm leaving, do you?" He walked back to her and stood, confronting her face to face. A little taller than she, and considerably broader. "You accuse me of not caring? Don't you realise that it is a curse to be born like this? Don't you understand that I would love to feel what you feel? To wake every morning and know that I belong? You misunderstood me from the first, Rhillian. You attribute false motivations to my actions, and false thoughts to my words. And now you wonder why I distrust your judgment of humans?

"I will tell you this one piece of wisdom, Rhillian, and listen closely, for it may save many serrin lives. Serrin are only good at understanding serrin. The *vel'ennar* binds us to each other, yet in doing so, it blinds us. Or at least, it blinds *you*. Humans cannot feel *vel'ennar*. I cannot. I could not describe it to you if you asked. And yet you presume to comprehend human feelings as though they were your own."

"Errollyn," said Rhillian, choosing her words carefully. "I'm sorry that you feel left out. I have always valued your insight, as I value the insight of many of my *talmaad*. We each have unique skills, and I would utilise them all. But I cannot be riven by such self-doubt, Errollyn. My judgment tells me our course is sure. I can do no better than listen to my better judgment. The eternity equipped me with nothing more.

"Now, you profess to understand human concepts better than I. It's possible, I admit. So understand this concept. I order you to stay at this post. Lacking perception of *vel'ennar* is no excuse for disobeying orders. Humans don't. Humans obey discipline. It is their greatest advantage over us. Now we must do the same."

"Humans obey discipline in their various parts," Errollyn agreed, unflinching. "But they have variety, Rhillian. They all fight each other. It's a tragedy, yes, but not a weakness. They have many views and many values. But now, you ask all serrin to follow just one. Yours."

"Not mine," said Rhillian, with temper. "I listen. My opinion is informed by others. We are collective, Errollyn. We stand together."

"And are condemned by it. We need division, Rhillian. It may save us. I'm sorry."

Rhillian's stare was unwavering. "If you leave now," she said, "don't come back. You won't be welcome."

"I've never *been* welcome." Errollyn turned and strode for the stairs. Behind him, he heard Aisha's upset, disappointed exclamation . . . at Rhillian, it seemed. Footsteps followed him down the stairs.

"Errollyn, stop." Aisha was fast, and caught his arm. "Errollyn, she doesn't mean it. Forgive her."

"This isn't a question of forgiving. It is a question of symmetry. Rhillian's is not mine."

"Errollyn, it's just . . . you baffle her sometimes." Aisha's look pleaded understanding. "No serrin acts as you do."

"And instead of tolerating my difference, she fears it. Aisha." He put a hand on her shoulder. "You are half human. Do *you* find me so strange?"

"No."

Errollyn smiled at her. "You're human enough to lie, but serrin enough to be awful at it."

"Errollyn, she has a great responsibility. No serrin has carried such responsibility before. The threat we face is vast. The old ways of serrin will no longer serve. She seeks the new. I do not envy her in that, Errollyn. She needs our support, not our criticism."

"Even if the only support I have to offer is a lie, and the only truth I see is criticism?" Aisha sighed and hung her head. "You think just like her. You think I do this just to be difficult. I don't. I do it because it's what I am."

"What we are, Errollyn, is of the serrinim." Aisha's voice was firm. As though her feet were finally steady upon the only solid ground she'd yet found in the whole argument. "I am half human, yet even I am drawn to it. That is what we were meant for. I believe that more strongly than I believe in anything."

"I know you do," Errollyn said softly. "And that is why there is no longer any place for me within the serrinim." He kissed his friend gently on the forehead and continued down the stairs.

"Errollyn," Aisha said plaintively from behind, "you *are* the serrinim! Whether you feel it or not, that's what you are!"

Errollyn did not stop his descent. Nor did he look back.

The night was alive with danger. Errollyn could smell it on the wind as he moved, a dark shadow through the alleys, paralleling the upper ridgeline as close as safety allowed. He paused often, and listened to the distant crackle of flames and the ringing of bells. Carts clattered up cobbled roads—wealthy folk on the move, protected by many guards, eyeing the shadows with weapons at the ready.

Once, he heard an approaching whisper of footsteps, and whistled warning in the darkness. The answering whistle revealed Nasi-Keth, three of them, well-armed and moving in the opposite direction. The passing was friendly, but neither party revealed their destination. When they were gone, Errollyn wondered which of the three Nasi-Keth factions they belonged to— conservative Alaine, serrin-friendly Gerrold, or progressive Kessligh.

As he moved between crumbling walls, scanning the ground for trip-wires, he considered the situation. It appeared that Steiner had sent carts to Halmady Mansion to transport prisoners. Normally, the route between Steiner Mansion and Halmady Mansion was simple—a short distance along the Sawback Road with mostly grand mansions on either side. But on nights like tonight there came a complication—Family Ganaron. Family Ganaron was a Maerler ally, surrounded by a cluster of Steiner-friendly mansions on Sawback Road, midway between the Steiner and Halmady residences. Most northern families were Steiner, and most southern families were Maerler, but not all. To have a position so near to the enemy's heart was valuable. Steiner would not risk transporting valuable prisoners past Ganaron Mansion. So which route would they take?

Errollyn took a downhill path, descending a steep, winding stairway then dashing across a narrow road and advancing up one side, pressing close to the walls. He ducked into another lane until he reached one of the giant fig trees that loved the sandstone incline. He climbed up its gnarled, twisting trunk until he could see the uphill stretch of the Slipway, one of north Petrodor's two best roads, winding up to the ridge from the docks far below.

He could see the looming rooftop of Halmady Mansion on the distant ridge. There were no flames, unlike those on Halmady's allies downslope. Those houses were disposable, he supposed. Halmady Mansion was too grand to burn.

He waited a long time, but saw no traffic. He heard the clatter of horse and cart here and there, but no one dared the Slipway. The waiting did not bother him. He'd waited for long periods before, hunting in the wilds of the Telesil foothills in Saalshen.

A clatter of hooves and wheels broke the stillness. Finally, horses came into view, and a cart driver, pulling hard on the reins to slow the animals where the Slipway turned steep and treacherous. It was an open cart, Errollyn saw, filled with armed soldiers. In the light of the half moon, he saw blue and white—Family Steiner. The next cart was also open and full of armed men. Then passed three covered carts. Then two more guard carts. He waited a moment longer, knowing it would be slow going around the switchback elbow where a hundred years of wagonloads to and from the docks had smoothed the cobbles slippery. Horses hated it.

If Princess Alythia was alive, she could be in one of those carts . . . but which? Or perhaps there would be a second convoy. A decoy, in case of ambush. But which would be the decoy? Was it possible that . . .

A dark shape on the road caught his eye. Small and fleet, hugging the shadows in the wake of the carts. On four legs, not two. A dog, maybe . . .

but it was a strange looking dog, for certain. Errollyn strained his eyes. The dog paused against a wall, ducking this way and that. Errollyn had seen such behaviour many times before. It was scared, yet felt compelled to press on. It sniffed the air, seeking a familiar scent. Clearly it was following the carts. And this was no dog. It was a wolf.

Errollyn nearly smiled. A wolf, in Petrodor? Following some carts? Well, the merchant trade loved exotic animals and the families were known to keep exotic pets. There were plenty of wolves in nearby Lenayin. So Halmady had a Lenay princess, and a Lenay wolf . . . could it be that simple? No, surely not . . . Sasha had told him all about her sister Alythia. She ran squealing from *bats*. But this was just too, too odd. Odd things often required odd explanations. Perhaps he and the wolf were seeking the same thing.

He was climbing from the tree when he heard men yelling, and the clash of weapons. He leapt, bow in hand, and darted along the alley. Horses shrieked, and there came the crash of a cart overturning. An ambush. The ambushers would have blocked the downslope—upslope was the place to be. At the next junction, Errollyn turned left, taking some uneven steps three at a time.

Finally he came clear onto a stretch of the Slipway, perhaps sixty paces upslope of the elbow corner. The corner was in chaos, carts banked up, several turned half-around, but the Slipway was not quite wide enough for such a manoeuvre, and now they were stuck. Men fought, and random fires lit the scene, casting crazy shadows on neighbouring walls. Steiner soldiers appeared to have formed a perimeter about the last of the covered carts and were fighting hard to maintain it, while prisoners were unloaded.

Directly before Errollyn's position, crouched low against the flanking walls, were a pair of Nasi-Keth archers. Neither was firing. Probably they feared hitting prisoners, or their own men. Uphill, with a walled street before them, they had the Steiners trapped . . . unless heavily armed Steiner soldiers managed to fight their way free, of course. At such close quarters, shoulder to shoulder, it was certainly possible.

Errollyn whistled at the archers . . . both spun with alarm. He approached in a crouch against a wall, and the men relaxed to see that he was serrin. "We must move now," he observed grimly. "If their perimeter holds, they'll break into neighbouring houses, from there it's a maze through the city, and they may escape."

"There's no clear shot," the nearest archer disagreed, tersely. "What's a serrin doing here?"

"Helping. Just hit what you can, don't take any risks." With that he stood up, nocked an arrow, and loosed.

A Steiner soldier struggling with the horses fell, shot through the side. Errollyn walked forward as he reloaded, eyeing the cover of a doorway just ahead. His next shot killed a man guarding the rear, and pandemonium spread through the rear contingent, men yelling alarm, fingers pointing uphill. Errollyn reloaded, and saw several crossbows being brought to bear from the back of the rear cart. He pressed himself into the covering doorway, bolts whizzed past, and one cracked off the wall. He drew left-handed this time, to keep his right shoulder pressed to the doorway, and put an arrow through a crossbowman's throat.

One of the Nasi-Keth archers behind him loosed an arrow at a flanking target, and missed, but the most exposed men were now scattering, or pressing themselves low, or hiding behind carts or trapped, thrashing horses. Several were pounding on adjoining doorways with the hilts of their swords, desperate for escape. Unluckily for them, doors in Petrodor were secured against the night with very heavy locks.

Something dark and burning at one end fell from an overlooking rooftop onto the last guard cart and burst into flame. Men ran and rolled aside, one burning. The cart's horses went crazy, smashed into a wall at an angle, and wedged themselves as the burning cart half tipped, one wheel climbing a wall. Errollyn had more targets, yet refrained. He'd killed enough these past weeks. Beyond the flames, dark shapes leapt, swords flashing orange in the firelight.

Suddenly there was a woman running free, her skirts smouldering, arms bound awkwardly at the back. A big Steiner man pursued, sword in hand. Errollyn drew fast, but the running woman blocked his sight—she was not a good runner either, slipper-shod feet sliding on the cobbles, she could fall straight into his line of fire at any moment. He stepped clear of the doorway, risking crossbow fire for a better angle . . . and blinked as a dark shape rushed past his legs and tore downhill at tremendous speed, trailing a leash.

The wolf shot past the running woman and leapt at her pursuer, who fended with a yell, losing his balance. His sword swing was wild, the wolf dancing clear then leaping at him again. An arrow fizzed past Errollyn's ear and struck the soldier in the shoulder. He fell, as the woman also fell, slipping and exhausted, to the cobbles.

Errollyn ran to her, an arrow ready, searching the firelit confusion behind . . . but the Nasi-Keth were breaking through now and the last Steiner soldiers were either surrendering or dying. He arrived at the woman's side as she struggled to sit. Her pursuer screamed and yelled, having lost his weapon in his fall, a shaft protruding from his shoulder while he tried vainly to beat off the leaping, snarling wolf that savaged his legs and arms.

Errollyn took a knife to the woman's bonds and her arms came free. She had long, dark hair that had once been lustrous, and large, beautiful dark eyes. Now, the hair hung in matted tangles, and her lovely face was swollen about the left cheek and eye. Lips that had once been full and unblemished now bore a cut, and dried blood streaked from one nostril. Despite her exhaustion, she did not seem especially horrified. Instead, she stared at the screaming man barely five paces away and watched the wolf grabbing his leg, shaking him like a toy. She seemed mesmerised.

"Is that your wolf?" Errollyn asked.

"She's her own wolf," said the once-beautiful woman in a hoarse, emotionless voice. "But she's my friend."

"Don't you think you'd better call her off?"

The woman gazed up at him. Screams filled the air, loud and panicked, but the lovely dark eyes registered no alarm. "Why?" she asked.

Thirteen

SASHA STOOD IN THE MIDDLE OF HER CELL and closed her eyes. Outside the slit window was a pale blue dawn. She could hear the distant swell of the ocean, rising and rushing against the rocks at the base of the promontory cliff. A gull muttered and cawed. She raised her arms and began a slow taka-dan with an invisible sword.

Balance. Symmetry. Serrin thoughts, both. Serrin obsessed about them, and humans wondered why. With feet in primary stance, the arms were limited in range of motion. Change the feet, and the arms changed, motion with motion, stance with stance, balance with balance. Power flowed in lines through the body. The power of balance, the power of symmetry. Universal powers. One did not impose them upon the universe. The universe imposed them upon her. If she flowed with them, she would harness their power. And no mere weight of muscle, nor strength of arm, nor thickness of armour, could stop her.

It seemed so clear, this morning. Perhaps this was what isolation did. Kessligh insisted so. This was what he sought when he meditated. Stillness. Her bruises ached, and she had not slept well, but somehow, the tiredness seemed to help for she could not think straight at all. Thoughts cluttered the head. The best svaalverd, Kessligh always said, was reflex. The conscious mind could be your enemy. Train it. Do not be a slave to it. Make it serve you.

The patterns of svaalverd were so beautiful, sometimes they took her breath away. Like one of Aldano's sculptures, but in constant, shifting motion. Sofy had asked her once what she saw in such a sweaty, macho activity. Sofy, who loved her arts above all other pleasures . . . and who, reluctantly, had begun to see the error of her ways.

A hard cross met an upward-slashing counter—a shift of the left foot back would create room for a downcut, the left foot to the side would lead to a low-quarter slash, the left foot forward would bring her inside the attacker's reverse and kill him. Little motions of the foot, barely half a paving stone between all three, and the possibilities altered radically. Each possibility branched out into many extra possibilities, and all of those had many branches too. Be careful which way you go. Know your centre. Never abandon it, or you'll get lost.

Angles intersected, and the better angle won. Shapes and patterns. All the universe was shapes and patterns, making forces and counterforces. Even people. Krystoff pressed hard, and died. Force and counterforce. Sofy did not press hard enough, and so others shaped her future. Insufficient force, a weak stance. Sasha needed to find a middle. Kessligh tried, and pleased no one—a step too far back, poor range, poor contact with the opponent's blade.

Find your centre. Stand on it. Make them come to you. Step into the swing. Use their power against them. Let them dash themselves against the rocks, explosions of white spray against the cliff.

Sasha blinked, realising that she'd abruptly found a connection between two unassociated moves. Her hands replayed the thought, her body shifting in time. Threads slipped into place, a beautiful sensation that made her smile, whatever her recent pains. Symmetry, the likeness between things one had previously assumed unconnected. The footwork was dissimilar, but the transition, and the philosophy of attack, were identical. That move would now kill, whereas before, it had merely defended. And so she grew a little wiser this still morning. A little deadlier. If only she were free.

The day passed slowly. Sasha ate bread and soup, paced her cell, stretched and performed taka-dans. She had always been bad at doing nothing, and soon enough, she was climbing the walls—literally. First she manoeuvred her bed once more to look out the window, and discovered that no matter how she angled herself, she saw nothing but sea and cloudless blue sky. The cell became hot, which was fine for her legs, but the dress sleeves and shoulders clung tight to her arms. Surely Petrodor seamstresses made few dresses for girls built like her.

She entertained herself for a while by tearing the sleeves off with her bare hands, after stripping bare to her waist. The sound of ripping cloth brought looks from the guards outside her door, who pulled the plate aside to see . . . and closed it just as fast, when confronted by the sight of a topless woman. But the door remained closed. Sasha wondered where the temple drew its guards from. Holy-minded Petrodor youth who for some reason could not become priests? Or just random, hired thugs? More likely the former, she decided. Surely the latter might have at least favoured her with a lewd remark or two by now. Or worse.

Her back hurt where she'd been kicked, and her bruised jaw made eating difficult. Her left ear seemed to ring a little, like a perfect bell that had been struck hard some time ago. She hoped that would not be permanent. By early afternoon, she was down to reciting a Tullamayne verse out loud, straining her memory to recall the blood-rousing third and fourth acts. With that accomplished to the best of her ability, she began translating it into Saalsi. Which proved actually quite interesting, and very challenging. "And by his fiery eye he did see, a vision beheld in glory gold . . ."

Glory? No such Saalsi term. "A vision beheld" . . . one *beheld* an abstract concept like glory? In Saalsi, it could be said in the literal, the figurative, the active and inactive, or if one were very clever, the dryly ironic or the highly suggestive. Choose the wrong one and serrin listeners would get the wrong idea entirely. But none of them really fit. How did one translate between the glorious passion of Tullamayne and civilised, sophisticated serrinim? Serrin, of course, did not bother trying—if they wished to understand such writings, they'd learn the entire language and read it in the original. But did that mean they truly understood it better that way? Errollyn didn't think so.

That over, and more exercises done, she was mentally and physically exhausted, and it was still only midafternoon. Any more of this, and she would scream. Evening brought dinner—a bowl of half-decent stew—and the relief of cool air. And a priest, after she had eaten, who threw her a robe and told her it was time for a bath.

He led her down the stairs and into the archbishop's chambers, which were empty and lit with candles They continued into a vast hallway with a vaulted ceiling and grand tapestries and paintings. Sasha could not help but look up as she walked—she'd never imagined to see the inside of the Porsada Temple. Not as a Nasi-Keth, and certainly not as a woman. The huge hallway was eerily quiet, save for the footsteps of their four guards. Had they emptied the hall lest anyone spy a woman in the temple? Or was it always this quiet?

Outside Sasha had only a moment to observe the spectacular night lights of Petrodor stretching far out around the harbour, before she was led down some stairs cut into the side of the cliff. The stairway was lit with lamps, steps smoothly hewn with the sharp-edged precision that seemed natural to sandstone. To the right and below, she could hear the ocean swell heaving. Only now did she realise exactly where she would be taking a bath. Probably the priesthood were scandalised enough at a woman in residence at the temple—the idea of her stripping off and bathing there was too much to contemplate. She was struck by a sudden image, as they descended, of a small army of priests hand-scrubbing the stones of the cell in her absence until their knuckles bled. She nearly laughed. Just as well for them it was not yet her time of the month.

After a long, switch-back descent, they reached a small cave, within which was a landing. Lamps lit the rocky ceiling to ghostly effect, as the swell roared in and climbed the landing's broad steps, and cast an ankle-depth of water across the flat flagstones.

"I'm bathing in there?" Sasha asked, as they paused on a ledge several steps above the awash flagstones. "That's salt water, I'll need a bath after my bath."

"Salt water will do fine," said the priest. His voice was thin and reedy within his hood, and she had yet to see his face. "There will be fresh water to wash your hair later, and soap. In case you are thinking of swimming to escape, there are permanent posts for holy guards just beyond the cave, one on the rocks to either side of the cave. They use crossbows extremely well. Should you miraculously be only wounded, and not killed outright, the swell is large tonight, as you can see. It should surely dash a wounded swimmer against the rocks."

And many healthy ones, Sasha thought, watching the next surge come roaring through the cave, and rush up the barnacle-covered steps. What an amazing place. The ocean had mesmerised her ever since she'd first laid eyes upon it two months ago. It was strange, and fearsome, but she was Goeren-yai, and loved all things wild and beautiful. Surely there were ancient spirits here, deep in the depths.

The guards retreated from the cave, and the priest followed. They had not bound her arms, perhaps considering (correctly) that she was not as formidable as a man barehanded, and that her recent bruises would slow her even further. And there were four of them, all big, and armoured with shields. Even she wasn't quite that stupid.

Sasha pulled off her dress and underwear, and stepped onto the slippery flagstones. The water was cold on her feet, but in Lenayin, she'd swum in water far colder than this. The swell surges were not so strong on the far side of the cave, she saw, and splashed her way across the landing, observing the wooden posts driven into rock where small boats, on calmer seas, would tie up to allow passengers to disembark for the temple. And she wondered how many visitors the priesthood received, in the dead of night, direct from ships from foreign lands.

Bathing was a challenge, and several times she had to jump up the steps to avoid a pummelling swell. But, in between surges, the water stayed calm enough for her to get thoroughly wet. The chill seemed to help her bruises and she emerged feeling refreshed. Certainly, she thought as she splashed her way back to her clothes, it was much nicer down here than in her cell. Perhaps they'd let her stay a while longer. The waves made such an amazing, echoing roar as they came in, and the patterns of lantern light reflecting off the water, and dancing across the ceiling, were truly beautiful.

She was drying herself with the robe she'd been given when she sensed movement from the corner of her eye and spun. It was the priest. Sasha stared at him, warily, and continued drying herself. Her nudity was a weapon against men such as these. Damned if she'd try and hide it.

"I'm not dressed yet," she stated the obvious. "Come down to observe your holy vows?"

"I've got something for you," said the priest, and reached inside his robe.

Oh great, I bet you do, Sasha thought with exasperation. Another horny priest, as in all the Goeren-yai jokes. Well, she might struggle bare-handed against four holy guards, but she was pretty sure she could handle this scrawny little idiot.

When he pulled out her sword in its scabbard instead, she was completely astonished.

"You can have it," he continued, his face still hidden within the hood, "but you have to swear something first."

Sasha stared at him. And realised that some clothes might actually be good, right about now. She pulled on the robe and tied the sash at the waist. "I'm not swearing anything. Who the hells are you?"

The priest pulled back his hood, and revealed the face of a small man, bald and bearded, with lively eyes now earnest and . . . anxious. The face of a man who was up to something. "My name's not important. What I'll do for you is very important. I'm going to help you escape. All you have to do is listen."

Sasha nodded warily. Escape was good. Just keep him talking. "I'm listening."

"My brothers are being murdered," the small priest said. "The archbishop has taken sides—and his chosen side is that of Family Steiner. He is behind the murder of my brothers, I am sure of it. I expect I shall be the next victim, or close to it, so it's very important that you listen very closely.

"Something very big is coming. The archbishop and Patachi Steiner have made plans, I'm certain of it. Halmady were a threat, and I'm not entirely sure why—maybe they really *were* plotting against Family Steiner, it's possible, but I simply don't know. Now Halmady have been eliminated, and—"

"Eliminated! When?"

"Last night. Eight families in all, most of their patachis are dead, and the Dukes of Danor, Coroman and Vedichi lent soldiers to the fight. The Steiner alliance has purged their ranks, and something far bigger looms. I do not know what to do. Fear lurks the temple halls, and the Holy Guard are supposed to provide protection, but there are rumours that some are bought men. Family Maerler would challenge Steiner on these murders, but a threat to the archbishop would give Steiner all the excuse they need to eliminate

Maerler, and many of the dukes may join them, in the name of defending the archbishop."

"And Steiner's alliance is the northern stack," Sasha half murmured, aghast. The little priest frowned at her. "They're closer, Father. They can blockade the temple if need be. Or capture it. Maerler can do neither from the south."

The priest nodded impatiently. "Yes, yes. I fear that the archbishop merely ploughs the field for decisions to come, decisions that require holy blessing. The other fathers can be troublesome, they have a voice in the council and they are drawn from all the families . . . it has always been a balance before, but now the balance is tilting. Do you understand?"

"You . . . you think that Patachi Steiner will strike at Maerler for good, with the archbishop's blessing?"

The priest shrugged hurriedly. "Perhaps. I cannot speculate, I am a man of the gods, not of politics. All I know is that the archbishop has violated his holy vows and approved the murder of those who should be most beloved to him. He is no longer an agent of good, but an agent of evil. I cannot allow him to succeed. Should I do so, I could never face my gods again."

"And how will my escape aid you?"

"It will unbind the hands of Kessligh Cronenverdt, whom the archbishop fears. And something else that shall become clear later. How well do you swim?"

Sasha frowned. "Well enough for a Lenay. Where am I swimming?"

"Out there." The priest pointed out beyond the mouth of the cave. "I have arranged with loyal men to have a small boat waiting, beyond the light. If you can reach it, they will take you to Dockside."

"What . . . tonight?"

The priest nodded. "Now. This very moment."

"And the crossbowmen?"

"The far emplacement is only for show, it's rarely ever manned. Tonight it is not. I have just visited the men of the near emplacement, and they now sleep." He held up a hand, displaying a familiar-looking ring. On its inside protruded a slim needle, just like the one Marya had used. "But you must go now, or they will be discovered."

"They'll be discovered anyhow!" Sasha exclaimed. "Or they'll tell what happened to them . . . unless you . . . ?"

"No." The priest shook his head and gave a little, helpless smile. "My vows do not allow murder, and the gods despise a hypocrite. They will catch me, and I will probably die. Such is life."

"You could come with me," Sasha suggested.

The smile grew a little broader. "I can't swim. It was not meant to be. Here, take this as well." He reached into a pocket within his robes and withdrew a leather pouch. "You will need both hands, so fasten this about your neck. It has a clasp, make it tight, for the sake of all the holy spirits do not drop it."

"What's in it?" Sasha asked dubiously, taking the pouch.

"There's no time. Don't unwrap it, I packed it tight. Just be certain you tell Kessligh Cronenverdt what I've told you, and give that to him. The rest will explain itself. Now you must go. The guards wait further up the stairs, they will grow suspicious."

Sasha fastened the pouch about her neck as suggested and took her sword from him and tied the leather bandoleer together where it should clip to her belt . . . which she now lacked. Slipped the bandoleer over her shoulder. And paused on the step down to the landing, looking back at the small priest.

"Look," she attempted, "if the boat's just out there, you could make it. You just stroke and kick, like this . . ." she demonstrated.

The priest smiled more broadly. "It is not my fate, Sashandra Lenayin. May the gods look upon you."

"I'm Goeren-yai," Sasha objected.

"The gods are generous."

Sasha nodded and descended the steps. "Thank you," she said. And splashed across the landing to the barnacled steps. A swell crashed on the lower steps and rushed on, water spraying about her shins. Staring out into the dark beyond the cave, she was struck by sudden, frightening doubt. Perhaps it was a trick. Perhaps they needed to dispose of her in some manner that did not look like cold-blooded murder. Here she was, making an escape attempt with a stolen object of some description, only to be shot by vigilant archers. She stared up at the small priest suspiciously.

"Have faith, Sashandra Lenayin," he said. "And know this—if you do *not* escape now, you shall be disposed of eventually. You have been a troublemaker all your life, I know. In Petrodor, the powerful dislike troublemakers. They'll never let you go alive. Take your chance while you have it."

Still eyeing him warily, Sasha made first the Goeren-yai spirit sign, then the Verenthane holy sign, in quick succession. The priest's smile grew wider, and he repeated her actions. Sasha had never, ever seen a Verenthane priest make a pagan spirit sign. Most would never risk it, for fear of their souls. It was good enough for her.

The next swell rushed up the steps and, as it came to its peak, she dove into the water. The water churned as the receding wave rushed back down the steps, and spun her into the middle of the cave. She splashed hard, and the bandoleer strap immediately slipped from her shoulder and dragged at her arm. Kicking to keep her head above water, she adjusted it . . . and found herself being swept dangerously close to the cave side. She put her head down and tried swimming again, but the bandoleer was slipping around now, the weight of the sword pulling down, alternately banging an arm and then a leg. And now a new swell approached, heaving her upward and pushing her back into the cave mouth despite her struggles. Already her arms were aching, and her breath coming hard, and she began to wonder if this were such a smart idea after all.

But then the backwash from the second swell swept out of the cave, and took her out with it. Suddenly she was in deep, cold water, and could see brief glimpses of cliff face through the salt that stung her eyes. There behind her, a small, square guardpost with arrowslits. She swam harder, heart thudding, telling herself that if she just survived the first shot, she could dive, and swim underwater, and come up for air only briefly. But now, her lungs were beginning to burn. She was extremely fit, she knew, but swimming was not an accustomed activity. Fitness meant different things for different activities. Worse, the sword was trying to drown her. Probably, the thought occurred to her as she struggled and gasped and splashed, that was some kind of divine, poetic justice.

At least she hadn't been shot. She clung to that optimistic thought as the swell heaved her up once more, and forced her to swim uphill. She tried not to think about the vast, dark, gloomy distance that now stretched below her, within which all kinds of strange and usually hungry creatures she knew to dwell. She simply made stroke after stroke, and tried to find a rhythm despite the frustration of the sword, justifying that swimming must surely be like running, where rhythm was everything.

Finally she stopped and trod water, and looked about. She couldn't see any boat. Well great, just fucking wonderful. Out into deeper water, she could see the lights of ships at anchor. There was no way known she was going to make it out that far. She should head back, only westward, back toward Petrodor. If she could get ashore just downshore of the cave, she might be able to make her way down the cliff face, hopping along the rocks, until she reached the Cliff of the Dead. If the waves didn't smash her against the cliff first. But she didn't see that she had any choice—too much longer out here and she would drown.

She'd barely begun stroking again when she heard a splash nearby. She looked about and saw with shock the bow of a boat coming straight at her. It pulled alongside and a man in a hood shipped his oar and leaned over to offer her a hand. Sasha grabbed it, hauled, and embarrassed herself by barely managing to get her arms over the edge. The man grabbed her about the waist and pulled her over, and she fell gracelessly onto hard wood and bench seats. And lay there, gasping. Whoever that little priest had been, she owed him in a big way. And she hoped that his gods would save him from an ill fate.

"I . . . I didn't see you," she gasped, heaving for air. "I thought I'd have . . . to swim back." The boat was moving now, steady strokes of the oars. She propped up her head to look, and found that the wet robe had ridden up as she'd come overboard, exposing her from the waist down. Thankfully, the two oarsmen now had their backs turned as they rowed, and in turn blocked the view of the man at the tiller. She'd hurt her hip coming into the boat, and she rubbed at it, pulling the robe into some kind of modesty. One more bruise to her collection.

She struggled up, and took a seat at the bow, pulling off the dangling sword and putting it aside. She remembered suddenly to feel at her throat and found the leather pouch still in place. They were headed into deeper water now, but roughly back toward Petrodor. Behind, Porsada Temple loomed, white and shimmering in torchlight. Strange how the whiteness of the exterior made no impression inside. Strange to think that she'd been there at all.

The oarsmen stroked on as the boat rose up on the heaving swell. Sasha blinked her eyes clear of sea water and gazed back at the men in the boat. All hoods and cloaks. She clambered back a bench, to look between the oarsmen at the tillerman.

"Thank you," she told him. "Are you priests too?" There was no reply. Nor, she observed, the prospect of receiving one about anything. "Sure, I understand. No questions. Fine with me. Thank you anyway."

They were good oarsmen though, she reckoned, having seen enough of small-boat seamanship to be a judge of that. She doubted they were priests. Possibly they were simply men for hire. In which case, she should sit still and shut up, before they realised she might be worth more money to someone else than whatever the little priest in the cave had paid them. Possibly they didn't even know who she was.

She passed the time examining her sword for damage and watching the passing ships at anchor. The sword looked fine, though she would need to polish it soon—serrin steel rarely rusted but salt water wasn't good for anything. And she'd need to rewrap the handle binding.

Eventually the boat brought her alongside a pier at Dockside, and Sasha jumped off onto a tied-up fishing boat. The men rowed off immediately, leaving her to climb across two more boats and then up a ladder to the pier. The pier was mostly empty, as was the dockfront. That was unusual. The air seemed tense with danger, even here in Nasi-Keth heartland. She crouched where she was, knowing that it would be near impossible to see her amidst the rigging of tied boats against the black background of the harbour. She searched the docks with her eyes. She'd been away two days, she had no idea what had happened, nor how far the Halmady trouble had spread downslope.

Seeing nothing, she unfastened the strap about her neck and poured water from the leather pouch. Then, figuring that it would be best to be prepared, before bringing Kessligh anything of value, she undid the pouch. It took a while, as the fastener string was tied with tight knots. Once opened, there was another bag made of silk. She undid it and pulled out a hard, round metal disk. Even this far from the dockside houselights, the glint of gold was sharp.

Expensive, then. It didn't excite her particularly—if she'd wished nothing but wealth in her life, she'd have remained in Baen-Tar and been a proper Princess of Lenayin. It was a Verenthane star, she realised. A star had guided Saint Tristen to Mount Tristen, and in the blazing light of that star, the word of the gods had been proclaimed to him. Stars marked the holy path, and such stars had eight points, for justice, truth, love, brotherhood, and . . . and . . . damn, she forgot. All archbishops had a new star forged upon appointment, and each star became a unique signature of that man's life and order. The stars of the saints were legend, and said to be imbued with powers granted to those saints by the gods themselves.

This star . . . she peered at it closely, trying to discern its features in the dim light. This star had eight shallow points, the spaces in between encrusted with precious jewels. It was smaller than some, fitting within the hollow of her palm. It had a slim, gold chain, to be worn about the neck. And it had writing on the back in a circle about a central gemstone—a ruby. The writing looked to be in some Bacosh language, most likely old Enoran. She knew a little, as much of the Torovan tongue borrowed from Bacosh religious terms, and thought she could make out a couple of words . . .

And her heart nearly stopped. No. No, surely not. Surely the priest had not given her *that* one? Had that little, smiling, bearded man gone completely and utterly mad?

Fourteen

"DEAR LORDS, IT IS." Alaine leaned over the table, staring at the golden object on its surface. His narrow face was pale beneath falling curls of dark hair and he made the holy sign to his forehead repeatedly. Gerrold had not left his chair, his eyes were troubled, but not reverent. "It is the Shereldin Star. The holiest of the holy. The gods favour us beyond measure."

"They unleash upon us a calamity," Gerrold said sombrely. "This will cause upheaval through all Petrodor. Through all Torovan, in fact. We must give this back."

"Give it back?" Alaine rounded on his elder companion. "Good gods man, can you not see what a gift this is? This is the first and oldest of the Verenthane holy stars, forged upon the founding of the Enoran High Temple in the presence of the first saints! The single most sacred object of the faith! With this, we can rally the faithful to our cause! We can instruct the priesthood to leave off their foul war. We can be certain that the will of the gods is with us, and we shall surely be victorious!"

The meeting was held on the second floor of the Velo Family household, Alaine and Gerrold had each brought two supporters. Sasha sat on a bench behind Kessligh, with Bret. She wore a change of clothes from her room, and a borrowed pair of boots. Only the nine people in this room knew of the treasure that had fallen into their laps. Or ten, if one counted Mari. Kessligh had told him, for courtesy, and invited him to be present at the meeting, as head of the household. Mari had declined, and looked ill and gone to his room to pray.

"The archbishop will say this was stolen," Gerrold replied. "He will call us thieves. He will mount a holy war on Dockside to retrieve it. He will unite all Verenthanes against us."

"No," said Kessligh. Of all three leaders, his expression was the most unreadable. "Father Terano told Sasha that the archbishop plots with Patachi Steiner." Those who knew the priesthood well had recognised the small, bearded priest from Sasha's description. Father Terano Maerler. Patachi

Maerler's brother, no less. Sasha now doubted if he would be killed for his actions. To kill the holy relatives of lower families was one thing, but Father Terano Maerler's death could turn the dukes to Maerler's side in the Maerler–Steiner conflict.

"It is unclear whether Father Terano acts from divine outrage," Kessligh continued, "or if he is merely a partisan, furthering his brother's interests. Either way, it seems clear that all power was accumulating to Patachi Steiner's hands. The archbishop was with him, the obstacles within the priesthood were being removed. The archbishop has declared that he shall not rest until the Shereldin Star has been returned to its rightful place in the Enoran High Temple, following the liberation of Enora and all the Saalshen Bacosh from the serrin. It is the symbol of this crusade, the rallying cry of the holy army. If Steiner becomes the leader of this crusade, with an army of Torovan at his disposal, he shall become a ruler of Petrodor unlike Petrodor has ever seen, answerable only to the archbishop, and possibly not even to him. Father Terano gives us the star to remove Patachi Steiner's authority to raise that army. There is no way that Patachi Maerler will help Patachi Steiner regain it. I think he'd rather we keep it. Better it lie in neutral hands than opposing ones."

"Then why not give it to Patachi Maerler?" Gerrold asked. "If Patachi Steiner is so power hungry?"

"What, and let the holy warriors rush to Maerler's side instead?" Alaine said. "Don't be fooled just because your beloved Rhillian has befriended him, Gerrold—he'll be every bit as bad as Patachi Steiner, given the chance. Perhaps worse."

"I agree," said Kessligh. Alaine gave him a look that was part surprise, part wariness. Gerrold looked down, his lips pursed. Kessligh took his seat and gestured for Alaine to do the same. There was an eerie silence in the little room, as though a great weight made even the air feel heavy. "We will keep it. The archbishop may not even know where it went."

"Try keeping that a secret around here," said Bret.

"Word will spread soon enough," Kessligh agreed. "We will let the archbishop and Patachi Steiner decide their next move. There may be a falling out. We shall see."

"Wait, wait," said Alaine with an intense smile, leaning forward in his chair. "Hold on just a moment. You're not giving the orders here. Just because your girl got lucky enough to sneak away with this doesn't suddenly make you the ruler of the Nasi-Keth."

"I didn't sneak," Sasha snapped. "I swam. Father Terano gave it to me, and told me to give it to Kessligh. He said specifically that the archbishop feared Kessligh. He did *not* say that the archbishop feared Alaine Endaran."

"Yes, well Father Terano is not Nasi-Keth," Alaine retorted, "and as far as I know, he doesn't get a say! Besides, for all we know, you've lied about it anyway—how you got it, what Father Terano said, if anything, all of it. Maybe you were in league with Maerler and his priest all along!"

"Maybe if you were a slightly bigger fucking fool, we could put a cap on your head and watch you dance for entertainment."

Alaine came out of his seat at that, his eyes wide and angry.

Sasha remained seated, glaring, knowing that he'd never get past Kessligh anyhow.

"You watch your tongue!" Alaine blazed at her.

"Anytime, anywhere," Sasha said darkly. She let the implication hang. They would not let her fight Liam. Now, surely they would not let her fight Alaine. She thought them cowards, and they knew it. She was not above using it to advantage.

"Alaine, sit," said Gerrold, his eyes shut as if suffering a headache. "She has a coarse tongue, but you did accuse her unfairly. How you could expect anything else in reply is beyond me."

Alaine sat, reluctantly mollified. Gerrold's views did not find universal appeal within the Nasi-Keth, but his age and manner made him a figure of respect nonetheless. If only, Sasha thought tiredly, he had a few more interesting ideas than just following Saalshen's lead in everything. The man loved the serrin to excess.

"The star will stay here for now," Kessligh said calmly.

"Why here?" Alaine retorted.

"Because moving it elsewhere will cause disagreement. I submit that we all agree not to move it anywhere. This stretch of dock is one of the most defensible, and the neighbours are all devout Verenthanes and loyal friends to the Nasi-Keth. If it pleases everyone, and should the moment arrive when word has spread, we can call a priest. Father Berin is a good man, and sympathetic to our cause. We could consult with him about the keeping of the star. He is neutral in our disagreements and will not play favourites."

Gerrold nodded slowly. "Father Berin *is* a good man. Though I submit we should call on him immediately. He will not betray us—he is the last one to call down any trouble on our heads, he loves his flock too dearly."

Sasha left the men to their debate and climbed the rickety staircase in the hall. Before the nearest door, she paused. Raised her fist to knock on the door, and paused again, her heart beginning a hard, unpleasant thumping. She had slept little last night and her head remained filled with Alaine's irritations. Perhaps this was not the best time.

But then, some things simply could not be put off. She knocked. When there was no reply, she turned the latch. No sooner had the door creaked open a handsbreadth, there sounded a vicious, snarling growl from within the room. "Tashyna!" came the irritated reply. "Tashyna, no."

There were footsteps and the door pulled open a little . . . and there, sullen-eyed and swollen-faced, was her sister Alythia. Sasha stared. This was not the Alythia she knew. There was no life in her eyes, no confidence, no sparkling flash of self-importance. The left side of her face was swollen and she had a cut on the right side of her mouth, perhaps a knuckle long. Her hair fell in tangles and she looked out at her long-lost little sister with only the barest hint of recognition.

"What do you want?" she asked, sullenly.

Sasha nearly lost her temper immediately. She'd been planning to make an effort, to be nice, to try consolation, and now Alythia gave her this. She swallowed it with difficulty. Alythia had always had that knack. "To come in would be nice," Sasha suggested.

"So you can laugh at my misfortune?" Alythia muttered. "Go away."

"Laugh? For the spirits' sakes, Lyth, who around here's been doing any laughing lately?"

Alythia looked uncomfortable. She looked at the floorboards for a moment. Then, "Wait a moment, I'll get the wolf." And she disappeared. Sasha blinked at the empty space, trying to put that last phrase into some kind of logical context. It didn't work. The universe, she concluded, was taking a turn for the absurd.

Sasha waited, then pushed open the door.

Alythia's room was much like all the others in Mari Velo's house—brick walls, two small windows overlooking the docks from the third floor, and creaking floorboards. There was a simple bed, upon which Alythia now sat, her legs folded to one side. She wore a plain dress, such as Dockside women wore, with no adornment whatsoever. Beneath her right arm, grey–brown fur bristling, was a Lenay timberwolf.

Sasha moved very slowly to the room's one chair and sat. Kessligh had told her about this, too. Kessligh hadn't found it any easier to conceive than she did. The wolf watched her, ears flat, front lip edging back in the beginnings of a snarl. Snarling at *her*, while protective of Alythia. If she'd ever imagined this scene in her youth, she'd have surely imagined it around the other way. Obviously this wolf was very confused.

"She's very pretty," Sasha observed. "She's about . . . oh, five months old? Maybe six?"

"I think." Alythia tightened her arm about the wolf, protective and comforting. The wolf relaxed a little, more comfortable now that Sasha was sitting.

"Her name's Tashyna?" Alythia nodded and gave her a surreptitious look. Sasha smiled, with genuine humour. "I remember. Master Islyll. He never liked me."

"He had to put up with you," said Alythia, as if that explained it.

Sasha refrained from retorting with difficulty. "She slept in here last night?" Alythia nodded.

"She's housetrained?"

"No. I cleaned it up." With no grimace, or sense of great horror. Another amazement. "I think I'll try and teach her though."

Sasha shook her head. "You can't do it, Lyth. That's a full-blood wolf, they just don't train. And even if she were a dog, she might be too old now anyway . . . I mean, look how big she is. Five months! I'm amazed she hasn't started tearing things apart just for fun—they do that, you know. You're not the first Lenay to try and domesticate wolves, it's never worked. Even half-breeds are hard."

"Aye, well maybe I'll surprise you," Alythia said shortly.

Sasha shook her head. "It's not about you, Alythia, it's about the wolf."

"Of course it's about me," Alythia snapped. "It's always been about me. You never liked me, you've never missed a chance to attack or humiliate me, you gleefully ruined my wedding send-off from Baen-Tar! Well, are you happy now? I'm a widow, at twenty-two summers. Does it please you?"

"I didn't come in here to fight, Alythia," Sasha said coldly. "You can fly off into your selfish fantasies all you like, but believe it or not, I've had problems of my own to attend to. I've been trying my best not to think about you at all, and generally, I've been succeeding."

"Fine," said Alythia, her lip trembling. "Just fine. You can go now."

"No," Sasha said firmly. "I can't go. I live here, a guest of the Velos. Now you do too. It's not right that we bring our private arguments under their roof. They're proud people and they deserve our respect."

"I just watched my husband and his family butchered before my eyes!" Alythia's wide eyes were incredulous. There was a horror there, of depth and substance previously unknown to the most glamorous princess of Lenayin. "You're telling me to just forget it!"

"I . . . damn, Alythia, I never said that!" Sasha held up her hands helplessly. "Why do you always confuse everything, always turn it into an attack on me? On something I did wrong, on something I should have done differently . . ."

"I don't care a pile of shit about you!" Alythia screamed. "Get out of this room! NOW!"

Tashyna lurched backward, frightened, ears suddenly back and snarling in Sasha's direction. Sasha sat very still. Alythia sat on the edge of the bed, breathing frantically, agony etched wide-eyed on her face. Pain seemed to claw at her throat, constricting it, making the tendons stand out. Sasha had never seen Alythia like this. Alythia's tantrums and tempers were nearly as famous as Sasha's own, but they were always of the minor kind—something someone had said to her, something someone had or had not done, a wine cup spilt, a thread frayed, a mess left uncleaned. Now her eyes had witnessed a horror so great, it seemed she was unable to even sob.

For the first time, it occurred to Sasha what the past night must have been like for Alythia. Shut in this room, sleepless, with only the wolf for company. Reliving the horror in the dark, over and over. She had that look, sleepless and stretched thin, her hair a mess, her nerves jangling. One remark could set her off. Much like the frightened wolf, snarling at everyone, insensible to considerations of friend and foe.

"Alythia," Sasha said quietly, "you're scaring the wolf. Please don't. I don't want to get eaten."

Alythia looked across at the wolf. Immediately Tashyna stopped growling and whined. She lay flat on the bed, grovelling. Sasha blinked in amazement. Alythia recovered her breathing, slowly. Hands rigid like claws began fidgeting in her lap.

"She thinks you're angry at her," Sasha observed. "They feel your emotions. Don't give them an emotion you don't want them to have."

"I know that," Alythia muttered. She held out a hand. Tashyna licked it, then crawled into Alythia's lap and began to lick her chin. Alythia hugged her, and held tight while Tashyna squirmed. There were tears in her eyes. Utterly unexpected, Sasha found that there were tears in her eyes too. Two lost, frightened souls. Somehow, they were perfect for each other.

Sasha took a deep breath and tried again. "You know that the little Halmady girl is alive?"

Alythia nodded, face half buried in Tashyna's thick fur. "Elra. How is she?"

"Well. Errollyn cares for her. There's no more room in this house, so she's several houses down, the Giana Family. They're good people."

"I heard she was burnt." Hoarsely.

"Only a little. Errollyn thinks she'll be fine."

"I saw a maid burn alive. In your Nasi-Keth attack. They threw things that burned. She screamed for a long time. I started running just to get away from the screams."

"I'm sorry," said Sasha. "Kessligh told me what he did. He doesn't have enough people, Lyth. He had to use burning bottles, otherwise you'd all be prisoners of Patachi Steiner."

"You weren't there."

No, Sasha nearly said, *I was almost drowning in the harbour off Besendi Promontory, hauling the holiest Verenthane artefact.* But she didn't.

"Lyth . . . look," she began instead, "we're not really talking here, are we." She said it as a statement, not a question. Alythia stared blankly at the base of a wall, somewhere to Sasha's side. Tashyna settled into her lap—the front half that could fit, at least—rested a wolfish muzzle on Alythia's knee, her eyes warily on Sasha. "We're just talking *at* each other, not *to* each other. We have too much history. But all that history belongs in another place, in another time. It doesn't do anyone any good here, certainly not either of us, not Tashyna, and sure as shit not all the poor folk here who'll have to put up with our bickering.

"We're both very stubborn people, and we can both be very difficult. I think I've grown up a little, I'll be the first to admit I can be a pain in the neck sometimes. But . . . I don't know, can't we just draw a line under everything that's been written in our history to this point, and start something new? That old history is getting pretty stale."

"I tried to help Gregan," Alythia said faintly. Her eyes remained fixed on the wall, but she was seeing only her memories. "I had a sword, but I hadn't any clue how to use it. There were so many soldiers. They had a . . . a big ram of some kind. They knocked the main gate down. There were hundreds of them. Gregan organised a defence of the main floor, and then the upper storeys when they fell, but . . . but they climbed through the windows when the stairs were blocked. They were prepared, I think. Some had ropes.

"A lot of Halmady men were killed. I saw them falling. The lead Steiner men had shields, they'd . . . they'd attack the Halmady soldiers, and press them, and . . . and I don't think they could handle the shields. Gregan grabbed my arm at the end, tried to run me to the main hall stairs, and fight through with a small guard. But the stairs were blocked. They stabbed Gregan eight or nine times before he died. He was brave. He screamed, but he fought too. He took two Steiners down. I screamed at them for mercy, that he was valuable, that there could be ransom. They didn't listen. They just kept . . . stabbing. He bled so much."

There was a chill on Sasha's skin, at odds with the warmth of the morning sun through the shutters. Alythia's stare was vacant, her voice thin, trembling. Remembering all. Sasha had seen horrors, death and bloodshed . . . but she had not watched someone she loved butchered before her eyes.

For all her youthful ignorance, Sasha had always been certain that she was far wiser in the ways of the world than Alythia. Now, for the first time, she was not so sure.

"The guards were all killed," Alythia continued, softly. "They just . . . murdered them, even once they'd stopped fighting. I . . . I tried to fight them, but one just knocked the sword from my hand. They dragged me downstairs. I saw maids being raped. I thought they would rape me too, but a senior man claimed me for a prize. On the patio, I saw little Tristi. They'd killed him." Alythia's voice finally broke, a strangled sob. "He was just a little boy, but they killed him. I couldn't see Elra. I thought they'd killed her too."

Heirs, Sasha thought, past the lump in her throat. Girls could not inherit. Boys could. Patachi Steiner had wanted the Halmady name erased. It seemed he'd succeeded.

"I don't know where Tashyna was. She must have hidden and followed me later." Her eyes met Sasha's, struggling for composure. "Gregan wasn't a wonderful husband for most of our marriage. But he died like one. All my life, I wished for the day I was wed to a dashing, handsome man like him. Two months I was married, and in much of that time he ignored me. Only at the end, when I finally won him back, he was killed. Some fairytale."

"I'm so sorry, Lyth," Sasha said quietly. "I don't know what to say."

Alythia sniffed and wiped at her eyes. She stroked Tashyna's head. "Well, I still have Tashyna," she said, attempting lightness.

"Elra will need you, once she's woken," Sasha added. "Errollyn's made her sleep for now, he says she'll heal faster that way. But she'll need a familiar face when she wakes."

Alythia nodded. "I'll be there. Can you help look after Tashyna? She's not good with most company, and Elra's scared of her. I thought . . . I thought if anyone could help me look after a wolf, it'd be you."

Sasha blinked in astonishment. A compliment. Of sorts. It was the first she could remember in . . . well, ever. "Of course," she said. "Of course I will."

"There were rumours that you'd met with Marya," said Alythia with a dark, level gaze. "Did you?"

Sasha nodded. "She stuck me in the back of the neck with a needle. I should have seen it. We're now her second family, Lyth. Steiner are her first. The ones that matter."

"I'm going to kill her," Alythia said in a low voice. "If I ever get close enough again, I'm going to slit her throat." Sasha had heard Alythia offer threats before, usually in high temper at the top of her lungs. This was the first time she believed Alythia really meant it.

Sasha didn't reply. She didn't hate Marya like that, despite what had happened. Marya was who she was—a good mother, a devoted wife, the perfect woman of the household in Lenayin or Petrodor. Alythia might have seen death, but she'd never killed. Killing enemies was hard enough. Killing sisters . . . dear spirits. She didn't want to think it. Marya had been the other great friend of her childhood, besides Krystoff. One did not banish such memories easily. And Krystoff's spirit would never forgive her. Nor her mother's. Nor all her other, still living siblings. Everyone loved Marya. Or had done, before the sides were chosen.

Tashyna squirmed in discomfort and tried to lick Alythia's face Sasha noticed that the water bowl by the bed was empty. "Here," she volunteered, "I'll get her some more water."

When she returned to Alythia's room, she placed the bowl on the floor. Tashyna waited until Sasha was sitting once more, then jumped from the bed and drank thirstily.

"Look," said Sasha, as the idea formed, "she'll need some exercise, I don't imagine she got much in Halmady."

Alythia shook her head. "Just a small pen. She ran lots of circles, it must have driven her mad."

"Well, I can take her on my run easily enough. She just needs to trust me. The first step's easy, here." Sasha got up and sat on the bed beside Alythia. Tashyna paused drinking and looked at them with big, yellowish eyes. "See?" said Sasha to the wolf, putting an arm around Alythia's shoulders. "My sister. I'm a part of your pack too. See?"

She put her head on Alythia's shoulder. Alythia felt stiff and uncomfortable. Tashyna cocked her head, ears pricked. Sasha smiled—she could see the wolf thinking. Reasoning. Doubting. Alythia seemed to relax—Sasha looked, and saw she was smiling too. And put her arm, too, around Sasha.

Tashyna went back to drinking, still watching from the corner of her eye. "Don't think this makes us sisters or anything," said Alythia. A joke, Sasha realised after a moment. With heavy irony. She was trying. Lords, it couldn't have been easy.

"Perish the thought," she replied, smiling. "Lyth, you're safe here. Or as safe as you could be in Petrodor, anyhow. No one here will hurt you in any way. Just . . . just know that."

Alythia nodded, biting the inside of her cheek. "Thanks" did not quite escape her lips. But that was fine. Sasha could wait.

Tashyna finished drinking and looked at the sisters. She stepped forward, wanting Alythia's lap once more, but pausing. Sasha eased herself slowly to the floor and, kneeling, held out her hand. Tashyna sniffed, cautiously, but no longer with such obvious worry. She licked. And lowered her head, paws braced, observing this new person from several angles.

Sasha planted her hands on the floor and imitated the wolf on all fours. Whined at her. Tashyna's ears pricked. Her tail wagged, then stopped. "Sasha, what in the world are you doing?" Alythia asked, a trace of that old, imperious tone returning. Sasha ignored her and risked a small jump, bracing her arms straight out in front, head and shoulders low. Tashyna jumped as well, backing a little. Sasha repeated it, several times. Then panted. Tashyna jumped at her, then backed away.

Sasha jumped at the wolf and Tashyna sprang up onto the bed. And then, to Alythia's exclamation, jumped straight onto Sasha from that height. Sasha rolled and Tashyna sprang aside, darting to the far wall and crouching. Her tongue was lolling now, excitedly. Sasha laughed.

"Oh, Sasha, stop it," Alythia complained, half wearily as if having expected no better. "That's undignified, even for you. You shouldn't go down to her level, she's just a wolf!"

"That's no way to speak of a friend," Sasha retorted and sprang at the wolf. Tashyna leapt sideways, with far greater agility, then jumped on Sasha's side. Sasha grabbed her and wrestled. Tashyna was nice enough not to bite hard, and jumped away, tail wagging madly.

Soon even Alythia was having to smother a smile behind her hand. Sasha had worked up a sweat by the time Kessligh pushed open the door, to stare with some concern at the cause of all the noise. Tashyna immediately backed away from the door, nervously. Sasha put a comforting arm around her and scratched her neck. "Oh look, Tashyna," she said brightly, "it's the dominant male!"

Kessligh raised an eyebrow. "Just checking. I thought maybe someone was dying."

"Oh, come on, if Alythia and I were fighting, it wouldn't last very long."

"Oh that's charming," said Alythia drily.

Kessligh squatted opposite Tashyna and offered a hand. Tashyna stretched forward hopefully, tail high and curled. "She's at least known *some* good treatment," Kessligh observed, "or she'd be impossible." Tashyna sniffed his hand. "She looks like a northern wolf. She's a little lighter on the chest and her coat's thicker."

"Aye," Sasha agreed, still on her haunches by the bed, breathing hard. "She's probably Hadryn. Which would make her the most agreeable Hadryn I've met in ages."

"Just as likely Taneryn," said Kessligh. Tashyna stopped sniffing and went to take a drink. Which was remarkable in itself, Sasha reckoned. Some new people, at least, no longer terrified her into demanding her full attention. Some could safely be ignored. "Better hope it's a cold winter, or she'll be hot in her new coat."

The wolf jumped back onto the bed and nudged at Alythia's shoulder. New friends or not, Alythia would remain her best friend. And deservedly so, Sasha conceded to herself thoughtfully. Wild animals did not give loyalty lightly. Alythia must have earned it.

"Come on Lyth," said Sasha, rising to her feet. "There's breakfast downstairs, we'll see if we can find some scraps for Tashyna."

"Give her a few more months and she'll need a lot more than scraps," Kessligh warned, leading the way to the stairs.

"Oh but Kessligh!" Sasha complained, in her best, well-remembered little girl voice. "Can't we keep her? Please? She won't be any trouble, honest!"

Behind her, fixing a lead to Tashyna's collar, Sasha could have sworn she saw Alythia smile.

Taking a young wolf on a leash for a run was not as simple as Sasha had thought. Tashyna reacted to *everything*, sometimes with fear and, at other times, with uncontainable excitement. She leaped from one side of the alley to the other, avoiding strange-looking people who stared, then bounding toward doorways from which wafted interesting food smells. Her ears would prick pleasantly upon the sight of children, tail raised, her whole posture alert and positive. And then she would halt, go sideways, or retreat at the sight of a man with a sword at his hip. Then Sasha would have to halt and yank her onward, and say reassuring words while she growled and slunk past the man in question . . . who usually pressed himself against the opposite wall for good measure. Thankfully most men with hip-worn swords were sailors who rarely ventured far from the docks.

Running up the incline paths and stairs was also a challenge, as Tashyna tried to bound up four steps at a time, only to be yanked short and entangle Sasha's legs with the leash. Worse yet, several times on the incline they encountered stray dogs. At the first one, Tashyna nearly tore Sasha's arms from the sockets . . . but within five strides, the other animal's nature-given instincts seemed to alert it to the fact that this was no big dog, but in fact a wolf, even though it had surely never seen a wolf before in its life. It ran baying with terror. Tashyna looked a little crestfallen.

Sasha laughed. "Don't worry," she said. "You're not missing much."

By the time Sasha ran her final leg along the dockfront, Tashyna didn't seem particularly tired. Instead, she leaped and snapped at the leash as Sasha laboured along. Surely Tashyna was unfit after so much captivity, spirits forbid she came into good condition, there weren't many Nasi-Keth runners who could keep up. Perhaps they'd have to send her on consecutive runs.

Dockfront crowds stared and pointed as she ran. Some men setting up their market stalls called out, "It's the Lenay wolf girl!"

"She's not mine, she's my sister's!" Sasha called back, cheerfully. And was amused by the thought of the rumours that would now spread along the dockfront of a Lenay warrior princess even bigger and meaner than the first, who befriended wild wolves.

Arranging for an extra supply of meat scraps was not hard—she simply took Tashyna to The Fish Head and said hello to Tongren. Tongren and his three sons greeted Tashyna as though she were a long-lost relative, giving her water, bacon rinds, and bones with scraps from the kitchen, promising better to come.

At a lane off Fishnet Alley, Sasha rapped on a warped old door, then opened it without waiting. A brick lane led through a dark corridor and into a small courtyard surrounded by several floors of old, brick building. Through some window shutters, Sasha could see people moving.

She tied Tashyna's leash to a small tree in the courtyard and gave her a final pat—Tashyna seemed to get the idea, and lay down with a yawn. Remarkable wolf, Sasha thought as she walked to the door. Maybe it *was* possible to train her.

She knocked and entered. Inside a small room was a bed, in which there lay a little girl with light brown hair. There was a paste on her left arm, which rested on the sheet that covered her. She looked flushed as she slept, and the young woman at her bedside wet her forehead with a damp cloth from a basin. At the bedside sat Alythia, holding the girl's good hand. By the end of the bed, Errollyn stood with another woman, whom Sasha recognised as a Nasi-Keth healer. Errollyn was explaining something. His green eyes met Sasha's as he talked.

Sasha put a hand on Alythia's shoulder. "Lyth, Tashyna's just outside," she said quietly. "Best warn these people there's a wolf in their courtyard."

"Thanks," Alythia murmured, her eyes not leaving little Elra's face. The last surviving child of Patachi Halmady . . . unless Vincen had somehow survived, which didn't seem likely.

Errollyn finished his conversation and hugged her, hard. Sasha hugged him back, and held on for a long, long time. She felt suddenly exhausted, wanting nothing more than to burrow her head against his chest and stay there forever. Finally Errollyn released her and took her face in his hands to look at her. "The spirits favour you," he said with a smile. "You make more trouble than a bear in a beehive."

"Just once in my life," Sasha murmured tiredly, "I'd like to be compared to something other than wild animals."

"You don't need to do this, you know," Errollyn told Sasha as they climbed the lower slope from Dockside. Sasha did not reply. "Yulia made her own choices. You aren't responsible for what happened."

"I'm not discussing this." Again the familiar, winding road, its sides cluttered with ramshackle brick buildings.

At the lane that led to Yulia's aunt's residence, Sasha nearly stopped. But she didn't, and walked up to the little side door and rapped. There was no reply. Sasha rapped again. Finally, it opened. Looking out at her was a young girl, perhaps ten.

"Hello Marli," Sasha said. Her voice was steady, which surprised her. She would push through it, she thought. Like diving into cold water, you pushed through the shock, safe in the knowledge that the sooner you began, the sooner you could climb out and begin drying. "Is your mother home?"

Marli shook her head. "She's out. Making preparations."

"Preparations?"

"The funeral." Marli's eyes were lowered.

Sasha took a deep breath. "When is the funeral, Marli?"

"Tomorrow. The rites say within three days." As if Sasha, a Lenay pagan, might need that explained to her.

"Is it at Angel Bay?" Sasha asked. There were cremation pyres there. In the strict Verenthane faith, bodies had to be buried, but cemetery plots were beyond the means of lower-slope residents and so the lower-slope priests had resurrected cremation.

Marli nodded, sullenly. "You're not welcome," she muttered. "There's no Nasi-Keth welcome."

Sasha stared down at the girl. Took a deep breath and tried to retain her composure. "Marli," she said quietly, "I'm very sorry about what happened to Yulia. It was my fault. I shouldn't have asked her to come. I should have gone on my own."

Marli met her gaze for the first time, with incredulous eyes. "You admit it?"

"Of course I admit it. Marli, do you understand?" She gazed at the girl hopefully.

Marli stared back, her wide eyes unreadable. "Responsible?"

"Yes, responsible. I'd like to be at the funeral, Marli. I have to be there."

"Mama wouldn't like it."

It was a less hostile response than it could have been. Sasha's hopes rose further, desperately. "I know that, Marli. I'm very sorry about that. But I knew Yulia too, and I know she didn't always agree with what her aunt thought. What do *you* think?"

"Me?" Marli blinked. "You actually ask what I think? Yulia's mother is dying, did you know that? She's not just sick, that's what Yulia always told people. She's dying. She was always my favourite aunt, and Yulia was my favourite cousin. We were always friends. I know I shouldn't have been happy that Yulia came to live with us, because she only did it because her mother was dying . . . but I was happy. I had to take care of the babies. Mama's always toiling, and she doesn't have time. My brother works as staff for a midslope Family. He's a groundsman, I never see him. It's just me here now.

"It *was* me and Yulia. Yulia helped with the babies. She helped Mama cook, and fetch water. She took care of Grandpa when he fell ill and took six months to die, I don't know how we'd have managed without her help. She taught me to read after the Nasi-Keth taught her, even though Mama said I was wasting my time. We played games together. I never played games before Yulia came to stay. I had someone to talk to, for the first time in my life.

"Now she's dead, because you thought she might be useful to your stupid Nasi-Keth games. But that's the way it always is, isn't it? Wealthy folk always use up poor folk like firewood, don't they? And now you come around here, and *demand* that you be allowed to come to the funeral, and say how you want to become even *more* involved with this family . . . doesn't it even occur to you that you're the *last* person in the whole world we'd like to see right now?"

There were tears running down Marli's cheeks, and an awful, hollow pain in her eyes. Sasha stood rooted to the spot, unable to move. She wanted to run, but her honour would not let her. She wanted to never have come, but her principles had demanded it. Most of all, she wanted to have been smarter than she was, and more sensitive of other people's lives, and to never have asked Yulia to come with her to the Cliff of the Dead. But she had, and all the wishing in the world would not change it.

"Marli, I'm so sorry," she whispered. "I want to help, Marli. Please, let me help."

"You murdered my best friend in the whole world!" Marli sobbed. "We don't need your help! Don't you *ever* come back here! I hope you burn in hell!"

She slammed the door. Sasha stood, stunned. She could not think, or speak. The situation demanded something, but she had no idea what that was.

It was Errollyn who finally put a hand on her back, and steered her away from the doorway and off down the lane away from the road. She had no idea why they were going that way, which was the longer way, but she walked regardless.

"Well," she managed to say, past the thickness in her throat, "I suppose that couldn't possibly have gone any worse." She tried a hoarse laugh, but that sounded stupid and callous. For a brief, horrible moment, she hated herself. It was the first time in her life she'd ever felt that way. She wondered how Errollyn could possibly stand her company.

Errollyn said nothing, continuing to steer her with a hand on her back. They'd rounded a narrow bend in the lane when the tears finally escaped her control. Now she realised why Errollyn had steered her down the lane. Here, she had privacy. She collapsed into his arms and sobbed as though her heart were being torn in two. Errollyn held her.

It was still only midmorning when Sasha and Errollyn arrived back at the Velo residence, and already there were crowds gathering. She counted perhaps three hundred people clustered across the dock, blocking the path of frustrated passers-by. Stall owners were shouting at them, waving their arms, trying to clear a space for their business. Cart drivers pushed through regardless, horses or donkeys skittish amidst the clustered bodies.

Mari wasn't going to be very happy, Sasha thought as she pushed through the crowd. There was a whispering in her wake and furtive glances searched her face, suspiciously, hopefully, disdainfully. Many of the crowd were old men and women, some leaning on sticks, too old to work. But not too old to hear a rumour, and come. The Dockside faithful. She felt uncomfortable in the press, but not threatened. Not yet. That, she was certain, would come later.

Two young priests guarded the entrance to the Velo household, barehanded in plain, black robes. Caratsa, they were called in Torovan—priest apprentices, boys in whom the fathers saw potential. Not so different from Nasi-Keth umas really, Sasha reckoned. These two seemed barely more than sixteen summers, and looked nervous in the face of the crowd, but they were a better choice of guards than armed Nasi-Keth. Even Dockside, there were those who distrusted Nasi-Keth, as peddlers of pagan serrin ideas. If a big crowd were to become angry, a few Nasi-Keth would not stop them. Two unarmed, innocent caratsa, however, just might.

The boys knew her and let her in, though she had to vouch for Errollyn.

On the second floor, she found Father Berin and two younger priests kneeling before the small table in the centre of the main room. One of the younger priests held a large, silver-bound book for Father Berin, who mumbled prayer and made symbols with his right hand at the appropriate moment. On the table, propped against the base of a candle stand, its chain hung over the stand's arms, stood the Shereldin Star.

Only one of the two windows had its shutters open, spilling in the overcast midmorning light. Kessligh stood by the other, gazing through a gap in its slats upon the crowded dock below. Sasha walked to him, eyeing the kneeling priests warily as she passed. Verenthane rituals made her uncomfortable. It was a prejudice, she knew, and she tried her best to smother it. Yet she could not deny it, all the same.

She joined Kessligh at the shutters and peered out. "How big is that going to get?" she asked quietly, so as not to interrupt the holy matters at their backs. And in Lenay, to avoid being understood. Educated priests in Petrodor were more likely to speak a little Saalsi than any Lenay.

"I'm afraid to say," Kessligh murmured, also in Lenay. His expression was no more readable than usual. He looked tired and drawn, but that was nothing new. Yet somehow, he did not look as concerned as she might have expected. His eyes were slightly narrowed, a thinking look. He saw an opportunity in this, she guessed. And, quite possibly, he simply preferred the prospect of an approaching climax, no matter how bloody, to interminable waiting. Knowing her uman as she did, Sasha was not particularly surprised. "Petrodor is a city of believers, and the poor are the most devout. Not like the rich, who follow the priests only for the power of holy blessings and the archbishop's goodwill. It's real faith here on the lower slopes, Sasha. It's not to be toyed with lightly."

"You're telling me it'll get huge out there, aren't you?" Sasha said.

"Probably," Kessligh agreed. "There's no helping it."

"Is this the best place for . . . for *it*?"

"Where else?" Kessligh asked.

Even as Sasha watched, she could see more people joining the massed crowd below. Word was spreading.

"How far will the archbishop go to get it back?" she asked Kessligh.

"No limit," said Kessligh. Sasha glanced at him. "He'll be frantic. The star is the symbol of this coming war. The holiest relic, long separated from its rightful home. Now it's gone. I don't know what he'll do."

"I met him," Sasha said grimly. "He didn't strike me a reasonable man."

"It's not his unreasonableness that bothers me," said Kessligh. "It's his stupidity. He doesn't understand the real world, only the priesthood. He sees that only Patachi Steiner is powerful enough to lead the Torovan army, but has no idea of how to handle Patachi Maerler's rival claim. So far he's been as subtle as an ironmonger's hammer, and about as cunning."

"Men with faith in the gods have no need of reason," Sasha said with certainty. "What use is reason when heaven is on your side?"

"Or when the spirits guard your flanks?" Kessligh countered, with a raised eyebrow.

Sasha snorted. "That's different. The Goeren-yai follow no dogma from a book."

"Only silly tales from campfires. People substitute all kinds of things for reason, Sasha. We use different names for it, but it's all unreasonable, just by a different name."

Behind them, the prayers stopped and Father Berin climbed gingerly to his feet, assisted by one of his companions. Berin was a broad-faced and usually cheerful man, of brown beard and hair, and a wide girth. He walked with a limp from childhood disease, and grasped now the cane a younger priest handed to him. "Yuan Kessligh," he said, coming across the creaking floorboards. The Lenay title—typical of the man, always interested in foreign peoples and their doings. From the first day she'd met him in the sculpture studio out the back of the North Pier Temple, Sasha had found him far more pleasant and interesting than she'd ever thought possible in a priest. "May I ask, what you have decided to do?"

"I was thinking to ask you that question, Father."

Berin licked his lips, pale and nervous. "Please, Yuan Kessligh, I am just a humble father of the lower slopes. It is not my place to make decisions . . . decisions regarding such as this." His voice lowered at the end as if he feared the star would overhear.

"But you take instruction?"

Father Berin spread his hands in defence and forced a strained smile. "Yuan Kessligh! The archbishop pays me no attention at all! I am a bug beneath his shoe."

"He never had cause to find you interesting before," Kessligh agreed. The sharp eyes narrowed. "What about now?"

Berin took a deep breath and glanced out at the harbour. He shook his head shortly. "I have received no instruction from him."

"And what would you say, should you receive instruction?"

Father Berin met Kessligh's eyes gravely. "I could not tell you if I did."

"Ah," said Kessligh, nodding slowly. "Now we come to the truth of it." Kessligh gestured at the window behind. "There are many people out there who would like to see you take possession of the star yourself. Would you desire it?"

A short shake of the head, eyes staring at the floor. "I am not worthy of such an honour," Berin muttered.

"And yet you come here, and give blessing and perform ritual. And verify."

Father Berin looked up, his eyes desperate. "Yuan Kessligh, I do not spy against you, nor against the Nasi-Keth! I . . . I have heard how this blessing came into your possession, and while I cannot conceive of it, I can only surmise that the gods must have had their purpose in bringing it to you. It is not my intention to work against the will of the gods."

"I understand, Father," said Kessligh. "You are caught between two worlds. Long have the priests of the upper slopes ignored their lower-slope brethren. They preach that the Nasi-Keth are a pagan influence opposed to Verenthane teachings, yet you live here and you have seen differently. Now, these two worlds come into conflict. Your order says you must obey the archbishop, yet in your heart, you cannot do anything to betray your flock. You do not know whether to work with me, or against me."

Father Berin shook his head and managed a small smile. "I could never call the Nasi-Keth pagan, Yuan Kessligh, when they produce from their ranks men as wise as you."

"Whatever wisdom I have, Father Berin, comes mostly from knowledge of my own limitations. I have no knowledge of this artefact, nor its meaning to the people of Petrodor. Tell me what you think I should do."

Berin looked at Kessligh for a long moment, his head faintly to one side. "And how is it that you became so lapsed in your faith, Yuan Kessligh?" His manner suddenly wise and assured, as though he now found his slippered feet upon confident ground. "I know a little of your upbringing amongst these alleys. Your childhood was hard, but no harder than many others."

Kessligh folded his arms. Sasha watched curiously. Searching his face for signs that she alone might notice. "The faith and I had a little disagreement," Kessligh said simply.

Father Berin nodded, lips pursed. "Please tell."

"The Nasi-Keth offered solutions. The priests offered prayer. I preferred solutions."

"But prayer itself is a solution, Yuan Kessligh. And most of your Nasi-Keth brethren insist that Verenthane and Nasi-Keth teachings each complement the other. The Nasi-Keth teach knowledge that improves people's lives, and prayer gives the Nasi-Keth members a sense of how to implement such knowledge so that it shall best serve the will of the gods."

"Exactly," Kessligh said firmly. "There should be no division. The Nasi-Keth are not just a society of useful skills, Father Berin. We are not merely a collection of scholarly learnings on medicines and advanced trades. We exist to expand minds, Father. What is the use of wise and clever hands, when the head remains as clumsy and stupid as before?"

"Ah!" said Father Berin, the twinkle returning to his eyes. "So this is the source of your contention—your brethren should believe what *you* believe, or else they are stupid. How does this make your beliefs more enlightened than my faith?" Sasha grinned, and smothered it behind her hand. Berin glanced at her, smiling. "Your uma is familiar with this train of debate, I see."

"You have no idea," said Sasha, with feeling.

"Of course they should not believe what I believe," Kessligh replied, as calmly as he'd ever instructed his argumentative uma. "The Nasi-Keth have no dogma, that's the whole point."

"No dogma except that they should ideally not be Verenthanes," Berin countered. "Which is a dogmatic view, no?"

"A philosophy of tolerance cannot be tolerant of all things, Father," said Kessligh, with an edge to his voice. "A philosophy of tolerance cannot tolerate intolerance. A philosophy of freedom cannot tolerate slavery. A philosophy of plenty cannot tolerate starvation and a philosophy of abstinence cannot tolerate gluttony. That would be to welcome the wolf into the chicken coop, to encourage the very thing that would be the philosophy's destruction. I promise you, the day that the leaders of the Verenthane faith can prove to me that the faith need not be dogmatic, I shall become more tolerant of your beliefs. Until then, we are helplessly at odds."

"Tell me, have you seen the beautiful paintings Master Berloni puts on the ceiling of my temple?" asked Father Berin. "Ah, they are marvellous. Such free expression, such unrestrained artistry and creativity. There are freedoms of expression within the faith that you fail to credit us with."

"They are very pretty," Sasha agreed. Father Berin favoured her with a smile.

"And they would not exist should the high-slopes priesthood care even a little what goes on in a lower-slopes temple, and what adorns its ceiling," Kessligh said firmly. "And they should not exist had the inspiration not first arrived from the Saalshen Bacosh, where the faith and the serrin have mingled so much more forcefully than here."

Father Berin shrugged. "Even so."

"Could you refuse the archbishop?" Kessligh asked, bluntly. "Could you defy his instruction, in any matter?"

"The archbishop rarely gives such instruction," Berin replied, somewhat less ebullient than before. "Such is not how the parishes function, we are—"

"You could not," Kessligh answered for him. "He is your lord, and you owe him your obeisance. And you claim an absence of dogma in your faith? A freedom of thought? Do you see why I can't let you have the star, Father Berin? Why it would be profoundly foolish of me?"

Father Berin sighed and scratched at his beard. From the docks below, the sounds of human commotion seemed even louder—argument and conversation, and many people pressed close together.

"The people grow restless, Father," said Kessligh. "What do they want?"

Father Berin pursed his lips. Tested the grip upon his cane, adjusting his weight and stance. "To know why," he said at last. "Fate is a precarious matter in calamitous times. They wish to know their fate. They wish to know if they have been blessed, or cursed. They fear for their families, especially for the little ones. And so they look for a sign."

"And of course, I have to give them this sign," Kessligh added, with evident sarcasm. "As if it were from the gods themselves; who are evidently far too tardy and bored with human concerns to offer one themselves."

Another priest might have taken offence. Father Berin smiled. "The gods will show what the gods will show. If you feel the need to make a sign, that is their will. If you feel no need and curse them to the stars, that is also their will."

"My will is my own," Kessligh replied, irritated.

"If you say so," said Father Berin, still smiling. "Yuan Kessligh, do not fear the flock at your door. Neither insult them, nor patronise them as you now patronise me . . ." and he paused for an impish smile. Kessligh looked unimpressed. "And nor should you think them stupid or unwise. They follow their path as you follow yours. Is it not a serrin saying that two paths, separated by half the world, may still arrive at the same destination?"

"No," said Kessligh. "If two paths continue for far enough, they will *inevitably* arrive at the same destination. The world is round, Father Berin."

Father Berin blinked at him. "Round?" And shook his head briefly in bafflement. "A figure of speech, no doubt. Serrin are so clever with their wordplay, no?"

"If you say so," said Kessligh, with a faint smile.

"I'm sorry about Kessligh," Sasha told Father Berin as she helped him down the narrow stairs. "He's not always subtle."

"He is a man who says what he means, and does what he says," Berin replied. "The gods admire such a man, whether he follows them or not."

Downstairs was filled with Velo relatives and neighbours, seated about the dining table or standing, while Mariesa and her daughter Frasesca served them with grapes, cheese and bread. Sasha knew grapes and cheese did not come cheaply to the Velos. But most of the relatives seemed unconcerned, talking loudly amongst themselves, mostly about the crowd outside. It occurred to Sasha that not everyone would view the coming of Verenthane's most holy artefact as a curse.

All rose as Father Berin entered and he blessed the household, and in particular the agitated Mariesa. The Velo boys, Valenti and Rasconi, were probably out preparing the boat for the afternoon trip. The boat stuck in Sasha's mind. A memory of Yulia seated by the mast on that last trip to the Cliff of the Dead, the sun across her face.

On an impulse Sasha took Father Berin's arm just as he was about to open the door. "Father," she said quietly, "can I talk to you about something?"

"Of course, Sasha," the priest replied in surprise. And added, as it occurred to him, "Would you like to speak in private?" Sasha nodded. Father Berin excused them both and walked to the rear door beneath the stairs. Some odd looks followed them, but animated conversation continued as before.

The rear door led to a dark little courtyard between neighbouring buildings. No one else moved in the lanes—Kessligh had posted Nasi-Keth guards at the ends, locals who knew other locals by name.

Father Berin looked at Sasha expectantly as she pulled the door closed behind her. Sasha took a deep breath. "I'm . . . I'm not very good at this," she admitted. "I haven't seen a priest in . . . well, not since I was little."

Father Berin nodded slowly. "But . . . you think of yourself as Goeren-yai. Do you not? I mean, that is what I'd heard and everyone . . ."

Sasha rolled her eyes. Everytime she had to make that a formal declaration, to a man of authority like Father Berin, it still felt like a risk. Or a dangerous blasphemy. "Yes, it's true," she said shortly.

Father Berin folded his hands before him. "Then why do you need a priest?"

Sasha blinked at him. "Oh no, wait, wait . . ." she held up both hands. "I don't need a priest." Father Berin just looked at her, mild and curious. "I mean, I *do* . . ." she stopped, took another breath and looked away down a lane, hands on hips. "Yulia Delin. She died."

"I heard," said the priest. "I knew her and her family only a little. I'm very sorry."

"I killed her."

Berin just looked at her. Waiting for her to amend the statement. Clearly he didn't believe her. Past the lump in her throat, she felt a surge of affection for the plump, limping priest. "She shouldn't have been there. I asked her specifically. I knew she lacked confidence. I knew she wasn't all that good, honestly. But I needed a partner to cover my meeting, and she was all that was available. She thought highly of me. I knew she'd agree, if I pushed. She shouldn't have been there, and now she's dead, and it's my fault."

Father Berin sighed, and leaned on his cane. "I'm not certain I understand what you need a priest for."

"I said I don't need a priest," Sasha retorted.

Berin gave a small, helpless smile. "Then why am I here? Why not talk to someone else?"

"Yulia Delin is dead, Father!" Sasha snapped. "One of your flock, and this pagan holds herself responsible. Doesn't that mean anything to you? Don't you . . . I don't know . . . don't you have something to say about that?"

"Sasha," Father Berin said gently, "what do you want? I mean truly. You feel guilty, and that is good. You *should* feel guilty." Sasha swallowed hard. "Not because you are to blame, but because it shows you have a good soul. Do you wish me to absolve you? I cannot do that—we each must live with our sins, Sasha. And besides, you declare you are Goeren-yai . . . that makes you answerable to your spirits, not to my gods. Of what use to you is absolution from me?"

"I don't *want* absolution!" Sasha insisted. "I didn't ask for it."

"Then what do you want me to tell you?"

"I don't . . . I don't know." She tilted her head and stared despairingly at the small slit of sky between the uneven brick walls overhead. Small windows looked down, old shutters faded, plaster crumbling. "I'm not used to this. Kessligh is. He's ordered thousands of men to their deaths."

"Do you think *he* feels guilty?"

"No. Or . . . not guilty. Sad. But Kessligh, he's a fatalist. He thinks the world is a sad place. Maybe I'm . . . I don't know. Maybe I expect too much."

"Or maybe he expects too little," Father Berin countered. Sasha shrugged and wiped at the corner of her eye. "Perhaps you are frightened that this is the life you are born to. You were a princess by birth, Sasha, however revoked that title now. You were born to command. The gods willed it so, I believe."

"Did they also will that I should reject them?"

Berin shrugged, helplessly. "Who can say? The good shepherd always welcomes the straying sheep back to the flock. Perhaps that shall be your fate too."

"I wouldn't count on it."

Berin smiled. "Trust me, I'm not. Fate is nothing to be taken for granted. Do not the Goeren-yai believe in the fates too? I know a little of the old Lenay ways, they are not so dissimilar to my own faith. But please don't tell the archbishop I said so."

"I won't." Sasha managed a reproachful smile. "You've tricked many Lenay pagans before with those words in the past."

Berin snorted. "And a great many priests were put to the sword for saying so too loudly."

"Shouldn't have been there in the first place," said Sasha. "We never tried to convert *you*."

"No, you only rode down from the mountains every few months to rape and slaughter entire villages. How you bunch of bloodthirsty ruffians manage to claim persecution with a straight face is beyond me."

Sasha saw movement across the courtyard to her left and half spun . . . but it was Rhillian, moving warily, with a serrin at her side whom Sasha did not recognise. Father Berin looked across in surprise. Rhillian straightened and considered them curiously.

"Have I come too late to witness the conversion?" she asked mischievously.

"Who let *you* in?" Sasha retorted, but she was smiling.

"I promised the young man guarding the lane a night of wild debauchery," said Rhillian, all green-eyed amusement beneath the brim of her hat. Eyeing Father Berin, hoping to shock him. "And I let him feel my thigh. Astonishing, isn't it? A woman's thigh, such a strange and unsighted thing, subject of so many rumours."

"No, no, Lady Rhillian," said Father Berin, jabbing his cane at her, "it's what lies *between* the lady's thighs that makes for the rumours."

Rhillian gave a little shake as she approached, like a cat with a brief chill. "Brrr. Such excitement! So many to be educated, but so little time." She gave Sasha a hug. Sasha returned it, hard. "I heard you were having adventures, nearly getting killed, making crazy escapes."

"Just another day," said Sasha.

"One observes. I'm so glad you're safe." Rhillian gave her a kiss on the cheek. "Now, you two seemed to be having a religious moment, which this pagan, unbelieving serrin would surely not comprehend, so I'll go inside and leave you your privacy. Good day, Father, stay out of trouble."

"Said the wolf to the lamb," Father Berin said slyly. Rhillian flashed him a smile as she entered the house. "That girl is trouble," said the priest, but the amusement remained. "I shall have to bathe twice tonight and beat myself with birch leaves."

"That *girl*," Sasha replied, "has nearly forty summers."

"I know." Father Berin shook his head and made the holy sign. "She looks barely older than you. Like I said, trouble."

"The archbishop certainly thinks so."

Berin shook his head impatiently. "No, no, not that sort of trouble. Trouble like the small child with the stick that never stops poking things that have no business being poked. The serrin, they think themselves so wise, but I see them as innocents. Children, marvelling at the world. We should forgive them their innocence, they are no more dangerous than any child."

Sasha smiled. "They see us the same way. They think religion is a child's game—an interesting game with fascinating characters and wonderful drama, but a game nonetheless. Or a stage play. Only not so harmless."

"Sasha, Sasha." Father Berin put both hands on her shoulders. "There are those in my faith who say that the world does not matter, only the Scrolls of Ulessis matter. Only the writings, and the word. I say differently. I say that the gods gave me eyes with which to see, and ears with which to hear, and a mind with which to think. To me, all the things that happen in the world are all the will of the gods. That means that the serrin are who they are because the gods willed it that way, and you are who you are because the gods willed it that way, and all this crazy complexity happens for a reason. The holy fathers of the scrolls, they say the world should be simple like the scrolls. But I look around, and I see what the gods have made, and I see no simplicity anywhere.

"Have faith in the fates, Sasha. You yourself are impulsive. Even in grief, you laugh and make jokes, then go back to grieving. You are full of life, and feel many things at different times. Perhaps your friend's death was a message, one that had meaning in itself, but also meaning to you. Perhaps you are destined for great leadership and the gods merely wished to show you the weight of the burden. Yulia Delin's death is only in vain if you allow it to be. But perhaps, if you learn from tragedy, and grow strong from it rather than allowing it to destroy you, Yulia's death, and her life, may yet serve a far greater purpose than any of us could have dreamed."

Father Berin had nearly reached his temple when a dark-robed man stepped away from a fish stall to walk at his side. "What do you want?" Berin snorted as he waddled along the dockfront. His two companions fell back, making space for the man in robes.

"Is it real?" asked the man. He had a grim face and short beard, hard with knowledge, but not with piety. Such were the men who surrounded the upper-slopes priesthood these days.

"You know it is," Berin said shortly, puffing hard. "Now see what you've done. You family fools, playing your games in the halls where no games should be played."

"Such is not your concern, preacher," the robed man said darkly, edging past the intervening crowd.

"Such is *obviously* my concern," Berin retorted. "I am a man of the gods, it gives me little cheer to see war between priests! We serve the gods, not your blasted families! Now see where it has taken you, involving even the holiest of symbols and stirring the passions of all the devout in Petrodor! Madness."

He edged his way between the stalls that sprawled across the temple entrance, and limped his way up the stairs. "You should have these people moved," the robed man observed, eyeing with distaste the beggars on the temple steps—two skinny men in rags, heads bowed and hands outstretched. "They show disrespect for the house of the gods."

Berin pushed through the big wooden doors. "If the house of the gods offers no good for even beggars, then what are we here for? Michelo, see to them, if you please." The younger of his companion priests walked across the steps to the beggars, withdrawing a pouch of coins from the folds of his robes. "They must be from upslope, or new arrivals from the country," Berin explained, waddling down the aisle of his temple. Overhead, men were once again at work on the ceiling. Pews had been pushed aside or covered with drop sheets, now that the morning service had finished. They had until evening service to put everything back, or there'd be trouble. "We work with the Nasi-Keth to offer food and shelter for those who would otherwise be beggars, most have no need of it."

"The archbishop disapproves of such collaboration," the robed man said, eyeing the overhead painting with suspicion. "He has spoken with you of it before."

"Nonsense," Berin snorted, stopping before the altar to confront the visitor. He kept his voice down with difficulty, lest the painters overhead strain their ears to catch an echo. "The archbishop has not set a foot on Dockside in more than thirty years, he sends men like you instead. Not even a priest. Dare *you* instruct me on how best to serve the gods?"

"I am a messenger, Father," said the robed man. "Nothing more."

Father Berin waved his hands in exasperation. "Well, message your superiors this—if they can think of a better way to assist the poor than to work with the Nasi-Keth, who have made that their mission in Petrodor for the past half century and more, then I'll be very open to suggestions. We train the destitute with trades and skills, and those without families who cannot or do not wish to join the Nasi-Keth, we try and convince a patachi to take them in."

"You play with the fabric of Torovan society," said the robed man impassively. "You destroy the nature of family, of marriage, of the people with their priests. You paint lewd scenes on the ceilings of your temples. You associate with godless serrin and those who worship them. You walk on very thin ice, Father Berin."

"You fool!" Berin hissed. "You think to flex your muscles with me now? Now, as the devout crowds gather on the docks and wonder how their guiding fathers have let so precious an artefact fall through their fingers? You have no idea how much the patachis are hated here! The only thing stopping them from hating the priesthood just as much is that they blame the patachis for corrupting us, not the archbishop! Gods forbid they ever learn the truth!"

"Would you be making a threat, Father Berin?" the robed man asked, dangerously.

"No threats!" Berin jabbed at the man's chest with the hand holding the cane. "When you walk out of here, Master-whatever-your-name-is, take a good look around. You will see many people who are not as poor nor as ignorant nor as helpless as they were when I was new to the priesthood. They have grown and they are not a force to be taken lightly. I have helped to make them our friends, and to make certain the faith is not lost to their hearts. I am one of them, and they trust me. I warn you—if you dispose of me, you will have trouble."

The robed man gave a small smile. He reached into his robes and withdrew a small scroll. "Father Berin," he said. "Let me be certain that I am understood. Tomorrow morning, at your sermon, you will address the contents of this scroll. You shall be precise, and you shall be specific. The archbishop shall be watching. As shall the gods."

He handed the scroll to Father Berin and then swept off down the hall. Muttering, Father Berin removed the seal and undid the scroll. He read the first passage, angrily. The second with growing disquiet. And the rest with cold dread.

"Father?" asked young Father Michelo anxiously from alongside. "What does it say?"

"I am not going to preach this," Father Berin muttered. He rerolled the scroll with tight, shaking hands. "I will *never* preach the likes of this." He stuffed the scroll into his robes.

"Father? What does the archbishop instruct?"

"Nothing, boy," Berin muttered. "Nothing at all. Now go and attend the gods' work. I need to pray."

"Oh dear," said Rhillian, peering over the edge of the rooftop. Below, the dock was a seething mass of people. Some people held large eight-pointed stars on poles, others held small drawings or engravings of saints. They spilled all the way out to the waterfront and onto the piers, blocking all traffic. Strangely, they made less noise now than when their numbers had been fewer. They gazed up at the plain bricks and shutters of the Velo house, and waited.

Sasha sat on one of the small stools upon the flat rooftop, and placed the tray she'd been carrying on the edge of a small, bricked flower garden. She poured herself some water from an earthen jug and drank thirstily. Rhillian took the stool beside her and accepted a bowl of soup. "Mmm. This smells delicious."

"Mariesa makes great soup," Sasha agreed, taking her own bowl. "What did you and Kessligh talk about?"

Rhillian shrugged, sipping her soup. "I'm surprised you weren't there."

"I can't be around for every one of Kessligh's meetings," said Sasha. "He's in charge, not me. I was shoring up the protection through the back lanes, making sure we're well covered."

"I would think you might need more than two archers on the roof," Rhillian suggested. At each corner of the rooftop crouched a single Nasi-Keth archer, his longbow strung and ready. Further along, on adjoining rooftops, were several others—it was all one rooftop, really, here along the dockfront, broken by rows of washing, small rooftop gardens and half-mended boat sails.

"If this lot gets out of hand," said Sasha, "a few archers won't stop them. We're guarding against family men, not worshippers."

Rhillian sipped another mouthful, then half stood to peer over the edge once more. It seemed a compulsive act. When she sat again, she looked troubled, almost bewildered. "This artefact," she said. "This star. It represents the Enoran High Temple?"

Sasha nodded. "Every temple has a star when forged. And every new saint. This one was forged upon the founding of the Enoran High Temple, the oldest in Enora."

"Itself two hundred and forty years after the revelation on Mount Tristen," said Rhillian. "Shereldin is a small village in Enora, near Remel. There was a great war there, where the first Bacosh king to follow the Verenthane faith, met and defeated the last pagan king. This Shereldin Star, this great symbol of peace and virtue, is named after a battlefield. A battlefield not far from the High Temple itself."

Sasha dunked bread in her soup and chewed. "You know the history far better than I, yet you ask me questions," she said around her mouthful.

"What I know as facts," said Rhillian, "and what humans understand as faith, are two completely different things."

"I know," said Sasha. In truth, she was more interested in consuming her lunch than entering into another semantical serrin debate over the varying natures of truth.

"Is this star supposed to hold special powers?" Rhillian pressed.

"I suppose," said Sasha with her mouth full.

"Of what kind?"

"The stars of the saints are supposed to hold those saints' holy favour, long after their deaths. I don't know what kind of power the founding star of a temple would hold."

"But people believe they can gain positive energy by being near it?"

Sasha gave an irritated shrug and swallowed. "Rhillian, I make a very poor expert on Verenthanes. I think they're crazy too."

Rhillian shook her head faintly. "I don't think they're crazy," she said. "I just try to understand. I mean, look at them all. What are they thinking? What can they possibly expect to gain?"

"You mean they're crazy," Sasha summarised.

"Emotion is a fact unto itself," said Rhillian, fixing her friend with an emerald gaze. No doubt Rhillian intended the gaze to be mild. Somehow, with Rhillian, that intention never entirely translated. Beneath the shadow of her hat, her eyes burned in the shadow. "I may not comprehend the cause of the emotion, but I cannot deny that it exists. Serrin take existence alone as proof of meaning. We seek only to understand, not to ridicule, nor to discredit."

Rhillian's Saalsi was so much more eloquent than Errollyn's, Sasha reflected, and realised that she'd barely even noticed Rhillian had switched to Saalsi.

"Changes the balance of power somewhat," Sasha suggested, nodding toward the dock as she ate. "Doesn't it."

Rhillian shrugged. "A little. Not greatly." Beyond the docks, the sea shone silver beneath the overcast sky. Behind the high cloud, the sun was not so strong today. Perhaps the long delayed winter was finally on its way.

"You wait to see how the play moves," Sasha continued, watching her friend warily. "Kessligh has more power now."

"Does *he* control the star?" Rhillian asked.

"It was granted to him, through me."

"By a rogue priest."

"Father Terano Maerler is not so much a rogue. Last I heard, he's still alive."

"How long will that last, I wonder?" Rhillian murmured, gazing at the silver horizon. "The Steiner alliance have purged their discontents. Perhaps the priesthood is next."

"If that happens, the checks on Steiner's power will grow even less."

Rhillian nodded sombrely. "That is why Maerler must be supported. Patachi Maerler is no friend of Saalshen, I am not such a fool as to believe so. But he remains today the only power in Petrodor capable of opposing Patachi Steiner and his friend the archbishop. In human societies, power works. This lesson I have learned in my time amongst you. It troubles a serrin's sensibilities, but slowly we learn to accept the truth. To have influence, amongst humans, one must have true power. The means to kill in large numbers. And so, we learn."

There was a hole in the back brim of Rhillian's hat. Sasha recalled the crossbow bolt at the Garelo Temple. Rhillian had nearly died saving Yulia. Mercy was the serrin's instinct. Now, she spoke of slaughter.

"Rhillian," Sasha ventured after a moment, "does it occur to you that perhaps the great powers have been reluctant to push too hard in Petrodor for a reason? I mean . . . the great houses are split roughly north and south, and that is a logical division, yes? A balance. A symmetry, even."

"To human eyes, perhaps," Rhillian said doubtfully. "Myself, I would hesitate to call the balance of terror and ignorance *symmetry* . . . but I quibble."

"The provincial dukes have been reluctant to choose sides until now," Sasha continued. "The balance in Petrodor serves them well. No one patachi has too much power, and the priesthood is neutral between them. Arguments over wealth and power hold no monopoly on one or another man's support. But now, the argument is religion. Faith. And faith can only ever have one side."

Rhillian stared at her.

"Faith can have many sides," she said eventually. She looked . . . disturbed. As though Sasha's words had shaken her. "Many of these people below, they are both Verenthane and Nasi-Keth. In the Saalshen Bacosh, interpretations of the scrolls are very liberal. Belief is not such a simple thing as you describe."

"To serrin, no." Sasha matched Rhillian's gaze as best she could. "You're not in Saalshen, Rhillian."

Rhillian's eyes narrowed and she made an expression as close to a dismissive snort as Sasha had ever seen a serrin make. "You sound like Errollyn."

"Serrin seek many truths," Sasha insisted. "Humans seek one. It is our weakness, and our strength. Our diversity ensures that one truth shall never entirely triumph. Serrin have little diversity, yet your very nature ensures you do not need to."

"We are diverse enough," Rhillian said quietly.

"Errollyn insists not."

"The very fact of which surely supports my assertion," said Rhillian, a little testily.

"And that he's the *only one* who disagrees with you supports Errollyn's," Sasha said firmly. "Rhillian, from the human perspective, that's just . . . odd. A little scary, even. I don't understand the *vel'ennar*, Rhillian. Neither what it is, nor how it works. But look at the Nasi-Keth. Or my native Lenays. They split in so many directions over the simplest of things, they are almost too numerous to count. Serrin all move together like a tide. I find that a little frightening, Rhillian. In truth."

"We find your need to massacre each other in order to express a diversity of opinion somewhat frightening," Rhillian said coolly.

Sasha nodded vigorously. "Indeed. Me too. But here, in this city, you've picked the one issue that might unite the people. Faith. North or south, rich or poor, Dockside or Backside or Riverside, they're all Verenthane. Not as many distrust the archbishop as ought to, for he's been held in check for so long by the stalemate of priesthood neutrality. The issue of the day is Saalshen and its occupation of holy sites. The Enoran High Temple, no less. You intervene and support Maerler to maintain a balance. But your very engagement in such a debate only works to the archbishop's advantage. You are serrin. You are pagan. With your presence, your interference, however well-intended, you only prove him right."

"And your alternative is that we retreat, cease our influence and allow Steiner to win anyway?" Rhillian's stare was disbelieving.

"Rhillian . . ." Sasha leaned forward, elbows on knees, her soup bowl suspended in one hand. "If Maerler concedes to Steiner's power and gives Steiner command of the Army of Torovan, as the archbishop surely wishes, it would be a negotiated settlement. These are merchants. They would make a deal. Such is the way of power here—threat, violence and bluff, followed by a negotiated deal. But all such deals are temporary, and difficult. Maerler would remain a power and a threat, if Steiner should falter. Patachi Steiner knows this all too well, I think. It would be a nightmare for him. There are worse situations for you, Rhillian. For Saalshen."

"You have no idea of my nightmares," Rhillian said quietly. "I see the war reaching Saalshen. I see a slaughter for which none of my tongues have yet devised words to describe."

"Perhaps you try for too much," Sasha pleaded. "If you support Maerler now, Steiner may feel he has no choice but to attack. Perhaps some of the dukes will follow him. By forcing the battle, you could destroy one or the other and force a final solution. The balance of power would end, and that would be a tragedy for Saalshen."

"And if I do nothing, Maerler may back down and Steiner may win, and the Army of Torovan marches to slaughter my people. Are you saying that is now unavoidable?"

Sasha hung her head. "I don't know. Maybe. We tried, Rhillian. But already the balance has shifted too far with the archbishop choosing his side."

"Perhaps he has not." Rhillian's voice was calm now. Distant as she contemplated the horizon and the rigging of moored ships. "The priesthood has just now seen one rebellion. Perhaps there will be others."

Sasha gazed at her with dawning dread. "Rhillian," she said softly. "Please don't do anything you might regret."

"There is nothing in this life," said Rhillian, "that I may choose to do that I might not possibly regret." She sipped at her soup and glanced sideways at Sasha, the slant of a lovely eyebrow beneath her hat. "Have you bedded with Errollyn yet?"

Sasha blinked at her, caught completely off guard. "Bedded?"

"A strange concept, I know. It happens sometimes between men and women. Surely it never crossed your mind."

Sasha took a deep breath and straightened, seeking dignity. "I've been rather busy."

"I wouldn't have thought it would take a whole afternoon." Rhillian's humour, like her stare, and her swordwork, was utterly merciless. "He insists it was his conscience that led him in this direction. I think perhaps it was his groin."

Sasha snorted, trying hard not to blush. She was not often prone to embarrassment. "Like I'm such a catch," she murmured. Rhillian grinned, then nearly laughed outright. Sasha scowled at her. "What?"

"You think yourself unattractive?" Rhillian's entire manner had changed. Now, her eyes shone with fascination. Spirits she was beautiful. Beside her, Sasha felt like a mule beside a purebred desai mare.

"No," Sasha retorted defensively. "I'm just . . . different. Like always."

"To a serrin, there are few combinations more intriguing than dark hair and dark eyes. There is subtlety, you see." She peered at Sasha's face, searchingly. "You see, the shading, so faint, so varied." She made a form with one hand, fingers shifting. "Serrin colours are so obvious, so bright . . . the shades of human form are such *res'ahl en*, the mystery of the *than'ath rheel* darkness, that shapes the *ash'laan* of . . ."

"Wait, wait, wait," Sasha said in Lenay. "I'm lost. Stop. I make it policy never to talk arts with serrin, especially not in Saalsi. My head will burst."

"Really?" said Rhillian, now back in Torovan, all bemused innocence. "I wasn't even speaking dialect."

"And of course you're terrible with languages," Sasha added, exasperated.

"Absolutely awful." It was an old joke. And by serrin standards, not so untrue. "Sasha, every serrin man I've heard remark on the issue thinks you're gorgeous. I'd be absolutely astonished if Errollyn felt differently."

"And you serrin spend lots of time sitting around talking about whom you'd like to bed?" Sasha asked incredulously.

"Every spare moment. Sasha." Rhillian straightened and looked her very firmly in the eye. "As your friend. You live a very dangerous life. I'm delighted that you've survived this far. Time may be short for all of us. Take the man to bed. I assure you, it's worth the effort."

Sasha stared a moment longer. And her mouth dropped open as she realised the implication. "You . . . you mean . . . you and Errollyn have . . . ?"

Rhillian outright laughed, a pleasant, warm sound. "Oh, and that surprises you? We're serrin! We have no morals, Sasha, and when we die, we're all going straight to the hells!" Sasha wanted to reprimand her that she really shouldn't joke about such things, but her mouth would not cooperate. "I have thirty-eight summers, Sasha, I've bedded rather a lot of men. I recommend it. Errollyn in particular."

"But you hate each other!" Sasha burst out.

Rhillian laughed again . . . and nearly lost control of her bowl of soup. She saved it just in time. "Oh no," she sighed. "Not at all. I . . . look," and she held up her free hand helplessly, "I can't explain it, it's just a serrin thing. I don't hate Errollyn. I'll never hate Errollyn."

"Because he's serrin?"

"No, that would be prejudice, you shan't trap me that easily." Very amused. "Are you really sure you want to go down this path with me? We could be here until sundown."

"No, right, forget it," Sasha said sarcastically. "Sanity before curiosity."

"Just trust me. On serrin matters at least, I'm quite sure I know what I'm talking about. I hope I haven't made you jealous. I'm quite certain I don't intend to marry him."

Sasha saw the amusement on Rhillian's face at that prospect. She had to laugh. "No. Bloody hells. It just seems that everyone's having sex except me."

"And who's fault is that?" Rhillian retorted expansively. "Take the man to bed, Sasha!"

Sasha sighed in disbelief and shook her head. She didn't know *what* she felt, or whether she'd take the advice. Everything was so complicated. She envied the serrin. In some things, they were endlessly complicated. But in others, the simple pleasures, they were so attractively simple.

"You know," she said, "I once thought Errollyn was the strangest serrin I'd ever met. But now I think it's probably you."

Rhillian smiled, not at all offended. "Well, you're *easily* the strangest human I've ever met," she returned playfully. "I suppose we're even."

Fifteen

THE FIELDS BESIDE THE ROAD INTO ALGERY were barren after the harvest, and men pulled ploughs behind teams of oxen to loosen the soil. The cart rattled over pavings, here on the gentle downslope into town.

Jaryd sat behind the driver's board in the covered cart, and peered past Teriyan and Sofy's shoulders. The road was so familiar. Ahead, past rows of fruit trees, the winding Hathys River ran between walled banks before the city. A stone bridge crossed where the river met the road.

Along the riverbank, Algery rose in a swarm of stone buildings, haphazard tiled roofs and narrow alleys. A great arch at the end of the bridge marked the entrance to the city, whereafter the road vanished beneath the roofs. He knew, however, that it headed toward the grand temple spires that soared from the city's heart. Beyond and to either side of the city rose the enclosing hills of the Algery Valley. Downstream, another quarter-day's ride, lay Pyrlata, and the Nyvar residence . . . now the property of Family Arastyn.

"Oh, it's so pretty!" Sofy opined, predictably. Tyree's capital did look pretty, Jaryd had to concede, however poor his mood for noticing such things. It helped that the sun was shining, the sky blue streaked with white, and the green orchards made lovely patterns in the midafternoon light against the rowed poplars and pines. "Here, what's this building?"

Jaryd saw where she was pointing, to a small domed roof on the riverbank, upstream of the bridge. "That's the skywatcher. Dastry Urelvyn built it. He was the father of Lord Urelvyn. He was Verenthane, but followed the old astrology; he built the dome to watch the skies at night. He had the star charts painted all across the ceiling and watched through his windows as they moved."

As the road wound down to the bridge, traffic passed them on the way up. Sofy made no effort to conceal herself as carts passed, or farmers walked the roadside tending to orchards. A Goeren-yai farm driver, his daughter and a nephew on their way into town two days before a big wedding attracted little attention, and very few people this far from Baen-Tar had any idea what the Lenay royal family actually looked like. Sofy had seen some of the likenesses which sold in town squares on market day and laughed. Dressed in plain travelling clothes with a cloth tied over her hair she was in little danger of being taken for a princess.

"Oh I wish I'd found more time to travel," Sofy said wistfully as they approached the bridge. "Only now that I'm about to leave Lenayin forever do I have a chance to see what my land actually looks like."

"This is just a city," said Teriyan, unimpressed. He did not look particularly comfortable on the driving board, his long knees sticking out, his hands grasping the unfamiliar reins. "Your actual *land* looks somewhat different."

"Oh tosh," Sofy snorted. "I've seen plenty of beautiful land lately, now it's time to see a city. You know what I mean."

Teriyan had tied his hair back in a knot in the style of the eastern Goeren-yai of Tyree. Long red hair was common enough, but there was still a chance of recognition—many men of Tyree had ridden to the Udalyn Valley, although fewer from the cities and towns. There was always a chance of coming across a recent comrade-in-arms, particularly amidst the crowds that promised in Algery.

Encounters with travellers on the road had informed them of the wedding in Algery, on exactly the day that Aeryl Daery had said. Galandry No-Name, once Nyvar, was to be wed to Family Iryani, close allies of Family Arastyn. It was the last, loose end of the Nyvar Family, the elder sister Dalya already wed, and the brother Wyndal adopted into Family Arastyn itself. And it was the best chance for access to Wyndal, in a big crowd for a big occasion, away from the private defences of the Arastyn Residence, aware of threats upon their house. Whether Wyndal would cooperate or not was another question entirely.

They rattled across the bridge, beneath the arch and into Algery with a loud clatter of hooves and rattling wheels. The road was busy with people, and colourful flags hung from windows above the way. People were carrying baskets of vegetables, rolling barrels of ale, or hauling legs of lamb or pork.

After slow going on the crowded road, they emerged into the square opposite the temple. Jaryd stared, suppressing a shiver. He recalled the services, walking at his father's side up the broad steps behind the priests. He'd liked the dressing up and the showing off. The services had been a bore, but he'd liked feeling important. Like a fool, he'd believed it his gods-given entitlement.

Now, the top step about the temple door was decorated with a small pavilion, garnished with blue ralama flowers and green poplar boughs. Flags and colours hung about the square—the colours of Arastyn House, red and blue, in four opposing squares . . . and the other, green and white, he supposed must be Iryani. Truthfully, he'd never cared enough to recall.

He gave Teriyan directions around the square's central fountain, into a narrower street. Near the opposite side of the city (for Algery was not large like Baen-Tar) they found the inn they were looking for and pulled the horses up outside.

"Wait here," said Teriyan, leaping from the cart. Sofy got down to see to the horses, something she fancied she knew a little about now. It seemed to Jaryd that she found delight in being useful. It was a quality much unlooked for in a princess. Jaryd stayed where he was and watched the inn across the road. In the narrow gap between buildings, he could glimpse open fields beyond and a lane that would lead to the stables. This was the quarter for inns, all on the city perimeter, where stables had lots of space and carts laden with fodder, and lords coming from the western valley would not have to pass through town before finding their destination.

The innkeep came out, talking loudly with Teriyan, and Teriyan unstopped a barrel for the man to have a taste. Satisfied that the horses were well, Sofy climbed back up to the driver's board.

"Over there," Jaryd murmured, nodding toward the opposing inn's verandah. "That's Dysmon Frayne. Younger brother of Lord Frayne. They have a property not far from Nyvar Holding. I've played lagand against him. His son was good in the youngsters' contests."

Sofy saw a tall, thin man with close-cropped hair. He was speaking with a Torovan merchant, colourful and long-haired, his broad hat in one hand. A young lady appeared from the inn's interior. Sofy seemed to stiffen.

"What?" Jaryd asked.

"Nothing," said Sofy after a moment, relaxing a little. "I thought for a moment it was someone I knew."

"Who would you know out here?"

"Um . . ." Sofy thought for a moment, "Maryel Tasys, Elynda Iryani, Pyta Paramys, Rosarya Pelyn and Alonya Redyk. Oh, and Emylie Arastyn, of course. All were in Baen-Tar. Maryel I know returned to Algery three months ago. She's certainly here. Elynda I'm not sure about, though I'd guess she's returned just for this wedding, since it's her brother. And of course Emylie will be here."

"Ladies-in-waiting," said Jaryd, understanding. This was Sofy's life in Baen-Tar. Many of the lords sent daughters to Baen-Tar in search of education, sophistication and, of course, husbands. While Jaryd knew many of Tyree and Lenayin's future rulers through play on the lagand field, Sofy knew many of their prospective wives through embroidery, scripture, dance and language classes. "You might have said so before we set out."

"I've far less chance of being recognised than you have," Sofy snorted, adjusting the cloth tied beneath her chin.

"Which is why you were holding your breath just now."

Sofy gave him an annoyed look. "I was not. Or maybe just a little. You can never be entirely sure." She looked up and down the street at passers-by and flags hanging from windows. A cart squeezed past their own, hooves clattering. "All this fuss for a wedding," she mused.

It seemed an odd thing for Sofy to say—she'd seen far grander weddings than this one. Then Jaryd realised. "Your own will be a lot fussier," he said.

"I know." Sofy seemed to gaze at nothing for a moment. Jaryd had never really thought about it before. Men got married, and unmarried girls became wives. Wives obeyed their husbands, and the natural order continued. He'd never . . . well, he'd never even considered looking at it from a woman's perspective. Especially not from the perspective of a woman who disliked her prospective husband, even though she'd never actually met him. She hated what he stood for, and what her marriage would be in aid of. War against the Saalshen Bacosh. It reduced her to a tool in other people's plans. A pawn.

It seemed unfair. She had no say in her own life, and her fates were mapped out for the interests of others. For the first time, Jaryd felt something toward a woman that he'd never expected to feel. He empathised.

"Maybe he'll be a good man," he offered, uncertainly. "Regent Arrosh's heir."

Sofy shrugged. "Perhaps." And said nothing more. That was most unlike her usual bubbly, cheerful self. Jaryd didn't like that. Strangely, it seemed he'd come to enjoy Sofy's good humour. Her sunshine kept him buoyant when all he saw were dark clouds. He clasped her arm briefly. It was forward of him. Should her royal minders have been present, it would surely have earned him a loud rebuke. But Sofy looked over her shoulder at him and smiled.

The innkeep accepted one barrel of ale of the four they carried, he and Teriyan lifting it from the back with some attempted help from Sofy. Jaryd remained in the back, wrapped in a cloak and feigning illness. They drove on, avoiding the fancier inns where nobility were quartered who might perchance recognise one or another of their party, and found accommodation at a cramped little place down an alley.

Teriyan took the cart and horses to see if he could find separate stable lodging, while Sofy and Jaryd carried their bags up several winding, narrow flights of stairs. The room was small, with two beds and enough space on the floor for a third. A crate made for a step up to windows that could be ducked through, and onto a small terrace amidst the sloping roof tiles, with a view of the little lane. Jaryd thought the place inadequate, considering what he'd been accustomed to when staying in Algery. Sofy, on the other hand, seemed intrigued, especially with the terrace and its view.

"Sasha would love this!" she said, gazing about. "When she was little she used to climb on the palace roof sometimes. She says she's still a good climber, I'm sure she'll get to use it in Petrodor. I think she could get from one side of this city to the other without touching the ground."

That gave Jaryd an idea.

A tile gave way beneath Jaryd's boot, clattered down the roof and broke with a *crack* in the middle of the street below. Jaryd pressed himself flat atop the apex, repressing a curse between gritted teeth. Voices from the inn rose in drunken pleasure, and from the sound of boots thundering on the verandah, it seemed the dancing had taken to the streets. No one noticed a falling tile.

Jaryd continued carefully. There was less light than he'd hoped up on the rooftops and the overlapping shelves of loose tiles were treacherous.

He climbed a new slope, trod lightly across a terrace, past a table and chairs, beneath some washing, and up onto the tiles again. Ahead and below was the inn. It looked no different from the rest of the undulating rooftops, but Sofy and Teriyan had counted streets and strides, making certain he knew exactly where it was. Jaryd was now glad they had, despite his protestations at the time. He knew Algery well, but he'd never seen it from this perspective before, and certainly not at night. Now if he could just find the right room.

Sofy had helped there too. She had followed inn staff down to the river with their baskets of laundry, posing as a water carrier herself, and had simply started conversations. Before long, she'd known not only which inn and room lodged Master Wyndal Arastyn, but what he'd had for lunch, which serving girl's backside cousin Dylis Arastyn had pinched, and all about the appalling table manners of Lady Arastyn. Sofy had seemed quite cheerful in her espionage. Jaryd had suggested that perhaps treachery came to royals naturally. Sofy had laughed.

Jaryd skirted a courtyard, paused briefly beneath a window, then climbed across to the terrace he'd selected as his target. There was no table here, no chairs, no washing line. Thick curtains were pulled behind the diamond-shaped glass panels. He crept forward and put an ear to the glass, but he could hear nothing. He waited, listening to the music and laughter down on the street. Wyndal would almost certainly be downstairs with the other nobles, but he had to be sure. He waited.

Finally satisfied, Jaryd pulled his gloves from a jacket pocket. One he pulled onto his right hand, and into the other he inserted the hilt of his knife.

Thus muffled, he selected a glass pane near the door handle and broke it with a sharp blow. Pieces fell, and clattered, but would surely attract no more attention than the falling tile had. He reached his gloved hand in and pulled the door open enough to slip in and peer past the curtains. The room was bare and small, with a single lamp burning on a small table.

Jaryd eased the terrace door closed and pushed back the curtains. He would have to hide under the bed until Wyndal returned, in case servants came to attend to the lamp. But first, he pulled his sword and practised a few swings, testing his reach within the small room. Better to focus on that, than wonder at the reception Wyndal might grant him. Better to think on that, than any confrontation with family. With family came thoughts of his younger brother Tarryn. Wyndal was clearly not as angry at Tarryn's death as Jaryd was, or he'd have killed his host family by now . . . or died trying. Or escaped, to plot revenge in the wilds like Jaryd himself. Wyndal was still here. He'd always been a thinker, though. Jaryd lowered his blade with a last, grim look around. Perhaps he should not pass judgment too quickly. Perhaps Wyndal was plotting something.

The door opened. Jaryd stared, frozen in place—there was no time to slide beneath the bed, it happened too fast. Just as quickly, he found himself staring down the snubbed muzzle of a loaded crossbow, cocked and ready to fire. The crossbowman entered the room, muzzle aimed unwaveringly at Jaryd's chest. Behind him, in the doorway, stood another man. He was young, with blue eyes and shoulder length blond hair. He would have been very handsome indeed, were it not for the horrific sword scar that caved in his right cheekbone, and took a slice from the bridge of his nose.

"You," Jaryd snarled.

Rhyst Angyvar smiled coldly. "You really *are* just as stupid as everyone always said, aren't you, Jaryd?"

It was a Varansday. Alexanda Rochel hated Varansdays. Varansday morning in particular, which required him to be out of bed at an ungodly hour, to dress up in his dukely best and walk the short distance across the house grounds to the Cochindel Temple for service. Worse, a light rain was falling and a chill wind blew from the north.

"Really, Alexanda," said Varona at his elbow, "we needn't walk. We could have taken the carriage."

"Nonsense," snorted Alexanda, his polished boots scraping on the garden path. "Ridiculous to mount up just to cross a stream. Hurry up, boy!" he growled at the servants behind them, struggling to keep umbrellas above the heads of their duke and duchess. "If I have to keep ducking your blasted contraption, I'll be sitting all service with a crook neck!"

Ahead of them walked a contingent of twelve Pazira Guard, dry enough beneath wide hats and coats over armour. Behind walked Bryanne, with several earls' daughters huddling beneath their own umbrellas, and trying not to get grass stains on the hems of their good gowns. Behind them, three earls and their wives, including Varona's brother Redolcho. Trustworthy men, of families interwoven with the Rochels for many centuries, and a long history of friendly relations in trade, war and marriage. These, Alexanda invited for company at the house. The others, especially those from foreign provinces, he was becoming thoroughly sick of.

"The gardens do look lovely in the rain, Varona," called Tiscea, Redolcho's wife.

"Oh, don't they just?" said Varona. The green lawns were lush and wet, and the green trees dripped, and the carefully rowed flower gardens seemed to drink in the moisture and glow with pleasure. "There is so much that is beautiful around Cochindel. So much that I have been unable to see." With a sharp glance at her husband.

"Quit your griping, woman," Alexanda retorted. "Isn't it just like a woman to admire the beautiful garden, and never a thought for the high walls and guards that protect it from ruin."

"I'd swear you thought we were all about to be assassinated," Varona replied, eyeing the armed escort to their front. At the rear of their little column, a similar number of armed men made a line. "Have your negotiations been going poorly, my love?"

Alexanda grunted. "Perhaps your rough tongue could be moderated by a woman's softer tones?"

"I try to secure safety and prosperity for Pazira," said Alexanda. "Not bargain a better price for a Xaldian carpet."

"Really, Alexanda," Varona sniffed. She withdrew her hand from the crook of his elbow. Alexanda reclaimed it and replaced it on his arm. He gave it a firm squeeze, whatever his gruff expression. Varona sighed. After twenty-six years of marriage, one learned to recognise an apology when offered, however fleeting it might appear to others. She gave him a thoughtful look. "You look so much nicer when you brush your hair properly. It no longer sticks out like a squirrel's tail."

"Thank you, dearest," said Alexanda. "How nice of you to notice." Varona smiled, and gave his arm a squeeze.

The eastern gate was overgrown with ivy and manned by a small guard-post atop the wall. Several more guards withdrew metal braces from the wall and pushed the gate open with a heavy squeal. Alexanda wondered for the dozenth time if these walls were really fooling anyone. The Pazira House defences deterred petty criminals and unprofessional assassins, nothing more. Like everything in Petrodor, it was a game of appearances.

Some of the village folk waved and called greeting as the column walked by. Varona waved back, and nudged Alexanda on the arm. He waved too. The villagers seemed to like that and called traditional Varansday blessings in their broad eastern accents. Most were peasants, but there were some local smallholders too. Some dukes refused to allow nonnobility to hold title, but Alexanda did. If a common peasant could make enough coin to buy his own plot, then he was clearly a good farmer and should be rewarded. In the Bacosh, of course, such notions would cost a man his head.

"I'm so proud to be married to a duke who is so well loved," Varona remarked with a smile as they passed.

"That there are so few who are is proof alone that the world is full of fools," he replied. "These people are the source of all a ruler's wealth, and all his power too, if war should come. Treat them well, and they shall grant him the world. Treat them poorly, and nothing shall save him when the troubles come. It's the simplest equation in the world, yet so many lack the faculties to grasp it."

"Oh, Alexanda, you *also* treat them well because you like to make people happy. Don't you?"

"A luxury," said Alexanda dismissively.

"Alexanda Rochel, you can't fool me. You're not half as hardhearted as you like people to think you are."

Alexanda spared his wife a small, wry smile. "If you say so, dearest."

About the temple crowded most of Cochindel and the remainder of Alexanda's earls.

There on a white horse beside the temple steps sat Captain Faldini, with a metal breastplate over chain mail and a helm instead of a hat, with a lance pointed skyward from its rest upon one stirrup guard. He and ten more horsemen kept a clear space before the steps.

"*Must* he bring his horse to Varansday service?" Varona wondered. "What does he think to do, ride it down the aisle?"

"He does his job, dearest."

"And makes a spectacular show-off in doing it."

"That is the nature of the man," Alexanda admitted.

The crowd parted as the column approached and earls doffed their hats to the duke and duchess. Captain Faldini dismounted.

"Your grace," said Faldini with a bow. He had dark eyes and prominent cheekbones, features sharp and angular beneath his helm. Some ladies thought him dashing, as he no doubt intended. Alexanda knew that Varona found him, in her own words, creepy.

Many earls, and some of the duke's own family, disapproved of Faldini's promotion to Captain of the Pazira Guard. Alexanda's cousin Redal, for one, had been furious. Lieutenant Redal could have accepted being passed over for some high-born noble, but to be passed over for the second son of a Luchani wine maker was a personal insult, at least in Redal's eyes.

Alexanda cared not. Skill, in his eyes, came from passion. He admired men of passion, something he'd learned from his father, and his grandfather before him. Alexanda loved to spend time at the vineyards, watching the master growers go about their tasks. He loved to watch a talented blacksmith hammering dark, sooty metal into a gleaming blade, or a wheelwright crafting a perfect circle from a straight length of wood. The best craftsmen, his father had shown him, had a passion for their work. And so it was with soldiers, too. Faldini had a weakness for crazy riding, was an unashamed egotist, and could have probably been a first-rate, bloody-handed butcher in the service of some other duke. But he loved his work with a passion, and he was the best available in Pazira. Promoting him to captain meant that Alexanda had to live with certain irate relatives. But overlooking him for one less talented would have meant living with his irate self. As his lovely wife often contended, that was difficult enough when there was nothing to be mad about.

"What news?" he asked Faldini in a low voice, as his wife and their guests, mingled with the surrounding crowd.

"Fast messages travelling between Cuely and Steiner Mansion," said Faldini. "They rode all night. I think perhaps Patachi Steiner and his dukes plan to attack Dockside and reclaim the star. If Dockside truly do have the star."

"Oh they have it all right," Alexanda muttered. "My reports tell me the crowds on Dockside grew all through the night. Gods know how it shall stand this morning. But no, a war against the Dockside is the last thing Patachi Steiner wants. For one, it would unite all the Nasi-Keth factions against him, probably under Cronenverdt, since he's by far the greatest warrior. Right now, they're happily disunited.

"And an attack on Dockside would obviously involve the serrin. The archbishop may have no qualms about offsiding Saalshen, but the patachis have plenty. They can afford to lose Saalshen trade if they win the war for the Bacosh, but not before. And Saalshen has been reluctant to cut trade early for fear of losing leverage, and thus inviting an attack they know they could not survive. An attack on Dockside would be crazy without an attack on Saalshen's properties, the way the serrin fight . . . and an attack on Saalshen's properties may even bring Patachi Maerler into the fight on Saalshen's side, with whatever dealings he's been making with Rhillian lately."

Captain Faldini looked mildly impressed. He shrugged within his armour. "I believe you. I'm just a captain. I cut heads."

"You'd be a much better captain if you knew *which* heads," Alexanda remarked.

Faldini smiled. "That's your task, Your Grace. Just point me at them."

"I'm hoping to avoid pointing you at anyone. We number four hundred, but reports now lead me to believe that Danor and Coroman have brought at least eight hundred each, whatever their claims. We dare not declare ourselves too soon."

Faldini scratched at his chin. "Word about the barracks is that Maerler is finished. The archbishop favours Steiner, it's clear. Why not declare with Steiner and be done with it?"

"Patachi Maerler," said Alexanda with heavy sarcasm, "commands ten thousand plus, and most of southern Petrodor. Any assault into his territory would be a military nightmare. He has Saalshen on his side. His holy brother has just deprived the archbishop, and thus Patachi Steiner, of their greatest rallying cry—the Shereldin Star—and placed it most cleverly into the dragon's mouth. Patachi Maerler is cunning, Captain—he gives the star to the dragon, and now Patachi Steiner must go and fight the dragon if he wants it back. Patachi Maerler will sit back and watch them maul each other, and smile. Had he kept the star himself, Patachi Steiner may have fought *him*. This way, he loses nothing and his enemies decline.

"Furthermore, I will not leap on board this crazy ship of war unless I am convinced Pazira has absolutely no other choice. You are young, and you have seen battles, but you have not seen war. I have. This war that looms shall be slaughter on a scale that would make even the highlanders cringe."

Alexanda walked to the head of the column moving up the stone steps to receive a blessing from the priest before the doors.

It was a nice little temple, Alexanda reflected. His builder's eye studied the stonework and appreciated the symmetry, the precision of supports and strongpoints that might be hidden to others. Footsteps echoed in a gathering volume as the temple slowly filled. Alexanda and Varona reached the end of the aisle, and sat together on the left, Bryanne joining her mother, further from Alexanda. Alexanda removed his hat, and continued his examination of the ceiling. The wood support beams looked interesting—rel wood, perhaps. Rel was usually too heavy for such beams. He wondered how the craftsmen had done it, craning his neck . . .

"Dear, sit still," his wife scolded in a low voice, as the benches beside and behind them were gradually filled. "It's not dignified."

"I promise you, dear lady, this ceiling is vastly more interesting than anything some priest might say this morning."

"We have this conversation every second Varansday," replied Varona, on the edge of temper. "You are the duke and it is your obligation to sit here and suffer with the rest of us."

"Oh tosh, what are you talking about? You enjoy it."

Infinitely more refined, Varona raised her eyebrows. "I happen to be a good Verenthane."

"And I'm not?"

Varona smiled, and patted his arm. "Don't worry, dearest. I pray for you."

"Why is it an interesting ceiling, Papa?" asked Bryanne.

"Oh, Bryanne," said her exasperated mother, "don't encourage him."

Alexanda smiled broadly at his daughter. Bryanne grinned. "I'm so glad you asked, petal. Now look up at this beam here, this one right at the end above the wall. That's called a brace."

He was still explaining the intracies of construction and weight-bearing loads, when the priest ascended to his altar. Varona slapped her husband and daughter on the leg to make them shut up. Alexanda did so, grumpily, and as the priest began to drone, he busied himself with thoughts of Petrodor and its circumstances.

If there was one good thing to arise from the current mess, he thought, it was that the power of the provinces and their dukes had been reinforced. Now the squabbling patachis realised they needed them after all, and for more than just decent wine and a good cheese. Most of the men who would march to war would be drawn from the provinces. But they would only obey the instruction of the archbishop, not any fat, greedy patachi. Fathers and mothers would only part with their sons if the gods decreed it. Priests and patachis, so mutually necessary, and such an equal curse upon the land.

Danor was with Patachi Steiner and had participated in the recent attacks against Family Halmady and their allies. So had Vedichi . . . but that was no surprise; Duke Belary was a leech, sucking the blood from all within his borders until Pazira towns were bursting with poor peasants escaping from Vedichi's harsh masters and harsher taxes. Coroman's support was a given— Petrodor was within Coroman's historical borders and, while Duke Tosci was no fool, Steiner's allied families owned many of Coroman's best lands, and the loyalty of his wealthiest earls. No, Patachi Steiner had Tosci by the balls, and Alexanda could hardly blame the man for his capitulations. Pazira, thank the gods, had distance between itself and Petrodor. That and a healthy, regional contempt that went back many centuries.

Songel was a prospect. Alexanda had met with Duke Abad just the other night. He was clearly unhappy with the Steiners and was leaning Maerler's way. Maerler, it seemed, had offered him terms of trade more favourable than had Steiner . . .

In addition to Songel, the province of Flewderin was only interested in being left alone, and Cisseren were . . . well . . . ambivalent. Add it all together and Patachi Steiner only had three provinces firmly behind him. Four remained, as the serrin Rhillian never failed to point out whenever they met. Four weaker provinces, it was true, but add Saalshen and the balance was just about even. Maerler were not out of this race yet, not by a long way. Now Alexanda just had to think of some way to help extend the deadlock indefinitely. In that sense, his sympathies lay clearly with the green-eyed, white-haired beauty and her strange flock. If only he could find a way, before it drove him mad.

And what of this strange business with Halmady? Who knew that Halmady were plotting against their allies? Patachi Halmady had been known as a most unambitious man—a praiseworthy quality, if one were Patachi Steiner and looking for a safe right hand. Alexanda did not know what to make of it all. Could it have been true? Or were Halmady inconvenient for some other reason? Adding to the strangeness, he now heard that Princess Alythia of Lenayin had survived, and was with her sister in Dockside. Steiner had ordered the others killed, it seemed, but not the princess. Well, hardly surprising, if one were to reckon with the temper of her father, the King of Lenayin. But the king's temper would be sorely tested anyhow in this slaughter of his daughter's betrothed family. Something had arisen within the halls of Steiner Mansion to make such a drastic action seem well worth the risk. As to what that could be, Alexanda could only wrestle with the uncomfortable feeling that he was missing something. Something very big, and very obvious to everyone who knew the secret, and completely puzzling to everyone else . . .

The temple was very quiet, he realised. The priest was still talking, and usually there were rustles of fabric from the ladies' dresses, or creaks from the benches as people shifted their weight. Now, nothing. Alexanda looked at the priest. He seemed very . . . well, tense. A bald man in a black robe, his face an even paler shade of white than usual, reading from a scroll upon the lectern.

". . . and have the blasphemous gall to call this slander 'philosophy.' They creep through our city in the dead of night, promising murder and mayhem to all who oppose their malicious intent. They spread their misgotten wealth, corrupting those whose souls can be easily bought—the traitors, the blasphemous, the bastards and the fornicators. These evil collaborators have sold their souls for a few golden coins, and now, they are servants of the demons of Loth.

"Trust none who would serve these demons with the glowing eyes. Like demons, they have no morals. They fornicate with whomever they choose, their women have no concept of feminine virtue, and they have even been known to fornicate with their own brothers and sisters—even with their children. Through their human servants, they seek to spread their vile ways into our midst, to excuse them before our revulsion as 'philosophy,' and other such evil words that pretend know no good nor evil. They seek to devour human souls, as they have no souls of their own. It is the moral, godly duty of each and every true Verenthane in Petrodor—nay, in all Torovan—to resist these evil, twisted creatures with every fibre of our being. So have the gods decreed, and so does our blessed archbishop declare to we, his humble supplicants."

The serrin, Alexanda realised, with horror. This shaven-headed son of a goat was talking about the serrin.

"Chief among the crimes of these wretched animals is blasphemy." The priest spoke with little of the spontaneity or passion that the words might have appeared to describe. Instead, he read with the air of a man giving a prepared recital before a troupe of learned scholars, determined to get every word correct lest he be later reprimanded for his omission. "Let us consider the principle 'philosophies' of Saalshen. Chief amongst them is the *shal'ans neel*, what these evil ones declare as describing the absence of truth. Not only do these pagans disbelieve in the gods, they disbelieve in everything! There is no love, they declare. There is no peace. There is no right, and no wrong, and therefore all actions are excusable! By this alone, we can see that the only guiding principle of Saalshen is immorality itself. The inhabitants of Saalshen are guided in their course here in the world by the principles of immorality, of evil, of decadence and greed and lust. Surely such a plague could only be visited upon us by demons of Loth and their servants."

Alexanda's initial shock gave way to fury. He thought of leaping to the altar and throwing the lectern to the ground. He thought of beating the priest to a pulp with his bare hands. He thought of drawing his sword and running the man through as he surely deserved. This was worse than playing with fire. This . . . *this* speech, was something that for all his faded faith, he had never thought to hear from the mouths of priests. This was evil.

Alexanda got to his feet. Now there was a stirring in the temple. The priest continued, glancing up from his scroll, wavering for the first time in his diatribe of filth. Alexanda reached for his wife's hand, expecting her protest and well prepared to berate her before the entire temple. Instead, she rose stiffly, reaching in turn for Bryanne. Alexanda gave the priest a long, deadly glare. The priest continued reading, recovering his rhythm with grim determination. It was clear he had not written these words himself.

Without a word, Alexanda turned and walked down the aisle. Guardsmen by the doors scrambled to open them and alert the guard beyond. Varona and Bryanne followed. Behind him, Alexanda could hear others following. The priest's voice droned on, with determined perfection on every syllable.

Alexanda walked out into the light rain to a town grey and deserted, save for the Pazira Guard now scrambling into position in the small courtyard before the steps. Up these steps now ran Captain Faldini, alarm on his face. He met his duke halfway down.

"Send a man to find the groundsman Adrian," Alexanda told the bewildered captain. "Tell him to send a message by bird. Tell him it's urgent."

"We have birds?"

"Something a groundsman knows that a captain might not. A gift from Rhillian. They will fly direct to her, or to Saalshen's properties, at least."

"Yes, Your Grace. What should the message say?"

"Tell her that the archbishop uses the morning sermon to incite fury," Alexanda said grimly. "Tell her that she should expect a riot, at the very least. This sermon will be identical, the length and breadth of Petrodor. Gods forbid they hear it in Riverside, though I'm sure they will. Gods curse that bloody-handed tyrant of an archbishop."

Others were filing down the stairs now, donning furs against the rain. A number were scowling in fury as evident as his own. Some others seemed bewildered, as though they did not know why their duke had stormed out of the sermon, but had felt obliged to follow. Yet more appeared uncomfortable, and hesitated on the wet steps as if wondering if he would now go back inside. Walking out on a sermon would not look good if word got back to their holdings . . . or indeed to the archbishop himself. Many others, it was clear, remained inside the temple, keeping their seats for reasons of faith, etiquette, dislike of their duke, or outright agreement with the priest's words. Well, Alexanda thought darkly, as Captain Faldini rushed to give orders, at least now he'd know for certain who was who.

Varona took his hand on the steps, and squeezed. "I'm sorry, my love," she said quietly. "You were right, I should have let you stay in bed."

"Not at all," said Alexanda darkly. "It's well that you dragged me out in the rain. Now, we must be prepared for anything. That blasted archbishop has no idea of what he's just done."

When Sasha climbed to the pier from Mari's boat, a box of crabs on her shoulder, she found Errollyn running with long strides along the planks toward her. He looked alarmed, dark grey hair flying, unconcerned of his footing on the wet pier. Sasha lowered her box.

"Father Berin is dead," Errollyn announced as he arrived, his green eyes hard. "Murdered."

Sasha swore. "Mari!" she called. "I have to go, there's trouble!" From down on the boat's deck, Mari waved her off impatiently, toiling with several more boxes.

"What do you know?" she asked Errollyn, as their boots thumped on the planks.

"The sculptor Aldano found him in the workshop after morning sermon," said Errollyn. "His throat had been cut." Sasha cursed again. "Sasha, the morning sermon was trouble. Elsewhere there's uproar, apparently the archbishop wrote a speech saying nasty things about serrin."

"Not Father Berin, surely?" Their boots hit the paved dock, and they turned right. There were few stalls this morning, partly thanks to Varansday and partly the rain. It fell light and cold from a grey sky, but Sasha was already sodden from a morning exposed on deck. A few sailors and locals walked the dockfront but most seemed intent on business, not wandering the sparse stalls in search of a bargain.

"No, not Father Berin," Errollyn agreed. "Those who attended his sermon said he spoke of tolerance. A passage from the scrolls where Saint Tyrone encounters a starving pagan and gives him food and water although he was starving himself."

"Oh aye," Sasha muttered as she ran, "I'm sure the archbishop's men would have loved that."

There was a crowd around the temple doors when they arrived, a forlorn cluster of men and women standing in the rain, and praying. A pair of caratsa let them in and they walked fast down the aisle, beneath the ceiling scaffolding. Several Nasi-Keth were guarding the door to the workshop, Sasha recognised them as Alaine's men. Beyond the doorway, standing amidst statues and ragged blocks of uncarved rock, stood Alaine himself, arguing furiously with another three of his men.

"I don't care if they protest!" Alaine was shouting. "I want every man, woman and child who attended morning service questioned, and their person and residences searched!"

"Alaine," said Marco, a wide man with long hair, "it is most unlikely to be one of the common folk who did this thing . . ."

"In the name of the good gods, man, how will you know until you start asking questions?"

"It will require the consent of either Kessligh or Gerrold," another man warned him.

"Damn Kessligh and Gerrold to the hells!" Alaine exclaimed. "Gerrold's too busy licking the serrin's boots to care what happens to our poor Father Berin, and Kessligh cares only for the greater glory of Kessligh!"

Marco looked at Sasha as she approached, and then others did too. Alaine turned. Sasha ignored his glare and looked to the left. Father Berin's body lay before a magnificent statue of Darshan, the Verenthane God of Fire. He had fallen forward, hunched on his knees, as if in prayer at the feet of the gods, and the statues, he had loved. A round, brown bundle of cloth, the pavings before him awash with blood. Darshan towered over him, strong and beautiful, as his follower had been weak and stunted.

"Take good care of him," Sasha wished the statue, swallowing hard against the pain in her throat. "He was one of the very few of you lot I ever liked." No wonder the others had killed him.

"Father Berin did not read the archbishop's prescribed sermon this morning," Sasha bluntly told Alaine and his men. "It seems he made the archbishop angry."

"You're very quick to assign blame," Alaine snarled at her. "I'm sure the notion appeals to your pagan notions of Verenthanes."

Errollyn paid them no attention, and walked slowly around the body of Father Berin, green eyes searching.

"You'll search the homes of hundreds of local worshippers before you suspect the archbishop of wrongdoing?" Sasha asked Alaine. "You'd blame your own people before that perfumed lunatic on his clifftop?"

"This is *our* faith!" Alaine shouted, dark eyes blazing, his jaw tight. "We shall not be dictated to by highlanders, pagans or little girls! Where the hells *is* Kessligh, anyhow? Does not the murder of Dockside's most loved father concern him enough that he should make the journey here himself?"

"Kessligh has the concerns of Petrodor on his shoulders," Sasha retorted, "as did Father Berin."

"I think it quite likely that your great uman did it!" Alaine said. "To then point the finger at the Torovan holy father and sow division amongst Verenthanes! Nothing would please Kessligh better than to convert all the Nasi-Keth to his pagan ideologies and win support away from me!"

"Is this another of those childish accusations that you know you'll never have to back with cold steel?" Sasha asked him. Alaine's words did not sting or anger her as they might. "So brave you men of Petrodor become when you know you'll never have to suffer the consequences of your accusations."

"If it were up to me," Alaine snarled, "I would revoke that rule in an instant!"

"And you'd die as much the fool as you were born."

"The murderer was left-handed," came Errollyn's voice from the foot of Darshan's statue. Both Sasha and Alaine turned and looked. Errollyn was crouching alongside Berin's body, examining the wound on his throat. "The cut begins on the father's right, then across. It's a clean cut, the mark of someone who has experience. I've seen murders committed by common thieves, they lack precision, sometimes they make a terrible mess, their hands are shaking so. This assassin is an expert. There are also no signs of struggle, no bruises on the face or neck, although there may be some on his body."

"So he knew the killer?" Sasha wondered.

"Perhaps," said Errollyn. "Also, his neck chain is missing. There *is* a mark here that suggests it might have been torn."

"Someone thought he no longer deserved it," Sasha said darkly.

"Whatever evidence you find, your mind is already made up," Alaine snorted, turning away in exasperation.

Sasha looked at the other three men, Marco in particular. He looked uncertain. Wary. "What do you think, Marco?"

"I think all these dead priests make a trend," said Marco. "I think there shall be a special hell reserved for whomever has been killing them." Sasha gazed at him, almost pleadingly, wanting more. Marco looked uncomfortable.

"It's sad," said Errollyn, sombrely, gazing down at Father Berin. "He dies amongst the statues of his gods. His faith was free, open to reason, to art and interpretation. I think whoever killed him found that offensive."

"We should have posted guards," Alaine muttered, running a hand through his hair.

"Father Berin would never have accepted," Marco replied. "We could never have anticipated that the archbishop would . . ." He stopped himself short. Alaine glared at him. And then beyond, as Errollyn made a holy sign to his forehead, and rose.

"You!" Alaine demanded. "You have no business making that sign in this place! You have no idea what it means!"

Errollyn regarded him coolly. "Wear your sword at your hip and no longer fight with svaalverd, Master Nasi-Keth," he replied. "You have no idea what *they* mean."

"That's completely different!" Alaine bristled.

"Most serrin would be intrigued at the debate you propose," said Errollyn, returning to Sasha's side. "I find you boring, Alaine. Tedious and predictable. Come," he said to Sasha, "let's go. If that sermon was as bad as I hear, we'll be needed elsewhere."

"I don't *know*!" Sofy exclaimed in anguish, pacing in the little inn chamber. Teriyan stood by the curtains that had been pulled across the patio windows, leaving only a little of the morning light spilling through. Byorn sat on one of the two single cots, and Ryssin leaned by the door, one ear to the outside. "I don't know how they knew!"

It had been Ryssin who'd seen them bundling Jaryd out the rear exit of the inn. Ryssin was a tracker and hunter who lived in the woods a short ride from Baerlyn. He was a skinny, weathered poker of a man, who Teriyan insisted could turn invisible in the faintest shadow. He and Byorn had taken a different route to Algery than the others. He'd been watching the inn from the stables, suspecting any dangerous activity would come through the rear way, not the front, where half the guests were cavorting. They'd taken Jaryd down a narrow alley, posting several guards behind. Ryssin had tried to skirt around, but his quarry had disappeared. The tracker was apologetic, not liking to hunt in cities half as much as he did in the wilds.

"Sounds like they took him without a fight," Byorn said grimly. "Considering our boy's state of mind, I'd say they had him trapped from the beginning. Otherwise he'd surely have died fighting."

"Like I said," Teriyan said. "A trap." His stare was fixed hard on Sofy, his arms folded. "And so I'll ask again, Your Highness . . . how did they know, do you think?"

"You're accusing me?" Sofy stared at him. "If it weren't for me, you wouldn't even have known where Wyndal was!"

"Haven't seen him yet," Teriyan said flatly.

Sofy felt a surge of fury. "I am a princess of Lenayin!" she said hotly. "And you'll not take that tone with me!"

"I'm a warrior of Baerlyn," Teriyan retorted, "and a Goeren-yai, and I'll take that tone with whomever I damn well choose. *Think*, girlie. I'm not accusing you of treachery, I'm suggesting someone's been playing you like a reed pipe. Think for a moment. Who might that be?"

"Listen here," Sofy retorted, trying desperately to gather her wits. Attempting to pull rank had been stupid, the kind of mistake a naive noble might make—how many times had Sasha told her that it never worked in Lenayin? "I might not be able to fight with a sword, but I know things that you'll never know. I know people, and I know maids and servants, and I know when people trust me and when they're lying to me. And I'm telling you,

Wyndal is here! He was staying in that room, and the servants had seen him there!"

"There's more ways to skin a rabbit than that," said Ryssin. "You ask them and they tell you what they think is true. But what if someone was fooling *them*?"

Sofy stared at him. Somewhere deep in her stomach, a little knot began to twist.

"Look, who bloody well cares?" Byorn said in exasperation, smacking one big fist into his other hand. "All we need to know is where's Jaryd now? He's got only nobles defending him, we can take those chicken-legs any day . . . we get him out, and . . ."

"Kill another bunch of Tyree nobility?" Teriyan retorted. "Aye, there's a fine plan. That'll make the king right happy with us, he'll probably order Koenyg to wipe Baerlyn off the royal maps!"

"Then what are we going to do, just let them have him? We were well within our rights to come here, we weren't attempting to hurt anyone, we were trying to rescue Jaryd's brother from treachery . . ."

"And you're going to stand out in front of Prince Koenyg's cavalry charge in the Baerlyn Valley and argue that when they're all thundering down on you?" Teriyan asked.

"Koenyg!" Sofy exclaimed, horrified, as it occurred to her. "Oh dear gods." The men all looked at her. "Don't you see?" she told them. "It could only have been Koenyg. He *knows* I know all the servants, he *knows* that's where I get all my information from."

"What, here in Algery?" Teriyan asked, frowning.

"No, in Baen-Tar! He must have . . . must have planted a rumour, or . . ." She put a hand to her forehead, staring hopelessly at a wall. She felt so stupid, and so ashamed. Maybe she'd even got Jaryd killed . . . or would do when Great Lord Arastyn was finished with him. She wanted to cry.

"Now hang on a moment," Teriyan cautioned, "all your information can't be wrong. I mean, someone did try to kill Jaryd in Baerlyn, and you rode to tell him of that plan."

"Yes, but they can have different sources," Sofy replied in a small voice, a hand to her mouth. "It's possible that tale was real, while the other was false. Perhaps the plan to kill him came from some other lord, someone not involved in *this* plan."

Teriyan frowned at her for a moment longer. "What is this plan?"

"Koenyg hears about me asking questions, knows I'm concerned for Jaryd, and plants the story about Wyndal where he knows I'll find it," Sofy said quietly. "He knows I'll ride to Baerlyn, since a princess has no men of her own to command. Maybe that was why it was so easy to get away. He knows I'll tell Jaryd, and Jaryd will come here. All Arastyn need do is make sure Wyndal's room is watched and guarded, and wait for Jaryd to climb through the window."

There was silence in the room. "Well let's not leap to anything hasty," Ryssin cautioned finally. "We don't know that's what's happened."

"You don't know Koenyg like I do," said Sofy. "Not many people can fool me in this kind of thing. But he could."

"You're saying there was *no* plan to kill Wyndal?" Byorn ventured. "Koenyg just made it up?"

"To lure Jaryd here," said Sofy, with a sad nod. "And let the Tyree lords put him on trial."

"Worked," Ryssin said glumly.

"I wouldn't jump to that conclusion either," Teriyan warned. "The one about Wyndal being safe. No reason Koenyg wouldn't plant a true story, it works just the same."

Sofy banged her fist against her thigh in frustration. "I'm getting really, really sick and tired of that brother of mine. What are we going to do?"

Sofy pressed through the crowd that lined Algery's main road. She wore a colourful headscarf and held a small bundle of blue ralama flowers, traditional for wedding celebrations. Men on horses were riding up the road now, bedecked in their finest, swords swinging at their belts. Heralds lofted great banners, while the women of each house rode behind on painted carts, horses' bridles dangling with colourful decoration and jangling with bells.

At intervals along the road sat soldiers astride. Falcon Guards, Teriyan had noted. It was surprising to see them here, but only a little—the wedding, like so many other manoeuvres of late in Tyree, was an attempt by Great Lord Arastyn and his allies to patch over past differences, and pretend that certain controversial events had never happened. Well, they had, and Teriyan's idea was to exploit the fact.

Sofy edged through the crowd, smiling sweetly and clutching her flowers. Nearly everyone here was a Verenthane; the only Goeren-yai she'd seen were Falcon Guard, or craftsmen and traders here for business. All cheered and applauded the passing nobles, in a scene that not long ago, Sofy might have found delightful. Now, she repressed a frown as she walked. Didn't they know what this wedding was in aid of? Didn't they care what their great lord had done to gain his present position? Or were they merely relieved to see life return to normal once more? This procession, of course, was still a day before the wedding itself, but it was tradition to gather at the temple and ask the gods for blessings.

She finally reached the corner where the road turned into the main square before the temple. A Falcon Guard lieutenant sat tall astride his horse, surveying the crowd with a hand conspicuously near his sword belt. Between him and her, Sofy saw only a wall of people. She took a deep breath and began shoving through, apologising all the way.

"Excuse me, sir?" she called to the lieutenant on his horse, thinking that wiser than just tugging on his pants leg. She'd seen what armoured cavalry did to people who grabbed them from the ground in battle. The man did not hear her over the cheers and the thunder of drums from the temple square. She risked a touch on his leg and the lieutenant spared her a disdainful glance. "Excuse me, sir, I have a problem, can you help me?"

The man resumed his surveillance of the road. For a moment, Sofy thought he was just going to ignore her. But then, he swung from the saddle. Sofy took a further step from the crowd to stand beside him—only she could have made such an approach. Teriyan or another man could never have come close enough.

"Hello, Lieutenant Hamys," said Sofy, close by his shoulder. "Do you recognise me?" Lieutenant Hamys looked at her properly for the first time. He was a young man, noble born, one of the Falcon Guard's best warriors. He was not especially handsome, with a grim disposition. Now he startled with recognition. "Do not exclaim," Sofy said firmly, her voice well-obscured beneath the noise on the road, "do not bow, do not kiss my hand or do anything to give me away, or I swear I'll kick you in the balls."

Hamys blinked. Astonished, perhaps, to hear the delicate Princess Sofy use such language. Well, she was somewhat astonished herself. "Aye," he said then, nodding slowly. He forced his face back into its previous disinterest. "Aye, what's the problem, then?"

"Great Lord Arastyn has Jaryd Nyvar hostage," said Sofy. A long, flat stare from Hamys, directed at the crowd and the passing horsemen. No one paid them much attention. "He heard his brother Wyndal's life was in danger, so he came, but it seems that was a trick to capture him. We do not know where Arastyn might be holding him. Might you know, by some chance?"

Hamys said nothing for a long moment, his lip twisting wryly as he thought. A grimace, not a smile. Sofy could guess at his thoughts. The Falcon Guard had all received the king's pardon for riding in the rebellion. Jaryd had been their commander then, in name at least. Their true commander, Captain

Tyrun, had been killed in the battle of Ymoth. Many Falcon Guard had also died. Teriyan had been there, and Byorn. So had Sofy, and though she had not fought, she'd tended the wounded until her hands and dress were red with their blood. Hamys remembered. Hamys had seen her and knew her face. But having received the king's pardon, he was sworn to make no more trouble, least of all on the behalf of Jaryd Nyvar.

"Can ask," Hamys said finally. "You know the Taryst Market square?"

"No," said Sofy, "but I can find it easily enough." There weren't more than two or three market squares in Algery, it couldn't be hard.

"There's a tavern on the corner called The Cavalryman. Good place. I'll send someone there by midafternoon if I find out."

"Thank you," Sofy said with feeling. "Thank you very much, Lieutenant."

"Welcome," said Hamys, with a faint smile. He remounted and Sofy stepped back to the crowd, turning to push her way through. When she glanced back, Hamys was signalling to another mounted man nearby.

Sofy turned down a narrow side road. There, loitering in an alley mouth, she found Teriyan. "An inn called The Cavalryman," she told him. "Taryst Market square. And don't be a boneheaded man and refuse to ask for directions, yes?" She left without waiting for a reply as they'd agreed it was better that they split up.

Halfway across the town square, Sofy began to suspect she was being followed. She stepped through the crowds as briskly as she could, as bassyrn drums thundered about the temple steps, where a cordon of cavalry held back the townsfolk. As she spared glances toward the temple, she thought she could see a figure behind her, always at about the same distance. Her heart thumped, and she wondered if she dared walk down the narrower road alone.

Food stalls were doing a roaring trade about the square's perimeter, and she stopped at one for a handful of roasted nuts. The seller pointed the way to Tarys Market square, warning that it would be empty right now. Sofy nodded, giving a coin from her belt purse (exposed, as theft was rare in Lenayin) and looked about. She saw no one obvious, just a throng of people, most with their backs turned, more interested in the lords and ladies dismounting before the temple. There was a flash of fire there, and gasps from the crowd. Fire-breathers, no doubt. Above them all walked a man on stilts . . . surely a travelling lowlands troupe, no Lenay man would sully his dignity for jest.

For a moment, Sofy hesitated, dry-mouthed. Should she wait here for a little, for the safety of crowds? Hamys surely couldn't find out Jaryd's location *that* quickly? But then, perhaps he could. What if a messenger arrived at The Cavalryman and found no one there?

She took a deep breath, and strode past a stall selling roast duck wings and another baking potatoes in raal, and turned down the narrow, cobbled road to which the stall owner had pointed. She walked fast, her boots echoing. The lane ahead was dark despite the sunny day, and she could not resist a short glance over her shoulder, but no one appeared to be following. She considered ducking into a narrower alley to see if someone did indeed come down after her . . . but what would she do if he saw her? What could a girl who could not fight do, face to face with such a man?

The lane twisted several times at cross streets, and then she entered Taryst Market square. It was not so large, perhaps fifty strides from one end to the other, and utterly deserted, save for a prowling cat.

On the corner to the left, an inn with a sign in Kytan, Tyree's predominant tongue after Lenay. She couldn't read it, but it was accompanied by a picture of a man on a horse. The Cavalryman, surely. Sofy approached, looking furtively around . . . and wondered what in the world an eighteen-year-old girl, alone, could have for business in an inn. She thought furiously, but as she pushed in the doors, had thought of nothing.

Astonishingly, the inn was half full. Not of locals, but of Goeren-yai, mostly men, but a few women too. They sat at their tables and drank ale and talked loudly. Several younger boys were with them . . . and one girl, no more than six, sitting with her parents. Sofy smiled, suddenly realising why Hamys had sent her here. A big wedding attracted Goeren-yai traders and craftsmen from all over, but most would rather find an inn and down a tankard or two than attend a wedding parade. The Verenthane townsfolk were all aflutter, but the rural Goeren-yai couldn't have given rat's arse.

"Will you have a drink, lassie?" asked the innkeep behind his bar—a Verenthane with a big moustache, looking quite pleased to have customers on such a day. Sofy was for a moment astonished . . . a drink? For a young woman, in a Verenthane city? But then she realised—he thought she was Goeren-yai too.

"I'll have your lightest ale, thank you," she said.

"Oh aye," said the innkeep, unstopping a barrel and holding a mug under the stream that poured out. "We do that nice here, with some lemon water for the ladies."

Sofy paid for her mug and took a seat by a window, near three men, a woman and a young girl. She'd hoped to be ignored, but amongst Goeren-yai, that wasn't always likely.

"You waiting for your pa then, lass?" one of the men boomed, loud enough for the whole inn to hear. As if it were everyone's business.

"Aye," said Sofy, with a conscious effort to remove the Baen-Tar education from her speech. "We brought ale from Eyud. We're headed back this afternoon, Pa's just asking after other business, for the next time he comes down this way."

"We're leatherworkers from Malry," another man added. "All the lords and ladies riding into town today on their pretty horses, we were up to late evening yesterday making the final touches on the bridles."

"Eyud's a long way to bring a pretty girl on a trading trip," said the woman, eyeing her curiously. Something about her expression made Sofy nervous. Like she suspected something. "Do you not have any brothers, then?"

"Three," said Sofy. "But one's not well, and the other's just recently married, and Myklas . . . he's too lazy and Pa always spoils him." It sounded right to the group, they nodded and smiled knowingly. She was becoming a good liar. It nearly worried her.

"So," said the woman, slyly, "your pa has a man lined up for you? Is that why he *really* brought you all this way, to meet some boy?"

Expectant looks from all present. Sofy smiled coyly, and sipped at her ale. "He's not a *boy*," she replied finally.

"Ah!" said everyone, in unison. There were footsteps on the verandah, and the inn's doors swung open. Sofy looked, and her heart nearly stopped. Noblemen entered the inn, Verenthanes with a dashing cut to their shirts and jackets, swords prominent at their hips.

One scanned the room, saw Sofy and pointed. He and two others marched over. Behind them, more gathered in the doorway. At the table to Sofy's side, the Goeren-yai men turned to look. "That's the one," said the leading man. "That's the one who was asking nosy questions down by the river. My maid pointed her out to me in the square, she swears it's the same girl."

Sofy sat frozen. She'd thought she'd been so careful! But there were spies everywhere, and all through the crowds. Of course there would be! There were no great lords in Lenayin as paranoid as Great Lord Arastyn right now.

"You, girl, up," said another man, gruffly. "My lord will want to speak with you."

"Hey," said a Goeren-yai man from the neighbouring table. "You watch how you speak to the girl. She's Goeren-yai, and she ain't your servant."

The noble pointed a black-gloved finger at the leatherworker. "You, shut it," he said, dangerously. "This is our town, you yokels are here on the lord's forbearance. You'll mind your business and do what you're told."

"Hey, friend," said the second leatherworker, "I *paid* my way here." He rose to his feet. The other Goeren-yais followed. "I don't need any lord's forbearance, I work hard for my coin and I'll come and go as I please." The woman collected her daughter and pulled her aside, wary but not afraid. She grasped Sofy's arm, and Sofy got up and edged backward.

"This is Algery, you peasant!" the noble spat. "This is Verenthane land!"

"This here's *Lenayin*, you pissant, and I'm a Lenay." About the inn, other Goeren-yai men were rising to their feet. In the doorway, the remaining nobles were coming forward to face the threat. It looked to Sofy an even fight.

"This here is your girl?" the noble demanded, pointing at Sofy.

"Aye," the leatherworker lied, tossing long hair from his face. "What's it to you?"

"Then you're under arrest too!"

"Arrest!" Several Goeren-yai men laughed. "You've got no more power to arrest someone than I've got power to flap my arms and fly to Saalshen!"

"Aye, well you're about to learn differently," fumed the noble. "Girl! You're coming with us!"

"Over my dead body," said another man, from a different table entirely. All were armed. Goeren-yai men always were.

"Then we'll come back and get her later," the noble suggested, with a dark, nasty smile. "With cavalry. We'll see how you like that, you stupid pagan goatfucker."

The first leatherworker didn't bother drawing his sword, he simply punched the noble in the face. With a roar the two sides leapt at each other, bare-handed, and the face-off disintegrated into a brawling mass of flying fists. Tables collapsed, chairs were picked up and hurled, bodies went crashing and wrestling to the floor. A Goeren-yai tried to throw a townsman through a window, missed, and crashed him headfirst into the wall instead. Another townsman dropped a Goeren-yai out cold with an impressive left, only to be crash-tackled into the bar by his companion.

Sofy scampered into a relatively safe corner with the woman, the two of them shielding the little girl. Sofy watched in disbelief as several of the younger lads danced about the perimeter of the fight, yelling encouragement to their fathers and uncles, and handing them chairs at need. No one had yet gone for their blades, however, in which respect the riotous confusion held to a remarkable discipline. If it weren't so completely preposterous, Sofy might have sworn that many of the men seemed to be . . . *enjoying* themselves.

"Oh how ridiculous," said the Goeren-yai woman at Sofy's side, wincing as a man toppled backward over a table nearby. "I can't take my men anywhere. This is the third brawl this year." The fallen man leapt back to his feet . . . he was Verenthane, and the woman reached out her foot and tripped him as he sprung forward. He stumbled, and his opponent took advantage, hurling him bodily into a wall, then pummelling him with fists. Sofy blinked at the woman, but she seemed far more interested in following the fight. Sofy wondered what Sasha would do. Probably the same as the other women, she decided. Against men, Sasha fought with her blade, or not at all.

A new arrival barrelled in through the door, a tall man with red hair flying. Teriyan. He grabbed a townsman, locked an arm with an athletic twist, spun whilst falling and *threw* . . . the townsman went shoulderfirst through the bar, wood splintering as the innkeep ducked for cover. Another townsman came swinging, but Teriyan blocked, ducked, then lashed, lightning fast, catching his opponent in the jaw. The man staggered, caught Teriyan's boot in the groin, then an elbow smash to the side of the face that dropped him like a sack of vegetables.

"Oh, he's good!" enthused Sofy's companion. "He's an expert, you can tell."

Indeed, Teriyan's arrival seemed to swing the fight and suddenly there were more Goeren-yai standing than townsmen. Another townsman was outflanked and dragged down, and a big Goeren-yai simply grabbed one smaller man and threw him out the window . . . which was closed, naturally. Glass crashed and fell, and then the remaining townsmen were backing away, making a dash for the door, or the broken window. The Goeren-yai men let them go, followed by much cheering and shouted abuse at the retreating men's backs as they ran, holding several hobbling injured between them.

The Goeren-yai woman abandoned her daughter to Sofy's care, dashing forward to assist one groaning, half conscious Goeren-yai on the floor. A Verenthane townsman was hauling himself up, his face bloody, legs refusing to cooperate as he clutched to a table. One of the leatherworkers went to him, and the townsman's hand went to the knife at his belt.

"Hey!" said the leatherworker firmly. "None of that, stranger. You put up a good fight and you lost, no shame in that. Now don't be a damn fool and spoil everyone's fun."

The townsman's hand retreated from his belt. Even through the blood, he looked a little shamefaced.

"Did you see my daddy hit that man?" asked the girl in Sofy's care. She was beaming with delight. "He hit him so hard his face broke!" Well, Sofy supposed, Sasha had always said she should get out sometime and see the real Lenayin. Now she had. And she was learning why her people made lowlanders nervous.

"Hey there, M'girl!" said Teriyan, spotting her and striding over, sweaty and enthusiastic, yet not so triumphant as the others. "Is he here yet?"

The messenger, Sofy remembered. "No!" she replied, anxiously. "Maybe this will have scared him away!"

"Well he better get here fast before the real soldiers get here. What happened?" Sofy told him. Teriyan looked grim. "Damn, they'll be back then. For any old brawl they wouldn't bother, but if he was after you . . ."

"I don't think he . . ." *knew who I am*, she nearly completed, but silenced herself with a glance down at the little girl.

Teriyan crouched before the girl. "What's your name, petal?"

"Rassy," said the girl.

Teriyan tipped her nose with a calloused finger. "Did you like that fight, Rassy?"

Rassy looked uncertain, her face screwed up with conflicting emotions. "No. But . . . well, we won."

"Aye we did!" Teriyan beamed at her. "Goeren-yai always win when we stick together. Don't forget it!"

"Excuse me," came a nervous voice to their side. Teriyan and Sofy both looked, but the young, swordless lad of perhaps fourteen years had eyes solely for Sofy, wide like saucers. He smelled of horses. "Are you . . . I mean, M'Lady . . . are you . . . ?"

"Oh *there* you are!" Sofy said happily, put a hand on his shoulder and steered him out to the verandah as though he were an old friend. The men in the inn were preoccupied with settling their mess. "I'm just a common town girl," she told the boy in a low voice once outside, "and you'd best remember it or my friend here will get angry." Teriyan had followed them out, and loomed alongside.

The boy nodded hastily. "M'Lady, I was sent by Lieutenant Hamys . . . I was working in the stables as usual, and he comes to me, and he says—"

"Does he know where Jaryd is?" Sofy interrupted impatiently.

The boy nodded. "There's a small place on the edge of the main square, only you don't enter from there, you get in from an alley at the back. It's . . . it's where the lords keep their secret liquors and weed for big celebrations, the ones they don't want the priests to know about . . ."

Oh aye, Sofy had heard of *those.* Rumours were that Myklas and some of his stupid friends liked to keep such a place somewhere in the palace, to the scandalised horror of their elder brother Wyldred. A place with servants would never do, because servants always gossiped.

"Then it'll be small and dark with probably a few guards," she said to Teriyan, guessing what the big man would want to know. "Probably there'll only be one way in or out, it has to be isolated, Jaryd's still plenty popular with enough people, Arastyn couldn't risk putting him any place where lots of people might have access . . ."

"Perfect," said Teriyan.

"Oh, no wait," said Sofy, recognising that look immediately. "Isn't there some way to do it quietly? I mean . . ."

"It'll be quiet enough," said Teriyan. "But if there's only one way in and out, it's not like there's lots of options."

"Tomorrow, the lieutenant says," added the boy, anxiously. "During the wedding when everyone will be in temple."

Teriyan beamed at the lad. "Sounds like a plan!"

Sixteen

To find trouble on the midslope, one needed only to follow the sound of the yelling. Sasha and Errollyn climbed along alleys and darted across narrow streets, seeing men and women running, and children being ushered inside. There was tension in the air, as thick as the sky was grey.

Sasha pressed herself to a street corner and edged a look each way—the street turned downhill to the left. To the right, it opened onto mostly abandoned market stalls. She listened for the familiar city sounds—the cry of a water carrier, the clatter of wheels on cobbles, the clangour of a smithy. Today, there was nothing but the yelling, coming from somewhere upslope, very near.

Errollyn yanked her sharply backward, and a hiss cut the air, a bolt striking the stone by her corner and clattering away. Errollyn thrust her behind him, drew an arrow and aimed around the corner. "Several windows," he said. "I see no target, it could have been any of them."

Sasha's heart recovered, and she heaved a deep breath. "It was a crossbow. He'll take time to reload. Let's go."

They dashed across the street to the opposing lane mouth and sprang up a short flight of steps. Sasha rounded a bend cautiously, and heard a warning hiss. She flattened herself to the wall. Behind her, Errollyn gave a whistle. Ahead, another whistle answered.

"Have you ever tasted eel?" came a whisper from ahead, in Saalsi.

"I've tasted every foul, slimy thing that swims and farts and shits in that ocean," Sasha muttered in reply, also in Saalsi, unpeeling herself from the wall. "Get me a steak and I'll marry you."

A man stepped from behind a crooked wall, blond and thin-bearded. Bret. "Done," he said with a grin. "I'll enjoy being husband to a princess."

"The way I'm going," Sasha said as she joined him, "all you'll inherit is a sore head and an early grave."

"I expect those anyway." There were another three men with him, Sasha saw, crouching along the lane ahead. The sound of shouting was barely beyond the next line of houses now. And she could smell fire.

"Where's Kessligh?" Sasha asked Bret.

"Preparing defences," he said, grimly. "You didn't see him?"

"I saw lots of people running around Dockside putting up barricades," said Sasha. "I didn't know he was directing it, I just got back from fishing and found this."

"You heard Father Berin is dead?" Errollyn asked. Bret stared at him. A younger lad further along gave a small cry of dismay.

"Shit," said Bret, fuming. "So much for the negotiated solution. Some of us were hoping the archbishop would seek to resolve this quietly. Instead, he's declared war."

"Nothing that dignified," Sasha snorted. "He panicked, like a small boy in his first stick fight. He lost his advantage, events took an unexpected turn and now he's gone completely wild."

"It's to be expected from fanatics," said Errollyn. "King Leyvaan did it in Saalshen—he thought he was divine, so he ignored martial common sense and paid for it. Fanatics always defeat themselves in the end."

Sasha gave him a cynical look. "Surely not always?"

Errollyn exhaled hard. "What happens here?" He gestured up the slope to the sounds of turmoil. "That's House Gesheldin under attack?"

"Attack is too strong a word," said Bret. "Some worshippers from a nearby temple tried to storm the house with rocks and tools, but there's ten *talmaad* in there with bows, so they haven't had much luck. I've suggested to Daerlerin that he should evacuate while he has time, but he says otherwise."

Errollyn made a face. "Daerlerin is stubborn. If it remains just this mob, he can hold out indefinitely. What more do we know?"

"Our knowledge of anything beyond the ridge is slight," said Bret. "There may be many gathering in Backside and Riverside, but we won't know until they get here."

"The patachis could block them from crossing the ridge," Sasha said hopefully.

"And stand before the archbishop's holy mob?" said Errollyn. "Why should they?"

"It's too early for the patachis to declare war on Saalshen. They can't afford it."

"They can afford to lose the archbishop even less," Errollyn said grimly. "They'll watch the bodies pile up, and offer sage advice afterward. There's no time, we have to convince Daerlerin and the other *talmaad* to evacuate to Dockside. I'll go and talk to him."

"That could be a problem," Bret remarked.

Errollyn gave him a cool, almost surprised look. "Surely not?"

The lane climbed up several broken steps and emerged onto the higher road at an angle, above which a tall building rose. Errollyn crawled up the steps as Sasha waited back, anxiously watching. Arrowfire whistled, and a bolt clattered off the building below a window. Rocks followed, bouncing harmlessly. Sasha could hear individual words in the shouting, now. It was obscene, the language of bigotry. She'd never actually heard it herself.

As Errollyn approached the top step, a man with a crossbow ducked into the lane just above Errollyn's head. The man took aim at a window but was immediately struck by an arrow, and fell tumbling backward down the stairs, crossbow clattering. He rolled at Sasha's feet, head bloodied and unconscious, a shaft through his shoulder.

"Poor shot," Sasha remarked to Errollyn.

"An excellent shot," Errollyn disagreed. A second man darted into the alley and fell with a shout as Errollyn simply yanked him down the stairs. He sprawled awkwardly across his comrade's legs.

Sasha levelled her sword at his neck. "There's a reason most townsfolk don't risk even a peek down the alleys," she told him. He stared in terror, clutching his arm.

"We can't take prisoners," Bret complained.

"No problem," said another man, hauling the injured man to his feet and punching him in the head. He fell hard . . . possibly too hard. Sasha gritted her teeth and looked elsewhere, disliking the necessity, but reasoning that there were people in Petrodor far more deserving of her sympathy than rioting bigots.

Errollyn peered around the corner. "Twenty paces that way," he said, pointing left, loud enough to be heard above the yelling and clatter of stones. "Around forty of them, about half with some kind of weapon. I couldn't see much that way . . ." pointing right, "the road bends uphill, but I'd guess about the same. There's some blood on the street, but no serrin arrows. The archers can hold them off from this side, the real trouble will be at the back of the house."

Sasha suddenly saw what Errollyn meant about shooting-to-wound being an excellent shot. A wounded man took two others to carry him away, robbing any momentum. It would also surely be disconcerting to a bunch of Verenthane fanatics that the evil demons refused to kill despite every provocation, and spared those lives with remarkable, if painful accuracy. Not that it would gain them any love from this crowd. Just a healthy dose of fearful superstition.

"I'm going to get in and speak to them," said Errollyn, remounting the stairs.

"Me too," said Sasha, following.

Errollyn turned on her. "No."

"Why the hells not?"

"I'm faster. Your legs are short."

"They are not! They're fast enough for short distances . . ."

"Sasha," he said with a pained expression, "there's no one for you to kill between here and the house. All you'll make is another target, there's no point!"

Sasha didn't like the look on his face. Errollyn had been distracted lately. Withdrawn, almost moody. His argument with Rhillian sat heavy on his mind. Sometimes, he seemed lost. "I'm going," Sasha said determinedly.

"No!" He shouted at her. "Look, Bret, keep her here, you can't afford to lose Kessligh's uma on some pointless risk. Sit on her if you have to."

"Oh sure, easy," said Bret, and took a firm hold of her shoulder. Sasha threw his hand off, spinning on him, but then Errollyn was gone, racing out across the street. Sasha spun back to watch him, clutching against the stone alley side, heart in her mouth as stones hurtled past him and pelted off the road cobbles. Then he was gone, up the side alley beside the house, before any shots could be fired.

She exhaled hard and slumped a little against the wall. Bret was looking at her, an eyebrow raised. "What?" she snapped.

Errollyn seemed to be gone a while, though in reality, Sasha knew it was probably not so long. The rioters settled into a steady rhythm of chants and sporadic stone throwing. Occasionally Sasha fancied she could hear more yells and fighting from further upslope. Probably there were rioters trying to attack the rear of Gesheldin House. Ten *talmaad*, equally skilled in archery and svaalverd, could easily hold off an untrained, poorly armed rabble like these.

Finally Errollyn reappeared, only this time, he was walking. Immediately the cries went up and stones flew. Errollyn ran several steps, paused as the stones flew wide, smoothly drew his bow and fired a shot. Then ran again as more stones pelted down. He reached the alley mouth unscathed, as calm as if he'd strolled to the markets.

"What was that?" Bret asked, meaning his unorthodox retreat.

"They had a crossbowman waiting against a wall where Daerlerin's people could not hit him. Safer to kill him first."

Whistling arrows made them all glance back, then shrieks not ten paces from the alley mouth. More yells, and the sound of a weapon clattering to the cobbles. Several had tried to charge the alley mouth it seemed. Bad idea.

"What did Daerlerin say?" Sasha asked, weapon ready in case some crazed fool appeared.

"He's not leaving," said Errollyn with frustration. "It's eleven *talmaad* including him, and another ten household staff. I wouldn't rely on any of those in a fight."

"Not all humans are completely useless with a blade," Bret said sourly.

"Yeah, well a lot of these don't have full use of their limbs," Errollyn retorted.

Saalshen employed many such folk in their properties, of course. Dear lords. "Look . . . we can help Gesheldin House at least. We can go around upslope. They're being pressured from there. We can relieve that pressure and probably disperse the mob . . ."

"Get to close quarters with these idiots?" Bret said dubiously. "We'd kill rather a lot."

"Errollyn," Sasha said quietly, "Bret's right. If we kill a lot of them, it might only make things worse. Most of midslope are shut up in their homes, they have no desire to get involved in this. But if many of their neighbours are slain, it may rouse them."

"And if the numbers become that large," Bret added, "there's nothing any of us can do. Best to leave things as they are and allow the rage to die down, I say."

Errollyn glared at the Nasi-Keth man, green eyes burning. Bret nearly flinched. "And if huge mobs from Backside arrive, do we just let them all be slaughtered?"

"If huge mobs from Backside and Riverside arrive," Bret replied, "then Daerlerin's fate rests with Daerlerin. If he comes to our sanctuary on Dockside, he and his people will be saved. If not, they'll die. Saalshen's properties are too spread out to withstand such an assault. Individually, they are defensible, but not collectively, and not on this scale."

"Saalshen relied on the trade for defence, just as you've said," Sasha said sombrely. "They failed to think ahead to the day when the trade would no longer protect them."

Errollyn slumped against the alley wall and rested his head against the wet stone. Light rain fell gently into his face. He looked in pain. "Rhillian," he murmured. "What have you done?"

Aisha burst into the hearth room, panting and wet. Rhillian, Kiel, Terel, Patachi Gaordin and his sons looked up from a table where a map of Petrodor had been unrolled. Patachi Gaordin and his sons were all armed. Of Lady

Gaordin, the daughters and children, there was no sign. All furniture had been pushed to the walls, and buckets of water positioned in the corners, in case of fire.

"They're coming," Aisha panted, in Torovan, for the humans' benefit. "A great column up the Saint's Walk. There are priests with them, holding stars on poles. They carry fire and chant words of Verenthane greatness and other, filthy things I shan't repeat." She accepted a cup of water from one of Gaordin's sons and drank thirstily. The others exchanged looks. "They appear quite well armed, there are hoes and scythes, in addition to the more usual weapons."

She leaned on the table and stared at the map, calculating distances in her head. There was not enough time. Fear gripped her, worse than any time since Enora.

"Hoes and tools do not make them quite well armed," Kiel said coolly, his clear grey eyes impassive. "We should not overestimate the capabilities of ignorant peasants with farming implements."

"How many, Aisha?" Rhillian asked quietly.

"Thousands," Aisha whispered. "I've never seen so many thousands. I had quite a good vantage on the temple tower, the column stretches all the way up the Backside slope." When she met Rhillian's eyes, her gaze was haunted. "It's just like Enora, Rhillian. Like the day the mob came to Charleren, and burned all the houses, and killed all the . . ." she broke off, looking at Patachi Gaordin. He looked scared. So did his sons. "We must get the families out. Rhillian, we cannot hold back so many. We should concentrate our defences on those properties that can be defended. In Charleren, they came with knowledge of all those families who were most friendly to serrin, and most especially where the half-castes lived. Those got the worst of it."

Aisha had seen the aftermath of that, in her not-so-distant youth. Pretty Charleren, a typical, picturesque Enoran village, close to her parents' farm. She had gone with her parents or her siblings to Charleren on many occasions, to buy or sell at market, or to call on her uncle and cousins. Charleren had had pretty stone cottages, a lovely old temple, a bustling market, and a view from its low hill across rolling green and yellow fields of maize and wheat.

Aside from her uncle, aunt and cousins, Aisha had known and liked many of the villagers. Gruff Tazian the mayor, who liked to dress in his old infantryman's surcoat and strut around like an officer, but would reduce children to squeals and giggles when they marched in his wake until he would turn and chase them, growling like a monster. Fat Romaldo, the butcher, who called all little girls "princess," and whose bellowing laugh and dangling sausages were Aisha's most prominent memory of the old market. Old Mrs. Ishelda, always tending her flowers in her cottage garden, or baking sweetcakes that she would give away to village children. And her cousins' friends, with whom she would play games, and take turns riding her uncle's two fat ponies.

The mob had risen from Andulan, a larger town, and had been driven by a gang of infiltrators from Larosa across the border, it was later found. Why Charleren, it was never discovered. Perhaps being small, relatively undefended, and near the border, its availability alone made it a target. Aisha recalled the alarm in the night, and the sight of fires aglow on the dark horizon. Her father had raced off, forbidding his wife or eldest son to follow. Both had fumed, but had stayed behind with Aisha and her siblings. At the first light of morning, word came that the mob had gone, and local riders were pursuing them into the fields. Aisha's mother had determined to take her children to Charleren, so that they could see the enemy's face.

She recalled walking the streets, smelling ash and smoke, seeing the remains of cottages—just bare, blackened walls about a pile of charred and smoking beams. Bodies on the street, some laid in rows where others had collected them for dignity, and others yet unclaimed. Blood on the paved road, as thick and red as after Papa had slaughtered a sheep. Mayor Tazian, hanging from the market courtyard tree by his neck, with several others, like some strange, horrid fruit. The ruin of Mrs. Ishelda's cottage, and the blackened, twisted corpse amid the beams, the carefully tended flowers twisted and brown from the heat. Romaldo the butcher had been the worst. Mama hadn't let her see him, for his cottage remained mysteriously unburned. Only later had she overheard children from another village telling how he had been tied to a chair, and forced to watch as his wife and children had been slaughtered before his eyes with his own butcher's knives, before suffering a slow death of many cuts. Romaldo had married a serrin lady, just like papa. Like Aisha and her brothers and sisters, Romaldo's children had had colourful hair and shiny eyes.

Of her uncle, aunt and cousins, only Dashi, the youngest, had survived. Mama and Papa had adopted him as their own, and from that day, he'd become Aisha's newest brother. He'd cried every night for months, and sometimes Aisha would take him into her bed and hold the little boy until he slept.

"We will stay," said Patachi Gaordin, without conviction. "We will defend our home."

Aisha stared at Rhillian. Rhillian looked down at the map, her eyes moving fast over the winding lines of streets, lanes and landmarks. "You must go," she told Gaordin. She turned to the small man and put both hands on his shoulders. "Your family have been loyal friends to Saalshen for more than a hundred years. Your grandfather was a good friend to the first *talmaad* to arrive in Saalshen. We have done much for your family since then, my friend, and we would fight to defend your home if it were possible. But it cannot be done, not if we had ten times the *talmaad* that are available. Not against the numbers that march against us."

"Where do we go?" Gaordin asked, anguished. "Where will be safe?"

"Dockside," said Rhillian. "Take your family to Dockside. The Nasi-Keth prepare defences there. The lower slopes will resist with everything they have."

"We have properties across southern Petrodor," Kiel observed, eyeing the map. "Most of them will have little chance of reaching Dockside before the mobs arrive. Perhaps we should call in our debts with Patachi Maerler and see if his pledges of friendship are anything more than just words."

"Can you run some more?" Rhillian asked Aisha.

Aisha nodded. "I'll be quick." She'd always been a good runner, preferring that even to horseback on her parents' farm. The cold, rain-wet stones of Petrodor seemed suddenly a world away from that old life, and she wondered quite how she had managed to come from there to here. Serrin, an old saying went, never stopped travelling long enough to be homesick. Well, aside from her recent detour to Lenayin, Aisha had been in Petrodor for three years now. She had stopped travelling for long enough. She only hoped to live long enough to see Enora, and her family, once more. The column moving up the Backside slope had been enormous. She didn't like her chances.

Alythia rolled the broken old cart wheel down the Dockside lane, past running men with weapons both formidable and improvised, past mothers with anxious expressions ushering their children, past old folk watching from their doorways with grim, wary eyes. Others too were carrying old refuse, or dragging it, toward the edge of the flat ground, before the Petrodor Incline began to rise.

At the end of the lane, a barricade was forming. At its base was an old, lopsided cart, over which were stacked broken stones and bricks, old wooden beams, a disused fishing boat mast, broken furniture, and piles of old barrels and crates. Fishing nets had been draped to hold the debris in place, and those nets in turn were tied to neighbouring window frames. Alythia's wheel was quickly tossed on the barricade by a young boy. He wore a short blade on his back, as did two others, and an older man gave directions. All Nasi-Keth, and all local Dockside folk.

On the roofs above, a man with a bow watched the incline, a dark figure against the cold, grey sky. Further up the slope, Alythia could see smoke rising. Occasionally, she could hear distant cries and fighting. She thought of

Gregan, and her knees threatened to shake. She could not go through that again. This was not what she was meant for. She was a princess of Lenayin, though little chance that anyone would recognise her for such with her plain dress and bruised face. She thought wildly of escape, of running along the dock to North Pier where the wealthy families guarded their warehouses and loaded their big ships . . . but Steiner ruled North Pier, and Steiner had killed Gregan.

Or she could head to Angel Bay where House Maerler and their southern allies ran a similar dock mostly out of sight behind Sharptooth . . . but there was no way around Sharptooth at sea level. She would have to climb, and that would take her straight into the mobs and the fighting. Perhaps she could grab a boat and sail out across the harbour . . . but that was crazy, she had no idea how to sail. If she had money, she could surely pay some sailors to take her, but she had not a single copper to her name.

Sasha had money, came the desperate, bitter thought. Sasha and Kessligh had money, stashed away somewhere. Not that they'd ever tell *her* where they kept it, nor let her have any if she asked. She was a prisoner here, amidst these rough, smelly common folk. Of course, she'd been a prisoner in Halmady Mansion, too, but at least those had been people of class and breeding.

A hand grabbed her arm, startling her. "You, girl." She looked, and found a middle-aged woman with a worn yet strong face, and rough-curled hair streaked with grey. "Do you know medicines?"

"I . . . I can nurse," Alythia said reluctantly. Even Lenay princesses had to learn to tend wounded men.

"Here," said the woman, and handed her a small waterskin from the bundle she carried. Alythia saw that the woman wore a blade at her back and carried a broad leather satchel on one hip, opposite the waterskins. "I need strong young girls behind the barricades when the fighting starts, we'll have wounded men falling back and they'll need water. The older women are stocking cloth and medicines further back, but you'll need to help the wounded get to them. We won't have any men to spare once the fighting starts, do you understand?"

Alythia nodded mutely, accepting the skin, yet still thinking of escape. There were priests leading the mobs, it was said. Priests! Surely a priest would wish no harm to a Verenthane princess of Lenayin? But how would they know her for a princess? Surely it wouldn't matter? Surely a Verenthane mob would not kill Verenthanes? They were attacking and burning *serrin* properties upslope, after all . . .

The Nasi-Keth woman gave her a pat on the shoulder. "Don't be frightened, girl. I hear Yuan Kessligh himself has taken charge of our defences.

Those Riverside idiots don't stand a chance." She departed, with a final tap of the eight-pointed Verenthane star about Alythia's neck. The Nasi-Keth woman, Alythia saw, wore a similar star.

Verenthanes, it dawned on her, staring at the commotion of people around her. All were Verenthanes, including the Nasi-Keth. The mobs came to clear Petrodor of serrin, and reclaim the Shereldin Star from the Nasi-Keth of Dockside. But . . . didn't they *know* that the Docksiders were also Verenthanes? Didn't they care? What kind of Verenthanes were these, who would kill their own kind?

Beyond the barricade, midslope families were hurrying down the hill, frightened women clutching children, men carrying clubs or kitchen knives, or the occasional sword or spear. The Nasi-Keth man in charge of the barricade waved them through and asked for news of the mobs. Alythia heard only a little of the replies. She only heard the word "thousands," repeated over and over.

She made her way back toward the Giana Family's residence, where Elra rested by the little courtyard. She'd barely gone ten steps when she saw one of the Giana daughters pointing her out to a tall man. He had long black hair, a bushy moustache and familiar-looking tattoos curling across his forehead. He wore a big sword at his hip, with a plain pommel and leather binding—big and brutal, with none of the decoration and lightness Gregan and his peers had preferred. Worst of all, he was now striding her way with something approaching glee in his eyes.

No . . . not worst of all. There was a small crowd following him, and Alythia realised in shock that they all seemed to be of a kind with the big, heathen man. For surely heathen he was, the tattoos gave him away, to say nothing of the sword and long hair. Highlanders, like herself. The sort of men whose company good, high born Verenthane women were supposed to avoid. There were perhaps fifty in all, and even strong Dockside men gave a wary sideways step to let them pass, for they looked fierce indeed as they came.

"Princess," said the big man, halting before her with a bow. The other men did the same. "I am Tongren Deshai'in. I am a friend of your sister Sashandra. We here are men of the highlands, Cherrovan and Lenay alike, former enemies united to fight for a common cause. You are a princess, highland royalty. We bow to you and ask you to bless our banner, and to command us in our battle to come."

Alythia gaped at him in absolute horror. "Me!" she nearly shrieked. "You . . . you . . ." She stared across the line of watching faces. There was no worship in their eyes as they regarded her, only a hard calculation. Alythia swallowed hard. "Master Tongren," she said, in her most composed yet slightly trembling voice, "I fear you have me confused with my sister. I am no war leader. I cannot wield a sword, and I am quite certain that if I commanded you in battle, not one of you would survive to see tomorrow."

There was laughter, at that. "Quite likely anyhow!" one man said cheerfully. "I hear there's *thousands* of 'em!"

"Just bless the damn banner, girlie," said a squat, round man with a bull neck and blond braids. "Give us your Verenthane prayer and look pretty for us, and give us a kiss if we get killed, that's all we ask."

Alythia glared at him. Highland pagans never had learned how to speak to royalty. "What my friend says," Tongren explained patiently, "is that it is a formality, nothing more. But we are all a long way from home and it would gladden our hearts all the same."

His accent was strange, unlike any Lenay accent she'd heard. "You're . . . Cherrovan?" she guessed.

"I am, as are my sons," with a gesture to a pair of strong-looking lads, "and perhaps half our number. The rest are Lenay."

Alythia made a helpless gesture. "Why . . . why would Cherrovans even want to be led by a Lenay princess?" she exclaimed. "I mean, we're supposed to be mortal enemies, aren't we?"

Tongren shook his head. "After a time in Petrodor, Highness, I've come to realise just how close Cherrovans and Lenays truly are. We are highlanders, with highland honour and highland beliefs, whatever our distance from home. It is the tradition of all highlands peoples to seek the blessing and leadership of the greatest amongst them before battle. Now, of the three Lenay princesses currently in Petrodor, you're the only one who isn't a self-confessed pagan, or currently fighting on the wrong side. Plus you're actually here."

He seemed, to Alythia's consternation, unaccountably cheerful. Highlander though she was, she had *never* understood that in Lenay men. Now, she failed to understand it in Cherrovans. "But I'm Verenthane!" she pleaded with them. "I mean, you're not even . . . are you?"

"Jory's a Verenthane," said one of the lads Tongren had claimed as his sons.

"But we don't hold it against him, much," said another, and others laughed.

"Goeren-yai men are preparing to march to battle in the Bacosh for your father," Tongren added, "and he's certainly a Verenthane, last time I looked."

Alythia knew she was trapped. She spun around to stare at the barricade behind. There were many others, blocking all lanes and streets in and out of Dockside. They seemed to her less like barriers of defence than walls of a newly erected cage. The world conspired to trap her, to burden her with responsibilities she had never called for, to fight for people she had never loved against those she had no reason to hate. The Steiners had killed Gregan and ransacked Halmady Mansion, not impoverished mobs of the faithful from Petrodor's worst slums. If it were the men of Patachi Steiner and his allies who now marched upon them, she had no doubt she would have manned the barricades herself with whatever weapons the locals would entrust her with. But this . . . this was not fair. This was not the life she had chosen, nor the person that she was.

But if she refused these men, she would offend them. When trapped in a cage with angry beasts, she reasoned, it was safest to befriend them, if only to preserve one's self. And besides, she had to protect Tashyna. And Elra. She turned back to the hard, highland men and struggled to regain her most princessly decorum.

"Please understand that I am not uncertain for doubting your honour," she said sweetly. "I am terribly honoured. I only fear that I shall do you a disservice. I have never fought a battle before, and I am not a warrior like my sister."

"You fought when the Steiners attacked Halmady," Tongren countered. "You bear the bruises." Alythia's eyes dropped, and she swallowed hard. "And you befriended a highland wolf. I hear she runs only to the sound of your voice."

Alythia heaved a deep breath. She was a widow. She had nowhere to go but back to her father. One day soon, she would be with him again, back with her Lenay family. Then, she would be a true princess once more. Until then, she would grit her teeth, and suffer whatever burdens the gods laid upon her.

"I accept," she sighed at last. "Please, what do you wish of me?"

The men had a banner with them, a black wolf's head against a blue background, fastened to a spear. Alythia kissed it and said a prayer over it, and then the men all dropped to one knee and she said a prayer over them too. Many Torovans stared as they passed, no doubt wondering what ill portent would follow these highland ruffians and their rituals.

Tongren then insisted that she carry a knife, even though her only previous use of one had been cutting steak at meals. Strangely, that notion offended her less than she'd thought it might. He showed her how to hold it and which part of her attacker was best to stick it into. Alythia watched with cold curiosity as men from her little highland army dispersed toward the barricades, leaving just Tongren and his two sons.

"Say," said Elys, Tongren's eldest son, "why not bring out your wolf? She'll be a more dangerous weapon than any knife, I'd reckon."

"I don't think so," said Alythia. "She'd just run around in circles and get in everyone's way."

"Ha!" laughed Tongren, giving the knife an expert, dangerous twirl. "That's what battle is, girl."

Palopy was a grand old building, built high on the slope overlooking the first U-bend in Maerler's Way. It had four floors of yellow limestone, and two main faces, one looking down onto the harbour, and the other facing the outer bend in Maerler's Way. A high wall, lined with spikes, separated the lawn and courtyard from the road, its gates barred with steel-reinforced beams. Behind Palopy, the slope rose into a vertical cliff, protecting it from the rear. Downslope, and to the north, were large, heavily defended properties belonging to Families Gelodi and Vailor, the former of the Steiner alliance, the latter of Maerler. The only access presented to the mob was Maerler's Way, and they were giving it everything they had.

Rhillian crouched behind the low wall that lined the roof as her archers waited patiently for the raging mob to charge again. There were two groups, from this vantage—one on the upslope stretch of the Way, the other downslope. The curve of the bend itself was littered with bodies, nearest the archers' range. Now there were shots flying across the road from the building directly opposite, surrounded within the bend. Men had stormed that building, neutral though its residents were, and Rhillian had seen men, women and children dragged protesting into the street. One man had fought, and been hacked with an axe. The others had been swallowed up by the receding mob. Now, Palopy and its *talmaad* defenders were constantly under fire from the building.

"Here they come again," said Terel, peering above the wall, his bow in hand.

"They coordinate through the back alleys," said Rhillian, watching with narrowed eyes. "The upslope group with the downslope. They'll blow the horn this time, both will come at once."

At the head of the upslope mob there was indeed a man with a horn. They milled, yelling and chanting, waving weapons in the air. The road was not nearly wide enough, and the crowd stretched out of sight as the Way bent. Many of their number would be rushing off elsewhere, Rhillian knew. Thus the armed crowds had been spreading across Petrodor, congregating at one serrin property, or the property of a serrin sympathiser, and burning and looting until it all became too crowded, and then moving on. So far, the *talmaad* had managed to stay ahead of the tide. But the tide continued to build.

The horn blew, and with a roar, the forward part of upslope and downslope mob broke free and sprinted toward the Palopy wall. Rhillian rose with her own bow in hand, strained and loosed, knowing that despite not favouring the bow, she could hardly miss. She ducked to fit another arrow as shots from across the road sang past, or clattered off the wall. On her second shot, she could see men falling as they charged, perhaps forty *talmaad* firing rapidly across the road face of Palopy, from rooftop and windows. Bodies fell in tangles, tripping men behind, cutting swathes across the cobblestones.

A yell came nearby as a serrin took a crossbow bolt through the arm, and then the mob reached the wall. The *talmaad* continued firing, loosing arrows judiciously into those trailing behind—here a man with a sword fell, there a strong-looking man with an axe screamed and tumbled on the cobbles, while skinny lads, older men, and crazed howlers armed with naught but their fists continued unscathed. The rhythm of blows upon the gates began once more, as the new arrivals took up the hand-carried ram that the previous waves had brought. Those men had held shields, evidence of preplanning, but when the remnants had turned and run, the shields had been left behind.

Down on the garden courtyard, and safe from crossroad fire, three serrin armed with glass bottles ran to the wall. Into the neck of each bottle, a flaming rag had been stuffed. The men reached the wall, braving the occasional flying stone, and lobbed the bottles over the wall-top spikes. Humans made oils that flamed in battle and caused terrible burns, but they were nothing like as hot as serrin oils. The flames that burst and roiled above the wall were blue and green and terrible screams rose with them. The hammering on the gates stopped and now there were men running back the way they'd come, some unscathed, others burning and thrashing. Some stumbled and rolled on the ground, screaming, although they did not appear to be afire at all.

"Save your arrows!" Rhillian yelled, and firing at the retreating mob ceased. In truth, they had more than enough arrows for many days of siege, but it was not mercy she offered. Traumatised men who had seen their comrades burned alive by unholy blue–green flames would spread tales of terror amongst their fellows. Fear drove the mobs. Fear was the archbishop's weapon in sending these fools against the serrin. But fear could be her weapon too.

To Rhillian's left, Kiel risked a brief aim above the wall and loosed a last arrow. A running man took the arrow square between the shoulder blades and fell, his staff and Verenthane star clattering to the road.

Rhillian gave Kiel a glare beneath the wall. "I know you heard me," she reprimanded him.

"That one was a priest, I think," said Kiel, coolly fitting another arrow. His grey eyes were calm, as though killing these men troubled him less than plucking flowers. Well, Rhillian thought drily, perhaps it did. "Their gods do little to save them," Kiel mused. "How interesting. The last one, too, that I killed fell with a most satisfying thud. No hand reached down from the heavens to divert my arrow. I think I'll kill another, just to be sure."

"That's unworthy, Kiel," Rhillian muttered. "Even for you."

Kiel's expressionless grey eyes appraised her as he knelt. "How so?"

"There is such a thing as decorum, even under threat of death."

"And under threat of the total annihilation of one's people," Kiel asked mildly, "what does decorum dictate then? I say that we should adopt a new decorum. One more befitting our circumstances."

"I *know* what you say, Kiel," Rhillian snapped. "It's the same thing you always say." The wounded serrin was moving herself to the nearby trapdoor, cradling her impaled arm. Rhillian wondered how much longer until the ballista downstairs was working. Surely not long now.

Kiel gave a small smile. "I'm nothing if not consistent," he said.

"If the serrinim are not the brightness that keeps the dark at bay," said Terel, calmly testing his bowstring tension, "then we shall become the black hole that drinks in all the light."

"Terel," said Kiel, sardonically. "Such poetry. What poetry do our enemies compose, do you think?" He cupped a hand to his ear and listened to the screams of agony from the wall, and the chanting fury of the crowds beyond. "Such blissful music. We should first survive, my friend. Poetry can wait."

Terel gave Kiel a blunt stare. "To be adequate, Kiel, we might measure ourselves to a deer or an elk, a noble grazer on the grassy plains. To be great, we might measure ourselves to the great hunters, the cats or the wolves and bears. You measure us to the worms, Kiel. If you are lucky, you might one day make a toad."

Most serrin would have given some reaction, perhaps a smile, a shrug, or a furrowed brow of concern, a prelude to a long and continuing argument. "We shall see," Kiel said instead. His grey eyes were like still pools on an overcast day, betraying nary a ripple of emotion. "We shall see who is right, my friend. And perhaps sooner than later, I feel."

Rhillian ran crouched to the long trapdoor, and descended the stairs into an ornate hallway. Suddenly her world was all glossy carpets and intricate wall hangings, the screams of the burned and the whistle of arrows far away. Three years she had spent in Petrodor, off and on, and still the crazed extremes of the place made her head spin. She turned into a sitting room, which had been converted into a space for the wounded. Master Deani cared for just two *talmaad* and Hendri the groundsman, who had been struck in the head by a stone in the opening attack. The woman was Shyan, Rhillian saw, now tended by two human staff who poured her poppy-flavoured water while examining where the crossbow bolt had gone straight through her bicep.

Master Deani seemed more concerned for Yeldaen, who had taken a bolt through the middle and lay mercifully unconscious. Rhillian crouched at

Deani's shoulder as he worked, preparing the bolt for removal. And repressed a wince, to see the damage.

"Will he live?" she asked.

"The fates are halved," said Master Deani, drenching a cloth in a pungent bowl of solution, then pressing it around the protruding bolt. "I shall do all I can." His aged face was grim, his hands sure and fast. Deani was no Nasi-Keth, but he knew medicine like one. Palopy was not his house—Saalshen owned it—but Deani might as well have done, for how he ran the place. His father had been a friend of Saalshen's in the old days, when such friends were rare, and he had accepted Saalshen's employment since his earliest years. But Deani was no convert to serrin ways and philosophies, however skilled at medicines. He was simply a good man of Petrodor, a devout Verenthane, dedicated to his family and as loyal to his employers as any family soldier to his patachi. "Do they press us hard? I will need more hands if our number of wounded grows."

"If we spare too many hands we shall be overrun," Rhillian said grimly. "Best hope our good neighbours defend their neutrality by force if needs be. If the mob gain access to those houses, we'll have them pouring over the walls on two sides, and we've not enough archers to hold them then. These people are crazy, losses deter them not."

"I can hear," Deani said drily as he worked. "I doubt our neighbours will fold, however much they love their archbishop. It would be like inviting a rabid beast into your house to solve a mouse problem."

"The Armadis across the road have discovered so," Rhillian agreed. "One man caught an axe to the face, I couldn't see who."

Deani hissed through his teeth. "I sent gifts to Patachi Armadi at the birth of his son. Who are these fools? Riverside?"

"They seem ragged enough," Rhillian said dubiously. "Aisha says they came mostly up the Saint's Walk, that's close enough to Riverside."

Deani made a face. "There's only one place in Petrodor to make so many crazy people, and that's Riverside. Backside's big, and plenty poor, but not so poor to make for crazed desperation. And Backside are mostly folks who've been here some years, and know enough to tell a foul, bigoted lie from the word of the gods. Riverside are rag-picking blow-ins, the lot of them. They've got the smarts of old boots and the charm of rotting manure."

"Our properties were assaulted before this lot even arrived by crowds from *midslope*," Rhillian countered.

"Bah." Deani made a dismissive gesture. "Every crowd has its fools. The problem with you serrin, you're too polite for your own good. Riverside are slime, the Nasi-Keth would have had better luck setting the place on fire than trying to convert them. The damn archbishop got there first, only he didn't waste his coin on clean water and medicines—he's a smart man, that archbishop—he built *temples*. And those poor, stupid fools loved him for it, they've got so much more hope of the next life than this one. My advice—send them there as fast as you can."

Rhillian left Master Deani to his work and crossed the hallway into the opposite room facing Maerler's Way. From the outside, the door would have appeared to lead to an innocuous bedchamber, but, instead of a bed, the room housed a great ballista—a giant crossbow elevated at its nose by two wheels. Now, the room stank of a strange, sickly solution. Two serrin were mixing the stuff in a wide basin, empty buckets nearby filled with water, along with other bags and buckets of strange-smelling, bright-coloured substances that Rhillian could not identify. Serrin oils did not keep well in large volumes, and were stored in premixed portions that would not catch fire. Only now, the final mix was made.

The two serrin filled a bucket—careful not to get the sticky, oozing substance on their gloves—and poured the solution into a leather pouch the size of a stonemelon. The pouch was sealed and placed into the ballista's firing sling. The man and woman then began winding the winch handles at the rear, pulling back great arms, each as long as a person. The thick cord groaned, and began to tremble.

"What's first?" asked the man, Arele.

"The Armadi House," Rhillian said grimly. "Burn it down."

The winching stopped. The woman, Calia, opened the shuttered windows to the grey day outside. There was no need to aim. Armadi House lay directly ahead, across the wall and the corpse-littered bend of Maerler's Way. Bolt and arrow fire whistled toward them and clattered off the walls. One impaled a neighbouring window shutter with a thud. Arele poured a spoonful of the sticky mixture over the leather pouch and lit it with a wrist-flick of his metal flint. Flame bloomed green about the pouch, and Arele pulled the firing rope. The ballista kicked and leaped like a wild thing. Armadi House disappeared in a brilliant flash, and Rhillian shielded her eyes. When she looked again, a portion of the house's second floor was engulfed in flame. The fire appeared to have mostly missed the windows, but that would soon change. Armadi House was only small compared to Palopy, but Rhillian was glad as she gazed at the blaze that humans did not possess the means to make the oil.

"Once more," said Rhillian, closing the shutters and locking them, as Calia and Arele set about preparing another shot. "Those walls will get so hot the stone will crack."

"I'll find a window with the next shot," Arele assured her, pouring into the next leather pouch. "It'll burn fast enough." Arrowfire thudded into the shutters. They were heavy, reinforced for the purpose, and even the crossbow fire did not penetrate. Rhillian risked a quick glance around the neighbouring window frame . . . and she frowned, as her eyes found a new commotion on the upslope stretch of Maerler's Way.

On the last visible portion of road, before it disappeared about a bend, the crowd parted enough to reveal a wooden, cartlike contraption. Only then did Rhillian see the firing arm and the tension ropes.

"We have a new target," she announced urgently. "They've brought artillery."

"How big?" asked Calia, sealing the pouch, teeth gritted and nose wrinkled against the stench.

"They're a hundred and fifty paces away, and I think they'll hit us with plenty of room for accuracy."

"Some weight to haul all the way up Backside," Arele muttered.

"Oh they've been quite well organised," Rhillian said darkly, ducking back from the window as a bolt shot through and punched into a big armchair. "If one were suspicious, one might wonder how long something like this has been planned." She peered again around the window rim. From the Armadi House came desperate yells and the glimpse of figures running past windows. A man leaned out a higher window to dump a bucket of water, and was immediately impaled with four arrows. Rising smoke obscured the view somewhat, but Rhillian could see the winches being worked on the catapult, bare-chested men heaving on the spoke handles.

"How far across?" Arele asked, placing the shot as Calia wound on the winch handles.

"Five hands left," Rhillian judged, and Arele straddled the ballista body, lifting across even as Calia continued winding. "Another hand. Good." Rhillian took a last look out the window, measuring distances with her eye. "Up a notch." She turned and helped Arele lift the front. Calia finished winding, the arms groaning with the strain, and the firing mechanism clicked into place.

Arele poured the igniter oil and lit it, while Rhillian unlatched the window shutters and flung them open. Arrows and bolts whistled through the window, cracking against the far wall, kicking over furniture, ricocheting off the ballista itself. Calia risked a look along the weapon's length as the incoming volley ceased.

"Good," she said.

Arele pulled the rope. Rhillian ran to a side window this time and peered out in time to see the flaming projectile strike the house wall to the down-hill side of the catapult. Flames erupted, and perhaps thirty men disappeared in that terrible glare, a sea of fending arms and desperate dives for cover. But the flames roared mostly past the catapult, decimating the crowd to one side and behind, but barely singeing the artillery men. And now, those men were lighting a flame of their own.

"Artillery!" Rhillian yelled at the top of her lungs. Fire flared on the end of the catapult arm, and then the arm unwound with a rush. The projectile arced toward them, burning against the dull grey sky. Falling short, Rhillian saw, with satisfaction.

"Come on, reload!" she called to Arele and Calia, who were already doing so. "We'll get one more shot at—"

A mighty flash of flame cut her short, roaring up from the courtyard below. She ducked low, feeling the heat of the rising fireball through the open windows. From the streets beyond, the mob roared its bloodthirsty approval. As the heat died, Rhillian risked a stare down at the courtyard gardens below. They were a mess, bushes and trees ablaze, flowers withering in the heat, and smoke rising everywhere. Another roar, and the mob were charging once more; only this time, she could barely see them come. Again, a storm of serrin arrows resumed from the Palopy rooftop, now a question of aiming and hoping. Many would hit, no doubt, but now the mob had a chance.

Rhillian slammed the shutters closed once more.

"Where did a ragged mob of crazed worshippers acquire serrin oils in that quantity?" Arele muttered as he worked, a new urgency in his hands.

"I don't think it was serrin oil," Rhillian said grimly, running to the back of the ballista and working the winch herself. "The colour was different. I think they made this themselves."

"Errollyn warned of this day," Calia said quietly. "He warned that one day humans would match us in our crafts."

Rhillian gritted her teeth and winched fast. She could hear new shouts from above, dim though they were above the howls of the crowd at the wall and the resumed hammering at the gate. She finished the winching, and dashed from the room, up the hallway stairs, and up in a crouch on the rooftop. Acrid smoke darkened the air, and there was a foul smell to every breath. Serrin, carrying buckets, dashed behind the *talmaad* at the firing wall, keeping low as occasional return fire still flew from Armadi House. They were dashing west, upslope . . . Rhillian looked that way and stared.

Bottles, burning at one end, were falling from the top of the western cliff face. As they hit the flat, tiled roof, they broke, and burst into flame. Already there were lakes of flame burning across the western Palopy roof. The property above was that of Family Gershelden . . . an old Ameryn Family, and allies to Family Maerler. She had not expected treachery from that quarter. But loyalty to Maerler, of course, did not necessarily dictate complete obedience. There seemed no end to the steady fall of bottles.

Talmaad threw buckets of water on the fires, yet the flames clung with unnatural persistence. More were erupting every moment. Tiles would crack with prolonged heat. Roof beams beneath would burn. If not extinguished, the roof would collapse and the fire would spread below. She could move *talmaad* from the firing wall to help extinguish the flames, but every archer was needed or the wall would fall. There was so much smoke now in the air that some of the mob could possibly scale the wall without being seen and open the gate from the inside. She had forty *talmaad* in Palopy, and thirty human staff, most of whom weren't much in a fight . . . that seemed short-sighted now. But hiring cripples and other unwanteds had won them such goodwill from their families. Had she been wrong to continue the policy? What good had goodwill done them? Who amongst the locals would rise to save them now?

Aisha could smell smoke on the wind as she ran, ducking fast along a winding alley. She was south of Sharptooth. Above her The Crack ran upslope toward the high Petrodor Ridge. She caught glimpses of grand mansions lining The Crack as the slope began to rise, a ridge intersecting the Petrodor Incline. She paused only to listen at the way ahead and avoid the mobs. The roads were swelled with armed men, mostly Riversiders to look at them, but not always. Saalshen's properties were ablaze from one end of Petrodor to the other. She had caught a glimpse of the roads around the old Saalshen house of Tiraen—heard the furious chanting of a thousand angry voices, a song from her darkest nightmares come to life. All the smaller Saalshen properties had been abandoned to the defence of Tiraen, Palopy, Cresfel and Edana. All the *talmaad* of Petrodor defended those four properties now. Now, she doubted that all the *talmaad* in Petrodor would be enough.

Her breath came desperately hard, and her legs cried protest at the sight of a new slope rising before her, but she could not have stopped if all the elders of Saalshen had demanded it. Terror drove her, and picked her back up after she missed a step and fell. She dashed across the next winding road, and ran along the shadow of a wall until she found a new alley entrance and darted within.

Before Tiraen, she'd stopped at House Berendani, one of Maerler's main allies. There she had met not Patachi Berendani himself, nor one of his sons, but a common soldier. Her pleas had fallen on deaf ears. No Berendani soldier would move against the mobs, he'd said, with stony formality. The mobs marched in the name of the archbishop. They wielded the Verenthane star. No Berendani man would stand against the will of the people of Petrodor and their gods. Saalshen, alliance or no alliance, was on its own.

They'd lost, Aisha realised, as she panted up the steepening slope. Two hundred years of Saalshen's presence in Petrodor was at an end. This game of powerful houses had been just that—a game, until someone had invoked religion. There, the game of calculation had ended. Now it was a rabid, mad orgy of violence that threatened to destroy everything, friend and ally alike. No wonder the patachis all retreated into their mansions and locked the gates. No patachi could withstand power like this. The archbishop had shown them all their place. The archbishop's weapons were not elegant, but they could crush everything and everyone, if he chose. Now, they all learned.

Patachi Maerler was her final hope. The Nasi-Keth were confined to Dockside, well aware that they would be next once the serrin were dealt with. They would be barricading Dockside for the attack that would follow, the attack that she knew the archbishop, and some others, had been urging Patachi Steiner to make for some time. Patachi Steiner had sensibly refused, and now events propelled the archbishop to mobilise his ragged army of the faithful to reclaim what had been displaced by the previous political games. The Docksiders stood a far better chance than did Saalshen's properties, that was certain. If she could not convince Patachi Maerler himself to help, then Saalshen would soon be receiving news that its entire Petrodor *talmaad* was dead. A slaughter to foreshadow the slaughter in the Saalshen Bacosh . . . and then, perhaps, within the borders of Saalshen itself.

She came upon a pair of dead men in the alley, recently killed. One had been cut nearly in half by a single stroke. Riversiders for certain, Aisha saw, leaping quickly over the vast pool of blood. They had that raggedy, unwashed look about them, even in death. And slope-dwelling locals avoided these alleys for a reason; at least it seemed there were still some other nightwraiths out on this grim afternoon.

Ahead, the slope became a cliff, rising like a single, yellow tooth from the harbour. Aisha stopped and counted the pyres of smoke across southern Petrodor. She counted nine. There were ten Saalshen properties south of Sharptooth. Tiraen, she guessed, was the last one left. Below were the many ships docked at the port of Angel Bay. Here, below the looming cliffs of Sharptooth, smaller trails of smoke made a black smudge against the ocean. Even in calamity, the funeral pyres burned. The dead waited for no one.

The last lane along The Crack emerged onto the road to Maerler Mansion. It was a deadend, well chosen and well exploited—a single, narrow road overlooked by the walls and archery positions of friendly houses. Any large force advancing this way would be annihilated one piece at a time. Whenever Aisha had visited before, she'd come the back way, up the passage from the base of Sharptooth cliff, but if she took that route today, Palopy and Tiraen could easily fall before she reached Patachi Maerler.

She took a deep breath and emerged from the lane mouth. Atop the walls, men with crossbows manned battlements not unlike the old castles of Enora. Aisha saw their weapons pointed down at her and wondered if she should say a prayer. Papa had. Mother had never entirely swayed Papa from his Verenthane beliefs, although she had tried. Helen hadn't thought that fair, and they'd argued.

Serrin were supposed to be completely accepting of human faith, Helen had said. Mother wasn't doing that. Mama had replied that she had no problem with Papa's faith, but as serrin, she would challenge any inconsistency that troubled her. To which Helen had accused her of completely misunderstanding the nature of human faith. To be faithful, she'd insisted, was not to question, but to accept. Mama hadn't liked that, and the argument had gone on long past dinner, until the coals had begun to dim on the fire grill, and Papa had gone off to bed. Papa had never been interested in such debates. He worked his lands, and if it did not help with farming, Papa wasn't interested. That, ironically, was why Mama had fallen in love with him in the first place. Mama said that he listened to the music of his own soul.

Approaching the Maerler gate, Aisha realised that she did not need to pray. If she were about to die, impaled by human arrows far from home, she would die with thoughts of her family in her mind, and love for them and her fellow *talmaad* in her heart.

The grille on a small side gate slid open before she could knock. "If I let you in," a low voice growled, "Patachi Maerler will have your hide. You're supposed to use the *other* gate, serrin."

"If you don't let me in," Aisha replied, "it's unlikely my hide will last the day regardless." Silence beyond the grille, then a muttered conferring. "No one saw me come, except your loyal allies here." She jerked her head back along the street. "But you can trust them not to tell who's been visiting you, surely?"

The gate squealed open and Aisha slid within. Immediately opposite was a second gate, from which came the sound of many bars being released. Soldiers opened the inner gate, and Aisha entered onto a stone walk between gardens of carefully raked gravel. Above loomed the great limestone face of Maerler Mansion.

More soldiers at the huge main doors swung them open as Aisha trotted up several flagstone steps, beneath huge, square pillars made from piled granite pieces and mortar. Whatever Maerler's claims of greater sophistication than their Steiner enemies, there was little sophistication about the mansion's exterior. While Steiner Mansion was reputed to be a pleasure palace, this was a fortress pure and simple.

Within the main doors, however, the effect lightened. Guards escorted Aisha along the grand central hall, where chandeliers shone light on tapestries and paintings.

The hall opened into a great circle, above which towered a perfect dome. More guards, and hurrying servants passing. From somewhere distant, echoing through the halls, the sound of raised voices. Aisha strained her ears as she followed the guards but could not make out the words.

"Wait in here," said a guard, opening a door. She found herself in a sitting room, with two tall windows overlooking the sea. She walked across, as the door shut behind, and gazed out at the view. Below, there was nothing but ocean, the mansion walls making a sheer drop. Here below to the right, Angel Bay, the funeral pyres and the docks. The docks, at least, looked empty, many tall ships abandoned in their bays, and the decking cleared of merchandise. Beyond was mostly warehouses. The Southern Stack had never allowed many dockworkers and fisher folk to set up house directly beside the water, and so the docks culture had never truly developed south of Sharptooth. Thus, the Nasi-Keth held far less influence there. In the south, people were more conservative, and the families still ruled the poor folk's loyalties. Perhaps if Sharptooth had not divided those people from the north, there would have been more ideas exchanged, and things would be different. Geography was destiny, it seemed. Amongst humans, anyhow.

Her eyes moved to Alaster Promontory beyond, and the waves heaving against its rocky shield. Then across the teeming slope to the many fires. She could see Tiraen from here, one large mansion, though small at this distance. Nothing looked amiss, as surrounding buildings blocked all view of the roads. Nothing seemed to be burning, yet.

To help relieve the cold tension twisting her stomach, Aisha tried the adjoining door, but found it locked. She paced for a while, then went back to the windows. She should have been back there, fighting with her friends. She had never felt so helpless.

The door clicked open and it was Patachi Maerler himself, tall and elegant in green leggings and a black satin shirt, buttoned all the way up to his tight collar. The patachi's stride was fast, and his manner held none of the playful sparkle of previous occasions. He stopped in the middle of the room, his expression blank, and watched her with lidded blue eyes. Four guards lined the wall behind him, swords but no halberds.

Aisha bowed low. "Great Patachi," she said in her most eloquent Torovan. "Saalshen's agents are besieged. My mistress Rhillian sends me to invoke your promise of allegiance. She seeks assistance, kind sir, in the name of the friendship between you and her, and of our great future to come."

"She promised me trade," said the young patachi, inexpressively. "She promised me power. That is impossible now. Our mutual enemy Patachi Steiner has pushed the priesthood too hard and forced my brother to take drastic action. It was the only way he could preserve the neutrality of the priesthood. Yet the priesthood remains partisan still, and the sons and cousins of Maerler and her allies do not number enough amongst their ranks to make a difference. We could not prevent the archbishop from his sermon. He means to retake the Shereldin Star by force. I think perhaps he shall destroy it by mistake. Either way, he has stirred great hatred of Saalshen in the hearts of the people. Not even the greatest patachi can stand against this and live."

"Patachi," said Aisha, bowing once more, "the Nasi-Keth shall hold the Shereldin Star. Patachi Steiner has sensibly refused the archbishop's requests for an assault on Dockside for many years. Dockside is defensible, their people will fight to the last, and now Kessligh Cronenverdt leads their defences." She looked up, desperately. "Whoever holds the star can dictate terms to the archbishop! The archbishop has sworn to reunite the star with the Enoran High Temple. He intends to march the Army of Torovan into battle with the star at its head—"

"You lend me little confidence," Maerler interrupted coldly. "The archbishop has roused more angry men with his sermon than Patachi Steiner could dream of. I think you underestimate the scale of it, little serrin. From our heights here on Sharptooth, we have quite a good view of the proceedings, and we count well past ten thousand. Possibly twenty." Aisha could well believe it, having seen what she'd seen . . . yet still her blood ran cold. "Steiner has perhaps fifteen thousand in total, but he could never have used more than a third of them in any assault, given his defensive requirements. The Nasi-Keth can muster barely more than fifteen hundred fighters, the rest are many thousands but they are a rabble, and I think you overestimate their chances.

"Kessligh will most likely lose the star. If so, the mobs will doubtless take it to the archbishop, where it rightly belongs. Should Kessligh retain the star, he will bargain until the highest bidder, and his price will be no war in the Bacosh . . . which was perhaps feasible before today, but not after. Perhaps he will threaten to destroy the star, which will force all the great houses to join forces against him. War in the Bacosh is inevitable now. In trying to equalise the imbalance growing within the priesthood, I fear we have forced the archbishop's hand too far. That sermon should never have been delivered, and had the equilibrium existed, the other priests could have stopped it. But now, everything is tilted, and nothing shall be the same again."

Rhillian, Aisha recalled, had spoken of equilibrium. She'd argued with Errollyn about it. Aisha had spoken up once in support of Errollyn. Had she spoken loudly enough? Perhaps if she'd pushed harder . . . but to what ends? Rhillian was within her *ra'shi*. The pull of the *vel'ennar* was strong. But Errollyn did not feel it . . . He could stand against Rhillian, where Aisha found it hard. Was he then in the right? Had he been right all along? And had she, and all the *talmaad* in Petrodor, been blind to it?

"It's over, little serrin," said Patachi Maerler, suddenly tired. "The game is at an end. It was fun while it lasted, but perhaps the archbishop always had the final move in his keeping, and we were all fools for thinking we could play him. I do not know who will lead this Army of Torovan into the Bacosh, but I do know that the decision is no longer mine to make. I think I shall keep you, however, as a bargaining tool with Saalshen's new representatives, when they arrive. My spies tell me that you speak rather a lot of languages, and have much knowledge of the Saalshen Bacosh. Have no fear I shall mistreat you. I offer you safety and hospitality from the storm."

Aisha's fear subsided, as something else displaced it. And the patachi frowned to see the sudden change in the little blonde serrin's bright blue eyes. "I will fight to defend my people," Aisha said quietly, with menace in her tone. "I came to you freely, as a friend. I would leave as such."

"You are in no position to make demands, little girl," Maerler said crossly, but there was an edge of uncertainty in his tone. "I offer you your life. Most people would be grateful!"

"I am not most people," Aisha said coldly. "I may look like a little girl to you, my Lord, but I have seen thirty-one summers. Humans have misjudged serrin many times before."

The patachi began a retreat and Aisha took a deep breath as the four guards against the wall moved forward, encircling, hands fingering the pommels of their swords. "Just let me go," she told the patachi quietly. For the briefest, hopeful moment, she thought he might agree. But she saw the rapid calculation in his eyes as he realised he'd told her too much.

Aisha had no desire to kill these men. But her friends were out there dying, and these men sought to prevent her from joining them. "Dear girl," said the patachi, backing behind his guards, "please be reasonable. If you go back out to face those mobs, you will surely die."

Aisha barely heard him. She could feel the pull, the force of it like a tugging in her heart. *Vel'ennar.* Like a part of herself that did not belong solely to her. The pain of it made her ache. If she stayed here, trapped within the patachi's hospitality, she'd go mad.

She tore the blade from its sheath and leapt forward, swinging down. Her target sprang back, the other swords came out fast . . . she cut sideways at the closest before he could prepare his defence, and felt the blade go through mail and flesh. She sprang into the gap left by that man as he fell, defending two strokes in passing and nearly removing that man's head with a fast, one-handed overswing, the guard ducking just in time, stumbling for balance.

Aisha moved sideways toward the door, three guards and the patachi following, none quite prepared to stand between her and escape. She saw the fear on their faces, the uncertainty in their postures—wondering, trembling, if they dared try her blade. The men of House Maerler knew the *talmaad* better than most. Aisha knew her standard was not that of Rhillian, though Errollyn she could usually match. And Errollyn was formidable enough.

She reached for the door handle. A soldier edged forward, seeing one hand off her sword . . . Aisha replaced the hand fast, and took stance against him. The soldier backed up. Patachi Maerler moved in sudden frustration, striding across the room to the adjoining door. He too found it locked, and hammered on it in frustration. "Guards!" he yelled.

Aisha flung open the main door and tore through, the soldiers in pursuit. Two men were running down the hall, skidding into a stance as Aisha came through. She feinted left, sprang right instead, brushed the first man's side as his hurried blade missed, drove the point of her sword through the second man's middle, then dashed on as he fell, nearly losing her sword as she pulled it clear.

Servants scattered and screamed as she came, a maid carrying a lady's expensive dress fell to the floor and covered her head. A strong servant in black thought to tackle her barehanded, then changed his mind as Aisha aimed a running swipe at him, and he dived for the wall. She arrived back at the central dome just as more soldiers came rushing in from adjoining halls and yells echoed through the house.

One man threw his halberd directly across her path, seeking to entangle her legs as he drew his sword. Aisha leapt, as more soldiers tried to block her path, dodged left as one swung, parried his companion, spinning about as she ran to defend herself, then jumped onto a broad wooden bench that ran about the circular wall. She ran along it, ran two steps up the wall to jump a swiping halberd at her legs, then jumped for a large vase on a plinth as the bench ended, and sent it crashing to the floor, guards scattering from its flying shards. She hit the floor and stumbled, rolled awkwardly back to her feet, parried and killed the first man to attack, his body crashing into the wall behind.

Two more were on her fast, their blades sure and deadly. Aisha parried, ducked and spun desperately aside, using the one advantage her small stature afforded. She defended from another direction, aware she was being driven further from her desired route, and risked keeping her back to the man who approached from that way. She barely survived a head-high swipe, deflecting it upward, then turned at the last moment to drop low, and take the man behind's leg as he cut for her back. The leg severed in a shower of blood, and she was over his body before he could scream, and racing for the hallway, severing the halberd of the man who slashed at her side. With a many-voiced yell, perhaps twenty men pursued. It might have been more.

The end to this hallway was blocked by more soldiers, so she crashed through a doorway and into a room where many children were all dressed in costume, rehearsing a play. Several were gods, in white and tinsel. Several were pretty noble ladies. One, dressed all in black, held a great farmer's sickle, and a hood pulled over his eyes. Death. Maids and tutors leapt for the children, screaming, as Aisha came dashing across the floor, bloody sword in hand, headed for a door on the far wall. A young maid dived on top of little Death and covered him with her body. In her mind, Aisha saw little Dashi crying amidst the ruins of his parents' house, spattered with the blood of his brothers and sisters. She had to get back to him.

Aisha hit the opposing door in a shoulder charge, and it smashed open. Half stunned, she staggered onward, found a stairway and rushed down it. Halfway down, two soldiers arrived at the bottom and began to rush up. Aisha hurdled the railing from ceiling height, hit the flagstones and rolled, as the soldiers on the stairs reversed. She ran away from them, past barrels lining a limestone hall, and crates of leafy vegetables on top of those, and smelled the distinct flavour of the kitchens nearby. And near the kitchens would be . . . the cellar!

She turned left, nearly colliding with a smock-wearing servant who turned and ran away, and only managed to get right in her path. She dodged left, so did he, then right, as did he, with hands over his head and terrified . . . frustrated, Aisha kicked his heels, and he tripped and sprawled. Aisha hurdled him, and emerged into the huge, wide, kitchens—an open limestone floor and several long benches, big ovens blazing in the far wall. Most barely even noticed her as she entered, consumed with chopping and mixing and shouting, arms bare in the heat. The kitchens of a great house would pause for no calamity, and food was clearly more important than war. Aisha empathised.

She ran an aisle, tapped one cook on the shoulder and asked, "Which way to the cellar?" The cook pointed without even looking and Aisha ran off, ducking low as soldiers appeared, searching for her.

She slid out a small entrance in the wall and ran down a flight of stone steps, the way lit by oil lamps. There she arrived at a doorway, and found herself in the vast, familiar cellar, with a wood-beamed ceiling and more beam supports, surrounding which were stacked piles and piles of barrels and boxes. She ran down the stone steps to the cellar floor, sighting on her left the flight of steps she'd taken with Rhillian, Errollyn and Kiel to the isolated room where Patachi Maerler usually met his serrin guests.

There was no guard at the trapdoor—there was no need usually, as the guards at the tunnel's far end would signal if someone were coming by tugging a small cord that ran through metal loops on the tunnel's ceiling and rang a small bell that was located . . . somewhere. Was there a bell at the other end that could be rung from here?

She heard running footsteps coming from the kitchen and quickly undid the bolts holding the trapdoor shut. Soldiers arrived at the top of the cellar stairs as she pulled up the lid and jumped inside, letting the trapdoor slam shut behind her. Abruptly, she was plunged into blackness. There was only the occasional lamp along the tunnel, she recalled. As Sasha would say in her charming Lenay brogue—"Shit."

But Aisha remembered the stairs well enough, and recalled them to be uniformly even. She walked down at first, dragging her toes to feel out the length and shape of the steps. That done, she began to accelerate her descent. In total blackness, it was difficult to judge, but Aisha was trained in the svaalverd like all *talmaad*, and both footing and balance were intimate to her. She could balance on a fence rail in bare feet in the rain, she'd jumped from stone to stone across a stream from memory alone whilst blindfolded, and she'd been able to perform all the basic svaalverd stances since the age of eight. Running down stairs in the dark wasn't so hard after that.

To be sure, she removed a cloth she used for cleaning her blade from a pocket, wrapped it around her left fingers, and trailed them along the rough limestone wall. Behind her, the trapdoor opened, but then the stairs switched back on themselves and she was around the corner. Those men would think twice before following a serrin into the dark. They'd stop and find a lamp first. She used the burst of light from the trapdoor to locate and cut the warning cord that ran along the ceiling. Soon she found some light in the tunnel and descended all the faster, her feet a rapid patter on the stone. The more rhythm she found, the easier it became, even when the tunnel became black once more, around several more corners. Her soft boots made only a little sound.

Finally, she reached what she fancied was the last stretch of stairs—she had come down far enough and there was a lamp burning at the bottom. Had a warning reached the guards at the bottom of the stairs? There was no way of telling, and no way to make her descent safer. The stairs were a straight line with no cover. If one had a crossbow and she were caught halfway down . . . well.

She put the cloth back in her pocket, shifted her sword to her left hand and pulled a knife with her right. Then she began her descent as quietly as she could. Halfway down, she could see the rusted iron gates that led out to Dockside, dimly illuminated by the lamp above the guard's chamber. Just a few more steps and she'd be within knife range. Just a few . . . but then a man with a crossbow stepped from the guard's chamber, and Aisha knew the fates for frauds.

She hurled her knife anyhow, aiming high to make the distance—it hit the ceiling and bounced with a ringing crack . . . the crossbowman fired, and Aisha leapt, and felt her left leg kick away from under her. She fell crashing down the steps, somehow contriving to twist her small frame into a tight bundle and not decapitate herself on her own blade. The guard dropped his crossbow and pulled his sword. Aisha braced her arms and leg to stop her roll just short . . . her left leg screamed agony, her intended brace-stance collapsed and she barely managed to raise her blade in time to catch the full weight of the guard's blow. With no semblance of technique, it smashed her into the wall. Her head hit the stone, knocking her insensible, but her hands were moving of their own accord, her left hand snatching the second knife from her belt as she spun sideways to stab the man backhanded through the shoulder.

He screamed, and Aisha saw through blurred eyes a second guard in the guard room, his crossbow levelled at her chest. She sprawled forward, grabbing the wounded first guard, keeping him between her and the crossbow. The first guard swung around, trying to grab her. Aisha swung with him, ripping her sword across his leg. He screamed again, falling, Aisha catching his weight, or trying to, as her own leg gave way and her head spun, and she threw her sword in final desperation. It was a poor throw, and the second guard deflected it off his crossbow. He tried to re-aim, but Aisha tore the knife from the wounded man's shoulder, slicing her hand in the process, and threw that too. It was a worse throw, but the crossbowman ducked back behind his doorway.

The man at Aisha's feet grabbed her wounded leg and she screamed in agony, falling on top of the first abandoned crossbow. She grabbed it and swung arm-point first at the wounded man's head. It smashed into his helm, and his grip released. Aisha grabbed up his fallen sword, staggering to her feet, threw the crossbow at the emerging crossbowman who ducked back, and charged. Or tried to, as again her leg nearly folded.

The crossbowman fired in panic as she came through the guard chamber entrance, and Aisha felt a blaze of pain across her ribs, and a yank on her jacket that nearly turned her around. She swung in blind fury, but her hand was agony and her leg gave no balance, and he blocked the blow with his crossbow, then swung it at her head. Aisha tried to defend in the confined space, but her blade entangled with a wall, so she ducked instead and caught the full weight of the weapon on her shoulder, and a glancing blow off the head. She fell hard, face first on the stone and suddenly her mouth was bloody. The crossbowman was drawing his sword, backing around to the doorway for safety. Aisha rolled hard and slashed at his leg, and he leapt back, catching the tip across his shin.

He yelled, and hopped, and Aisha crawled for a desperate lunge, and stabbed one-handed through his thigh. He screamed and fell. Aisha was on him fast, as he collapsed on his back in the doorway, and she angled the blade across his throat. He got a hand on the blade's edge to try and stop its progress, but the steel was blunt on the reverse side and Aisha had a good, painless pressure with her left hand on the steel, while her right anchored the hilt. Blood flowed from the guardsman's hand. He sobbed and looked terrified. Humans were so dangerous when terrified. Aisha knew. She'd seen the ruins, the burned corpses, the strange fruit hanging from the courtyard tree. One shouldn't feel sorry for terrified humans. One couldn't.

She killed him, arterial blood spurting, drenching her face, an unspeakable horror on her victim's. Aisha left him dying on the floor, and crawled to reclaim her sword from where it had fallen alongside the guards' bunks. Then she sat and considered her leg properly. There was a crossbow bolt straight through her calf, just missing the shinbone. The pain was horrible, and there was a lot of blood. Her hand was cut, her head swam and throbbed, and her shoulder felt like maybe something was broken, where the crossbow had hit her. The man she'd killed was still kicking. He wasn't dead yet. Death wasn't fair. Death never was.

Somehow she hauled herself up and staggered to the iron gate. The wounded man there had found her first knife, the one she'd thrown. He sat propped against the gate, the knife held hopelessly before him, his hand trembling. Clearly he had no idea how to throw it, nor was in any condition to do so. His leg was bleeding badly, and his right shoulder was bloody. She shouldn't leave him that knife, with its serrin steel edge. Nor the other one that she'd thrown at the dead man. But she'd forgotten that one, and taking this one off a second terrified, wounded man seemed too much effort. She had to get out.

"Move," she said hoarsely. "Get away from the gate." He moved, strug-

gling, trying to keep pressure on his bloody leg with one hand, while shuf-
fling with the knife hand. Aisha lifted the gate's heavy bar with difficulty and
slammed the bolts open. The gate opened soundlessly as she pulled, its
hinges well oiled. She limped out into the thicket of redberry bushes that
obscured the entrance. Above, the high yellow cliff of Sharptooth soared
toward the grey sky. Opposite, beyond the bushes, dark walls loomed, windows barred and bricked up.

Aisha limped past the bushes, then collapsed on the narrow, paved lane
between wall and cliff as her head spun and her balance failed. She rolled on
her back, and found that the pavings were wet, and a light rain fell onto her
face. The tug in her heart did not pull so strongly, now. Perhaps, she thought,
if she lay here long enough, the rain would wash her back into the sea, where
the currents would carry her all the way to Enora eventually. She wished it so,
more than anything she'd ever wished in her life. In the distance, above the
gentle patter of rain and the cry of a gull, she could hear the sounds of battle.

"We're coming over!" Rhillian yelled. "We're coming over, and you'll have to
fight us if you want to stop us!" She stood atop a ladder at the rear wall of
Palopy House, yelling at Patachi Vailor. Patachi Vailor stood likewise atop a
ladder on his side, glaring at her between the tall metal spikes that lined the
wall. Patachi Vailor was an older man, white-haired and bearded, and on
those occasions Rhillian had met him previously, of gruff and taciturn
demeanour. Now he glared, and his nostrils flared outrage, but there was fear
in his eyes.

"You lead that mob into my house," he shouted, "and my family will all
die!" The air was thick with smoke, even as the rain tumbled down. Screams
and yells were fainter, but only because the crackling roar of flames drowned
them out.

"You swore allegiance to Patachi Maerler!" Rhillian shouted furiously.
"You are Maerler's man, and I have allegiance to Maerler, and you will let me
over or . . ."

"Or you'll what?" Vailor snarled. "I never swore any allegiance with Saalshen! I never swore to protect demon pagans and cripples with the blood of
my sons! Saalshen's time is finished, and I'll not sacrifice my family on the
altar of a lost cause!"

"You will regret this!" she hissed. "Do not sleep too soundly at night,
Patachi Vailor, for Saalshen's arm is long and her footsteps silent!"

She slid back down the ladder before the patachi could reply, and raced toward the house. Palopy was aflame. The entire western side of the upper floor facing the cliff, now burned like a bonfire on a happy Sadisi. Smoke billowed from the lower floors as the ceilings began collapsing, and the flames spread. The rear garden was filled with Palopy staff—humans all, men and women comforting each other, tending the wounded, covering their faces against the filthy smoke. Some dunked cloth in the courtyard fountain amidst the grass and flower gardens, and wrapped those about their lower faces.

Rhillian ran up a garden path and looked at the wall of Family Gelodi to the east. The spiked wall rose tall, and there was even less hope of escape that way for Gelodi were sworn to Steiner. Ahead, near what was left of the front garden, she could see serrin with bows and oil-shot pouches taken from the ballista, now abandoned upstairs as the smoke became intolerable indoors. Arele and Calia had brought the oil and leather pouches downstairs, where *talmaad* threw them by hand, to keep the fire burning where the wall had been breached. Artillery fire sailed in at regular intervals, not as accurate as the ballista, but accurate enough. The front of Palopy House was burning in places too, and the gardens were a flaming wreck. Most fire had been trained on the front wall, which had collapsed in two places, but the flames were so intense, none of the screaming mob had made it through. Some had managed to scale the wall with ladders or rope, and been shot. The others waited, chanting, for the fires to die.

There was not enough oil left to keep the fire at the gate burning for long. Arele had divided the oil and ammunition into two, one to the east side, and one to the west. Calia had been on the west side when an artillery shot had hit nearby, killing her and wounding two others horribly. Humans might have found someone to put them out of their misery, but serrin were very bad at that sort of thing. Master Deani had smothered their screams with cloths soaked in solution to make them sleep, and they'd been dragged to the rear garden and left to die. Nothing more could be done. Calia's oil had burned too, when the artillery hit, and that fireball had set much of the west wall on fire. Calia had had the fortune to be standing close. For her, it was quick.

Kiel approached Rhillian, strangely unhurried as stones cracked and bounced behind him—there were no archers atop Palopy's roof now, and the mob filled the street beyond, hurling rocks and firing the occasional arrow through the breach. Serrin fired back, and killed many, but the window of attack was small and the mob was vast. Some serrin had taken to firing almost straight up, to let the arrows fall sharply on the other side of the wall. It had some effect, but there was a wind blowing now, and rain falling, and a vertical arrow was no sure chance of a kill.

"Patachi Vailor?" Kiel asked her. His grey eyes were as calm and cool as ever. Rhillian shook her head. "Shall we attack him?"

"He has a hundred men and many archers," said Rhillian. "We'll be killed coming over the wall."

"We'll be killed here anyway."

"Make a suggestion," Rhillian said darkly, "or do something useful."

"We could leave the humans here," said Kiel. "Serrin alone and unburdened might stand a better chance. If we moved stealthily across the Gelodi wall instead of the Vailor, they might not be expecting us, and then—"

"You're joking!" said Rhillian.

"I'm not. You asked for a suggestion."

"Make another!"

"Rhillian, I merely suggest that—" An artillery shot erupted with a thud and rush of flame at the front of the house. Rhillian shielded her sensitive eyes. Kiel gestured back over his shoulder, with perhaps the first trace of real frustration that Rhillian had ever seen from him. "They're going to kill us, Rhillian. If I must die for Saalshen then I die gladly, but you in particular are important, and—"

"And our staff are not?" There was a desperation building in her. Had she caused this? Had she been wrong and Errollyn right? How could she be responsible for something so horrible? All her poor human friends with their families' long decades of loyal service to Saalshen . . . why had she not thought of them in her plans to save Saalshen's presence in Petrodor? What were a few buildings besides their lives? "Kiel, I don't understand you! How can you not feel for them?"

"I feel for them very much, just as much as you do. But they are not—"

"I don't believe you," Rhillian said coldly. "You speak like the priests, you say one thing and mean entirely another, and expect me not to know the difference. Is Errollyn the one truly corrupted by the humans, Kiel, or are you?"

Kiel just gazed at her, lips faintly pursed, as if considering a troublesome puzzle set for him by his scholarly uman. Neither her words, nor the flames and screams, nor the prospect of imminent death seemed to trouble him.

Terel arrived at their side. "An issue?" he asked, without preamble. The right arm of his jacket was burned. His angular face was tight, lips pressed thin as he loomed over them.

"Kiel wishes to leave our staff and run," Rhillian told him.

Terel did not look surprised. "You go, Kiel," he said, with mock kindness. "You leave the matters of substance to the adults." *Shland'eth rhmara*, he said. "Matters of substance." The context was philosophical, *tel as'rhmara*, "a strand on the web of truth." There were few things that mattered more to serrin minds. It was the fabric of the universe itself, truth made incarnate, through the acts of thinking people. Terel excluded Kiel from it all, as an adult might patronise a silly, irrelevant child.

Kiel's eyes darkened. Anger. Two emotions back to back, Rhillian was nearly astonished. "Clever Terel," said Kiel, with a voice that betrayed nothing of that which burned in his eyes. "Let us hope your sword is as sharp as your tongue."

Rhillian turned and ran back toward the rear garden, her bow in hand, her quiver feeling strange on her hip. Master Deani was tending wounded on the grass beside the courtyard. Rhillian crouched by the feet of the man he treated—Timon, she recognised, a nice boy with bright red hair, the son of a midslopes jeweller. The boy had slow wits and was too clumsy for jewellery, but he'd made a fair kitchen hand. Rhillian had always seen him cheerful, pleased to be a person of some importance in his community, and no longer a disgrace to his father. Now, he lay burned and moaning, his clothing blackened, the skin of his torso and arm coming away in black and red clumps.

"There's no escape through Vailor," Rhillian said through gritted teeth.

"I gathered," said Deani, putting soaked cloth and powder on the burns, cutting away the charred clothes where they stuck to the flesh. Timon screamed. "Can you hold them?"

"No. The wall is down and soon the fires will die. They will come through soon enough."

"Then we're dead?" Deani asked, still working. There was fear in his voice, yet he worked incessantly, as if striving to keep the fear at bay. A Verenthane man would wish to know if death awaited, Rhillian realised. He wished to make peace with his gods.

"No," Rhillian said firmly. "When they come through, they will be a narrow, scattered formation. They have never seen swordwork like the svaalverd before. These are not warriors of any note, they shall be slaughtered in their tens and hundreds. The sight should give even fanatics such as this a pause."

"You give the men of Riverside credit they do not deserve," Deani spat. "They're not human, they're animals. Listen to them!" Jerking his head toward the chants and yells. "They care nothing for their own lives, and even less for ours. You should go now, take all those who can move and risk a flight over these walls . . ."

"No."

"Even if you lose half of them, that's half more survivors than there'll be if you stay here . . ."

"Deani, who amongst us has the speed or strength to scale those walls, or run fast, or fight if necessary?" With a wild gesture across the smoke-blown garden, and the staff of misfits whom Deani had turned into one of the best and most dedicated household staffs in Petrodor. Attentive and kind and skilled . . . and yet here a deformed limb, and there a puzzled or childlike expression . . . all looking at her now, at the serrin lady who had ruled their fates for so long. Even now, there was trust in their eyes. And hope.

"Probably none," Deani admitted.

"You're telling us to abandon you?" Rhillian asked.

"Most of us dying is still better than all of us dying!" Deani snapped. "You should take those who can, and move now, while you still have a chance!"

"Not while there's still a chance!" Rhillian shouted. "Not while there's still a hope we might turn them with our blades!"

"Stubborn, crazy damn serrin . . . here's the reason you'll never win a conflict with humans! You always refuse what has to be done! Necessity offends you, and if you ignore necessity, you're dead! Listen to your friend Kiel, he knows! He alone of you all!"

"I'm not going to leave you to die!" Rhillian screamed, heaving to her feet. There were tears in her eyes, and she was trembling. "You don't understand the serrinim, Deani, we *can't* just leave! We'll shrivel up and die if we *go*!"

Deani got to his feet also, with emotion in his eyes, and embraced her. Rhillian embraced the small man back, and tried not to sob like a child. "You're too good to us, silly girl," he told her. He pulled back to pat her on the cheek, in the style of an older Torovan man to a woolly-headed but well-loved youngster. "You understand me? You're too good to us. Humans don't deserve you. We never will. And the sooner you realise it, the sooner you'll learn to save your own people."

Seventeen

SASHA RAN UP THE WINDING STAIRS of Tarae Keep, staying close to the wall to avoid others descending. She emerged onto the high southwest tower in falling rain, to find a small crowd there. This was the highest point on Dockside, affording a clear view across the vast expanse of Petrodor incline and the docklands along its foot.

Tarae Keep was perhaps three hundred years old—very old by the standards of Petrodor, where little of the present city had even existed prior to a century and a half ago. The keep had been built by the powerful Ameryn Lord Tarae, whose trading empire had ruled north and south along the Sharaal coast, to protect the road up the incline that was now called Maerler's Way. Today the keep served as a stable for the animals that hauled loads up the Way, and a trading warehouse and market for merchants big and small.

Directly below the tower ran the Dockside end of Maerler's Way, headed for the dock itself. Streets and lanes formerly bustling with trade now bustled with preparations for battle as the barricades were reinforced, buckets of water strategically placed and weapons distributed. If the barricades were overrun, Sasha knew, the keep would serve as a holdout position.

High up on the slope, Sasha could barely see the top of a building aflame, which several locals had assured her was the Saalshen house of Palopy. Smoke made a thick, dark plume in the leaden sky. Along the slope, many other trails of smoke joined to make a single, evil smudge across the horizon.

Beside the tower's western wall, Kessligh held court amongst a small crowd of Nasi-Keth and respected Dockside men. He spoke to them of the defences, addressing each man and assigning responsibilities. It was the first time since her arrival in Petrodor that Sasha had seen Kessligh so completely himself. His manner was firm, his gaze direct and men listened with rapt attention. Only Alaine looked unhappy, his dark curls plastered to his head in the falling rain.

Kessligh saw her through the crowd and beckoned her forward.

"South End has about twelve hundred men who might count as fighters," she told the gathering. "Not including Nasi-Keth, of course. But I wouldn't rate their weaponry as highly as we have mid-pier . . . I promised them I'd try to get some halberds or spears down there. They've not enough with reach to defend the barricades."

"We're short on long-handled weapons all along the dock," said a man she didn't know. "They'll have to make do."

"We're not likely to get hit at South End," said another. "It's too near Sharptooth, the roads are too steep."

"Depends how well they're led," Kessligh cautioned.

"Led?" Alaine said sharply. "This mob aren't led! They're a rabble, they'll come charging down wherever they will, the more direct the better."

"We've reports of artillery, rams, shield walls, oil fires . . ." Kessligh shook his head. "It would be naive to assume this was not planned. No doubt the archbishop foresaw contingencies. There are plenty of provincial militia or ex-militia who could have been gathered for such a task, perhaps paid, perhaps persuaded by their priests on instruction from the archbishop . . ."

"You're talking about the Holy Father!" Alaine growled. "I'd watch my tongue if I were you, highlander."

"I'm a soldier," Kessligh replied. "I win battles. I care little for convention, I care little for holy doctrine, and I care least of all for your precious feelings, Alaine. I can help you all to win this battle. The question you have to ask yourselves is 'How badly do I wish to win it?'"

"So you appoint yourself our commander now, do you?" Alaine snorted. "You who has barely set foot in this city but for the past few moons? Do you think to declare yourself emperor, is that it? Is this all it takes to demonstrate your undying love for Petrodor and its people? One battle, two moon's residence, and some pretty words?"

"You are hysterical," Kessligh observed, "and you whine like a child." Sasha had heard that tone all too often. It had the desired effect on Alaine—his eyes widened and his lips pressed thin with fury. "You have too little concern of our enemies, Alaine, and too much for your precious standing. I don't care a pile of horseshit for power in Petrodor. If we fail here, and the Army of Torovan is formed, I shall have no choice but to travel to the Saalshen Bacosh and continue the battle from there, far away from Petrodor. Then I'll be out of your hair entirely.

"I care only about the looming war. I fight to prevent it, and to save this light of freedom the serrin have offered us for future generations. Right now, that means saving the Nasi-Keth stronghold of Dockside Petrodor. Sirs, others may claim to love you more, or to know you better, but none can claim to serve you as well. I am the greatest warrior of the Nasi-Keth, and the greatest warrior in Lenayin, a land of great warriors. This is my uma. You know I do not idly boast."

His stare swept the surrounding men. They did not reply. But then, they did not need to. Alaine could read the expressions on their faces. He spat in disgust, turned, and pushed his way toward the stairs. One of his two followers present turned to follow, but the other stayed. The man departing looked at his fellow and paused. Then came back, and retook his place in the circle. Alaine strode alone to the stairs, and vanished.

"Sasha, what more?" Kessligh resumed as though Alaine had never spoken at all.

Sasha tried to regather her thoughts. "Very few archers, no more than fifty for the whole South End. I tried to correct a few positions, but a lot of the roofs down there are sloped, they don't make good posts, especially not in the rain. I don't think they're well practised, either."

"With the numbers that'll come," said Kessligh, "they'll only have to aim into the middle of a road."

"Oh . . . and one of their men had a good idea with fishing nets. He's weighted the ends and has found some women to throw them from high windows onto attackers below. I sent him to talk to a few people from midslope, to show them how it's done . . ."

"Our women should not be in the fight," said one of the Docksiders.

Sasha raised her eyebrows. "Oh *really*."

The man looked uncomfortable. "They are the mothers of our children," he said stubbornly. "Our children should not be motherless."

Sasha caught Kessligh's glance, reading his subtle expression instantly. It was the same argument as in Baerlyn. Some things in life are constant, Kessligh always told her. Now, once again, she saw his wisdom.

"I'm quite sure this mob will slaughter your women and *eat* your children, given half a chance," Sasha retorted. "Refusing to fight back will only kill them faster."

"Now look," one of Alaine's supporters protested, "Alaine had a good point. These are Verenthanes, and you should watch how you speak of them."

"*They* don't care!" Sasha retorted, pointing upslope toward the many trails of smoke. "To them, we're *all* pagans! I know this type well, believe it or not. In Lenayin, we've an entire north full of them. They say they're the only true Verenthanes and anyone who doesn't believe as they believe is pagan and deserves a horrid fate. Look around you, sirs. The Nasi-Keth amongst you follow the beliefs of un-human pagan demons! The rest of you associate with them! Your own archbishop has declared many times that associating with such evil pagan influences is a sin against the gods . . . why in the world do you continue to forgive him for that?"

Several men protested loudly, but Kessligh silenced them with a raised hand. Which was astonishing in itself. It was almost as much respect as he received from the commonfolk in Lenayin. So respectful the people become, Sasha thought sourly, when you hold their lives in your hands.

"What my uma means to say," Kessligh said, with a faint edge to his voice, "ever so tactfully I'm sure, is that in these circumstances, one must separate the man from the faith. The archbishop, my friends, is not a god. He is a man, like us . . . or most of us . . . and as such, he is fallible. You may believe it is a sin to question the gods. But it is no sin, surely, to question the man."

"How are we to know the will of the gods," came a defiant retort, "if not through the words of their appointed representative?"

"That is what the serrin call 'the eternal question,'" Kessligh replied with the faintest of smiles. "Life, my friends, is full of these eternal questions. Questions without answers, but ones that must be continually asked nonetheless. Truth is elusive. The archbishop cannot alone possess it, for he is just a man. Perhaps the answer lies in numbers. No one man can know all truths. That is why we have councils, so that many individual truths may work against each other, and find a common truth. Perhaps it is through our collective efforts that the gods shall reveal their truths. After all, we are the gods' greatest creations. Where else should their truths lie, if not in all of us, together?"

It silenced them for a while. Not that any were entirely convinced, Sasha reckoned. More that they realised it would take a great deal longer than the time available to reason such debates to a conclusion, and there were many more important things afoot.

"Crazy," Sasha summarised once the men had left, leaving her and Kessligh to observe the preparations on the road below. "We're about to be overrun by a bloodthirsty mob of murderers, and we're arguing faith and philosophy."

"It's not so crazy," Kessligh said mildly. "They need to be certain who the enemy is. If they question the need to fight now, morale could suffer."

"Hard to imagine anyone not seeing a need to fight," said Sasha, gazing at the smoke plumes on the slope.

"So far, they've only attacked serrin. Some have doubted the mobs will come down this far. They don't believe the reports of crowds chanting for the Shereldin Star."

Sasha sighed. "Even now, they cling to their Holy Father. They can't bear to see him as an enemy."

"There will be another archbishop one day. Perhaps he will be more amenable."

"You're defending them?" Sasha raised an eyebrow at him. "Kessligh the disparager of all that is not rational and proper?"

Kessligh gazed up at the slope, his hands on the wet stone of the wall. "The problem, Sasha, is not what a person believes in. Verenthane, pagan, Lisan Skyworship, the Kazeri desert mystics—it's all the same, all have the potential to be equally good or bad. The problem is not what things are believed, the problem is how people choose to believe them."

"Aye," said Sasha, leaning on the wall beside him. Somewhere in the conversation, they'd begun speaking Lenay. It was a reflex of comfort. Of home. From below drifted the hubbub of foreign voices, the clatter of weapons, the banging of barred doors. From the slope, the smell of acrid smoke. "Serrin are so moderate. They never do anything to excess. But even a mountain mystic preaching peace, love and happiness could take it too far, couldn't he?"

Kessligh nodded. "On his own, the mystic is harmless. He holds no power, and so his ideals remain just ideals. But say he converts the king to his beliefs. The king says peace, love and happiness are now his command. What does he do to those who refuse to be happy? Burn them?"

"*Val'er aie to'sho maal*," Sasha agreed. In Saalsi, "the attraction of opposites." Or nearly. "Ideals are figurative. Politics are literal. Ideals expressed through politics become political, and lose their idealism. Or become the very opposite of what was intended."

"Exactly." Kessligh nodded, once and firmly. "They *are* opposites. That's why idealistic leaders are so dangerous. An ideal in a debate is a curiosity. Wielding a sword, it can become a nightmare. The literal and the figurative, the ideal and the practical, they negate each other, sometimes violently. To combine them is to mix serrin oils with fire."

"But humans are most attracted to idealistic leaders," Sasha said with a frown.

Kessligh smiled. "Another eternal question," he said. "We believe in utopias. We think in absolutes. We should stop."

"So much simpler to just fight the stupid fight," Sasha muttered.

"Aye, but why fight at all, if you don't know why you're fighting?" Sasha made a face. "You understand more now than you did," Kessligh said approvingly.

"All this time amongst serrin," Sasha replied. "Errollyn's helped a lot. He and Rhillian are the only two serrin I've met who can say what they think without tying their tongues in knots."

"Where *is* Errollyn?"

"Down at South End, helping their archers prepare." She stared grimly at nothing. "Gerrold and his supporters have gone to help the *talmaad*. Errollyn feels guilty he does not do the same. He doesn't admit it, but I can tell."

"We can't spare the people, Sasha," Kessligh said sombrely. He stared at the fire of Palopy House, high on the ridgeline above. "It's a long climb up there. We could lose people on the way up and back. Only our best fighters would be useful fighting in the open streets and if we had losses, or became entangled or cut off by the mobs, Dockside would be vulnerable. Rhillian knew that when she embarked on her present course."

"You . . ." Sasha blinked at him. "You didn't know this would happen, though?"

"Saalshen has always been vulnerable to human enemies in Petrodor," said Kessligh. "Steiner or Maerler, or some combination of smaller houses, could always have wiped them out if they tried. Their main protection has never been their swords, Sasha, but their trade. Even now, all the reports are that Steiner and their allies remain firmly locked up behind their gates, despite some in the mobs calling on them to come out and fight the serrin. The Saalshen trade is too valuable. Steiner is now caught between offending Saalshen, and offending the archbishop."

"Rhillian did not count on the mobs, Sasha. Inside Petrodor, most of the populace are more or less controlled by those who owe some gratitude to Saalshen. But on the fringes, in the slums, and in Riverside in particular, the patachis have little sway. The archbishop himself has always been constrained by the divided loyalties of his lower priests, but now that balance too has swung. I never thought it would happen exactly like this. But I have warned Rhillian many times that this control that the patachis exert upon the people is merely a temporary illusion, and that it's only the wealthy, and the Nasi-Keth, who feel they owe Saalshen anything. This is not about faith, Sasha, it's all about power—faith is merely the tool by which power is attained. Like you said, faith may indeed be good, but the nature of power is ever unchanging. It corrupts any goodness faith may have had. Rhillian was always too clever for her own good, she always saw the complications, but missed the simplicities. Amongst humans, power rules all. Only now, perhaps, does she grasp what that means."

"I'm scared for her," Sasha said quietly. "She's my friend."

"I know. I fear for her too. But Errollyn was right, she should have left the games of power to humans. If she'd joined with me, this wouldn't have happened. But she thought she knew better. She was wrong."

"She's not a bad person," Sasha said stubbornly, fighting the pain in her throat.

"No," Kessligh said quietly. "They never are." He straightened and wiped back his lank, wet hair. "Best you get back down there. Try to get some semblance of basic formation behind those barricades, they need to know what happens *after* the first wave hits."

"Pandemonium," Sasha said drily.

"Yes. Tell them that. That's why the formations are so critical."

"This is formation fighting," Sasha complained. The thought of going back downstairs made her slightly dizzy. All those people, all rushing around. "Lenays rarely fight like this and, with all respect, you never taught it."

"No, this is street fighting," Kessligh corrected. "These streets make for small formations, and Lenays fight in small groups all the time. Remember the training hall drills, five against five."

"I never took part in those," she said doubtfully. "Too much pushing."

"Yes, but you watched them. Just the basics, Sasha—these men have basic drill, some of them are quite good. Just make sure they know when to move and where. I'm not sure they all understand the concept of a reserve yet."

Sasha sighed. "All right. I know that much." She looked at him. "You're confident?"

"I have no preconceptions," Kessligh said grimly. "That's why I win." He gazed across the cramped and cluttered docks, the squared brick and stone, the crumbling walls, all wet and grey beneath cloud and smoke. The place where he had been born, and had abandoned. Gerrold had abandoned the docks to defend his beloved serrin. Alaine held no appeal for people facing the prospect of war. Kessligh Cronenverdt had returned. He ruled here now.

Sasha ran back down the tower steps, onto the battlements where some archers were inspecting their arrows, and down the long steps inside the wall to the keep floor below. Within the shelter of buildings that had until recently served as stables, women now gathered piles of linen, water and medicines, ready to tend the wounded. Through a doorway, Sasha could see at least one Nasi-Keth woman amongst them, giving directions. She thought of Yulia, who had thought to become a medicine woman. She would still be alive had she done so. Sasha shook off unhelpful thoughts and strode to the main gate in the wall.

Near the docks was a straggly group of twenty men, in roughspun pants and sodden shirts, their hair plastered wet. Some grasped proper halberds and spears, and a few carried swords. There were quite a few axes and hammers, and most had fish knives in their belts. None had any more armour than the odd leather jacket. Dear spirits. But Kessligh was right, they drilled better than their appearances might have led her to expect, and all the long weapons were well placed at the formation's front.

Along the dockfront, numerous other groups had similarly gathered. Outside of Lenayin, this was what it meant to be militia—working men, of various trades, who occasionally fought. It offended her highland sensibilities. Men who went to war should at least know what they were doing. To send unskilled mobs of fishermen and paupers at each other's throats with improvised tools was not civilised. And to think the lowlanders called Lenays barbarians . . .

Before she could intercede, Sasha glimpsed someone striding hurriedly up the docks, holding what appeared to be a sleeping child in his arms. It was Errollyn—she'd have recognised that lithe, muscular stride anywhere. She ran to him, noting the hard concern on his face . . . and saw that he carried not a child, but a small woman. Her light blonde hair was wet not only with rain, but with blood, and there was the unmistakable shape of a crossbow bolt through her left calf.

"Aisha!" Sasha gasped as she arrived at Errollyn's side. He kept walking, as fast as he could without jolting the bundle in his arms. Sasha struggled to keep up, half jogging, noting that Aisha seemed unconscious. "What happened?"

"She was found near Sharptooth, the girl who found her said she murmured something about Maerler and treachery, then fell unconscious." Sasha had never seen Errollyn so upset, it radiated from his every tense muscle.

"Is she hurt besides the leg?"

"She's taken a blow on the head, her hand is cut and her shoulder seems damaged. Her head worries me most."

They strode past the drilling men, past piles of refuse from which children ran to and fro, lugging whatever they could carry down the lanes to the barricades.

They turned down Fishnet Alley, and soon into the Gianna house courtyard. Tashyna sat up abruptly where she was leashed to the courtyard tree, tail wagging warily. Her coat was a little wet, otherwise the rain seemed not to bother her at all. Sasha ran to push open the door into little Elra Halmady's room, and Errollyn carried Aisha to the neighbouring bed. The little girl was awake, her left arm above the covers and wrapped in wet, pungent cloth. She watched as Errollyn placed Aisha carefully down and began cutting away her pants from around the protruding bolt. One of the Gianna sisters came in, saw Aisha and dashed off, yelling for medicines and bandages.

Errollyn inspected the bolt, now thick with congealed blood where it stuck from Aisha's flesh. Then he felt at her throat, seeking a pulse. He began gently feeling her head around where the blood seemed thickest. He murmured something to himself in a Saalsi dialect that Sasha could not recognise. It sounded suspiciously like a prayer.

"Is she a serrin?" asked Elra from the neighbouring bed.

"Yes, she is," said Sasha.

"Is she going to be all right?"

"She's going to be fine." Sasha placed a hand on Errollyn's shoulder.

"Errollyn. She rode with us in battle against the Hadryn heavy cavalry, she can survive a little blow on the head. She'll limp for a while once you take the bolt out, but I've seen your medicines work miracles. She'll be fine."

"I should be with them." There was a strain in Errollyn's voice. Sasha saw the tears in his eyes. "I should be with them. Even if I can't feel it, I should be there."

"Errollyn . . ." Sasha shook her head in disbelief. "Can't feel what? What are you talking about?"

"It's a curse." He stood abruptly, fists clenched. For a brief moment, Sasha thought he might strike something. "It's said all that is strange is a blessing, but it feels like a curse."

"Errollyn." She touched his arm gently. "Aisha needs you here. She always respected your choices. Don't regret what she does not."

He looked down at her, his green eyes struggling. "I wanted to feel it, Sasha. I wanted to believe in Rhillian, and I wanted to believe in Saalshen, and I didn't want to doubt. But I've always been different. Ever since I was a child, I couldn't feel it, however hard I tried. Rhillian didn't understand that, and she made me so angry because she was the one who wanted a *du'janah* in this *talmaad* in the first place. A balance of truth, she said. She refused to understand, and she made me so angry, and now I've betrayed them all . . ."

"No!" Sasha grasped his arms firmly. "No. Rhillian made her own decisions, Errollyn. You were right, damn it. Kessligh tells me just now this proves you were right—"

"And you think this makes it any easier!"

Sasha gazed up at him. The pain in his eyes echoed the one in her heart. She took a risk, and reached to wipe away his tears. A Lenay man might have struck her for such an insulting gesture. Errollyn did not flinch. His gaze was almost . . . longing. Something occurred to her. "Errollyn. You've never told me your age." Aisha looked barely sixteen, yet she had more than thirty summers. Rhillian had even more. She'd always assumed that Errollyn must also be considerably older than herself. But something in his eyes now made her wonder.

"I'm twenty-three," he said. Sasha was almost shocked.

She managed a crooked smile at him. "Finally a serrin who looks his age." And acts it, she nearly added, but didn't.

Errollyn stared at her desperately. And kissed her full on the lips. The kiss lingered, deeper and deeper, and suddenly her heart was hammering and her arms were about him, and she wanted nothing more than to melt into that warm intoxication and never emerge . . . He pulled back, hands firm on her shoulders. His stare at this range was paralysing. Deep green, like the deepest ocean. "Don't die," he whispered. "You're all I have left."

He turned back to Aisha and Sasha backed up, blinking. Her knees wanted to give way. She had twenty summers, and it was the first time she'd been properly kissed. She could hardly complain of the intensity. Yet still . . . one *hell* of a time for it, she couldn't help think. She recalled Errollyn's last words, and was suddenly angry.

"No, I'm *not*!" she snapped at him. "You have Aisha. Look, you have Elra." Pointing to the other bed, where little Elra stared with wide eyes at the scene they made. "You have all the spirits-blasted Nasi-Keth! This whole dockside, in fact, those who aren't completely stupid. Don't you do this stupid, defeatist thing to me, I liked you much better when you were arrogant and annoying!"

She turned to stride out, heart still hammering, and realised that it was not the final parting she wanted, not after what had just happened. She spun back around, grabbed him, and kissed him as hard as she could. *Then* she stormed out.

Palopy House, fully ablaze, was beginning to collapse when the last of the oil ran out and the fires that had filled the gaps on the defensive wall began to die. The first of the mob to brave the dying flames fell instantly, shot through the neck or heart. Rhillian waited, in the smouldering wreckage of small trees and bushes that had once been a lovely garden, and tested the pull of her bow. She'd wrapped a cloth about her face, yet still her mouth tasted of ash and irritation rasped in her throat when she breathed. Her broad hat, too, she'd dunked in water to keep the burning embers from her hair. Behind, another wall collapsed with a great roar and a billow of thick, white ash that rolled across the fire-blackened front garden. At least now, with an attack imminent, the artillery had stopped.

More serrin crouched about the open yard, barely visible through a haze of smoke, drifting ash and falling rain. Stones sailed through the air and clattered on the pavings, or thudded on the black stalks that had once been grass. Beyond the wall, the chanting now rose to a frenzy: "Death to serrin." Rhillian had long since ceased listening to the words—it was only rhetoric, that most foul of human creations.

With a final roar, they came through the smoke—a torrent of men, the leaders carrying the shields from the first wave of fallen. Rhillian fired low and they fell screaming, clutching their legs. More hurdled them. Bows thrummed and arrowfire buzzed, men falling in a flail of arms and legs, punched off their feet by the power of serrin longbows. Others fanned out, running crazily, trying to clear the killing zone. Most fell, as Rhillian struggled to keep pace with the reloading speed of her comrades, pulled and killed a man coming down the gravel gate path.

Ahead of her, several serrin nearer the gate were forced to drop their bows and pull swords. Across the yard, several more did likewise. The volume of fire reduced, yet the numbers coming only seemed to increase. Rhillian kept firing, and killed another four. The next were too close, and she dropped the bow and drew her blade.

The rioters were no swordsmen. Most did not have swords. She killed more than seemed civilised, her precise, slashing strokes in brutal contrast to the thrashing lunacy that passed as attacks. Corpses and bits of bodies thudded to earth about her as she made new space for her footing, backing slowly across the yard. Swivel, slash, fade and cut, the improvised dance of master performer amidst a throng of clumsy pretenders, she laid a trail of gore and blood in her wake. Only now, the numbers grew greater and she was running out of space.

Not far away, she saw Arele hit by a wooden pole and stumble. He killed the next who lunged at him with an axe, hacked the pole in half, but off balance, failed to see the knife from behind. That man also died, but Arele fell to his knees, and two more simply threw themselves on him, and more piled on, striking and cutting.

Another attacker, barely more than a ragged boy, did not attack, but stood off and threw stones. Rhillian fended a spear thrust and took its owner's hand on the reverse, swivel-stepped into an onrushing club wielder and cut him nearly in half, then took a hard stone to the chest as the boy threw, cradling his armful and reaching for another. She parried a slashing hand-scythe, which caught about her blade and twisted the hilt in her hands. She sidestepped and missed the reverse, tried to lunge at the stone thrower but he danced back. A running madman tried to tackle her, but she spun away, his arm knocking her off balance once more. An axe-wielder tried to split her down the middle, and she rolled backward, recovering to kill another who came at her side, only to take a stone to the side of her head. Half stunned, she whipped a knife without thinking and killed the young stone thrower with a knife through the throat. And was fighting for her life before she could so much as pause and register the horror she'd just performed.

The heat of roaring flames seemed to singe her clothes, her feet stumbling now on debris from the collapsed walls. Her attackers were a sea of mad shadows in the ash and smoke, arms and faces and flailing weapons lit orange in a hellish glare.

She hacked another, then ducked and sprinted clear of a flanking move, her boots tripping on charred rubble. Ahead, falling back to the gap between the house and the western cliff, she saw several serrin fighting desperately. One fell even as she ran to them, yet the smaller space made it more defensible. She arrived at Terel's side, hurdling the half-dozen corpses of those he'd felled, and killed two more from behind as they tried to press Terel's flank.

Now they fell back along the western side, the cliff-facing wall of the house long since fallen, what remained of the stately building now a mass of flaming masonry and pancaked floors. Attackers darted through the gaps between defenders as they retreated, only to fall to crossbow fire from behind. Some of the house staff tried desperately to reload those few crossbows—not a preferred weapon of Saalshen, though its relative simplicity meant several of the staff could use it. The attackers were now not quite so suicidal in their charges, yet they pressed hard, thrusting and jabbing with spears, hook-poles, halberds and other long weapons, forcing the four remaining serrin on this side back step after step. Others with lesser weapons tried for the gaps that opened up. Rhillian knew that if the defence was pushed back past the end of the burning house, and into the open rear garden, all was lost.

Terel knew it too, and risked a spin past a thrusting spear to fell its owner and took the arm of another in retreating. But more took their places. One threw a spear at Rhillian, and she ducked aside just in time. She went low beneath a halberd swing, took that man's legs, and slashed open another who came at her side. A spear thrust grazed her ribs as she danced back. She saw a scythe come swinging, and cut it in two.

Terel made another forward dance, killed a pole wielder, yet caught a spear thrust to the arm. One-armed, he parried hard, but a blow sent him off balance. Rhillian leaped to his defence, but an axeman cut at her with a hack she had no choice but to duck, and then Terel was surrounded. He killed another, but a blow from a club sent him to a knee, and a flashing blade sent blood spurting. They fell on him like seagulls on rotten bread, stabbing and screaming. A gap opened in the line and then they came pouring through.

Suddenly, Rhillian was no longer being attacked. Men ran past her instead, howling at the top of their lungs. She saw the staff wielding crossbows go down beneath the surging mob. She saw Carla, the funny girl with the slow speech and a cheeky grin, trying to defend herself with her crossbow as the blows and thrusts came raining down. The mob poured over paved paths and gardens, leapt the little rocky steam, and sprinted at the pitiful little circle on the fountain courtyard, where terrified men and women who had no business in any fight made a futile defence about the wounded.

Even through the horror, Rhillian spotted something beyond the far wall. Smoke, rising above the Vailor residence. It came from the far side, where the Vailor gate opened onto another road. Vailor too was under attack. A tiny, faint hope dawned. She sprinted into the rear garden, leapt down to a paved path, beheaded a man who got in her way, and thrashed through a flower garden onto the main courtyard. Pick one, she thought. You'll only get one chance. Choose well, or there's no hope at all.

Deani was holding his own with his sword. Elesa the cook swung a blade with less assurance, pivoting on her one good leg. Big Anton the doorman had the smarts of an ox, but swung his halberd in huge arcs, felling several and sending others scampering sideways. But none could serve. Rhillian saw Teri, also swinging his sword. Teri was a dark-haired lad of fifteen, quick as a mouse and deaf as a stone. But he weighed little, he was fast, and he was quick-witted.

She ran for him like an arrow, cutting an arm off Deani's opponent in passing and hurdling several wounded. Teri was backing away from the courtyard, confronted by three attackers. Rhillian killed two fast from behind, danced aside the slash of the axe-wielding third, then sent his head bouncing across the lawn. She grabbed the terrified Teri by the arm. "Run!" she yelled into his face.

Teri ran, Rhillian clutching his arm, past the garden benches and through the lush bushes before the rear wall. The ladder was still there. Rhillian urged him up it. "Don't go over!" she insisted, making him look at her. His frightened eyes watched her lips. "Wait for me, don't go over yet!"

Teri nodded quickly, then scampered up the ladder. Rhillian dashed back, but over the bushes she could see the courtyard was a seething mass of armed men. She saw Deani, falling, then impaled by a scythe as he lay on the ground. She saw Elesa the cook pinned by several men, who began hacking off her limbs, while she screamed. She saw big Anton with a man on his back and another hanging to his arm, thrashing and punching whilst spears and blades sliced through his legs, his stomach and back. She saw their wounded hacked to pieces where they lay on the ground and a severed head stuck on the end of a spear, and thrust into the air. She saw many armed men running her way. Ahead of them, she saw Kiel, bloodied and limping. He was yelling at her and waving for her to go.

She backed up, waving Kiel past her. He got up the ladder fast enough, despite a bloody leg, and Rhillian followed. She leapt for the top of the wall just as armed men reached the ladder below. Kiel kicked the ladder away as Rhillian pulled herself up. Teri lay atop the wall alongside the spikes.

Rhillian squeezed between several spikes, eyeing a soft patch of dirt on the other side . . . movement caught the corner of her eye, and she saw a

Vailor man with a crossbow, barely fifteen paces away, aiming straight at her. She dived, clutching a spike to avoid falling, and the bolt whizzed overhead . . . and hit Teri, who was just rising.

He fell forward. Rhillian thrust herself back between two spikes, catching at him desperately. Teri hit the top of the wall and slipped from the edge. Diving forward, Rhillian caught his flailing arm and grabbed it with both hands. Teri hung there, staring up at her in disbelief. The bolt protruded from his side, beneath the ribs. Below him, the men who had chased them now came running to the spot beneath his dangling feet.

"Kiel!" Rhillian begged, hauling with all her strength. "Help me!" Teri was only a lad, but her arms were tired, and even the svaalverd could not disguise a woman's disadvantages here. Kiel crawled along the wall and reached down for Teri's other hand. Grabbed, and began pulling. Rhillian strained until her arms seemed nearly to dislodge from their sockets, finding no leverage in their position. But the boy rose and Kiel grabbed his collar with one hand.

A huge bailing hook atop a long pole swung up from below and tore into Teri's shoulder. The boy had enough time to meet Rhillian's eyes one last time, and show her his astonishment. The pole pulled, and Teri was torn from their grasp.

"NO!" Rhillian screamed, and would have hurled herself off the wall had not Kiel grabbed her by the hair. Somewhere in the fight, her hat had come off. "Rhillian!" Kiel yelled at her. "Live! LIVE, Rhillian!" She did not have her blade, she realised. It had fallen on the Vailor side of the wall. Beneath them, Teri was impaled by spear, then sword, then knife, again and again. There was blood everywhere.

Rhillian slid back, then jumped onto the Vailor side. She hit the dirt hard and rolled, then scrambled for her fallen sword. The crossbowman was still struggling to reload, that being rather the problem, with crossbows. Rhillian came out of the bushes and he tried to defend himself with his crossbow, but Rhillian took his hand off at the wrist. Then she pulled her second knife, just to make it personal, and thrust it hard up beneath the man's jaw. The horror in his eyes, the gurgling in his throat, the sticky blood that gushed over her hand, all were an intoxication. She'd never known herself so savage. She'd never known it would feel so good.

Rhillian remembered only a little of what came next. She and Kiel crept through the bushes against the walls, encountering several more guards with fatal consequences. The attack on the front of Vailor House seemed ferocious, and had drawn most of their defenders that way. Kiel and Rhillian had climbed onto a rear balcony, then onto the roof. From there, they watched the attack on Vailor's front wall, as thousands of rioters tried to storm the property, probably to attack Palopy from behind, and make sure none escaped. But the road on this side was narrow—only a few attackers could assault the wall at any time and there was no room for artillery.

Soon the mobs pulled back, no doubt informed by others that Palopy had fallen. Rhillian and Kiel waited until dark, then crept down to the ground. From there it was a simple matter to surprise two guards on a side gate, slit their throats and escape onto the road beyond. Soon enough they were creeping along a familiarly dark, winding route, boots splashing in puddles.

Eventually, they emerged onto an open shoulder between leaning walls. Kiel stopped to rest his wounded leg and tighten the improvised bandage. There was a view of Dockside below. Despite the gloom of the overcast night, there was light enough on the docks. Fires burned along their length, reflecting off the water and turning even the clouds above to a dull, orange glow, like coals in a dying fire. From far below, above the gentle patter of rain, there came the raucous sounds of battle.

Eighteen

SASHA HAD NOT YET SWUNG HER BLADE IN ANGER, and already she was exhausted. She surveyed one alley's barricade, the scene alight with burning torches and the more distant flicker of a burning building. Men rested in the respite between assaults, drinking water brought to them by women carrying buckets. Younger lads scurried forward to replace pieces of the barricade that had fallen in the fighting. Bodies of the enemy were pulled away from the barricade, so they did not make a set of steps for the next attack to climb. Several defenders were discovered to be wounded, and were eventually persuaded, with much shouting and handwaving, to fall back for treatment. Then another man would be hustled forward from the waiting cluster further down the alley, to take his place in the line.

Sasha pushed forward through the throng, yelling, "Who's in charge?" Eventually a man revealed himself—a great, pot-bellied ball of a man, wielding a big, blood-spattered axe. "Losses?" she asked him, without pre-amble. She was not bothering to identify herself, and most people seemed in little doubt.

"Four," the man announced, leaning a thick arm on his axe. "That last attack, they had long weapons to the fore, they seemed more organised . . . here, Feri says he saw a militia man . . ."

"Had to be!" the man named Feri declared, a big broadsword in hand, still wide-eyed and breathless from the shock of that last engagement. "He moved so well, he flicked out his damn spear like an expert, like he was fishing or something! He got Haleni right in the throat!"

"Aye, I know," said Sasha. "The front ranks are loaded with militia, they're not all crazed lunatics. It's the same right across the line. What about armour, are you seeing any more armour?"

There were head shakes all about. Tired men; dishevelled with rain, sweat and blood.

"Just the usual," said the big axe man. "How does the line hold?"

"Excellently," Sasha announced, loudly enough for them all to hear. "We've had not a single breach so far. They aren't—"

"Ware!" came a shout from above, and people ducked as an arrow clattered off a nearby wall. Some attackers had taken possession of empty houses above the foot of the slope and were firing from long range toward the torchlight. Mostly, it was a nuisance.

"They aren't able to deploy their artillery," Sasha continued, "that which they've managed to bring down the slope. Kessligh thinks we may see a more concerted attack on one part of the line—if that happens, we may need to redeploy some men. Those of you who are good runners, get ready to move if the order comes."

"We're winning?" another man said hopefully. It was the question of a shopkeeper who found himself in a battle for the first time in his life and wondering if he might actually survive. Winning? The night, Sasha knew, was very young yet. Yet she allowed herself a small, wry smile.

"Aye," she told them. "We're winning."

That got a cheer. Sasha turned and pushed away through the crowd as men returned their attention to the barricade. Once clear, Sasha rejoined Kristan and ran up the adjoining alley, headed north along the stretch of docks that Kessligh had assigned to her—from Maerler's Way all the way down to South End, she had effective command.

Kristan stuck close to her shoulder, not yet breathing as hard as she. He was a Nasi-Keth lad of nineteen, slim with a mop of curly black hair and freckles. The uma to one of Kessligh's strongest supporters, he was a good fighter and an excellent runner, and had been tasked to make certain Sasha was not ambushed by some sneak behind the lines.

The connecting alleys were barely lit, and occupied mostly by women or older children hurrying with bandages, food or water. Several alleys on, she came to Fisherman's Lane, its familiar length now a commotion of battle preparations like the others. Sasha pushed her way forward, and found the mood behind this barricade nearly raucous, men talking loudly and with great enthusiasm, some even laughing at a battle-crazed joke.

Immediately behind the barricade, she discovered why. The highlanders had taken over. Tongren stood atop a portion of the barricade, in all contempt for long-distance archers, and was yelling animatedly at the others, instructing them on formations, and what had just happened in the last attack and should not happen again. He made shapes with his hands, pointing with his sword and describing men's movements. His manner reminded Sasha of the captain of a lagand team, discussing a change in tactics during a break in play. His blade was bloody and his arms were bare, black tattoos spiralled down his biceps to trail delicate patterns about his thick forearms. Sasha had not seen those tattoos before. They were the markings of a great warrior, for certain. In Lenayin, Goeren-yai men had them added as they fought in more battles, and won more victories. Cherrovan, she knew, was not so different.

She recognised Ydryld the ironmonger, another big, wide-muscled man. Ydryld was Lenay, but Verenthane, and indistinguishable from the local Torovans . . . save for his size. Very few Torovan men had such size about them, particularly in the shoulders. Only now did it truly strike her. She herself was a little below average size for a Lenay woman—but in Petrodor she was above. Tongren, no doubt, was a moderately tall man in Cherrovan, but here he was huge.

"You did well," Sasha surmised to Ydryld. Ydryld smiled a gap-toothed smile and pointed proudly to the lane before the barricade. The bodies piled there were twice the number of any other lane. Ydryld's huge sword looked familiar to Sasha's homesick eyes—it had Lenay workmanship, nothing fancy and a little battered, but big, well-balanced and deadly sharp. She could well see the horror of it, here amongst the clubs and spears and half-sized thrusting swords of Petrodor.

"Sasha! Sasha!" It was Elys, Tongren's eldest, shaking her arm. Sasha almost didn't recognise him, his long black hair tied into a warrior's braid, a highland sword in his hand. He pointed at Tongren atop the barricade. "That's my father!" he proclaimed. There were tears in his eyes, and he seemed ready to burst with pride. "My father's a warrior! I'm going to have tattoos like him too, one day. You watch."

"Were you pressed hard?" Sasha asked Ydryld.

"That pack of chickenshit fools couldn't threaten us in their dreams," Ydryld retorted. "Look at us! Only two men hurt, those barely scratches, and look at this pile of dead filth at our feet! We're invincible!"

The men about him gave a roar and weapons were thrust into the air.

"Hey!" yelled Tongren over the top of them. "Pay attention, damn you! They'll come harder next time, this was just a probe! Listen to me and we'll kill even more of them! Sasha!" As he spotted her amongst the taller men. "How holds the line?"

"Well!" Sasha replied and pushed through to him.

Tongren jumped down from the cart he'd been standing on. "What does Kessligh think?"

"You mean you haven't had a runner?" She stopped before him, looking up.

"Aye, he came, looked, and said carry on." Tongren grinned. "Kessligh knows this alley at least is safe!"

"And that's a problem," said Sasha. "We're too strong here. You were right, that was a probe in strength, whoever's commanding this doesn't mind losing a few hundred Riversiders if it shows him where our strengths and weaknesses are. Fisherman's Lane has shown itself our strength, so he probably won't come this way again, not seriously."

"Aye," Tongren nodded. "Where do you think?"

"Oh hells . . . there's really no telling. Kessligh might have a better idea than me, the line is fairly much the same all the way along. And however much command is had over there, I'd bet it's not *that* good. Commanding that mob would be like herding squirrels."

"Aye, he'll just pick three or four weakest spots, and concentrate on those," Tongren agreed. "If they get through in several places at the same time, we're in trouble."

"We can't let that happen," Sasha said firmly.

Tongren nodded. "So what d'you want some of my men? They won't like it, Sasha—this is the first damn time in centuries Cherrovan and Lenay have fought together for something!"

"No," said Sasha, gazing over the top of the barricade. Even now, youngsters were throwing dislodged pieces back on top, making it higher. In the flickering torchlight, she could see a catapult at the foot of the slope, its wooden frame studded with arrows. She glanced up, and saw the dark shape of a bowman crouched on a roof above the lane. Most of the Nasi-Keth were archers tonight, not swordsmen, by Kessligh's command. Fighting down in the alleys was at close quarters and cramped; a wheelwright with a hammer could be as useful as a svaalverd fighter in such conditions. A Nasi-Keth could kill as many attackers as he had arrows in his quiver.

Tongren followed her gaze and grinned. "They can't fire the damn catapult on the slope!" he said gleefully. "One shot, and the weight of the swinging arm knocks it over! That or the shot goes way short, and that's oil-shot they're using, could end up anywhere. So they wheeled this one down onto the flat, only they're right within archer range and your boys on the roof cut them all down before they could fire."

"There's people moving over there," Sasha observed, seeing shadows flitting about the catapult.

"Our archers are holding fire," Tongren explained. "Gaeryld and his son are over there scouting."

"Out there?" Sasha stared into the flickering gloom of the lower slope. Amidst the cluttered houses, torchfires burned, but the chanting and yelling was not so strong here as elsewhere. Still, there were many thousands of armed, bloodthirsty men arrayed just above the flat of Dockside. Spirits knew what they were organising, or what help they were getting from supposedly neutral sources.

"Gaeryld's from Valhanan Lenayin—your part of the world," Tongren explained. "He's not been here more than three years, he was a woodsman there. He had some trouble with another man's wife, I gather, and that family's sworn to get his head, so he came here instead. His son's a little rat-bastard cut-purse, half of Dockside would wring his neck if they could catch him, so it seems only fair we're putting his talents to use."

Sasha gazed up at the big Cherrovan, wonderingly, and could not help but ask, "And what about you, Tongren? Those are interesting tattoos."

"Ah, you like them?" He examined his arms, smiling. "I was a chieftain's son."

Sasha blinked at him. "You're joking."

Tongren laughed. "Village chieftain, not provincial. A little place called Raeshald, in Alsfaynen Cherrovan, in the high country just to the west of—"

"I know where it is. That's just north of Hadryn."

"Aye, we share the same enemies, you and I! And a right mess you made of those bloody Hadryn, too."

Sasha withheld comment, still staring. Most Cherrovan had little compunction killing any Lenays—Hadryn or otherwise. But she did not want to divert Tongren's tongue. "What happened?"

"My father wanted me to marry the wrong girl. I wanted to marry the right girl. We ran away together, to the only place my relatives couldn't come and kill me."

Sasha's mouth dropped open. "You mean . . . your wife . . . ?"

Tongren grinned. "Aye, the dragon lady herself. Don't let her fool you, Sasha, she's the sweetest woman ever born to the breast of the spirits."

"And Elys doesn't know?"

"No hiding it now. I'd thought it best not to talk, lest word escape back to my family. But my father died just recently, my eldest brother rules Raeshald now. He sent word, he'd like to see me. He talks of a pardon." He sighed, his eyes wistful. "I would like to see my homeland once more. I've lived here for sixteen years now, since Elys was a babe. But at night, Sasha, I can still hear the mountains calling, deep in my soul."

"Do you fear a trap?"

"I'm only a little stupid, girl, not entirely. Of course I fear a bloody trap! But my brother has enemies, and it's the Cherrovan tradition for brothers to share power. My brother needs me." An arrow whistled somewhere abouts, then a more distant clatter on a rooftop. "But come, this pause won't last forever. How many of my men do you need?"

Sasha took a deep breath. "I think I'll leave you together," she said. "But I'll pull the Torovans here off the line, and send them to reinforce the neighbouring lanes. This will be a highlands affair."

Tongren grinned, a dangerous light in his eye. "I'll give the order. I like it so far."

"There may be a point," Sasha continued, "where a major thrust will come down either to the north," and she pointed right, "or to the south," and she pointed left. "At that point, if they manage to break through, all of their momentum will depend upon a constant flow of men into that breach. This rabble are not fighters, Tongren, you've discovered that." Nodding to his bloody sword.

"Aye," Tongren agreed, listening intently.

"Success for them will only come through sheer weight of numbers. If you see a thrust coming through beside you, I want you to charge into its flank."

Tongren looked astonished. Then his eyes lit up. "Charge?" he exclaimed. "Burning bullshit, you've got more balls than a lagand tournament."

"These streets are narrow," Sasha insisted. "A small group of good fighters, well motivated, can cut off an entire road and stop the flow of many times that number of enemy. If you can get in amongst them, then you can buy us time to deal with the breakthrough, without having to worry about the torrent that comes through behind."

"What about leaving Fisherman's Lane undefended?"

Sasha shrugged. "It's a risk, but like I said, they probably won't come through here again. And do you think that mob could respond quickly to a new opportunity? Are they that sophisticated?"

Tongren whistled. "Bloody hells," he said. "You really are Kessligh's uma, aren't you?"

"I only seem brilliant because you Cherrovan wouldn't know strategy if it bit you on the balls," Sasha retorted with a dangerous grin.

Tongren roared with laughter. "Fair enough, girl," he said. His eyes blazed with anticipation. "A charge! Bloody magnificent!"

Sasha pushed her way back through the crowd to join Kristan when she saw a young woman leaning against a wall, looking cold, wet and frightened. She held a spear with a curious banner—a black wolf's head on a blue background. It was as bedraggled in the misting rain as the dress that clung to her shoulders and breasts. Strangely for a non-Nasi-Keth, she had a knife sheath tied to the sash about her waist. With a blink of astonishment, Sasha saw that the woman was Alythia.

Sasha made a gesture for Kristan to wait, and went to her. "Lyth?"

Alythia looked at her, dark eyes waif-like behind a matted fringe of tangled black hair. She straightened immediately, no longer shivering, wiping hair back from her face. Shoulders back and breasts out. They'd always been her proudest asset, Sasha thought sardonically.

"What's the banner for?" Sasha asked when Alythia gave no greeting.

"Apparently I'm a princess of Lenayin," Alythia said shortly. "I was given it. By them." With a curt nod down the alley.

"Oh," said Sasha, realisation dawning. She fought down a smile. She *wanted* to laugh out loud. Perhaps, several months ago, she would have.

"I *was* helping," Alythia continued, acerbically. "I was carrying things and helping to prepare for more wounded, but *no* they say, I'm a princess of Lenayin and I must stand here in the freezing rain and hold this stupid banner."

"I think it's a rather nice banner," Sasha said mildly. Alythia had always loved to remind Sasha of how she, noble elder sister, had chosen the great burdens and duties of princesshood, while Sasha, irresponsible brat, had gone running off to play with horses and swords in the wilds. Evidently Alythia's notion of a royal burden had been one too many boring feasts and dances. Standing in the rain with Lenay soldiers on the battlefield had never entered into her equations.

"They're barbarians," Alythia said coldly, rewrapping her free arm about herself. She nodded toward the barricade. "They scream and howl louder than the mobs. After the first attack failed, they screamed all kinds of horrible things at their backs. One of them . . . *relieved* himself on the dead." She shuddered.

Sasha nodded. "Aye, all very intimidating, I'm sure. They'll think twice before attacking down this lane again."

"Good Verenthane soldiers would not conduct themselves in such a manner."

"About a quarter of them *are* Verenthane."

Alythia looked uncomfortable. "Not city-bred Verenthanes they're not."

"Oh aye, all you city Verenthanes shit jewels and your farts smell like flowers." Alythia glared at her. Sasha took a deep breath. "Look, Lyth, these are your people. Our people. For better or worse, richer or poorer, these are our blood. For the spirits' sake, be proud! These are the best fighters on the line, no contest . . . better even than many of the Nasi-Keth."

"It takes more than an easy aptitude for killing to impress me," Alythia said coldly. "Culture and civility are the makings of a modern man. Of course, some people are more easily impressed."

"You could always go and stay with Steiner," Sasha retorted, her tone hardening. "If you find present company beneath you."

"Maybe I will," Alythia snapped. "Maybe they'll be much more civilised!"

"Aye, maybe you could marry one of them!" Sasha suggested sarcastically. "Then some other house will kill that husband, then you could marry his murderer, and so on, leaving a trail of dead husbands right across Petrodor!"

She'd never seen Alythia so furious. For a moment she thought Alythia might try and strike her. Surely only the realisation that Sasha was much better at that kind of thing prevented her. Sasha knew it had been an incredibly cruel thing to say . . . but hells, she'd never been able to deal with Alythia. And now Alythia was insulting not just Lenayin, whom she was supposed to represent and champion, but the rural Goeren-yai in particular. Alythia was impossible, and cruel, and she deserved it.

"I'm leaving," Alythia said hoarsely, her voice shaking, angry tears in her eyes. "I'm going some place warm. Someone else can take this stupid banner and stand here in the rain. I've had enough."

"No, you haven't," Sasha replied, her voice hard. "You *are* a princess of Lenayin. That title is all you have left. If you leave your place here, behind your very own people, and leave that banner lying in the rain, people will know you're a fraud. And then you'll have nothing."

She stalked off, beckoning to Kristan, and ran down the adjoining alley. She did not look back. She did not want to see her sister standing cold and miserable in the rain, lost and alone, with tears in her eyes. She did not want to feel sorry for her. There were other things to worry about.

By the time she reached Tarae Keep, she was breathing very hard. Some Nasi-Keth umas, three boys and a girl, stood about the arched door leading inside. Even now, a young runner came pelting at high speed past Sasha and Kristan, skidded to a halt before one of the waiting youngsters and recited a breathless message. The other youngster took off within the keep, heading for the stairs and the tower high above. Sasha and Kristan accepted some water from the bucket by the door, then ran for the steps up the inside wall.

"Wait, wait," Sasha gasped after Kristan. "I . . . I can't . . . just wait." She walked the stairs, heaving deep breaths.

Kristan walked slowly in front. "I hope you fight better than you run," he remarked, a typical, cocksure young Torovan man. Sasha grabbed his boot and pulled. Kristan gave a yelp and fell face-first on the steps.

"There's a reason you Petrodor men don't arm your women," Sasha snarled as she walked up over him. "Within two weeks, they'd have killed every last one of you!"

Atop the tower, Kessligh stood with several more senior Nasi-Keth and some prominent men of Dockside, surveying the scene. Three more young umas stood back, waiting for a new message. Kessligh glanced back at her.

"It's good," Sasha surmised, as men made room for her against the wall. "They fight well, there was nothing even close to a breakthrough. It won't last, of course, but I didn't tell them that."

Kessligh nodded. "Aye, best not. Weakest barricade?"

"There's three—Aerelo Road, Calachi Lane and Rani Lane. Nineteen dead between them, another ten wounded. The average was about three dead at other barricades. I redeployed some men, and the local Nasi-Keth are keeping a close eye on it . . . but I can't break up those defences without lowering morale even further. Men will fight hardest for their own neighbourhoods."

"Aerelo Road is too far into South End," said Kessligh, gazing south toward Sharptooth. "It would make a good feint, but they'll never get the numbers into that breach to threaten us. The approach to Calachi Lane is exposed, there's water reservoirs and market gardens, no cover from archers . . ."

"Our archery positions there are excellent," Sasha agreed. "They left maybe thirty dead on the road in what was a quite brief attack—a larger assault would lose them many more."

"These madmen don't care about losses," one Dockside man remarked. "Ours or theirs."

"No," Kessligh said, "but anything that breaks up the numbers pouring into a breach is bad for them. Men falling to archery on a narrow road will trip up those running behind, and block the many hundreds behind them. If I'm them, I'd concentrate on Rani Lane, with a diversion toward South End. They'll bet we're worried enough for our flanks to defend South End, but in truth, I think it's the ones who attack South End who'll be easily flanked and cut off by us. Rani Lane is closer to Maerler's Way, so they'll have plenty of men ready to pour into a breach . . . but it's only two lanes from Fisherman's Lane. Sasha, how fare our valiant highlanders?"

Sasha managed a faint smile. "It's murder before the barricades," she said. "They looked a little bored, but I found something for them to do. Charge and flank, if the attack comes down Rani Lane."

Kessligh nearly smiled. "You and your brutal streak, Sasha. Tongren will make chieftain himself on the back of those stories."

Sasha blinked at him. "You *knew* about Tongren? He only just told me!"

"Of course I know about Tongren. Fisherman's Lane is central between this keep and South End, it's the perfect place for that highland rabble led by a Cherrovan chieftain's son with a point to prove." Sasha stared. "Don't look at me like that. I know everything."

The southern end of South Pier covered, attention returned to the northern end up to the warehouses at North Pier. Sasha had no illusions as to why Kessligh had assigned her the southern half—it was surely the easier half to defend. Further north was the Corkscrew, a major road up the slope just like Maerler's Way, and down it had come more chanting rioters than anyone had dared guess. There was no old keep guarding the mouth of Corkscrew, the Corkscrew being a much younger road, built after the age of Ameryn

Lords. Instead, there was the largest barricade Dockside's residents could possibly erect, and the better part of five hundred fighters equipped with all the real and makeshift shields and armour available.

North and south of the Corkscrew, the many lanes and alleys leading from the slope to the dock had likewise been barricaded. They'd recently been probed by a wide and apparently ineffective wave of attacks. Most troubling of all, the North Pier warehouses were heavily guarded by very well-armed and armoured soldiers from all the major North Petrodor houses.

"If those decide to join the rioters and move on us, we're dead," Sasha observed.

"Aye," Kessligh agreed, "but then who will defend the warehouses from the rioters? These are mostly poor folk from Riverside and those warehouses are crammed with the richest trade in Torovan. Which of the families would leave their treasures unguarded now?"

"If this lot sweeps us off the docks," another man added, with a jab of his finger toward the slope, "the next thing they'd do is not only raid the warehouses, but grab our damn boats and head out to the ships at anchor. Lots of rich pickings there."

Kessligh nodded. "Patachi Steiner would love to be rid of the Nasi-Keth, but he's not such a fool to think that this is the way to do it. He knows the balance in Petrodor better than most, he knows his own house would suffer. The patachis exercise power in the most controlled and, to their eyes, civilised manner possible. One assassinates one or two opponents to make a point. One doesn't invite crazed mobs to lay waste to half the city. I'm sure he's horrified."

"How nice of him," Sasha said drily.

"What matters," Kessligh emphasised, "is that our north flank is safe, thanks to them. The mobs will not get any men onto the docks past the guards defending their warehouses."

"Still . . . you're keeping an eye on them?" Sasha pressed.

"Always," Kessligh said grimly. "But we don't have the fighting strength to hold a reserve just for that eventuality."

"Damn. No word from Gerrold?"

"We hear several of Saalshen's houses are still holding out in the south," another Nasi-Keth said. "The last we heard, Gerrold's men were crossing the Crack. Some have taken boats and sailed around Sharptooth, hoping to evacuate survivors."

"They're needed here," muttered a local man. "Damn traitors."

"Gerrold and his followers have made their choice," Kessligh told them. "Their loyalties have always lain with Saalshen."

"Not all of them," said Sasha. "I met quite a few of Gerrold's former followers out at the barricades. A lot have not followed him." Nor Alaine, she did not need to add.

"Yuan Kessligh!" came an urgent call from behind. All turned to look, and Sasha saw the Nasi-Keth girl from below, breathing hard and a little frantic. "Up the stairs behind me! There's . . . well, there's . . ."

A figure emerged from the shadow of the doorway behind. Several men half-drew their swords, then paused in relief as it became clear that the figure, and the one behind, were serrin. Sasha saw the gleaming white hair, and the green eyes, and her heart leapt for joy. She took two steps forward, thinking to rush and embrace her friend, but something made her stop.

Rhillian's face was taut and hard. Her hair was a most uncharacteristic mess, only half of her customary braid remained, the rest matted and tangled from rain, ash and blood. Her clothes were bloody in places. The man behind her was Kiel, and his condition was similar, save that he limped on an injured leg.

"Yuan Kessligh," said Rhillian. Her voice was hoarse, almost unrecognisable. She coughed heavily, clearing her throat. To Sasha's distress, Rhillian did not spare her even a glance. Her emerald stare fixed entirely on Kessligh. There was nothing of warmth or humour in those eyes. Nothing, indeed, of humanity. They burned with the fire of some strange and dangerous animal, hunting its prey from the shadows. "Palopy is fallen."

"One hears," said Kessligh. "I'm sorry."

"Have there been other serrin survivors come to Dockside?"

"Several. From some of the smaller northern properties. Gerrold's followers brought some down."

"How many?" Rhillian asked, tightly.

"Perhaps five last I heard. And some of your human staff. There may have been more since then."

"Last you heard." Upon the wind came the sound of distant chanting, growing louder. "We met several of Gerrold's supporters upon the slope. They said that you'd ordered all Nasi-Keth to stay here. Many of Gerrold's people remained behind."

"That's correct."

Rhillian's eyes narrowed. "We are worth that little to you?" she asked, her voice strained with new emotion.

"Dockside is worth more," Kessligh said bluntly, folding his arms.

Rhillian swallowed hard, and stared away across the flickering lines of torchlight where Docksiders manned the many barricades between buildings. "I hear that several houses still stand south of Sharptooth," she said with difficulty. "I ask permission to borrow some boats and sail to Angel Bay and beyond, and see if we can find some survivors escaped along the shore."

"No," said Kessligh. "I can't allow it. We may need those boats to manoeuvre our own forces. If a breakthrough occurs, the women have plans to load all children onto the boats and row them out to the ships, or outside the harbour entirely. If any more serrin have survived, they will have to keep to the alleys and make their way here as you did."

"The Crack grows increasingly impassable." Rhillian's voice was trembling. "They may be wounded, or cut off. Please. I beg you."

"I'm sorry," said Kessligh. The hardness of his tone shocked even Sasha. She better than anyone knew Kessligh the warrior, but she also knew the compassion that lurked beneath. She yearned to round on Kessligh and beg Rhillian's case . . . surely they could spare just a few boats? But she could not question Kessligh in front of others, not now.

"He planned this from the beginning," said Kiel. His pale grey eyes were narrowed with pain. "This is the footsoldier who rose to become head of the armies of Lenayin. A master of political manoeuvres. Three great opponents he faced in his bid to secure power in Petrodor for himself—Alaine, Gerrold and Saalshen. Now, all three are removed from his path."

"You watch your tongue," growled one of the men by Kessligh's side.

"I'm not going to stand here and argue paranoid fantasies," Kessligh said firmly. "I have far more important matters to attend to."

"When I awoke this morning, there were more than two hundred *tal-maad* in Petrodor," said Rhillian. "And over three hundred human staff in our employ. Right now, I think those numbers combined might equal fifty. If we cannot rescue those who hold out to the south, by tomorrow morning, it shall be but a handful. The serrin of Petrodor are nearly all dead, and you cannot bring yourself to raise a *finger*?"

"If we lose this battle here," Kessligh said, "then all of Dockside shall share your fate. Would all our deaths help to ease your pain, Rhillian?"

"Your defences are strong!" Rhillian shouted. "You held off their first assault easily, you will—"

"It was a probe!" Kessligh shouted back. "I can't take the risk, Rhillian!"

Rhillian stared at him. "We aren't worth *anything* to you," she said, as if it were suddenly obvious. "All this talk of saving Saalshen from the great war, but all this time—"

"Don't." Kessligh lifted a sharp finger, his temper fully roused, and jabbed it at her chest. "Don't you even start. I tried to warn you, Rhillian, I tried to warn you what would happen—"

"Oh, so it's all our fault now?"

"Yes!" Kessligh snapped. "Yes, it's your own damn fault! The balance of power was always the only thing protecting Saalshen, and that was exactly what you started playing with! You don't understand how humans function, Rhillian—Errollyn warned you as much, as did I, as did—"

"You mean you saw this coming? Well we would have liked to know!"

"I don't know, Rhillian, one can never know for certain. That's the point! I never assume I know all possible outcomes, and I always make certain I've covered my back! Your properties were exposed, you relied upon people needing you too much to try something this drastic . . . and you assumed you knew enough that this would never happen! I've lost count of the number of times I tried to warn you of exactly that . . . but you stupid, stubborn girl, you never listened!"

Rhillian moved in a flash and drew her blade. About and behind Sasha, more blades came out, and Kiel's followed. The flickering torchlight atop the tower caught Rhillian's eyes—they dazzled and flashed past the gleaming edge of her blade. Sasha stood stunned, perhaps the only person atop the tower who had not drawn. Serrin never did such things, whatever the provocation. She could not believe it.

"Rhillian." She walked forward, slowly. Rhillian's expression struggled for calm, a thin veneer laid over a seething mass of rage and grief. Her face twitched, her eyes ablaze in the torchlight, she seemed almost incomprehensible. "Rhillian, no." Sasha stopped just beyond the poised tip of Rhillian's blade. "I'm so sorry for what's happened. But it's not Kessligh's fault. He doesn't mean to hurt you. He's just like that. Trust me, I know. I can't let you hurt him. Please don't make us enemies."

Rhillian stared straight past her, eyes fixed with murderous intent on Kessligh.

"Rhillian," Sasha tried again, "Aisha is here. She's hurt, but not badly. Errollyn says she will recover soon enough." Something in Rhillian's expression seemed to change at that. Still her eyes did not move, but she was listening. Sasha braced herself and took another step inside the arc of Rhillian's blade. And stopped, the lethal edge poised two fingers-width from her neck. "Rhillian, whatever serrin are left will need you. Think of them."

She reached for Rhillian's face. Trailed gentle fingers down her cheek. They left a clean trail through ash and blood. Finally, Rhillian's eyes found Sasha's, and abruptly filled with tears. As though she'd been avoiding Sasha's gaze for precisely that reason. Her lip trembled and, for the only time since Sasha had known her, Rhillian seemed utterly incapable of speech. Sasha stared back in horror. Dear spirits, Rhillian. What did you see?

Rhillian lowered her blade to one side. Sasha kissed her on the cheek and embraced her gently. Rhillian's body was stiff and trembling. She rested her cheek in Sasha's hair and murmured, "I'm sorry too, my friend."

She turned and left, Kiel following, descending the tower stairs as she sheathed her blade. Sasha turned back to Kessligh as men slowly sheathed their blades. Kessligh, she saw, had never drawn his. His jaw was tight and his fist clenched. He was upset, she realised. One did not see that often.

"I didn't have a choice," he muttered in Lenay. About him, men gave him puzzled looks, wondering what he said. Only Sasha understood. He, too, had never seen a serrin draw a blade for no more reason than fury. It had shaken him. "She was *incapable* of understanding. I can't explain to her what she's not capable of hearing. All of our languages, and we didn't have enough words."

"Kessligh," said Sasha, also in Lenay, walking to his side. "It wasn't your fault."

Kessligh took a sharp breath. "No. It's never my fault. But it's always my responsibility." He turned back to the view and resumed the previous conversation.

Alythia heard the blast of horns echo across the slope, and it seemed to foretell the end of the world. The horns were followed by a roar, arising further away, then flooding across the entire Petrodor incline, a moving wave of sound. Men ran down Fisherman's Lane toward the barricade as youngsters and women who had been up the front ran back to the rear. Alythia clutched her spear banner tightly, and felt so sick with terror that she thought she might faint. It would have been a relief. But lately, she had rarely been so lucky.

The barricade was obscured behind a wall of waiting men. Their number seemed barely half what it had been during the last attack. Alythia heard the blood-curdling shrieks of their attackers growing closer, and knew for a certainty that, this time, the defences would surely fail.

Archers were firing now from the surrounding roofs, arrow fire flashing into the uphill road, a flicker of lethal motion in the dancing torchlight. Alythia's heart pounded, and she found herself standing on her tiptoes, as if that extra height might help her see over the heads of the men at the barricade. About her, to her astonishment, came harsh yells from the women, urging their men to stand firm. Most cried in Lenay or Cherrovan tongues as many warriors' wives had followed their husbands to this lane.

Then, atop the barricade, a tall figure stood clear of the crowd, his long, black hair falling wild down his back. He thrust his sword into the firelit sky and roared. The answering roar from the highland defenders echoed between tight stone walls and, for a moment, she could not hear the attack coming at all. The man then began yelling to the onrushing mob. He seemed to be taunting them, daring them to come. The others joined in. There were few spears or other long weapons raised now in the defence, most had been sent away to reinforce neighbouring barricades. Here the men fought mostly with swords, as highland fighters would.

The attack reached the barricade with an audible crash of bodies on piled debris. A new wave of men appeared atop the pile, scrambling on all fours to ascend. The defenders cut their legs from under them and bodies crashed and tumbled forward or back, or fell where they were and added to the height of the defences. Now Alythia could see archers standing on the roofs above the barricade, silhouettes against the red overcast, firing straight down into the crowds as fast as they could draw and loose. They were shooting any men trying to dismantle the barricade rather than climb it—she'd heard others discussing that tactic after the last attack.

Still the attackers hurled themselves up the barricade. Some seemed to throw themselves off the edge, crashing bodily down on the men below. Seeing that tactic, some highlanders were now climbing the barricade on their own side and striking down attackers before they could even clear the lip. A wounded highlander stumbled clear of the rear ranks, clutching a slashed arm, and two women rushed forward to intercept him. The rear ranks moved forward to fill the gap. Then again, as another wounded man came, only this one looked worse, cut across the side, a comrade half carrying him.

There were flashes of flame and smoke beyond the barricades, and then it seemed there was fire coming from the windows of houses further down Fisherman's Lane. "They fire the houses!" one of the women exclaimed.

"Aye, they'll burn the roofs out from under our archers," said another. Already the thick, black sheets of smoke obscured the archers' view of the battle below, but they stood their ground and kept firing.

"Still no crossbows," said a Lenay voice at Alythia's side. It was a middle-aged woman with a creased face and grey-streaked hair, grimly surveying the battle. Her accent was thick Isfayen. "Your sister was right, they don't mean to break through here. Otherwise they'd have sent crossbows to pick off our archers. This is just to keep us busy."

From the adjoining north alley, a young Nasi-Keth girl came sprinting, yelling at the top of her lungs, "They break through on Rani Lane! They break through on Rani Lane!" The girl went racing into the rear ranks of the highlanders, pushing forward, seeking a commander.

The Isfayen woman by Alythia's side ran back, shouting to the women treating the wounded, "Quickly, gather up everything! I want strong girls ready to lift the wounded, we may need to carry them clear!"

"I can walk, damn it woman!" snarled one of their charges, but the women ignored him. From the north alley came the unmistakable sound of battle, audible even above the racket directly in front. Smoke billowed into the sky, above where Alythia thought the Rani Lane barricade would be. She stood paralysed, clutching to her spear banner, her heart hammering. This defence would be outflanked, she realised. If she stayed here, she would die.

Ahead, there came a roar of massed voices, but this one was from the defenders. And now the wild Lenays and Cherrovan were pouring over the barricade, heading *into* the attack. More and more clambered over, and seemed to find plenty of space on the other side. The mobs were retreating, she realised in disbelief. And now, her only defenders were running away. A forceful, astonishing realisation struck her: she felt safer with them around.

Before she knew what she was doing, Alythia took off after them, past the north alley and up to the barricade. Smoke roiled from neighbouring windows, stinging her eyes as she clambered over crates, broken furniture and wagon wheels. A body came loose as she scrambled over the top, and slid down the barricade, loose-limbed and heavy and horrible. Alythia bit back a scream, and climbed down the far side, her wet dress catching on debris. She hauled the fabric clear, tearing it, then something sharp scraped her shin. She snatched her leg away, seeking alternative footing, and her shoe came down on something both firm and springy . . . she looked and saw she was standing on a man's chest where he had fallen backward off the barricade, head down and legs entangled. The warm wetness about her ankle were his intestines.

Alythia flailed away, lost her balance, and fell heavily on a pile of bodies that thudded and wheezed beneath her. One of them moved, a bloody hand reaching, pleading. Stumps of limbs protruded from the pile, some still pulsing blood, bone stark and white amidst the flesh. She stumbled frantically to her feet, nearly tripping on her spear, then again on more bodies, these felled by archers, and some still groaning. The entire lane beyond the barricade was a carpet of horrors, many shrieking and sobbing. This was what happened when highland warriors were challenged to a fight by those unworthy of the privilege.

The banner dragged at her arms, and she held the spear aloft, so that the banner flew out behind as she ran. She turned right and went up the crumbling alley. Her breath came hard, her wet dress clung awkwardly to her legs and the spear ruined her balance. It occurred to her, rather oddly, that she could not recall the last time she'd actually run. Ladies and princesses did not run, nor even stride. Only serrin and crazy tomboys like Sasha. She half twisted her ankle in a dark hole in the pavings and, for the first time in her life, wished to the gods she was wearing pants. Worse, her breasts bounced, and that was uncomfortable almost to the point of pain.

Alythia emerged into the alley mouth, and onto Rani Lane. Rani was wider than Fisherman's. Left and right, highlanders had made a defensive wall. Beyond those walls were masses of Riversiders, flailing weapons and fists and banners decorated with holy symbols, hacking away at the barrier of highland tattoos, wild hair and steel. To the right, dockward, the highlanders were pushing the larger numbers backward. To the left, slopeward, the highlanders' line slowly gave ground, screaming and hacking and leaving tangled knots of bloody corpses in their wake for the next line of attackers to stumble upon.

Even Alythia could see what had happened—a huge surge of men had rushed down this lane, until the highlanders had stepped into the middle, like a gate into an irrigation trench. Now, some of those who had gone past the highlanders had stopped and come back to try and clear the blockage. Beyond them, the lane was increasingly empty, save for the bodies, the flames that poured from the windows of several buildings, and the remnants of the barricade, now strewn across the lane.

To the left, slopeward, the pressure bearing down on the highland line was huge. If they kept giving ground, in just a few moments they would be forced back past Alythia's alley mouth . . . and then the mob would be on her. Her legs were jelly, she could not outrun them. She took a deep breath and stepped out into the middle of Rani Lane, her banner held high. She stood in the clear space between the two moving highland lines as men screamed and fought to either side. A gust of cold, misting wind caught at the wet banner, unfurling it enough to show the wolf's head, its teeth grinning in the firelight.

Not all of the highland men were fighting. The slopeward line was three deep—men would fight hard, then fall back and allow the next in line to take his place, whilst those behind took some deep breaths. The dockward line was only one deep, with several reserves darting behind in case a gap would open. Some of the back ranks noticed her, and the banner, and gave a huge cheer. Others looked, and the cheer grew to a roar. Those fighting had no time to look, but they heard the roar, and seemed to take it for encouragement, for the Riversiders died at an even more furious pace after that.

Alythia spun back and forth, walking as the lines moved, careful not to trip on the bodies the dockward line were leaving behind as they advanced. One of the dockward line fell to a spearthrust, and Alythia pointed frantically with her spear, but the next reserve was already moving to fill the gap. Alythia grabbed the fallen man as she reached him and tried to pull him up—if he were left to lie there, the moving lines would roll over him and leave him to the mob. He staggered upright, slowly, clutching his bleeding stomach. Alythia tried to support him.

Something strange was happening, she noticed. Dockward, the distance between the highlanders and the Riversiders seemed wider, and strikes more sporadic. The Riversiders' lines seemed thinner too, as though some had peeled off the back of the formation and run elsewhere. It was fear, Alythia realised. Perhaps the mob was not quite so fanatical after all, she thought, with a rush of hope. Perhaps the most fanatical ones had charged first and died. Perhaps these were the followers, who now wondered at the wisdom of certain death beneath the swinging blades of battle-crazed, snarling pagans.

Even slopeward, the highland line was spread out, giving each man room to swing. She'd seen the Royal Guards practising shield drills in Baen-Tar, packed like fruit in a barrel, each line pushing on the other in a giant contest of strength . . . but here, few men on either side had shields. If the mob would just rush them, the line would be overwhelmed, the highland swordsmen deprived of their superior technique and driven back by sheer weight of numbers . . . but now, the mob was not pressing, and the crowd behind was not pushing as hard as they might. It had been a long day; many had died. Perhaps the righteous fury was fading. Now they hung back, finding poor footing on the bodies of their fallen, and tried to exchange blows or defend with what weapons they had. Most took a terrible wound in short order, and the next-in-line appeared distinctly less enthusiastic in turn.

Now the dockward line were pressing forward faster and the Riversiders backing up. Some stumbled, and the highlanders were onto them in a flash, hacking the fallen, then driving into the gaps created in the Riversiders' line. Spaces opened in the highland line as those men charged forward and, for a heart-stopping moment, Alythia feared some Riversiders might take advantage and spring through the holes. But the whole momentum had shifted, and suddenly, the Riversiders, still eight-to-one greater in numbers at least, tried to turn and flee toward the docks. Those at the front collided with those behind, men fell in tangles and panic spread. The highlanders howled in delight and sprang into their midst, hacking and slashing with wild abandon. Entire ranks of unarmoured men dissolved in bloody, screaming ruin and the rest fled for their lives.

Some of the older heads yelled for order, holding men back from pursuit. Some highlanders ran back to the slopeward line, past where Alythia stood with the wounded man clutching her shoulder for support, and formed a fourth rank behind the others. The remainder began picking up weapons the defeated Riversiders had dropped and began hurling them into the mob upslope. Several spears flew low and flat, doubtless impaling someone further back, then a scythe was hurled with a vicious flat spin, raising more screams and mayhem. Some swords followed, also with a flat spin, then a sickle, a club and a number of knives. Into an unarmoured mob, packed too tight to dodge, they couldn't miss. With no weapons to spare, and their own being their only means of defence, the mob threw nothing back.

Suddenly there were arrows whistling about and Alythia ducked in horror, but they were falling into Riversiders. She stared up and saw Nasi-Keth archers perched atop the walls above—at least ten, with more arriving now above the south wall. Arrows flew thick and fast. With no protection, the Riversiders began dying in scores.

It was too much, and the survivors broke and ran. With a roar, the highland ranks charged, and scores more Riversiders who could not run fast enough, or were blocked by those behind, or tripped on fallen bodies, also died. Through the press of running bodies, Alythia thought she saw several Riversiders fall to their knees and beg mercy. And were decapitated where they knelt, to Alythia's hot satisfaction. They had to be joking. Mercy? After what they'd done?

A dozen men did not charge, but held their ground and formed a new line, watching both ways along the lane. Mostly older men, Alythia saw, and some others with wounds. Instinctively, they seemed to understand the tactics that their situation required and deployed themselves to achieve it, without needing to be ordered. But of course they would. Highland men drilled for war all their lives. These men, especially the older ones, understood warfare like Dockside fishermen understood sailing.

"All clear?" called a voice from the wall above. Against the deep red sky, Alythia saw the unmistakable dark grey hair and handsome build of Sasha's friend, the serrin Errollyn. He held that strange serrin bow, with elbow joints in its arms, that just *looked* dangerous. Even at this range, his eyes were visible, two penetrating green spots in the shadow of his face.

"Aye!" shouted up one of the men, above the groans and screams of the wounded and dying who now made a ghastly, writhing carpet along the lane. "Good timing!"

"Sasha told us they'd come this way." His eyes scanned the lane. "And so the highland legend grows," he remarked.

"We're just getting started!" came the retort.

"Good. There's plenty that broke through. If you move back fast, you could get some more." And he vanished, as did the others.

"Highness," said another man in Lenay. His long, matted hair and thick beard were spattered with blood, some of it his own from a forehead gash, but just as much not. His eyes burned, the left one within a maze of intricate tattoos, and he fell to one knee. "You were magnificent. It was an honour to fight beneath your banner."

Alythia blinked at him. "It . . . I was?"

Another repeated the gesture as the first man rose and kissed the banner fiercely. Others repeated the gesture. Alythia stared at them and . . . wondered. She was a widow. She'd thought she had nothing left. But *this* . . . this was something. Despite the fear, the blood, the wet and the cold, her shoulders straightened, just a little.

"Highness," said another man, upon kissing the flag. "You were glorious."

Alythia managed a small smile. "Of course I was," she said.

Kessligh had given up trying to command from the tower as the messengers had ceased getting through and the view below showed him nothing but chaos. Sasha ran at his side as he pointed and yelled to small groups of disorganised defenders, directing them to cover the major approach lanes to where the breakthrough had been thickest. Within that zone, behind Rani Lane, many Riversiders had broken through. Now, they looted, burned and killed, but so far they had not spread much beyond. Most of the other barricades had held and another large attempted breakthrough to the north had been thwarted. Sasha did not dare feel too optimistic given the chaos before her, but surely, if the other barricades were holding, this should be little more than a matter of mopping up.

There were more Nasi-Keth on the roads now—climbing to the rooftops with bows was time-consuming and, with the targets more dispersed, it was possible to do more damage on the ground with a blade. Some senior Dockside men had joined Kessligh's side, and they moved fast about the new perimeter, attempting to contain the breakthrough. Sasha took several Nasi-Keth with her and dashed to the docks to see if she could form a defence there.

Down several lanes and alleys to her right as she ran, she caught a glimpse of running figures, weapons, fires and fighting. The fighting would be all across Fisherman's Lane now. She hoped the children had been moved in time. She hoped that Mariesa and the Velos were out as well, and that Mari had not been a fool and tried to defend his home alone. And she hoped that the star had been moved safely.

She emerged onto the docks, and found hard fighting. Some houses were on fire, lighting the massed boats at their moors with a leaping, hellish glare. Before the fires, dark figures clashed and screamed, weapons waving. Women ran from doorways clutching children and, further along, someone jumped, or was thrown from a high window onto hard stones below. Sasha looked left toward the North Pier, and saw mostly shadow, lit by the occasional lamp, and no fighting.

"Get in there and kill all these maggots on the dock!" she yelled at the men with her. "Don't go into the houses to flush them out—make them come out, we'll trap the bastards! DOCKSIDE!"

With a yell, the men charged past her. They fell on those closest, killing two who foolishly stood to fight, saving a local man who wrestled with another to keep a knife from his throat, and then the confusion grew thicker and Sasha could no longer see where everyone was. In the firelit chaos, it became difficult to tell friend from foe—there were no uniforms, no rich raiments or armour, and makeshift weapons on both sides. Mostly, Sasha determined, the ones who were yelling and chanting were the enemy. And they usually saved her the trouble of guessing—one sight of a woman with a blade and they knew she was an infidel.

She killed several, a sidestep here, a feint there—the Riversiders were easy to fool and left themselves ridiculously exposed to her blade. Then she saw three Nasi-Keth ahead, blades out and backs together, warding off perhaps a dozen Riversiders who circled and lunged, many with longer weapons. Sasha did not even think, instinctively noting their positions, the mob's weak spots, and how it might all unfold in a rush if she hit it just like . . .

One man saw her coming, spun and lashed with his halberd, Sasha ducked beneath it with a spin that split him across the middle. Another did not turn in time—she lashed one-handed to extend her reach, taking his arm whilst holding ground to spin back the other way, and cut past the next man's defence before he could bring it to bear. Three men attacked her at once as their comrades fell, one was obstructed by his own companions, Sasha took a half-step back from a club swing that whistled past her nose, then held her arms vertical to deflect the big cleaver that swung down from above—a quarter turn, a quarter step back and a downward flick of the wrists, her blade sliced her attacker from shoulder to rib cage.

The club wielder tried to knock her skull into North Pier, but Sasha stepped inside it and took both his hands off at the forearm, then contemptuously knocked aside a sword blow to her head from the third man, and slashed. That man staggered, then sank, blood drenching his front. The other six—there *were* only six now—turned and ran, horrified at the carnage this new arrival had wrought. The three cornered Nasi-Keth had not even a chance to attack, one being wounded, the other two having been merely preoccupied with surviving. All blinked in disbelief, staring at Sasha amidst her six new victims. Sasha didn't really know what they were staring at—against such opponents as these, with surprise on her side, such martial feats were nothing special, certainly far easier than an average training session against Kessligh. That these three Nasi-Keth had allowed themselves into such difficulty said rather a lot more about *their* swordwork, however.

One of the Nasi-Keth, she realised, was Liam, exhausted and dripping sweat. Sasha walked straight up to him, knowing that she acted rashly, but she was Lenay, and Goeren-yai, and young, and her enemies lay dead at her feet. Rashness was made for such moments. Liam was staring at the bodies behind her. He was facing her. He'd seen it all.

She laid her blood-stained blade on his shoulder, the killing-edge toward the side of his neck. "Who's the greatest swordsman on this dock?" she demanded, her eyes blazing. His own blade was free beneath her guard. He could slash up and kill her if he chose . . . and risk that she would not have time to remove his head before she died. She could see the thoughts running through his darting eyes—the anger, the confusion, the disbelief . . . the fear.

"You are," he said hoarsely.

"Louder!"

"You are the greatest swordsman on this dock!"

Sasha lowered her blade, with an evil smile. "Good Torovan boy. You finally learn honour. Now fight with me, and I'll bring you some more."

Soon, the dockside was cleared. Unarmoured and poorly skilled, the Riversiders were cut off and deprived of the overwhelming numbers that had won them through the breach. Some ran in panic as their circumstance began to dawn on them, while others tried to organise an orderly retreat, to little avail. More bodies piled on the bloody pavings, and the last resistance ran for the lanes and alleys, desperate to find a retreat back up the slope. A few tried to surrender, and begged mercy. Neither gods nor Docksiders heeded their pleas.

It became a great rout, and Sasha contented herself to walking at the rear of it as triumphant men rushed ahead, pursuing the last Riversiders through the narrow spaces, into doorways and up rickety staircases, where some tried to hide in the houses they'd previously looted. Soon, the greatest danger came from the falling bodies of Riversiders thrown screaming from rooftops and windows. The men of the Dockside thrust their weapons in the air and yelled, and rushed eagerly to fulfil her various instructions, the damp air vibrating with the excitement of victory.

Sasha felt relief, but no triumph, nor even satisfaction. Victories in combat against such poor swordwork as these would bring her no honour. This had been crazed and brutal, the hysterical against the desperate.

The yells and celebrations grew more raucous. Soon there were more celebrations than battles, man embracing man, exultant in the manner of men
who had never truly thought to be warriors and were astonished to find themselves not only alive, but triumphant. It was honour of sorts, Sasha thought
dully, wondering if she ought to quiet them and redirect efforts into putting
out the various blazes that burned. It was Petrodor honour, the honour that
one found simply by living while so many others lay dead. It might be
enough for them, but it was not enough for her.

"Sashandra!" cried a Nasi-Keth man she did not recognise. No one was
hugging *her*, perhaps from simple decorum, or perhaps the dark look on her
face . . . she turned that dark expression on the new arrival. "Best come
quick," he said and ran back the way he'd come.

Sasha followed, wondering what was so urgent with the battle won. Perhaps there had been a breakthrough further north . . . spirits she hoped not.

He led her into Rani Lane and there was a small group of people gathered near one wall. Sasha felt her gut tighten and accelerated to a sprint past
her escort. Skidding to a halt, she thrust past the outermost of the group . . .
and found Kessligh, sitting with his back to the wall, one leg thrust awkwardly out before him. Protruding from the thigh was a crossbow bolt, and
the pants leg was bloody.

Sasha swore in fright and scrambled to his side. His head leaned back
against the bricks, his hair bedraggled, his face tight with pain. He looked at
her now through slitted eyes and managed a faint, pained smile. Sasha stared
down at the bolt . . . this was all wrong, this could not have happened. Not
to Kessligh. Kessligh was invulnerable. "How?" she finally managed to ask,
stupidly.

"Oh, hells . . ." Kessligh managed a weak, despairing wave, toward
somewhere up the lane, "some fool with a crossbow. I didn't see him, I was
giving instructions somewhere else. He got lucky."

Crazy, was all Sasha could think. She knew it happened. She knew that
battle was as much fortune as skill. But Kessligh had fought through more
battles than nearly any man alive. He bore precious few scars for his troubles—indeed, the worst she'd seen was on his left arm, and that she'd given
him herself whilst training.

"Sasha." Kessligh clasped her hand and gave her a firm stare, whatever
the pain. "I've been lucky, Sasha. So damn lucky. It had to end some time. In
truth, I was due."

"Oh horseshit!" Sasha exclaimed. "You've *never* believed in fate!"

He shrugged, not bothering to repress an agonised grimace. "It's my first
rationalisation," he hissed. "I'm due one of those, too."

"It's not too bad," Sasha tried to reassure him. "I mean . . . it looks like it'll heal fine. It's not . . ."

"Don't talk horseshit," Kessligh replied, "it's straight through the main muscle. If I were twenty years younger, I might be all right. But after this comes out, I'll have a limp like a cripple."

"No! With serrin medicines, I'm sure it'll—"

"Sasha, look around you. We won, Sasha, and there's a lot of people dead. Be pleased for everyone who's still alive. My leg is a very minor tragedy tonight."

"Yuan Kessligh," said one of the women, hovering near, "we've called for a healer, she should be here shortly."

"Sasha." Kessligh put a rough, callused hand to her cheek and gave her a wan smile. "You're my uma. Go and help the people. They need you."

Nineteen

WHEN PATACHI MARLEN STEINER STEPPED into the arch-bishop's chambers, he found a vision splendid seated on a throne atop a small altar. The Archbishop of Torovan wore his full black robes, with the finest, most intricate silver filigree embroidered into the sleeves. He held his silver-ornamented staff in his right hand, and a leather-bound copy of the holy scrolls with the left. Atop his head, he wore the tall black hat of the Torovan archbishops, flat on the top, encircled with gold like a crown.

To his sides and against the walls stood young caratsa, brown-robed and anxious; about the room were the Holy Guard, in full silver and black. Marlen Steiner's cold blue eyes flicked to the spot where a table and chairs usually stood before the wide, open windows . . . but the tall windows were latched firmly shut and there was no table.

Marlen Steiner walked before the phalanx of Holy Guards, and wondered where all the other priests were. Porsada Temple's grand hall had been deathly silent, with only the sentries to break the uniform stone arches and hallways. Marlen's son Symon followed at his father's side and, with them, their loyalest provincial allies, Duke Tarabai of Danor and Duke Belary of Vedici. There was no need for more patachis now. Patachi Marlen Steiner, of the great house of Steiner, was the only patachi in Petrodor now worthy of the name.

"Your Holiness," said Marlen, walking slowly with the help of his cane. He passed between the Holy Guard, and knelt on one knee. He kissed the archbishop's extended hand, where the large gold ring bulged on the finger. His knee hurt as he rose, a familiar ache. Marlen considered the archbishop, he looked tired. Marlen doubted the man had slept much. From his windows, he must have had a grand view of Dockside all through the night.

Greetings done, the archbishop clapped his hands and the caratsa filed for the door. They moved quickly, Marlen noted. Their manner spoke of fear. The Holy Guards retreated several steps.

"Your Holiness," Marlen said once more, with as low a bow as his aching joints would allow him. "How good of you to see me at such short notice."

Archbishop Augine managed a thin smile. "How remiss would it be if the archbishop did not listen to his people?" Fear. Again, Marlen smelled it. Guards everywhere. No priests in sight. The archbishop's private chambers rearranged for most intimidating effect. The man had rolled the dice, and lost. Now, he feared. Perhaps he had cleansed his fellow priests too thoroughly. Perhaps those priests now forgot their holy vows in turn, and sought revenge, providing access to the temple for armed men of their respective families. So long as the archbishop seemed strong and commanded the respect of his allies and his guards he was safe. But the cold light of this fine morning had shown Augine's failure.

"I have news, Holiness," Marlen continued, resting his weight heavily upon his cane. "I have spoken with Patachi Maerler."

Augine's eyebrows raised with attempted off-handed interest. "Oh yes?"

"The patachi sees that his position has changed. He informs me that he no longer claims command of the great Torovan army. He concedes that Family Steiner is the logical choice for such a command. I feel that the issue is resolved."

Augine blinked at him. His chin rested in one hand, gold-ringed fingers tapping nervously on his jaw. "Resolved, you say? Resolved how?"

"Patachi Maerler concedes to my authority," said Marlen Steiner, his stare firm and level. There could be no mistaking his meaning.

"I . . . see." The archbishop replaced the hand on his leather-bound book. "And how shall you recover the Shereldin Star? This matter seems . . . much unresolved."

"There are ways," said Marlen.

"Ways?"

"Yes. Ways."

Augine's jaw trembled in rage. "I shall not be kept from your plans like a child! Without the star, you shall have nothing! No Verenthane holy warriors shall follow you on a crusade while that symbol remains held to ransom by pagans on Dockside!"

"Perhaps," said Marlen Steiner, cooly, "you might have thought of that. Before you launched your mob."

"I will not be lectured to by a—" Augine cut himself short with difficulty. Marlen was surrounded by armed men, yet he did not fear. The archbishop needed him. Family Steiner was perhaps the only protection the archbishop had left.

"Your Holiness," Marlen said grimly, "I shall be brief." He took a measured step forward, his cane creaking. "The mobs are the crudest of weapons. They have destroyed Saalshen's presence here, and made an enemy of Saalshen far earlier in the game than was either wise, or safe. Trade shall suffer from Saalshen's retribution. Trade that pays for weapons, you understand, and soldiers. Saalshen's warriors strike from the shadows, Holiness. Be assured that the mobs did not kill them all. Guard yourself well."

The archbishop paled.

Marlen continued, with dark satisfaction. "Worse yet, you have united Dockside against us. Where before the Nasi-Keth were split, I now hear that Kessligh Cronenverdt has emerged a leader and a hero."

"He was gravely wounded!" Augine snapped. "I have spies too, Master Steiner."

"Not gravely," said Marlen, shaking his head. "Serrin medicines heal fast. Be assured that Kessligh Cronenverdt is most difficult to kill. Many thousands have been killed. Yes, *thousands*. Most of them poor folk from Riverside. These were your most willing followers, Your Holiness. They were your coin, and you have spent them unwisely. There is discontent amongst the dukes. Our good dukes need men of strong health and loyal hearts to work the land. They are alarmed to see commonfolk transformed into a raging mob at the deliverance of a mere speech. They feel a precedent has been set. They wonder if the serrins' mansions were only the first, to be followed by their own castles and holdfasts."

"The country folk are not like the Riversiders," Augine muttered, in great discomfort. "The Riversiders had nothing."

"And you offered them eternity." Marlen spread his hands and gave a small, sarcastic smile. "How generous." The archbishop glared. "The dukes' fears may not be well placed, but they are roused all the same. They do not seek the leadership of priests, Your Holiness. Yours is the dominion of the heavens. The dukes seek the leadership of men in this earthly realm, and no other."

Augine looked at Dukes Tarabai and Belary. Neither said a word. Each of these men could raise thousands of soldiers and had declared their intent to do so as soon as a leader for the army had been chosen. What was the archbishop's power now beside the weight of thousands of armed men? Real soldiers, unlike the mob?

The archbishop took a deep breath. "What do you propose?"

"That all future dealings in these matters be left to me, and to me alone, in consultation with my loyal friends. You have gambled and lost, Your Holiness, and you have weakened the authority of the priesthood. Now, the question shall finally be solved. My way."

At first, Jaryd heard a muffled thump. He sat on a small chair by a window overlooking the square, hands behind his back, chained about the chair legs and in turn to his ankles. Rhyst had made sure he had a good view of the square and the wedding of his sister. The last loose end of Family Nyvar, Rhyst had said, with a nasty smile. Or the second-last, rather. That would come later.

About him were boxes and barrels, and a lot of dust. The room was narrow, barely more than an afterthought between apartments. He'd never been here before, but he knew exactly what it was and had no doubt benefited from the fine stash now stacked around him.

Jaryd heard another muffled thump. Someone was moving up the stairs, perhaps. He stared out at the sunlit square, at the crowds of townsfolk and the cordon of guards holding them back from the temple entrance. Galyndry would probably be an Iryani by now. He wondered if she went willingly. He wondered if she even believed the tales of who'd killed their little brother Tarryn. Galyndry was not a brave soul. In fact, she'd been a girlish fool for most of Jaryd's memory, but he knew himself well enough now to doubt his own judgments, particularly about people he'd thought he'd known well. Possibly he was wrong. But if he was not, why was the wedding progressing? Surely she could have protested? Fled? Schemed . . . he didn't know, *something*? Women, in Jaryd's experience, would scheme as hardened warriors fought—tenaciously and without mercy. And yet here were the crowds, and the flags, and the carnival fools and cavorters. Delya was down there somewhere too, already wed to Family Arastyn, Tarryn's murderers. And Wyndal, whose life he'd thought in danger. Fancy coming all this way, to suffer this fate, for the ungrateful likes of Wyndal.

Another thump and a muffled crash. The lordling on guard was Gyl Ramnastyr . . . Rhyst had wanted to guard Jaryd himself but the others hadn't let him. No one trusted Rhyst Angyvar alone in a room with the man who had sliced open his face. They hadn't beaten him badly, nor even hurt him much. Perhaps Great Lord Arastyn had other plans in mind. But Gyl was now on his feet, listening at the door.

Crash, thud, and the unmistakable ring of steel. A yell of pain. Then another thud, and a rumble that might have been a body falling down stairs. Jaryd struggled to shout out against the cloth that gagged his mouth, but made little sound. A thump of footsteps up the stairs, then a clank of keys at the door.

"Who's there?" shouted Gyl, sword drawn, eyes wide.

"Friends!" came the reply.

"On your honour, man, name yourself!"

There was a muttering from the other side. "Damn you and your blasted honour, how dare you talk honour with me?" A key rattled in the keyhole. Gyl stuck the point of his sword between door planks and thrust hard. The sword went partway through, then stuck. The door clanked open, then was smashed inward by a heavy kick, Gyl's sword still in the door. Gyl stumbled backward, whipping a knife from his belt, but it was Teriyan coming through the door, tall and swaggering, his wild red hair only making him seem larger and more fierce.

And he was wielding a sword. "What are you going to do, lad?" he asked Gyl. "Beg for a fair fight? You'd not win that one either." Gyl stood for a moment, paralysed. Then he put the knife on the floor and backed off against one wall.

"Jaryd," Gyl said quickly, his voice trembling as Teriyan tried the keys in the lock for Jaryd's chains. "Jaryd, you know I've never treated you poorly, I never said those things behind your back that Rhyst and the others did, honestly, I swear it . . ."

"Sweet spirits," said Byorn, emerging in the doorway, sword in hand, "don't they start begging real quick in Algery?"

Teriyan found the right key and the lock fell open. He opened the manacles and began applying keys to the ankle lock as Jaryd removed the gag, gasping.

"What happened?" came a familiar voice from the doorway. "Is he . . . ?" Sofy squeezed into the room behind Byorn.

"You let her come?" he asked Teriyan.

"Not much choice in the matter," Teriyan retorted, "given that there's horses waiting and we leave immediately."

Gyl was staring. "Princess Sofy? What are you . . . ? I mean, Your Highness, what brings you . . . I mean . . ."

Byorn stepped over to him. "Kid," he said firmly, "that's not Princess Sofy. You're delusional." He punched Gyl in the head and the lordling thudded limply to the floor. "A blow to the head will do that to a man."

"Great," said Teriyan as the last lock came off. "Finally one person who recognises the princess."

"I think he's been to Baen-Tar," said Sofy, blinking at the unconscious Gyl. She did not, Jaryd observed, seem particularly surprised or alarmed at Byorn's actions.

"Are you hurt?" Teriyan asked Jaryd as he stood.

"No." He walked to Gyl's fallen body and undid his sword belt and scabbard. Byorn yanked the sword from the door and Jaryd sheathed it. "Let's go!" He ushered Sofy and Byorn ahead of him, descending the steep, narrow stairs whilst buckling the belt where his own had been, before his captors had taken it. The steps were partially blocked by several unconscious guards, one of whom groaned and writhed. Jaryd found Ryssin guarding the doorway, and gave the long-haired woodsman a slap on the shoulder in passing.

Ryssin gave him a toothy grin. "Where've you been, lazy boy?" It wasn't especially funny or clever, but Jaryd laughed all the same. These were some of the most irreverent men he'd ever met and their manner was growing on him.

They ran across the narrow street and into a narrower alley. Then a new street, and here were five horses, saddled and waiting, held by a nervous stableboy. Jaryd ran to the lad, the others close behind.

"These for us?"

"A . . . Aye, M'Lord Jaryd," the boy stammered, and gave a little bow. Jaryd looked at the boy for a moment. Not everyone in Algery had forgotten, it seemed.

Sofy took the horse nearest his, and Jaryd quickly moved to help her mount, but she was swinging herself up before he could do so. He swallowed his surprise and leapt quickly astride. His bruised face hurt, and his ankles and wrists ached where the metal had pressed, but there was a surge of fire through his veins now. So close. He'd been staring down at the town square since the morning, studying the guards, noting which of them might be friendly, guessing at the placement of men within the temple . . . and wishing he had a horse and a sword.

"This way," said Teriyan, pointing down the street away from the square, "there's a perimeter road along the river to the bridge, the bridge has Falcon Guard on it, they'll let us past and then—"

"You go," said Jaryd. "I'll catch up."

"And where the Verenthane hells do you think you're going?" Teriyan demanded.

Jaryd's horse seemed to smell his rider's mood, for she stamped and skittered, tossing her head. "I came here with business to attend to," Jaryd said grimly. He was so close. "And I'll attend it."

"Listen, you little snot," Teriyan snarled, "I didn't just risk my neck getting you rescued so you could go and get yourself killed!"

Jaryd wheeled his mare, but it was Sofy, to his astonishment, who caught his bridle. "What are you doing?" she asked, brown eyes wide with horror. "You can't do this to me!"

"To you?" Jaryd shook his head. "What the hells does this have to do with—"

"I came all the way from Baen-Tar to save you!" Sofy cried. "Me, a princess! Have you any idea what I risked for you?" The desperation in her voice surprised him. He'd shouted like that himself. At Tarryn, in his dreams. "Come back!" he'd cried. "Don't leave me!"

But the temple . . . the wedding . . . and the sword at his hip. He wrenched his mare's head away from Sofy's hand. "I said I'll catch up!" he insisted, with a final glare, this time at Teriyan. "Don't you follow, you've a princess to look after, and she's far more important than me!" He turned and pressed his heels to the mare's flanks. The streets were mostly empty and he moved at a trot, not daring a gallop on slippery cobbles. He knew the way well enough, ahead was the square, and revenge. He could smell it.

The square opened up before him as he burst between food stalls, scattering alarmed townsfolk. The temple loomed to his right, its spires awash in golden sunlight. Guards' helms gleamed about the main steps, the clustered townsfolk nearest the temple all in their Ranasday best. It was, of course, impossible. But when Jaryd Nyvar had a horse and a sword, nothing was impossible. In his life, it seemed now perfectly clear, a horse and a sword were the only things he'd ever truly had. The only things to be relied upon. He kicked the mare hard and accelerated.

Jaryd drew his sword and held it high so that it caught the fall of sunlight and gleamed. The crowd split, screaming and shoving. Then he was amongst them, slowing so as not to ride them down, pushing through as though the mare were fording a river. He heard yelled orders and warning shouts from the guards, and one rider coming at him . . . he swung the mare, her shoes slipping on the cobbles, nearly falling . . . switched hands to lash at that man's approach. He met a firm parry and urged the mare fast toward the temple steps, only to be cut off by another rider. Jaryd ducked low as Iagand had long ago taught him, twisted the mare about once more, judging where her hindquarters would find the steps, and used that height to come down on the new attacker with a hard slash. The man parried and replied, but Jaryd tapped heels at just the right moment, allowing him the angle to parry sideways and swing straight into a hard cut that took the other man clean from his saddle.

The first man was back, and Jaryd simply charged the mare into his path . . . the other horse reared, shying away. The rider lost balance momentarily, and Jaryd did not. He slashed, and that man went straight down with a scream and smashed into the pavings.

Two more were careening across the base of the broad temple steps toward him . . . only the nobles, Jaryd realised with a jolt. The soldiers just watched. They were Falcon Guard and he had once fought at the head of their column.

"Ha!" he yelled, urging the mare toward the attackers. From several guardsmen, he could have sworn he heard a yell of encouragement. Jaryd charged between the two horses, pure suicide, then he feinted left, pulling up as if in fear . . . the man on the right swung out a little to round his rear, and take his blindside while the other hit him from the front . . . only Jaryd dug in his heels once more, and charged straight at him. The man on the left tried to close the gap, but it was suddenly too big, and his horse's hooves slipped. Too fast, Jaryd was inside the right-man's swing before it had even begun, striking him to the face with the sword hilt.

He rounded on the other man, slashing once and twice. The defender parried with skill, urging his horse to leap forward, gaining space while twisting in the saddle to guard his rear. Jaryd jostled the other horse's hindquarters, pushing, not allowing it to steady . . . a sudden skid and the other horse went down, its rider crashing to the pavings as his seat disappeared from under him. A yell from the guardsmen, clear now above the screams and confusion of the crowd,

Jaryd dug in his heels and the mare sprang forward up the steps, skipping unevenly to find her footing on the broad flagstones. The two noble guards at the temple doors took one look at him and scrambled to safety. He reared the mare before the doors, her hooves lashing . . . and the doors crashed open.

Within, all eyes turned to look. Algery Temple was huge. Sunlight spilled through stained glass high above, scenes of the suffering of Saint Ambellion, of the mercy and justice of the many Verenthane gods. All pews had been cleared away for the wedding. The crowd of lords, ladies and their children stood along the centre aisle, stretching their necks to see what happened before the altar. Now they shrank aside, staring in disbelief as the ex-heir of Tyree, a blood-stained blade in hand, rode a frothing warhorse down the temple aisle.

Jaryd rode erect. Let them see his fury. Let them see his contempt. He wanted them all to know how little he cared for their ways, and their respect. The mare began to prance. He'd had no idea she could do that, but it seemed his legs and hands had unconsciously demanded it, and the horse had responded. Good girl. All around him, he saw more than disbelief and incredulity. He saw fear.

Ahead, before the altar, all of Tyree's most wealthy lords and ladies were gathered, garbed head to toe like preening birds. They, too, turned to gawk. Musicians stood to the altar's sides, instruments stilled. All mouths were open in silence. The mare's steel-shod hooves rang clear through the temple, echoing off the high ceiling like the march of vengeance herself.

A slow, mesmerised fading began, women pulling children back to the safety of the columns that lined the temple's sides. Before the altar, men pulled swords and blocked his way. Beneath the altar itself, Jaryd saw now his sister Galyndry, surrounded by a clutch of of women.

Opposing her was Harvyd Iryani—older and taller. Jaryd spied his father, Lord Iryani, nearby and recalled him dining at the Nyvar table, sharing laughter and wine with his father. Other men, other lords, their sons, their daughters . . . all had dined at his table, or played lagand with him and his brothers, or gossiped with his sisters.

Jaryd halted the mare before them and she reared, wary of all the drawn steel.

"Jaryd!" his sister cried. "Have you gone mad!"

Jaryd's eyes searched the crowd as he whipped the mare into several tight, wheeling turns, sending men scampering back from her dangerous hindquarters. This was a warhorse, and she'd been trained to kick when men with swords came too close. Then he saw him—Great Lord Arastyn—behind several armed cousins, staring in disbelief.

"You!" he snarled, pointing with his bloodied sword. "Treacherous scum! You can have your great lordship, you can wear that golden cloak, no matter how blood-spattered it be, I care nothing for the title now. But I demand revenge! *You murdered my little brother*!"

"Jaryd!" came Galyndry's sobbing cry. "Jaryd, no he didn't! It was all a big mistake, Jaryd . . ."

Jaryd whirled the mare once more. "How much did they pay you, bitch?" he roared at her. "Does all that gold and finery lessen the pain? Do golden coins truly soak up the pools of a brother's blood? Will you cry with pleasure tonight as you're fucked by a man whose hands are red with Tarryn's blood?"

Galyndry collapsed into the arms of her wedding brood, sobbing hysterically. The priest and his assistants, clutched their books and holy symbols, silent and pale.

"Jaryd," came a new voice, more measured. Wyndal stepped into the open between the horse and the altar. He was grandly dressed like the others, slimmer than his elder brother, not as tall, and nearly blond against his brother's light brown. "Jaryd, you've no right to do this. A girl is married once in her life. You can't ruin it."

"I came for you," Jaryd said thickly. His voice caught in his throat. "I heard they were going to murder you too. But it was a trap. Wasn't it, brother?"

Wyndal's eyes darted. His tongue licked his lips. Jaryd stared in disbelief. Cowardice was something for tales and stories. An insult to be hurled in good humour or in bad. It was something that happened to other people. In the tales, cowardice afflicted the least honourable, the most arrogant, or the one who, in some other way, broke with the code. Cowardice did not happen to good people. It did not happen to one's brother, not unless that brother was a villain from the tales . . . which Wyndal, for all his and Jaryd's differences, was certainly not.

Jaryd wanted to throw the accusation in Wyndal's face, to scream at him, to berate him as he'd berated Galyndry . . . but somehow, suddenly, it seemed pointless. He was wailing at the wind. This was the world of lords. He'd never understood it. Wyndal, Galyndry and Delya . . . one moment they'd been of Family Nyvar, the most powerful family in Tyree, and then Nyvar's loyal retainers had abandoned them. They had no loyal peasantry, no standing army to defend the family name, just a loose affiliation of friends and allies kept strong through intermarriage. Lose a key ally, and have all the others switch their allegiances to *him*, and there was nothing to break the fall.

Jaryd could fight. Fight, and ride. It was all he'd ever been truly good at. Wyndal had the skills, but not the passion. And the girls . . . were just girls. What was he asking them to do? To die fighting? To surrender their necks to the chopping block? To add their corpses to Tarryn's and give him more siblings to avenge?

"You leave him alone," said Delya, emerging from the wary crowd to stand by Wyndal's side. She was tall, his eldest sister, and wore shimmering scarlet, bare at the shoulders and lined with fur. Her voice was trembling. "Jaryd, it's not as you think—Great Lord Arastyn had no choice, the other lords would *never* accept you as heir."

"Then kill *me*, not Tarryn!" Jaryd stared around at the sea of faces and the drawn steel. "Which of you has the balls?" He pointed his sword at Arastyn. "I've challenged you to a duel already, and you refused! I repeat my challenge! Prove to your people that you're a man, and not just a killer of small boys!"

Only the presence of his brother and sisters was keeping him alive now, Jaryd knew. There were enough capable warriors surrounding him, swords in hand. They could cut down the mare, and he would follow. But they would not do it before his siblings. The fear in their eyes was not fear for themselves but for their position and their allegiances. It was precarious to be a lord in Lenayin—to look powerless was to invite ridicule, to look tyrannical was to invite rebellion. Jaryd's lip curled in contempt of them all.

"Why don't you get down off your horse, boy," came Lord Paramys's voice, "and we'll talk like reasonable men."

Jaryd laughed. "Aye, I'm sure that's exactly what'll happen once I get down off my horse." He whipped the mare into another fast circle, sending men once more scampering for distance. "Look at you all. Frightened little fools, each clinging to your precious titles like a drowning man to a log in a spring flood. The flood swallowed my family, and washed the earth bare, as if they'd never been. If the great Family Nyvar can disappear, how much faster can yours? I'd laugh at you if the spectacle weren't so pathetic. I've *seen* the real Lenayin. I've seen how men lived before wealth and titles and lust for power came and took their honour, and their courage. Those Lenays know you for the frauds that you are. One day soon, even your Verenthane countrymen will share that contempt, and then you'll have nothing."

His stare settled back on Arastyn. The hatred was not so intense now. He wanted very badly to kill him. But he also wanted . . . What did he want? Come to that, why was he even here? Why come crashing into this temple to ruin his sister's wedding? Were all these fools worth his blood and sweat? When he'd left the only people who meant anything to him standing in the lane, cursing him for an ungrateful fool? He invoked their name, to drive the point home to these thick-headed idiots, to tell them of the perspective he'd gained out in the wilds of Valhanan . . . but only now did he realise how much that experience had meant to him.

They were leaving without him. Heading back to Baerlyn, and Lynette, who would surely be sad if he did not return, whatever her complaining. Andreyis too. And Jaegar, who would shake his head and think of something wise to say, no doubt. And the village girls who had whispered and giggled when he came near. And a princess who'd watched him leave in the alley just now, with something close to tears . . .

Jaryd blinked. The fury was fading fast. Sofy had said *what* to him? Dear spirits, what was he doing *here*?

He wheeled the mare about once more and kicked with his heels. There were yells from behind, and men ran to close the temple doors, but they were too late. He clattered out into bright sunshine, and slowed the mare so that she did not slip too badly on the steps. There were fewer townsfolk present now, but enough remained to scatter in panic from his path. Again, Falcon Guards stood their horses still, making no effort to pursue. About the edge of the square, Jaryd glimpsed more men on horseback, not in armour or guard colours. They were heading away, back toward the inns and the stables. That was worse, Jaryd knew. He had little time.

He rode the mare as fast as he dared on the streets, holding her wide and diving into the corners so as to lessen the skid of her hooves. Even so, she staggered and slid so hard he swore he would fall . . . only she recovered, avoided collision with the wall and continued. Random townsfolk darted aside, and then there was the bridge before him, with fields and orchards across the river and Falcon Guardsmen blocking the way. Yet, even as he rode, they reined aside, waving him on.

"Go, M'Lord!" one of them yelled and, as he flashed by, Jaryd recognised none other than Sergeant Garys of the Udalyn campaign. "They're ahead of you!"

Jaryd cleared the bridge's rise, then cut alongside the road to where soft turf made galloping easier, sparing a wave to Sergeant Garys as he did. The turf was torn from previous hooves, freshly made. He was not far behind.

He rode the gentle slope out of town between the stone wall and the paved road, occasionally risking the pavings where the gap between stone and an irrigation ditch became too narrow. The mare shied and flinched, but she seemed to get the idea. Soon he was flying along a flat stretch between barren fields and thriving green orchards, Algery lost behind green folds of trees and pasture.

He flashed by several carts on the road, then some travelling horsemen and then the pavings stopped and he could race down the road's centre without fear, tearing up clods of earth in his wake. To his left now came Chereny Wood. Up ahead would be the little stream he recalled. Sure enough, here came the small bridge, and he slowed the mare, to the horse's snorting surprise, and turned her off the road and onto the stream bank. It was wide enough for a gallop, until it emerged back onto the road, saving time.

Past some obscuring hedges that lined the road, he caught a glimpse of a horse's backside at a gallop. An acceleration, and several bends, and he was on them. Teriyan saw him first, riding at the rear, red hair flying. He grinned, waved, and gave a whoop of delight. Jaryd grinned back, closed alongside as the road took another gentle bend past a farmhouse, and clasped the older man's hand.

Ahead was Sofy, skirts pulled high to clear the saddle, but riding mostly on her stirrups anyhow. Jaryd was somewhat astonished at how well she held her balance—big horses like these ones were vastly different to Sofy's little dussieh, especially at speed. She peered back at him through a blowing veil of hair, and grinned also. Jaryd took her hand, at full gallop, and leaned to kiss it. Sofy laughed. Jaryd thought she might have hugged him, but was wise enough not to attempt it.

He exchanged happy greetings with Byorn, then assumed the lead from Ryssin and took them off the main road, down a narrower way between pasture walls. They were close to the southern edge of Algery Valley, where folded slopes lifted from the valley floor, blanketed with trees, and emerged at points above in sheer, rocky outcrops. For a while he set them a steady pace, allowing the horses some respite. The trees came down into the valley, and he took them along a well-remembered horse trail that ducked down to a low stream that poured off the valley side. There he bid them halt for a moment and water the sweating horses. Amidst the trees, and in a sheltered fold of land, there was no chance of being seen.

"Well?" Teriyan demanded.

"Well what?" said Jaryd, examining the mare for any sign of lameness.

"Well, did you kill anyone?"

Sofy, too, had briefly abandoned her horse to come and listen. She leaned against the mare's side with less eagerness than Teriyan. It was a more mature, pained expectation than Jaryd might have anticipated from the girl he'd first met in Baen-Tar, and come to know on the road to the Udalyn Valley.

"Several," Jaryd said flatly, feeling a foreleg that had surely bruised, on pavings, collisions with opposing mounts, or temple doors. "No one I immediately recognised, and all trying to kill me at the time. No one inside the temple, though."

"You got *into* the temple?" Teriyan asked.

"Aye."

"On the horse?"

"Aye."

"With the wedding still in progress?"

"Aye," said Jaryd, a touch irritably. "What's your point?"

"We're fucked!" said Teriyan, with feeling. "That's my point! You made Arastyn and company look like a right bunch of turkeys now! They'll send everyone they've got after us!"

"Aye," Jaryd said shortly, and shrugged. "Maybe. They won't have the Falcon Guard helping them, that's for sure."

"That's still every damn nobleman who can sit ahorse, and a bunch of townsmen too!"

"For sure, but can they track?" Jaryd pointed ahead. "Another twenty folds and the valley turns north, then we're into the horse trails straight to Valhanan. Once there, we can find a stream, ride up it, climb out on some rocks—this lot can't track in the woods to save their lives, they're city folk."

"They've dogs," Teriyan objected.

Jaryd shook his head. "Good for game but bad for horses, and in poor shape too."

"Why not go south into the forest here?" Sofy asked, pointing upstream into the thick trees. "Why stay in the valley where they can chase us?"

"Because thirty folds south," said Jaryd, "is Talyekar Ridge, which is pretty much impassable, so we'd have to go east anyhow. If we go east through this forest, we'll do it slowly, while our pursuers in the valley will do it quickly. They'll get well ahead of us, then cut us off. Best to make fast ground while we can, it's easier to lose them while they're close behind than it is to avoid them when they're already ahead of us, setting up ambush."

Sofy nodded, biting her lip.

"Sounds like a plan," Teriyan said roughly and smacked the younger man on the shoulder. "Glad you decided to join us after all!" He said it with a reprimand that promised retributions to come, but with humour all the same. Jaryd smiled and set to adjusting his saddle.

Sofy put a hand on his shoulder. "You didn't get your revenge?" she asked.

Jaryd shook his head. "No. But some Goeren-yai say that revenge is the only sustenance that will not perish with age."

Sofy did not look particularly amused at that. "Then why come back?" she asked.

Jaryd looked at her. Her long hair was tangled and windblown, yet it did not suit her ill. Her big, dark eyes were earnest. Questioning. "Since Tarryn was killed, I've been thinking only of reasons to die," he said simply. "Lately, I thought of some reasons to live." He kissed her on the cheek.

Sofy stared at him, astonished.

"Mount up," he told her. "We have to move. And don't tell anyone I did that, or I'll have Prince Koenyg joining the long line for my severed head."

"Oh, you'll have many more than Koenyg!" Sofy said brightly, retreating to her horse. "You'll have the archbishop for one, he'd be furious. And my brother Wylfred, he'd be most upset." All of a sudden she was bubbly again.

"All right, I get the idea."

"Oh, and Damon! Damon would kick your backside if I told him!" She mounted swiftly enough that Jaryd had to wonder if her little dussieh was the only horse she'd been riding, as she'd claimed. "And probably Father too. He's the King of Lenayin, you know."

"I heard," Jaryd said drily.

"And Lord Terfelt of Valhanan, he visited again last month, he's got *such* a crush on me."

"You don't think I could take *him*?"

"Silence," Sofy said primly, "I'm compiling my list. Now let's see, there's . . ." Jaryd pressed heels to the mare and forded the stream before she could continue. "I'll have it all memorised by the time we stop again!" Sofy called after him, unperturbed. "You'll be so thrilled to learn of all the people who love me so much they'd want you dead! I'm very popular, you know."

"I used to think Sasha was the craziest princess," Jaryd said to Teriyan in passing. "But she told me some stories about Alythia and, now I know Sofy, I'm beginning to think Sasha might be the sanest."

Soon the forest trail became farmland once more, broken by rows of trees and bushes, and increasingly steep, rolling terrain. They passed farmers tending animals, ploughing fields or pruning orchards, and others on the road with carts. The party attracted many strange looks, but there wasn't much anyone could do about that now.

At a bend about a gentle slope, Jaryd reined his mare to a halt. Down to the right, along the base of the forested hills climbing up from the valley, ran a small stream. Ryssin rode up beside him. "What's the problem?"

"I know this way well," said Jaryd, edgily. "The Daeryn Road arrives ahead, it's a fast ride from Algery if you gallop."

"Fast enough to cut us off?" Ryssin asked, guessing Jaryd's concern.

"Aye, maybe. There's about ten good routes to get to where we're going, but it's not like there's any shortage of chasers. They'll split up and follow the lot. I'm not worried about those behind us, we can outrun them . . . but if any got ahead . . ."

"You think we should go around?" Ryssin asked.

"Maybe," said Jaryd. "But it'll be slow, and then we might really get caught."

"Sitting here's pretty slow too," said Ryssin. "Your choice, lad, pick one."

Jaryd exhaled hard. "Go back and tell them—if we strike trouble, ride *at* them. There'll be no guardsmen following, it'll all be nobles, and they'll not have had much time for armour. The only ones wearing armour were at the wedding, and I don't think any of those will be chasing."

"Aye," said Ryssin. Jaryd nudged the mare forward and rounded the bend. Ahead, hedges and poplars lined the fences at the Daeryn Road intersection. The greenery was thick, but not so thick that it could hide horses and riders. No, if there were going to be an ambush, it would come from the barn he saw on the left. He rode further, and the barn came into view past a rise. He could not see anything. But then, that was why they called it an *ambush.*

He glanced behind to see that everyone was following, then checked to the right where Daeryn Road continued downhill to a little bridge over the stream . . . and glimpsed movement from the corner of his eye. His head whipped around, and there, charging from behind the barn, were four horsemen . . . no, six . . . no, *nine* horsemen.

"Ride!" he yelled, and slammed in his heels. The mare bolted, and he tore across the intersection risking a glance behind . . . Ryssin, then Byorn, then Sofy, skirts flying. He had to turn back before Teriyan came into view, but he guessed he would be there too, guarding the rear. He held the mare wide right, then cut into the left-hand bend ahead, as he'd learned in many reckless races along such roads in his youth . . .

A glance behind showed Ryssin following his line, then Byorn. He made a similar line at the next right. Probably, he thought grimly, the wind rushing in his face, whoever was chasing knew these roads equally well. Probably it was someone who knew him well, to have guessed he might come this way. Having Teriyan at the rear had seemed a reasonable precaution before—he was the best warrior astride after Jaryd. But fighting from horseback was not the same as regular swordplay. Had they all been afoot, Jaryd had no doubt the nine nobility would have little chance against the four swordsmen of their party. But horses were expensive, and nobility had vastly more riding experience than even Teriyan.

Jaryd knew how to lose them . . . or at least, some of them. It was an old trick, in these parts, and doubtless his pursuers knew it too . . . but now, there was Sofy to worry about. She had the least riding experience of them all. Perhaps . . . perhaps it would be best for her to turn and surrender? They'd never harm a princess of Lenayin. But what if she never got the opportunity to open her mouth and they killed an insolent country girl for conspiring with a traitor? Teriyan was right—he'd made these men mad. Likely whomever they caught would not live long enough to make pretty explanations.

Trees, then fields, then farmhouses all flashed by as the road wound back and forth, and Jaryd searched impatiently for a suitable location. Then he saw it—an orchard, sloping toward the stream. Beyond the stream, the rising, forest-covered slope of the valley side. He pointed hard with his right arm and hoped to the gods that Sofy would be able to muscle her horse off the road if it baulked. The orchard was surrounded by low stone walls, but one corner fronting the road was missing for access . . . Jaryd urged the mare sharply through the hole. The mare didn't like it, but he left her no doubt and she went, hooves uncertain on new footing, rushing past fruit trees. He ducked some branches and then he was in the lane between planting furrows and the mare accelerated once more, liking this new road better.

Jaryd glanced behind and saw Ryssin, Byorn . . . then Sofy . . . good. He slowed the mare again and cut right, ducking branches. A hanging fruit hit him in the head, and he raised an arm to protect his face from another branch. Soon he cut left again, onto a wider lane, checking behind . . . again, Ryssin was there, but he had no time to see the others. The ground beneath the trees was thick with long bullgrass, which would hide the horses' tracks. Certainly they could be tracked, but slowly, and the pursuers would have no choice but to split up.

After a while of zigzagging toward what he thought was the centre of the orchard, Jaryd stopped. Ryssin appeared between the thick branches, but there was no space to stand two horses aside, so he rounded the nearest tree. Byorn came past also, then Sofy, who stopped in the lane between trees. Then Teriyan, squeezing his horse against a tree's branches, leaning low in the saddle amidst the leaves and fruit.

"Good thinking, lad," he said, breathing hard. From somewhere behind, Jaryd could hear yells; hooves thundering one direction, and another.

"They'll split around the perimeter," said Jaryd. "About half of them. The other half will come in through the trees and try to flush us out."

"Couldn't they dismount and crouch down?" Sofy asked, looking dubiously at the surrounding trunks. "Can't they see the legs of our horses?"

Jaryd was impressed—it was exactly what they'd done, sometimes, hiding from irate farmers, or opposing teams in boyhood games. "In a younger orchard, yes. But this is mature, see how the branches hang down?" Sure enough, many fruit-laden boughs were pressing the grassy ground. "You can't see more than two or three furrows in any direction."

Sofy was breathing hard and clearly a little frightened, yet she looked remarkably composed for all that. Her hair, though, was now thoroughly tangled, and she bore a red scratch on one cheek.

"What now then?" asked Teriyan. "Do we split up?"

"Better to stay together," said Jaryd. "Splitting up just increases the odds they'll find one group or another. They've got holes in their formation now— if we can find one, best we get all of us through it." Teriyan nodded. "They'll think we'll be heading across the stream into the forest . . . I reckon we keep going across the valley, they won't expect it, there'll be less of them guarding that side. I'll ride down on my own and be seen, draw them into chasing me back into the orchard, while you lot take off to the east. I'll follow as I can."

"Wait, wait!" Sofy protested. "You said we'd stick together!"

"I said *you'd* best stick together," Jaryd retorted. "I know these idiots chasing us, I know this country, I've escaped mobs chasing me before and I can do it again—my biggest problem is other people slowing me down." With a firm stare at the princess. Sofy's return stare suggested she didn't believe him. "Ryssin, scout forward near the edge of the orchard . . . when you hear my diversion, ride like a demon."

The woodsman nodded. "We'll head for the trees further up," he said, "and risk the slower trails."

"Aye," Jaryd agreed, "I think we're far enough east by now anyhow."

"Head for the highest point along the ridge if we're split up," said Ryssin. "I'll find you."

Jaryd nodded, turned and rode downslope, the mare ducking and weaving uncertainly through the tangling branches. He heard the others moving off. Then other hooves, somewhere more distant, horses moving through the trees. He unsheathed his sword. If he came upon one of the nobles in this thicket, there was not going to be much time to react.

He paused, several furrows back from the edge of the orchard, and stood in the stirrups, but the trees were tall and he couldn't see through the branches. After a moment he caught a glimpse of movement on the perimeter . . . and then, as he peered, a man on a horse, moving sideways, searching the trees. Jaryd readied his arm, steadying his breathing. These men meant to kill him, he had no doubt. His siblings were not here now to restrain their swords.

He thumped the mare's sides and burst from the orchard. The rider reacted with shock and the horse reared, Jaryd cutting past its hooves to lash at the rider's back . . . only the noble's guard was fast, and steel clashed in defence. Jaryd wheeled, and saw three more coming at him from the left, two from the right . . . they were yelling, too, drawing others. He plunged back into the orchard, branches tearing at his face and arms, weaving for whatever small gaps he could glimpse through the greenery.

Suddenly there was a horse and rider before him . . . his mare reared, half colliding with the other horse, whose rider swung hard. Jaryd barely got his sword up in time, but the impact jolted him in the saddle. Swinging branches displaced by the horses snapped back, and the next thing he knew, he was falling, twisting to roll and not fall on his sword. He hit, but the ground was soft, and he rolled fast to avoid the other horse's trampling hooves. He rolled into the base of a tree and scrambled up, looking for the mare . . . but she was off.

Jaryd tried to run after her, but the other man spun his horse after him. Jaryd leapt sideways into a gap between trees, the horseman not reining up in time and finding no space to manoeuvre as he stopped alongside. Jaryd saw his chance and lunged upward and felt his sword drive home. A shriek from the rider, his horse suddenly fighting a pull on the reins. Jaryd was about to drag the wounded man from the saddle when hooves thundered behind, and he ran instead, having no time to claim the horse.

He ran fast, weaving between trees, hearing the thunder of hooves and the crashing of heavy bodies through branches. At least the others would be away by now, he found time to think—these men were only interested in him. He scrambled beneath heavy branches and put his back to one gnarled trunk, gasping for breath as several horses came past. He glimpsed the glint of drawn swords through the trees. He ran then not for the centre of the orchard, and safety, but downslope . . . he could hear riders shouting that he was off his horse. They knew he was on foot. No longer would they bother maintaining a perimeter around the orchard. Perhaps if he could find an adjoining fence-line, he could crouch low and run, and they'd never see him . . .

He reached the eastern edge of the orchard and crouched, staring across the open, recently ploughed field. No fencelines. No irrigation trenches, no hedge rows. He'd have to head back upslope to the road. Or . . . he crouched lower as hooves thundered nearby. Then a horse crashed into the open field, barely five trees upslope, and cut directly past him. His rider did not see.

Jaryd moved fast, took four running steps and slashed with his sword before the rider could respond. The sword cut deep, the rider clutching his side, reins pulling the horse around in a tight circle. He fell, a horrid, shoulder-first thump upon the turf, and rolled, finally losing the horse's reins. Jaryd ran for the horse, but already there were hooves thundering behind . . . he grabbed the dangling reins, but the horse shied away, making him grab again. The hooves behind were too close, and he spun, seeing another rider coming down on him fast, blade drawn. The riderless horse scampered away, Jaryd running after, as much to use its bulk as a shield than to grab the reins. The attacking rider came past, too far out, and wheeled, losing all speed before a new charge.

Jaryd ran straight at him, coming in low, blade first. Warhorses *hated* that when they weren't running. This one reared, and Jaryd feinted left, then ducked right, and cut up at the right-handed rider from his weaker left side—the harder, low angle to defend from the saddle. The rider's desperation saved him, his blade slashing hard downward, deflecting the blow . . . thus exposing an arm low, which Jaryd grabbed and dropped his entire bodyweight onto. The rider crashed from the saddle, face down on the turf.

Jaryd came up fast, ready for the finishing blow. The other rider half rose, holding an arm awkwardly, face dirty where it had planted the turf . . . and Jaryd recognised Rhyst Angyvar, blond hair, cut face and all. "You again," he observed. "Do you need another twenty men in support before you'd dare try and take me?"

Rhyst scrambled back cringing, blade wavering in panicked defence. "Help!" he screamed. "Somebody help me!" More hooves were thundering from several directions. Both riderless horses had galloped off in fear. Jaryd was tired of hiding in the orchard. He turned to meet the nearest horseman, blade at the ready . . . and saw that this horse was coming at him from across the open field, not the orchard. On its back was Sofy, hair and skirts streaming in the wind. And now, she was actually slowing, leaning down with one arm as she'd surely seen cavalry practise . . . only she hadn't taken her near boot out of her stirrup. Dear lords.

Jaryd sheathed his sword fast, took several running steps as she slowed alongside, and ignored her arm entirely, not wanting to pull her slight weight from the saddle. He leaped, and grabbed the saddle horn between her legs, and the rear side, and somehow managed to drag himself half onto the galloping animal's back. A further struggle, his face buried against Sofy's waist, and he got a leg over, grabbing Sofy and the saddle horn to pull himself into position behind, as they cut downhill alongside the orchard. And here ahead, another rider was coming past them on the left, sword ready for a backhand cut that would take both their heads off with one stroke.

"Down!" Jaryd roared, shoving her forward onto her horse's neck with his left hand, drawing with his right and smashing the stroke away just in time. Sofy recovered, steering them around as Jaryd held her about the middle with his left arm, his right free to ward off anyone else who tried to kill them. A glance back showed the man who'd nearly decapitated them was slow in recovering, holding his jarred right arm.

"Where the hells is Teriyan?" He shouted, trying to keep Sofy's hair from his face. "He was supposed to look after you!" It angered him that she should risk herself so. It angered him worse that he was the cause of it.

"We . . ." Sofy seemed breathless. Jaryd realised that that would be the first time anyone had swung a blade at her. "Another two men chased us!" she replied, finally, when she had enough breath. "We separated from Ryssin and Byorn, but then these two chased us . . . Teriyan killed one, but the other was persistent . . . I thought you might be in trouble, so I thought I'd come back!"

"You stupid girl, you're worse than your sister! You're a princess, you can't risk yourself for me! What were you thinking?!"

"Hey listen, *boy*," she retorted, "if I hadn't, you'd be dead! I'd quit while I'm ahead if I were you!" Jaryd blinked. He hadn't exactly been expecting her to burst into tears at his rebuke, but he hadn't expected *that*.

Abruptly he laughed, hysterically, and gave a whoop. It was good to be alive. He hugged her close with his left arm, for which he had plenty of excuse, because balance was hardly easy on the back of her saddle.

A glance over his shoulder showed at least four riders in pursuit, though none was terrifyingly close. Well ahead, beyond the wall of the next field, he saw the small figure of another rider. This one had long red hair and a drawn blade. Jaryd waved him on harshly, shouting at him to move on—no doubt the big warrior was mortified at having lost the princess, whatever the threat to his own life. (Though it seemed the second man pursuing him had met an ill fate as well. Perhaps, Jaryd thought, he'd underestimated Teriyan's skill on horseback.)

Teriyan took off, though Jaryd doubted he'd go far—probably just to clear the way ahead. But he was heading too far along . . . Jaryd was pretty sure he knew a better way.

"Down here," he said, pointing with his sword down toward the stream on their right. "There's a shallow crossing here, I think, and then a trail beyond it."

"Don't point that thing everywhere around me," Sofy retorted, turning them right. "It's unnerving."

Jaryd grinned. "Listen, Princess Cavalryman, the next time you come in for a fast pickup, leave me a stirrup, huh? How the hells am I supposed to get into the saddle without a stirrup?"

"Damn!" Sofy exclaimed. "I was certain I'd missed something . . . I've only seen them do it a few times!" She tugged at her dress about the saddle horn—it was riding rather high up one leg, Jaryd noticed. "One thing's for certain, I'll never make fun of Sasha's fashion choices ever again! This dress is trying to get me killed!"

As they approached the stream, Jaryd grasped her more tightly. "Ease up! Ease up!" As Sofy tugged back on the reins. "Not too much, don't walk or they'll catch us! Just there, now . . ." The horse cantered into the stream and spray went everywhere. Then they were coming out the other side. "Good, now go!" Sofy kicked with her heels.

"Left!" said Jaryd in her ear. "Stay on the bank. Now, see the break in the trees past this big vertyn?"

"I see it!"

"Turn right there, there's a trail!"

Sofy turned and then they were galloping up a narrow path through the trees. Already, the land was beginning to rise. Jaryd looked around but saw nothing behind . . . the pursuers had fallen back. Probably their horses were the more tired—to have made that intersection in such rapid time from Algery would have required a flat-out gallop. "Slow down a little, there's some sharper corners here!"

Their own horse was tiring and frothing wet with sweat, but it wasn't far now. After a time on the winding trail, the path dipped and Sofy slowed further to take them down into a little fold in the forested hillside. Here ran a stream.

"Straight ahead!" said Jaryd, pointing up the stream. Sofy kicked the horse to a canter along the stream bed, water erupting in their wake. It was rocky in places, but Sofy steered them onto the bank, and, further up, took them skilfully over a fallen, mossy tree trunk. Then, on the left, there was flat bedrock along the stream bank.

"This one?" Sofy asked. She'd heard enough tales of pursuits and hunts, Jaryd reckoned, to know what was up.

"No, there's plenty more," said Jaryd. "Let's confuse them." Sure enough, they passed several more spots where bedrock met the stream bank. At one such, Jaryd finally directed them left and out of the stream. The horse's hooves left no trace on the rock that any but an expert tracker would see.

Then they were riding uphill, twisting through the dense forest. After a long period of climbing, Jaryd was finally convinced that their pursuers were no longer on their trail.

They rested the horse for a moment by a small stream, allowing the tired beast a long drink while Jaryd checked it for injury. Sofy watched, standing close behind, curious to learn more.

"How far do you think we are from Teriyan and the others?" she asked, tugging at her dress in some discomfort.

"Not far. They'll be heading up one of these ridges too. Hopefully we'll find them ahead." He replaced the horse's right foreleg to the ground, content that the shoe fit well and no stones were caught beneath. "Why did you come back for me? Seriously?"

"Seriously?" Sofy repeated, with some incredulity. "How can you ask 'seriously'? All of you heroic young men with delusions of grandeur, taking ridiculous risks whenever there's a woman around . . . I thought you were going to get yourself killed, and I was right!"

Jaryd straightened and stretched an aching shoulder. And he almost surprised himself when he smiled, a little cockily, and said, "In my case, Your Highness, they're not delusions."

Sofy half gaped at him. From the old Jaryd Nyvar, such a statement would have been expected. But from the new, the humour had been rare. Something had changed. Jaryd was not entirely sure what. Well, he had a journey back to Baerlyn to think about it. With Sofy.

"The biggest annoyance with this whole thing," Sofy remarked, her eyes lively, "is that I'm not going to be able to tell anyone about how I saved your life! Probably I'm going to have to deny I was ever here!"

"Half the Falcon Guard know you were there," Jaryd replied. "No stopping those rumours once soldiers start them."

"True." Sofy seemed pleased at that.

"And you'll have this vicious red scar to explain," said Jaryd, indicating her cheek.

"Is it really that bad?" she asked in dismay. "I thought it just stung a little." She felt at it with her fingers.

"Let me look." Jaryd peered close. Very close. He was half aware of what he was doing, the old, reckless reflexes kicking in. He knew it was stupid, but he had to test the reaction. He had to see . . . had to see if what she felt was like . . .

As he peered, he could feel Sofy's breath on his face. She smelled sweet. Her eyes were fixed on him, her breath tight, her body suddenly rigid. He hadn't really expected that. Or maybe he had. Or maybe . . . somewhere in the midst of his indecision, their lips touched. She tasted sweet too. The force of it stunned him. She was just a girl, really, and not even his type anyway. And he'd had women who were . . . well, who were . . . but it was no good, he couldn't think straight, and his heart was thudding like a wild thing.

His hands went to her back, and he kissed her more deeply and passionately than he'd ever kissed any woman before. Sofy's hands were against him, clutching as if in indecision. She made a low moan, that might have been protest, and might have been something else entirely. But her body pressed close, and then her hands were at his back, clutching his shirt, pulling him closer. It seemed to go on forever. The way it felt, that would have suited Jaryd fine. Only now, his hands were wanting more, a reflex slide on the back of her dress, searching for a lace. Wondering what the smooth white skin beneath would feel like, bare beneath his hand. Wondering what her body would feel like, pressed skin to skin with his own.

They parted. And stared at each other, clutching to each other's arms. Sofy's lovely eyes were big and dark, wide with hungry disbelief. Slowly, her fingertips went to her lips, as if savouring the memory of the kiss. And, perhaps, in a gesture of simple shock. Sofy, who was betrothed to the heir of Larosa. Sofy, upon whose marriage a great war hung, and the fate of multiple civilisations. Sofy, who was staring at him now in the realisation that all of these things, however difficult they'd been before, had just become enormously more complicated still.

"Oh dear lords," she murmured. "We're really in trouble now, aren't we?"

Twenty

RHILLIAN STRODE THE DOCK as a cold wind gusted off the ocean and the boats heaved and tossed at their moorings. Grey clouds hung low, foretelling an end to summer. Halrhen and Shathi walked at her sides, serrin from the three Saalshen trading ships at anchor in the harbour, the last refuge of Saalshen on this bleak, forsaken shore. Halrhen cradled Aisha, half conscious and in pain, barely larger than a child in the big man's arms.

Smoke swirled across the debris-strewn and puddled pavings, and the stink of burning flesh. Pyres lined the dockside, at least fifteen, with several more under construction, piled high with the wood from half-demolished buildings. What little oil Dockside possessed was being spent to dispose of thousands of corpses, before disease set in. Raggedy men and women worked in groups, piling bricks to form a retaining wall, then hauling bodies by the cartload. Men wrapped themselves in dirty old cloth and leather to ward the blistering flames, wrestling stiff bodies onto the blaze. Priests and caratsa blessed the cartloads of stiffening corpses with holy water and prayers, mouths and noses covered with cloth to ward the smoke and smell.

They needed pits, but there were none on Dockside—the dead were normally disposed of at Angel Bay, but passage across Sharptooth remained treacherous as some of the Riverside mob continued to haunt the alleyways. There had been some suggestion that fishermen could haul boatloads of corpses out to sea and dump them, but the boats were needed for fishing, spare men to sail them were few and far between, and the winds now prevailed onshore, not only making sailing difficult but threatening to blow the terrible cargo back onto the docks regardless, all bloated and floating.

The uniform line of Dockside buildings was broken in places, where a blackened hole appeared, and a pile of collapsed masonry and charred wooden beams. Men and women climbed amongst the ruins, collecting valuables or anything salvageable. The dock markets had reappeared, stalls hawking wares amidst the carnage and smoke. People needed to eat and life went on. Rhillian knew that they would rebuild—humans had been killing and destroying each other's civilisations for as long as serrin had been recording their history, and yet the sum total of humanity never ceased its upward march. Once, she might have found some admiration for their tenacity. Now, she saw only bleak futility. They regenerated like rabbits, or like weeds. They *needed* to destroy each other, it was how they progressed, from one era to the next, in successive waves of creative obliteration. Serrin had thought to try to restrain this impulse in humans, to control it, to teach them better. Now, she saw it was pointless. This was what they were, and to wish it otherwise was to teach wolves to eat cabbage, or deer to lust red meat. She'd come to Petrodor three years ago, with dreams of finding a symmetry between humans and serrin. But humans and serrin, as Kiel had always warned, were fundamentally incompatible. Now, there was only survival.

They turned onto a pier as frothing waves rushed against the pylons below. Masts waved back and forth, and rigging whipped and clacked against the sail arms. Then Rhillian heard footsteps thumping on the pier planks behind. She turned.

"Errollyn," she announced to the others, for warning. They kept walking. Rhillian fell several steps back, but did not stop.

"Rhillian." Errollyn seemed out of breath. "Where are you taking Aisha?"

"Out to a ship, where else?" Rhillian said coldly. She did not look at him.

"You can't just grab her without telling anyone!" He was upset. "I didn't know where she was! I thought she'd been kidnapped, or—"

"She is serrin," said Rhillian, "and she belongs with serrin. We're taking her home."

"You asked her?"

"I don't need to ask her. Those of us who matter, just *know*." Silence from Errollyn. She could feel his hurt, radiating like heat from the fires. Barely a day before, she might have been shocked at herself. Now, she barely cared.

"At least let me say goodbye."

"You had few such compunctions with those at Palopy. Many are dead, who departed without your farewells."

"Fuck you," he said in Lenay.

They reached the end of the pier. A rowboat was moored there, its oars shipped, two more serrin waiting on its heaving deck. Halrhen simply held Aisha to his chest, an arm beneath her backside as she grasped his shoulders, and began climbing down the ladder. The serrin in the boat held it steady as best they could, and called warnings of an approaching swell.

Rhillian turned to Errollyn. The wind tossed his shaggy hair about a face marked with soot. There was a defiance there, and a pain, and a confusion that perhaps only Aisha would have understood. Rhillian was beyond caring about that either.

"You'd best change her dressings as soon as you're aboard," Errollyn said. "I've done my best, but Dockside is short of clean dressings today. Also her fever is a little higher than it should be, despite my medicines. I've been mixing fenaseed and gilflower in her tea, so don't let her eat bread, they don't mix well—"

"We've healers aboard who surpass your skills," Rhillian said. "She'll be better cared for there than here."

"She hates boats. She'll be sick."

"It won't kill her." Errollyn stared at her. Rhillian could see the retort forming on the tip of his tongue. She knew what he wanted to say. All the deaths he wished to blame upon her. He refrained, with great difficulty, and heaved a deep breath. His judgment, however unspoken, did not make her angry. Rhillian felt beyond that. "You could come with us," she suggested, bluntly.

"No," said Errollyn. He reached within his jacket and withdrew a folded parchment. It had been sealed with a cord, tied in a bow. "I want you to deliver this to the council. I wrote it by Aisha's bedside this morning, when I could not sleep. They are my reasons for staying. In case anyone is interested."

Rhillian tucked it into a pocket within her own jacket. Below, Halrhen stepped into the boat with Aisha. "You can write what you like," said Rhillian. "Humans have better words for what you have done than we. They call it betrayal."

"You can call it whatever you like," Errollyn said coldly, "but you can't disguise your disaster here. I warned you, you ignored me, and now look. Go back to the council. Impress them with your pretty words and excuses. Fool them, like you've fooled everyone else. Like you've fooled yourself, most of all. And then soon enough we'll all be dead."

They stared at each other, two old friends atop the furthest pier from shore, as the wind blew and the air smelled more for a moment of salt and freshness than death and charcoal. Rhillian had always known the serrin indivisible. Now, that certainty seemed shattered.

She climed down to the waiting boat and the company of true serrin. Errollyn watched, forlorn and alone, as she found a bench and the sailors pushed the boat out into the swell. He stood and watched for some time as the boat rowed steadily out into the harbour, lifting and slapping on the rolling swell. The only living serrin left in Petrodor, the last in a continual habitation lasting at least three hundred years. Then, finally, he turned and walked back toward the line of fires.

Rhillian took the parchment from within her jacket and considered it. The cold water heaved and splashed just to her side. It would be such a simple thing to toss the parchment away and allow the waves to claim all of Errollyn's vaunted wisdom. His writing would no doubt speak ill of her. It would no doubt make his own stance seem wise and reasonable. Things would be simpler if the parchment were to disappear.

Instead, she tucked it back into her jacket. Whatever had happened, she was still serrin. She would never betray her heritage, nor the justness of what she knew to be true. The rowers' arms were strong, and drove the boat hard through the waves. Beside her, Aisha sat wrapped in Halrhen's supporting arms. Her eyes were half closed, her head bobbing as the swell took them up and down. Rhillian clasped Aisha's hand. The fingers tightened faintly in return.

"Soon," Rhillian promised her. "Soon you'll be home."

The Velo household was all blackened stone and charcoal. The fire had engulfed the neighbouring residences too, the wind swirling a haze of ash amidst the smoke from the pyres. Sasha embraced Mariesa Velo, her hands and dress black from searching through the ruins, and gazed at the desolation.

"We'll rebuild it," she assured the older woman. "Everyone will help, you'll see. It'll be better than before."

"I have my family," said Mariesa. "I have not lost any of my beloveds, thank the gods. I am happy." She'd been repeating it like a mantra since the blaze, Valenti had said. Sasha could see Mari, Valenti, and brothers and sisters climbing over the piled black stones, moving what surviving possessions they could find into small, charred heaps. It would have broken her heart, had not her heart already been broken by sights many times more grievous than this.

Mari saw her and climbed down from the rubble. His right eye was swollen shut and there was a cut across that brow. He embraced Sasha hard, like a father.

"You did it, huh?" he exclaimed, considerably less distraught than his wife. "You beat those bastards! You and Kessligh . . . just look at this, you make us heroes!" He waved a sooty hand at the pyres.

"You did it," Sasha told him solemnly. "You are heroes, by your own making. They'll tell tales in Lenayin of the Dockside's defence."

Mari beamed and clapped her on the arm. He'd fought armed with nothing more than the hook pole he used to haul in crab nets, to hear Valenti tell it, insisting that he used it better than any Nasi-Keth used a blade. The better weapons, he'd left to his sons. Deaths along the Dockside stood at between two and three hundred, though it would probably be days yet until the final tally was known. The Velo family had not lost anyone, though there was a dead cousin and an uncle wounded, in the balance.

"So where is it?" Mari asked in a low voice, with a wary glance at the surrounding commotion. "Some folk, they see our place burned down, they think it's lost. I tell them it's not lost, but I don't know where it is, and they don't believe me."

"It's safe," Sasha assured him. "Kessligh knows where it is. He's not telling anyone."

"And . . . Kessligh is well?"

"Kessligh is very well," Sasha said firmly. "One other person knows. Tell that to anyone who asks."

Sasha continued her way across the dock, answering questions, giving comfort to some and advice to others. Men and women hailed her heartily and several stall owners insisted she accept hot food in passing.

She put on a riding glove to stop the handful of fried octopus from scalding her, and chewed as she walked. Amidst the tragedy, she could see hope. Family helped family, and complete strangers exchanged food and water, and comforted the grieving. Dockside had always been close, by Petrodor standards, but this calamity had forced them closer. These people had been the lowest of the low, before the arrival of the desperate Riverside masses, at least. The Nasi-Keth had raised them and brought them together, and now events had strengthened those bonds. Further north, where the big ships docked at North Pier, she could see the bustle of the trade had resumed, although perhaps not at its previous intensity. Much of Dockside worked at North Pier, another reason the patachis had been reluctant to support the archbishop's bloody gamble. This morning, the Docksiders went back to work and repaid the debt they owed the patachis for holding the northern flank, however selfishly motivated.

There were no pyres burning near North Pier Temple, and were it not for the lingering smell of smoke, it would have seemed that all here was normal. Only the foreigners were absent, sailors not game to leave their boats or their upslope inns, and venture down to Dockside so near to the calamity.

Inside the temple, Sasha found the pews replaced by bedding for perhaps a hundred wounded. Women walked amongst them, carrying trays of food or water. Nasi-Keth healers knelt to administer medicines, and rewrap bandages, while a few priests and caratsa comforted others. The air smelled of sweet and pungent herbs, and various pots were stirred above makeshift fireplaces.

Sasha made her way carefully between the wounded . . . the most serious, she noted, had been lain to the right, directly beneath the painted ceiling and its scaffolding. The scene there was grim indeed, and the air smelled more of blood than herbs. To the left, seated against the base of the wall, she found

Kessligh gazing up at the painted ceiling. A heavily bandaged man Sasha did not recognise sat by his side, his head lolling.

Sasha knelt at Kessligh's side and clasped his hand. "How do you feel?" she asked. She felt a little nauseous just being here, truth be known. She hated to see him in this place. She knew how he disliked crowds and cities, even more than she.

"Don't look at me like that," Kessligh reprimanded her, mildly. "I'm fine. The leg is not infected."

"Look . . . I could move you. Father Horas has given me an upstairs chamber, there's room enough for—"

"No," said Kessligh. "My friend Peteri here was just telling me about the painting . . . before he went to sleep." Indicating the man at his side. "I haven't had time to really look at it before. And the healers here use different techniques than I've seen; I learn by watching them work."

He looked quite serene, Sasha thought. He'd always had an ageless face, hard and sharp. Sasha wondered how he could be so calm. Probably he would never be the same swordsman he had been again. Yet he sat with his bandaged leg outstretched, his head against the stone at his back, and gazed up at the scaffolding and the half-completed figures of gods, angels and their followers.

Tears welled in her eyes, though she could not say precisely why. Kessligh looked at her. And frowned, predictably. "What?" With exasperation in his tone. He'd never been able to accept emotion as a rational response to anything. Certainly he'd never made allowances for her gender. Previously, she might have found it infuriating. Now, she smiled through the tears.

"You're such a grouch," she told him. Kessligh frowned some more, not understanding. "I love you," she said simply, and kissed him on the cheek. And got up to leave, knowing better than to think Kessligh would appreciate any extended display of softness.

"Hey, get me some fried chicken legs or something," Kessligh called after her. "That stall owner by the mouth of Ashetel Lane does great chicken. I'm sick of seafood."

"Aye, mighty Yuan!" Sasha said sarcastically in Lenay. "Whatever you command." Kessligh watched her go with a wry smile, then turned his eyes back to the ceiling.

In the temple's studio the statues stood silent. Sasha climbed the staircase up the end wall, pushed open the creaking wooden trapdoor and emerged into a dusty hall, daylight falling cold through a series of windows.

She opened a door into a small, paved chamber with two beds. On one lay a saddlebag, containing the few possessions that she had not left at Pazira House—some changes of clothes, her washing oils and other serrin things that a girl did not like to go without. Some thoughtful soul had moved them when they'd taken the Shereldin Star from the Velo House. She had not asked them to, but she could not help but be glad.

Another old, slightly warped door led to the washroom. She knocked, but there was no reply.

"Errollyn?" She pushed the door open. Errollyn sat on a small stool, clad only in pants. His hair was wet, tousled about his neck and brow, and rivulets of water ran down his bare back. He sat with an elbow on one knee, staring at the far wall. He did not look at her, nor speak, nor move.

Sasha pushed the door open more fully and stepped into the washroom. His sword and bow leaned in one corner, and his belt with knives, and the quiver of arrows. Last night, he'd spent much time collecting his arrows from the corpses of his many victims. The fingers of his left hand now rubbed absently at the calluses on his right.

Sasha stepped before him and squatted, hands on his knees. Tears streaked his cheeks. His deep green eyes seemed to shimmer, swimming with moisture.

"Rhillian's leaving," Errollyn whispered. "They're all leaving. She took Aisha."

"I heard," Sasha said solemnly. "Would you rather go with them?"

He stared at her. His eyes were almost frightening. "I can't. My path is here. I cannot betray myself."

Sasha took his hand awkwardly. And squeezed. "I'm glad. For myself, I mean," she amended quickly.

"I cannot betray myself, so I must betray my people. She was right about me. She named me a traitor."

"She said that?" Sasha couldn't believe it, it was not a serrin concept, and never had been. Only . . . she recalled Rhillian last night atop the Tarae Keep. Recalled the horror in her eyes. Sasha had often wondered just how far a serrin might need to be pushed in order to cease being reasonable. Last night, she'd looked into the eyes of a woman pushed far beyond any limit. "Errollyn . . . they're saying Palopy was a massacre. I don't know how she and Kiel survived, but it must have been horrific. She doesn't know what she's saying, Errollyn—"

"Doesn't she? I am *du'janah*. To be born *du'janah* is to be born a traitor."

"I don't understand . . . what does that mean? Not one of you serrin has actually explained to me what a *du'janah* is."

Errollyn touched her face gently. He ran a thumb over her cheek. It tingled, and Sasha felt her heart beat faster. His face twisted in a grimace. "I can't explain. There are no words. You'd need to be serrin."

"Damn it, Errollyn, that's an excuse, nothing more." Somehow, with her, a racing heart threatened to unleash a temper, no matter what had brought it on. "How can I help if you just keep pushing me away?"

Errollyn hung his head with a sigh, and offered no answer. His hand slipped from hers. His despair was one sad sight too many. The Errollyn she knew was full of mischievous, irreverent intellect. He found everything interesting, but took nothing too seriously. Now, he seemed a sad wreck of a man. Sasha hated morbidity. She had to do something, because this . . . this was all getting too much.

Her heart thudding madly, she stood, and pushed him upright as she straddled him. Then, she sat in his lap. Errollyn stared at her. A shiver went up her spine. She put her forearms across his shoulders and locked fingers behind his neck. "I've had a hard day," she told him, awkwardly. As if that explained everything. Dear spirits, she hoped Rhillian had not just been teasing her, or this was going to rank among the most embarrassing moments of her life.

Errollyn took a deep breath. Wiped at his eyes. "This is unmanly, I suppose?" he said, with a crooked smile. And what a smile. Her heart nearly stopped. Errollyn could cry as a Lenay man rarely would and, yes, a part of her thought it most unbecoming of him . . . and yet he had eyes like a predator and a body not unlike one of the statues downstairs. With a bow in his hand, he was surely more dangerous to his enemies than even she was with a sword.

"It's only unmanly when it becomes a habit," Sasha replied, a little breathlessly. Errollyn took another deep breath, finished wiping his eyes and tousled his wet hair. Dear spirits, she liked that too. It hung about those impossible green eyes, grey and wild.

"I apologise for being a pale shadow of the many great yuans you've doubtless known."

"Not many great yuans have bested as many in battle as you have," she pointed out.

Errollyn made a face. "Aye, but that's archery. A coward's cheat. Even you think so."

"I do not."

"Oh yes you do. You've said many times that you hate archers."

"I didn't mean it."

"Do you always say things you don't mean with such conviction?"

"Always. Most things I say with great conviction I don't mean. I'm like that."

"And why would that be, do you think?"

"Errollyn!" Sasha burst out, finally losing patience. "I gathered all my courage just to sit on your lap! Do something!"

Errollyn smiled, gazing at her calmly. His eyes were so close. If she looked into them directly, she would freeze. "Why does it fall to *me* to do something?" His breath was warm on her cheek. "You have two arms, two legs . . ."

"I . . . well, look, it just does!"

"In Lenayin, where women are submissive and await the advances of passing men like the virtuous maidens they surely are?" He was teasing her, she realised. Like a cat playing with a mouse. She got off him before she could succumb to the urge to hit him . . . but he caught her about the waist and pulled her back down.

"Don't play with me!" she said hotly.

"I thought you wanted me to play with you?" She hit him, hard in the shoulder. He winced, but laughed. "You're beautiful when you're angry."

"You're a pain!" She really *was* angry now, she disliked feeling so helpless. And yet . . . and yet his hands on her waist ran up her sides, admiringly, and her breath came very short.

"I'm serrin," he said reasonably. "Of course I'm a pain." And dear spirits, as if she hadn't learned the truth of *that* lately. "You're sure you want to do this? Your priests will tell you it'll send you straight to the hottest hell."

Sasha snorted. "I'm Goeren-yai, I don't care a puddle of piss what some priest says."

"Watch your mouth," Errollyn teased, touching her lips with a finger. "We're in a temple."

"A temple full of sexy nude statues," Sasha replied, stifling a giggle.

"Sasha?"

"Hmm?"

"Thank you for sitting on my lap. I've been hoping you would for quite some time." Before she could think of a reply, he kissed her.

It felt as wonderful as she remembered from the day before . . . only this time, she could stay where she was and enjoy it at her leisure. She kissed him back, but evidently not very well, because he smiled, took her hair in both hands and showed her how to do it better. That became a game and soon she was laughing between kisses, and feeling . . . spirits, better than she could ever remember feeling, with the possible exception of the first time she'd bested Kessligh in a sparring session as a girl.

She undid her bandoleer and put the sword aside, while Errollyn's hands moved up over her hips to a breast . . . "I'm sorry," she quipped at him, feeling a little cocky all of a sudden, like a girl riding a horse for the first time who thought she was doing pretty damn well. "I don't have much there."

"The rest of you more than compensates," Errollyn replied, and pulled off her jacket. Sasha ran her hands over his bare chest, the first time that she'd not bothered to try to hide her delight at the view. Errollyn put his hands up her shirt, moving to pull it over her head, but instead found . . .

"What in the hells is this?" He pulled off the shirt and stared at the gold chain about her neck. Or, more precisely, what hung on the end of it. "Well that's an anticlimax," he remarked. "Of the many things I was looking forward to finding under here, *that* wasn't one of them."

Sasha bit her lip. The Shereldin Star felt cold against her skin. With her jacket on, no one had yet noticed the chain beneath its collar.

Errollyn stared, then looked up at her. "You're wearing the holiest artefact of the Verenthanes beneath your shirt."

Sasha shrugged. "There was nowhere else. Kessligh didn't trust the new hiding place. He wanted it well guarded, and . . . well, I am the best swordsman in Petrodor now."

Errollyn's amusement was turning into a grin. "It doesn't concern you that some might consider it improper to hide the star against bare, female skin?"

"Should it?" Sasha retorted. "What's more important—holding to silly superstitions or keeping it safe?"

"Look, I think you can do without this for now . . ." he took the chain up over her head and placed the star atop her discarded shirt and jacket. "It kind of spoils the mood."

"Doesn't it!" she agreed, and kissed him again.

What followed, Sasha thought later, was rather like a memory of battle, its recall dimmed through a haze of frantic, heart-thudding action. Or rather, she tried to make it that way, but Errollyn restrained her, told her firmly to slow down and laughed at her when it became clear that she could not. Slowly it dawned on her that she was completely out of her depth. Errollyn was *experienced*. Like most serrin. He seemed almost as confident of her body as he was of his own.

He finally got her to a bed, shedding clothes as they went, and pressed her onto the mattress. He tried to settle her down to his pace, kissing and feeling her, and that felt wonderful for a while. But inevitably, she became impatient . . . it was slightly embarrassing to be so frantic, while he remained so calm. She wanted him to be frantic too, but had no idea how that might happen, unless he was inside her. Even serrin men were supposed to go crazy then, surely?

Errollyn didn't go crazy. He watched her, in turns curious, affectionate and intense. She tried desperately to match him, to be as cool, as controlled as he, but it wasn't working. Worse, he drew her out, as though he was pulling back on his bowstring. Finally, at her moment of greatest pleasure, he gave her a great, athletic burst that fairly set the bed to shaking. What followed was indescribable.

"Good?" he asked her when she had recovered a little, gasping and swearing against his shoulder. Cocky, arrogant serrin. It wasn't fair. He read her well enough, and grinned, nuzzling her hair.

"I'd . . ." she managed, when she could get a functioning word out. "I'd thought it would hurt, or . . . or something."

"Doesn't always." He kissed her ear, and progressed down her neck. "Would you like some more?"

"I . . . I don't know that I can. Can you?"

"Always."

She tried to give him a hard look but it turned into a laugh, and then they were kissing again. He did some things to her that she'd only heard described, and those by disreputable sources. Worse, she loved it. Perhaps her critics were right, and she *was* depraved. It was nothing she hadn't imagined doing, if only she could have found the right man. Or, as seemed more likely the case with Errollyn, the wrong man in the right circumstances. This time, when she climaxed, Errollyn came with her.

After they'd lain together for a while, warm and a little sweaty, Sasha remembered something else. "Damn, I have to take my powder."

"There's no rush. It works even after a few days."

The powder was a habit with Sasha. She did not know if she would have the opportunity to swallow the stuff if she were captured again, certainly not all captors would be as considerate of her dignity as the Archbishop of Torovan. But she'd always considered it worth carrying, just in case. This was the first time she'd considered taking it for amorous reasons.

"You seem to know a lot about this," she remarked.

Errollyn shrugged. "Serrin are educated young."

"How young?"

Errollyn smiled, a dazzling blaze of green eyes. It sent a thrill up her spine . . . and through her loins. "I was taken aside by a nice girl in my fourteenth year. She had sixteen years, and she decided my time had come."

Sasha shrugged. "That's not so young. In some parts of Lenayin, girls marry and bear children younger than that."

"Serrin women cannot conceive younger than yourself. Sometimes not until twenty-five."

Sasha blinked up at him. "Truly?" Errollyn nodded. Sasha had known that serrin women had few children compared to humans, but that was all.

Another thought occurred to her. "How do you know it isn't the male seed that's weak?" she challenged.

Errollyn shook his head playfully, so that his thick grey hair fell on her face. "Serrin women have the same difficulties with human men."

"And human females conceive quickly when mounted by the virile young men of Saalshen?" It was by far the oddest conversation she'd ever had—naked on her back with a man between her legs. Something about it was wonderful, beyond the simple eroticism. All her life, she'd been the crazy tomboy who wore pants, rode horses and broke things. She'd rarely had the chance to be a woman, in truth, and she hated all of the things that in the eyes of most Lenays, would have made her one. All except this . . . but she'd never had the chance to do *this* before. Not safely, with someone she'd have trusted with far more than just her virginity. Now, she felt . . . womanly. She flexed her legs more tightly about Errollyn's waist, and liked the way that felt.

"Virile old men too." Errollyn ground himself against her, sensuously. Sasha winced, biting her lip, but trying to look defiant. That didn't work either. "It's instantaneous."

"I'd better take my powder then."

"No. Stay." He kissed her, gently. "There's no rush. Two days after is fine."

Sasha sighed and reached for a blanket that had come loose in their love-making. She drew it over them both. The air had a chill, most unlike the warmth of recent weeks. "I have to go soon," she told him. "There's work to be done."

Errollyn studied her, one hand toying with her hair. "You're sad."

Sasha smiled, and wrapped her arms around his middle. "Only out there," she said.

"Kessligh will be fine," Errollyn assured her. "He'll be a better swordsman on one good leg than most people manage on two."

"I know." She shook her head against the pillow. "It's not just Kessligh. It's . . . all this suffering. Is . . . is this my life? Do you think?"

"Do *you* think?"

Sasha rolled her eyes in exasperation. "I . . . damn, I shouldn't be thinking about this now. I don't want to spoil it."

"I'd like to think I mean more to you than just a good fuck," Errollyn remarked. Sasha blinked at him. They'd been speaking Lenay, of course. It astonished her how that was just an unconscious habit with people she trusted.

"I didn't mean *that*," Sasha retorted.

"I know," Errollyn said mildly. "I'm just saying that if I wanted to bed some girl who was pretty and said nothing of substance, I'd pay some mid-slopes whore for a night."

Sasha smiled. "Oh, I doubt you'd have to pay." She brushed shaggy hair from his face. "It just struck me today . . . walking past these piles of burning corpses." Errollyn stroked her hair. She took a deep breath. "I've always had this . . . very simple equation. Every time Kessligh's training became too painful, every time I hurt myself in sparring, or fell off a horse, or awoke one morning feeling just so stiff and awful that I couldn't possibly rise from my bed, I told myself that if this weren't my life, then it would have to be Baen-Tar, and Alythia's life, all pretty dresses and gossip and marriage. And suddenly, my present situation wouldn't seem so bad.

"Today on the docks, I thought about that equation once more, and . . . and suddenly pretty dresses and awful gossiping twits didn't seem like such a bad life after all. You know?"

"I know." Errollyn nodded. "I was raised in the foothills of the Telesil Mountains. My uman was Dahlren." Sasha gazed up at him wonderingly. Errollyn did not speak of his childhood often. "She was an old thing, and unimpressed with people, human or serrin. The world of wild things was her world. She was too old to take an uma, but she took me nonetheless. I grew up mostly alone, save for Dahlren, and she wasn't much for conversation. I learned the ways of animals, I learned the herbs of healing lore and I learned to hunt. Sometimes I look around in this city, and wonder what I'm doing here. I dream of greenery when I sleep. I dream of trees, Sasha. Do you dream of trees?"

"There's an old vertyn tree," Sasha murmured sadly. "It grew at the back of our house on the hillside. I climbed it many times when I was younger, and later, Andreyis climbed it with me. It always amazed me that I could be so high, and yet the mountains were so much higher. It made me think about the scale of things, and about the Goeren-yai saying, that one could never trust a human judgment of size and power, and how all the greatest warriors of history were as nothing compared to the mountains. I dream of that tree sometimes."

"Dahlren died when I had just thirteen summers," Errollyn continued. He looked sad and thoughtful. Sasha took the hand in her hair and entwined her fingers with his. "That was terrible. We lived mostly alone, there was just a little village down from the shoulder of the hill where we had our small farm. I had help with the va'eth aln, the funeral rites, but not much else. I insisted on staying on after that, on my own . . . I was stubborn, you would say. I continued my own learnings, as Dahlren had done. I think it changed me. I sometimes wonder what my life might have been like had I taken a different uman. But I am who I am, and wonderings will achieve nothing."

"Dahlren was *du'janah*," Sasha said sombrely. "Wasn't she?" Errollyn looked surprised. "That's why you were sent to be her uma."

Errollyn slid off her with a sigh, to Sasha's regret. She worried that she'd said the wrong thing. But Errollyn lay close, a hand propping his head. "She was *du'janah*," Errollyn confirmed. "It was discussed, between my parents and various elders." His brilliant eyes darkened. "I wished they'd just leave me alone. My elder sister had taken an uman who was a master of woodcraft. I wanted to learn woodcrafts too, but it was insisted that I should take a *du'-janah* uman. Dahlren was unsuitable, and too old, and unfriendly and fit to die on me before I could complete *useen*, but that did not matter to them."

Sasha put a hand on his chest. He was nearly hairless below the neck. It seemed a natural condition of serrin. "Did you love her? Dahlren, I mean."

Errollyn smiled faintly. "I grew to. I helped with small tasks that her fingers found difficult, or her arms lacked the strength for. And I did love her lore, and grew to love the forests and hills more deeply than anything. I took Dahlren's small affections where I could."

Sasha smiled. "You learn to recognise them after a while, don't you?"

Errollyn raised an eyebrow. "You with Kessligh?" Sasha nodded, with no small exasperation. Errollyn shook his head. "No, Kessligh is a veritable eruption of love and joy compared to Dahlren. She could spend days, and not speak a word to me. But I learned to love her anyway. Love is not always a good thing. It hurt all the more on the winter morning when I woke and found that the previous night's chill had taken her life. I blamed myself for years, but it was so fast, and she'd insisted her cough had been nothing."

Sasha ran a hand through his hair. Her heart ached to hold him, and she knew that he probably would not mind . . . but she was Lenay, and one did not embrace or comfort a man in pain. Not if one valued his dignity, and his honour.

"I met some of her family at the *va'eth aln*," Errollyn continued. "They insisted she'd left them, and had not been cast out as Dahlren sometimes told me. They were all baffled by her. They said it was an unfortunate thing to be *du'janah*. After a short while of conversation, I think I began to understand why she left."

"Errollyn," Sasha said softly. "Tell me. What is a *du'janah*? Precisely, in your own words."

Errollyn gazed at her. Exasperation built to a faint wince. "I . . . I don't know, Sasha, it's so difficult to explain to a human . . ."

Sasha straddled him. Pushed him onto his back, and lay on his chest, nose to nose. She kissed him gently, and pressed herself to him, a pleasant warmth of skin on skin. And was pleased to feel him harden once more against her. She propped herself on her elbows. "Look," she told him, "I can't get any closer than this. If you can't tell me now, then you probably can't tell anyone. *Sel ath'avthor shalma'ta mai, el'ath dael baer'il shoen.*" "And if it cannot be said in words, it probably doesn't exist."

Errollyn made a wry smile. "You can get closer," he suggested.

Sasha kissed him again. "I can?"

"You can."

"Ah." Sasha reached down and slid him inside her once more. She was a little sore, but she didn't care at all. "Now tell me," she breathed on his lips. Errollyn ran his hands up her bare sides, over her back, making every rib glow, and every small hair tingle.

"To be *du'janah*," Errollyn said simply, "is to be without *vel'ennar*."

Sasha stopped making love to him and gave him a very blunt stare. "If that's all you've got for me, I'm kicking you out of this bed."

Errollyn grinned then laughed. Kissed her deeply. Sasha resisted a little, waiting warily for an answer. Errollyn considered her, sharp-eyed and penetrating. "Have I told you how beautiful you are?"

"Several times."

"You have an amazing shape." His hands found her hips. "Serrin women tend to be slimmer. But these hips are extraordinary. And your eyes, so dark and exotic . . ."

"Yes, yes, yes," Sasha said impatiently. "I know, dark features are so exotic to serrin. Big deal. Give me an answer or you're lying on the floor."

Amusement flashed in his eyes. "You try to be tough, but you're just putty in my hands."

"Oh yeah?"

Errollyn's arms came about her, and he moved firmly against her, up between her thighs. He kissed her, a hand coming up into her hair, and suddenly she was struggling for breath.

"Errollyn . . ." she managed, barely freeing herself. "Look, stop it, I'm serious!"

"You don't look serious," he whispered to her, not stopping at all. "You look excited."

"Oh spirits . . . no, look, just . . ." He rolled her over, effortlessly, half pinning one arm. He weighed so much more than she and, at this range, his power was daunting. She ought to have been alarmed, she knew. She disliked being helpless. And yet, for all her warning instincts, she'd never been so desperately pleased to be overpowered in all her life.

She cried out as Errollyn made love to her. Her heart thudded madly against her ribs, and she could no longer breathe but gasp. Right when she felt herself on the early road to her third climax of the day, Errollyn paused.

"To be serrin is to be one, Sasha," he murmured, gazing into her eyes. "To be one like this." He moved against her. Sasha retained barely enough dignity to feel embarrassed that her only reply was a half-muffled squeal against her bitten lip. "This is the *vel'ennar*. It is the oneness. We do not know each other's thoughts, and we cannot read each other's minds, but it is close. When King Leyvaan invaded, serrin from everywhere came immediately. They did not wait for a message, they simply knew something was wrong. They *felt* it, Sasha, as you feel me."

Oh dear spirits, she certainly did. She kept her mouth shut, not trusting herself with words.

"To feel the *vel'ennar* is to never feel alone. It is to never feel insecure in company. It is to never hate those who think differently. That is why we don't kill each other, Sasha—or not for a thousand years, at least. That is why we are collective, as humans are not. That is what makes us different from you."

"Except that you . . ." Sasha managed, with a struggle for composure. "You don't have it?"

"No." His eyes gleamed, though whether it was from anger, or arousal, Sasha could not say. "I am the throwback. I am what serrin were, a thousand years and more ago, back when we *did* still kill each other. Sometimes I think they fear me. The entire, collective philosophy of the serrinim rests on the assumption of *vel'ennar*. They depend on it, especially in this conflict with humans. They look to our differences, and cling to them. They see the likes of me as threatening the balance. So they send me out into the wilds, like they sent poor Dahlren, before they made her so bitter that she abandoned them entirely to seek a solitary life and death in the foothills.

"That's what made me so mad, Sasha. I grew to love Dahlren, but I feared that this wretched, bitter person would be me, given enough time. I want to feel the *vel'ennar*, I've always wanted it, as badly as I want you now, so badly it hurts. But I could not. Other children would exchange smiles at the unspoken humour, and I wanted to know what the joke was. Others would form bonds, the nature of which always baffled me. They knew I was different, and they were kind, but their kindness smothered, as though they thought I suffered from some terrible, incurable disease, when, as far as I knew, I was perfectly healthy.

"In time, I learned to turn it to a strength. I debated the philosophies in councils in ways that few had ever heard before. All judged that my differences gave me a unique insight and I became valuable to them. I joined the *talmaad* and was posted here to Petrodor. But Rhillian, for all her kind words, never respected my insights, nor understood them. And if she cannot understand one of her own kind, how can she possibly understand humanity?

Vel'ennar is a blindness, Sasha. It makes serrin safe from themselves. But it is the sword that humans shall use to strike off serrin heads."

Sasha put a hand on his cheek and smiled at him. "Thank you," she said. "But Errollyn . . . tell me what you *feel*. What does it feel like? I want . . . I want to get inside you. I want to know who you are." Even as the words left her lips, she knew that she was falling in love. It wasn't wise, she knew, but like the passionate lust that drove them to such craziness beneath this blanket, there was nothing she could do about it.

Errollyn kissed her, long and lingering. "Right now," he said softly, "I feel only you. And in truth, I prefer it that way."

Rhillian leaned upon the ship's railing and watched the small boat struggle against the wind and swell. Two men worked the oars, and a smaller figure waited in the bow. That would be Adele. Adele was good at sneaking. Like Aisha, she'd been running messages at the time of the attacks. It was the main reason she was still alive.

The wind blew the smoke from Dockside's pyres back onto the slope, wreathing the city in the ashes of the dead. An orange sun set upon the ridge, shrouded in black. Yethel would have thought it a magnificent image, and sought his easel and paints. But Yethel was dead. Feshaan. Ylith. Reshard. Terel. All her friends. Her *talmaad*. Her responsibility. Rhillian wanted to cry, but the tears would not come. Her heart had broken. Crying now would break her soul. She had to be strong. The storm was coming.

Adele climbed over the railing and made her way along the rolling deck. Several of the human staff watched blankly from where they sat about the mast. They had come from properties in Angel Bay, the only places to have survivors. Some had nothing left, and departed their home with the only family they'd ever known. Adele's blue–black braids tossed in the wind, her lean face worn with lines that had not been there a few days ago.

"Neither Patachi Maerler nor his people would see me," she said tautly as she reached Rhillian's side. "It's over. Patachi Steiner will take command of the Torovan army and march on Saalshen."

"I believe the human word is 'cowardice,'" said Kiel, in Torovan. He had appeared out of nowhere, but Rhillian barely blinked. She was accustomed to that. Kiel's calf was heavily bandaged, but he walked well enough, and held his balance on the rolling deck.

"Cowardice," Rhillian corrected in Lenay, gazing at the smoke-wreathed hills. "It sounds better in Lenay." With all its inflections of honour and blood. It suited her mood. Sasha would know what she meant.

"Patachi Maerler feels he has nothing more to gain, and everything to lose," said Adele. "With the priesthood standing so clearly against Saalshen, he cannot side with us any longer. Not if he wishes to avoid displeasing the archbishop. The balance has shifted."

"This archbishop's days are numbered," Rhillian murmured. "One way or the other, he has overestimated his power and has become a liability, for everyone. For the priesthood most of all. But the new archbishop, when he comes, will not be able to undo what has been done. His favour now rests with Patachi Steiner, and the coming war shall make Patachi Steiner even more powerful than before. Or so he hopes."

"So it's over," said Adele, with what sounded something like regret, and a lot like relief. "Do we sail?"

"Soon," said Rhillian, faintly. "Very soon."

"We cannot just run away," Kiel said firmly. "We cannot let any human see Saalshen so easily defeated."

"Soon also, my friend," Rhillian assured him. She took a deep breath. "Very soon."

"We must stand firm," Kiel insisted. "There is a storm coming."

"No," Rhillian said softly. "The storm has arrived. And it is us."

Twenty-one

"ENOUGH," SASHA GASPED, pushing weakly at Errollyn's shoulder. "Dear gods, enough." Errollyn nuzzled at her ear, kissed her neck and then finally slid off her. She turned away from him, and he pressed close against her back, pulling her to him. Sasha bit back a happy grin . . . it felt improper to feel so good, when so much else was bad. But it had always been her philosophy to take her pleasure where and when it came, and devil take the consequences. A lamp flickered on the table by the door and their clothes lay together on the floor where they'd tossed them. Their weapons arrayed carefully against the wall.

"You appeal to the gods now?" Errollyn murmured in her ear.

"What?"

"Just now. You appealed to the gods. And several times before. Somewhat more loudly."

Sasha tried to frown at him over her shoulder, but that was hard. She knew he was teasing her, again. Errollyn found these things amusing. "I was born Verenthane, they won't mind."

"That implies you're no longer Verenthane, in which case they probably will."

"You can be quite annoying sometimes, do you know that?"

"You don't seem to mind too much." His hand strayed down her flat stomach. "If you prefer my less lucid thoughts, we could make love again."

"No," she protested. "I can't. Damn it, Errollyn, that's five times in a day. It hurts."

Errollyn put his arms around her and rested his mouth against her hair. "And how does it feel to be no longer a virgin?"

From a human man, the question might have been insulting. But from a serrin . . . Sasha smiled wryly. "I was only ever a virgin in body, never in spirit."

Errollyn laughed softly. "Good answer. Almost serrin, in fact."

"I suppose if pressed, I could take that as a compliment."

For a short moment, she was content. He made her forget about all the killing, and the fear. She found a moment to wonder if that was a good thing . . .

A new shroud of gloom threatened to settle, but Errollyn's lips found her neck and his hand explored her thigh, and the gloom lifted. She turned within his arms, kissed him some more and then settled against his shoulder.

. . . and was woken by a horrid, acrid smell. Her head spun as though she were falling, even lying in bed. She pressed her face hard to the pillow, trying to hold her breath. Hands grabbed her, a knee pressed to her back, her arm twisted to prevent her reaching for the knife beneath the pillow. Something hit her from the side, perhaps Errollyn fighting back . . . but she dared not lift her face and risk a lungful of the acrid stench.

The next thing she knew, she was still facedown on the bed, not knowing how much time had passed. She reached for Errollyn with a hand, and found only sheets. Beneath her pillow, the knife was missing. She risked a sniff of the air, and found the smell strong, yet not overpowering. She pulled the blanket up, pressing it to her face . . . the air stung her eyes, and someone had put out the lamp. Stumbling off the bed in the dark, she felt for the weapons along the wall, finding nothing. Her impulse was to rush out the door and after Errollyn . . . but she was naked, weaponless, and her eyes were stinging. What could she do in such a state?

She reached instead for the washroom door and pushed inside, fumbling on the cold stones for the water bucket. She dunked her hands and washed her face and eyes, and blinked blearily around in the darkness. The room seemed to lean sideways . . . she took several steps and her bare foot kicked something familiar. She bent and her hands found . . . her sword. Not stolen, then, but placed in the washroom. Who would . . . ? Who . . . ?

She swore in Lenay, and heard a distant crash from downstairs. Taking a deep breath, she dashed back through the sleeping chamber, then out the door. The trapdoor to the stairs was open and she ran down fast, the night air chill on her bare skin. Her nudity might have bothered her, were it not for the blade in her hands. The sword gave her more comfort than any number of clothes could have done. Beyond the softness of her own footsteps, she heard a muffled grunt and a harsh whisper of voices.

Sasha reached the base of the stairs by the wall, and slid the sword free, placing its scabbard silently on the pavings. Statues loomed about, poses softly outlined in the dim light from overhead windows. Hands reaching for the stars, clasping in fury, wide open in exclamation, or grand gesture. Stone faces stared, mouths gaped silently, hard eyes watchful in the dark.

Sasha held her blade low, two-handed, and took one careful step after another. Her eyes slowly searched the dark, wide and unfocused as she tried desperately to stop from blinking lest they tear up once more, red and irritable. She stayed close to a row of statues, ready to dive for cover in case of an archer, or to parry hard. Somehow she doubted either eventuality. If they'd wished her dead, surely they'd have slit her throat in bed. But neither was she in a mood for generosity.

She heard movement over by a far wall, something heavy. She took a careful step around a great figure of a winged god, and found a shadow near the leg of another statue had come to life. The shadow was all blackness, save for a pair of luminescent emerald eyes and a motionless silver blade. The eyes were familiar. Sasha stared in disbelief.

"Rhillian?" she whispered.

"Sasha," came the quiet reply. "Go back to bed."

Sasha took a deep, quivering breath. When she spoke, there was a painful lump in her throat. "Not without Errollyn."

"You are a beautiful woman, Sasha. You can have any man you like. But not this one."

"You . . . you've gone mad. What in all the hells are you doing?"

"Restitution," said Rhillian softly. There was something faintly odd in her stance. A slight sideways edge to her position, a barely perceptible backward slant to one shoulder. Her sword was not raised, held only in one hand, but it was bare. Clearly Rhillian was defending something. Perhaps Errollyn had put up more of a fight than expected, and several strong serrin were having difficulty carrying him. Perhaps one had been injured. For the first time in her life, Sasha found herself hoping so.

"Get out of my way," she demanded. She edged a step forward, then another. Rhillian took in the posture, with the recognition of one who read such things as a scholar might read a text. Sasha's head still swam, and her knees were weak. She would not need clothes to take Rhillian, but balance would be useful. There weren't many opponents she was uncertain against, face to face. Rhillian was one.

"Would you kill me?" Rhillian asked. Her tone was not wounded, as Sasha might have expected. It was bland. Almost cold.

"Kill you? You attacked me!"

"You are still alive."

"In my culture," Sasha retorted through gritted teeth, "that makes no difference. You had no right. Now, I do."

"Ah," said Rhillian flatly. "Lenay honour. So, go ahead."

Sasha stared at her. To either side of the winged god's legs there was clear space until the next statue. Sasha stepped left, and Rhillian came across to block her. Still Rhillian did not raise her blade. Sasha moved right, and again

Rhillian blocked her path. Somewhere in the dark beyond, serrin were hauling Errollyn, probably unconscious, out onto the dock. Sasha braced herself to feint one way and dash past the other . . . but that was bare steel in Rhillian's hand. She might dodge Rhillian's grasp, but not her blade. If Rhillian swung, she would have to swing back. Very few svaalverd exchanges ended in disengagement. If strokes were exchanged, most likely one of them would die.

"Damn you, Rhillian!" Sasha shouted. She was trembling. She couldn't do it. She was leaving Errollyn to his fate.

"He is dangerous to us, Sasha," said Rhillian. "He knows so much about us. The workings of the councils, the likely actions of various people, even the composition of the armies of the Saalshen Bacosh. He has made clear that we cannot trust him. And so, he must be removed."

"He's with the Nasi-Keth, Rhillian! You think *we're* the enemies of Saalshen now?"

"We have relied on others for our defences. No longer. The line has been drawn. If Saalshen needs something done, we do it ourselves. The actions of others have disappointed."

"Horseshit!" Sasha retorted. "Your actions, your choice, Rhillian. Always."

"We *have* no choice," Rhillian said shortly.

"No! You chose!" Sasha levelled her blade furiously. "You could have worked with Kessligh, but you thought you knew better! You could have listened to Errollyn, but you thought you knew better! Now, you make another mistake! Your record is not very good, Rhillian! Don't you think perhaps a *wise* serrin might learn from this pattern?"

"I can't let you pass," Rhillian said softly. "I'm sorry, Sasha. You do not understand."

"That's not a reason, that's an excuse. A childish one at that. As well I might excuse the actions of King Leyvaan, or Patachi Steiner, as a matter of understanding."

"If you cannot see the difference between my actions and theirs," Rhillian said, "then truly you are lost."

In utter frustration, Sasha put her blade on the ground and walked forward. Rhillian tensed, but did not move. Sasha stopped before her, head tilted back to look the taller woman in the eyes. Rhillian's gleaming eyes were narrowed and cautious. For a brief moment, Sasha felt the overwhelming urge to strike her, bare-fisted. Rhillian held her blade off to one side. One swing would end it, and sudden movements on Sasha's part were probably not wise.

"Rhillian, what happened to you?" Sasha touched Rhillian's pale cheek. Rhillian flinched back. Serrin never did that. It was the reaction of the frightened, or the traumatised. The emerald eyes were haunted, distant. "Rhillian . . . I've seen horrors too. Wars are horrible. People die in their hundreds. You can't . . . you can't just dismiss an entire species because of one such incident . . ."

"I saw the thing that will destroy my people," Rhillian said. "I saw the hatred. I saw . . . I saw the truth that will accept no other truth. I saw the death of reason, the death of debate, the blind rule of singularity, as all humans pursue their own singularity. Even you."

"You're wrong."

"You can't reason with the unreasonable, Sasha," Rhillian said, this time in Lenay. She looked older, there was a hollowness to her cheeks. "That is the nature of the unreasonable. We tried reason. We've tried it for a long time. Look where it got us."

"And you think being unreasonable will be an improvement?"

"I don't care if they think me unreasonable. I want them to fear me."

"I don't fear you," Sasha said quietly.

"You should." For the first time, emotion struggled in Rhillian's eyes.

"And should I grow to fear you, and even to hate you, will you then consider your work a great success?"

The cold façade nearly cracked. Rhillian caught it just in time. And struggled, her eyes moist. "If it must be."

"You know I'm a bad enemy to have, Rhillian. Best that you kill me now."

A tear spilled down Rhillian's cheek. "You know I won't."

"Then I'll never fear you, and you'll have failed."

Rhillian nearly smiled. Her lips twisted faintly. She took a deep, trembling breath. "You're impossible." She leaned forward and kissed her on the forehead. "Goodbye, Sasha. Farewell. Try to understand."

Sasha embraced her. Rhillian returned it, one-armed, leaving her sword-arm free. "If you hurt him," Sasha said fiercely against Rhillian's shoulder, "I'll kill you."

"I know," said Rhillian. "You won't need to, I promise."

"Don't think for a moment this is over."

"Nothing is ever over, Sasha," Rhillian said sadly. "Endings are only the beginnings of something else."

It was only after Rhillian had departed into the dark that Sasha realised she did not know where the Shereldin Star was.

Patachi Maerler awoke to the realisation that he was not alone in his chambers. A silver blade reached nearly to the tip of his chin, gleaming in the dim light from beyond the high chamber windows. The hand about the hilt was gloved in black. Above a silken handkerchief, emerald eyes shone bright in the darkness.

At first, Alron Maerler thought he must be dreaming. These were the things of nightmares, the ghost stories about the demons of Saalshen and their ability to walk through walls. Alron knew the defences of Maerler House, and knew that it was impossible for any intruder to sneak through with nary a sound. And yet, here she was.

Alron's sleep vanished in a rush of fright.

"M'Lady Rhillian," Alron ventured. "You look displeased." From his side came a soft stirring.

"If she screams, you die," said the serrin, cold and hard. The girl in Alron's bed turned over, blinking sleepily from beneath the covers . . . and her eyes widened. Alron's hand clamped hard over her mouth, stifling the scream.

"Do not speak, do not move, do not think," Alron told her firmly. "Understand?" The girl only stared. "Understand!" Finally a terrified nod. Alron removed his hand slowly and propped himself on his pillow as the sword retreated a fraction. Some fools refused even now to recognise the martial skills of serrin women.

He stroked his long, brown hair back into place and made a smile at the demon-lady. It had worked so often before on ladies of all kinds. This particular demon-lady had seemed somewhat affected on previous visits. He saw no reason why he could not reverse this situation also.

"M'Lady Rhillian," he said, fluffing a lacy sleeve cuff languidly. "An unexpected pleasure. Pray tell me, what takes your fancy on this lovely evening?"

"You betrayed me," she said. From her posture, and the angle of her sword, it seemed to Alron Maerler that this one would be a little more difficult to charm than most.

"Betrayed?" He gave her an astonished, hurt look. "Surely not. We had an arrangement of convenience, dear lady, nothing more." The blade moved; a slow, deliberate shift of weight. At Alron's side, the girl whimpered. "Quiet, fool," he told her. She was the daughter of a cousin of Patachi

Haldera, nothing of great significance. And now it was her misfortune to hear everything that was about to be said. Such words could not be allowed to spread. Surely Cousin Taberi could think of a . . . quiet solution. Delicate, unlike the head-chopping heathens of the north slope. A drop of silverleaf in the soup, perhaps. Or a nasty fall down the stairs.

"We had an agreement," said the she-demon. "We were on the same side."

Alron nearly laughed. He bit it off in time, and struggled for a moment to contain his mirth. "Please," he finally managed, "you must understand my position. I can only fight the fights that I can win. I assure you, it pains me to see that horrid buffoon Steiner gain command of the Army of Torovan, and with the archbishop's blessing at that. The coming years shall be dark indeed for my house, as we shall be forced to pay obeisance to uncultured heathens at every turn. House Steiner's power in Petrodor shall grow, and there shall be very little I or my allies can do about it . . ." he shrugged, "I have struggled very hard to prevent such an eventuality.

"And yet, here we are. The archbishop beseeches the people to make war on Saalshen, and I cannot very well go against the archbishop, can I? He says the serrin are the enemy, he makes the believers of Petrodor and Torovan believe the serrin are the enemy . . . should I sacrifice my house, my family and partners in trade for Saalshen? Would you sacrifice Saalshen for me and mine? I think not."

"They say in Petrodor, it is death to break a deal."

"My Lady," Alron said with exasperation, "you are not being reasonable. House Maerler required an alliance with Saalshen in the short term because, although it pains me to admit it, the southern stack is a lesser stack than the northern one. Then, that alliance served some useful purpose. Now, it simply cannot be. I am very sorry that you feel betrayed, but . . ." again, he shrugged, "this is Petrodor, my Lady. The archbishop was nicely contained until he and some other assorted thugs of Steiner's started murdering the counterbalancing priests, and so he comes to this, the incitement of the crazed and desperate masses. You have suffered their wrath, my Lady, and I am sorry for it. Surely you could not expect me to volunteer for the same fate?"

It seemed that the serrin actually smiled beneath her silken handkerchief. Her snow-white hair was covered too, leaving only the green eyes visible, hovering in the dark.

"Fear not, dear Alron," she said. "All is not lost." She reached into a hidden pocket and withdrew a gleaming, golden object. Tossed it to him. A weight landed on Alron's middle. He looked with a frown . . . and his eyes widened. It couldn't be. "It is yours now," she said mildly. "You can do with it as you please. Should you proclaim to lead the Army of Torovan to replace the star in the Enoran High Temple yourself, I am sure that many would follow."

"You utter fool," Alron breathed. He did not reach for or touch the golden object. He wished to, but his hands refused to move. "What have you done?"

"I have given you power, Patachi Maerler. Power such as Marlen Steiner does not possess. Nor, indeed, the archbishop."

"You've started a war." Alron stared at her in disbelief. "Steiner and the archbishop will rally the dukes and burn the southern houses to the ground when they hear of my possession. They . . . they've . . . damn it woman, look what they did to Dockside, all to reclaim this one golden trinket!"

"Fear not the archbishop," Rhillian said softly, almost pleasantly. "His days are now finished. Another shall soon take his place, and if we do not like his propositions either, perhaps another, and then another."

Alron shook his head slowly. His heart galloped like a frightened horse. "You . . . you didn't."

Rhillian shrugged, a faint motion of the silver sword in the dark. "I sent my most capable person. I am standing here before you. I assure you, these days the archbishop is far more lacking of faithful protectors than you are. Many of his own people liked him not." The sword-tip tapped the golden star, gently. "So surprised, Patachi Maerler? So shocked? What's another little assassination between Petrodor adversaries? One of you would have done for the archbishop soon enough."

"That is a business between the men of Petrodor!" Alron insisted angrily.

Rhillian nearly laughed. "Oh, but you invited us to play, Master Maerler! Do not be such a poor sport. One can hardly complain if one invites an acquaintance into a game of dice and the acquaintance ends up taking all of your money. And please, do not think of denying you have possession of the star. You have on your staff several agents of Steiner, as you surely know, but one of them is actually an agent of ours. Already she has told Steiner that she has seen you in possession of the star."

Alron stared down at the golden weight on his chest. Beside him, a girl with only a little time left to live watched on in mute disbelief. Rhillian sauntered closer. "Think of the *power*, Master Alron," she whispered. "Long have you chafed at the brutishness of the Steiners. You fear to lose, but what if you win? What if the faithful rally to your cause? What if it is you who leads the victorious Army of Torovan into Enora and returns the holy star to its rightful place after two hundred years of absence?"

Alron wanted to touch it. He wanted to feel its weight so badly that his fingers itched. "I have Duke Abad of Songel," he said slowly.

"You have Duke Abad," she agreed. "He told me of his loyalty himself. And the Duke of Cisseren."

Even in the dark, the symbols on the golden disk seemed to glow enticingly. Alron Maerler's fingers traced their outline in the air above . . . Ancient Enoran. The Scrolls of Ulessis themselves were written in Ancient Enoran.

"Flewderin are disinterested," he said slowly. His heart was beginning to pound, but for a different reason than fear. His father and grandfather had dreamed of great prestige for Maerler and the southern families of Petrodor. The prestige of respect and glory, not of wealth and gaudy trinkets. Would his forebears have flinched should providence have delivered such a gift into their hands? Were they looking down from heaven even now, damning him for his cowardice? What a gift this was! The she-demon was a pagan, after all, and surely had no true concept of its significance. "You yourself have talked with Duke Rochel of Pazira?" He looked up, eyes burning with possibility.

"I have. Many times. Duke Rochel is most displeased at the prospect of war, and dislikes Patachi Steiner intensely, as you know."

"Neither is he a great friend of mine," said Alron with a frown.

"It is well known that the proud blood of Rochel takes unkindly to the perceived usurpers in Petrodor, be they northern or southern. But it is clear, Patachi Maerler, that if there were one patachi alone to come to prominence in Petrodor, he would prefer it to be the least powerful of the two. As you have so honestly admitted to me just now, that is you."

Alron nodded slowly. "He feels he can control me more easily than Marlen."

"But you will have the star. Such power is difficult to control. The champion of the masses, you will be. Think on it."

Patachi Maerler took a deep breath. He looked up and smiled. "M'Lady Rhillian," he said. "I thank you. You may go."

His fingers closed on the cold metal chain. Immediately, the trembling stopped.

Alexanda Rochel threw his mug of tea at the wall. It struck the stone and bounced, splashing tea over a garden painting, then across an upholstered chair. The messenger—a soldier of Captain Faldini's—stood in the doorway, and said not a word. Alexanda put both hands into his thick, untidy hair and tried to come to terms with the calamity of the message. A teacup was not enough. He picked up the whole tray and threw it with a clatter and crash of breaking crockery. Then he threw a chair.

Varona entered, wide-eyed, her hair falling haphazardly from her half-completed style, tied up with curlers and pins. A pair of young maids hovered behind, anxious with hot irons in hand.

"Alexanda?" Varona looked angry at first then dismayed as she saw the broken crockery. Her husband could be ill-tempered, but he rarely broke things. Then, as she gazed at him, she began to feel frightened. Alexanda stared at her, bleakly and rubbed at his face.

"Patachi Maerler has the star," he said at last, tiredly.

Varona stared at him for a moment. "I'd heard . . ." she ventured. "I mean, Elisa was just saying that she'd heard . . . someone saying that the archbishop was dead?"

Alexanda let out a long breath. She didn't understand. She was a damn sight smarter than many of the men who thought to advise him, but she was from a different world.

"Yes, the archbishop is dead," he said wearily, leaning heavily on the tabletop. The table was all set for breakfast, rows of ornate plates and cutlery gleaming in the morning light. A breakfast with his favourite earls and their wives, a rare pleasure. He should have known better. "Of course he's dead, our girl Rhillian is sweet and civilised on the surface, but she's certainly no saint. If someone had ordered a massacre of my friends and family, I'd have done the same and worse."

"You think Rhillian killed the archbishop?" Varona looked shocked.

"Her or one of her *talmaad*. It makes no difference, dearest, that's not what's important here . . ."

"Rhillian could never do such a thing! She's . . . she's such a sweet girl, and she respects human customs all too much!" Alexanda sighed and looked at the ground. Varona came close, upset and clutching the Verenthane medallion about her neck. "I . . . I heard that he'd been killed horribly, Alexanda! Elisa heard . . . she heard that he'd been . . . that he'd been . . ."

"He was found in very small pieces piled into a bucket, yes," Alexanda said flatly. "The bucket was found on his bed, the archbishop's hat perched on top. There were guards standing watch outside his chamber. They never heard a thing."

"There won't be enough for a proper burial coffin," Varona breathed, horrified. "The rites will be . . . I mean, his soul . . ."

"Whatever soul that man had deserves hellfire and damnation for what he ordered," Alexanda told his wife grimly. He took her hands in his. "He was not a true Verenthane, my sweet. Do you understand that? He was an impostor, and he betrayed every true believer with what he did."

"But . . . but to kill a man of such stature in that way . . . I'd . . . I'd have thought the serrin had more *principles*!"

"The serrin are pagan, my dear. Principles mean different things to them. Just because they're well-behaved in polite society doesn't mean we should mistake them all for saints. They're also very frightened. The forces arrayed against them are formidable, and set on the annihilation of their entire people. Worse yet, Rhillian's friends were massacred before her eyes. Imagine you should see such a thing happen to me, to Bryanne, to Carlito and—"

"Oh Alexanda, *stop*!" Varona glared at him, horrified. "I will *not* contemplate such a thing!"

"What would you want to do, dearest, to the man who ordered it?" Alexanda gazed at her firmly. There was fear in his wife's lovely eyes. Fear and concern. Dear gods, he loved her so much. "Varona, Patachi Maerler has the Shereldin Star. I have no idea how, but perhaps some suspicions. He has declared himself its rightful guardian, and invited all who follow its cause to unite behind him as leader of the Torovan Army on the grand crusade."

"And what will you do?" Varona asked fearfully.

"I will do what I have to do," Alexanda said. "I will do what I've been desperately trying to avoid since the first moment I arrived in this gods-forsaken city. I will pick a side."

Barely had the barricades been abandoned than they were being manned again. Grim, tired Docksiders stood in rows, improvised weapons at the ready. As late afternoon shadows fell across the incline, upper Petrodor was burning. Sasha sat atop a Dockside roof and polished her sword. There were fires everywhere. Famous houses were ablaze. Smoke blackened the sky and, when the wind shifted, there would come loudly the screams, shouts and clashing steel of battle.

A man climbed out the trapdoor nearby and sat beside her. It was Bret, his previous thin beard now shaved to allow easy access to a shallow cut on his jaw. He gazed up at the battle.

"They're not fighting with sticks and knives up there," he observed.

Sasha kept polishing. The blade was so brilliant now she could see her reflection.

"They say Rhillian gave Maerler the star," Bret added when Sasha did not reply. "Makes you wonder why Maerler didn't just have his brother priest bring him the star, if he wanted it so badly."

"Some priests have morals," Sasha said darkly. "Some serrin don't." Bret just looked at her, long and wordlessly. Sasha kept polishing, crosslegged on her chair. "Maerler's a damn fool. Even Patachi Steiner didn't try to take possession of the star directly. He at least knows no one will ever confuse him with a saint."

"Patachi Maerler has always been a proud and vain man," Bret agreed. "Patachi Steiner is just greedy. Rhillian must have decided to chance Maerler's vanity."

"Her opinion of humans is at its lowest ebb," Sasha muttered. "And we keep fulfilling her expectations."

"What do you think she intends?" Bret asked, nodding toward the conflagration. It would take months, Sasha was sure, for the smell of ash to wash from the Dockside. "I mean . . . what does this gain her?"

"She wants to see Petrodor bleed. She sets humans at each other's throats. She hopes there'll be nothing left with which to fight a war."

"She's mad," Bret said softly. "All she'll create is a single victor. And then we'll have tyranny."

"She doesn't think it could get any worse."

Bret shook his head sadly. "These serrin, they think they know everything. She hasn't seen anything yet."

More to the left, a new mansion was on fire. Nearer to Sharptooth, now. The fighting seemed to be heading that way. Perhaps Patachi Maerler was losing, but Sasha knew that it was rarely so simple. More likely, the two sides would batter each other to a bloody draw. Just taking one ridgetop mansion would cost the lives of many soldiers. By the time Steiner's forces managed to smash their path all the way to Maerler House atop Sharptooth, most of the army would be dead.

A mansion's roof caved in, followed by a rumbling crash of collapsing masonry and a billow of sparks. Gasps and exclamations went up from the neighbouring rooftops. Some children sounded excited and their parents were not discouraging them. Many Docksiders seemed happy to see the upper slopes burning for a change. Sasha wondered if they'd be quite so pleased when Bret's prediction came true.

Bret looked at her for a moment longer. "Kessligh has forbidden it, you know." Sasha gave him a blank, questioning look. "Going after Errollyn."

Sasha returned her attention to her sword. "I'm not going after Errollyn."

"And you'd never lie to me, would you Sasha?"

"If you're so unsure that you need to ask the question, what possible use would my answer be?"

Bret took a deep breath. "Rhillian won't hurt Errollyn, Sasha. She hasn't gone that far yet."

"Kiel would."

"But Kiel's not in charge, is he?"

"They're serrin, stupid," Sasha muttered. "They don't understand the concept. Kiel follows Rhillian on the big picture, but on smaller matters he does as he pleases."

"Sasha . . . wouldn't it just be better to let it all end here? Everyone's suffered enough."

"There was a great warrior in Lenay legend named Tragelyon," said Sasha, still polishing. "He led his people to a new land and settled them in an uninhabited valley. His neighbours didn't like it and gathered a warband to attack. Tragelyon challenged them to single combat, and drew a circle in the dirt around him with his sword. Every attacker who entered that circle died.

"That's where we get the tachadar circles from today. Tachadar in old Taasti means space, but more than space. A personal space, to which every man's honour entitles him, no matter if he is in his homeland, or travelling in a strange land. That's why we don't hug and kiss so much as Torovans do. You only enter that tachadar when invited. When stepping into the circle for sparring, we always ask permission on the other person's honour.

"I have my tachadar, Bret, even in this city. And Errollyn has his, even though he's not Lenay—he speaks it well enough, and he fought for Lenayin, he's earned Lenay honour. Rhillian didn't just spit on it, she pissed on it—mine and his. It's unacceptable."

"But Errollyn is more than your friend," Bret said quietly. Sasha didn't look up. "And maybe Rhillian felt, by taking him into your bed, you crossed *her* circle."

"No," said Sasha, very firmly. "You can't claim another person unless they want you to. Errollyn came into my bed by choice. He left Rhillian's service by choice. She pissed on that too."

"Sasha . . . here in Petrodor, we also have tales and legends. There is one of two sisters who loved each other very dearly and both married powerful men from different families. Those families have a falling out, which turns to conflict. The carnage is great and, with each family member killed, the two sisters grow to hate each other more and more. Finally, one day, they find that all of their families are dead, and only the two of them remain . . . and yet, despite their families having been the only cause of their hatred, they still cannot bring themselves to reconcile."

Sasha gazed at him. For the first time since Bret had sat down, she stopped polishing. "What happened to them?"

"They died together, each impaled on the other's sword." Sasha swallowed hard and gazed up at the flames. "It is a terrible thing, Sasha, to fight a friend."

"And is a friend still a friend," Sasha asked quietly "when she destroys those things I most care for?"

"Errollyn is not dead, Sasha. Nor will he be."

"Yesterday Errollyn. Today Petrodor. What tomorrow, Bret? For how long must she desecrate my circle and expect me to sit here on my hands and do nothing?"

Alexanda Rochel strode up the winding, firelit road and tried not to look too hard at the bodies of the dead. Ahead, a wall had collapsed, spilling brick and stone across the cobbles. Amidst the debris lay men in the colours of several southern-stack houses, and others in the maroon and gold of Pazira. Some lay locked together where they'd fallen, arms about the other like old friends. Several soldiers tried to bind the wounded arm of a sobbing comrade. Burning buildings lit the men, walls and bodies in a dancing, hellish glare, and smoke seared at the back of Alexanda's throat.

Alexanda paused before the wounded man. "Hold on, lad, you'll be home soon. This is but a moment in time, be brave and it will pass." The man tried, but Alexanda could see the arm was half severed. He strode on, repeating his own words in his head. Be brave, and it will pass. The lad had been about Carlito's age. Dear gods.

On a bend ahead, crouched against a wall, a Pazira soldier sheltered behind a huge wooden shield. He gestured wildly at the duke, urging him to caution . . . already the shield was peppered with at least ten bolts. Another flashed by, skittered off the wall and clattered around the bend, men jumping aside as it came. Alexanda, a sergeant and four personal guard hugged a wall, then ran quickly up and over piled bricks to a huge hold in the wall opposite.

Within was the rear yard of a grand mansion, its lawns and patterned gardens strewn with debris and bloody corpses. Ahead, doors and windows had been smashed in and entrances were now guarded by Pazira soldiers. Alexanda walked inside, down a grand hall littered with broken ornaments and furniture. There were sword cuts in the wall plaster. Here, a spray of blood from a severed artery. There, a body.

Up a flight of stairs, then another, and through more ruined rooms until he reached a balcony. There, behind an ornamental pot large enough to hold three men, crouched Captain Faldini in animated conversation with a lieutenant.

"My Lord!" Faldini said cheerfully, his eyes sharp with enthusiasm. "Hell of a fight, yes?" His breastplate bore a great scar and his chain mail sleeves were spattered with blood. "A great shame young Carlito is not here to see it, he would have made you proud!"

"Thank the gods for that mercy at least," Alexanda muttered, taking a knee beside his captain. He had to adjust his own breastplate as he did—it did not fit half so well these days as it had, the buckles tight at his shoulders, and always seeming to slip to his hips. "Where the hells are we?"

"Nearer to Sharptooth than nearly anyone else!" Faldini exclaimed. "Look, now we have this place, our men secure this road here . . ." Faldini gestured to the dark shadow of street directly ahead, then pointed to the leather map unrolled on the balcony before him. "I don't know what it's called, but it leads right to The Crack, just south of Sharptooth. We're nearly there!"

They were on the Backside-side of the ridgeline, both Alexanda and Faldini having concluded that it was the softest route to Sharptooth. Those fools Belary and Tarabai were thrusting straight along the ridgeline road, and were nothing like as close as this. Probably they were up to their necks in the bodies of their own dead by now. Duke Tosci of Coroman had taken an even more downslope route—to Alexanda's south up the Backside slope, thrusting to clear the ridge squarely into the middle of the southern stack.

Steiner and his patachis were pressing through midslope, knowing that maze of winding roads far better than the Torovan dukes. There was talk of a seaborn attack as well, and a landing upon the southern docks. With no view of the ocean, Alexanda had no idea if that was just talk or not.

Abad of Songel, it was said, was fighting for Maerler, but Pazira had not yet met him in battle if that were the case. Of Flewderin and Cisseren, there was no word, only rumour. Clearly Maerler was badly outnumbered. But in this city, the odds of any battle were stacked so heavily with the defender that numbers were meaningless. The serrin had held out for much of a day with just a handful of *talmaad* against thousands.

"We're getting lots of white cloth hung over the walls," Faldini continued. "Many of them don't want to fight."

"Doesn't help us much if they won't let us in," Alexanda grumbled. He peered through the balcony railings onto the narrow street below. Pazira men were mustering in formation, shields to the front, rams, hooks and grapples behind. Captain Faldini had done his work well, preparing for this even while Alexanda strove his utmost to try to ensure it would never happen. There were even draught horses held in reserve. They'd brought down several defensive walls so far, and would surely be needed for more.

Faldini was not bothering with the artillery some of the other dukes were using—it took too many men and horses to haul, he'd insisted, was difficult to manoeuvre in close corners and nearly impossible to fire accurately on sloping ground. Better yet, Pazira forces now took short cuts between roads by smashing through mansions—"in the front door and out the back," as he'd put it. No artillery worth its use could fit through a doorway.

"How many men have we lost?" Alexanda asked.

"I haven't been counting," Faldini admitted. "Perhaps thirty?"

"More likely fifty," Alexanda growled, giving his captain a dark stare. "I've been counting the bodies on the way down the road."

Faldini shrugged. "That's why they love you more than me," he said with a grin. Were Faldini not such a competent officer, Alexanda was certain he would love him not at all. It was one of the great ironies of life that often the most bloodthirsty and cruel commanders suffered the least grievous losses. Bloodthirsty commanders won quickly. Quick victors suffered fewer deaths. A cautious officer could become bogged down, his indecision prolonging the fight, and thus killing more of his own men. In war, as in so many things, the gods displayed their foul sense of humour.

Longbow fire thumped and whistled from a neighbouring balcony, then from the roof above the two men's heads. Arrows fled into the firelit night toward the mansion at the road's end where the crossbow fire seemed to be coming from. Longbows would do little good at such range, but the object, Faldini explained, was to put the opposing archers off their aim and jangle the enemy's nerves with incoming fire. Good longbow men could fire six or more times to a crossbow's every one, suiting them better for the purpose.

"They'll know how close we are now," Alexanda muttered. "Several more mansions like this one and we'll cut through to Sharptooth. They'll pull up some reserves, perhaps make a flanking move downslope to our right, and come at us from there."

"Let them flank to our right," Faldini said. "If they grant us the height and attack from downslope, we'll slaughter them. Better yet, the defensive advantage becomes ours, we've these magnificent big shields you had the foresight to bring in such large numbers . . ." Alexanda snorted, recalling Faldini's protests at the big ugly things, "we can make a wall across the road and dare them to scale it.

"Besides which, I've seen no indication these city fools actually understand concepts like 'reserve' and 'flanking attack.' So far most of them have been defending their own property and no one else's. Only Maerler's staunchest allies are fighting, the rest are sitting quietly behind their walls waiting to see which way the wind is blowing."

"Captain Faldini, if I can persuade you of just one thing that my advancing years have taught me, it is this—things can always get worse, and usually do. If one expects it, then one can avoid the indignity of surprise."

"I always liked surprises," Faldini remarked, watching the preparations for the battle's next phase with eager anticipation.

"Then you're a fool. In battle, surprise is usually followed swiftly by a painful death."

"My Lord, if I might suggest . . . maybe I just enjoy this more than you?"

Alexanda shook his head in disbelief. "Truly you are a man of great insight. Carry on, Captain, do your worst."

"You know I always do, my Lord."

Twenty-two

ERROLLYN SAT IN THE CARGO HOLD, chained to the mast, and listened to the commotion up on deck. He could hear the ballista firing, and feel the thumping vibration through the decking. The thick mast trunk shuddered and creaked with the strain of billowing sails, and he could hear the yells and instruction, the rapid winching of ropes and the squeal of pulleys.

He sat with his knees drawn up, his ankles chained and his arms flexed back to embrace the mast behind. His wrists were chained together around the mast, and the manacles dug into his hands. His ankle chains, in turn, were tied to the base of the mast so that he could not stretch his legs. It hurt. His previous injuries stiffened and throbbed, and the air down here was foul, a thick stench of old grain, livestock, manure and rot. About him, crates and sacks made looming shapes in the gloom, creaking each time the boat rocked over a wave, or turned against the wind. He had never particularly minded the movement of boats, provided he could be on deck with the horizon in sight and the fresh ocean breeze on his face. Now, he felt ill. He hated enclosed spaces. Rhillian knew he did. Yet she ordered him tied down here anyway.

And now, it seemed, they were under attack. Whoever it was unsurprisingly seemed to be having difficulties catching the Saalshen vessel. He judged that they were still in Petrodor harbour—with a wind this brisk, surely an open ocean swell would move the boat more than this.

A movement to one side made him look as light flickered through the gloomy hold. A figure appeared, small and unsteady, moving slowly. The lamp in her hand turned Aisha's short, pale hair to orange, and her blue eyes to shimmering amber pools. She limped to him, wrapped in a blanket, clutching a waterskin and a bundle. Errollyn took a deep breath and tried to will his uneasy stomach calm. Here, at least, was one person who felt significantly worse than he.

"You shouldn't walk on that leg," he told her as she knelt alongside. His voice was hoarse and his throat dry.

"Shut up and drink," Aisha told him in Lenay—his preferred human tongue. Aisha had always been better at tongues than everyone. She even spoke Edu, though she'd only been in the Valley of the Udalyn a few days. She unstoppered the waterskin and poured into his mouth. Through thirst and discomfort, Errollyn did not fail to note that her hands were shaking.

"What have they done to you?" Aisha half-muttered, half-despaired. "Errollyn, why do you always have to be such a pain in the arse?" The expression held a humour in Lenay that most other tongues lacked. An affection behind the insult.

Errollyn swallowed the last of her water. "Let me out," he said.

Aisha just gazed at him, pained, pale and unsteady. She hated boats, whether above decks or below. "Aisha, Rhillian's gone mad. She's lost all sense. Just let me out of these fucking chains."

Aisha put the waterskin and the bundle down, and moved around the mast, out of Errollyn's sight. He felt her hands on his, feeling the chafing where the metal bands pressed hard into his skin. Again he heard her muttering to herself. Overhead, the ballista fired again, and more shouts as others watched the projectile's progress. They were firing *ashlro'mal* up there—liquid fire. Doubtless their targets were not enjoying the experience.

"Look," said Aisha, reappearing at his side, "I've found some good grapes and some plums, all fresh, and some blue-tinge cheese from Halsradi to the north, it'll help you—"

"Damn it, Aisha, I need escape, not cheese!"

"It's excellent cheese," Aisha ventured, attempting humour.

"You and your fucking cheese!" Errollyn snarled. "I saved your life, isn't that worth something?"

Aisha sat on the deck with a thump, and winced as she pulled her wounded leg clear. She stared at Errollyn helplessly. "Errollyn, I . . . I can't."

"Then fuck off and take your cheese with you!" His heart was pounding, and his head spinning. He could barely feel his hands and the numbness was spreading up his arms. His back and shoulders screamed for relief, and his lungs despaired for clean air. Some people thought Aisha younger than him, but she was nearly ten years his senior. He didn't need another lecture.

"Errollyn . . . they said . . . one of the shipmates said you hurt Tasselryn. With a knife."

"When being abducted by force in the night," Errollyn said coldly, "it is customary practice in human lands or in Saalshen to fight back. Tasselryn was clumsy, and I got a hand free long enough to grab for his belt. I *could* have slashed his throat, but these days Rhillian seems short on gratitude."

"Errollyn, no serrin has purposely slain another for more than a thousand years!" Aisha's pale blue eyes were wide with horror. "Has . . . has it occurred to you even once what you nearly did?"

"What *I* did?" He managed a half-crazed laugh. "Rhillian hits me in the face, and I'm to blame that her knuckles are bruised?"

"Errollyn, you nearly killed another serrin!"

"His arm is a long way from his heart, Aisha."

"How can you make jest of this? I . . . I don't believe that you . . ."

"Aisha, it makes absolutely no fucking difference," Errollyn told her coldly. "So what if one serrin kills another? That would only make us normal. We're the odd ones, Aisha, the ones who fail to understand the world. Every other species kills its own kind, or would like to if it could. But we . . . we cling to matters of little import as though they were all that mattered in the world. Let a million of us die, but please, don't let just one of them be slain by his fellow serrin . . . what a joke. This species has no perspective. I'm sick of you all."

"We strive to make the world better by holding ourselves above it, Errollyn," Aisha whispered, horrified. "If you can't understand even that, then . . . then you are beyond me."

"How can you make the world better when you can't even think for yourself?" Errollyn retorted. "Let me free, Aisha!" Aisha just stared at him. "You can't, can you? The *vel'ennar* is the wind that fills your sails, and you will go wherever it blows. You could not contradict your fellows if they were butchering small children!"

"Unlike you, Errollyn," Aisha said coldly, "I have seen small children butchered. Do not speak of that you do not know."

"And when Kiel impales his first human newborn on the point of a sword, what shall you do, Aisha?"

"Kiel would never—"

"He damn well would and you know it!"

Aisha stared at him. Above, the ballista thumped again. The boat leaned again, the vibration of flapping sails through the mast as they changed direction. Aisha's eyes dropped to the boards.

"You can't answer the question, can you? You can't let me free. You can't contradict Rhillian. You can't move. You are half human, yet I am less serrin than you. I am tied to the mast, yet it is you who are in chains."

"It got me out of Maerler's mansion," Aisha said softly. "The *vel'ennar*. It pulled me free, Errollyn. I felt it calling me, tugging at me. I had to be back amongst my own kind. I did not wish to die alone, amongst strangers."

"I can love a stranger, Aisha," Errollyn said hoarsely. His throat hurt, but this time it was not for dryness. "I can want her safe and happy, even though she is not of the serrinim, nor connected to it. Can you?"

"My father is human," Aisha replied.

"No," Errollyn said firmly. "He is within your *vel'ennar*. As the household staff at Palopy were within Rhillian's, human or not. I mean someone else. Could you love them that much, Aisha?"

"As much as you love Sasha?" Aisha ventured. Errollyn just stared at her, demanding an answer. "I don't know," she said, very softly. "I'd like to think so. But . . . I don't know."

"So where lies the serrin claim to universal tolerance when you look at me like a stranger? When you see me tied to the mast like an animal and cannot set me free? When you know me for all these years, and you still have not a clue why I am like I am, or what it feels like to walk in my shoes?"

Aisha fixed him with a direct stare. "You're feeling very sorry for yourself, Errollyn," she said warningly.

"No," said Errollyn, "I'm feeling very sorry for you. At least I can feel my chains and understand that I am a prisoner. You cannot even see the cage around you."

"Errollyn," Aisha said despairingly, "why do you do this to yourself? You push others away, you reject their assistance . . ."

"I see you offering cheese, not assistance."

"You attack and humiliate them . . ."

"We serrin call it debate, if we're not impossibly thin-skinned . . ."

"And then you point in triumph, and say, 'Look! She doesn't understand me! My arguments are fulfilled!'"

"Would you ever choose to be without the *vel'ennar*, Aisha?"

"No." Decisively.

"Why not?"

Aisha did not reply.

"The *vel'ennar* is about inclusion, Aisha. You fear you wouldn't fit in. I'm telling you you're right. I was farmed out to an old uman on the verge of death, when I was still a child. No one else could understand me, they said. She was bitter and cynical. I am not so bitter yet. But as time goes on, I see that perhaps she was right. There is no place for those without *vel'ennar* in a society whose entire ethos is inclusion. As there is no place for animals on two legs amongst those who walk on four."

Aisha placed a gentle hand on his brow and brushed back his untidy hair. "It hasn't been that bad amongst us, surely?" she asked sadly.

Errollyn took a deep breath and swallowed hard against the lump in his throat. "The worst thing," he said quietly, "is that I can love you all as much as I'll ever love anyone . . . and yet I know that what other serrin feel for me is less than what they feel for others."

"Oh Errollyn," Aisha said gently, taking his face in both hands. "It's not like that at all. You said it yourself, you do not need to feel *vel'ennar* in order to be a part of someone else's! If humans can be within a serrin's *vel'ennar,* then surely you can be too!"

"Then why am I chained to the mast?"

Aisha closed her eyes and rested her forehead against Errollyn's.

"And why have I somehow felt, my entire life, that it was always coming to this?"

"You're overreacting," Aisha assured him gently.

"Kiel wanted to kill me," Errollyn murmured, repressing a shiver. "I saw it in his eyes."

"He's upset." Aisha sounded unsettled.

"He's dangerous. He's what we could become, Aisha. All of us. His logic is impeccable. He embodies the truest heart of what it means to be serrin. And he is capable of barbarism, like what he did to the archbishop. He is our future, Aisha, if we allow it. And Rhillian walks his path more and more every day."

Aisha kissed the younger man on the forehead with great affection. "Be strong Errollyn. Know that however lonely you may feel, you are never truly alone. I love you as a brother."

"Then let me free."

"I can't," she said simply.

"Then our friendship has limits."

Aisha's eyes filled with tears. She opened her mouth to reply, closed it, then stared at the dark hullside, and piles of surrounding cargo.

"Here," she said, finally unwrapping her bundle and revealing a plate of fresh fruit and cheese. "Open wide. Try not to spill any, this is excellent quality."

The Pazira shields made a line so hard and tall that the fight had become more like wrestling than swordwork.

"Push!" Captain Faldini yelled, in unison with a heaving grunt from the front line. Men leaned into their shields like sailors into a howling gale, boots scrabbling on the debris-strewn cobbles for balance. On the flanks, men held shields over their heads, trying to give protection from the archers firing down from the mansion wall. The front gate had collapsed when the first thrust had thrown hooks over it and run the ropes down to the draught horses downslope . . . archers had tried to sever the ropes with crossbow fire, but the ropes were too thick. Oilfire had been wasted trying to burn the ropes, but it went out too quickly, and ropes did not burn without encouragement. Now the mansion's defenders were out of oilfire, and without half a wall and half a gate. Cityfolk built defences for city threats, and forgot how powerful four enormous country plough-pullers yoked together could be. The top of the wall lay smashed across the road, one gate hanging askew. Beyond this mansion (whose ever it was, Faldini neither knew nor cared) lay the mouth to Sharptooth, and glory for Pazira.

Sword and spear thrusts found the edges of the shields, men pushed side-on, keeping their bodies as narrow as possible to that threat. The rank behind pushed in turn upon the front rank's backs, and thrust with spears and swords over the top of the shield wall.

The man directly before Faldini fell to a crossbow bolt from the wall. Faldini leapt over him into the second rank, and put his shoulder into the back of the man ahead's breastplate, wielded his spear high for space, and waited for one of those on the shield wall's other side to raise his head. None did, but one of their second rank tried a spear thrust that deflected off the shields. Faldini noted where it had come from, leapt and thrust his own spear . . . it made firm contact, grating on metal, and seemed to stick. Someone screamed, one more scream above the animal grunts and groans of men, the clash of steel and the howls of the wounded.

"You city-bred, perfumed sister-fuckers have never *seen* a real war!" Faldini roared. "Die screaming, you arselickers!" Something crashed off his helm. They pushed some more and the line crept forward another arm's length, then another. The broken gate hung barely fifteen paces more down the road, and their enemies were now struggling for footing on smashed rock from the wall.

A man behind him took a bolt through the neck and fell . . . Faldini glared up in time to see the bowman crouch back down behind his battlement. "Georgi!" he yelled, still pushing, searching around him in the crush . . . and he saw the lad, aiming his crossbow up past the defensive shields. He fired, and a man atop the wall took a bolt through the face. "Good lad! Soldier, grab Georgi for me!"

He was moving backward now, his back to the shieldman, pushing hard while looking behind. Hands grabbed the young crossbowman and shoved him through the armoured crush.

"Give me that, I'll help you . . ." Faldini shouldered his spear, grabbed the crossbow's winch handles and began winding fast. Georgi fumbled in his pouch for a new bolt . . . a shot from the wall struck a man's breastplate. A spear thrust jabbed past Faldini's shoulder and hit Georgi in the chest . . . Faldini grabbed it and pulled sharply down. On the other end, the spear's owner tried to pull back down, reaching upward, and with a yell, a Pazira spearman took that chance to kill him. Georgi had only been knocked back into the man behind, and was now bending trying to recover his fallen bolt . . . "Get another one!" Faldini hauled up the crossbow and handed it to the lad. Georgi grabbed it, fitted a new bolt, his freckled face anxious beneath the rim of his steel helm. "Aim on my shoulder, I'll point him to you!"

Faldini turned, felt the clank as Georgi rested the crossbow on his shoulder . . . a surge of pushing and suddenly everyone was going sideways, Georgi struggling for balance. Then the crossbowman raised his head once more above the parapet, a new bolt fitted. "That's the swine!" Faldini roared, pointing straight. "Kill him!"

The crossbow thumped against Faldini's shoulder, and the man atop the wall fell reeling, a bolt beneath his jaw. Faldini howled triumph. Suddenly the shield wall surged forward several places, several defenders falling on the loose footing. The shieldmen ran over the top of them, and the second rank killed them where they lay. An uneven gap opened to Faldini's left between two shields and Faldini switched his spear to the backhand, took a sighting and thrust hard at the first target he saw. It deflected off a city man's smaller shield, but rocked him backward. Faldini dropped his spear and charged through the gap, pulling his short sword and driving it through an unsuspecting man's neck. He reversed right, dropping low to slice through the back of another shieldsman's leg. The man he'd tried to spear attacked, Faldini grappled him bodily, and they both lost balance on the sliding stones. Suddenly free of opponents, his own shieldsmen were surging forward, trampling their captain to make ground over the stones.

Faldini saw his first shieldsmen were already pushing through the broken gate. Some took shelter in the arch to try to open the second gate door and double the space. Others pressed into the mansion to establish their position, while shieldmen stood at their backs, warding crossbow fire from above. Only now, Pazira's second rank of crossbows had gained enough space to set up their own rank down the street behind a shield wall, and were peppering any defending crossbowman who raised his head.

Faldini scrambled over broken stone and shattered mortar. Then he was in through the gate, adding his own shoulder as the second gate began to swing, six men pushing with all their strength as more piled through behind. Ahead, he saw, it was all over—Pazira soldiers were pouring across the courtyard, into the mansion, up stairs and ladders up to the defensive wall where crossbowmen threw down their weapons and begged for mercy. Glass broke, pots crashed and, somewhere distant, the inevitable screams and cries of women—servants or ladies of the house, it made no difference to Faldini. They were between him and Sharptooth, and would yield, one way or the other.

On the rooftop of a neighbouring mansion, he could see crossbow-armed guards crouched and watching . . . damn fool cityfolk, he thought as he leaned on a wall removed his helm and wiped sweat from his brow. If they all stood together to defend the weak points, they'd make an impossible wall . . . but which patachi would order his own house abandoned to help defend a neighbour's? No, here they each defended their own house, and thus divided themselves into small groups that were excellently defended from other small groups, but not from the rampaging Army of Pazira. Worse, these were city-bred merchant scum without a trace of breeding, and no concept of honour or dignity—barely one house in five was actually fighting; most were just watching their neighbours getting slaughtered, and feeling glad it wasn't them. Petrodor had harboured fractious rivalries for so long they'd come to believe it a virtue. Now they discovered otherwise.

There were local men running into the courtyard now, hands over their heads, some bleeding from wounds, all terrified and expecting to die. Then women, mostly servants, then several ladies in gowns and fancy hair. Faldini refastened his helm.

"Captain! Captain!" He turned, and found Sergeant Drosi scrambling up the pile of masonry past the twisted gate. "Captain, one of the houses opened its gates and attacked! They had a white sheet over the wall, but they opened their gates anyway and hit our flank . . ."

"Which house!"

"The . . . the big one with the pillars!"

"They've all got fucking pillars man!"

"Come and see, Captain, the duke was leading the defence!"

"The duke?" Faldini spun and yelled at the nearest officer, "Prepare the next assault! I want the horses brought up, shield walls formed, and every man to have a drink and some food—we're going to need it!"

"Yes, sir!" came the reply, and Faldini was already off and running as best he could over the masonry and bodies. The duke had been a passable warrior in his day, but that day was long past. Oh, he understood strategy well enough, but there had never been a warrior's fire in his belly. It had been on Faldini's own insistence that the duke had not been leading the main force through the streets. He was a man of advancing years, Faldini had said, and his men would understand if he moved with the main body, not at the head.

The Duchess Varona had agreed vehemently. It was perhaps the only time in Faldini's memory that he and the duchess had agreed on anything.

He ran in pursuit of Sergeant Drosi, his weary legs struggling for pace on the cobbles. He passed Pazira soldiers running forward, some more tending wounded fallen in the recent assault, and dodged around a team bringing up the draught horses.

The road bent downhill and he could see the commotion—a big mansion on the inner bend, now visible, flames licking from its upper windows and men rushing across its courtyard. Faldini and the sergeant rushed into the rear guard—a chaos of wounded and dying, men dragging fallen comrades, and leaving others not in Pazira colours to bleed and scream where they lay.

Inside the wall, a Pazira crossbowman told his captain what had happened. "No warning," he said, still searching the upper balconies and the rooftop for targets, "just a squeal of gates and a roar of men . . . they lay into the back of us, we lost maybe twenty before we could reform and get the shields up." He wiped at a bloody nose. "We were moving downslope when the duke arrived with the middle reserve . . . he didn't even bother with the men attacking us, he went straight through the gates and in there." A nod toward the mansion.

"Good man," Faldini growled approvingly. Not a failure at strategy at all, his duke. These city soldiers would defend their properties first and foremost. Attacking their mansion would force them to pursue, straight back through the gates they'd come out of, and expose their backs to their enemy. "That was the end of them, then?"

"Only a handful got away, out of maybe a hundred. The duke's finishing the house."

The crash and yells of battle resounded from somewhere within, but were dimmed by the gathering roar of the fire. Men on the garden were beginning to shout, waving at others to get clear before it all collapsed. Servants and ladies ran into the yard, clutching a few children. A small, yapping dog ran frantically about the patio, barking at soldiers, barking at flaming embers, barking at the world. A few Pazira soldiers appeared at ground-level windows and doors, but they appeared to be waiting, shouting within for comrades to follow, and quickly.

"Where the hells are they?" Faldini muttered as the flames leapt higher. Windows exploded with a shattering crash and debris fell to the ground.

Finally, Faldini spotted Pazira soldiers emerging. Several supported wounded, while others merely cleared the way. Then came a cluster, like a procession, holding a limp body on their shoulders. The fallen man's helm was missing, and thick, untidy grey hair spilled onto the shoulders of his men.

"Oh mercy no!" the crossbowman beside Faldini exclaimed. "Oh please gods!" The cry crossed the courtyard in a rush, soldiers ceasing whatever they were doing to stare and exclaim, and make holy signs to the deities.

The men of Pazira laid their duke on the patio, his head lolling, his eyes gazing sightlessly at the fire-strewn sky. Faldini walked forward, helm under his arm, staring down in disbelief. The duke's breastplate was covered with blood from a cut through the throat . . . though the cut itself was invisible beneath wads of soaked cloth his desperate men had applied as they sought to defy the facts of war and flesh and sharp steel.

Some men fell to their knees and sobbed. A lieutenant called for order and dignity, but his voice was quaking. Faldini wondered if there would have been such a reaction for him, had it been his own body lying there amidst the falling, burning rain. For the first time in his life, the certain knowledge of the answer troubled him.

"I did tell you they loved you more than me," he murmured. More loudly, he said, "Can anybody tell me the name of the family who owns this property?"

"Telrani," came a reply, from a grim and wizened old corporal. "This be the house of Family Telrani."

"From this moment," Faldini announced, "there shall be no more Family Telrani in Petrodor! Where you find a Telrani, kill him! Where you find a relative of a Telrani, kill him also! Burn their property, kill their women, I want them *erased*! Sergeant Drosi!"

"Captain."

"Kill these people." He pointed to the huddled lords and ladies in the courtyard, watching their mansion burn. "Leave only the servants and children."

"Yes, Captain." Sergeant Drosi pulled his blade and went to see that done.

Children. Faldini spat. That much I grant to you, he thought silently in the direction of his fallen duke. Only you wouldn't have even killed the women, would you? Torovan was about family, first and always. Family stood together, and family died together. Old, eccentric, wealthy dreamers like Alexanda Rochel might have managed to forget that fact, but the lowborn likes of Faldini knew better. He'd see about the children another day. But not here, with his duke's body still warm.

Errollyn awoke with a pain-dazed jolt as his hands fell free. Blood rushed back into his arms, and pain crackled as though he'd driven his arm into a fire. He hissed, flexing his hands, and noticed then that the chains had been separated midlength, as though by a sword. And now the ropes about his middle were coming undone.

"Who's there?" he asked hoarsely.

"Who do you think?" came the familiar retort. "Who else would be crazy enough?" It sounded as though her teeth were chattering. Errollyn did not know whether to laugh or swear.

"Sasha, you're mad. How did you get on board?"

"When we've time enough for tales, I'll tell you. Now how in all the hells am I going to get these chains off your ankles?"

Errollyn let himself fall sideways onto one arm, and gasped with relief to lie on the decking, his back no longer cramping, his shoulders suddenly free. His feet, however, remained manacled to the base of the mast.

"Perhaps a key would be civilised?" he suggested.

"Aye, but I'd have to take that off someone, wouldn't I?" Sasha retorted, prowling about the mast, a shivering shadow in the darkness. "They're not likely to be obliging." She squatted by the chains. "I broke my first sword on chain like this, only it didn't fracture properly until the middle of a great bloody battle."

"I know, I was there." Sasha looked at him. Errollyn struggled to sit up, caught her arm and kissed her on the lips. "You're cold." The arm of her jacket was sodden beneath his hand. "You swam out?"

"Mari's boat. He swore he knew a way, which end of the ships casts a shadow from the deck light. Ship thieves sneak aboard all the time, whenever a ship is shorthanded or otherwise preoccupied." Errollyn nodded as it dawned on him. After the casualties the *talmaad* had suffered, and with the running battle in the harbour, the ship crew would be both preoccupied and shorthanded. "Mari seemed to know quite a lot about it. His misspent youth, I think."

"The battle's stopped?" Errollyn listened hard, but he couldn't hear the ballista firing.

"Some of Steiner's ships were chasing, it seems everyone's suddenly declaring themselves the rightful possessor of the Shereldin Star, and that means attacking serrin. Damn nuisance, mostly . . . three of them got burnt out and sunk, they can't exchange fire like this ship's got." She laid her sword across the ankle manacles, measuring the blow. "I can sever the chain, but you won't be able to walk, and I sure as shit can't carry you."

"Look, Sasha, you're freezing . . . you'll cut my foot off in that state. Only one person's been down here all night, and she wasn't supposed to come—get your jacket off and warm up a bit."

"No time, damn it, Mari's waiting . . ."

"Sasha, I can barely move my arms." It was true. If he tried to wield a sword he'd most likely drop it. "Jacket." He pulled at her jacket and was mildly surprised when she yielded. "Here, sit," he said as the jacket came off. Sasha sat with her back to him, knees curled up, as Errollyn rubbed her as vigorously as his weak, throbbing hands could manage. "Why come for me?" he asked.

"Didn't trust Rhillian to treat you well," Sasha replied through chattering teeth. "Looks like I was right, huh?" Her shirt was also sodden, and her skin cold beneath. Errollyn got his hands under the shirt and rubbed hard.

"I put a knife in one of them," Errollyn explained sourly. "They didn't take it well."

"Most people don't," Sasha reasoned. "Is he . . . ?"

"No. If I'm in any history books, it won't be for *that*."

"You haven't done anything wrong, Errollyn," Sasha said more forcefully, and the trembling of her jaw seemed to lessen. "You can't let people get away with gross injustice, even when they're otherwise decent. It's the principle."

"It's *your* principle."

"And not yours?"

Errollyn spared a moment to wrap his arms about her and press his cheek against her wet hair. She slumped against him, as though that embrace were enough reason to let every other concern and tension vanish for a short while. Errollyn felt his heart soar. "I'm glad you came, crazy fool," he murmured in her ear.

"I had to come," she replied, a touch desperately. "You're the only one who really understands me." The words might have come from his own lips to her, Errollyn reflected. To hear her say it back to him . . . well, they had to get out of this alive, he thought. Because he wanted to take this amazing, energetic, wild, exasperating, beautiful, crazy person to bed and make love to her for about a year.

Sasha took another look at the manacles that bound Errollyn's ankles. They were thick and heavy, impenetrable save for where the tightening bolt joined the two halves together. The gap between the two parts was about the width of a sword.

"I can hit that," Sasha observed.

"On a good day you can hit that," Errollyn reassessed.

"Every day's a good day." Sasha took up her blade, readied herself, and measured the blow. Errollyn winced, took a deep breath, and shut his eyes. And waited. And opened them once more to find Sasha had lowered her blade. "I can scarcely see it," she admitted. Errollyn realised that if his own vision was poor down here, Sasha must be nearly blind. She might have been wielding by far the sharpest blade known to steel, but she'd have to hit the bolt with tremendous force to split it. Good svaalverd could impart force, but mostly it was a form designed to turn an opponent's strength against him. Inanimate objects were another matter entirely. And if she missed . . .

"Sasha," Errollyn tried again, "go and get a key."

Sasha stared at him for a moment in the gloom. "I don't want to have to hurt anyone."

"Then don't. Not permanently, anyhow."

Sasha sheathed the blade over her shoulder and heaved a short breath. "All right. Don't go anywhere." She slid between the piled cargo and vanished. Errollyn knew what bothered her. It was easier for him to fight without swords. She was a strong woman for her size and, with a blade, neither size nor strength proved any hindrance to her formidable technique. Without a blade, however, her options narrowed. But Errollyn had confidence in her. She was . . . well, remarkable.

Soon enough she was back, a bunch of keys dangling from a silver ring in her hand. She knelt by his feet and began trying one after the other, grinning in the dark. "That easy?" Errollyn asked.

"I'd thought serrin many things, but never forgetful," she said. "These were just lying on a table in the big quarters up that way." She nodded toward the bow. "Everyone seems to be on deck."

She found a key that fit, the manacles clanked and fell away. Errollyn tried to rise as his ankles came free, but his legs were weak. He waited a moment, squatting with a hand to the mast for balance.

"I'm sorry," Sasha told him, "I couldn't find a blade for you."

"Yours is enough for two," Errollyn assured her.

"In this ship, I doubt it. There's no room at all in the corridors." She looked worried again. "Look, beyond the hold, there's a passage that goes—"

"I know, I've been on these ships before." His legs throbbed as blood flowed through his veins. His arms felt heavy, as though made of lead.

"You'd best lead, you can see better in the dark . . ."

Errollyn shook his head. "You know the way in, you know the way out."

"No, I don't want to—"

There was a noise amidst the piled cargo. Sasha moved fast to her feet, blade drawn.

"Errollyn?" came a familiar female voice. "Look, I found some—" Aisha halted in midlimb. In her hands was a tray, holding various fruits Sasha did not recognise and a clay jug with some cups. She stared at Sasha, unmoving. Errollyn recognised the expression and rose to his feet.

"Aisha," he said in Gethania dialect, "don't be frightened. She came to free me, that's all."

"Frightened?" Sasha repeated, in Saalsi. Evidently she knew a little more dialect than she let on. "*Frightened?*" Her tone was disbelieving. "You're scared of *me?*"

"You're holding a sword in my face," Aisha said warily, in Lenay. She stood on one leg, leaning on sacks for balance. Even standing had to be agony for her. "Why, if you're not prepared to use it?"

"You left him tied up like *that*?" Sasha's voice was nearly trembling with anger, pointing with her blade to the base of the mast. "You were just going to leave him there? Have you any idea what damage that can do?"

Aisha stared at her mutely. Then looked down at her tray. More food. Aisha's answer to everything. Errollyn might have laughed, were he not so sad for her. He put a gentle hand on Sasha's shoulder.

"It's all right, Sasha," he said quietly. "It's not her fault. She just can't think for herself. None of them can." Aisha's eyes flashed angrily. "Remember the pull, Aisha? Remember how it got you out of Maerler's mansion?" The anger faded. "You can't resist it. Nor can you deny it. As one serrin goes, so go you all."

"I just thought . . ." Aisha tried, and stopped, staring down at her tray. "I mean, I can't just . . ."

"Aisha," said Sasha. Now there was emotion in her voice. Almost tears. "Please, don't raise the alarm. Just let us go."

Aisha just stared, mouth half open. She seemed almost paralysed. Errollyn swore, pushed past Sasha and gently removed the tray from Aisha's hands.

"Get off your feet, silly girl," he told her, easing her down to the floor. He rested her back against the sacks, then checked the bandaging on her leg—it was firm, clean and smelled of strong potions. Then he checked the swelling on her head, mostly invisible beneath her pale blonde hair. Aisha leaned her head back on the sacks and breathed deeply.

Sasha crouched alongside. "Aisha? Are you well?"

"Just . . . a little dizzy."

Errollyn caught Sasha's sideways glance and returned a meaningful look. Here it was, the dilemma of the serrinim, all wrapped up in Aisha's paralysis. Sasha's eyes were more comprehending than they might have been a few days before.

"Aisha . . ." Sasha tried again, "spirits, look, you're nearly out on your feet, you couldn't lie down when you knew Errollyn was suffering, you tried to help him however you could, short of actually untying him . . . Aisha, you know this is wrong. Don't you? You know this isn't what the serrinim are about?"

"Just . . . just tie me up," Aisha said breathlessly. "Just tie me up, and then I can't . . ."

"Damn it, can't you make just one decision for yourself?" Sasha retorted, exasperated. Aisha's glazed look was almost pleading. She didn't want to decide. She couldn't.

Suddenly Errollyn felt as frightened as he'd ever felt in battle. We're all so helpless, he thought. That's why we need those rare ones like Rhillian and Kiel. The ones who can make decisions; who can decide between greater and lesser evils. And if those rare ones get it wrong . . .

Sasha was staring at him, her expression incredulous. Finally, she was understanding. She shook her head faintly, and put a gentle hand on Aisha's forehead. "Aisha, I can't tie you up. You're hurt. Possibly no one will come down here for some time. Just stay down here for a while, and don't move. Can you do that for me?"

"I . . ." Aisha swallowed hard, sweat sheening her forehead. "I have to tell . . ."

"No." Very firmly. "You don't have to tell anyone, Aisha. It's your choice."

"It's not." Feebly.

"Yes, it is."

"No . . . you don't understand."

Sasha took Aisha's hand in hers. "How hard do you feel it pulling, Aisha?" she asked gently. "What does it feel like?"

Aisha's pale blue eyes seemed to stare straight through her, as if she could see through the hull and up at the stars beyond. "It's all the world," she murmured hoarsely. "I can't resist it. You act against the serrinim, and therefore I must . . ."

Sasha put careful fingers on her lips. "It's all right, Aisha. I understand." She kissed the smaller woman on the forehead. "I love you, my friend." They embraced, gently. Then Sasha gestured to Errollyn with a free hand. "Errollyn, carry her. We'll take her back to her bed."

By the time they got there, Aisha was fast asleep in Errollyn's arms. "That's not a natural sleep, is it?" Sasha whispered to Errollyn as he tucked her carefully in. The small quarters was lit by a single lamp, bare wooden beams all around. Everything creaked in rhythm with a gentle swell.

"Natural enough for serrin," Errollyn replied. "She was already exhausted. It was too much."

"Can she do *anything* to contradict Rhillian?"

"It's not just Rhillian," Errollyn said. "It's the situation. We all feel the peril. Like animals in herd, once the herd moves, we must move with it. Rhillian is only the first herd animal of many. It's impossible to resist."

"More so than . . . than lust?"

"More so than fear," Errollyn said quietly. And Sasha looked almost afraid at that.

"I'm glad you're *du'janah*," she said quietly. "You're free."

"Freedom is frightening," Errollyn said simply.

They moved down creaking wooden steps into the cargo hold once more, and Errollyn could hear noises from on deck, distant shouts and ropes being pulled. They crept along the central passage between crates and sacks, past the mast and its abandoned chains. Toward the stern, a doorway led to a narrow wood passage. Sasha crept first, blade ready, and flattened herself to a wall when footsteps thumped above their heads. Light came dimly from a hanging lantern, high up where it could not be bumped by passing sailors.

The footsteps passed. Sasha cautiously climbed a ladder and peered onto the floor above, then pulled her feet up and vanished. Errollyn followed. This floor was sleeping quarters, rows of hammocks strung between wall hooks, all empty.

Sasha crept up the next ladder, holding her sword low as she climbed one-handed. Errollyn followed, his arms and legs throbbing. The possibility of discovery put his muscles on edge, but rather than tensing they trembled and wobbled, like an old man's arm on a walking cane. Sasha peered onto the deck, and Errollyn felt the cold breeze of the ocean.

Suddenly Sasha twisted on the ladder, dropping so that she could whisper in his ear, "To stern against the side rail, there's a coil of piled rope, four paces away. If you lie down within it, you're hidden." He nodded shortly, hoping that her eyes were keen enough to know the difference between four paces and five.

Suddenly Sasha was gone, a brief push and the barely audible creak of deck planking. Errollyn pushed himself after, a hand low on the deck as he ran, his legs nearly giving way in the crouch, but four steps brought him to the coiled rope with Sasha already inside.

Peering over the top, Errollyn found himself looking toward the bow across the open deck. Overhead, the great triangular sail was furled, and in a clear space at the bow, there rested a great ballista, surrounded by many serrin. Round leather shots waited in small wooden crates, and about the deck were numerous buckets of water. Errollyn could smell the acrid scent of burned wood and varnish, and singed leather.

Beyond the bow, the light-speckled slopes of Petrodor Harbour rose from sparkling black waters. Atop the slopes, the lights were burning, a series of bright orange flames that spread enough light on the hillside for Errollyn to recognise Sharptooth. It did not surprise him. No one had told him what Rhillian had done the previous night, but he'd guessed all the same. They knew each other that well, Rhillian and he.

A wind came brisk from the north, rustling at the furled sail above, swinging the boom and singing through the rigging. A patch of water nearer the shore was ablaze . . . Errollyn stared harder, and thought it possibly a ship, though the mast and ropes and people about the ballista made it difficult to be sure.

"There's a watch on the stern," Sasha whispered, "but she got called down to help fix an anchor. That's when I climbed the rudder. They've got the boat fixed across the wind, anchors to stern and bow so they can keep their artillery fixed to the shore in case of pursuit."

And they did not expect small boats to circle out into deep water and come at them from the dark behind.

"We'll have to go soon anyway, watch or no watch," Errollyn whispered. "We can jump from the stern and swim." Mari's boat would be waiting out there somewhere. Far enough into the dark that serrin eyes could not see it. A long way, in the cold, dark ocean. And how would Mari be able to see *them*?

"And if they shoot us in the water?"

"I'm serrin. Killing a serrin is no small matter for another serrin."

"Aye, and what about me?"

Errollyn gritted his teeth. His eyes searched the deck for Kiel . . . there were Hael and Shaliri, restringing bows and fastening full quivers on the railings. And closer, tying off loose ropes near the mast, was Halrhen who had carried Aisha from her Dockside bed. Several others, and a few surviving human staff from the Petrodor residences. But no Kiel. Even so . . . Kiel would not order another serrin killed . . . but Sasha?

"Perhaps we should kill the watch," Errollyn murmured. From beneath him, Sasha twisted to give him a hard look. "Isn't it what humans would do?"

"Only if I have to," Sasha snapped.

Errollyn heard the whistle just before Sasha and hurled himself hard down on top of her. The arrow hit the top rope with a thud, directly before his nose. It hit almost vertical, and he stared up . . . there, riding high on the mast, was a dark-haired figure with a bow. Kiel.

Sasha swore. "I looked *up*!" she insisted. Into a confusion of rigging in a black sky, with human eyes.

"Follow!" Errollyn hissed, leaping off her and running for the steps to the raised stern. Yells came from the bow, joined by shouts from up the mast as Kiel called the alarm. Errollyn cleared the steps and came face to face with Triana, piercing blue-grey eyes, a blade in her hand. The stern watch. "What are you going to do?" Errollyn half snarled, half laughed at her. "Kill me?" Triana stared at him in consternation. Errollyn spread his arms, daring her, and half preparing to tackle her bare-handed. "Would you be the first of a thousand years?"

Her eyes darted past his shoulder, alerting him that Sasha had mounted the stairs. Triana moved to go around Errollyn, but he danced across, keeping himself between the two women. "You leave her alone."

Triana backed up. Errollyn circled, Sasha at his back, and saw figures running across the deck toward the stern. Kiel was descending fast as a cunning system of pulleys and ropes sent him soaring down to the deck. Even now, he was fitting another arrow. "Rhillian!" Errollyn yelled at the figure with gleaming white hair that ran toward him. "You call him off right now!"

He pointed at Kiel. Kiel fitted his arrow, in middescent, and pointed it at Errollyn. Only not quite . . . Errollyn saw where it was headed, saw the muscles lose tension on Kiel's forearm, and leapt. The arrow hit him as he dived across Sasha's path. Blinding agony tore through his shoulder and the world turned colourless.

He heard Sasha's scream. He heard Kiel's shouts for Triana and Halrhen to get her . . . and opened his eyes to see Halrhen, a large and formidable swordsman, leaping his way . . .

Sasha moved. Blades flashed, clashed, and bodies flowed in lethal motion. Lying on the planks, dazed and insensible, Errollyn could recognise only shapes. The serrin fighters made beautiful shapes, with perfect form. And Sasha's shapes . . . were less perfect. She cut the corners off, crude and blunt, and devastatingly effective.

Halrhen fell first, slashed across the middle; then Triana, throat severed, blood spurting. She fell right near him, and squirmed and kicked as she died. Then he felt Sasha's hand grasp his arm and pull him toward the stern rail. He rose, consciousness returning . . . it was just the shoulder, he told himself firmly, struggling for strength. Just the shoulder. You're weak from the chains, that's all.

He dragged himself to the railing, feeling for the shaft . . . his hand brushed it and the pain made him wish he hadn't. Serrin were thundering onto the raised stern now, falling back as Rhillian took the lead. Her blade was naked and there was horror on her face. She crouched, first by Triana, then by Halrhen. When she looked up at Sasha, her eyes were filled with grief and rage.

Sasha stood between him and Rhillian. Her naked blade was barely bloodied, so fast had been her strokes. Errollyn could not see her face, but her stance alone was lethal. The thought drifted across his dazed consciousness that if Rhillian attacked, she would die. He'd thought them evenly matched before—his human lover and his old serrin friend. Now, he saw otherwise. Rhillian was serrin. Serrin perfected the form. The same form, always the same, where the only deviations came from the form's own complexity. Sasha made new forms. Or took the old ones and shaped them to her needs. She was human, and pragmatic, while Rhillian was serrin, and artistic. Rhillian fought with superb precision and artistry. Sasha fought to kill.

If all humans learn serrin ways, he thought, and copy serrin skills, surely we're doomed. Surely we cannot be humanity's enemy, and expect to survive.

Rhillian took her own stance. Blood covered the deck. Rhillian's emerald eyes blazed, her sword poised for attack. Sasha stood, and waited to kill her. Errollyn wanted to speak, but could not. If he spoke, he might distract Sasha and give Rhillian an advantage. Even as he thought it, he realised he was wishing Rhillian to die. It shamed and horrified him. He'd never wished it before on someone he loved. But he loved Sasha more.

Rhillian did not attack. Perhaps she feared. Perhaps she saw reason. Perhaps she knew herself outmatched. Errollyn could not tell. He only saw from the stance of the two women and the look in Rhillian's eyes, that all trace of regret or restraint had vanished. The friendship was passed. Now, they were enemies.

Finally, Rhillian spoke. "Get off my ship," she said, very quietly. Her voice dripped with menace. "Get off before I kill you both."

"You and which army?" said Sasha in Lenay, blunt and contemptuous. A Lenay warrior to the last. Errollyn eyed the semicircle of naked blades around them and thought it a poor choice of words.

The next thing he knew, he was very cold, very wet and in more pain than seemed reasonable. The world moved strangely, breath came with difficulty, and then not at all . . . he choked, gasping, trying to breathe through his nose as the air refused to pass down his throat. Hands rolled him over and his shoulder screamed agony. He was struck on the back, hard, then vomited water. And gasped again, to little effect. He thought he was going to die.

Then the air came, slowly, and he could breathe again. After a long time of gasping and coughing, he rolled back. Above him, through salt-bleary eyes, he saw Sasha. He was in Mari's boat, he realised. It was moving toward the shore. Away from the serrinim. Away from Saalshen. Toward foreign lands filled with cold and hostile people who did not understand him, and wished all his people dead. Strangely, that thought did not bother him, either, as much as it might.

Sasha was talking to him, but he couldn't hear much—there was a rushing, buzzing sound in his ears. Possibly they were full of water. He lifted his good arm and felt her hand clasp his. Most humans might have wished the serrin dead, but this one didn't. This one would fight to save him. It seemed the least he could do to return the favour.

"Hold on, Errollyn," she was urging him. "We're almost home."

Home. Now, he had no home. Home would be wherever she was. And that thought did not bother him very much either.

Twenty-three

THE WIND WAS CHILL atop the North Pier Temple. Sasha pulled her coat tight as she sat on the small terrace above her quarters. Below, men hauled baskets and donkeys pulled carts filled with trade—cages of noisy chickens, ducks or geese; huge bundles of green, leafy vegetables; bags of potatoes and cauliflower; bags of flour and grain; and sometimes livestock tied into long trains of rope. Transportable items, for the docks.

Right on the southern edge of North Pier, the temple was always surrounded by a cacophony of activity. The new father, Father Recheldi, was a decent enough man, quieter and less well loved than Father Berin, but perhaps that would change in time. He had returned five days before from the grand mass to elect a new archbishop, and had had little to say about the process, save to shrug and murmur, "Time will tell."

A man named Tietro was archbishop now. Few had ever heard of him, save that he came from a northern Torovan town in Danor, and Family Tietro were said to be close allies to Duke Tarabai of Danor. The days of fatherly neutrality, it seemed, were over. Few had been surprised.

Sasha had been pleased, though, that Father Recheldi had not returned with instructions from higher up that she and Errollyn could no longer be quartered in the temple. Most of the Torovan priesthood did not know that the North Pier Temple even existed . . . or not until recently, at least. Dockside temples were unaligned, the families of their priests neutral in broader Petrodor alliances, and their fathers thus unable to trade favours and climb the ranks to the higher slopes. Perhaps those higher ranks now thought to offer Father Recheldi favours to spy on her, or worse . . . Sasha did not know. She remained alert, and trusted no one but her closest friends. She'd been in Petrodor for long enough now that that was more a reflex than a conscious decision.

From back toward the dockside, she could hear the rush of waves against the dock and the creaking of boats at the pier. From the North Pier, yells and shouts, the trundling creak of heavy wagons, and the squeal of pulley ropes hauling loads. Further south, toward South Pier, the cries of the marketplace

. . . and a more recent sound, the clinking and hammering of tools. Dockside was being rebuilt.

As she gazed up the vast, shambling slope before her, the bells were tolling once more as the upslope temples joined in the celebrations. The North Pier Temple did not have a bell. Father Berin had had better things to spend money on.

The trapdoor behind her creaked and Sasha turned in her chair to see Errollyn pushing up through it. His left arm was in a sling, yet he wore his sword all the same. The bow, of course, he left in their quarters.

"I wonder if they'll ring the same when the demons of the apocalypse come flying through," he remarked, seating himself in a nearby chair. He pulled some grapes off the small table between and stretched with a wince. He looked tired, his hair in even greater disarray than usual, yet to Sasha's eyes he seemed healthier each day.

"I think maybe this *is* the demon of the apocalypse flying through," Sasha said.

Errollyn smiled. The bells were tolling because Torovan had a king. Following the announcement of the new archbishop, the archbishop had then turned around and declared a sole ruler for Torovan—a king, as there had never been a king in eight hundred years.

King Marlen Steiner.

"He had us all right from the beginning, didn't he?" Sasha sighed. "Probably from when he first heard of the coming war."

"Royalty is a strangely attractive notion for humans," Errollyn remarked, shifting to seek a better position. He was always stiff, always getting aches in strange places. Worse, he tried to exercise as though he'd never been hurt, until Sasha had threatened to tie him up like Rhillian had. Kessligh was little better, though somewhat more patient. Between the two of them, Sasha sometimes felt like a nursemaid.

"Probably he was the one who started Archbishop Augine and the others table-thumping about the war in the first place," said Sasha. "Marry a Lenay princess, start a war, destabilise your enemies and claim all the spoils when they collapse. That's quite a list, even for Patachi Steiner. Even his worst enemies underestimated his ambition."

Marya had been the key. Lenay royalty. It had long been agreed that marrying into Lenay royalty did not confer royalty upon a Petrodor family. Marya had been a princess, yet that did not make Symon Steiner a prince . . . nor Patachi Steiner a king. It was a status symbol, nothing more, like the fancy jewels that Family ladies wore—a Lenay princess was an exotic status symbol for powerful Petrodor men. A fashionable accessory, like a necklace, or a jewelled dagger. Or a pet wolf. Only now, the new archbishop decreed that such a marriage *was* enough to make Patachi Steiner a king, and the entire Family Steiner a royal family. And it became so because there was no one left of sufficient power and resolve to prevent it. Torovan had a king, because those who mattered decided that it should. Sasha had read and heard told of enough old, romantic Torovan tales to know that it wasn't supposed to work this way— always in those tales there resided the notion of *entitlement*, that one ascended to such things because it was right and proper, and decreed by the heavens. But then, that was why the archbishop existed, to decree on the gods' behalf. No one ever questioned who put the *archbishop* in power. The gods did. Of course.

Obviously her own father, King Torvaal, hadn't seen this coming either. He'd interfered by marrying Alythia to Family Halmady, and thus unknowingly creating a rival claim to the throne of Torovan. Steiner's claim would be superior, of course, because Marya was elder, but the Great Families of Petrodor were nothing if not insecure. Claims could be extinguished as easily as lives.

It was all so silly. Sasha had never been a great lover of royalty, but most of that had been for personal reasons. She'd never, until now, been quite so disgusted by the entire concept. She was revolted by it. Was this how kings were made? Through greed, murder, intrigue and villainy? Some kind of king Patachi Steiner would make, she was certain. Now, as Kessligh had predicted, things were worse.

"There's not going to be enough space on the old Maerler Mansion plot to build his new castle," said Sasha.

"He won't stop at the old mansion plot," Errollyn said grimly. "He'll build on all of Sharptooth."

"Three of those families conceded rather than fought," Sasha reminded him.

Errollyn shrugged. "You think that'll matter?"

Sasha thought about it. Then shook her head. "You're right. He'll demolish the lot."

"King of Torovan," Errollyn said, as though the words tasted foul on his tongue. "I'm sure he'll adopt the grandest trappings of royalty he can find. He'll keep all his trading empire, all the ships, all the warehouses. He'll turn all his allies into lords, give them holdings . . . not high enough to offend the dukes, but high enough."

"Make the relationship formal," Sasha agreed, nodding. "Formality has an odd way of changing people's behaviour."

Errollyn raised an eyebrow. "As a Lenay, you'd know." Sasha shrugged. "That castle atop Sharptooth will dominate the city. I'd think it'll take him fifteen years to build, at the least."

"Ten," said Sasha, popping a grape. "Petrodor grows so fast, and the stonemasonry here is excellent. There's unlimited labour, probably Riverside will be restocked of desperate souls in a year or two, they'll do anything for a few coppers."

"Possibly." Errollyn gazed up at the slope with eyes narrowed by pain. "We made a mess, didn't we? Serrin and human both."

"A king will make Torovan an ambitious power to contend with, well into the future. That means more wars, more trouble, more suffering."

Sasha gazed past Errollyn toward where Sharptooth jutted up from the Petrodor Incline. Yesterday, the last of the fires had finally stopped smouldering. Reports said there wasn't much left. "Fortunate maybe Rochel didn't live to see it," she murmured. "He'd have hated it. Maybe enough to have done something stupid. He could get away with a few insolent remarks toward patachis. Kings are a different matter."

"All considered," Errollyn said, his green eyes upon her, "you don't seem that upset."

Sasha shrugged, tossed a grape in the air and caught it in her mouth. "Torovan's right next to Lenayin," she explained. "We'll keep them in line. How much trouble can they be?"

"Ah, the smug arrogance of bloodthirsty power."

Sasha smiled. "It has a lot going for it, you can't deny."

Errollyn did not reply. He leaned back and gazed up at the crowded slope. Sasha watched him with mild concern. He had been quiet, the past week. Partly it was just physical exhaustion, constantly dealing with the pain of his injury. But sometimes she would find him on South Pier, gazing out to sea at a harbour now empty of serrin vessels. He was the last serrin in Petrodor. Sometimes Sasha wondered if it saddened him to be so alone, or if he were more saddened that he felt little changed.

She grasped his hand, and felt a pressure in return. They had not made love for a week, and that too was instructive. It demonstrated that there was far more to their relationship than lust. In the week past, they had spoken of many, many things.

"Winter comes," said Errollyn, watching the dark clouds speeding by. "The lords of Torovan and Lenayin have all winter to prepare their forces. Spring is marching season."

Sasha nodded, thinking of Sofy. This winter would be her last as an unmarried woman. Come the late spring, or perhaps the early summer, she would be married. And Sasha's world would be transformed once more.

"A whole winter," she mused, "stuck in this place." Smells filled her nostrils, familiar but still strange, even after so long. Animals, foodstuffs, cooking, foulness and sweetness in equal measure. Smoke from fires, and the omnipresent whiff of ash that had not yet left the dockside. Yells and loud conversation, hammering, trundling wagons, protesting animals, crying children and the upslope clangour of bells. "I might go mad."

Errollyn gave her a wry smile. "You're already mad. You'll survive."

Sasha smiled, pulled her chair alongside his and rested her head upon his good shoulder. Errollyn put his arm around her. To be a highlander in Petrodor, Tongren had said, was to be lonesome. She knew what he meant. But she did not feel alone.

Tashyna paced. The cage was small and it rocked back and forth alarmingly. It set her nerves on edge. There was little air beneath the blanket, and it smelled bad, of human children and their doings. She curled up once more and tried to rest, but the jolting made that impossible. It upset her, this change of fortune. Things had been improving. Now, there was this nightmare.

She whined and growled, but there came no response from beyond the blanket. The plodding of hooves continued and, occasionally, the rattle of a wagon passing the other way. She settled once more and tried chewing the bone the Nice Lady had given her. It was big and had had lots of meat, now devoured. The Nice Lady had hugged her and cried. Tashyna hadn't understood that, and had thought maybe she'd done something wrong. She'd licked and whined, and tried to understand . . . but the Nice Lady had helped the Big Man put her into this cage, and then the blanket had come over, and that was the last she'd seen of them both.

The bone smelled of the Nice Lady . . . and of the Other Nice Lady too, the one who'd brought it. She seemed to defer to the Nice Lady, and her hair was shorter. In Tashyna's eyes, everyone deferred to the Nice Lady. And so they should. Tashyna gnawed on the bone, savouring the smell of humans who were good to her, and hoping they would take this blanket off soon and let her out of the cage so she could see them again.

Finally the trundling stopped. The blanket was removed and Tashyna blinked in the rush of light . . . only there was less light now as the sun was sinking. All the world smelled different. There was water here, and trees, and grass, flowers, and big, strange animals in the nearby field. She could smell them, and everything else, all at once. She stared around, unable to decide what to look at first. It was all too much.

The Big Man patted her cage and she growled reflexively . . . then remembered he had fed her many times, and stopped. She got confused, sometimes. She didn't know who to defer to, save for the Nice Lady. The Big Man only laughed.

"Now, now," he said, "I don't blame you for being mad after we locked you in this damn cage for so long. But here, see, there's no one around now. We'll take a side road, you can run alongside for a while."

Tashyna stared at him, uncomprehending, and watched as he gathered a long rope lead, and poured a wooden bowl full of water from a skin. He placed the bowl on the ground beside the wagon's wheel, then opened the cage. Tashyna jumped out . . . and smelled the two big animals pulling the wagon. Fascinated, she ran forward. They had big shoulders and horns, and they snorted and tossed their big heads as they looked at her, eyes rolling. But there was a Smaller Man with a similar smell to the Big Man, she recalled he'd been very nice to her too, and he was now holding the big animals' heads still. She ran around them for a bit, smelling and looking, and decided that they were probably too big for her to kill on her own. But such an interesting smell! Her mouth watered, and she realised she was thirsty.

She ran back to the bowl the Big Man had put on the ground and eyed him warily . . . but he was walking away, heading back to the Smaller Man. She drank, and it was good. Then she heard the Big Man coming back, but it didn't matter, he was nice. He hooked the rope lead to her collar while she drank, but that didn't matter either—the Nice Lady did that too.

"Good girl," said the Big Man, ruffling her coat. It was growing thicker now, and it was good to have some breeze to cool her down. There was a second wagon behind, she realised, and she smelled the Big Man's Woman, and the Children. They'd been in the underground place where she'd sometimes been fed, and they'd always been nice to her . . . although she thought the Big Man's Woman was afraid of her. Which was good. All the wagons were piled high with all sorts of things, a whole new profusion of smells.

In the distance, something looked vaguely familiar. Tashyna raised her head. They were on a small rise, and the lower farmlands lay aglow with orange and green in the late, angling sun. And there, beyond the farmlands, a long, high ridge formed the horizon against the sky. The ridge bristled with stone. Smoke smudged the sky and she sniffed the air . . . but the wind was from the wrong direction.

Home, something said in her mind. The Nice Lady was there, and the others. But . . . the wind came brisk from behind, and she turned once more and sniffed. Trees, she smelled. Water, and grass, and dirt and mud, animals and manure. Fresh smells.

Home, something else said in her mind.

She turned back toward the distant ridge and whined.

"I know," said the Big Man at her side. "It's a shit hole, but it's a hard place to leave. I've got roots there, perhaps too many damn roots." He spared a glance at the piled wagons. "But it was never meant to be. I don't belong there. I've got the mountains in my blood, like you. I want to see the earth thrusting skyward once more. I want to smell the clean air and wade in the wild rivers, and hear the spirits talking to me in my sleep. Lenay or Cherrovan, we're all highlanders. We're going home, girl. You can smell it, can't you?"

Tashyna stared at the distant horizon until the building urge grew too great, then she threw back her head and howled. Someone over there had to hear her. She'd never howled before in her life, but now, it was irresistible.

Tashyna howled until the urge had fled, knowing that something had changed forever. She felt loss. She felt a deep, yearning sensation. And yet, on the breeze, there blew from the west the smell of freedom.

The Smaller Man whacked the big animals on the flanks, and the wagon began trundling once more. Tashyna trotted alongside, liking that much better than the cage. More big animals in neighbouring fields stared at her. Some ran away. She tried chasing them, but the rope brought her up short.

Soon some other travellers came past headed the other way. Tashyna crossed over to look at them, and their big animals nearly went crazy.

"Crazy damn fool!" one shouted as they passed. "That's a real bloody wolf!"

"Of course it's a real bloody wolf!" the Big Man bellowed back cheerfully. "And I'm a real bloody Cherrovan! And if you've got a problem with that, you'll be a real bloody corpse!" The other travellers made off in all haste, and there was much laughter from the wagons.

The landscape changed as the road continued and the stone-covered, smoky ridge behind faded from view. Soon enough, Tashyna began to forget all about that place of stone and noise and crowds of unfriendly people. She was of the highlands, and she was going home.

About the Author

J OEL SHEPHERD was born in Adelaide in 1974. His first manuscript was shortlisted for the George Turner Prize in 1998, and his first novel, *Crossover*, was shortlisted in 1999. He wrote two other novels in the Crossover series, *Breakaway* (2003) and *Killswitch* (2004). *Sasha*, the first novel in *A Trial of Blood & Steel*, was published in 2007.

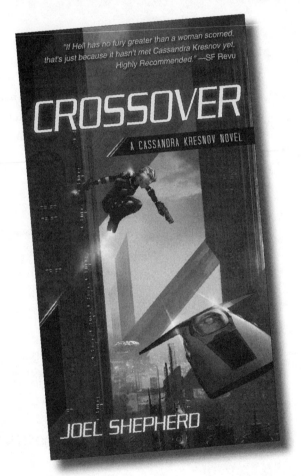

ALSO AVAILABLE

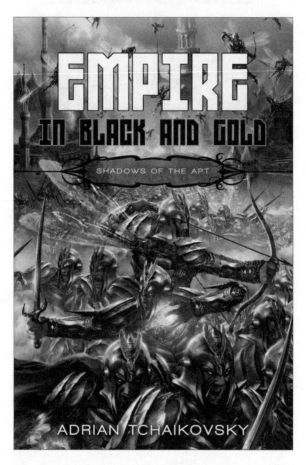

EMPIRE
IN BLACK AND GOLD
SHADOWS OF THE APT

ADRIAN TCHAIKOVSKY

"A remarkably strong fantasy debut."
—Book Spot Central

Pyr®, an imprint of Prometheus Books
716-691-0133 / www.pyrsf.com

APRIL 2010

"A good and enjoyable mix between a medieval-looking world and the presence of technology."
—*Starburst*

Pyr®, an imprint of Prometheus Books
716-691-0133 / www.pyrsf.com

MAY 2010

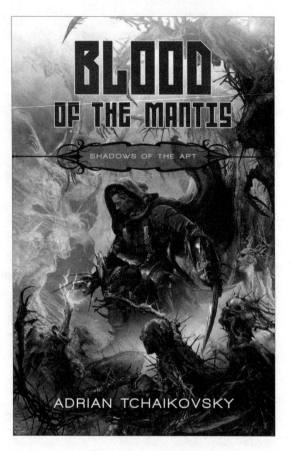

"*Full of colorful drama and nonstop action involving mass warfare and personal combat.*"
—**Fantasy Book Critic**

Pyr®, an imprint of Prometheus Books
716-691-0133 / www.pyrsf.com